I0760433

The Looking-Glass Curse

The Complete Series

Eva Chase

The Looking-Glass Curse: The Complete Series

First Digital Edition, 2020

Cover design: Yosbe Design

Case illustration: Julia Oosterloo

Ebook ISBN: 978-1-989096-62-8

Hardcover ISBN: 978-1-998582-12-9

Created with Vellum

Wicked Wonderland

The Looking-Glass Curse
Book 1

CHAPTER ONE

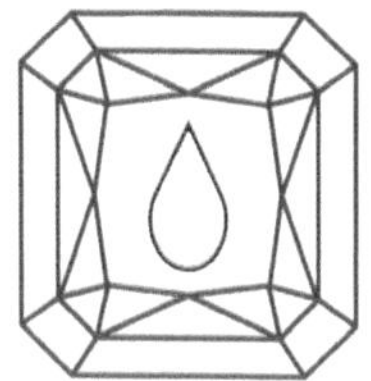

Lyssa

I should have known something was wrong the second I tripped over Brian's jeans coming in the door. He could be a bit of a slob, sure, but he didn't usually leave his pants… and shirt… in a heap in the apartment foyer.

I caught my balance, which was a pretty impressive feat considering I was clutching a heavy bag in each hand, and my first naïve thought was that he'd had some kind of accident, gotten sick on himself, and peeled off the mess as soon as he'd gotten in the door—

Then my gaze snagged on the silky midnight-blue dress that was also crumpled on the floor, a few feet into our living room. Brian definitely hadn't been wearing *that.*

It wasn't one of my dresses either.

My mind glazed over with an uncomfortable prickling that seeped down into my chest. I walked through the apartment on autopilot, rounding the corner to where I could see through the open bedroom door just in time to get a stunning view of my boyfriend's naked ass as he plowed into an equally naked woman on our bed. She gasped, he groaned, and my fingers went slack around the handles of the bags I'd been holding.

One jar of pickled eggs and four bottles of kombucha hit the floor with a thud and the crackling of shattered glass. Brian flinched and jerked away from—out of—oh, God, I might hurl—the other woman.

"Shit. Shit," he said as he scrambled off the bed. The woman gave a little shriek when she saw me and groped for her slip.

Somewhere in that moment, I split down the middle. One part of me kept my mouth clamped shut so I didn't actually puke from all the horror churning in my stomach. The other part zipped off far, far away to watch from a detached numb distance.

Brian had obviously been looking for something very different from me. The other woman's dark brown hair was almost as far as you could get from my pale blond. Tall, curvy. Maybe that was the problem? He'd wanted a bigger handful of boobs?

My stomach lurched harder. The other woman darted past me toward the door. Brian stood there raking his hand through his hair, still swearing.

"I didn't know you'd be home early," he said finally.

A laugh sputtered out of me. Which side of me had that come from? Maybe both. Because my boyfriend—correction: *ex*-boyfriend —was apparently such an asshole he thought that was some kind of excuse. Because this was the perfect cap on an already awful day.

"I had a meeting with my supervisor right before lunch," I said. "The call center laid me off."

How many times had he brought women over while I'd been sitting in my little cubicle taking repetitive customer service calls on other days? He'd moved into the apartment three months ago. Had the cheating started right away? Had he been screwing around even *before—*

My horror collided with the numbness, and my brain derailed in a burst of sparks. I jabbed my hand toward the door.

"Get out. Now."

"Lyssa, come on. We should at least talk about—"

"*Now*!" I snapped in a voice that didn't sound like mine at all. It must have been convincing, because Brian hopped into his boxers and fumbled with a shirt faster than I'd have thought was humanly possible. Then he was hustling through the apartment, dodging the bags of shattered glass, stopping for just long enough to scoop his PSP off the table. For fuck's sake.

He nearly fell on his face as he hauled on his jeans, which would have been satisfying, but sadly he managed to catch his balance. Before I had to turn on that sharp voice again, he'd ducked out the door. It closed behind him with a thump. His lady friend had already fled, taking her dress with her.

I dragged in a breath, and my chest hitched. A sour vinegar-y smell filled my nose. I looked down at the plastic shopping bags leaking kombucha and pickling juice onto the hardwood floor.

I didn't even *like* that crap. It was Brian's favorite drink, Brian's favorite weird little snack. After getting the news about the lay-off, I'd just wanted to do something to make someone else happy, because accomplishing that would make me feel better too.

Why did I have such shitty luck with boyfriends? Maybe Brian had been a little rough around the edges, but I'd shown him I didn't mind that. I'd thought he was in it for the long haul. How many signs had there been that I'd missed?

I rubbed my forehead and left the mess, flopping down on the linen couch instead. Deep breath in; deep breath out. Over and over, until my feet felt steadier where they were braced against the floor.

The apartment was in my name. Brian had kept forgetting to set up a meeting with the landlord to get on the lease. He'd have to come back and get the stuff that belonged to him, but I could put it in boxes near the door so I hardly had to see him. Or give him a time to come and be somewhere else so I didn't have to see him at all.

A year and a half. A year and a half, and he— In *my* bed—

He'd have to leave behind his key. Then I'd be done with him. It was weird how it really would be that easy to untangle him from my life in every practical way. Our lives hadn't gotten all that entangled in the first place, had they?

I'd thought it would take time. I'd thought—

It didn't matter now. I was never wiping that image out of my head, and I wasn't giving him a chance to repeat it. Melody might tease me about being a pushover, but I wasn't *that* much of a doormat, thank you.

My hand went to my purse to grab my phone. I could call my best friend right now, and she'd put this whole rotten day in perspective. Melody was good at that. Though she might have to stretch her skills beyond their usual limits today, given the catastrophe my life had turned into.

I was just reaching my thumb to tap her name when my ringtone warbled. For a second, I thought my best friend had psychically picked up on my distress and decided to pre-emptively call me. But it wasn't her number on the screen. It was my mom's.

Oh, no. Had Cameron gotten into even more trouble? It would figure if today's nasty surprises weren't over yet.

I answered, gripping the edge of the sofa cushion with my other hand, preparing for news of my older brother's latest exploits. "Hi, Mom. What's up?"

Mom's hesitant voice traveled over the line. "Oh, well, not much with me, but— Is this a good time to talk, honey? I know you're probably at work."

I bit my tongue against another rough laugh. "That's not a problem. What is it?" She wasn't talking with the obvious quaver I associated with Cameron problems. It could be he was still keeping his nose clean after all.

"It's all very unexpected," Mom said. "You remember your grand-aunt—Aunt Alicia?"

"Of course." Aunt Alicia had been my dad's aunt. When he'd gotten sick and for a while after he'd passed on, she'd come by the house to check in on Mom, Cam, and me. She'd always brought the best picture books and let me sit on her knee while she brought the stories to life with her bright voice. My clearest memory of her was us tucked together in Dad's old armchair, her hair, always pinned neatly back, shining blond and silver in the light from the living room window.

I hadn't seen her since I was eight or nine, around fifteen years ago. She and Mom had gotten into a fight about something or other, and she'd stopped dropping in.

"Well, it seems she's no longer with us. And she left a will—she didn't have any kids of her own, you know, and she never married—and… She's left everything to you."

My grip on the phone loosened. I recovered myself at the last second before I dropped it. "What?"

"I guess you were the person in the family she felt closest to," Mom said with one of her faint twitters. "I'm not sure exactly what you'll want to do with it. There's a little money, not a lot, and then there's the Tenniel property. It's quite an old house… Your father grew up there, and his parents inherited it from his grandfather… I'm not sure what state it's in after your grand-aunt was living there all that time alone."

Aunt Alicia was dead. A pang ran through me, but it was muted, both by the more direct blows I'd just taken today and by all those years since she'd shown any interest in me. She must have lived an awfully lonely life if her best choice to inherit was someone she'd only known when I was a little girl.

A flutter of excitement rose up under the pang. I didn't want to be *here* anymore, and now I didn't have to be.

"I'll have to go take a look at it, right?" I said. "Who do I need to talk to?"

"Oh my God, Lyss, this place is freaking amazing!" Melody leaned forward to peer through the windshield as I parked just outside Aunt Alicia's house. Which was now, according to the deed stuffed in my suitcase, *my* house.

My best friend had given the place an accurate assessment. I stepped out to get a better look at the building, and it took me a second to catch my breath.

The old Victorian stood on a couple acres of overgrown fields tangled with wildflowers. Three stories of dusty pink clapboard and carved wooden lintels loomed over us. A covered porch stretched across the whole front, and a tower jutted from the middle of the house with gable roof that pointed toward the stark blue sky. The narrow windows gleamed, revealing nothing but darkness on the other side.

So, this was the place where Dad had grown up. His parents had died in a car accident not long before I was born, so I guessed Aunt Alicia had inherited the property then. It was only a couple hours' drive from the city. Why hadn't she ever brought Cam and me out here?

Why had she given it to me now? There hadn't been any explanation in the will, and her lawyer hadn't been able to tell me anything useful. I was hoping the answer to that mystery lay somewhere inside. She wouldn't toss me a house without some kind of personal message, right?

We headed up the front steps to the double front doors. The key Aunt Alicia's lawyer had passed on to me looked like something out of a museum. It must have been ages since they'd changed the locks. But it turned smoothly, the door opening with just a faint creak.

We stepped inside onto the hall's soft runner. A mahogany table with bowed legs squatted by one wall; a matching grandfather clock ticked by the other. Ahead of us, two arched doorways led into the main floor's rooms before a grand staircase rose up to the second floor. At the flick of the light switch next to the doors, a brass chandelier blinked on high above our heads.

Aunt Alicia had looked after the place right up until the end. Only a faint layer of dust had settled on the furniture from the several days she'd been in the hospital before her death last week. A delicate smell like dried lilac perfumed in the air. A few framed charcoal sketches hung on the walls—country landscapes and town scenes that I recognized as Aunt Alicia's own work. I still had a sketch she'd done of me as a kid, tucked into a memento box somewhere.

Melody glided from doorway to doorway, her eyes lighting up behind her chic glasses. "Holy crap. Can you imagine the photoshoots you could have in this place?" She clapped her hands with a wide grin.

"You mean, the photoshoots *you* could have," I said teasingly. My best friend was an aspiring fashion photographer-slash-designer. She'd just gotten her most recent collection accepted into one of the independent boutiques downtown for the first time. The dress she had on right now, a bold pattern of purples and golds that set off the black bob of her hair to amazing effect, was her own work. "If you want to set something up, you know I'll be all for it."

She waggled a finger at me. "First I want you to agree to model some of my stuff. You'll look great in it, Lyssa. I promise."

"I'm pretty sure it'll look better on a professional model," I said. "At least now I can help by providing the set."

We'd had this conversation about a gazillion times. My five-foot-five frame was hardly model height, and while, sure, I was thin, it was in an awkward way rather than gracefully slender. Melody maintained that gawky was "totally a thing" in the high fashion world these days. I didn't have a complex about my body or anything—I was pretty happy with it, most of the time—but I didn't see any need for it to be splashed across catalogue spreads for all kinds of strangers to evaluate.

Like usual, Melody let out a playful huff. "I'll convince you one of these days. You've got to let loose, girl! Especially now that you're done with that drag of a job."

"It's more like they were done with me," I pointed out. "And it wasn't that much of a drag. I don't know why I was one of the ones who got laid off. Everyone else complained all the time, but I kind of liked it, helping people get the info they needed. There weren't *that* many jerk customers. I was pretty good at it too, you know."

"Of course you were," Melody said. "You never saw a problem you didn't want to fix. Don't you need a little break from taking care of everyone around you?"

I wrinkled my nose at her. We'd had this conversation lots of times too. "I don't have to take care of *you*."

"Not anymore."

Maybe there'd been a bit of that element to our friendship when we'd first clicked in ninth grade. Melody's parents had just gotten into what she now called "The Shouting Era," a five-year lead-up to their eventual divorce. So I'd encouraged her to hang out at my place as much as she wanted, which ended up meaning nearly every evening. *You're always so together*, she'd said to me once back then.

Whenever I'm around you, I feel like anything that's wrong, it's got to be fixable.

In return, I could thank her for introducing me to my first alcoholic beverage (wine coolers, which I still liked), my first joint (which had also been my last), and my first party make-out session (with Tommy Milton, who hadn't stuck around, but he'd been a really good kisser). I grounded Melody, and she pushed me to spread my wings. The balance worked just fine.

"Anyway," Melody said now, as we wandered through the dining room and into the kitchen fitted with appliances that looked like antiques, "that's not even getting into the *real* deadweight you just cut loose from your life. Adios, Brianito!"

"I know you didn't like Brian that much," I said. "But you could *pretend* to be sad we broke up."

"Why bother? He showed his true colors, didn't he? Good riddance. I'm glad you know what an asshole he is so you can move on."

"I think I'm going to take a break from dating for a while."

She laughed. "Who said anything about dating? Have a fling, a one-night-stand or two. It's about time you lived it up. You've got a place to live and money to last you a little while. Just this once, you don't need to worry about anything except what you want—and then go for it."

I raised my eyebrows at her. "And what if what I want is to curl up on that velvet sofa over there with a steady supply of ice cream and binge-watch all of Netflix for a month?" I pointed toward the living room—or maybe that was the family room, or the sitting room. It was hard to keep track.

Melody brushed past me and tugged on a strand of my hair. "I know you've got more wildness than that in you, Lyss. Sometime you've got to let it out, or else you're going to explode from bottling it up so long. Come on, let's see what's what upstairs."

As we headed up the staircase, a small furry body tumbled onto the landing. A black kitten that couldn't have been more than a few months old peered at us and meowed piteously. I clucked my tongue at him and scooped him up. Melody gave me a curious glance.

"The house came with pets included in the deal," I said. "There should be a tabby named Dinah around here somewhere and a couple other kittens. Aunt Alicia hadn't named those yet."

"Are you going to keep them?" Melody asked.

I rubbed the kitten's head between his swiveling ears. There was something comforting about the warmth of his soft little body. "I don't know. I guess I'll see what I end up deciding to do with this place. My apartment has a two-pet limit. I could put them up for adoption if I have to—it's only Dinah I had to agree to keep."

The second and third floors held a total of four bedrooms, a music room with a grand piano, a library, and a bathroom where the pipes hummed in a slightly unnerving way when I tried the sink faucet. If I decided to keep the whole house rather than sell it, I might want to invest in a few updates.

Every room held new mysteries—a closed wardrobe, a chest of drawers, a secretary desk. My heart beat a little faster with each one, even though we were just doing a quick survey of the place. I could explore the house in more depth once I'd gotten my bearings. Even though I'd never seen Aunt Alicia here, I felt her presence in the elegance and the neatness of the place. She deserved to have her belongings handled with proper care, not rummaged through as if I were looting the place.

So far I hadn't come across any indication that she'd anticipated my arrival, though.

In the middle of the third floor, a wrought-iron spiral staircase led up into the high tower I'd seen from outside. We scrambled up and emerged into a small room much messier and shabbier than the ones below.

A couple of bookcases stood against the walls, the books on them strewn about haphazardly between dusty figurines. A few pieces of clothing had been flung over the rocking chair in the corner. Next to it stood a full-length mirror with a silver frame that was shaped like a leafy vine winding around the glass.

Melody let out a low whistle. "I guess she didn't make it up here very often. Maybe those stairs got to be a bit much for her."

"Yeah," I said, only half listening. My gaze was stuck to the mirror.

I stepped closer to it without thinking, and a quivering sensation raced over my skin. The hairs on the back of my neck twitched.

I froze, hugging myself. "Did you feel that?"

Melody cocked her head. "Feel what?"

She didn't look at all disturbed. I shook my head. Taking all this in must be starting to overwhelm me. My heart was still beating even faster than before, but almost… eagerly. At the same time, my body balked at the idea of staying in this room with Melody one moment longer.

I turned toward the stairs. "That's the whole house. I'd better get my grocery shopping done before the store closes. A town that small, they might not even stay open past five."

"Hmm," Melody said, following me down. "One potential downside to getting to live in a fantastic old house—can you even get pizza delivery here?"

We both laughed as we reached the bottom of the spiral stairs, and the tension inside me broke. But when I glanced back toward the tower, a faint tingling crept back up my neck that I couldn't quite shake.

CHAPTER TWO

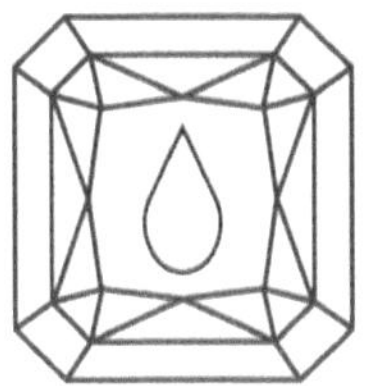

Lyssa

It felt strange having a huge house to myself after a few years in pokey apartments, dorms before that, and my childhood bungalow before even that. Even when I'd lived in that last apartment by myself for the first several months before Brian had moved in, I'd always been able to hear my neighbors around me, thumping across my ceiling or hollering to each other on the other side of the walls.

Aunt Alicia's house was out in the middle of nowhere. Other than the rumble of an occasional car passing by on the country road, I might as well have been the last person on Earth.

The pipes hummed, and the floors creaked—sometimes even when I wasn't walking on them. The kittens scampered around with the rasp of their little claws. But somehow the space still felt vastly quiet from the moment Melody headed home. Even when I tucked myself into bed in the smallest of the six bedrooms, snuggling under my beloved feather duvet that I'd brought with me, the emptiness of all the other rooms echoed around me.

Maybe it'd been a little ridiculous, running right out here just a few days after I'd kicked Brian to the curb. I'd wanted a change in scenery, not to be hit over the head with my aloneness.

When I woke up the next morning, sunlight was already streaming through the thin curtains on the bedroom window, and the black kitten was tumbling across my duvet. Noticing I was up, he gave me his usual plaintive meow. I ruffled his fur and pushed myself out of bed.

Time to get into the deeper exploration. There had to be something there that would explain why Aunt Alicia had wanted me to have the house at all.

The black kitten had definite ideas about where I should begin my survey. As soon as I walked out into the hall in my lounge-wear of lacy tank top and yoga pants, he darted toward the spiral staircase that led into the tower's attic room. I hesitated, watching him hop from step to step.

"Are you sure you don't want some breakfast first?" I called.

He paused, peered at me between the wrought-iron steps, and then kept bounding up.

I would have liked some breakfast. A cup of coffee would clear some of the just-woke-up mugginess from my head, and my stomach pinched, empty as all these rooms. But something drew me to those stairs anyway. Maybe it was the kitten's determination to see his mission through. Maybe it was curiosity driving me to sort through the contents of at least one room.

Or maybe there was more to it, a tug on a level I wasn't even conscious of.

I walked up the spiral stairs, gripping the cool metal railing. The small room at the top of the tower looked the same as it had yesterday other than the light coming in the windows slanting at a different angle. The air tasted dry and a little stale, but not musty, at least. The general disorder still struck me as odd. Aunt Alicia had kept the rest of the house so tidy. Was Melody right and the climb up the stairs had just gotten too hard?

I couldn't help straightening out the books on the shelves, blowing the dust off them before setting them upright and in even rows. They were mostly children's books, I realized: Narnia, Oz, Kipling, and more. My gaze fell on a wooden chest that I'd missed yesterday, tucked behind the railing at the top of the stairs. A toy box? Had Aunt Alicia stuck all the artifacts from her and Dad's childhood up here?

To reach the chest, I had to pass that tall standing mirror. The sunlight glimmered off both the glass and the silver frame. Not a streak of dust had settled on its surface. That was a little weird.

The quivering sensation that had come over me yesterday crawled up my back. I couldn't help glancing at my reflection as I walked past. That was some great bedhead I'd woken up with. I combed my fingers through my shoulder-length waves, walking on—and jerked to a stop.

I'd disappeared from the mirror. I wasn't standing right in front of it anymore, but I was close enough that I still should have been able to see myself. With one step, the whole reflection of the room had blurred, and I'd faded away completely.

I stood stock still, staring harder. None of the shapes in the suddenly hazy glass would come into focus. None of them looked like me. What the hell was wrong with the thing?

The quivering ran over my whole body. My heart thudded, but I eased closer to the mirror. The blurred shapes shivered and swirled before my eyes. All at once, the thump of my pulse felt exhilarated rather than nervous, as if I could sense I was on the verge of an incredible discovery. So close. If I just—

My hand reached out of its own accord. My fingers grazed the slick glass. I leaned forward, peering at the blurred image, and my hand slipped right through that smooth surface. I only had time to let out a squeak of surprise before the rest of me toppled after it into the mirror.

I spun head over heels, plummeting downward so quickly my hair whipped across my face. A twisted version of the room I'd left shifted around me. Bookshelves curved, closing me in. Wrought-iron bars like the railing of the stairs crisscrossed over them. I groped for something to catch my fall, but my fingers never connected with anything solid. I careened on down and down, another cry slipping from my throat, toward darkness that was broken by a glint of light.

I flipped again and plunged into a thicker darkness that closed around me with the cold wet texture of… water? All of a sudden, I was surging upward instead of falling, even though I hadn't gotten any impression of turning around. The faint light was expanding over the rippling surface above me.

I kicked my legs and swept my arms through the water, my lungs starting to burn. The currents coursed around me faster and faster…

With a gasp, my head broke into the open air. I sucked as much as I could into my lungs and got half a mouthful of salty water at the same time. As I sputtered it back out, I swiped at my eyes to take a clear look at where I'd ended up.

The salty flavor of the water had made me expect a broad expanse of ocean. What I saw looked more like a pond. I could make out the entire shoreline, from maybe twenty feet ahead of me to fifty feet on either side and a hundred or so behind me. Dark stones glittering with mica jutted along the water's edge. The fronds of enormous ferns and huge waxy leaves from hunched trees shaded them. Over the top of one of the ferns ahead of me, I thought I made out a daisy bigger than my head.

Where the hell was I? How the hell had I fallen into a mirror? I couldn't wrap my mind around anything that had happened in the last few minutes, but I definitely didn't feel secure treading water here over unknown depths.

I swam for the nearest shore, up ahead, my feet never touching the ground. I had to haul myself out of the water onto one of the twinkling boulders. Drenched and dripping, I scrambled over the rocks onto a grassy path that led between the towering foliage. A rich floral scent wafted over me.

My clothes were soaked, but the beaming sun warmed me enough to keep me from getting chilled. I wrung as much moisture as I could out of my top and my pantlegs while I watched and listened. Nothing much changed.

I took one cautious step down the path and then another. After a few more, the foliage thinned enough for me to spot more gigantic flowers like the daisy protruding between the ferns. There was a lily I could have worn as a dress—and a decently modest one too. A tulip I might not have been able to wrap my arms all the way around. A begonia I could have used as an umbrella.

The head of the daisy turned toward me. Its petals bent to form a sort of mouth.

"Did no one ever tell you it's rude to stare?"

My jaw dropped. If I'd been staring before, my eyes must have been just about popping out of my head now.

The tulip curled its… lower lip? "My goodness, they don't teach the walking ones much in the way of manners these days, now do they?"

I managed to stammer out a few words. "I—um—I didn't—"

The lily ruffled its petals and said in a matronly voice, "Now, dear, we'll never understand each other like that. If you have something to say, do get on with it."

My legs wobbled under me. I stiffened them to hold myself steady. "I've never met flowers that could talk before," I said. Had I hit my head somewhere in that fall? Or before? Everything since I'd touched the mirror might be a bizarre hallucination. None of this could be real… could it?

"Well, it isn't as if it's all that strange," the daisy said, sounding offended. "Why shouldn't we talk? You can."

"Never thinking about anyone but themselves," the tulip murmured, with a disapproving shake.

I pressed the heel of my hand to my forehead, but the pressure felt completely real. Pinching my arm only made me wince. No, wait, that was for dreaming, not hallucinating. How did you wake yourself up from a hallucination? Could you?

I couldn't think of anything I'd ever read about that. But the longer I spent talking with giant flowers, the more my head was spinning. I could at least move the hallucination along.

"Are there other people like me around here?" I asked. "The 'walking ones'?"

"Oh, I suppose we aren't good enough company, then?" the daisy said with a sniff.

"What did I tell you?" the tulip put in.

"You look rather out of sorts," the lily said. "Perhaps it would be better if you put down roots for a little while."

Not here. I sidestepped farther along the path. "I think I'll go have a look for myself. It was very nice to meet you. Uh, goodbye!"

Then I swiveled on my heel and hurried away. The flowers' voices carried after me, one or another remarking about how polite I'd managed to be when I was leaving. I tapped my ears as if they might be the problem, but I could still hear them.

The path opened up to a wider road cobbled with red and blue stones. Trees lined the road, their leaves so vibrant green—this one lime, that one more of a mint—that I had to blink as if a bright light had flashed into my eyes. I looked down the road to my right, saw nothing but more road and more trees, and then turned in the other direction.

A figure was standing there, several paces down the road: a man in a deep violet suit with a matching top hat. The shirt underneath the jacket was white, but his tie gleamed a rich olive green. The outfit should have looked ridiculous, but somehow it fit him perfectly, from his broad shoulders down his otherwise lean frame.

He was poised as if he'd stopped in mid-step to stare at me like I was staring at just about everything. As I took him in, he recovered himself. He strode forward with a swift grace that I wouldn't have expected from his top-heavy physique. His eyes stayed fixed on me.

I crossed my arms over my chest, abruptly self-conscious. I hadn't bothered with a bra for puttering around the house when I didn't have much to hold up anyway, and my wet tank top was clinging to the unimpressive curves I did have. If I'd known I was going to be conversing with flowers and dudes who shared their fashion sense with Willy Wonka, I'd have picked my clothes a little more carefully.

I didn't have anywhere else to go, though, and this guy didn't look threatening, just intense. So I stood and waited until he came to a stop a couple steps away. Spiky tufts of dark blond hair poked from beneath his hat, and he had at least a couple days' scruff on his narrow jaw. His eyes, still studying me, were nearly the same rich shade of green as his tie. I'd never seen any depiction of Willy Wonka I thought was hot. This guy was definitely several steps up, weird clothes or not.

"It looks as though you got yourself rather drenched," he said in a light tenor that had a little bite to it. His lips formed a thin smile that didn't quite reach his eyes. I got the feeling he wasn't all that happy to see me.

"I, um—there was a pond—" I waved vaguely in the direction of the water. Okay, Lyssa, time to get a grip and find your tongue. "I don't know what I'm doing here. I'm not really sure where here *is*. So, any help in that department would be hugely appreciated."

"How exactly did you come to be here, then?" the guy asked.

Good question. "Ah, there was this mirror, and I touched it, and I… fell into it somehow." I peered at him, gauging his reaction, but really, how insane could that explanation sound to someone who lived in a world with giant talking flowers? He was either used to craziness, or he was part of my crazy hallucination.

"Hmm." The man adjusted his hat, his own gaze searching. I couldn't tell what for. Then he held out his hand with the same tight smile. "I'm Hatter. Pleased to make your acquaintance."

Interesting name, but I couldn't say it didn't fit. I gave his hand a quick shake, hoping mine was dry enough. "Lyssa."

"Lyssa," he repeated. Something about the way he rolled the two syllables over his tongue, as if tasting them, sent a giddy shiver through me. He spun away from me in one smooth movement, motioning for me to follow him at the same time. "Why don't you come to the city, and I'll see what I can do with you. You never know who else you might run into wandering around out here."

I wasn't sure running into *him* was the best luck ever, but at least he sounded like he was trying to help. I hurried after him, swiping my damp hair away from my face. "Thank you. I didn't mean—if you were on your way somewhere else—"

"Just taking a stroll," he said. "I'd have ended up heading back this way anyway."

We passed more trees with their radiant leaves. Buildings came into view up ahead, some short and stumpy and others stretching several stories high, all of them a little odd. One had only windows on its first floor and what looked like a front door up on the third, doorstep and all. A bungalow there appeared to have been flipped right upside down. Another, taller structure shot up narrowly toward the sky with a bulge around its middle where one floor jutted out twice as wide. Farther in the distance, a silver spire of a tower glittered with the sunlight.

The closer buildings were all painted in hues just as vibrant as the trees and the road and Hatter's clothes: this one mauve and robin's egg blue, that one crimson and daffodil yellow. Just looking at them made me feel dizzy.

"People really like their bright colors here, huh?" I said when I couldn't keep my mouth shut any longer. In my pale peach top and gray pants, I stood out like a sore thumb. A very drab sore thumb.

"It keeps us entertained," Hatter said in an inscrutable tone.

Some of the other people that "us" must have referred to ambled past us as the road veered into the city. A lot of them looked normal other than their flashy clothes, though no one else I saw wore the full suit-and-hat ensemble my companion had opted for. And some…

My legs locked at the sight of a figure with a man's body and a frog's head, topped by a little wool cap. And there, a couple storefronts beyond him, was a sheep in a lavender sundress walking on its hind legs, a purse slung over its shoulder. My mouth opened and closed and opened—and Hatter tugged me off to the side by my elbow.

"This way," he said, the bite in his voice more obvious. I yanked my gaze away from the strange figures and followed him through the doorway of a shop that gleamed orange and turquoise, but at least had the doors and windows approximately where I'd have expected them to be.

Hallucination, I reminded myself. Or else this place was simply crazy. Frog-dudes and walking sheep weren't any weirder than me having a conversation with a daisy.

The building we'd come into was a shop. Hats of all colors and shapes perched on display ledges and counters around the room. Hatter's place of business, I guessed? He led me past all that to a door at the back, where a flight of stairs led us up to an apartment.

Maybe I should have been a little more worried about going into some stranger's home, but I felt a whole lot safer in here than I did out there with the animal-people. Especially when we stepped into the open-concept living-dining room, and I could breathe again.

The wooden furniture was painted in a variety of colors but faded with time so the cacophony wasn't anywhere near as stark as outside. The walls were a tame beige. Hatter motioned for me to sit at the little dining table, which had four seats around it: a bar stool, a beach chair, a beanbag cushion, and a velvet wingchair.

"Let me get you something to dry yourself off with," he said, "and then we can determine what to do with you."

CHAPTER THREE

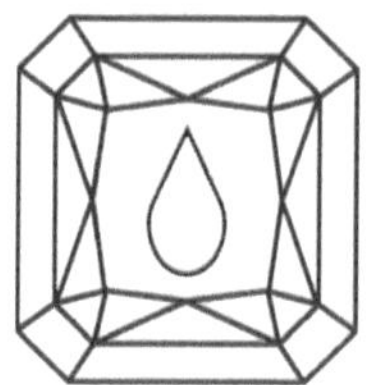

Hatter

I wasn't in the habit of giving a tremendous amount of thought to my supply of towels. The stack of them in the cupboard next to the bathroom came in a rather large number of sizes, colors, and patterns. For a few seconds I stared at them in something of a daze, as if one of them might be particularly more suited than the others for the task of drying off a recent arrival from the Otherland. Shaking myself, I grabbed the polka-dotted one on the top.

After a moment's hesitation, the young woman—Lyssa; of course, almost the same but not quite—had picked the beach chair to sit down on. When I came back to the main room, she was running her fingers through the damp strands of her hair, such a pale blonde it was almost ivory. Her head jerked up at the sound of my footsteps. I could see hints of resemblance in the soft curve of her cheeks, the straight slant of her nose, but only when I looked closely.

Hearts take me, I had to keep my hat on straight. I'd been picturing this scenario—or one like it, in any case—for so many years I'd lost track. I didn't take strolls past the Pond of Tears Lane for no reason. So why did nothing I'd ever imagined saying feel remotely appropriate?

She was too fucking real. Too real, and too unaware of what she'd stumbled into. How could I be angry with her?

Even if I also was, unreasonably, a little.

"Here," I said briskly, handing her the towel.

She rubbed it over the flexible pants that hugged her slim legs and then wrapped it around her shoulders like a shawl. I schooled my gaze carefully above her neckline. I really shouldn't be affected by the sight of other parts her wet clothes had been hugging. No, letting my mind stray even one inch in that direction would be the most unwise thing of all.

"Are you all right?" I asked, as perhaps I should have back when she'd first mentioned her encounter with the pond.

"I guess," she said, staring around her with those wide blue eyes. "I mean, I still have no idea what's going on. This place is so crazy, but… it feels so *real* too. Are hallucinations supposed to last this long?"

Her stomach gurgled loud enough that I could hear. She clapped her hand over it, a delicate flush creeping over her cheeks. "I didn't eat breakfast. Maybe I fainted or something."

She was hungry. I could at least offer her a little hospitality. I grabbed a couple of teacups off the shelves and filled them from my pot which was always fresh and hot no matter how often anyone poured from it. Nifty bit of magic, that.

"Cream or sugar?" I asked, setting the cup in front of her.

She eyed the clear brown liquid as if it might be more salty pond water. "Um, a little of both, please."

I set the creamer and the sugar bowl on the table along with a plate with the scones I'd picked up from the bakery down the street this morning. Lyssa considered those with some wariness too, but when her stomach grumbled again, she lifted one and took a bite. Her eyes widened even more as she chewed.

"What flavor is *that*?" she said.

"Honey pineapple coriander," I said. "One of my favorites."

"Oh. Er. It's an interesting combination."

She did keep eating it, though. I dropped into the wing chair and tipped back my hat so I could study her with my eyes unshaded.

"First things first," I said. "This is not a hallucination. Wonderland is perfectly real, even if it seems strange to you."

Lyssa paused in mid-chew. "Wonderland?" she repeated.

I swept my arm to indicate everything in this building and the world beyond. "Wonderland. A wonderful place where all are welcome." Had I let a little too much sarcasm creep into that pitch? Lyssa mostly looked bewildered.

I took a sip of my tea—dark and sharp, exactly right—and leaned my elbows onto the table. "Most of your sort who visit arrive through dreams, but occasionally looking-glasses do the trick. Where was this mirror that you say you fell through?"

Lyssa swallowed the rest of her scone and licked the crumbs off her thumb. Very few weren't won over by honey pineapple coriander once they gave it a try. I might have been more satisfied by her reaction if the motion hadn't drawn my attention to her full lips.

Had it really been necessary for her to be quite this pretty? I couldn't see how.

"It was in my Aunt Alicia's house—well, really she's my grand-aunt," she said. "I was just looking around, and the reflection on the mirror turned all weird, and when I reached for it…" She made a whirling motion with her hands.

Grand-aunt. The years really had blurred together, hadn't they? "You were visiting this grand-aunt?" I said, keeping my voice even.

"No." Lyssa knit her brow. "She died, about a week ago. I hadn't seen her in a long time, though. For some reason I haven't figured out yet, she left her house to me."

She died. Lyssa said the words casually enough, but they hit me like a finger-jab to the gut. I opened my mouth and closed it again, momentarily lost for words.

"I'm sorry," I managed.

"Like I said, we weren't close. Just some good childhood memories. She's not around to explain why her mirror turned into some kind of portal." Lyssa paused. "If I can even get back. How do people who end up in this 'Wonderland' through a mirror head home? Do I go jump in the pond again?"

"No," I said. "There are other ways, I'm sure. There always are. I'm afraid I'm not the best person to advise you on that matter, though."

She hadn't meant to end up here. She knew nothing about any of us or our struggles. Nothing I could have been angry about was her fault.

Yet at the same time, her presence in this world would appear to certain parties as a threat. The longer she stayed in my home, the more likely I incriminated myself if those parties discovered her.

Two very good reasons to send her off from my life to those better equipped to handle her.

"Who *would* be a good person to 'advise' me?" Lyssa asked, snatching up another scone.

"I believe I know just the one." I pushed my chair back from the table, and right then Doria poked her head into the room. My back stiffened.

"Hey, we've got company!" Doria said, bounding into the room with a swish of her skirts and her long brown hair. She was wearing one of those tiered black gowns she'd become enamored with lately, with just enough dramatic ruffling and lacing to offset the lack of color to any outside observer's critical eye. She draped her arms across the back of my chair. "Who's your new friend, Pops?"

I forced a smile. She knew I hated that nickname. Which I supposed to a fourteen-year-old meant all the more reason to use it.

"My new friend is just about to leave," I said, standing up. I slipped my hand under Doria's elbow and guided her back toward the hallway. "And I don't think you're quite finished upstairs." She normally slept later than this, or I wouldn't have brought Lyssa here at all.

Doria had enough sense to lower her voice, but not enough to stop her from asking, "What's the big deal? You can't blame me for being curious. She's an Otherlander, isn't she?"

"She is," I said, stopping by the doorway. "And more trouble than you need on your plate."

Doria rolled her eyes. "I think I can handle a Dreamer. I've talked to one before, you know. They're kind of hilarious. Why should you get to have all the fun?"

"Because I'm not having fun, and she's about to leave. Can you trust me on this one thing?"

I held her gaze for a long moment. Doria pouted, but she also sighed in resignation. "If it means that much to you, Pops."

She raised her hand to give Lyssa a little wave goodbye, and the frilly sleeve of her dress slipped down from her wrist to reveal a shape inked on her pale skin. A small black spade.

My heart lurched. I snatched her arm and turned it so her hand was palm up, the shape still exposed. "What in the lands is that? What were you *thinking*?"

"Geez, Dad, calm down. It's pen. It'll wash right off. Watch." She popped her finger into her mouth and rubbed it against the skin. The ink blurred, turning into a faded smear. A breath rushed out of me.

"Happy now?" Doria said archly.

"A little more than before," I muttered. "Don't you *dare* leave the apartment with anything like that on you, all right? Why don't you go upstairs and wash it all the way off, and by the time you're done, this lady and I will be finished here."

Doria grimaced at me, but she ducked her head in acquiescence. I gave her hair a ruffle that I knew she'd hate about as much as I hated her calling me "Pops." It was a fair trade.

"Thank you, Mouse," I said.

She replied with a light punch to my shoulder that was as close as she got to hugging me these days and scampered back upstairs.

When I turned back around, Lyssa shook herself out of a stare. "So, ah, that was your…?"

"Daughter," I said, and immediately saw the gears spinning in her head. I spent enough time in front of mirrors in the shop below to know I didn't look all that old by Otherworld standards. Even if that wasn't an accurate representation of my age, I might as well save her wondering. "Adoptive daughter, technically speaking. She was orphaned when she was two."

Doria had held on to her early memories for a few years after that, but these days, I was the only parent she'd ever known other than the stories I'd told her.

"Oh." Lyssa rubbed her face. Her hair was starting to dry, the strands of it falling around her face fine as thistledown. "I'm sorry. I'm still finding all of this very confusing. This is a place called Wonderland. Sometimes regular people come here when they're dreaming? And for some reason this mirror in Aunt Alicia's house—"

She looked so lost that my throat constricted. The floor creaked over my head as Doria paced in her bedroom. I had to handle this quickly, in a way that was best for everyone.

"Look," I said, cutting Lyssa off. "All that really matters is that you'd like to get home, isn't that right? I think I know someone who can arrange that. We can get it sorted out right now. Then you can return to your life and forget all about this wondrous place."

If past examples were anything to go by, forgetting us wasn't hard at all.

"Okay," Lyssa said. She took another gulp of her tea and stood up. "Home. That sounds good."

"Come on then, looking-glass girl."

I led her back downstairs and through the shop. The thought of her reactions when we'd entered the city made me hesitate.

"Try not to stare too much at anything—or anyone," I said. "Act like you think you're dreaming, and this is all par for the course."

"Like I'm dreaming," she repeated. "I'm still not totally sure I'm not."

Hopefully no one else would realize she wasn't either.

We headed down the street and around the corner to the park. It was only mid-morning, but a couple of guys in neon panda suits were dancing around and chugging glitzbeer by the gate. A few actual pandas in neon overalls were sprawled on their backs on the grass, soaking in the sun and puffing cigars. A couple wearing very little at all ran their hands over each other's bodies beneath the meager shade of a sapling.

A group of sprightly old women dashed by, shrieking with laughter as they tried to catch the gray-haired gal in the lead to mash her face with a coconut cream pie. I tipped my hat to them and managed not to wince when they tackled their target.

It was hard to blame Lyssa for wanting to go home as quickly as she could. These days, this place was a little much even for me.

"I don't have a direct connection to the guy who's most likely to know your fastest route home," I said. "But I'm acquainted with someone who does. Chess is… a little odd."

Lyssa raised her eyebrows at me.

"Even by our standards," I added. "But he's a decent fellow. You'll be in good hands. Just don't take anything he says too seriously. Around this time of day, I'd expect to find him… here."

We came to a stop at the edge of a vast game board of red and white squares painted on the neatly trimmed grass. A man with an owl's head was shoving his red bishop, which was about the height of his waist, into place with his feathered arms. We were standing by the white king and queen. The other white pieces were scattered across the playing field, but there was no sign of Chess. Which didn't mean he wasn't around, of course.

Lyssa eyed the game. "Is this why he's called Chess?" she said. "Because he loves playing it?"

I shook my head. "Just a coincidence. It's short for Cheshire." I craned my neck to scan the distant hedges, and a lilting voice spoke just behind me.

"And where are you trying to get to today, Hatter?"

CHAPTER FOUR

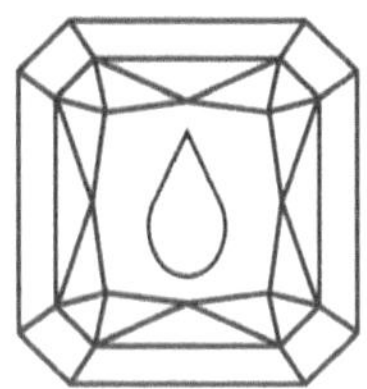

Lyssa

I spun around, expecting to see the guy who'd spoken to Hatter standing right there. The stretch of lawn behind us was empty. What the hell?

Then the sun caught with a flash on teeth in the curve of a wide grin. A wide grin that was floating in the air a few feet away from me, not attached to anyone at all.

I blinked in a double-take, and the rest of the guy shimmered into being around his grin. The broad smirk didn't falter for a second. I clapped my hand over my mouth to hold in a yelp of surprise.

"Chess," Hatter chided. "I know *you* think that trick is funny, but it gives everyone else a heart attack."

"Nothing they won't recover from," the guy who was apparently Chess said with a careless shrug. He turned his grin on me. "My deepest apologies, lovely."

He didn't sound the tiniest bit apologetic. His rumpled auburn hair slanted across his head as careless as his shrug had been, and his light blue eyes glinted with mischief. The shape of them and his prominent high cheekbones gave him a feline look, which was only compounded when his grin stretched a little wider and I noticed the sharp points on a few of his teeth. The dude had *fangs*.

Well, Hatter had said Chess was odd, and coming from someone like Hatter, that meant really fucking strange. He'd also said I could trust this guy to help me get home. So, I guessed what I did next depended on how much I trusted Hatter.

Hatter lifted his hat just long enough to rake his fingers back through the dark blond tufts of his hair. "This is Lyssa," he said in a low voice as he set the hat back down. His gaze fixed on Chess as unwaveringly as it had on me when we'd first met. "She's an Otherlander but not a Dreamer. She came through a looking-glass. I thought your man in the Tower might have some idea how to get her back home. Which is where she'd like to be, ASAP."

"From a looking-glass," Chess said, giving me another once-over. "You must have all kinds of stories."

"I'm not sure how many of them are all that interesting," I said. "Especially compared to what you must see all the time around here."

He chuckled. "To the mad, wouldn't sanity look like madness?"

"Chess," Hatter said. His jaw twitched.

Chess gave him a baleful look. "I'm on the job. Next time bring me something I get to keep, all right?" He flashed another grin and then tilted his head to me. "Let us make haste to the Tower, lovely."

"It's Lyssa," I said. I meant to walk in the direction he'd indicated, but my body balked.

Hatter tipped his hat to me. "Just think of getting away from all this actual madness to the comforts of home."

Good point. "Thank you," I said to him, and forced myself to set off next to Chess.

Chess crossed the park with a languidly muscular prowl. He pointed to the gleaming silver spire I'd noticed earlier. "That's our destination. I hope you're not afraid of heights."

"As long as I'm inside that thing and not clinging to the outside, I think I'll be fine," I muttered.

Another short laugh spilled from Chess's lips. He gave me a smile that looked a little less wild and a little more genuine because of that.

"I believe we're going to get along. What do you think of your jaunt through Wonderland?"

Oh, God, how to answer that? My gaze swept over the park. All the vegetation here was as vividly colored as the flowers and trees I'd seen when I first stumbled out of the pond. Over by the hedge, a woman with a golden retriever's head in a sun hat was tossing a stick for a little dachshund that giggled like a baby. A giant turtle and two girls in dresses that looked like they were made out of pieces of disco ball stitched together were splashing around in the marble fountain, the water painting their skin in a rainbow of colors. Beyond them, a few figures sprawled in a ring, two of them kissing, another bobbing her head up and down over the one guy's— Okay, looking the other way now.

Up ahead loomed even more of those off-kilter buildings. Maybe I shouldn't have made that joke about the outside of the Tower. For all I knew, the front door was thirty stories up.

"It's, um…" I bit my lip. "A little overwhelming. But also, I guess, kind of amazing. I mean, I've definitely never seen anything like this before."

"And you haven't seen everything yet," Chess said. "It's nighttime when Wonderland *really* comes to life."

I wasn't sure this place could be more lively without suffering from a coronary. It could be these people would all die of boredom back in the real world—the Otherworld, as Hatter had called it.

That thought reminded me of Melody's comment about how I needed to go wild. I sucked the rich scents of the grass and the flowering bushes into my lungs and tried to "loosen up."

Was this place actually real? Was I hallucinating? You couldn't really trust your hallucination to be upfront with you on that subject, right? But either way, what I'd said was true. This place was so bizarre it took my breath away, and that didn't have to be a bad thing.

There was no Brian here, no Mom, no Cameron, no anybody who knew who I was. When in Rome, do as the Romans do—and what the Wonderlanders seemed to do best was whatever the hell they wanted without a care about who was watching.

"So, everyone acts like this all the time?" I said, jerking to a stop to stay out of the path of a couple of kangaroos in evening gowns who bounded out of an alley and across the road in front of them. "They just run wild?"

"Fantastic, isn't it?" Chess said. "What's the point in wonder if you can't revel in it? People have everything they need. All they have to worry about is what gets them off most right now, or the moment after that, or—"

"I get the point," I said, but a little thrill shot through me at the same time. I wasn't sure I'd *ever* only worried about what would make me feel good. My responsibilities and commitments had always been there looking over my shoulder.

They hadn't followed me here, though.

"Just be careful," Chess said with a waggle of his eyebrows. "Indulgence is a gateway drug. Once you get started, you may find you're as mad as the rest of us."

He dipped into a sudden bow, sweeping his arm toward a gleaming silver doorway. "Ladies first." Somehow I hadn't realized we were getting that close to the Tower.

I pushed open the first door, only to find a second door beyond it, and then a third … and suddenly I was stepping out into a narrow space about the size of the bathroom in my apartment, with more silver glinting all around and the ceiling so far above my head I couldn't make it out. Was I looking up the height of the entire Tower?

"Elevator," Chess said in a singsong voice. "Twenty-seventh floor. Cheshire coming calling with a guest."

There was a brief pause, and then an invisible force beneath my feet heaved me upward. I gasped. Chess, who was gliding along beside me, caught my arm to hold me steady.

"What the heck is this building even for?" I said. It didn't really look like somewhere you'd come to get yourself off—unless my companion had included getting off elevators in that statement.

"Oh, even a land of wonder requires a certain amount of management," Chess said, in that tone that made it hard to tell how serious he was being about any of this. He flicked his fingers toward an arched doorway we were soaring past. "Department of Balloon

Animals." Another. "The Committee for Midnight Snacks." Another. "The Flower-Painting Division. You get the picture."

"Yeah. Who are *we* going to see?"

"The twenty-seventh floor belongs to the Inventor. You could say he's our White Knight." Chess gave me one of those sly smiles. "Don't tell anyone I told you that. I'll deny everything."

"Right," I said. "I'll try not to spread the word to the many friends I've made here—all one of them." And I suspected Hatter would have backed away from calling me a 'friend.'

Chess could obviously figure out who I meant. "Hatter's good," he said. "Hatter knows, even if he likes to pretend he doesn't. Whether he cares, well, I'm not sure if even he could tell you for sure."

"You know, you have a confusing way of explaining things sometimes," I said.

Chess grinned wide enough to show off those pointy canines. "What a lovely thing to say, lovely."

The invisible elevator quivered to a stop. All four walls around me held a door, this one gold, that one silver, another bronze, and the last one iron. I glanced at Chess, but he just slung his hands in the pockets of his teal slacks. "They'll all get you to your destination. Is it really a choice when every option gives the same result?"

I didn't know how to answer that, but thankfully I didn't think he expected an answer. My hand reached instinctively for the bronze door. I grasped the handle and shoved it open.

My steps rang out on a polished white floor. Everything around me was white, from the walls to the desk at one end of the room and the sleek high tables near the other wall—the surfaces so glossy a vague impression of my reflection wavered on them. After the chaos of color I'd been wandering through since I arrived here, the starkness was a completely different shock to the senses. I felt dizzy all over again.

As I regained my bearings, I realized not quite everything in the room was white. The white shelves mounted on the wall near the high tables held bits of metal and wire and glass, as well as some contraptions that looked as if they'd been built out of similar bits. I stepped closer to investigate, and a door I hadn't even noticed, it blended so seamlessly into the wall, opened behind the desk.

The man who strode into the room was the kind of guy your gaze would snap to the second he entered any room, even if there were a hundred other people already in attendance. He stood taller than Chess, and if not as brawny, his frame had plenty of muscle under his collared white shirt and pale gray slacks. His penetrating eyes and his curly hair were the same shade of dark chestnut, the latter slicked back from his high forehead. The slight crook in his Roman nose only made his face even more compelling for its minor imperfection.

Most of all, though, what drew my eyes to him was the aura he carried with him in his stance, in the way he considered the room, as if he could have commanded anything around him to do his bidding and known it'd comply. This was a guy who got things done.

If this was Wonderland's version of a White Knight, they could sign me up for saving right now.

"It's good to see you, Chess," the guy said in a smooth baritone, his authoritative eyes settling on me. The sensation of receiving all the attention at his command momentarily stole my breath. "Who's your guest?"

"Allow me to present Lyssa of the Looking-Glass, my good knight," Chess said with a grand gesticulation of his arm in my direction. "Hatter found her and brought her to me to bring to you. She's looking for a way home."

Something shifted in the guy's expression at Chess's first words, so quick and subtle I couldn't read it before it vanished.

"Lyssa," he repeated, with a similar care to the way Hatter had tested out the name, as if both of them had thought they might find something deeper inside it. He stepped out from behind the desk and took my hand in one of his. His grasp was firm and warm and made my pulse flutter. "Let's set aside titles—call me Theo. I can understand why you'd be eager to return to the Otherland. I hope your experiences here haven't been too unnerving?"

"No," I said, drawing myself a little straighter with the urge to prove something about myself to him, even if I wasn't totally sure what. "I'm all right. It's been kind of an exciting adventure, really. I'd just like to know that I *can* get home."

"I'm sure we can arrange that." Theo glanced at Chess. "There hasn't been any trouble?"

Chess shook his head. "Hatter would have mentioned. Clear to us and opaque to them."

"Good." Theo rubbed his square jaw, which had a five o'clock shadow even though I was pretty sure it was still morning. Who knew what kind of time Wonderland operated on, anyway?

"There aren't many doorways to the Otherland left, and most are difficult to reach," Theo said. "But there is still one in the basement of the club for Caterpillar's use. Few will even know about it, so I doubt he keeps it all that tightly guarded these days." He squeezed my hand and dropped it. "We can see you home tonight."

CHAPTER FIVE

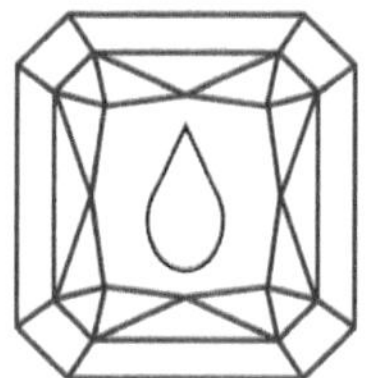

Lyssa

By night, Wonderland's city flaunted its bright colors in streaks of streetlamp light, shifting as some of those lamps bobbed or swayed. I wasn't sure I preferred the moving muting of the vivid hues over their vibrancy at full sunny blast.

As I walked down the street next to Chess, who was escorting me to the club and would be helping me get to my doorway home, I pictured the building layout Theo had shown me. My chest constricted with nerves. The hallways that made up the club's inner depths had veered up and down and around without any clear logic. Theo's instructions had included comments like, "Take the stairs up until you reach the bottom."

I was going to be on my own once I started down those halls. What if my Otherlander brain couldn't follow Wonderland architecture all the way to my goal?

How did the White Knight even know about this apparently secret doorway? I glanced over at Chess.

"Who *is* Theo, anyway?" I asked. "What does he do in that huge office when he's not helping out stranded Otherlanders?" He'd given the impression of being someone important, but it wasn't clear to me that authority had much of a place in this world.

"He does whatever he can, and some things he can't too," Chess said with his playfully enigmatic grin. "Dispensing advice. Constructing inventions. Planning plans. A figure highly respected by all who know him and many who don't."

Inventions—I had seen those contraptions on the shelves. Chess had called him "the Inventor" when he'd first told me about Theo. I might have pushed for more information, not that Chess was likely to give me a straight answer, but then he motioned to a building up ahead with one of his dramatic gestures.

"The Caterpillar's Club."

For a second I could only stare. A building shaped like a huge spinning top squatted over on a wide lot at the edge of town, as tall as the nearby three-story buildings and equally wide at its thickest. Beams of light in a rainbow of colors flashed from its outer walls.

It was also literally spinning.

Chess set his hands on his hips as he took in the whirling structure too. "It's the most popular establishment in the land. If you dance where no one can see you, do you even exist?"

A jangling song that sounded like a blend of funk and country filtered out into the night. Several locals walked past us right up to the building. With a flicker, they vanished from view. I caught my jaw before it went slack.

"Um. How do we get in?" If there was a door, the building was spinning too quickly for me to identify it, let alone have a chance in hell of stepping through it.

"You will get to where you want to go by going there," Chess said. "Assume there is a door. Decide to walk through it. And in you go! Shall we?"

He offered me his elbow. I slipped my hand around it, taking a little comfort in the solid bulk of his arm beneath my fingers. Chess might take some getting used to, but if I had to pick someone to have by my side, I was happy to go with the brawny dude with fangs. Not that I'd seen any reason to worry about my safety so far. Everyone seemed to be too busy enjoying themselves to bother hassling anyone else.

"Once you're inside, just act as if you belong there," Chess said in a softer voice that soothed some of my nerves. "You've got at least an hour. Relax. Enjoy yourself. Pretend it's all a dream, no worries, no consequences. Why not make the most of what Wonderland can offer while you're here?" He winked at me. "Just avoid the mushrooms is all I'll say. You'll need your sense of dimension on straight to find your way home."

"Got it," I said. "Thank you."

We ambled together toward the spinning building. My stomach started to tighten as we got closer to its blurring walls. The lights glanced off my eyes. I focused my gaze straight ahead, imagining an open doorway there. I'd fallen up into a pond and ridden on an invisible elevator. I could believe I could walk right through a wall.

My pulse stuttered, my feet almost stumbled, and Chess gave me a little nudge. With a popping in my ears, the building sucked us in. An instant later I was wobbling on a slanted dance floor, surrounded by revelers and lights and that twanging song. A crisp smell filled my nose, like dried herbs and pomegranate juice. Just breathing it in, a shiver of excitement raced over my skin.

Chess leaned close to murmur by my ear. "Have fun, lovely. You deserve it. I'll be back for you when the time is ripe."

I watched him disappear into the air with a tug of my heart. He had to scout out the club and make sure my way would be clear, but I missed his warm presence at my side instantly.

Have fun. Relax. Act like I belonged here. A rainbow of strobe lights that matched the flashing ones outside wavered through the dark room. The dancers undulated beneath them, the crowd seeming to rise and fall in time with the beat of the music. The first song I'd heard had faded into a thumping house beat with a screech of heavy metal guitars.

I was getting the feeling that *nothing* in this world was ever totally normal.

Even if screechy guitars weren't really my thing, the bass reverberated through my body. When was the last time I'd really danced? Melody dragged me out to clubs back home every now and then, but I always felt a little stiff going through the motions there, all those observers either finding me wanting or deciding they wanted something from me.

None of that mattered here. Nothing at all from my real life mattered here. I'd never see any of these people or their wacko Wonderland again.

A smile curled my lips. I followed the slant of the floor down into the crowd, letting gravity and the mass of bodies sweep me along.

I spun and swayed with my hands in the air. The music wove around me, urging me on. After a few minutes, I realized the crowd wasn't undulating—the floor did, rising and falling like waves all across the room. The frenetic drumming of the next song sent me whirling up over one shallow hill; the staccato rhythm of a violin brought me down into the dip on the other side.

All around me, the other dancers churned with total abandon, some of them flailing more than dancing, not looking as if they cared what anyone thought of that at all.

A rush of exhilaration shot up through me. I moved faster, weaving my limbs with the beat, letting out all the panic I'd felt arriving in this world, all the anger and hurt of Brian's betrayal, all the weight I'd been carrying.

I couldn't leave the weight of my responsibilities completely behind. I had plenty to still worry about in the real world. But right here, right now, I was no one but Lyssa Tenniel, a dancer in the crowd. The realization was so freeing that tears sprang to my eyes. I swiped them away and threw myself into the next song.

A few figures circulated through the throng wearing white shirts with a black graphic like the club symbol in a deck of playing cards emblazoned on the front. Clubs in a club? I laughed, watching one server hand out tall glasses of a pearly liquid, another extending a platter covered with slices of pink and purple mushroom.

Chess had told me to avoid those. I wasn't sure having one of the drinks was a good idea either. A guy near me knocked one back and let out a whoop so loud it split the music. A little of that pearly gleam washed over his eyes as he bounced on his feet. There was wild, and then there was right over the edge.

Speaking of wild… One of the dancing couples near me was going at it with tongues and hands all up in places I wasn't used to seeing exposed in public. Along the walls, other couples—and a few trios and quartets—were undulating against each other in movements that set off a flare of heat between my legs even as the voyeurism made my cheeks flush with embarrassment. Discretion obviously wasn't a common concept around here.

Toward the other end of the vast room, a bunch of the dancers were clambering into a human pyramid, somehow continuing to bob to the rhythm while they balanced on each other's shoulders. I swayed toward them with a laugh and found myself face to face with someone I knew.

Hatter wore the same violet suit and top hat as before, and he wasn't dancing, just drifting through the crowd with a stiff expression. When our eyes met, he stopped in his tracks. I grinned at him automatically, high on the feeling of freedom, and his mouth curved into a full-out frown for a second before he forced it flat again.

I sidled close enough for him to hear me. "What are you doing here?" I shouted over the music. He didn't look like *he* was enjoying himself.

"I should ask you the same thing," he said. "Decided to go local, did you?"

"This place is apparently my ticket home," I said. "At least I'm *trying* to blend in. Why'd you come to a club if you don't want to dance?"

"Because everyone comes," he muttered, low enough that I barely made out the words. Then he added, "I'm trying to keep an eye on Doria."

Oh. Yeah, it was easy to picture that girl with her flyaway hair and her goth-y dress cutting a rug in this place. And easy to imagine Hatter going all Mr. Protective on his daughter like he had when she'd interrupted us in his apartment. Though what he'd been protecting her from then I wasn't really sure. Maybe Otherland-ness was contagious?

Even if he was being a wet blanket, I didn't want to just wander off. Now that I'd met a whole lot more Wonderlanders, I could tell there was something different about Hatter. His presence didn't overwhelm me the way everything and everyone else here, including Chess and Theo, did. For a second, I didn't feel off-balance. Even though he was still hot in his scruffy be-suited way.

That must have been what gave me the courage to grab his arm. "Let's dance, then, and maybe we'll run into her," I said. "You can't know fewer moves than I do."

Something about that comment made his lips twitch in the other direction this time. Not quite a smile, but close—and a real one. "Oh, I do know a few," he said. He shifted his arm to clasp my hand. Raising it in the air, he spun me with a graceful flick of his wrist. My hair fanned out around me.

I didn't know how to top that, at least not by dancing. A glint of mischief lit inside me. I snatched the hat off his head by the brim, set it over my own hair, and shimmied away into the crowd.

"Hey!" Hatter protested, but he sounded at least as amused as he did annoyed. I'd count that as a win.

I moved with the beat, the basic shuffle and sway I'd been doing before, scooting just a little to the side when Hatter caught up with me, slipping this way and that as he followed. I didn't have to move too quickly, because he obviously didn't want to make a big scene out of his chase. His gaze tracked me, his eyebrows raised as if to say, *Really?*

I risked whirling around, and he caught me by the waist from behind. "I'll be taking that back," he said by my ear, lifting the hat from my head. His breath grazed my cheek, and the heat of his hand bled through my top. I resisted the urge to lean back into his body. I wasn't sure he wouldn't jerk away.

"If you've got no hat, do you stop being Hatter?" I asked instead.

"Only if I lose my shop as well, I suppose," he said. His fingers adjusted against my side, sparking a tingling that spread to my core, and suddenly I wanted more than anything for him to move that hand —upward or down, either would do. We'd fit right in, wouldn't we? A fresh blush flooded my cheeks just as he continued, "Your grand-aunt once asked me the same question, you know."

A cold smack of shock shattered every other emotion I'd been feeling. I whipped around to face him. "What?"

Hatter's expression shuttered. He gazed back at me blankly, like he was going to pretend he hadn't just said that. I grabbed the lapel of his jacket before he could consider retreating. "You talked to Aunt Alicia?" Something clicked in my head. He'd said I wasn't the first person who'd fallen into Wonderland through a mirror. If the one in her attic had worked as a doorway before… "She *came* here?"

"It was a long time ago," Hatter said, in a way that made me wonder just how old he was. He didn't look past thirty.

I'd thought he'd reacted a little oddly when I'd mentioned Aunt Alicia's death, but I'd assumed it was just the awkwardness of dealing with my potential grief. It hadn't been that at all. He'd known her.

I opened my mouth to demand more details, and the booming of a gong echoed through the room. The dancers jostled toward the bar that had just lit up by a distant wall. My pulse hiccupped.

This was the cue Chess had told me to wait for. The club delivered the night's special drink at a specific time, and while security was busy managing the line for a sample, they'd be more lax around the doorway I needed to get through.

Chess himself materialized beside me. I let my hand drop from Hatter's jacket. He shot me a look that might have been a little apologetic and said, "Safe travels." Then he let the crowd streaming past us carry him away.

"And he thinks he's already gotten where he'll never get," Chess said with a smirk. He held out his hand to me. "Now's our chance. Are you ready?"

CHAPTER SIX

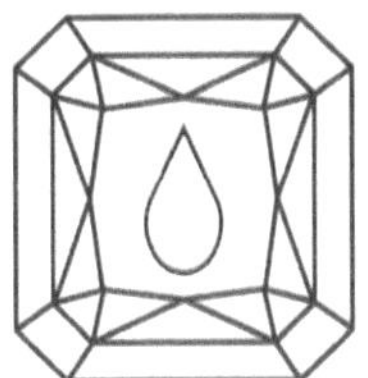

Chess

Lyssa looked so out-of-sorts that I had to wonder what in the lands Hatter had said to her. He could be provoking with people he didn't feel the need to hold his tongue around, but I wouldn't have thought our Otherlander had reached that point of familiarity yet. She accepted my hand, but her brow stayed knit.

"Did you ever talk to an Otherlander who came here the way I did, through a mirror—someone named Alicia?" she asked.

Was that one of the earlier girls? Had Hatter said something about that phenomenon? The name sounded familiar, but then, so had Lyssa's for the exact same reason, and I'd never spoken to her before.

I could certainly say with all honesty, "I have not, but I'm not always present wherever I am, so that says little about whether she's been here."

That answer appeared to satisfy Lyssa enough that shc let the subject go. She shook herself as if casting something off. "I guess this isn't a great time for twenty questions."

"We'll keep dancing," I said, stepping closer. "Pretend we've already drunk our fill, hmm?"

A poppy song with an underlying wail of wordless vocals swelled around us. I bobbed with the beat, pulling Lyssa a little closer and letting her ease away, then whirling us both around. The sparkle I'd seen when I'd caught glimpses of her dancing in the crowd came back into her bright blue eyes. A flush of exhilaration colored her pale cheeks.

Her clothes were far from spectacular compared to the other dancers, but lit up from the inside like that, she was striking in her own way. Maybe more so because she wasn't quite like any of the others, and their flashy fashion statements all blended together after a while.

It'd been a long time since I'd seen anyone in the club who appeared to be finding something they needed rather than trying to lose everything they could.

Of course, right now what Lyssa most needed was to find her way home. I kept a sliver of my attention on the door at the opposite end of the room from the bar, where a couple of Caterpillar's goons were still standing. There'd been four earlier, but two of them had gone over to keep order as everyone grabbed their nightly special. Bit by bit, never in a straight line and never quite facing them, we made our way toward that exit.

I switched hands, drawing Lyssa to me for a quick dip as we scooted over one of the rises on the rippled floor. Her hair swished past my face, a delicate scent like a spring breeze there and then gone. She wasn't the steadiest on her feet, but she followed my lead well enough. A little smile came over her face. She slipped under my elbow and spun out to the farthest length our arms would allow, as if daring me to bring her spiraling back to me. I did it with a grin.

"You dance better than you explain things," she told me, and I laughed. The spin back had brought her right in front of me, just an inch of space between us. I deliberately didn't close that gap, but I couldn't say I wasn't thinking about it. Hatter wouldn't have shown her that good a time. I could manage to leave an impression before she left Wonderland.

"You only say that because the explanations of how things are and how we'd like them to be are so seldom lined up," I said glibly, and sidestepped, turning us in a slow circle. Lyssa rolled her eyes, but her smile had widened.

It really was refreshing having a new face around here—a new face and a new personality that hadn't already been bent by the circumstances we all lived within. I had to say I rather regretted that she had to leave us, at least so soon. But keeping her here would have been purely selfish, especially when she'd have no idea what she was truly getting into.

No, selfishness wasn't my aim at all. I released any regret I felt about her departure with the fall of her hand from mine. Then, on an impulse to extend the moment just a few seconds longer, I snatched her fingers up again and pressed a quick kiss to her knuckles.

"It's been a pleasure meeting you, Lyssa. May the path you take lead you to where you're meant to be going."

The flush in her cheeks darkened. I took one last good look at her for my own collection of impressions before I swayed around and stumbled into the nearer of the guards by the door.

"Hey there," the boxy man said in a stiff voice, clapping his hand on my shoulder. "Keep your feet, friend."

"Are you my friend?" I asked, gazing back at him as if in a daze, amusement tickling in my belly. "Well, if you say you are, then you must be until you say you aren't again. Friend, I have something wonderful to show you!"

I clutched his forearm and made to drag him with me. "That's enough of that," the guard said gruffly. He didn't know I already had him.

He moved to detach my hand, and I tripped over my own feet in a spectacular explosion of limbs, so powerful I hauled him right over with me. We collapsed onto the ground, him face down and me sprawled across him.

Completely by accident, of course.

I thrashed in dramatic fashion as if trying desperately to recover myself and failing epically, sputtering a vapid line of apologies at the same time. The guard beneath me cursed and struggled. The second guard dashed over to haul me off of him. As he yanked on my wrists,

Lyssa grasped the doorknob and ducked through the exit I'd distracted them from.

In an instant, with a flash of her flaxen hair, she was through. I coughed and sputtered to cover the click of the door closing behind her. This whole escapade really was one of my finest performances. The goons hadn't had any idea how much that oddball Chess was capable of.

I staggered on my feet for good measure, since it wouldn't do for them to see me suddenly steady.

"Sorry, so sorry, every apology I could possibly mean and then make," I said, although I couldn't mean any. As long as they didn't know that, I could say it truthfully. Then I bounded off with a sway here and a wobble there to join the crowd that was flooding back across the dance floor. A more frenetic energy than before coursed between my fellow dancers, spurred by tonight's beverage of choice.

My gaze slid back to the door Lyssa had disappeared through. It remained closed, the guards stationed as they'd been before, no sign that they'd realized anything was amiss. A grin curled my lips.

My work here was done. Now I could party with everyone else like nothing in the world mattered.

I wove between the bodies across the dance floor, flickering in and out of visibility, sometimes flashing just my smile when someone stared. Eventually I made my way to the bar and grabbed one of the frothy red drinks that remained. I tipped it down my throat, and a jittery tingling rushed through my chest.

I spun around, not minding if I got dizzy. This was what the Caterpillar Club was for. Shed it all like so much loose fur, feel it wisp away. I didn't know how anyone survived otherwise. We all lost ourselves here.

Except Lyssa.

As I merged with the sea of dancers, I found myself wondering what exactly it was she'd found here. Whether it was anything worth finding, or only what we'd already discarded. Then I grabbed another drink and a slice of mushroom, chewing it until the room seemed to shrink around me, and the rest was a blur until that final inevitable fall of darkness.

I woke up on my back on the flattened grass, the thicket looming around me. It wasn't the most comfortable surface I'd ever slept on, nor the most appealing shelter, but I supposed I could have had a lot worse the day when everything got stuck. If you could look on the bright side or the dark, why in the lands would you choose to fall down into the depths?

A twinge shot through my side as I sat up. My heart skipped a beat. It couldn't be anything left over from times past—that was impossible. Sometimes I got odd aches and pains if I ended up turning over oddly in my sleep. But that spot, right between two of my lower ribs—it brought back too clearly the way the pain had seared through my flesh and my lungs had heaved and blood had dabbled the ivory tiles—

I jerked myself away from that memory and onto my feet. With some careful prodding, my hands opened a gap in the thicket so I could make my way out into the park.

Everything looked as it always did at this time in the morning. The red and white chess pieces were toppled and scattered across the painted board as if someone had given in to a temper tantrum last night over a loss. A torn strip of sapphire-blue silk drifted in the breeze where it had snagged on the low branch of one of the looping trees. The warble of chipper voices drifted from the patio tables by the gazebo, a lusty moan from near the fountain. Morning people.

Hmm. Not everything was quite the same. Hatter was striding across the lawn looking aghast. I couldn't remember him ever coming to call quite this early. He must not sleep as well as I did.

He came to a halt, breathing hard as if he'd run most of the way. The precarious angle of his hat—a bowler today, and the same persimmon hue as his suit—added proof to that impression.

"Why, Hatter," I said, "are you in an awful hurry to see me, or am I just seeing you in an awful hurry?"

He grimaced at me and made a brisk beckoning gesture. "Come on." Then he spun on his heel and started hustling back the way he'd come.

I kept pace, eyeing his angular profile, curiosity tickling up my spine. This was all rather bizarre. What excitement had Hatter somehow gotten himself into so early in the day? He certainly appeared very worked up about something. And that bright suit—from my observations, he always went more garish the more out-of-sorts he was feeling.

"I believe it's customary when requesting someone to attend to you that you give them the gist of where you are taking them and what for," I remarked.

"I'll show you everything when we get there," Hatter muttered. "We can't talk about it here unless you want us both losing our heads. Besides, it'll be clearer if you see."

After he turned onto the street, it soon became apparent that we were heading toward his shop and home. My gaze skimmed over the displays of hats as he hustled me through the main floor and up to his apartment. He lifted his hand toward the table without a word.

A teacup and a scattering of crumbs sat at the end where the beach chair squatted. I looked from them to Hatter, wondering if he'd already lost his head in the metaphorical sense.

"You brought me along to show me you've made a bit of a mess with your breakfast?"

"I haven't eaten yet," Hatter said. "That's— Yesterday, before I brought Lyssa to you, we came back here. She was hungry, so I gave her some tea and a couple of scones. I didn't bother to clean up because, well, I never do. You know how it is."

I did. No matter what we did, no matter what changes we tried to make to the world around us, no matter where we ended up, when the clocks reached midnight everything snapped back to exactly where it had been the minute past the midnight before. I could have gone to sleep amid the queen's rose bushes and still woken in the city park. Hatter could have smashed every dish he owned, and the next morning they'd all be back in the cupboards.

Except…

"That's her cup," he said, a little hoarsely. "Those are the crumbs she left. The things she touched—the things she changed—they *stayed*, Chess."

I studied the table for a long moment, wetting my lips. "Did that —the last time we had one through the looking-glass, did the same thing happen?"

Hatter's mouth tightened. "The last one was before the freeze."

"Ah." I rubbed my chin. My skin twitched with the urge to swish a tail I didn't have. A grin slowly stretched across my face. "This could change everything, you know."

"I know," Hatter said quietly. "If she comes back. If she doesn't, what does it matter?"

The image of Lyssa giving herself over to the music last night swam up in my memory. "I have the feeling she will," I said, "In the meantime, we'd better talk to the White Knight about this. Will you come along? It'll be better if he gets a firsthand account."

"I don't want to be roped into any schemes."

"The Spades aren't in the business of forcing compliance, Hatter," I said. "That's the other side's modus operandi."

He tipped his head. "I know. All right, I'll come. But let's make it quick."

CHAPTER SEVEN

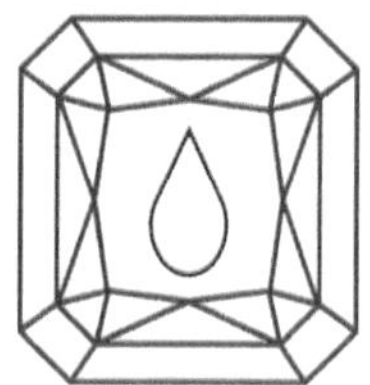

Lyssa

The second the door clicked shut between me and Chess in his tumble with the guards, the club's music cut out. I found myself in sudden dim silence with a hall stretching out seemingly endlessly on either side. The abrupt transition shocked me even more alert. The directions Theo had given me ran through my mind.

First right, until the hall splits. Back up into the side passage and then go forward.

Okay. I could do this. And I'd better do it fast, in case Chess hadn't managed to distract the guards enough.

I set off to the right. The dim light streamed down from some invisible source high above. My finger ran over my knuckles where Chess had pressed that brief kiss to the back of my hand. A gesture so sweet that I couldn't blame the speedy thump of my heart just on the perilous task ahead of me.

A few minutes before he'd turned up, I'd been getting all hot and bothered over Hatter. Well, they were both something to look at. And maybe I needed a fling with one hot guy or another to remind me that the break-up was Brian's loss, not mine.

My recent ex had definitely never set off sparks that electric in me. I'd been missing out, trying to make things work with him. Melody would enjoy getting to say, *I told you so*.

A thinner hall branched off to my left. I stopped. *Back up into it and then go forward.* There was nowhere to go on the other side.

But Theo had sounded sure, looking at the plans, and it wouldn't be the weirdest situation I'd encountered here.

I eased one foot backward and then the other until I'd stepped completely into the side hallway. The light fell differently across the opposite wall at this angle, revealing a sliver of a passageway just in front of me.

Go forward. All righty then.

I hurried across the main hall and into the narrow passage I'd just discovered. My shoulders brushed the chilly walls. A wordless whispering rose up with each graze of my skin. My pulse raced faster.

The floor slanted up and angled into a series of stairs, like Theo had said it would. They were so tiny I had to take two or three at a time. I leapt from one to the next, my breath getting short.

And then, all at once, they swung around, flinging me onto my hands and knees onto ground that felt like hard-packed dirt. When I looked behind me, the stairs I'd been climbing veered upward away from me as if I'd been hurrying down them all along.

I pushed myself onto my feet. The ceiling was so low that even at my not particularly impressive height, I had to hunch or my head would have bumped the ceiling. An earthy smell saturated the cool air. Theo had said someone he called "Rabbit" used the mirror I was searching for to pick up ingredients for the club's refreshments. I wasn't sure how literal that name was, but this tunnel sure could have passed for a rabbit hole.

Go left of the stairs until you're back where you began, then right, and you're there. If I'd managed the rest of this journey, I could handle that.

The light that had seeped down the stairs faded away as I ventured down the tunnel to the left. My fingers ran over the wall, jumping over bumps that I couldn't help thinking must be tree roots. Where the hell was I now? I wanted to say I couldn't possibly still be beneath the club building, but on the other hand, it wasn't even possible that the club building could have been spinning like a top, or that I could have walked into it by just deciding there was a door, so what did I know?

I slid my feet carefully over the floor, afraid I'd trip over something in the darkness. The tunnel split, the walls falling away on both sides. I turned left and followed that branch as it curved.

A faint glow came into sight up ahead, growing as I approached. The stairs. They looked like the same stairs, anyway, although I couldn't figure out how I could have gone in a complete circle when I hadn't encountered any other branches in the path. Maybe it was better not to question things here.

I was back where I'd begun, anyway. I was just about to pass the stairs and head down the other tunnel when a rustling sound reached my ears. A thin voice was muttering somewhere in the distance.

"Just a little more. Just a little more, he always says. It always is a little more, but never enough. And now I'm late again."

My stomach flipped over. I scrambled backward deeper into the passage where the darkness was thicker and flattened myself against the wall.

The rustling came louder. A stout figure with a rounded belly and a rabbit's head, his fur gleaming pure white, hustled out of the tunnel I'd meant to go down. I braced myself, but to my relief he dashed up the stairs instead of continuing toward me. I waited until the patter of his footsteps dwindled, and then I let out my breath.

If I'd gotten to this junction even half a minute earlier, I might have already been too far down the tunnel to avoid him. I'd have been caught.

What would the Caterpillar's people do to me if they found me wandering around in their sort-of basement? Theo hadn't mentioned that. Neither had Chess. The guards upstairs hadn't seemed all that threatening, but I didn't think I wanted to count on anyone's mercy.

I listened for a moment longer and then darted to the tunnel Rabbit had emerged from. It veered sharply and ended in an earthen hollow of a room, only slightly wider than the tunnel had been. A tall mirror like the one in Aunt Alicia's house, this one oval and framed with tarnished gold carved into the shape of roses, reflected the shadows.

I hesitated, just for a second. Theo had said a looking-glass doorway in Wonderland should take anyone traveling from here to wherever they intended to go, as long as they'd been to that place before. Rabbit wouldn't have been passing through to Aunt Alicia's house, but I should be able to.

Stepping toward the mirror, I pictured the little attic room—the messy shelves, the rocking chair, the toy chest. The railing of the wrought-iron staircase disappearing into the floor. The staleness in the air. With a deep inhale, I brought my hand to the glass surface.

My fingers slipped right through like it was a pool of water. The rest of my body was yanked after them as if compelled by some new form of gravity. I shot through a rush of cold as if I'd fallen back into that pond, and for a second I was afraid I had, that this mirror had tossed me right back to the start of my journey in Wonderland. Then I tumbled onto the floor in Aunt Alicia's attic.

I rolled over and pushed myself into a sitting position. Everything looked the same. Everything smelled the same. It wasn't even night here—morning sunlight was still beaming through the room's little window. The black kitten pranced across the floor and swatted at my pant leg.

A giggle spilled out of me. All I could do was hug my knees and laugh and laugh, as if I was releasing all the insanity I'd just been through.

Wow, that had been intense. In both good and bad ways.

The kitten chirped a mew. I scooped it up and cuddled it against my chest. "This was all your fault," I informed it. "If you hadn't gone scampering up here…"

But did I really wish that it hadn't?

No. I glanced back at the mirror. Scary, yes. Intense, yes. But that experience had also been the most exciting thing that had ever happened to me—even if it was already hard to believe it had really happened.

I wouldn't have traded it for anything. Well, almost anything.

And now I had questions that needed answers.

My cell phone reception wasn't the best out here in the country. Mom's voice crackled over the line, occasionally fading out completely.

"Are you sure you're comfortable staying there on your own? You could always hire someone to pack things up."

"I don't want to pack things up," I said. "Not yet, anyway. I'm still looking through everything." I skimmed my fingers over the spines on one of the library's shelves. The bookcases here were a lot tidier than the ones in the attic had been. Aunt Alicia's taste in literature—or, at least, that whoever in the family had built this collection—had been pretty diverse. The shelves held everything from Victorian poetry to modern philosophy, and novels spanning two hundred years.

"I just want to be sure you're okay. Losing your job like that, and Brian—I know it's got to be hard—"

"I'm fine, Mom," I said, gently but firmly. "You know, I'm not even upset about Brian anymore. It was shitty the way I found out he was a total asshole, but I realized I never felt like I could totally be myself around him. So it's a good thing that I get to move on. And I've already got a couple of job prospects to look into."

That wasn't strictly true, but sometimes I had to lie a little so Mom didn't spiral off into her worries. I'd had a job of some kind since I was fifteen, and I'd always been careful with my money. I'd find something before I was in any financial trouble. There wasn't any reason for her to worry about me, but sometimes I thought she'd gotten so in the habit of having to worry about Cameron that she couldn't remember how to turn that part of her brain off when it came to her other kid, despite my best efforts.

The part about Brian *was* true. My mind wandered to the memories of those clubs Melody had dragged me off to before. Maybe I should give them another chance. See if I could find some hot dude who got my motor going here in reality. It'd be nice just to see what it'd be like enjoying myself, having fun with someone, not jumping straight to focusing on what kind of future we might have.

More of Aunt Alicia's charcoal sketches hung on the walls between the bookcases. I stopped in front of a larger frame that held a vast Tenniel family tree. She must have gotten this done herself, or at least updated it. It showed eight generations of my father's family, all the way down to me and Cam in the bottom right corner.

"Why do you think Aunt Alicia never had us visit her out here?" I said, easing into the subject I'd really wanted to talk about. "When we were still seeing her, I mean. There's tons of room, and it isn't that far from the city."

"Oh, Alicia was always a little strange about certain things," Mom said. Her voice got a little terse, like it often did the rare times Aunt Alicia had been mentioned since their falling out. "I suggested it once, and she looked outright horrified by the idea. Said something about how it wasn't really suitable for children, old furniture and antiques and so on."

I frowned. "I haven't seen anything that looks *that* fragile." Not so much that she couldn't have trusted a nine-year-old and an eleven-year-old around it, I didn't think. Well, maybe my brother was a different story. He might have broken something just to get a reaction. But nine-year-old me had been almost as cautious and neat as I was now.

If her concerns had anything to do with the mirror upstairs, obviously she hadn't mentioned that to Mom.

"Like I said, she could be a little strange." Mom sighed. "Sometimes I got the impression that there were parts of your father's side of the family she wanted to keep private, just for herself. He wanted to name you after her, you know, and she was *adamant* that she didn't approve. He and I settled on 'Lyssa' to try to compromise, but I don't think she was completely happy even with that."

I paused as I approached the nook with the secretary desk at the back of the library. "You never told me that before."

"Well, it didn't seem important. I didn't want to give you a bad impression of her when she was doing so much to help out."

"Was that what your big argument was about?" I ventured. "Her keeping stuff to herself?"

"No, it was… It started over such a silly thing. There's no point in digging up that history now."

Mom always brushed off any questions about how they'd fallen out. I sat down at the desk. Unlike most of the furniture in the house, it was cedar. A sweet woody smell drifted off it as I sat down on the matching wheeled chair and tugged open one of the drawers down the side. It held scattered pens in a variety of color and a stack of linen notepaper.

Before I could push harder about the argument with Aunt Alicia, Mom veered into a subject she had a lot more practice talking about.

"Have you heard from your brother at all recently?"

My stomach twisted. "No. He usually only gets in touch if he's trying to get money out of me, and since he's catching on that I'm done with that, he doesn't try very often."

"I just worry… He said some very unkind things to me the last time I saw him. I think he might have started with the drugs again. And after that fight in the bar last month… If you do hear from him, will you let me know right away?"

I checked the second drawer and found it empty. What awful things had Cam shouted at Mom this time? Memories of some of his vicious rants from the past ran through my mind, and I restrained a wince. "You know that if you bail him out, it just gives him more chances to screw up, right? At a certain point, helping becomes enabling." A lesson it had taken me a while to learn myself.

"Don't be too hard on him, Lyssa. It's been difficult for him, growing up without a father…"

Cam had gotten a father for two years more of his life than I had. He'd been expressing how difficult that was in the most spiteful ways possible for almost two decades. Somehow I'd managed to work through my pain without hurting everyone around me as often as I could.

As I tried to figure out something else to say that wouldn't make Mom upset, I eased open the lid on the desk, and my gaze fell on a wooden box about as big as a hardcover book. One of those linen notepapers was taped to it, with a scrawl of handwriting that started with my name.

Lyssa,

You won't understand until you've been there. Then you'll be ready to take the key.

A.

I stared at the note and tried the box. The lid stuck fast. "I know, Mom," I said. "I promise I'll call you if I hear from him. I'd better let you go and get back to the sorting."

After I set down the phone, I tugged at the box's lid again. It was definitely locked. A brass fixture with a little keyhole gleamed on the front. The cherry-wood was smooth and plain other than a simple border around the top and a carving in the middle there, like the outline of a multifaceted gem with a teardrop at its center. Interesting design.

Aunt Alicia had left this for me—how long ago? The paper didn't look particularly aged. Maybe right before she'd gone into the hospital, knowing she didn't have much time left. But where was the key she'd mentioned?

I looked at the note again. *You won't understand until you've been there.* After my adventure this morning, my first thought was Wonderland. Had she known I'd end up there?

And if that was what she'd meant… was the key to open this box back there on the other side of the mirror?

CHAPTER EIGHT

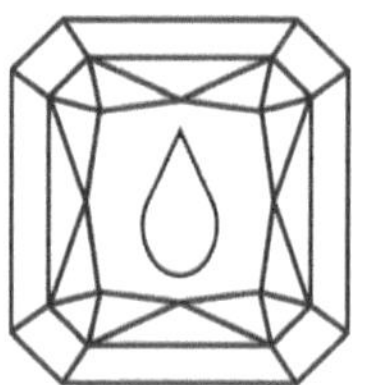

Lyssa

"So do you have the entire house catalogued and sorted into boxes already?" Melody asked. When I made a face at her, my best friend laughed. "Oh, come on. I know what you're like. You're happiest with a place for everything and everything in its place."

I speared a chunk of cantaloupe from my fruit salad. We'd met up for brunch at this quaint place in a small town about halfway between Aunt Alicia's house and the city. Red-and-white checkered curtains hung on either side of the front window, and the soft strains of a Patsy Cline song was piping from the speaker mounted in the corner. The smell of fresh-baked bread permeated the whole place.

It was mellow and cozy, the kind of atmosphere I usually would have sunk right into. So, why was I so on edge?

"I think it's pretty normal to feel more comfortable when things are in order," I said. "You can only be carefree until the moment you have to tear apart the house to find your electric bill or your power's going to go out."

"Hey, I'm not going to argue with you. You've definitely rubbed a few good habits off on me." Melody grinned. "I'm just saying there are levels of orderliness, and we know which end of the spectrum you're at."

"Fair. I have looked through everything now." Looking for that key, in case it was in the house after all, and for any other messages Aunt Alicia might have left behind. On both counts, I'd come up empty. "But I haven't moved much around. It just feels… right, the way she left it. Everything already has a place." I shifted in my chair, leaning back and then forward again. "How about you? Did you get started on the designs for next season?"

"Not yet." Melody sighed. "I want to do something really exciting and fresh, but it's hard continually pushing myself past what I've already done. And now that I've got the deal with that store… I think it's put this little voice in my head that's nagging me about whether *they'll* like the new line too."

"Of course they will," I said, waving my fork at her. "They love the stuff you've already done, and that's all totally you, and whatever you come up with next will be too. And if they don't love it, I'll go in there and tell them they're out of their minds."

My best friend shook her head, but she was smiling again. "I'd almost like them to turn it down just so I can see that happen." She paused, studying me as I fiddled with my napkin. Her forehead furrowed. "Is everything okay, Lyss? You seem a little agitated or something."

I groped for something to say and jabbed my fork into a sliver of pineapple. "I guess it's just weird, being in a new place, everything in my life so different all at once. I'm still settling in."

It wasn't just that, though. The flood of pineapple juice in my mouth brought back the mix of sweet and spice in Hatter's ridiculous honey coriander pineapple scones, which had also been somehow delicious. And more vibrant than the piece of fruit I was chewing right now.

Ever since I'd left the house, I couldn't stop noticing how much duller this world was compared to Wonderland. Every sensation was subdued. Every color was muted.

The slow pace of the everyday rhythms around me, the predictable patterns everyone around me was following—I should have been grateful to have them again. This was what reality was supposed to feel like.

All full of things I could label and stick into neat little boxes.

Maybe the reason I'd been able to let go in Wonderland was that it'd been so obvious I couldn't stick to my usual habits there. How could I let loose and go wild in reality when everywhere I looked, I was reminded of the rules I was meant to follow, the boundaries that defined what would be considered normal?

I couldn't tell Melody any of that. *Oh, I fell through a mirror and ended up in this wacky place where everyone acts crazy and only cares about having fun.* I hadn't even believed it myself until I'd been there for at least an hour. She'd laugh as if it were a joke and then take me to the mental hospital when she realized it wasn't.

That bizarre trip was the first major event in my life I hadn't told her about, and the lie by omission sat heavy in my gut.

"Are you sure that's all it is?" Melody said. "If you found something freaky—like, your grand-aunt's secret S&M playroom or something—you know you can tell me. I promise not to judge the dead."

I had to laugh at that. "No, I haven't been traumatized by any shocking sexual revelations." Just revelations of another sort. And not exactly traumatized. I stirred the last few berries on my plate. Even if Melody would never believe what I'd experienced yesterday, I could trust her to give me good advice. I just had to find the right way to ask for that advice without setting off warning bells that I was going 'round the bend.

"Mel, you've taken lots of chances other people might have thought were kind of crazy, but you've always made it work. How do you decide when to go for it and when it's really too risky?"

Melody's eyebrows shot up to her bangs. "Hmm. Sounds like there is a story here. What happened, Lyss? What have you gotten up to? Did you let loose a little after all?"

I rubbed my mouth, feeling awkward under her scrutiny when I couldn't really answer those questions. What was an easy story to give her?

"It's just a guy," I said. "One of the neighbors, a few properties over." *A quick step through a mirror, and you're there.* "I spent a little time with him, and it was… exciting. But I don't really know him. He was pretty off-the-wall—I never knew what he'd say or do. I'd kind of like to go see him again, but maybe it'd be stupid going over to hang out with this stranger—what if he turns out to be crazy in a dangerous way?"

"Already into the rebound!" Melody crowed with a gleam in her eyes. "Go, Lyssa. I knew you had it in you. You're really thinking about going over there for a booty call?"

"Something like that," I said. Ever since I'd fallen back out of the mirror, the urge had been gradually creeping over me to climb the wrought-iron stairs again, to dive back through into that startling world where for at least a little while I'd felt so free.

"Well, I do think it might be good for you." She tapped her lips with her spoon. "Did he do or say anything that made you nervous when you were talking to him before? Or are you just nervous now because of what you don't know?"

I thought back over my ramble through Wonderland. I'd been scared because I hadn't known where I was, and then disoriented because I'd been faced with so many strange things, but nothing there had hurt me. Even during my escape home, the guards in the club had been tame, and the more I remembered my close call with Rabbit, the more absurd my fears had seemed. He'd been, like, half a head shorter than me. I probably could have knocked him over and run for it if I'd needed to—if he'd even tried to stop me.

No, my worries had all been in my own head, not any outside menace. Like Mom's about me.

"I think it's just what I don't know," I said. "He was off-beat, but in a fun way, once I got on the same wavelength. If that makes sense."

Melody's grin could have rivaled Chess's. "I think you need to boink this guy. Maybe multiple times. You're always cautious about men, Lyss. If nothing he did gave even you bad vibes, I think you're good. Nothing ventured, nothing gained, right?"

"Right." A wave of relief swept over me. Suddenly I was grinning too. Some part of me had needed her permission to completely commit.

She motioned at me with her spoon. "I must also fulfill the gal code of mutual security. You text me when you're heading over there, and then text me when you get back. If I don't hear from you by twenty-four hours after that first text, I'll summon the National Guard. Deal?"

"Deal," I said, giving her a thumbs up. My full day in Wonderland had taken barely any time in the real world. I could make it back before she got worried no problem.

"Now tell me more about this guy," Melody said, leaning forward avidly. "I need a full body description."

Three different images popped into my head automatically: Hatter, Chess, and Theo. Well, they'd been a major part of my Wonderland experience, hadn't they? And all definitely appealing in their different ways. I could mix and match a little to satisfy my best friend's curiosity.

"He's got curly dark brown hair," I started, still smiling, "and intense green eyes, and this grin that's totally contagious..."

When I returned to the house, my nerves came back. I refilled the cats' food dish with kibble and topped up their water, even raised the toilet seat just in case I was gone for longer than expected. I pawed through the clothes I'd brought with me three times before settling on a casual teal halter dress that still wasn't anywhere near as flashy as usual Wonderland wear, but at least I'd blend in better, and the cotton should dry quickly after my swim in the pond.

My hand wavered over my make-up bag for a few seconds, but I didn't have anything waterproof. The three guys who'd been cycling through my thoughts for the last day and a half had all seen me bare-faced already. They didn't need to witness the raccoon-eyed version.

I walked out of the bedroom and walked back in a minute later. I wasn't sure if I could bring anything with me, but I could at least try. I tucked a cardigan and a change of clothes, plus deodorant and, after a brief debate, my toothbrush into a plastic bag that I knotted and then stuffed into a canvas tote I could carry over my shoulder.

Just in case. Just in case.

My nerves were still jumping. I bit my lip, wondering if I'd forgotten anything. I should probably have a snack before I left, to make sure I wasn't starving the second I made it to any of the guys. I'd probably looked like a pig grabbing two of Hatter's favorite scones yesterday. Should I bring some food *with* me? I couldn't think of anything I had in the house that would pack well.

Restless, I wandered through the house until I ended up in the library. I'd left the desk open, the box sitting where it'd been when I'd found it. The note said the exact same thing it had yesterday about having been "there" and the key.

It was simple. I'd hop into Wonderland and have a little more fun, prepared this time. I was almost certain now the key had to be there. Maybe one of the guys would know about it—it appeared at least Hatter had met Aunt Alicia whenever she'd gone through the mirror. I'd have to badger some more information about that encounter out of him too. Getting back home hadn't turned out to be hard at all, and I knew exactly how to do it now. If for one or two nights the situation at the club wasn't great for sneaking past the doors, no big deal. I was prepared for that too.

There really was nothing else to take care of. No reason not to go now. Other than my own mundane hang-ups.

I had to do this. I needed to know what Aunt Alicia had left for me in that box—I needed to understand why she'd left this place to me with that mirror for me to find.

Melody had been right. It was time Lyssa Tenniel went a little wild.

I raised my chin and headed down the hall to the spiral staircase. In the attic, the mirror drew my gaze immediately, as if tugging me to it. I paused just long enough to text Melody like I'd promised.

Off on my thrilling adventure. Wish me luck!

You've got this, girl! she wrote back a moment later.

I set the phone on top of the toy chest, slung the tote bag over my shoulder, and walked right up to the mirror. The reflection hazed, my image wisping away. My hand rose to touch the glass. The chill gripped me—and yanked me through so fast I lost my breath.

Wonderland, here I came.

CHAPTER NINE

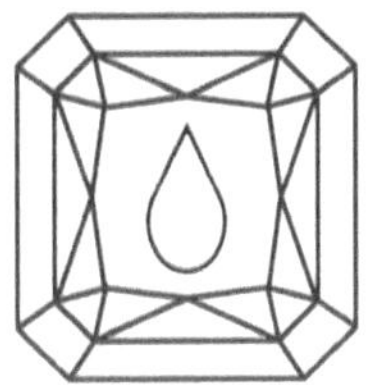

Theo

Over the years I'd determined the exact line around the palace grounds where the smell of roses would become too overwhelming and my lungs would clench, my mind start to fog. One benefit of an unchanging world: I never had to fear that this day the wind might shift in a new direction or that more flowers would have bloomed on the bushes to spill their fragrance into the air.

The Queen's tyranny did come with small blessings.

I adjusted my position on the tree branch I'd propped myself on, right at the edge of safety, tracking the movements of a few of the courtiers as they meandered through the gardens. The heart-shaped diamond brooches they all wore on their dapper suits and elaborate gowns glinted brighter in the sunlight than any other jewelry they wore. To fail to polish one's brooch enough was to risk being accused of treason.

The Queen's tyranny also came with plenty of downsides.

The device I held, like an elongated trumpet with its mouthpiece at my ear and its bell pointed at the gardens, swiveled as I tweaked its levers. The bell twitched toward the courtiers. I'd also long since perfected this particular invention. I could hear the strolling party's conversation through the hedges, over the high brick wall, and across the field and the sparse strip of forest between that wall and me, as clearly as if I were perched in the tree right above them.

"Wasn't that luncheon delightful?" one of the men was saying. "I swear, the Queen truly does have the most excellent taste."

"Oh, indeed," the woman next to him gushed. "I could have eaten that ham for *hours*."

Whether the meal had truly been all that exceptional was up for question. The speakers would be perfectly aware of the guards posted here and there around the grounds. *Come on now*, I thought at them. *Talk about something a little more important.*

"I expect the festivities tonight should be exquisite," a second woman said, fanning herself. "Tonight's musicians are among my favorites."

"Perhaps we could have a dance then," the man said, and the woman dipped her fan over her face with a coy giggle.

They didn't seem conscious of anything amiss. I scanned the grounds from my vantage point. The low hill this tree stood on the crest of gave me a decent view over this half of the palace grounds, but only half. On the other side of the sprawling scarlet fortress of minarets and domes lay the Glittering Lake and the woods for hunts. But most of the conversation happened on this side.

There. A couple of guards in their pleated red-and-pink uniforms had drifted together near one of the grounds' inner gates. I swiveled my listening horn until the bell faced them.

"No trouble so far today."

"None here either. We've no reason to expect any, do we? No sign of the Spades in some time."

"Oh, I'm sure they'll stir up more treachery. And just as sure we'll crush it. I expect they're still licking their wounds from the last time."

"May another day pass in peace, then."

"Thank the Hearts for it."

"Yes, thank the Hearts."

They ambled apart again. My mouth tensed as I pushed myself upright.

I supposed this status quo would look like peace to them. That was how they slept, wasn't it? Telling themselves no one would ever be hurt if we'd all just play our parts and stay in our places. Blaming violence on those who hadn't learned all the rules or chose to ignore them. Everything would be perfectly peaceful if all Wonderland's people could turn off all but their simplest desires.

Of course, an awful lot of its people had learned to do just that. I might find the royal approach horrifying, but I couldn't deny its efficacy. Not when I needed to see it fully and clearly if I were going to overthrow it.

There was still no conversation about any odd changes. No speculation about a girl who might have tumbled through a looking-glass into this world—or out of it. Hatter and Chess had done well enough by Lyssa. No one had noticed her passing through.

This time.

The Otherland's looking-glass, the one she'd have fallen through, seemed to have an irresistible draw. The earlier girls who'd come were before my time, but I'd heard about them, and they'd returned enough times to make an impression. Never enough of a difference to turn the tide, but the situation wasn't exactly the same this time. This time I *was* here, and I had my plans.

I folded up my hearing trumpet and tucked it into my satchel. My descent from the tree was perhaps not the most graceful ever. The thump of my feet sounded loud in the sparse forest. I'd only taken a few steps back toward the city when a distant rustling told me the sound hadn't gone unnoticed. Just my luck that some guard would have decided to be overly ambitious in his patrols today. The people still could chance their motions from day to day.

I strode on between the trees as if I hadn't noticed the pursuit. As if I had no reason to think anyone would take any issue with my stroll through the woods. Which, indeed, I didn't. These weren't royal grounds. They were open to anyone in Wonderland.

"Halt, please!" a voice called out. I stopped and turned with eyebrows raised in puzzlement.

The guard who hustled over to me stood at least a few inches shorter than me in his uniform. The stripes of red and pink followed the tunic's pleats, with a crimson heart shape embroidered on one of the pink strips, as if it weren't already clear enough which part of the land this figure belonged to. He was a young one—not much older than Hatter's daughter, I judged, relaxing a little more. Too young to cause much worry.

"Oh," he said when he reached me, his eyes going a bit round as he took in my own uniform-of-sorts. In a land so addicted to vivid color, white and gray made a bold statement of its own. "Inventor. I didn't realize it was you." He paused. "What are you doing out here?"

"Just taking a survey of the forest," I said in the authoritative tone that came as naturally as breathing. "For a new plan of mine. I thought perhaps a change in scenery would bring extra pleasure to the Clubber crowd. A dance festival out in the open air for a night or two, just to liven things up."

"That does sound nice," the boy said, with the awkwardness of one who'd never been to Caterpillar's Club or possibly even talked much with any of Wonderland's ordinary folk. He'd know that keeping them entertained and distracted was of high priority, though.

"I've seen all I need to," I added, letting just the slightest note of dismissal enter my voice. "I was on my way back to the Tower to work out the rest of the plan there."

"Yes, of course." The guard made a nervous gesture for me to continue on my way.

He was young but ambitious. I supposed that was why he'd ventured so far from the walls around the palace in the first place. After a minute, I heard the rattle of a pebble dislodged by one of his feet and knew he was following me.

The royal court respected me as Inventor. I'd proven my skills in keeping the city's people content and occupied. But those with power were always suspicious of others with power. The Knave had come sniffing around the Tower more often in the last few years. He couldn't tie me to the Spades, but he'd clearly have liked to.

It would take more than a fledgling sentry to topple what I'd built, though. Ambitious or not, the training of the guards remained the same, and their usual habits always seeped through. I had little trouble losing my follower with an abrupt detour through the city park and a pass through the cake shop.

The twins were standing outside the fondue bistro, which meant they had news. I shifted my satchel from one shoulder to the other as I passed. Just a few minutes after the elevator whisked me up to my floor of the silver tower, they arrived in my office. Both were smiling.

In this stark setting, the twins managed to look even more garish than most of their fellow Wonderlanders did. Though identical from the bright red hair that scattered their heads to their boyishly round cheeks, they took a strange enjoyment out of dressing as reverse reflections of each other. Today their stout frames were clothed in overalls—scarlet for Dee and moss-green for Dum—and ruffled shirts—moss-green for Dee and scarlet for Dum—with sneakers matching their respective shirts and jaunty scarfs matching their overalls.

"She came," Dee said. "Just like you figured she would."

"About an hour ago," Dum added. "She went to Hatter's. We were waiting for you."

"Good," I said with a smile of my own. Lyssa hadn't taken long to make the return trip at all. Which meant I'd better get to work. "Thank you for keeping an eye on the Pond of Tears and for informing me immediately. Dee, would you ask Chess to bring her around? She knows him now." The less additional strangeness we exposed her to while she was making her decisions about us, the better.

"On it," Dee said with an eager salute. He set off in the elevator, and I motioned Dum over to my worktables.

"There are some materials I'd like to try," I said, retrieving a list from one of the shallow drawers. "It's too late in the day for me to make much use of them, but you can determine where they're most easily and discretely procured and bring them around first thing in the morning."

Dum scanned the list with a quick glance I knew would commit the contents to his memory. "For the big effort?" he said.

"Yes. I'm hoping we may have our chance to go forward with it soon."

A pleased gleam lit in his hazel eyes, but it dulled a moment later. I knew a shadow of doubt when I saw one.

"What is it?" I asked. "You know you can bring any concerns you have to me."

"Of course, White Knight. You always guide us well." He rubbed his mouth, still hesitating. "It's only—the Otherlander. When they come, they always cause more turmoil than anything else, from the stories I've heard. Are you sure we want to bring that element into the mix, especially if we're that close to our goal?"

"We may be that close to our goal *because* she's here," I said. If Hatter's observations were correct… she might be exactly the missing ingredient our rebellion had needed. The leap to help us over that last lingering stumbling block. Now that she was here, I wanted everything else working as smoothly as it possibly could so we could seize our moment as soon as it presented itself.

"If the queen gets wind…"

"The queen doesn't have the faintest idea," I said reassuringly. "I was just out by the palace scouting before you came by. The faster we bring the Otherlander into our circle, the more easily we can make sure the queen *never* finds out, not before we're ready."

Dum nodded slowly. The tension that had come into his stance fell away.

"They say around the court," he said, in a tone that suggested the idea amused him, "that these girls from the looking-glass want to take Wonderland for themselves. What could they want with us?"

"That's the queen's paranoia for you," I said. Occasionally I was glad for the tight grip she kept on certain information. The full story would only complicate our rebellion. "She expects everyone to have an eye on her throne. I've met this girl already, Dum. The last thing she was looking for was some kind of war. Besides, how could one girl threaten the entire palace?" I shook my head with a wry smile.

"I would have said as much to the fellow I overheard, but I might have lost my head in the process. We'll see how the tables turn, won't we?" He took one last look at my list and gave me a sharp nod. "First thing in the morning."

When he was gone, I sank into the smooth leather of the chair behind my desk and gave myself a moment to breathe.

Chess would have Lyssa here soon. She'd seemed impressed by her first venture into this office. She'd seemed impressed by *me*. I'd keep building from there.

The White Knight before me, the man who'd mentored me for the role, had been the Inventor too, though perhaps not as successful. I'd watched him fumble with schemes and gadgets that couldn't quite live up to his ambition as many times as I'd seen him come through. But the one thing he'd faltered on was his belief in gathering all the available information before one went forward with a plan.

I knew what he'd have done if he'd been here for Lyssa's appearance. Perhaps it was time I took her to visit our own Queen of sorts, to discover what I could about what her presence might accomplish for us. Presented as a favor for her benefit, of course.

Lyssa might not be looking for war, but that was exactly what we needed her for. If I was going to lead my people to victory, I'd better win over her mind, heart, and soul before she left here again.

CHAPTER TEN

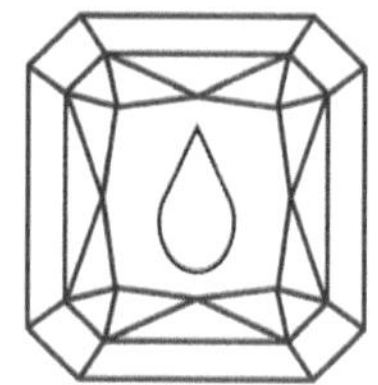

Lyssa

After the long fall, I was so braced for the shock of the water that the sudden gush of it over my skin and surge upward gave me a twinge of relief. Clutching my tote bag close by my side, I kicked and paddled with my free arm up to the glinting surface.

Now, prepared, the trip to the surface didn't take half as long. I wasn't even winded when my head broke from the water. I drank in the salty scent rising off the pond and the thicker floral aroma wafting from the vibrant foliage along the shoreline, and my face split with a grin. The beaming sun warmed on my hair as I set off for the closest bank with a lopsided breaststroke.

Was even the weather here always this bright, or had I just gotten lucky twice in a row?

On the bank by the shimmering rocks, I wrung a few cups of water out of my dress, tugged it straight, and headed down the path. The scents were even headier, the colors even richer than I'd remembered. How could the real world *not* look dreary compared to this? I spun in a slow circle, letting the scene flood my senses, giddy in a way I'd never felt before.

And as long as I had the mirror, Wonderland was all mine. A secret I never had to share with anyone.

I bounded farther down the path, as close to skipping as I'd come since I was a kid. The overgrown flowers with their petal-framed faces leaned together in conversation where I'd seen them before.

"Hello!" I called with a wave.

The daisy gaped at me, and the tulip started to sputter something about rude interruptions, but I'd already moved on.

No one was walking on the red-and-blue cobblestone road today, at least not right now. From the position of the sun in the sky, if it worked the same as it did in my world, it was about the same time of day as it'd been when I'd left Aunt Alicia's house: early afternoon. If Hatter's walks were a regular occurrence, he'd probably already taken today's. But it wasn't as if I needed him to show me the way into town.

My heart kept thumping eagerly as the bizarre buildings of the city came into view up ahead, but I slowed my pace a little. There was no need to rush this experience. I ambled along the streets, checking out the nonsensical structures with more thought than I'd been able to give them yesterday, surreptitiously noting the wide array of figures ranging from fully human to fully animal heading this way and that around me.

A woman in a layered silk dress with a head like a doe's was pushing into Hatter's shop as I reached it. I wavered for a second, watching from the edge of the window.

Hatter came out from behind the counter to point out a few possibilities to the deer woman. He was dressed in what I guessed was one of his usual suits, the jacket and pants the same maroon as the pork pie hat perched on his spiky dark blond hair, the tie bright orange. Not a combination I'd have expected to work on anyone, but like last time, he pulled it off somehow. He plucked one veiled confection off a shelf, and then nimbly swapped it for another when the woman shook her head, his hands moving with a swift grace that reminded me of how he'd spun me on the club's dance floor.

Which reminded me of the sudden spike of desire that had shot through me at his touch—and the shock that had broken through that heat when he'd mentioned Aunt Alicia.

I might have wanted to come back to experience this place again, but I also had a mission.

Since I was starting to feel like a stalker peering through the window like this, I gripped my tote bag tighter and reached for the door.

Hatter's head turned as I came in, his mouth forming a shopkeeper's welcoming smile in the instant before his gaze stopped on me. He stiffened, his smile faltering with a twitch of his lips.

Great to see you too, I thought with an edge of sarcasm. What actually came out of my mouth was a hesitant, "Hi."

"Let me finish with Ms. Forrest, and then I'll be right with you," he said in a business-like tone, recovering his cool. The deer woman was beaming at her reflection in one of the shop's mirrors. They exchanged a few more remarks—but as far as I could tell, no money—and then she sashayed out. Hatter whirled on me.

"Didn't you go to an awful lot of trouble to get yourself home a couple days ago, looking-glass girl?" he said. "What are you doing here again?"

Despite the exasperation in his voice, there was just enough warmth there and in his eyes to make me hope he wasn't *completely* unhappy that I'd shown up. "Getting home turned out to be pretty easy," I said. "And after I got back, I realized I ended up kind of liking it here. Also, I've got some questions you're not getting out of answering this time." I raised my eyebrows at him.

Hatter's mouth twisted, but he held my gaze. "Fair enough. In that case, let me invite you upstairs again."

He didn't bother locking the shop door or putting up a closed sign. Theft must not be much of a concern around here. "Has it just been two days since I left?" I asked as I followed him up the stairs to his apartment. I hadn't been sure how much time might have passed, considering how little had in the real world while I'd been here.

"Almost exactly," Hatter said. "Was it longer for you?"

"No, the same." I didn't know how to wrap my head around that. Did time slow down while I was here and then speed forward to catch up? I guessed it didn't really matter, as long as I could keep coming here without losing days at a time in the real world.

The upstairs apartment looked pretty much the same as yesterday, other than a few used plates and mugs scattered on the table. A sudden prickle of embarrassment ran down my back, thinking of how I'd accepted Hatter's hospitality last time without even thinking of politeness. I'd been overwhelmed, but I'd still imposed on him.

Well, I could make up for it today by cleaning up the mess he'd left for himself. I scooped up a couple of saucers and teacups and carried them to the sink.

When I'd started the water running and turned to clear the rest of the table, Hatter was watching me with bemusement, his mouth slanted at an odd angle that could have been moving toward a smile or a grimace. "What are you doing?"

"Atoning for the mess I left you with last time," I said. "And for dropping in on you two times without warning. Unless you prefer having dirty dishes all over the table?" I'd feel more comfortable sitting in a tidy room, but it was his home, not mine. Who knew what was normal for Wonderland?

"No," he said, with something closer to a smile. "By all means."

He was just sinking into the wingchair at the table when the stairs at the other end of the room creaked. Hatter sprang back up again as his daughter burst into the room. She was wearing another black dress, this one with a fluffy tulle skirt, and she'd woven black ribbons into the thin braids that mingled with her coffee-brown hair.

"She's back!" she said. "She's..." Her head cocked. "...washing the dishes?"

"Doria," Hatter started.

She breezed right by him to peer into the sink as if she'd never witnessed it full of bubbly water before. "Decided you like it here, huh?" she said, flashing a grin at me.

"I did, actually," I said.

Hatter snagged her elbow and eased her to the side. "Lyssa and I have a few things to discuss. Could you keep an eye on the shop until I can come back down, please?"

Doria folded her arms over her chest with a huff. "Fine. But you owe me. No complaining about the club tonight."

He tugged on one of her braids with a wry smile that crinkled the corners of his eyes. "It's a deal. Thank you, Mouse."

With obvious fondness, he watched her flounce down the stairs. The guy was hot even when he was being gruff, but seeing his face light up like that made my heart thump off-kilter.

"Mouse?" I asked as I set the last of the dishes in the rack. I hadn't noticed anything mousey about the teenager, literally or otherwise.

Hatter's expression shifted back to wariness as his attention returned to me. He settled into his chair. "An old nickname. We used to call Doria 'Dormouse' when she was tiny. After a while, the 'Dor' got dropped."

His 'we' brought out an itch of curiosity. Him and her birth parents? Had he taken her in because they'd been friends? What had happened to them?

But those weren't the kinds of questions you asked a relative stranger, not if I wanted him to answer the ones I'd actually come to ask him. I dried off my hands and decided to sit in the beach chair again.

"So," I said. "Since you're here to discuss things with me, are you going to tell me how you knew my grand-aunt Alicia?"

"There's not a lot to tell," Hatter said, steepling his lithe fingers in front of him. "She came through the looking-glass too. Presumably the same one you did. She visited Wonderland a few times, and that was that."

His voice was carefully flat, but I thought it got a bit sharp toward the end of that explanation. Had Aunt Alicia done something that had upset him while she was here? From his comment in the club, it'd sounded as if they'd been friendly. I had trouble picturing the regal silver-blond-haired woman who'd read me stories chatting with Hatter or any of Wonderland's other inhabitants.

"How long ago was that?" I asked. She could have been here as recently as a month or two ago, maybe. I wasn't sure how much her illness had debilitated her before she'd gone to the hospital for her final days.

Hatter's gaze turned vague. "I'm not sure," he said. "In Wonderland, we tend not to keep track of the years all that closely.

Judging from you, it's been a long time. The last time I saw her, she couldn't have been much older than you are."

"Oh." I blinked at him. Aunt Alicia had been fifty years older than me. "Then, how could you even—"

"You can't judge anyone's age by their appearance here," Hatter said, focusing back on me. "Once we're grown, wherever we start from, we only age in fits and starts, mostly at the end. And that end tends to be further off than Otherlanders can count on, as I understand it."

I tried to reconfigure everything he'd just told me around the man in front of me. "So, you're, like, at least seventy-something?"

He shrugged. "I told you, we don't keep track. Not a whole lot changes around here from day to day, year to year. Maybe that's why it takes so much longer for us to get older. If some conversion were possible between Wonderland and the Otherland, I'd imagine we're all about as old as we look to you in any way that counts."

Okay, I was getting diverted from the most important subject. Aunt Alicia couldn't have told Hatter anything about *me* or what she'd hoped for me when I hadn't even been born the last time they'd talked. But that didn't mean he couldn't help unravel the mystery.

"Did she ever say anything to you about a key?" I said. "I think she might have left it somewhere here in Wonderland."

Hatter's eyes flickered, and I knew before he spoke that I'd struck gold. "What makes you ask about that?" he said.

"She left me a note with the box that it's supposed to open. It sounded like… she wanted me to find the mirror and come through to Wonderland. And that once I'd done that, she thought I should have the key. I'd like to know what she left for me in that box."

"How strange."

I gave him a pointed look. "I can tell you know where it is. Why wouldn't you want me to have it if that's what she wanted? *I* wouldn't even know it exists if she hadn't nudged me in the right direction."

Hatter sighed. "It's a bit of a journey," he said. "If we left now, it'd be dark by the time we got there, hard to find the right spot."

Was he serious or just being difficult? Before I could push for a better answer, Hatter's hat shot right off his head as if blown by a brisk wind. It flipped over and landed in the air on top of a figure that was just shimmering into sight standing beside him. I bit back a startled squeak.

"I think I rather like this one," Chess said, tipping the hat at a jaunty angle on his rumpled auburn hair. "It suits me, don't you think?"

Hatter held out his hand with a scowl. "What have I told you about showing up unannounced—and invisible? Sometimes I think you want to give people a conniption."

Chess made a tsking sound. "Watch how you swing that temper around, or it might smack you in the face." He set the hat back on Hatter's head. "I did announce myself, to the young lady downstairs. A little surprise simply livens up the visit." He turned to me with a grin that only showed a hint of his cat-like fangs and dipped into a brief bow. "I heard our Otherlander friend was back in town and wanted to pay my respects. What brings you to this fine realm today, lovely?"

The grin, the compliment, and the memory of his lips brushing against my hand two days ago sent a strange flush over my skin. I willed it not to touch my cheeks where they'd see. "I was hoping to find something here. Hatter was just telling me that's impossible today."

"Ah, well, then you'll just have to stay until tomorrow. Hatter has a spare room—he can put you up, no problem at all. Isn't that so?"

Chess beamed at his friend. From the mischievous glimmer in his light blue eyes, I suspected he'd known exactly how Hatter would feel about that offer. The other man made a non-committal sound, scowling at Chess.

Guilt pinched my stomach at the thought of being an unwanted guest, but my need to find that key overrode it. If I was here first thing in the morning, I could make sure we got going, no more excuses.

"That sounds perfect," I said, and bobbed my head to Hatter as if he'd been the one offering. "Thank you so much."

He aimed his glower at me, but his expression softened a little. "As long as you're not expecting five-star treatment, you might as well use the room."

Chess clapped his hands. "What's settled is settled, then. What will you do for the rest of the day?"

I hadn't had time to think that far yet. "I guess I'd like to explore the city a little more. And…" My gaze slid back to Hatter. "Is there anyone else here you know my grand-aunt might have talked to?"

A shadow crossed his face. "No one you can still talk to now," he said.

"Are you looking for someone?" Chess asked. "Ah, that Otherlander you asked me about the other night, perhaps?"

"Yeah," I said, rubbing the side of my neck. "Well, sort of. I'd just like to know more about what she did here, what she was like then."

"I didn't know her all that well," Hatter said preemptively.

Chess tapped his chin. "You know, our White Knight makes it his business to hear a lot about all sorts of things. I'd say he knows at least a little about everyone and everything that's ever been part of this world."

My spirits leapt. I hadn't been sure if I'd have any excuse to see Theo again, but I definitely wasn't turning down the opportunity. "Do you think he'd have time to talk to me?" I asked. "I mean, it seems like he's pretty important—he must be busy, and he just helped me a couple days ago…"

Chess waved off my concern. "No one is ever too busy in Wonderland. And the Inventor got his second name because he makes it his business to champion all causes. We could stop by right now if you'd like."

CHAPTER ELEVEN

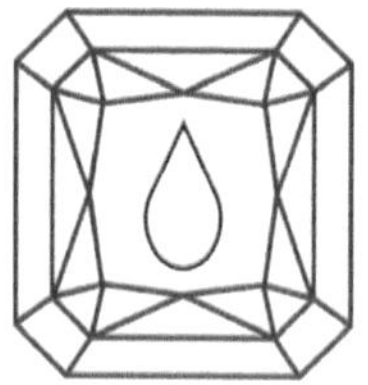

Lyssa

With Chess's habit of appearing out of thin air, it was easy to forget that he was a pretty substantial man until I was walking right beside him. He had to be around six feet tall, a couple inches taller than Hatter and several more than me. As he sauntered down the city street, his sculpted muscles flexed against his burgundy-and-yellow striped shirt and indigo slacks.

Studying his handsome leonine face surreptitiously, I couldn't help wondering how old *he* really was. I'd have pegged him as twenty-five or so, but from what Hatter had said, that didn't mean much. Did it even make him definitely younger than Hatter, or could people age at different speeds from each other here?

"You said you heard I was back in town," I said. "Who did you hear it from?" Not from Hatter or Doria, as far as I could tell. Who else would have noticed me?

"Oh," Chess said with an enigmatic air, "gossip always travels, and the flowers do like to gossip."

I could believe that. Were there more of those immense talking flowers here in the city? I glanced around as if I might see one strolling by us. No flowers, but I did spot a man in a particularly lurid costume that included a red-and-pink striped tunic and a bulging red… hat? Helmet? It was hard to tell. He strode out of a shop up ahead with his chin high.

Chess slipped a firm hand around my forearm. "We're going to take a little detour," he said with the same blasé tone, and tugged me into a winding alley between two of the nearby buildings.

"What's the matter?" I asked, glancing over my shoulder. Had he been worried about that weirdly dressed dude for some reason?

"A journey over new ground can unearth new thoughts. If we get where we're going, we're still getting there."

"Are you even capable of giving a straight answer to anything?" I muttered.

Chess grinned at me, amusement glinting in his eyes. "Certainly. With concentrated effort."

I groped for something else to ask in this moment when he appeared willing to make that effort. "How do you know Hatter?"

"By now, we all know just about everyone here," Chess said. "Few paths fail to cross."

"Well, sure, but you seem like…" Maybe *friends* was too strong a word. "…like you've spent quite a bit of time around each other."

Chess cocked his head, apparently giving that point even more concentrated effort. "I know I can trust him to be who he is, and he knows he can trust me to be who I am. It may sound strange, but that's more than either of us could say of most in this place."

"Is that why you work with Theo, too?"

"For the most part. The White Knight wears so many roles it's difficult to be sure quite who he is, but whoever he is, I'm certain he has our best interests at heart and the wherewithal to defend them."

"Defend them from who?" I asked as we emerged into a different major street.

"Whoever he might need to, I suppose," Chess said.

The silver tower shone to our left. In a second-floor doorway on a building between us and it, two men were, um, enjoying each other's company quite a bit, one pushing the other up against the doorframe. I tugged my gaze away, but the sight brought back the various PDAs and near-orgies I'd observed on my last visit.

"So... people here seem to 'get off' in the traditional way, with each other, quite a bit," I said awkwardly. "I'm surprised there aren't more kids running around." I hadn't seen anyone pull out a condom packet yet.

"One of the ways of our mad world," Chess said with a wink. "I gather in the Otherland you take a pill to avoid buns in ovens. Here you have to take one to make it happen. There are no diseases of any kind in Wonderland. Those who want to indulge have no reason to hold back."

"Oh." That sounded... very convenient if I wanted to follow Melody's encouragement into a quick fling while I was here. I didn't know if the pill thing applied to me, but my birth control implant would take care of that side of things.

Maybe that wasn't the best topic to be considering when I was standing next to one of the most attractive men I'd ever met, on my way to chat with another, though. At least, if I wanted to carry on a coherent conversation.

Chess ushered me through the Tower's doorways into its elevator chamber and announced himself the same way he had before, although this time he identified me as "Lyssa" instead of "a guest." The elevator launched us upward with a jolt that made me grab Chess's arm for balance. His biceps twitched with what felt like a flinch.

"Sorry," I said quickly, spreading my feet to steady myself that way, but Chess set a reassuring hand on my shoulder.

"Feel free to make use of me as often as is convenient," he said with a smirk that sent a fresh flush through me. Maybe he'd only been reacting to the sudden motion just like I had.

When we stepped into Theo's vast white office, the so-called White Knight was waiting for us, leaning against the front of his desk. He straightened up and stepped toward us, exuding the same potent confidence as before in every movement he made.

He had the sleeves of his white dress shirt rolled up over his forearms, and the open collar revealed a small V of his muscular chest.

For a second, possibly thanks to my recent conversation with Chess, my brain short-circuited from hotness overload. What was I doing here again?

Thankfully, Chess was not affected the same way. He gave Theo a cheeky salute. "Your Knightliness."

"Chess," Theo said with a nod, and his dark brown eyes came to rest on me, all warmth, a hint of concern, and no sign at all that he was irritated by the interruption. "And Lyssa. I hope you've returned of your own accord and that this visit is a wanted one."

"It is," I said. "I, um—I'm sorry to bother you."

"Lyssa came looking for information about another woman who made the trip through the looking-glass," Chess said, patting me with the hand he'd left on my shoulder. "I figured if anyone in the city might have answers for her, it'd be you."

The corner of Theo's mouth quirked upward. "A reasonable assumption. I'll do what I can."

"I'll take my leave, then." Chess gave me another little bow. "A pleasure as always, lovely."

I felt a weird twinge of disappointment that he didn't kiss my hand again before he left. But it was hard to linger in that sensation when Theo was ambling closer to me. He motioned me to the wall beyond the worktables. "This isn't the most comfortable space for a conversation. Would you join me?"

"Of course," I said automatically. My gaze drifted over the shelves of mechanical bits and assembled contraptions as I passed them. Curiosity nibbled at me. "What kinds of things do you invent?"

"That depends on what problems people bring to me," Theo said. "Yesterday I put together a device for locating lost puppies and a machine that could replicate identical cakes."

I caught myself just before I gaped at him. "Of course you could do that. This is Wonderland."

He smiled. "It still takes as much skill and practice as any devices built in the Otherland, I'd imagine. But there's something very satisfying about breaking a problem down into its base components and rebuilding it from the inside out."

I'd never heard anyone put the act of invention that way before, but now that he'd said it, I couldn't think of a better way to express it. "I bet there is. I don't think my problem should require a whole lot of inventing."

"Even if it does, I'm your man."

He led me into a smaller room with a shaggy rug and a cluster of boxy armchairs. The color scheme was less stark, all pale grays, beiges, and peaches rather than blank white. I sank into one of the chairs, finding it comfortingly cozy despite its shape. A crisp warm scent laced the air as if there'd recently been wood burning in a fireplace, but I couldn't see anyplace it could have come from.

Theo sat down across from me and leaned forward with his elbows resting on the chair's arms. His chestnut curls drifted across his forehead with the motion. "Why don't you tell me about this person you're looking for?"

"I'm not exactly looking for *her*," I said. "It's— The mirror I came through, it's in my grand-aunt's house. My late grand-aunt. But I've found things, and Hatter said something… She came through to Wonderland too, a while ago. Hatter said it was a few times, but that he didn't know her very well. Chess hasn't met her at all. She never mentioned anything about it to the rest of the family, as far as I can tell, and it was a long time ago, and I can't ask her now. I'd just like to find out anything I can about what she did here." Why she stopped coming back. Why she'd wanted *me* to come here.

"Of course you do," Theo said, with so much assurance that any qualms I'd still had about bothering him with this melted away. "It must be disorienting, stumbling on this place unexpectedly and then discovering someone from your family had experienced much the same thing without you ever knowing."

"Yes," I said with a rush of relief. He'd hit the nail on the head. "I think she willed the house to me so that I'd find the mirror and end up here, but she left me so little to go on… I just want to understand."

"I've heard tales of many Otherlanders who found their way into Wonderland, even those before my time. What was her name?"

"Alicia," I said. "Alicia Tenniel. Hatter said it was when she was my age—that would be around fifty years ago, in my world, anyway."

"Alicia." He drew out every syllable of the word as if it would summon his memories. And maybe it did. "I have heard mention of her. I don't believe anyone spoke of her doing more than arriving here and mingling with us for a short time, as you have. You said you believe that she intended for you to find your way here. What makes you say that?"

"Well, there's the fact that she left the house to me at all. I hadn't seen her in something like fifteen years—not since I was a kid. And I found a note she wrote to me, telling me that there were things I'd only understand after I'd been here. At least, I assume she meant here."

Theo nodded as if my rambling made perfect sense to him. "What sort of things did she want you to understand?"

"I don't know," I said. "The note was on a locked box, and she left the key here, so I haven't been able to open it yet. Which doesn't really make any sense, because how could she have written a note to me fifty years ago, when I wasn't even born yet, before she locked it and brought the key here? Or she came back again, and no one I've talked to saw her that time. But Hatter says he knows where the key is." I pressed the heel of my hand to my temple. "Maybe I should stop expecting anything that happens here to make sense."

Theo chuckled. "That might be wise. But I think I can tease out some sense for you. The box may contain an item that she knew anyone who went to Wonderland would find meaning in, and she secreted away the key before she knew who she'd want to give that gift to. Or perhaps there are other ways of opening the box that only she knew."

"I guess either of those is possible," I agreed. Hell, I could have taken the thing to a locksmith and asked to have the lock broken open. Somehow that would have felt like cheating, though. Like I hadn't earned whatever she'd left for me after all.

"Is Hatter going to help you find the key?" Theo asked, and suddenly I had the sense that if I said no, he was prepared to march right over there and command Hatter to do so. And that Hatter would hop to it.

"Yes," I said. "He said it's a long trip, so he'll take me there tomorrow. And then I guess I'll slip back home through the club tomorrow night if Chess doesn't mind distracting the guards by the door again, so I can use it."

"I'm sure we can arrange safe passage for you," Theo said, "if you do decide to leave us that early. You're welcome to stay here as long as you'd like to investigate your grand-aunt's activities further. I can arrange anything you might need. Just ask, and I'll find a way."

He held my gaze so steadily that my heart started to thump a little faster. "Thank you," I said. "I really appreciate how much you've helped me already. I don't want to impose."

"You're not," he said firmly. "Making sure every person in Wonderland is safe and at ease is my job."

He reached across the space between us and took my hand, so carefully I could have slipped his grasp before he'd closed it if I'd wanted to, but so smoothly my fingers instinctively curled around his in return. Determination rang through his voice. "You've come a very long way, Lyssa, and you deserve answers. I aim to see that you get them. There's one more thing I can offer, if you don't mind experiencing a little more Wonderland weirdness."

When he looked at me like that, talked to me like that, with his hand sending a shiver of heat right up my arm, I wanted to be someone who never backed down from anything, let alone a little weirdness. I'd survived plenty of that already. What had I come back here for if not to wallow in the weird?

"Okay," I said. "Sure. If you think it'll help. Do you have a lost-facts-finding invention?"

He smiled. "Not exactly. A colleague of mine lives one floor up. She has an… interesting way of looking at the world. The past and the future blend together with the present. It can be difficult to follow her observations, but she might be able to see more than anyone here could remember."

He stood up, still holding my hand, and I followed him to the elevator. He waved it open without a moment's hesitation. Walking that close to him, seeing how set he was on helping me, sudden emotion filled my throat.

"Thank you," I said when we stepped into the elevator. "I was kind of nervous about coming back here—not because anything bad happened last time; it's just so different from what I'm used to. But now I know for sure I made the right decision."

I beamed at him, and Theo went still as he gazed back at me. I might have thought I'd said something wrong if another smile hadn't crossed his face a moment later.

"I'm glad to hear that," he said. "I have to admit I was hoping I might see you again. I get the impression you're an interesting person to know, Lyssa Tenniel."

The words made my heart skip more than the brief hitch of the invisible elevator did. This level had only an open doorway leading into a small fore-room. Theo paused there and knocked on the door. "It's Theo," he said.

"Theo! Come in," a bright voice replied.

The room on the other side was a sprawling living room draped in softness. The pale blue-gray carpet under my feet felt like thick velour. Silk tapestries with swirling patterns hung across the walls. The space was scattered with plush furniture in a variety of shapes, all of it a slightly darker shade of blue-gray.

The woman who'd answered Theo's knock sat on a chaise lounge in the middle of the room, her fleecy white dress draped all the way down her legs and across its cushions. Glints of pins held her tawny brown hair in a heap of curls that crowned her head. She looked up at us without stopping her knitting. The silver needles in her hands hooked and jabbed in a rhythm that might as well have been a dance.

"Hello," she said to me in the same bright voice. "I'm sorry I wasn't prepared for company. I forgot that you were coming by."

"It's all right," I said. "I mean, we only just decided..." My voice trailed off as I remembered what Theo had told me. Had she known we were coming before we had? Had she seen our future conversation?

We hadn't even gotten into any talk about Aunt Alicia, and my head was spinning already.

"This is Mirabel," Theo said to me. "Though some people call her 'the White Queen' the same way they call me 'the White Knight.' Mirabel, this is Lyssa, come to Wonderland through a looking-glass."

"Of course she has," Mirabel said. She offered me a gentle smile.

"Please sit. I will try to order my thoughts. I don't always remember or follow… My mind is not what it used to be."

She made a vague gesture with one hand that drew my eyes to a ruddy twist of a scar on one side of her forehead, mostly hidden by her hairline. An accident—or someone had attacked her? Why would anyone here have wanted to hurt this woman?

"Your mind is still generous with its gifts," Theo said. At his prompt, we both sat on a sofa facing Mirabel. "Will you share those gifts with us today? Lyssa is seeking information about a woman named Alicia Tenniel who came through the looking-glass from the Otherland decades ago. Anything you can see from the past—or, I suppose, the future—we welcome hearing."

He'd lowered his voice, but his baritone still exuded passionate confidence. If anything, it was more gripping when he restrained himself.

Mirabel nodded. She set her knitting down on her lap, and her gaze slid toward the ivory walls. Her light brown eyes, like milky tea, clouded as if dashed with a fresh splash of cream.

"Alicia Tenniel," she murmured in a distant tone. "The key, it has been unearthed—it will be buried. So many secret meetings. Make her an honorary spade. Promises. She will mean them. She meant them until she didn't, slipping away, away—she doesn't know. The ruby was bleeding. It's still bleeding, drop after drop—"

Her words cut off with a sob. A tear trickled down her pale cheek. She buried her face in her hands, her shoulders quivering.

My throat had closed up. I hadn't followed any of that except the bit about the key, sort of, but whatever she'd seen, it'd obviously upset her.

"Mirabel." Theo scooted forward on the sofa to touch her back. His thumb rubbed up and down over her shoulder blade, his mouth twisted at a painful angle. "I'm sorry. I didn't know it would be painful."

"It's all right," Mirabel said with a ragged breath. She raised her head, and her tears had vanished. She wiped her mouth with the back of her hand. "What is broken is fixed and what is whole will be broken, and that is always the way of it, around and around. I'm only dizzy."

Okay. Maybe we should give her some peace and quiet now. I stood up. "Thank you for what you could tell me. It's a start." Hatter might know something about Aunt Alicia's secret meetings, or what the heck 'honorary spade' meant.

The movement of Theo's thumb stopped. Mirabel looked from him to me, and her lips formed another smile.

"Do you not want me to look for you as well?"

I hesitated. It was impossible not to ask now that she'd raised the question: "*Can* you see something about me?"

She peered at me with so much concentration that my nerves started to twitch beneath my skin. The haze came over her eyes again.

"You were dizzy too, dizzy with the drink. They saw the flowers. Bright, bright on your head. And the hands are spinning again. They're spinning!" Her voice turned into a gasp. Her gaze snapped back to me, her eyes clearing. Then she winced and touched her scar.

"Thank you, Mirabel," Theo said. "You've told us plenty. That's excellent." A thread of—was that *excitement*?—ran through his voice. I couldn't figure out what she'd said that was particularly meaningful. His hand stayed on her shoulder. "Would you like me to stay?"

"No. No, I'll go back to my knitting." She inclined her head to him. "We had dinner together."

"In that case, I'll make sure to bring around something good."

I snuck one last look at Mirabel as Theo guided me back to the elevator. She looked perfectly content again, humming to herself as she whirled her knitting needles.

"Trying to think that way doesn't, like, make her worse, does it?" I asked.

"She's been the same for as long as I've known her, which is many years," Theo said. "I tried, once, to avoid asking her anything for as long as I could, and as soon as she noticed, she yelled at me—the only time she ever has." He gave me a wry grin. "So I let her decide what she can handle."

The knots in my stomach loosened. I had to remember not to take anything too seriously here. It was still Wonderland.

"Did you understand anything she said?" I asked. It had seemed as if he had, enough to be happy about it.

But Theo shook his head. "It often takes a while before her comments become clear. She saw a lot, though. Keep her words in your head on your journey to find that key."

Yes. And what Aunt Alicia had left for me in that box might tie all those fragments together.

CHAPTER TWELVE

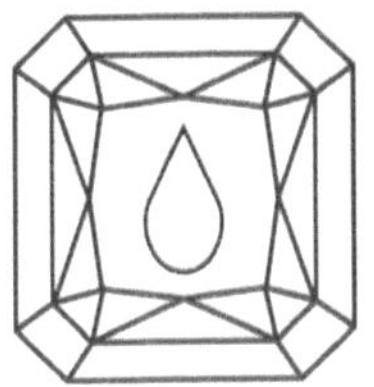

Hatter

Our Otherlander emerged from the spare bedroom about an hour after the sun came up. I had to admit she was pretty considerate as house guests went. I didn't hear a sound from her other than the faint hum of the pipes as she must have washed up and the slightest creak of the stairs. When she emerged into the main room and saw I was up, her stance visibly relaxed.

"Good morning," Lyssa said tentatively. Her face had a rosy cast to it from the recent washing, and her pale hair looked a bit rumpled despite her efforts at dampening it down. My heart gave an odd hitch. There was something undeniably intimate about witnessing another person first thing in the morning. It'd been more years that I could count since I'd had anyone spend the night here—other than Doria, of course.

I couldn't imagine she was affected in at all the same way by the sight of me. "Morning," I replied, glad that I'd happened to be up pouring myself another cup of tea. I leaned against the counter to watch her from a more distant vantage point as she approached the table. "I picked up an assortment of scones. Would you like a cup of tea?"

"Yes, please." Lyssa swiped at her mouth as if suppressing a yawn and perched on the leather-topped stool, considering the platter of scones. The bakery down the street produced five different flavors, so I'd gotten two of each along with the honey-pineapple-coriander ones I'd already eaten.

I poured her a cup and set the tea in front of her. She spooned a little sugar into it absently, her attention still on the platter.

"Are you going to tell me what flavors these are, or is this a test to see if I can avoid the one everyone in Wonderland knows is horrible?" she asked with the beginnings of a smile.

I couldn't stop my mouth from twitching upward in response. "I believe each of them is to *someone's* taste. I have no way of accounting for yours yet."

She picked up a scone with darker dough and purple flecks. "What's this one?"

"Licorice-rosemary-rye."

"Worth a try."

She bit in, and her whole face stiffened for a second as the flavors must have hit her tongue. I had to bite my own tongue to hold in a laugh. That type was definitely an acquired taste. Doria liked them every now and then after a particularly busy day—*Like a kick in the head to wake you up*, she'd told me once, rather gleefully.

Lyssa chewed slowly and managed to swallow without outright grimacing, but it looked like a near thing. I expected her to set the rest of the scone down on one of the plates I'd set out and reach for another. Instead, she kept nibbling at it with smaller bites interspersed with gulps of tea, until she'd managed to down the whole thing. Did she think I'd be offended by the waste if she didn't eat it? I supposed she had no way of knowing that waste was barely a concept that existed in Wonderland these days.

Perhaps it simply mattered to her to finish what she started.

I wasn't here to make a list of her admirable qualities. I absorbed myself in my tea and the familiar prickle of caffeine through my body. Lyssa bravely lifted another scone off the plate, without even asking what she was getting into this time. It was one of the vanilla-cranberry-pine ones. Her face brightened with the first bite, and that scone disappeared much faster than the first, leaving her expression full of contentment. She drained the rest of her tea.

"Should we get going?" she asked. "Since this is such a long trip."

Some small part of me had been foolish enough to hope she might have forgotten about her quest. If I were going to make a list of Lyssa's most *obvious* qualities, "stubborn" would end up close to the top.

Of course, stubbornness might be exactly what this land needed if anything were going to be done. If I'd even thought that risk was worth it. It clearly wasn't.

"Pick one or two of those in case you get hungry along the way," I said. "I have a lunch we can bring. It'll be around mid-day by the time we reach our destination."

Lyssa snatched up the other vanilla-cranberry-pine scone without a second's hesitation and bundled it in a napkin before tucking it into her bag. "How do we get wherever we're going? Does everyone just walk everywhere here?"

"Not many of us are generally interested in going very far," I said. And then there was the small matter of the queen having ordered every vehicle destroyed and every riding animal slaughtered, other than the few horses and carriages she kept on the palace grounds for her own use. She'd planned her oppression quite thoroughly. If we couldn't construct or produce it and then use it in the course of a day, we were shit out of luck.

But those weren't Lyssa's problems, and I wasn't going to court her temporary sympathies. She was here to vacation and locate her grand-aunt Alicia's key, and when she was done with both of those purposes, no doubt she'd wash her hands of Wonderland.

"Good thing I brought my sneakers, then," Lyssa said.

The sneakers in question were sky-blue, almost a perfect match for the flowy knee-length skirt she'd apparently packed, which teased around her bare legs as we set off down the street. She'd paired it with a pastel pink top with lacy straps—not quite the bold colors that were most popular here, but a closer fit than what she'd turned up in her first visit. She was a quick learner.

Alicia had been too.

Lyssa stayed quiet for the walk through the city, studying the buildings and the people we passed. Her gaze still stuck for a beat longer on the more unusual figures among my fellow Wonderlanders, but she'd also learned not to stare. I might not crave the constant excess so many had become fond of, but I had to think it must be rather monotonous living in a world where people were always people and animals only animals, and every house and shop stood itself in exactly the same way.

There is a certain comfort in knowing what to expect, Alicia had told me once, when I'd shared that thought with her. *Maybe the best world would be somewhere in between.*

I willed those thoughts away, letting my own gaze slide over the beauty and the decadence of our city. Leave the past in the past and focus on what I had today, that was the thing to do.

But just a few minutes after we'd left the buildings behind for the cobblestone road that led through the treed landscape near the Pond of Tears, Lyssa broke her silence.

"You obviously knew my grand-aunt at least a little bit. Maybe you can tell me… I talked to Mirabel—the White Queen?—yesterday, and she said something about secret meetings. And making her a 'spade.' And some other things, but they made even less sense. Do you have any idea what she meant by that?"

Theo had brought the Otherlander to the White Queen? What in the lands was he thinking? When I'd told him about the lingering teacup on Chess's insistence, he'd seemed interested but unmoved. I'd thought maybe he'd want to have her by to see if her influence would work on his inventions, not to dig into the lines of her past and future.

For a second, my pulse beat at a faster rhythm, the same way it had when I'd come downstairs two mornings ago and found Lyssa's cup still on the table. Had he seen a way—come up with a solution—

I clamped down on the flash of eagerness. *He* couldn't have any idea the risks he was running, drawing her further into our world. He hadn't been with us before—he'd never experienced the backlash firsthand…

"I'm not sure," I said carefully. "What did the White Knight have to say about it?" Whatever he was trying to achieve, it wasn't my business anymore. If he meant to enlighten her, then he could do the enlightening. I had no intention of stepping beyond whatever lines he'd drawn and becoming complicit myself.

"Not really anything," Lyssa said with a frown. "He was glad she'd said a bunch of different things, because there's more chance I'll stumble on something else that'll help me put those pieces together. But he didn't seem to have much idea of the bigger picture right now."

So, he'd avoided telling her much of anything. He must have had his own purposes for arranging that meeting. What audacious plan was our current White Knight dreaming up?

It shouldn't matter. It was nothing to do with me. As long as he didn't draw Doria in over her head… My jaw tightened.

If I got wind that he'd conscripted my daughter for any greater part in his schemes, *I'd* have his head.

Better that Lyssa knew as little as possible, so she went seeking more answers elsewhere. Preferably on the other side of that looking-glass.

"From what I saw, your grand-aunt made quite a few friends in Wonderland," I said. "She could have been meeting with any manner of them, secretly or otherwise."

"But she trusted you enough to tell you about hiding this key."

"Not just me. It was hardly a secret. She wanted to be sure if she sent someone looking for it, that it wouldn't be too hard for them to find one of us who knew."

Lyssa's clear blue eyes snapped to my face. "She told you that? That she might send someone looking?"

I exhaled in a rush. She might as well know this much. Maybe it would speed along her travels here. The sooner she returned to her home, the sooner my home was that small bit safer.

"This is all I know about it," I said. "I got the impression that she herself wasn't entirely sure what her plans might be. She said she had two keys, and she wanted to leave one here in Wonderland while keeping the other with her. That way, if she ever wanted to hide something behind the lock those keys opened without any risk of someone solely from the Otherland retrieving it, she could dispose of the Otherland key knowing one remained here for her—or any other looking-glass traveler's—use."

"There was another key," Lyssa murmured, as if that answered a question she hadn't asked yet. "I wonder—No. If she said that to you, and from the note she left me, she must have done something with that other key to make sure I could only use this one."

"Well, come on," I said. If I kept her walking fast enough, she wouldn't have the breath to ask many more questions—and we'd be done with this trip sooner. "Let's get you there so you *can* use this one."

The cobblestone road narrowed and gave way to plain old dirt. That path stayed well-trampled as it wound through the mushroom stands. Lyssa's eyes widened taking in the toadstools that loomed well over our heads, their flesh blotchy with lurid pinks and purples and reds depending on their particular species.

The occasional thump and holler carried to us from where some of Caterpillar's workers must have been on the job. From the giggles that also reached us, they were sampling the product while they collected it. I picked up my pace even faster.

Beyond the mushroom stands, patches of grass dotted the path until it was barely distinguishable from the fields around us. The green knolls on either side rose up in hunched and knobby shapes I'd imagined stories for as a child. This one might have been an elephant; that one a castle tower. Shrubs of fiery hues clung to their uneven slopes, and the breeze played a lilting melody through their whispering leaves.

It had been a long time since I'd come out this far. Doria had never seen the knolls. Maybe she was too old to get caught up in playing among them now. It might be good for us to take the trip out here anyway. I'd almost forgotten this side of Wonderland, wild but peaceful, unpredictable but hospitable.

No watching eyes. No judging glances. A thread of tension that had become such a familiar presence I'd forgotten it wasn't simply a part of me slipped from my chest.

Of course, I wasn't actually alone here.

"Hatter?" Lyssa said, in a tone that pulled that thread of tension tight again.

She was gazing over the knolls, her brow lightly knit. I had another feature to add to the list of the ways she was different from Alicia. I'd never seen her grand-aunt produce an expression anywhere near that pensive.

"Yes?" I said.

"If Wonderland is all about having fun and enjoying yourself, and no one has to do anything other than make themselves happy… why aren't *you* happy? I mean, you don't seem to be. Most of the time."

Her eyes flicked nervously toward me. I dragged my own gaze away. Hearts take me, how could I answer a question like that? It was a rabbit hole into a totally different Wonderland than she needed to observe. But she asked it so earnestly, as if she *cared* about the answer, that my stomach pinched as I considered a suitable lie.

I didn't think Alicia would ever have asked a question like that, either.

"Perhaps I'm a beacon of joy when I don't have stray Otherlanders to shepherd around," I said. "You've hardly had the opportunity to take a broad sampling of my moods."

Lyssa bit her lip. "I'm sorry. I guess I didn't really think about—you're taking your whole day to bring me out here—I *have* asked a lot, haven't I? I just didn't know… This situation is so strange. But that's not really an excuse."

The pinching sensation in my gut dug deeper at her obvious distress. It wasn't an act. She did care, at least in so much as she was impinging on a relative stranger. I hadn't meant to make her feel *bad*, exactly.

I groped for something else to say that would be true when barely anything I could have said felt utterly so, and a sight appeared over the top of the whale-shaped knoll ahead of us that sent a wave of relief through me.

"Never mind about that," I said. "I told you I'd bring you, and I have. We're almost there."

I pointed to the dark shape stretching up toward the sky. Lyssa blinked at it. "What *is* that?"

"It'll be clearer when we reach them."

We came around the knoll and into the midst of the giant columns. Lyssa's jaw hung slack for a moment before she recovered her voice.

"They're trees. Only… upside down."

"We called this the Topsy Turvy Woods when people came out this way often enough to need a name for it," I said, toeing the leafy branch that jutted across the ground from the base of the nearest tree. Its trunk rose so high into the air I had to squint against the mid-day sun to make out where it widened into twisted roots that nearly scratched the clouds.

"They all just grow like this?" Lyssa said. She wandered deeper into the strange wood, skirting the sprawled branches.

"As far as anyone can tell. There are tales about how ages ago some massive quake threw them onto their heads, but that sounds a little ridiculous to me."

A laugh sputtered from Lyssa's mouth. "Out of everything here, *that's* where you draw the line?" Her pensive expression from earlier came back as she peered at the spiderweb of roots splintering the sky overhead. "It feels different from the other parts of Wonderland I've seen. Ominous."

"I suppose you know why no one much comes out this way, then," I said briskly. "Now, let's see." I counted off the trees in my head, checking each trunk, until I spotted the one with the knot just above the level of my head. My feet stilled.

Decades had passed, as much as time had passed at all here, but that long-ago moment washed over me with perfect clarity. I'd stood just about here, with March and May and Carpenter and the White Knight whom Theo had inherited his role from, all of us watching Alicia brandish her brass key. The wind had ruffled her golden hair that she kept short, just to the base of her ears, and she'd grinned in that fierce way of hers, and I'd thought there couldn't be anything more beautiful in the whole of Wonderland.

The memory hit me with a pang that faded quickly. It was from long ago, yes, and a time when I'd been so much more naïve than I was now. I hadn't known what beauty really was. When March and

May had kissed at their wedding, when Doria had beamed her first infant smile…

Of all the things I'd lost, Alicia didn't even warrant a spot on the list. You couldn't lose what wasn't yours in the first place, after all.

Lyssa had come to a stop beside me. "The knot," I said, gesturing. "It'll pop out. The key should be behind it."

She nodded and trod gingerly over the more delicate branches with a care I couldn't help appreciating. When she reached the thicker branch that joined the trunk just a couple feet below the knot, she scrambled up it much like her grand-aunt had.

The knot gave way at the press of her fingers. Lyssa fumbled inside the hole and then turned toward me, her face lit up with victory. The key gleamed in her grasp. The wind whipped through her long white-blond hair, and my heart squeezed with sudden certainty.

We had to get her out of Wonderland before she turned everything here, both inside me and all around me, even more upside down.

CHAPTER THIRTEEN

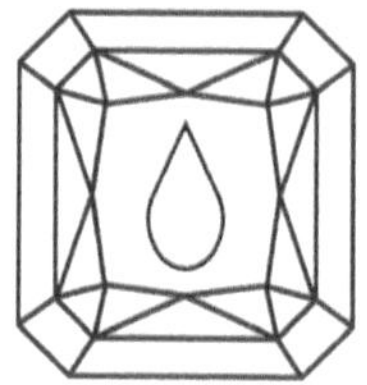

Lyssa

I turned Aunt Alicia's key over in my hands as we left the bizarre trees behind. The sooner we were out of the creepy Topsy Turvy Woods, the better.

A few bits of dirt clung to the key, but otherwise the brass surface gleamed as if it'd just been stuck in that tree yesterday. It looked like something from an antique store: a thin cylinder with a little notched bit protruding near one end and a circle of elaborate filigree at the other. The whole thing was about the length of my palm, and the filigree part took up half of that. The pattern of the lines and the indents at the top of the circle brought to mind a crown.

The key wasn't going to do me a whole lot of good here in Wonderland, though. I wiped the last flecks of dirt off it and tucked it carefully into my tote bag, on the inner side where I could feel the lump of it brushing against my hip as we walked.

I wasn't sure how much more walking I was up to doing right now. Even in my sneakers, my feet were starting to ache. Possibly my calves too. We'd already walked the whole morning.

Hatter strode along a step ahead of me, appearing for all the world as if he planned to march straight back to the city without a second's pause. Was he really in that much of a hurry to get rid of me? I hadn't been sure how serious he'd been about me causing his unhappiness—his wryly deadpan voice sounded an awful lot like his politely irritated voice—and he actually had looked kind of joyful being out here, which was the only reason I'd asked.

My stomach grumbled, and a fresh twinge ran up the backs of my legs. My body didn't care what he thought of me right now as long as it got a little relief.

When we'd come far enough into the stretch of small statuesque hills that I couldn't see the upended trees behind us anymore, I cleared my throat. The landscape here was still pretty weird. Just ahead of us a knoll with the shape of a gigantic human head was staring at me, and the scrawny bushes dotting the grass warbled as if their bright orange-and-yellow leaves were actual flames. But I was used to weird by now.

"Didn't you mention something about bringing a lunch?" I said.

Hatter was just glancing back with one eyebrow raised when a sound rippled over the hills that raised the hairs all up my arms and the back of my neck. It was a burbling sort of moan, like a rushing river in pain, cut off for a second with a ragged pant of breath that brought to mind razor-teeth. A thunderous crash sent the air shuddering.

"What the hell is *that*?" I said, my head jerking around.

Hatter had paled. "Nothing we want to meet," he snapped, and grabbed my arm. He dragged me off the path into the narrower gaps between the oddly shaped knolls. The burbling moan reverberated over the hills again, already louder.

I found my feet and dashed with Hatter around a huge grassy rooster, curled cat, and a splayed hand. He yanked me down behind a more distant knoll that weirdly looked pretty much like a little hill, just with a completely sheer slope on the far side.

"What—" I started to whisper, and Hatter cut me off with a finger to my lips. He stayed crouched next to me, his hand falling to my side, his eyes twitching with each new sound as he tracked them.

The thing we'd run from snarled and groaned. The ground shook under our feet. I edged a little closer to Hatter instinctively, and his hand shifted over my back in half an embrace, one I wasn't sure he was even conscious of. My pulse thumped at the base of my throat.

A flame-leafed bush clinging to the hill near us shivered, a smoky smell curling from its foliage that only increased the fiery illusion. There was a scraping sound like the scrabble of claws. Something hit the ground in a series of thuds. Teeth gnashed.

Hatter tensed as if to tug me away again, but the next moan reached us from farther away. The sounds dwindled until I was sure the thing was gone.

I sagged against the side of the hill in relief. "You didn't tell me there were *monsters* out here."

Hatter jerked his arm back to his side and moved to peer around the knoll. His face was still sallow.

"I didn't know there were," he said. "There never were before. That sounded like… like a jabberwock. They only roam the outer edges of Wonderland—which we're still quite a ways from. There shouldn't be…" He halted, frowning.

"Well, at least it didn't manage to have us for lunch, right?" I said, managing a weak laugh. A bit of grass and earth fell away under my hand as I straightened up, leaning on the hillside for balance. The gap revealed not more soil but a smooth section of stone, with a seam where it fit against another bit of stone. Huh.

I swiped at more of the earth, since really I'd rather give the jabberwock or whatever the heck had crashed through here plenty of time to get on its way before we returned to our path anyway. When Hatter glanced over, I'd already cleared off three whole stone blocks and the edges of those around them.

"It's not a hill," I said. "It's part of a wall. Or are they all made out of stone underneath?"

"Not in my experience," Hatter said. "Someone might have lived out here a long time ago."

The corner of some kind of carving showed on a neighboring stone. I worked the dirt off it. Who would have lived all the way out here instead of in the city with everyone else?

One large clod fell away, unveiling the rest of the carved symbol. My heart stopped. For a second, I could only stare at it.

"What?" Hatter said, sounding puzzled.

That image didn't mean anything to him at all?

I traced my finger over the lines. A faceted gemstone—*radiant cut*, I thought from my occasional daydreaming perusals of engagement rings styles—with a teardrop in the center.

"This symbol is carved onto the box Aunt Alicia left me," I said. "The one the key we just got is supposed to open." My gaze roved over the wall embedded in the hill. "What *is* this?"

"I don't know," Hatter said, his forehead furrowing as he examined it. "I've never seen that mark anywhere before."

I straightened up and stepped back, clutching my tote bag close to my side. The lump of the key pressed against my thigh.

I knew where I had to go to find my answers. The ache in my legs felt distant compared to that mission.

"Let's go," I said. "We can eat that lunch while we're walking. I've got to get home and find out what Aunt Alicia left for me."

"We'll play it a little differently this time," Chess said as we approached the flashing spinning top that was the Caterpillar's Club. "The guards didn't notice that anyone went through the door last time, so they won't be suspicious unless I try to pull the same trick. You can hang back, and I'll whisper invisibly in their ears. Lead them on a wild goose chase. When you can't tell what you're chasing, you can never catch it." He shot me his usual grin.

"Will we wait until they start giving out the night's special drink again?" I asked. The cooling night air licked over my legs. I'd changed back into my dress since it seemed to fit the club atmosphere better, and I hated to lose it more than the skirt and tank.

When I'd packed, I hadn't thought about how I'd bring the stuff back to me. My Otherland tote wasn't going to fit the club scene at all. I was leaving everything I'd brought with me behind—and bringing back Aunt Alicia's key, which was dangling under the dress's bodice from a brass chain Chess had found for me.

Doing without those few things wasn't a big deal. Besides, I wanted to get swept up in the dancing during this last chance before I headed home without worrying about holding on to anything.

"Acting at that point seems wisest," Chess said. "And while I may not always have the most level of heads, I can occasionally point it in the right direction. We'll get you home as many times as you need, lovely."

He tossed the compliment off his tongue so casually I knew it didn't really mean anything, but his words sent a flutter through my chest all the same. Hatter might have helped me begrudgingly, but Chess appeared to be getting plenty of enjoyment out of the subterfuge. I didn't get any sense he saw me as a burden.

Strains of violin mixed with a frenetic beat, filtering through the walls. The key slid between my breasts, a solid weight warmed by my skin. Maybe I wouldn't be letting *that* weight go while I danced, but it wasn't a burden either. It was a doorway into possibilities I hadn't discovered yet.

"Hey!" Chess said, and waved to someone he'd noticed down the road behind us. "Hatter."

We slowed so Hatter could catch up, although the slant of the other man's mouth suggested he wasn't overjoyed that he'd run into us. I wondered if I could get him dancing again. Melody would definitely tell him that he could stand to loosen up some.

I'd felt connected to him in that brief time when he'd shown a little playfulness. I found myself eyeing his hat, considering whether I'd be able to get away with stealing it a second time.

"Are you keeping an eye on Doria again?" I asked him. It'd been clear last time that he didn't go to the club to have a good time. "Didn't you promise her you'd cut her some slack?"

One side of his mouth curled upward at that. "I promised her she could run wild *yesterday*. Our deal didn't extend any further than that."

I suspected his daughter would be negotiating much more rigorously next time.

My heart beat faster as we reached the spinning walls, but I squared my shoulders remembering how easily I'd walked in last time. Picture a door. Believe I could go in, and in I'd go.

I took another step, and with a whine that whipped past my ears, I was standing on the undulating floor. The lights cascading over the room were all different shades of blue, green, and purple today, making the place look like some sort of underwater exhibit. A minty citrus smell tickled my nose. The dance floor was crowded, but not outright packed. We'd come early tonight.

Even if my feet protested after my long walk with Hatter, I'd wanted to squeeze as much joy out of my last hours here as I could, in case I didn't make it back to Wonderland. I knew without needing the experience that the pricks of pain in my body would fade away as soon as I was spinning to the music.

Chess leaned close to speak by my ear. "Caterpillar's here today. He doesn't always come out. He who watches prefers not to be watched." He made a slight tip of his head toward a tall, thick figure standing near the other end of the room.

At first, with so many people around us and the lights flickering this way and that, I thought the name Caterpillar was just an odd nickname for a totally human guy. Then the man moved, or more like waddled, around the fringes, his bulbous head bobbing out of time with the music, and I realized why he was so tall. His body had an extra segment in his torso, a second chest with its own set of arms just below the first. All of them were gesturing around him as independent limbs. That wasn't any Halloween costume.

My stomach lurched with horror. Walking animals and animal-human blends was one thing. An elongated dude with extra arms was a whole other level of strange. I jerked my eyes away.

"If we're lucky, he'll finish his chat with Rabbit and head back upstairs," Chess said. From the corner of my eye, I made out the white-rabbit head of the fellow I'd nearly run into in the passages under the club two nights ago.

I grasped Chess's arm, scanning the crowd for the thinnest patch where we could find a spot, wanting to get on with the dancing and wash the image of Caterpillar from my mind. My gaze caught on a startlingly white shirt flashing with different colors beneath the strobe lights while its wearer moved with the beat. Even if the shirt hadn't been unusual, I thought I would have recognized that powerfully assured form anywhere.

"Theo's here," I said.

Chess's eyebrows drew together and then arched up. "So he is," he said. "I suppose even the Inventor needs to blow off steam the old-fashioned way every now and then." His tone was oddly hesitant, but when I glanced up at him, he gave me his usual grin. "Shall we?"

Hatter's bronze-brown hat gleamed where he was circulating through the dancers farther to the right. Awareness of the three guys prickled over me with a faint tug, as if I were suspended between them, pulled in all directions simultaneously. I'd never been in the same room with all three of the men who'd shaped my time in Wonderland before.

How could my heart thump like this for *all* of them?

But Chess was the one standing next to me, the one with his solid arm slipping around my waist, the one who'd gone out of his way for me from the start. I shimmied with him into the mass of dancers.

My feet stung and my calves ached as I shuffled and dipped, but just as I'd expected, the discomfort melted away with the thump of the beat through my body in the wide room. Chess moved with me, a dreamy expression coming over his face. I gave myself over to that song and the next. Then Chess set his hand on the small of my back, drawing me closer to him with a deliberateness that made my heart pound faster than the music.

"Caterpillar's coming this way," he said, just loud enough for me to hear with his lips brushing my cheek, and my pulse skipped with a completely different emotion: panic.

"It's okay," Chess went on, his body still swaying with mine. "Just follow my lead. He might not even stop at us."

Caterpillar was stopping an awful lot of places. I caught glimpses as Chess turned us and edged a little deeper into the crowd. The overgrown man hefted his jointed body through the dancers, touching a shoulder here, an elbow there, bending his looming head to make some comment. It was pretty much only women he spoke to, I noticed. Just the club's proprietor making friendly with his clientele?

Chess spun us again, but Caterpillar veered at the same time. A smile pushed into his rounded cheeks as he looked down on the other man.

"Cheshire!" he said, in a booming voice that overshadowed the music. "Never quite as good a party without you." His beady eyes shifted to me, his gaze skimming down my dress. "I don't believe I've seen your dance partner around here before."

"I found myself a Dreamer today," Chess said quickly. "Lovely, isn't she?"

Follow my lead, he'd told me. Would it be a problem if Caterpillar found out I'd come through a looking-glass? Maybe he'd realize I might be aiming to leave through his?

Ignoring the heavy thud of my pulse, I forced myself to giggle. "Dreamer? What are you talking about? This can't be a dream. It's too fucking amazing!"

Caterpillar chuckled. "An attitude I approve of. I can make it an even better dream if you'd like."

I cringed inwardly at the thought of what he might mean, and Chess's hand tensed against my back. "No poaching, now, Caterpillar," he said, keeping his tone light.

"Oh, no, of course not," the club's owner said, with a puff of his chest that suggested he considered himself very generous to make that concession. "What do you think of Wonderland, my dear girl?"

I looked around the room as if still star-struck by it all, which wasn't that hard an emotion to fake. "It's so bright and flashy! I love it! If this is a dream, it's the best one I've had in a while."

"I can't ask for a better compliment than that." Caterpillar made a beckoning gesture, and one of the servers I'd seen two nights ago sauntered over with a platter of those vibrant mushroom slices. He plucked up a pink-and-violet one and offered it to me. "Don't miss the refreshments. You're in luck—we've got a particularly potent batch tonight."

Chess had warned me not to eat the mushrooms last time. He didn't seem to have any clever ideas for getting me out of this predicament, though. Caterpillar was watching me intently. It would be odd for a person who thought this was a wacky dream to refuse, right?

I accepted the mushroom slice gingerly. Suddenly I found myself thinking of Melody's old trick when teachers had caught her chewing gum back in high school.

Dear Lord, let this not be water-soluble. I popped the slice into my mouth and immediately pressed it hard against the roof of my mouth with my tongue. It stuck there, bleeding a faintly cloying flavor into my mouth, as I pretended to chew and swallow.

"Wow," I said, swaying with the music again. "I can already feel that kicking in."

If my voice was a little thicker because of the thing in my mouth, the Caterpillar didn't notice or assumed it was the drug's effect. He bobbed his head with a pleased expression and lurched on through the crowd.

Relief shot through me with a rush of exhilaration. I'd done it. I'd gotten through the conversation—fooled the guy who ran this whole club. And suddenly my head felt as if it were expanding, drifting up from my shoulders.

I jerked around and spat the mushroom slice into my hand before flicking it away among the bounding feet. The floaty feeling eased off with a shake of my head. Chess smirked and twirled me by the hand.

"You were perfect," he said.

"You better believe it," I said. "Now let's really dance!"

CHAPTER FOURTEEN

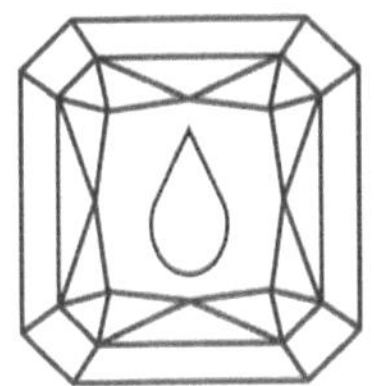

Lyssa

My skin was damp with sweat beneath my dress, and my spirits were soaring with the music when a much more welcome face than Caterpillar's appeared beside us. Theo gave Chess an affectionate clap on the back and smiled warmly at me.

"All's well here?" he asked.

"Everything's great!" I announced, spinning and reveling in the way my skirt flared out. I might have sounded a little loopy, but what did that matter? The whole point of this night was that it belonged just to me, an interval of brilliant freedom before I tumbled back into real life.

"Why don't you take over with this one for a while?" Chess said with a teasing glint in his eyes. "She's wearing me out." He squeezed my hand and then let it go as quickly as he'd taken it. "I'll see you when you don't see me."

Before I could say anything in response, he'd faded into the crowd. *Was* that the last time I was going to see him before I left? I'd have liked to at least say goodbye in case I didn't make it back… although, every minute longer I spent on this dance floor, I was imagining slipping back through the looking-glass for future visits.

If I dropped in once it was already evening, I wouldn't be imposing on anyone's hospitality. I could just pop right into the club and pretend I was having a recurring dream.

Theo leaned toward me and eased back with the rhythm of the music. His gaze held mine as if there wasn't anything else in this place he could possibly want to look at. Like in everything else I'd seen him do, every step he made emanated strength and confidence.

So fucking magnetic. My feet drifted nearer to him of their own accord.

"I saw you talking to Caterpillar," he said, dipping his head close to mine. "You handled him fantastically."

My lips twitched with a smile I couldn't contain. The approval in this man's voice felt like its own kind of drug. I suspected it was just as addictive.

"Chess helped," I said. "I didn't want anyone to get in trouble because of me. *Would* you get in trouble, if he knew how I got here?"

"You don't need to worry about that," Theo said, with so much certainty I didn't ask whether he meant because they wouldn't get in trouble or they'd be able to handle it if they did.

He swept his fingertips over my temple, brushing a few stray strands of hair back from my eyes. The contact sent a flare of heat over my skin even though he'd barely touched me. Maybe it was the intent focus with which he was meeting my eyes, as if there wasn't anything in the world more important to him in this moment.

No, *that* sensation was addictive.

"You're enjoying yourself here," he said, not quite a question. "Are you a party girl back in the Otherland?"

I had to laugh at that idea. "No," I said. "I'm not really a club person at all. But the ones back home, they're not—not like this. I've never had anything like this there."

He cocked his head, his intentness blending with warm curiosity. "What do you mean?"

I opened my mouth, and a nakedly honest answer spilled out before I could stop it. Maybe I didn't want to lie. Why shouldn't I be honest with him? That freedom was exactly what I craved in this place.

"Back home… I've got people who need me. People I care about, and I'd do anything for them, but it can still take a lot out of me. And everything I do, every decision I make, if I screw up or make a fool of myself, it could make the difference between having a job I need or not, it could freak out the people who care about me…"

"That's a lot of pressure to have on you," Theo said, so softly I only barely made out the words.

I ducked my head, choking up a little. "Sometimes the responsibility gets kind of suffocating, I guess. But I don't belong here, and that means I don't owe anyone here anything. They don't owe me anything either. I can just exist and be and do what feels good, without all that stuff weighing me down."

"Surely there's somewhere in the Otherland you could get that release?"

"I don't know," I said. "I've never found it. Maybe I just don't know the right way to look for it."

Theo's fingers glided under my chin, tipping my face up so I'd meet his gaze again. "I'm glad we could give you that here, then," he said. "And I suppose it makes sense. Maybe it's not all that easy for those of us who started here to appreciate this world the same way."

For an instant, an unexpected shimmer passed through his eyes, something like regret. Unless I only imagined that. It was there in a flash of blue light from above and then gone, replaced by his usual assured smile.

"We'd better make the most of the night, don't you think?" he said, his smooth baritone sending all kinds of tingles through me when his body was that close to mine.

I picked up my pace again, catching up with the beat. Theo sidestepped and swiveled, never moving too far away. As I let the music fill me once more, the motions of his limbs loosened a little. He tipped his head back to the lights as if drinking them in. There was something so vulnerable about the curve of his throat, the sense of searching in that pose, that my throat tightened for a second time.

I was starting to think there was a lot more to this guy than the measured power he seemed to live and breathe. A tenderness at his core that he kept well-shielded. How many other people had gotten even this brief glimpse of it?

The longing rang through me to delve into it even deeper, to discover everything there was to discover about the Inventor, the White Knight—this man of many names. Where had he come from? How had he ended up here?

But this wasn't the place for a delicate conversation, and I didn't really think he'd give me more of an answer than he already had anyway. What I'd said was true: I wasn't of this world. That might be the only reason he'd let his armor budge even that smidgen with me.

So I danced. The music reverberated through me and around me, and for a while everything fell away except the flow of my breath and the thump of my pulse in harmony. Theo stayed near me, matching my tempo with the occasional brush of his hand against my arm, my side, when he moved me with him.

The ache in my legs was only just creeping back into my awareness beneath my exhilaration when the clang of the gong rang out. The crowd of dancers surged toward the bar like they had the other night. Caterpillar was standing behind the bar waving a glass in the air.

I trailed behind the other dancers, keeping an eye on the basement doorway. Two of the guards had left it as before.

And three figures were striding through the club's entrance, steel batons glinting in their hands. I hesitated, eyeing them. They hadn't been here last time.

The three wore the same red-and-pink tunics and bulging helmets as the guy Chess had seemed to want to avoid the other day. The guy at the front had a tiger's head; the other two were fully human. All of them looked grim, their mouths set in flat lines and their eyes narrowed.

"What's going on?" I asked Theo, who'd stayed beside me. "Who are they?"

Before he could answer, one of them gave a shout and pointed to someone in the crowd. All three charged forward. I made out a woman with cascading black tresses groping to push a path through the crowd, but the other club-goers had stopped, stiff and still, at the shout.

One of the helmed guys snatched the woman's arm. The second caught her other wrist. They hauled her over one low slope and down another to a clear spot on the rippled dance floor. The club's music faded to a whisper.

"Traitor to the Queen!" roared the tiger-man who seemed to be the leader. "What was the meaning of this?" He brandished a rolled paper. I couldn't make out what was on it.

"I've never seen that before," the woman said, cringing. "It's not mine."

"Lies! We have three witnesses to your duplicity. Explain this message and tell us who you intended it for, and you may receive mercy."

"I don't know anything about it," the woman said raggedly.

Without a second's hesitation, the tiger-man whacked her across the head with his baton, hard enough to break the skin.

Blood welled on the woman's temple. She cried out, and the other men slammed their weapons into her ribs, her gut.

I jerked forward before I'd even realized my feet were moving. They were brutalizing her—they might *kill* her with those things. What could anyone have put on a piece of paper that would justify that?

The woman wasn't even fighting back, just huddling on the floor. I didn't know what I could do, but *someone* had to try to help, get her away from them—

Theo caught my elbow, yanking me back. When I stared up at him, his jaw was clenched, his expression as frozen as the club-goers all around us were. "You can't intervene," he said in a soft, strained voice. "They'll only turn on you too."

Part of me wanted to say, *Let them*, and run right in there to shove those guys off her for as long as I could. But Theo had an iron grip on my arm, and with each fleshy smack of the batons, nausea squeezed tighter around my stomach. The woman was slumped on the floor now, feebly shielding the side of her head with a bloodied hand, one eye swollen shut and one cheek bashed in. Her breath rattled over her lips as she sputtered for air between gasps. My legs wobbled as if the floor had tipped.

"Had enough?" the tiger-man finally growled. He knelt down beside the woman, waving the paper by her face. "What was your intent toward the Queen?"

"I'm sorry," the woman said, her voice not much more than a whimper. "It was only a joke. It made me laugh. I didn't expect anyone else to see it. I'm so sorry."

"Let's hope that's all this was," the tiger-man said. "We'll see if you've got more to say tomorrow, unless you want to go through this all over again." He motioned to the other two men. "Let's get her out of here so the *good* people of Wonderland can enjoy the rest of their night."

His cold gaze swept over the crowd. They dragged the woman out through the doorway, leaving a thin streak of blood on the floor.

"What are they going to do to her now?" I asked Theo. The crowd was already shifting around us, revelers drifting back across the dance floor. The music rose; the lights flashed faster. People threw themselves into the beat as if they hadn't just watched one of their acquaintances battered to a pulp.

My hands clenched at my sides. What was wrong with them?

"That depends on what else she says and what exactly was on that paper," Theo said. He still sounded strained, but not shocked. Was the scene we'd just witnessed *normal* around here? My stomach listed queasily.

"I don't understand. They were talking about 'the Queen.' They didn't mean Mirabel, did they?"

"No," Theo said. "They'd mean the Queen of Hearts, the woman those guards answer to. The ruler of Wonderland."

The ruler of Wonderland allowed—encouraged—vicious public beatings? Nothing about that or about the scene I'd just witnessed fit what I'd thought I'd known about this place.

Chess appeared in front of us as if out of thin air. He took in my expression, and his own tightened. "I wish I could have spared you seeing that, lovely. Are you all right?"

"No," I said. "Not really. I don't understand."

"You don't need to, looking-glass girl." Hatter had come up by my other side, Doria in tow and looking peeved. His voice was weary, his green eyes dark beneath the brim of his hat. "Get yourself home, pretend this was all a dream, and it'll have nothing to do with you at all."

"But why would your queen want— Why would she order— Why doesn't anyone *stop* her?"

Chess and Theo exchanged a look, Chess's gaze lingering on the White Knight for a beat before it slid to meet mine. "Simple to say has no bearing on simple to do," he said.

"Why don't we just tell her everything?" Doria demanded, jerking her elbow out of her father's grasp and folding her arms over her chest. "Why keep hiding it? I think she deserves to know."

"Doria," Hatter said sharply. He turned back to me. "This isn't your world. It isn't your problem. Go home and be thankful for that."

Chess tipped his head toward the basement door and leaned in. "The other two guards will be back at their posts in a minute or two," he said, his tone gentler than Hatter's had been. "If you want to reach the looking-glass tonight, we'd better go now."

Theo's hand eased up my arm to rest on my shoulder. He bowed his head next to mine from behind, his voice low and potent. "It's your choice, Lyssa. There'd be no shame in going home and forgetting. Or you could stay tonight to hear how things in Wonderland have gone terribly wrong—and how you might be able to help set them right."

His words quivered through me. I swallowed hard. I'd come back here looking for joy and freedom. But I'd also wanted answers—I'd wanted to understand, even if I hadn't known how much there might be I wasn't seeing here.

Maybe I *would* be able to forget if I slipped back through the mirror to my ordinary life, but right now the four figures standing around me were as solid and real as anyone I'd ever cared about. The woman whose blood was now being smeared under dancing feet was real.

What kind of person would I be if I turned my back on this place the moment things got scary?

I drew my spine as straight as it would go. “I’m staying,” I said. “So start explaining.”

CHAPTER FIFTEEN

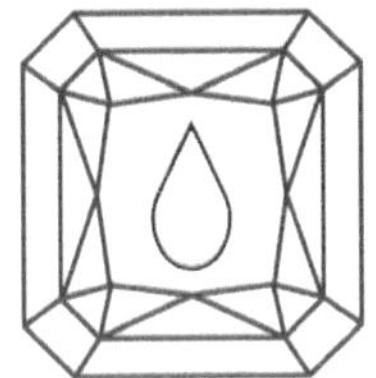

Chess

I would not have wished the story we had to tell on anyone, but our Otherlander had asked for it, so she would get it. And she'd get it from me, it appeared.

We'd slipped out of the club—Lyssa, the White Knight, Hatter, Hatter's daughter, and me—to escape the noise, but the hush on the darkened street outside felt far too exposed for the conversation we were about to have. In the end, we'd found ourselves at Hatter's house, mainly because it was twice as close as the knightly tower and I didn't entirely have a place of my own.

But Hatter didn't look at home at all, pacing the floorboards with their flaking creamy-yellow paint, his mouth tilted at a sour angle. When he lifted his hat for a moment to rake a hand through his spiky hair, I half-expected a thundercloud to peek out from underneath. It would have suited him in that moment. He clearly didn't want to be here, and yet he couldn't quite let the discussion happen without him.

He was as much a player in this game as any of us, no matter how hard he'd tried to place himself outside the reach of the board.

When his daughter started to say something, he motioned her

quiet. Lyssa, who'd sank onto the wingchair and drawn her legs up beside her on the cushion, glanced around our irregular cluster, anxious anticipation making her blue eyes shine even brighter than usual. The White Knight, who'd sat on the beach chair with such poise it might as well have been a throne, tipped his head to me.

I couldn't say why he didn't take the lead when I suspected he'd planned for this conversation, but why not me? Unlike him, I could remember the time before, when we'd had time.

I hopped onto the bar stool and leaned forward on my perch. "Here's the short of it, lovely. There's a palace not far from the city, and the royal family of Hearts rules from there. The Queen is the real power, and she wields that power like a tyrant. No one can say a word against her, no one can question her methods, or she's liable to call for one's head. Separate from one's neck."

Lyssa's face had already been sallow. At those words, it blanched even more. "Why does everyone seem so… *happy*, then?" she asked. "How can people go around playing and partying when those guards could storm in and start terrorizing them at any second?"

"Practice," I said. "Survival. To appear *un*happy can be considered an act of treason. If you don't learn to put on a good show…" I made a dramatic sweep of my forefinger across my throat. "And when you can't change what is, it's easier for many to put it out of their minds, to distract themselves whatever way they can."

There was no need to mention that oftentimes I was one of those many.

"Why *can't* you change things?" Lyssa said. "There are lots of you here in the city. How many guards does she have?"

"We do try," Hatter's daughter started. Hatter cut her off with a glare of warning. She huffed and flopped into the beanbag chair. Hatter continued his pacing.

The White Knight was watching me, his gaze approving, giving every indication he expected me to go on. "Well," I said, ignoring the brief urge to hunch my spine defensively, "there's a matter of time. Or lack thereof. We're hamsters on a wheel, running fast to end up exactly where we started." I made a looping motion with my hand.

"I don't understand," Lyssa said. "From what Hatter said before about how slowly you get older, it sounds like you have *more* time to organize some kind of rebellion than we would in my world."

My tongue and my natural inclinations always slipped away from the rawest answers. Even trying to summon the words brought back a flash of a different sort of rawness, pain radiating down to every bone—waiting, as I was stretching to breaking, for that wheel to flip over.

The White Knight picked up the thread where I'd hesitated. "There are certain kinds of magic possible in this land," he said. "Ways a determined enough person may bend what is to their will. The Queen was aware a rebellion was forming. So she captured Time. Without it, Wonderland cannot move forward."

"What do you mean, 'captured time'?" Lyssa said. "I've been here two days now—I came before that—time passed."

"We keep our memories," the White Knight said. "Our understanding can grow. But the rest, everything around us… It's the same day, reset, unchanging."

"We wake up where we woke the morning of the day she locked Time up," I expanded. "If I spill something on Hatter's poor floor, or he tries to touch up the paint, tomorrow it'll look the same as ever again."

"There's nothing wrong with my floor," Hatter muttered, stopping his pacing for long enough to glower.

Lyssa knit her brow. "Then how..." Her eyebrows leapt up. She jerked around to look at Hatter. "*That's* why you hadn't cleared the table."

He sighed. "There isn't much point when it'll clear itself overnight. After a while, pretending you need to just reminds you of the fact that you don't." His gaze lingered on her for a moment with a stark intensity. Thinking, perhaps, of the cup that hadn't cleared itself. My own eyes dropped to the spot where it had sat.

"Any device I create has disassembled itself the next morning," the White Knight said. "Nothing anyone builds can outlast the day. No supplies can be amassed. No traps can be laid. The only elements she couldn't contain were life and death themselves. New life can spark and grow where it's welcomed." He raised his hand to indicate Doria. "But if we lose our heads, we're gone."

Lyssa hugged herself. "Do you think they did that to the woman they grabbed in the club?"

"Not necessarily," I said. "Our situation allows for a rather brilliant form of torture. Batter us to the brink of death, and we spring back up good as new the next morning—when they can start all over again."

My tone must have gone a bit sharp, or else it was only the content of my words that made Lyssa wince. A thread of tension wrapped around my ribs. Were we laying too much on her? She hadn't been prepared for this. *We* hadn't prepared her. The bright and joyful Wonderland was falling down around her ears in one horrifying crash, and the brightness I'd enjoyed seeing in her was dimming at the same time.

But her head was still high, her jaw still set with determination despite her pallor. She'd stayed. I could have led her to an easy escape, to the comforts of home, but she'd stayed to hear what had befallen ours—and how she might help.

Underneath the soft, hesitant exterior, this girl—this *woman*—had a core of steel. It made me like her even more.

"So, anything you do to push back, by the next day it's like it never happened, except what people remember," Lyssa said. "That… would make a rebellion difficult."

"Especially when fewer and fewer people are willing to become involved," the White Knight said. His gaze slid to Hatter for a second before returning to Lyssa. "The Queen hasn't taken much comfort in the security she claimed for herself. Her reaction to any sign of dissention has become ever more brutal as the years go by."

"She takes every excuse she can to turn up the heat," I said. "When her youngest son died years ago, several heads rolled for that, even though the Spades had nothing to do with it, and she's been absolutely vicious since then."

The White Knight grimaced at the truth of those words.

"The Spades?" Lyssa repeated.

"That's how we refer to our group of rebels," I said with a swivel of my finger. "Only a Spade will know you mean the Inventor if you mention the White Knight."

Her eyes widened. "Mirabel mentioned—was my grand-aunt

involved in your rebellion? You acted like you didn't know what she meant." Her accusation shifted from the White Knight to Hatter.

"You were our guest," the White Knight said smoothly. "To tell you when you didn't need to know, when you couldn't be prepared, would put you at risk. I never met your grand-aunt. I'm not sure of the extent of her involvement."

"She associated with the Spades a little," Hatter put in with obvious reluctance. "Nothing particularly noteworthy. That was before the Queen captured Time. Things were different."

Lyssa dragged in a breath. She appeared to retreat inside herself, but only for a minute. "What are you going to do? Do you *have* a plan?"

The White Knight rested his elbows on the table. "We know what we need to do. We need to free Time from the Queen's grasp, so Wonderland can move forward again. All change will stem from that moment. But she has it caged in a pocket watch kept secure and guarded inside the palace. Reaching it has been the sticking point. Until, perhaps, now."

The intentness of his focus on her made my skin itch. I bit my tongue against remarks that wanted to slip out. The White Knight had always led us well—had been there for me when I'd had nothing.

I might like Lyssa, might feel uneasy about the situation we were placing her in, but I could very well owe *him* my life.

"You said in the club that I might be able to help," Lyssa said.

The White Knight nodded. "After your first visit here, we observed that you seem to carry a certain amount of Time with you from the Otherland. It rubs off on items you touch. The cup you drank from at this table four days ago didn't return to the cupboard overnight. We can't be sure how far that power will extend, but it could make all the difference to our cause. If you'll come by the Tower tomorrow morning, I can show you what I'm thinking. For now… You look as if you've had enough laid on your shoulders for one night. I apologize for the burden."

He pushed the chair back and stood up. Lyssa peered up at him—looking rather dazed, I had to agree. Dazed and exhausted.

"All right," she said, and stifled a yawn. "But I'm sure I'll have lots more questions when I can think straight again."

The White Knight gave her a wry smile. "I look forward to answering them as well as I can. Get your rest."

"We need to be careful with this," Hatter said. "The Caterpillar at the club tonight, and the Queen's guards— If they form any suspicion and pass it on to the Queen— They might have already." His jaw worked. He glanced at me. "Chess, you could… you could slip in and overhear…"

My shoulders stiffened. He trailed off completely at the grin I gave him, deliberately baring my sharpest teeth. "My ability to slip sight does not include slipping through walls," I said with deliberate firmness. "Where the doors are locked, I still can't go."

That wasn't what he'd been thinking of, and we both knew it. But he'd sworn to me to hold his tongue about that one thing—the White Knight didn't know, and I'd rather keep it that way, in regards to both him and everyone else in this room. It was the one piece of myself I still owned. The one piece no one was going to use, not again.

Hatter's mouth twisted in apology. "Never mind. I wasn't thinking straight."

I let my grin relax to show his contrition was acceptable. "The Caterpillar saw a Dreamer," I said, to set his mind more at ease. "The guards were occupied with their beating. No one even knows her name except for us."

Lyssa's attention snapped to me. "Should I not tell anyone else my name? Why would that matter?"

That was an entirely different rabbit hole. "It's just best if the bastards have as little as possible to work with, I'd think." I slid off the stool.

The White Knight nodded. "I've been tracking talk around the palace," he said. "If there's any reason for concern, I'll know." He paused, and let his knuckles brush over Lyssa's hair, so lightly the strands barely moved. "You're in good hands. And the moment you decide you need to make your way home, temporarily or for good, all you have to do is say so."

Hatter made a faintly scoffing sound. Lyssa just gazed at the White

Knight. Her expression, still dazed but with a hint of what looked like longing, made the niggling in my chest coil tighter.

Outside, he and I headed down the street together. It didn't much matter where I went in this last hour or so before midnight reset all our clocks. I might slink back around the club, just to taste the atmosphere. But first I wanted confirmation.

When Hatter's shop disappeared around a corner behind us, I pitched my voice low. "What did you offer Sealina to offset that beating?"

Credit given where credit was due: The White Knight didn't flinch or stare, or give so much as a twitch to suggest he was surprised by the question. Cool as a cucumber on ice. "Offer her?" he repeated smoothly.

"You planned that scene in the club," I said. I'd never seen the White Knight venture onto the premises without a specific purpose beyond enjoyment. "You set up all the pieces in a neat line and, oh, there they topple! You wanted Lyssa to see the other side of Wonderland."

He gave me a barely perceptible shrug. "I wanted what's best for Wonderland. She couldn't make a real decision without knowing. And wouldn't you say that simply hearing tell isn't enough to know?"

I would. His admission didn't sit entirely comfortably with me all the same. "So, how did you convince Sealina to go through with it?"

The White Knight turned his deep brown gaze on me. At times, it could look fathomless. This time, for example.

"I didn't offer her anything," he said simply. "She volunteered, because she wished to contribute to the cause. I guided her to ensure it wasn't a crime so great they'd take her head for it. She'll be well enough once they're finished with her. We *all* want what's best for Wonderland—to see its people freed, finally. Don't you?"

Damn him, he managed to work a note of concern into his voice even as he evaluated me. Concern for me, that I might be losing hope. He sounded as if he meant that concern honestly. Which sent a spike of guilt through me for nagging him on this subject at all.

"Of course," I said. "If you require my services again, you know you can call on me."

CHAPTER SIXTEEN

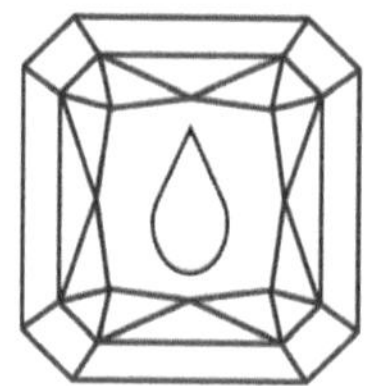

Lyssa

The dark history the guys had shared with me filtered into my dreams, merging with images from my walk with Hatter. Heads bounced across a dance floor soaked with blood that flipped me upside down and cracked the sky. A pack of playing cards with razor-sharp edges blasted at me with a burbling moan, hearts and spades tearing into each other. I kept waking up to the dark room and a frantic pulse.

Eventually, the dreams faded to give me a little peace, and I slept for a while. I finally raised my head groggily from the pillow to bright sunlight trickling past the mauve curtain. It had to be at least mid-morning.

I sat up on the feathery-soft mattress and stiffened to keep from swaying with momentary dizziness. My gaze fell on a little silver tray on the nightstand—a tray that hadn't been there last night. Two familiar-looking scones sat on it next to a teacup with its saucer set on top to hold in the heat. The porcelain was still warm against my fingers as I picked it up.

Hatter had put in exactly the right amount of cream and sugar.

And he'd left the scones I'd adored yesterday. I slid to the edge of the bed to eat the first one, reveling in the pine-y fruity taste, as if all of Christmas had been squeezed into a pastry the size of my palm. I didn't care that it felt like spring around here. In scone form, I'd take Christmas all year round.

I hadn't realized that Hatter had tracked my tastes that closely. I wouldn't have thought he'd go out of his way to cater to them. Leaving this meal here so I could fortify myself before I had to face the rest of Wonderland again… It was sweet of him.

I took another bite of the tangy sweet pastry and smiled. I guessed he didn't see me as a total hassle after all.

After I'd finished my breakfast, I carried the tray down to the living area with me. There was no sign of Hatter or Doria other than a few dishes they'd left on the table. I guessed they weren't breaking that habit any time soon. Since it niggled at me more to have them there rather than not, I took a couple minutes to wash them. Then I ventured down to the shop.

The display room was empty, but a tapping sound carried from a doorway beyond the stairs. I slipped past them to peer into the back room.

Hatter was standing at a table laid with felt and buttons and ribbons, twisting an elaborate bow at one side of a hat beneath a billowy feather. His deft fingers tweaked and secured each loop in a rapid dance. Something about the movement sent a tingle through me.

I took another step forward, and he glanced up. His hat—a bowler today, forest-green like his suit—had tipped low on his head. He fastened the ribbon with a swift press and nudged the brim of the bowler higher on his head, considering me with an oddly wary gaze. Maybe he just wasn't sure how I'd processed everything I'd heard last night.

"You still make hats, even though they'll only last until the end of the day?" I said.

"Wonderlanders still crave the occasional novelty," he said. "They give me their requests one day and pick them up the next."

"Oh. That makes sense." Why had I started with that opening? I tried again.

"Thank you for breakfast," I said, not knowing how to express my deeper gratitude for the consideration it showed without embarrassing myself or him, or both of us. I didn't even know how big of a gesture it was in this place with its standards, which were even more warped compared to my world back home than I'd believed at first.

"You enjoyed it?" he said with a slight twitch of his lips toward a smile. A real one, the kind that made the corners of his eyes crinkle. I had to drag my gaze away before I just stood there staring at him, waiting for the smile to grow.

"Very much." I picked up a half-finished hat from a shelf to the side, just to have something to do. "Keep a stash of those scones around, and I'll have no complaints about anything."

He chuckled. "I'll keep that in mind." Then he paused, his head shifting just a bit, as if he'd meant to look at me and thought better of it. "How long are you planning on staying?"

His tone was careful, but I didn't get the impression it was a hint that he was trying to kick me out.

"I don't know," I said. "I guess I should get going to see Theo and find out what *his* whole plan is that he thinks I can help with. From the way things worked the last time I came, I think I can stay at least a few more days before anyone starts to worry."

Melody had given me twenty-four hours before she went into panic mode about my supposed date. I didn't think a full day here would be more than a couple hours back home. If Theo's idea was going to require longer than felt safe, I should be able to slip back through the club's mirror to avert disaster there before popping back here, right?

The memory of Caterpillar looming over me with his segmented body and bulbous head made my skin crawl. I'd wondered before what would happen to me if his guards caught me sneaking to the mirror. Other memories from last night—the Queen of Hearts' guards, the stories Theo and Chess had told me—rose up with a lurch of my stomach.

Would Caterpillar have them beat me until I bled? Chop my head right off?

"You're leaving now?" Hatter moved to join me with a swish of his jacket and then hesitated again. "Would you want me to accompany you?"

"I think I can find my way to the Tower by now," I said. "It is the tallest building in the city. Unless… I should be worried about walking around here alone?" Nothing had gone wrong during my walk from the pond to Hatter's shop two days ago, but that might have been luck. I had to look back on everything I'd thought I'd known about Wonderland from a different perspective now.

Hatter was shaking his head. "The Queen's guards don't come into the city often unless they have someone specific they're looking for," he said. "And there's no reason they'd bother you."

"Just don't run around shouting out, 'Down with the Queen! Hurray for the Spades!'?" I suggested.

This time his mouth twitched downward. "You shouldn't even joke about that."

His voice came out so rough that guilt jabbed my stomach, even though I wasn't totally sure what I had to feel guilty about. "Right," I said. "Sorry. It's just a lot to wrap my head around. But I would like to keep my head, attached to my neck, and I say that with all seriousness."

"Good," Hatter said. "You know, whatever the White Knight is plotting, you don't have to get involved."

My throat tightened. I set down the hat. "Do you still think I should have gone home?"

It took him a moment to answer, his hand bracing against the tabletop. "I think you'd be safer there. This mess we're in is complicated, and you can't have been prepared to dive in. All I'm saying is you should be honest about what you can do and what's too much. It'll be better for us and for you. You don't have to jump just because he tells you to."

Did he think I'd never had to make the best I could out of shit? A flash of emotion from long ago, desperate and determined, darted through me. I raised my chin. "I have a pretty good idea of my limitations."

Then something clicked in my head, connecting this conversation to the one last night with his muttered interjections. Maybe his reluctance wasn't just about me. Maybe Hatter's offer of company hadn't been to shield me on the streets but at my destination.

"You don't totally trust them, do you?" I added. "The Spades, I mean." Or just Theo? But Hatter was the one who'd sent me to Theo in the first place.

His wary expression came back. "I trust their ends," he said. "The means… Different people draw the line between acceptable risk and way too fucking risky in different places. And sometimes even our own lines get blurry when the goal seems to be in reach. Just be careful."

"I don't think you have to worry about that with me," I said, remembering Melody's ribbing.

A shade of a smile crossed Hatter's face. It warmed me almost as much as Chess's grin could. "Maybe not," he said.

I left before I could manage to annoy him all over again. As I ducked out of the hat shop, a faint pattering sounded overhead. Doria scrambled from an outcropping of roof to a window ledge and hopped onto the ground. The fact that she'd managed her climb in one of those billowy gothic dresses made the maneuver even more impressive.

She tucked her dark hair behind her ears and trotted over to join me. "You're going to the Tower, right?" she said, a little breathless.

"Yeah," I said. "Are *you* supposed to be?"

She shrugged with a sly little smile. "I'm not a kid anymore. I've done a heck of a lot more than he knows. If I went by what Pops says, I wouldn't get to do *anything*."

I wasn't sure I liked the idea of aiding and abetting Hatter's daughter in her personal rebellion, but she *wasn't* exactly a kid, and it sounded like she'd go off to see Theo and his people one way or another no matter what I did. I wasn't so much aiding as observing the inevitable.

"You've been helping out the Spades?" I murmured. No one was walking near us, but after Hatter's warnings, I wasn't taking any risks about being overheard.

"I *am* a Spade," Doria said, quiet but fierce. "And I'm good at it. I don't go to the club to dance, you know. I listen to all the talk. I ask people questions no one would ask—or answer—if they were sober. I find things out."

I had the feeling between that enterprise and dancing, Hatter would have preferred she went to dance.

"Does it happen a lot—what happened last night?" I couldn't help asking. "The guards and… everything."

Doria bit her lip, which maybe was enough of an answer. "I won't get caught," she said. "I'm smart about it. It's not as if Dad never—" She cut herself off. "Whatever. It's my life, and I'd like to be able to have one where things don't just reset back to how they were no matter what I do."

"I can understand that." It was hard for me to even imagine living that way—for years and years. For Doria's whole life, I guessed. How long had the Queen of Hearts held Wonderland in her grip this tightly? Hatter had said Aunt Alicia had come before then, but that only meant it couldn't have been more than fifty years. Even five sounded like enough to drive a person mad.

Maybe the constant cavorting and whimsy weren't so weird after all. *Survival*, Chess had said. *Easier to distract themselves…*

Even the parts of this world I'd wanted to bask in were made out of pain rather than the joy I'd thought I'd seen.

Doria clammed up for the rest of our walk, which wasn't very long anyway. She'd obviously made this trek many times, and she knew which shops to duck between, which alleys to veer down, to cut straight across the city rather than taking the more winding route of the actual streets. When we reached the gleaming silver spire of the Tower, she let out a pleased sound and waved to a stout young man with bright red hair and brighter clothes wiping down a table outside a nearby café. "Dee!"

She bounded over to talk to him, so I went into the Tower alone. I hadn't navigated the elevator by myself before. Even though this was my third time stepping into that narrow but vastly tall space, my breath caught as I stared up past all those dozens of floors.

"Twenty-seventh floor," I said, the same way Chess had both times. "Lyssa coming calling."

The air pressure jolted me upwards. I started to wonder how a waft of air could understand language enough to know where to drop me off, and then I reminded myself that I was in Wonderland and nothing I thought I knew about physics or engineering applied here anyway.

When I stepped into Theo's office, he was standing by the worktables, a contraption about the length of his arm in front of him. "Lyssa!" he said, with what sounded like genuine pleasure. He finished screwing a bit of metal to one side of it and came around the table to meet me. "I'm glad you came. Last night must have been a lot to take in."

"It was," I said. Having him so close to me brought back the brush of his hand down the side of my face just before he'd left. My heart thumped in a heady beat. The White Knight had been captivating even before with that powerful aura of his, but knowing he supported the city not just with inventions and advice but also by leading its underground movement for freedom made his presence somehow twice as magnetic.

So much on his shoulders, and he took everything in stride with that warm assurance. It was hard to imagine him taking any risks he hadn't carefully weighed and judged worth it.

"You wanted to explain your plan to me, and how I'd fit into it?" I went on.

"I appreciate the enthusiasm." He reached for my hand as easily as if he'd taken it a hundred times, but he only held on for long enough to lead me over to the table. A gleam of passion came into his eyes as he looked down at the contraption.

"I've just been reconstructing my latest model of the pocket-watch retriever," he said. "I'm sure Chess will be able to come up with a much fancier name for it when I unveil it. Allies of the Spades gather the necessary parts each morning, the ones I didn't already have on hand. It's taken a lot of time and experimentation to create something with all the functions we need."

He ran his finger over a crystal sphere that gleamed in the midst of the contraption. "This was the crowning jewel that brought it all together, and it's the only one of its kind we've found, at least that we can reach. In some ways I've been lucky to have our daily resets, as it's rather fragile, and I've accidentally cracked it a few times."

"Yeah, I guess being stuck in time makes trial and error a lot more straightforward," I said. You always ended up back where you started… but you never lost anything either. "So that's the key to, well, retrieving the watch?"

Theo smiled. "Yes. Although this is only the second stage out of two. The first is how we make our way into the palace at all."

Of course. "There must be a lot of guards out there," I said.

He nodded without much evident concern. "But they too all find themselves reset when the day flips over. As I understand it, the Queen didn't bother to put any in place that first morning, knowing they'd always be able to reach it before anyone else could. She does like to keep her staff on their toes. The guards are rather lax about making their way there since there's never been any urgency before. We'll have an opening of about half an hour—if we're close enough to the palace already."

It wasn't hard to put the pieces together. "That's what you need me for," I said. "You're thinking that if I'm with whoever's running the mission, they *won't* be reset back to the city or wherever. We get as close as we can beforehand, and then as soon as the day switches, they can make a run for the watch."

"Exactly. Look at you, already three steps ahead of me." The approval in Theo's expression made me beam in return. He tapped the device on the table. "I'll also need you here when I construct this on the day of, so it doesn't reset into its pieces. We'll have to experiment some to see exactly how involved in its construction you need to be to make sure the effect sticks, but I can walk you through the proccss even if it comes to that. For now, would you just pick it up for a moment?"

"Sure." I eased my hands under the device. With its rods and wires, it looked almost like a skeletal arm. I held it gingerly for the space of a few heartbeats and then set it down. "That's it?"

"That's perfect," Theo said.

"What does it do, exactly?" I asked. "What do you need it for once you've made it to the room with the watch?"

"Well… the Queen has some unusual ideas about security," Theo said. "The room we can make it into isn't the room with the watch. *That* lies on the other side of a doorway too small for anyone to fit more than a forearm through, in a fortified glass case. Our retriever will be able to reach far beyond that doorway."

He flicked a couple of levers, and the device extended to four times its previous length. The crystal hovered in the center as if balancing the sides. When Theo ran his fingers over a dial at the end he was holding, the crystal flashed. An image of the room beyond the far end of the retriever appeared over the handles. "This will allow us to aim quickly and correctly. Then this will cut through the case and catch the watch with a magnetic pull." He pointed to a metal disc at the other end. "After that, all we need to do is pull the watch out."

Easy peasy, as my dad used to say. "All right," I said. "I don't even have to be there for that part, right? Just wherever you stake out the palace." That didn't sound like too much of a risk. If I did make the dash for the watch with them, I'd probably just slow Theo's team down. An athlete, I was not. "Do we go for it tonight, then?"

"As much as I'd like to see the Queen's tyranny ended, we can't afford to hurry this," he said, "Once we've shown our hand, we may never get another chance if we're unsuccessful. I'll be making a few final refinements on the retriever while checking how you've affected its stability, and we'll be going over the best current route across the grounds. I don't want to ask too much of your time, though. It should only take a couple days to be fully prepared."

I'd already been ready to stay that long. "I don't think that'll be a problem," I said. "As long as Hatter doesn't get tired of hosting me."

Theo's eyebrows arched. "Has he not appreciated having you as a guest?"

It wasn't really fair for me to complain after the bedside breakfast I'd gotten this morning. "He's been fine. It just has to be an imposition when he wasn't expecting any guests, right?" I said quickly, and groped for a change of subject. I ran my finger over the retriever's metal sinews. "Where did you learn to invent stuff like this? Or were you just born knowing how, some kind of Wonderland thing?"

"The White Knight before me took me through the ropes," Theo said, his lips curving fondly. "I suppose he must have seen some natural inclination in me to take me on as his apprentice."

I blinked at him. "Before you? There've been other White Knights?"

"It's just a code name, really," he said. "Or a marker of position as much as 'Inventor' is. There were Queens of Hearts before the Queen of Hearts, Hatters before Hatter." He cocked his head. "I'm not sure if there've ever been other Cheshires or if our Chess is one of a kind."

"Oh," I said. "Then how long have you...?" I gestured to the office.

He picked up another metal bit from farther down the table and started twisting it onto his device. "I've fully inhabited the position for more than twenty-five years now. Unlike Chess and Hatter, I was born into the freeze." He looked up at me, his deep brown eyes like a gulp of rich cocoa on a chilly day. "I was born into this world. I have to admire your dedication to our cause, to help us overcome our oppression. Where did *you* learn that compassionate fortitude?"

I'd never heard anyone put it in quite such a complimentary way before. It sounded a lot more heroic than Melody teasing me about being a pushover. My cheeks flushed, and a hollow formed in the pit of my stomach. I picked up a golden gear and turned it between my fingers, letting the nubs dig into my skin.

"I guess I was born into that position, in a way," I said. "My dad got sick when I was little—cancer. He fought it for three years, but he passed on when I was eight."

The hollow inside expanded with the uncomfortable mix of loss and bitterness that always came when I lingered on this subject. I'd barely known Dad as a dad, he'd spent so many of the childhood days I could remember hunched on the sofa or slumped in his bed, often without the energy to smile or say much more than, "Hey, Lyss," in that increasingly thin voice.

I soldiered on, because Theo was still watching me—because the attentiveness of his gaze told me my answer mattered to him. "My mom kind of fell apart. And my older brother, Cameron—he was just so *angry*. He kept picking fights, stealing things, getting into trouble any way he could... Someone had to hold the family together. Make sure Mom got to work, that the bills got paid, that there was food in the house. Be one solid thing in the middle of the chaos. So I made that me."

The gear slipped from my fingers and clinked on the tabletop. Theo set his hand over mine. "That's a lot for any one person to shoulder."

I didn't want him pitying me. His admiration was much more appealing. "I managed," I said, trying to exude the same effortless strength he did.

"My condolences, as belated as they are. I can't imagine... My father wasn't the most present of parents, but that hardly compares."

"I don't know," I said without thinking. "I can assume mine would have been a great dad if he'd had any choice in it."

Theo's gaze flickered, and shame clogged my throat. "I'm sorry. That was a horrible thing to say."

"It was an honest thing." Theo eased back, his face perfectly relaxed, his thumb tracing a tingling line over my knuckles. Had I imagined that flash of discomfort?

He chuckled. "I'd be surprised if you and Hatter don't get along quite well. I hope your family dynamics are less fraught now that you're grown?"

"Yes," I said. "Not peaceful, but definitely less dramatic." Now that he'd mentioned his dad, I couldn't help asking, "What was your mom like?" What combination of Wonderland parenting had produced this stunning man?

Theo's lips quirked with amusement. "Oh, she doted on me, gave me everything she could imagine I'd want. Unfortunately she rarely stopped to check whether her imaginings were correct."

I thought about Mom and her unnecessary worries. "I know what that's like. Well, not so much the 'gave me everything' part, but the rest. It's so frustrating when you know they love you, but there's so much they just can't seem to *see* about who you actually are."

"Yes," Theo said, with a thread of something in his voice that made me glance at him, but his expression hadn't changed. "That's it exactly. If they even see you at all and not just an idea of what they feel you should be."

"Or that they're *worried* you might be," I muttered.

"That too." His thumb slipped across the back of my hand one more time. "Well, as sorry as I am that you bore those burdens, I'll admit I'm grateful for whatever part they played in bringing you here to us. To me."

Those last two words in his soft baritone warmed me even more than his touch did. "Me, too," I said quietly, and drew on the fortitude he'd praised to grin at him. "Even if some of my life was tough, I decided a while back not to regret any of it, because who knows if I could do everything I need to do now if I hadn't learned all the things I did back then? You've just got to keep looking forward."

"Indeed," Theo said, smiling back at me. "Looking backward can be a treacherous thing. I—" He caught himself with a shake of his head. "I should let you go so I can get our plans organized, or I'll end up extending your stay even longer. Enjoy what you can of all Wonderland offers while I set the pieces in place."

"Just be careful?" I said, expecting a repeat of Hatter's cautioning.

"I know I don't need to tell *you* that," he said, as if he had absolute confidence in me. "Although I would advise staying close to the city while jabberwockies are straying farther from their usual grounds, since I don't have any vorpal swords on hand to lend you. Will you stop by again tomorrow, to see where we're at?"

"Of course," I said. I'd come just to see him.

He guided me toward the door, his hand warm on my back. "Let's hope for plenty of good news. And, Lyssa." He waited until I met his eyes. "If you should need a different place to stay, or you simply want a change of scenery at any time—my door will be open. No matter the reason, you can always come to me."

CHAPTER SEVENTEEN

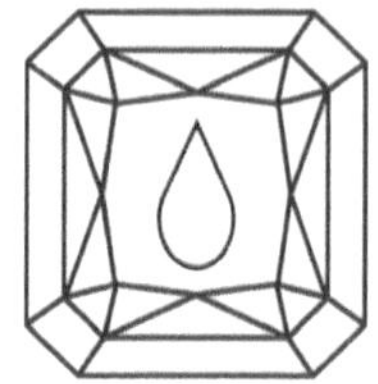

Lyssa

They'd cleaned the blood off the club's floor. I guessed that wasn't too much to ask. Swaying up and down the miniature hills and valleys made me more queasy than exhilarated tonight with those images in my head—with all the knowledge I'd gained.

Wonderland had come so much more starkly into focus in the course of a day, but not for the better.

I hadn't really expected to find the same sense of freedom I had before. That wasn't why I'd come. I snatched a shot glass full of swirling neon pink liquid from a passing tray and used that as an excuse to ease over to the wall with Chess, who'd volunteered as my dancing partner even though I wasn't planning on making a run for the mirror tonight. I could only picture the look Hatter would have given me if I'd asked him, and Theo had enough on his plate. Chess had actually appeared to enjoy the atmosphere here.

"Give me the whole run-down," I said to him now. I sniffed the neon drink and winced at the acrid mint scent. "How does Caterpillar fit in with the Queen of Hearts and her crew? It helps her the way he keeps this party going every night, right?"

Chess leaned his brawny shoulders against the wall with a languid nod. The flashing lights reflected off his eyes as he considered the crowd. The blare of frenetic bass covered our conversation. *I* could barely hear him standing right next to him.

"Caterpillar answers to the Queen," he said. "She gives him control over this establishment and various luxuries, and he keeps the Clubbers happy and hazy. He has to toe the line too. His head could roll as easily as anyone's if she took a disliking to it."

"Why does he have that mirror?" I asked. "What ingredients does Rabbit constantly need to get from *my* world?"

Chess made a whirling gesture. "Drugs stuck in time don't have the same potency. Rabbit retrieves a little substance, a little spice from the Otherland to ensure each night's batch of drinks and edibles will dope the dopes to the desired effect." He gave me a slanted grin. "We're hooked on you, you might say. Are you going to drink that?"

I handed him the glass, and he tossed it back. His grin stretched wider when he looked at me again. "Not bad. Don't worry—even if I lose my head, I'm very good at finding it again."

I made a face at him. "I'd rather you kept it to begin with."

"Ah, we'll all lose our heads the old-fashioned way if we can't take a little pleasure when it's offered." He grasped my hand and tugged me back toward the floor. "Dance with me, lovely."

He gave himself over to the music, his muscles rippling beneath his shirt and slacks. With his expression soft and open, he'd have looked cherubic if it weren't for the glint of fangs when his lips parted. A stray thought flitted through my mind. What would those pointed teeth feel like teased over my skin?

I still couldn't get caught up in the melody. Too many other thoughts were jostling for my attention. My gaze drifted over to the basement door across the crowd from us.

Could Theo take his inventions through the mirror into the Otherland to make them real? Or maybe they'd still reset, unless he could find the materials there.

"Rabbit has to collect new ingredients every day?" I asked Chess when I caught his gaze again.

"They vanish into the ether, I expect," he said.

And even if that strategy would have worked, there'd still be the matter of getting into the palace. Too bad I couldn't just bottle a bunch of Otherland time and bring it back with me for them to use however they wanted. They couldn't work any of this plan without me right there.

I still only had the vaguest idea where the palace even was. I kept up with Chess through another song, but that thought gnawed deeper until I couldn't ignore it.

When I shimmied closer, he set his hand on my waist as if to hold me with him. A flush spread across my belly. All three of the men I was counting on were way too fucking hot for their own good.

I bobbed up on my toes to speak by his ear. "I want to see the Queen's palace. Take me there?" It had to be easier to slip out to spy on it through the dark of night.

Chess leaned closer. His lips brushed my cheek, and my heart jumped. "Why on earth would you want to waste your time on that horrid place?"

For a second, I had trouble remembering my reasoning. "I'm going to have to see it sometime," I said. "I'd just—I'd like to have a better idea what I'm getting into."

Something about those words gave him pause. He peered down at me, his pupils dilated, and for a second I was worried the drink had affected him more than he'd shown at first. Then he nodded. "All right. We'll liven up the night royal-style."

He turned me so my back was to him, keeping his hand on my waist as we wove through the crowd of dancers. Was it wrong to be this attracted to three men at once? Maybe not in Wonderland. The club held plenty of trios and quartets along with the couples. Over there, three women were grinding on the same guy, this one with her hand up his shirt, that one caressing his face. Near the door, another woman braced herself against the wall with an ecstatic expression as one of her lovers kissed her neck and the other worked his hand between her legs.

No wonder I could hardly keep my hormones in check with all the sex in the air around here.

Chess ushered me through the doorway and out into the cooler night air. His stance became instantly more alert. "We go quietly until I find us a good vantage point, all right?" he said.

"Lead the way," I said. He hadn't guided me wrong so far.

We set off around the edges of town, buildings on one side of us and alternating trees or fields on the other. I ducked beneath the fronds of one of those enormous ferns leaning over the road, and Aunt Alicia's key, still on its chain around my neck, shifted with my movement.

She couldn't have left me anything intended to help with Wonderland's current predicament. The Queen of Hearts hadn't even captured Time yet when my grand-aunt had been here. But it might be useful in some other way. First thing when I got back, after Theo's plan had broken everyone from this repetitive cage, I was opening that box.

Chess stopped once, touching my arm. I stood stock still beside him, unable to hear anything that might have disturbed him. We stayed like that for a couple of minutes before he relaxed and ambled forward again.

When the street split, we took the branch to the right, away from the city. The cobblestones there glittered with mica like the rocks around the salty pond, even though only thin moonlight penetrated the scattered trees. The effect was like looking down into a slice of starry sky laid out on the ground. My stomach wobbled the way it had surrounded by all those upside down trees in Hatter's Topsy Turvy forest.

Okay, I was kind of looking forward to getting home, at least for a breather. There was such a thing as too intense.

Chess's fingers slipped down my arm to twine with mine. They squeezed my hand as a glimmer of light came into view through the trees up ahead. He halted, cocking his head and drinking air through his mouth. We walked a few paces farther and then veered off the road onto the tree-dappled hills.

Chess paused by a dense stand of saplings hung with vines with fluffy leaves like giant dandelion heads. He motioned me into their midst. "Stay here," he murmured. "I'm going to scout out our route."

Without waiting for an answer, he vanished before my eyes. He didn't make a sound as he slunk away, literally invisible in the night.

I rubbed my arms, more from nerves than from any real chill, resisting the urge to fidget on my feet. Minutes stretched by. A footstep crunched somewhere in the distance, and I froze even stiffer than I'd already been standing.

The steps rasped over the ground. They didn't sound as if they were coming toward me, but I also didn't think Chess would have let himself make that much noise. I held my breath, the muscles in my legs tensing to run.

The steps faded away. It took another few minutes before I could breathe normally again. Then Chess's light voice spoke by my ear.

"Time to go, lovely."

I startled and spun around in time to see his grin glint, floating in the air, just before the rest of him materialized. I smacked his chest, not hard enough to really hurt him. "You practically gave me a heart attack," I said, as forcefully as I could while whispering.

"I'm keeping you on your toes," he said. "It's a service I'm pleased to provide."

I made a face at him and swatted him again, and this time he caught my wrist and tugged me around so his arms wrapped across my chest. His whole solid body pressed against mine from behind. Heat flared from my core.

"I won't let anything happen to you, Lyssa," Chess murmured, so sweetly it melted me. For a second I thought he would kiss my cheek or the crook of my jaw. Then he let me go, taking my hand like he had before. "This way," he said, as casually as if he'd never touched me more than that.

We walked through the trees a while longer—long enough that my dizziness from his abrupt embrace had faded when an odd sound rose up around us. A thin, erratic chittering filled my ears, like someone trying not very successfully to stifle a cruel giggle. My skin crawled at it.

"What the hell is *that*?" I whispered to Chess.

He tipped his head to the trees around us, hunched shapes that rose several feet above us before drooping back down to kiss the grass with their thin quivering leaves. "The laughing trees," he said. "No one likes to come into this part of the forest—they say it's unnerving."

"It *is* unnerving," I hissed, but I had to agree that feature made it a good hiding spot.

Chess guided me to one of the trees and helped me climb from branch to branch until we reached a small platform at the peak of its hunch. "How did you make this?" I asked, tapping the bottom of the boards.

"I didn't," Chess said. "I found it. Someone used it before the freeze—maybe a Spade, maybe some curious kids. Funny how the two can act so much alike." He winked at me and held my elbow as I scrambled the rest of the way up.

At my first glimpse of the view over the trees ahead of us, my body went still, my breath catching all over again.

The vast property began maybe a quarter mile from where we were perched. It looked like a cross between a Christmas festival and an amusement park. Red and white lights twinkled across hedges and glided around posts as if they were droplets endlessly trickling down. A massive gazebo floated in the middle of the gardens as if on a glowing cushion, turning in a slow circle. Flamingos and peacocks strolled between the lights. An enormous rose bush dappled with scarlet blooms twisted and turned like a maze across nearly half of the gardens and beside the high wall. Its tart floral scent wafted over us on the breeze.

In the midst of all that stood a grand palace, its scarlet walls shimmering faintly in the night. Turrets wide and narrow sprouted up all around the domes that covered its center-point and each of the attached wings. Glazed pink tiles glinted in the garden lights where they framed the windows, some of which were shaped like six-petaled flowers and others like hearts. The Queen clearly didn't want anyone to forget her full name.

I spotted a couple of guards ambling past the palace. Closer, around the gazebo and throughout the rest of the gardens, strolled men and women, some more human and some more animal, clustered in groups of three or more as if in intent conversation. They all wore hats much fancier than anything I'd ever seen on Hatter, decorated with jewels and pearls as well as ribbons and feathers. The men had on tuxedos and the women ball gowns in various colors. Matching brooches sparkled on all their chests.

"Who are all those people?" I asked. "I haven't seen them in the city."

"You wouldn't," Chess said. He hunkered down and sprawled out on the platform on his belly, his chin propped on the back of his hands. My awareness of how exposed we were up here prickled over me. I copied his pose. I wasn't sure how much chance there was of our being seen through the darkness, but the lower profile we kept, the less chance there was anyway.

"Those are the Queen's courtiers," he went on. "The Diamonds, we like to call them, because of the diamonds she makes them wear to proclaim their loyalty to the Hearts family. They reside in the palace or on the grounds and pretty much never leave, living it up all day and all night. A lot like the Clubbers in the city, just in a much more posh venue. And they're no less terrified, in my experience."

His mouth had curled into the closest thing to a frown I'd ever seen on his face. I hesitated and then ventured, "In your experience?"

He let out a breath and recovered his grin. "I used to come out here sometimes to hobnob with the gentry. Diamonds have great appreciation for cleverness—or what they take for cleverness. If you can turn a phrase and a few tricks, play the wise fool, they'll beg you for more. Not a bad day's work for a little banqueting and lolling in the gardens."

Something about his tone gave me the impression he was trying harder than usual to keep up that playful demeanor. "But you don't go out there anymore," I said. "You said you only used to."

"The freeze hasn't ground down any of us into our finest shapes," Chess said. "I believe the spoiled go savage first." He rolled onto his back, switching his view to the stars. "I won't pretend we aren't all mad here, in our various ways, but I decided I prefer the Clubbers."

"And the Spades," I said.

He made a wordless noise I took for agreement. The subject

seemed closed. Maybe there wasn't much more he could say about it anyway. It wasn't my business how he'd passed his time before. The knowledge that he'd had access to that luxury and now passed it up in favor of risking his neck sent a wave of tenderness through me that I didn't know how to voice.

"I'm glad," I said, trying anyway. "That you picked the city over the palace, I mean. I'm glad you've been here to explain things even if I don't always understand and dance me through guarded doorways and all that."

He tilted his head toward me. His grin looked gentler now. His tone was too. "So am I."

My heartbeat stuttered. He turned his gaze back to the sky. I made myself focus my attention on the grounds.

Where would Theo want his team staked out before they made their dash for the palace, toward whatever room that pocket watch was hidden in? Did he have a way for us to get over the walls unseen, or were his people going to have to get across the entire garden in that half hour of grace?

My attention stopped on a spot on one of the towers where the garden lights reflected back especially bright. A symbol had been carved into the ruddy stone there—a heart surrounded by a sunburst. The Queen's mark? It reminded me of the gem-and-teardrop marking I'd seen on that old buried wall and on Aunt Alicia's box back home.

"Chess," I said, "I went out to the Topsy Turvy Woods with Hatter to get a key my grand-aunt left there. On the way, we came across a stone wall that looked like some kind of ruin. It had a symbol on it I've seen in my grand-aunt's things—like a multifaceted gem with a teardrop in the center. Do you know anything about that, or why there'd be ruined buildings all grown over out there?"

Chess knit his brow and hummed in his throat. "I can't say I've ever seen the symbol you mentioned," he said. "Or come across any ruin like that. But there was one time, when I was indulging in palace life, when one of the Diamonds went for a ramble outside the walls of the grounds and came back talking about seeing some sort of unusual old building."

Interesting. "Did they describe it?" I asked.

"The Queen sounded rather disturbed about it, so naturally I snuck out there to give it a gander myself the first chance I had," Chess said. "Whatever it'd been, the guards had already smashed it to the ground and carted off most of the rubble besides. An ever better disappearing act than my own."

"She was worried about people seeing it," I said.

"It would appear that way."

My hand dropped instinctively to the chain around my neck, testing the weight of the key. What people worried about showed where they had a weakness. "There must be something about those buildings she wants to keep hidden," I said. "Something that could hurt her."

Would the contents of the box back home give me any idea what that was?

CHAPTER EIGHTEEN

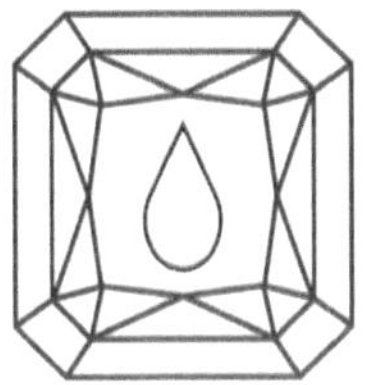

Theo

I felt a twinge of guilt knocking on Mirabel's door at this hour of the night, even though she kept the oddest hours of anyone I knew. Maybe it was simply the knowledge that I was the last person she'd ever turn away that nagged at me.

"Theo!" she said when she answered, with one of her dreamy smiles. "I'm always sad to see you go."

She was in one of her backwards moods again. Even with Time caged in the Queen of Hearts' pocket watch, the personal timeline in our White Queen's head twitched back and forth with no care for linearity.

I couldn't say I minded. If there ever was a time I wanted to hear about her memories of the future, it was now.

"I can't stay very long," I said as we drifted to her assorted seating options. I could never be sure how much or how clearly she recalled events I hadn't experienced yet. "I'm expecting a couple of people downstairs in half an hour."

"It's good to see you for however long," Mirabel said. She sat down at one end of one of her softly cushioned sofas, and I sank down at the other. "What can I do for you, White Knight?" Her lips quirked up a little at that title, as they often did.

"We're on the verge of a major move," I said. "One that will put lives on the line. I wanted to ask—when I came here earlier, with Lyssa, when you looked at her you said something about the hands moving again. You saw the hands on the Queen's watch, didn't you? You saw Time freed?"

Her gaze drifted. "Time can never be trapped for very long."

I supposed "very long" meant different things when you were barely bound by time at all. My entire life felt like a rather long time to me.

"Of course," I said. "From what you saw, will it be freed soon? Close to now, I mean?" Before or after this moment, whichever direction it looked like to her.

If I set this plan in motion, could she tell me it would succeed?

It might have been folly to hope for that sort of certainty at all. Mirabel's hand fluttered over the high heap of her golden-brown hair. Her thin eyebrows drew together. "The days will pass in a daze, and then—oh, she is angry. The shouts, the screams. I am glad I missed that. I see—I see—"

Her voice was turning ragged. I touched her arm to stop her. "It's all right. Never mind. I shouldn't have asked something that specific."

But the need to come up with something to even out the wavering of my thoughts still gnawed at me. There were too many factors beyond my control. For Hearts' sake, Hatter had passed on word about that jabberwock prowling around much closer than the borderlands. Our land was shifting in ways I couldn't predict. So many problems I couldn't tackle while Time remained trapped.

"What about Lyssa?" I found myself asking. "Have you seen any more of her since she came?" That was a more reasonable question, more pliant.

Mirabel's gaze traveled back to me, momentarily fully alert. Her mouth curled into a smile that looked almost sly. "It makes me glad knowing you didn't always keep your heart so closed off, Theo."

My chest tightened, as if my ribs were closing around that organ right now. Dear Hearts and hopes, what exactly had she seen?

She swayed on the cushion, her eyes clouding again. There was no way to hook onto specifics when she faded like that.

"I'm asking about Lyssa," I reminded her gently. "Lyssa… and the Spades, and our rebellion."

She made an amused sound. "Mmm. She's right to have feared them."

A chill tickled over my skin. "Who? Who should she fear?"

"They'll all come from the same line," she said, and her voice faded into a wisp. I couldn't even be certain she was still talking about Lyssa at all.

"Hey," I said. "Let's leave it there."

Mirabel tipped against the back of the sofa and sighed as if reflecting the disappointment I'd meant to hide. Her hair spilled across the padding. The angry pink botch of her scar glared where it marred the pale skin of her temple.

I reached out and grazed the back of my forefinger over the skin just under it. "She really injured you with that blow, didn't she?" I said quietly. "Inside and out. I would have liked to have gotten to know you before."

"So would I," Mirabel said. A giggle spilled out of her. She spread her arms wide. "But who would want a child around who contains not just a beginning but every ending there is?"

My mouth twisted. "It wasn't your fault."

"No," Mirabel murmured, her momentary amusement fading. "No, it wasn't."

I let my weight ease back against the sofa's padding too, just for a moment. "You're the only one who really knows me now," I said. That fact had been true since the moment the White Knight before me had met his end. Why was I feeling it now like a fresh wound?

Talking with Lyssa had stirred up more feelings than I'd bargained for. Feelings I couldn't afford to wallow in, not with so many things that mattered so much more than me at stake. I couldn't give her anywhere near the same openness she'd offered me so straightforwardly. I couldn't even really talk to Mirabel when her understanding of our lives was so skewed.

But I'd always been on my own, really, and I'd known I would be. At least I was doing some good now.

I shouldn't have come here at all, looking for certainties I knew no one could give me. If I needed certainty, I'd have to find it the only place I'd ever been able to generate it before: inside myself.

"Are *you* all right, Mira?" I asked. One last question, both absurd and necessary.

"I am," she said. "As much as I am not ill. It will get better and worse. Who can say different?"

"Very wise, as always," I said.

She leaned toward me, extending her hand, and I bowed my head automatically. Her lips brushed my forehead like a benediction. "It's always lovely to have you stop by, baby brother," she said, as if I'd just arrived.

I straightened my shirt collar in the elevator on the way down, though it hadn't been particularly crooked before. Then I tugged at the cuffs I'd unrolled.

It didn't matter if Lyssa's comments earlier today had affected me more than I'd have liked. I'd accomplished my goals with her all the same. I'd forged a deeper connection, and now I had her.

As long as I made sure to keep her.

I knew what I had to do. I knew what I had to say. It would be that simple if I let it be.

Hatter showed up at my office first, with a scowl and shadowed eyes. He took me in with a glance and propped himself against one of my worktables. "Do you have a whole closet full of that damned outfit, or do you just re-wear the same one every day?" he asked flatly.

I smiled, relaxing into my role. I was the Inventor and the White Knight. And Hatter was easy.

"It *is* always the same day," I said. "Are you offended I've never come shopping for a hat? It seems like a waste when I'll lose it at the stroke of midnight."

Hatter glowered at me. "I really couldn't care less what you put on your head."

"I'm glad you still feel you can be totally honest with me," I said.

He sucked a sharp breath through his teeth.

Chess diverted whatever acerbic remark might have left Hatter's mouth next by sauntering through the doorway. "You called, your Knightliness?"

"Good," I said. "Now we can talk."

"About what?" Hatter muttered. "I shouldn't have come at all. I don't jump at your whistle. Doria and Lyssa are asleep back at the apartment—there's no one there if anything should happen."

"Nothing will happen," I said. "If you thought it would, you wouldn't be here. But you raise a good point all the same. That's exactly why you both are here: to discuss Lyssa."

Chess grinned. "Always happy to discuss a pretty girl."

I ambled over to my desk and sat against the front of it, giving them a moment to consider what precisely I might need to address.

"The three of us are the only three people in Wonderland whom Lyssa both knows and will heed," I said, resting my hands on the slickly polished surface. "So I believe we need to be on the same page. I'd like all of us to commit, right now, to protecting her here, by which we're protecting all of Wonderland."

"It wouldn't occur to me to do anything else," Chess said breezily.

I fixed my gaze on him. "Then perhaps you should avoid taking her on any further excursions by the palace grounds."

"You did what?" Hatter snapped, spinning on Chess. "Are you out of your mind—more than usual, I mean?"

Chess didn't look particularly perturbed, but then, he rarely did. He couldn't be surprised that I kept a close enough eye on the area around the palace to have found out he'd ventured there with our Otherlander. It was my business to know everything that happened in Wonderland, or at least to give the appearance that I did where my reach faltered.

"The guards never got close," he said. "She asked me to take her—said she wanted to understand what she was getting into. A difficult request to argue with."

"Then don't argue with her," I said. "You're all but made of cleverness, Chess. You can produce a dozen excuses out of thin air as easily as you can produce yourself. Use them on her, not on me."

He had the loyalty to look chagrined. "Fairly stated and duly noted."

"*I'm* not your lackey to order around," Hatter said. "I've looked after her anyway. I kept my mouth shut when I thought that's what you'd want, for all of Wonderland. Why am I here?"

I looked at him without shifting my stance. "You've made her feel unwelcome."

A truly fascinating play of emotions crossed Hatter's face. Somehow he managed to look vexed and startled and distressed all at once. It was intriguing. He wasn't easy when it came to Lyssa. What exactly had been going on between them?

Lyssa had implied that he'd expressed some irritation about hosting her, but she'd dodged the subject when I'd attempted to learn more. I'd thought it was simply her apparent propensity to defend everyone around her, but perhaps the situation was more complex than that.

"Did she say that, or are you just assuming I'd be a poor host?" Hatter said after a moment. He'd managed to school his expression back to its previous disgruntled state.

"She expressed some concern that you might not want to continue sharing your apartment now that her stay has been extended," I said. "And I know you well enough to guess that she didn't make up that worry completely out of thin air."

"I'm not going to fawn over her," Hatter said. "She has a room; I've made sure she's eaten; I took her all the way out to the damned Topsy Turvy Woods. If she's not satisfied with that, the problem's with her."

"I don't think it is," I said. "She's a perceptive woman. I know you've divested yourself of any allegiance to the Spades. I know you disapprove of some of the activities we carry out. Your opinions are yours to own, and I won't waste your time trying to argue you out of them. But when it comes to Lyssa, you need to accept that she'll be working alongside us and at least act as if you're on board, or I'll have her move into the Tower and you can wash your hands of this situation completely."

Hatter wet his lips, his stance tensing even more. "I haven't tried to talk her out of it," he said. "I haven't criticized you. I just want what's best for Wonderland too. For Wonderland and for her."

"But you don't think our best route involves her aiding us in storming the palace, and you've no doubt let hints of that disapproval show. I heard you encouraging her to go home last night at Caterpillar's. You know what you're doing."

"Do you?" Hatter demanded. "You weren't here for the last looking-glass girl, but you must have heard stories, just like the stories I've heard of the two before that. The moment the Queen finds out she's here—if she finds out the Spades have drawn her in—we could lose lands more than just the passing of time."

"If we all commit to watching over her, there's no reason the Queen should have any idea," I said. "I know you can't want this endlessly invariable life to continue forever, Hatter. You can't want that for your daughter either."

Hatter's face flushed red. "Leave Doria out of this," he said. "You've drawn *her* in enough already. Why should I trust in your plans when none of them have gotten us unstuck before?"

"Because even I knew our attempts in the past were only parries to test our reach, to weaken the Queen's if we could. And I know with Lyssa's power we can see this one all the way through to freedom."

"Or maybe we'll see it through to dozens more heads rolling in the streets. The only certainty you have is a teacup and some crumbs! How many lives would you stake on that?"

"I'm not rushing in. I'm making all the observations I need first."

"Fuck your observations," Hatter bit out. "Are you even going to set foot near the palace this time? We all know it won't be *your* head rolling if it comes to that."

I eased myself off the desk, straightening up in a subtle motion, just enough to remind Hatter of the few inches I had on him. "Nor has it ever been yours. Let's stay honest with each other, Hatter. It's not me you're angry at."

I said the last words quietly and evenly. The fierce light in Hatter's eyes waned. He looked away and rubbed his mouth with the back of his hat, the tension in his shoulders deflating.

"Are you going to protect her too?" he asked, his tone no longer accusing, only weary. "In this grand scheme of yours, will you make sure she leaves this place with her neck intact?"

The image came back to me of Lyssa standing not far from where he was now, her gaze downcast as she talked about taking responsibility for her family at the delicate age of *eight*. The quiver in her voice and the iron set of her shoulders, fragility and resilience in striking combination.

So beautiful.

Seeing her like that, the thought had crossed my mind, *She deserves better than this.* It hit me again with Hatter's bald question. I didn't think he had any idea he was actually landing a blow.

The answer was the same as it had been then. Wonderland deserved better too, and I owed Wonderland first.

"I said the *three* of us needed to commit to protecting her, didn't I?" I said. "I include myself in that number. I'd like nothing more than to see her safely home when our work is done."

"All right," Hatter said. "I'll keep on as I have been, and I'll keep my judgments even more reserved. She won't hear any reason to doubt you or the Spades from me."

"Thank you," I said. "Now go get some rest, both of you. I'm sorry to have asked you in so late."

Chess bobbed his head and beat Hatter to the door. When they'd left, I retired to the small room down the hall that contained my bed and not much else. It was almost midnight. There was little point in attempting to sleep just yet.

I lay down on top of the cool sheets anyway. I'd never really gotten used to the faint jerking sensation that flinched through every nerve just before the day reset if one had any distance to travel.

I closed my eyes, and then they were popping open to the jangle of my alarm clock.

It quieted at my tap. One minute after midnight. Often times I went right back to sleep after it woke me. But I'd used that small bit of stolen time to rig it for days like this, when I had concerns that needed immediate attention.

If I hadn't done that, would I have still had some left now so that we wouldn't have needed Lyssa at all? It was hard to say. At the time

I'd thought I had as much stashed away as I could ever need. But I'd let personal feelings cloud my awareness of the greater good, and now it was all gone.

I would not let my people down again.

I padded back down the hall to my office. When I flicked on the lights, my bleary gaze shot straight to the pocket-watch retriever on the worktable.

It was still there. I approached it with a thump of my pulse, taking in the details, the bits still scattered on the tabletop or the shelves rather than attached to the device.

It had returned to the exact state and position it had been in when Lyssa had set it down there.

A smile curled my lips, and the twist of uncertainty that had driven me up to Mirabel's apartment loosened in my chest.

The rules of engagement were clear. All we had to do now was go forward, and I knew exactly the way.

CHAPTER NINETEEN

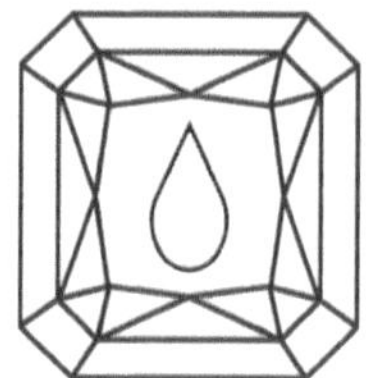

Lyssa

The sensation of waking up in Hatter's guest-room bed was starting to become familiar. I'd slept more times in it now than I had in the bed I'd taken back in Aunt Alicia's house.

From the thin sunlight that barely managed to creep past the curtain, it was still pretty early in the morning. I pulled the fluffy duvet back over my head and nestled my face into the pillow that gave off a faint whiff of chamomile tea. Part of me wanted to just stay there, hidden from the weirdness of Wonderland and the terror underneath the strange until I could fulfill the role Theo needed me for and then go home.

I'd never been very good at wasting a day away, though. After a few minutes, I exhaled in a huff and pushed myself upright.

The least I could do was help Hatter out a little while I was here. Maybe there was something I could do in his shop that'd be a little useful.

I looked over the dresses hanging in the room's closet. Hatter had told me there might be something around I could borrow so I wasn't stuck with just my two Otherland outfits, and then Doria had gone totally overboard, hauling in enough to last me a couple weeks. Anything in the apartment that wasn't black, I guessed. No one had said it in so many words, but from the way they'd talked, I'd gotten the impression these clothes used to belong to her mother.

The dresses had stayed here in my closet. Because I'd touched them? It was hard to imagine that if I'd been a Wonderlander, they'd have vanished overnight back to wherever Doria had dug them out from. She mustn't be able to get any new clothes, at least not any she'd keep. Maybe that was why she'd been so enthusiastic about the thought of me having these.

I settled on a smock dress with a pattern of blue and yellow overlapping triangles and not too many ruffles—whoever these had originally belonged to had *really* been into the frills. Then I slipped into the bathroom to wash up. When I emerged, my gaze drifted of its own accord toward the doorway at the other end of the hall.

The door to Hatter's bedroom had been closed when I'd gotten up the last two mornings. Now it was wide open. From this angle, coming out of the bathroom, I could see right to the back where he was slumped in an armchair next to a four-poster bed. I stepped closer with a flash of alarm that something was wrong.

No, he was just asleep. His head had tipped to rest against the wall, a sapphire-blue top hat I'd never seen him wear before leaning askew on his dark blonde hair, the tufts of which stood up in even more spikes than usual. The jacket of the matching blue suit he hadn't bothered to take off hung rumpled on his lanky body. His legs sprawled across the floor, one straight and the other bent.

His face had softened with sleep, but a hint of tension still held his jaw. A pang ran through me. Why was he sleeping there and not in the very comfortable looking bed? What troubles chased Hatter even into his dreams?

I had the urge to go over, ruffle his already mussed hair, and straighten his hat. Okay, and also the urge to lean in and kiss those thin lips to see if that would melt those last lingering worries. I didn't expect he'd react all that well to the first part, though, let alone the second.

I stepped backward, meaning to leave him be, and the floorboard creaked under my heel. Hatter flinched awake, his hat toppling right off. He snatched it with his nimble fingers and froze with it hovering over his head, his gaze finding me.

"Sorry," I said, my cheeks heating. "I— The door was open. I didn't mean to intrude."

He relaxed a little, setting the hat down on his head and rubbing his eyes as he straightened up in the chair. "It's always open," he said matter-of-factly. "In the mornings. Because I left it open the night before that day."

"The day when the Queen of Hearts trapped Time," I filled in. He nodded. I hesitated, and then added, "And you went to sleep that night in your chair instead of your bed? Without even taking your hat off? Or is that normal here?"

The last question got me one of those twitch of a smiles. "I didn't mean to fall asleep in the chair," he said. "I was waiting for news. That's why the door was open too. I just sat down for a moment…"

And he'd drifted off, and then the morning after, when he'd woken up like that, had been repeated every day since. Damn. "I guess things must have been pretty tense right before the Queen made that move, huh?" I ventured.

"That's one way of putting it." He hefted himself out of the chair. "If you don't mind… This suit has a day's wear already."

My cheeks flared again. I was totally standing here gawking at him when he just wanted to prepare to meet the morning. "Right," I said. "I'll just—"

I started to turn, and my gaze snagged on a piece of paper on the shelves that filled the wall on the other side of the bed. A white sheet, folded in half so it stood up, with a delicate charcoal drawing of a house scrawled across its surface.

Not just any house. The house I'd pulled up in front of something like a week ago. Aunt Alicia's house. And I'd know the texture of those lines anywhere. She'd drawn that.

When my eyes jerked back to Hatter, his expression had shuttered. "I asked her what kind of a place she lived in once," he said. "She drew me a picture. You were heading out?"

"I was." I grasped the knob and shut the door behind me for him. Then I hustled down the stairs to the living area, my face still hot, my heart thumping in a disjointed rhythm.

I'd seen Hatter fully clothed and sitting in chairs plenty of times before, but suddenly that encounter felt as much a private intrusion as if I'd walked in on him getting out of the shower.

I found the teapot and discovered it was both hot and full already. Some weird quirk of the time freeze or of Wonderland in general? I wasn't sure.

By the time Hatter made it downstairs, I had the table set with two cups of tea—Hatter's dark and unsweetened, the only way I'd seen him drink it—and what looked like some leftover fruit loaf that was the closest thing to a breakfast food I'd found in the fridge. He must have gone to get those scones fresh from somewhere around here every morning.

Hatter took in the spread with a flicker of puzzlement at the loaf as if he'd forgotten he had it. He'd put on a different suit, a mossy green that matched his eyes, and the tufts of hair that protruded from under his hat—a trilby, today—looked damp from the shower. Perfectly scruffily handsome.

Suddenly my mind was speculating about what I might have seen if I *had* walked in on him in the shower, which really didn't help me with keeping my composure.

"I figured it was my turn," I said, gesturing to the table.

"I suppose that's fair." Hatter sat down in the wingchair and took a sip from his cup. Then he gave me one of those rare real smiles that crinkled the corner of his eyes—warm enough that my pulse fluttered. "Thank you."

Note to self: The fastest way to Hatter's good graces was through his tea.

He cut a few slices of the loaf, and I took one. It was some kind of mix of pumpkin and cherries, and pretty damn good for a loaf that had to be a few decades old. I managed to wait until Hatter had made it through a slice of his own and about half his tea before I let myself open my mouth.

"You said you didn't know my grand-aunt that well. You've got one of her drawings in your bedroom." Implicit request: Please reconcile these undeniable facts.

Hatter's mouth tightened. He gulped some more tea. "I thought it was interesting, knowing what part of the Otherland looked like. And now that Time's trapped, I can't move it or get rid of it even if I'd like to."

That answer didn't completely sate my curiosity, but it did prompt a different line of thought.

"When the Queen did that," I said. "Trapping Time—it wasn't very long after Aunt Alicia came here?"

"No," Hatter said flatly. "Not very long at all."

I tried to fit together all the pieces of information I'd gained and the observations I'd made over the course of the last few days, but they still didn't quite form a picture I could comprehend. "Did you use to help out the Spades?" I asked. "Back then?"

"I'm not sure how what I did or didn't do however many decades ago is relevant."

Okay, I'd managed to lose his good mood almost as quickly as I'd induced it. Somehow I didn't think offering him a refill was going to cut it. "I'm just trying to make sense of everything," I started.

Hatter set his cup down with a *clunk* loud enough to cut off the rest of what I might have said. "Lyssa," he said in a weary tone. "All you need to know is whatever plan the White Knight gave you and how you fit into that. Could you please leave off the rest?"

The strain in his voice made my heart squeeze. I wasn't asking *that* much of him, was I? Just the barest basics of why I was even here staying with him, why he'd sent me to Theo, when his current connection to the Spades seemed to be mainly via his daughter and against his wishes at that.

The question fell from my mouth before I could catch it. "Why don't you like me?"

It sounded so pathetic that I winced inwardly. Hatter blinked, his jaw twitching. "Sorry," I said. "I shouldn't—"

"No," he said. "What makes you think I don't 'like' you?"

It was my turn to blink at him. "You wanted me to leave. It seems to make you grouchy that I'm here, that I want to talk about anything that's going on or anything to do with my grand-aunt. Sometimes I think we're okay, but then— I don't really know what I'm doing here, or what's normal. If I did something that offended you or I've crossed a line or something, I apologize. You could just tell me."

He was still studying me with an inscrutable expression. At least he didn't look pissed off anymore.

"Why would you care what I think of you anyway?" he asked.

I opened my mouth and closed it, my throat constricting. But that was a fair question. If I was asking him things like that, the least I could do was answer honestly first.

"I just—" I looked down at my hands. Oh, come on, Lyssa. Gripping the arms of the beach chair, I tugged it around so I was facing him straight on.

"Why *wouldn't* I care?" I said. "I like *you*, okay? I mean, as much as you've let me get to know you. I like… that you offer little acts of kindness without making a big deal out of it, and that you don't mind showing you're annoyed when you are, and how much you obviously care about Doria. I like that you can joke around when you let your guard down. Out of everyone in this crazy place, you're the person who feels the most real, and I need that, so if I've put my foot in it without realizing or—or…"

I lost track of my words when I met his eyes again. Something in his face had brightened without an actual smile, but those eyes had darkened to a hungry shade that touched me like fingers being trailed over my skin. A shiver of anticipation raced through me, even though he hadn't made any move to really touch me at all.

His voice came out in its usual light tenor, without the slightest edge. He sounded almost amused. "And all it would take to make you happy is for me to like you?"

My pulse skipped a beat. This wasn't that crazy, was it? Even if it was, didn't I owe it to myself to do at least one truly crazy thing in the short time I was here?

I scooted to the edge of my chair. "You know," I said, "I think I'll aim a little higher than that."

Leaning in, I curled my fingers around his silky tie and tugged him to me.

I didn't have to pull very hard. Hatter met me halfway, his mouth colliding with mine and his fingers teasing into my hair, and God almighty, I didn't give a shit whether he liked me or not if I could have him like this. No one had ever kissed me like Hatter before.

He kissed like he meant it, like he'd never meant anything more. His mouth was hot and sharp with the taste of his tea, and the smell of him, bright lime and dark wood-smoke, washed over me. The graze of his fingers through my hair sent sparks over my scalp.

If he'd been hungry, then apparently I'd been starving just for this. I wanted to inhale him, to devour him—wanted it even more as he kissed me again with his tongue searing over mine.

He was still too fucking far away.

Hatter must have agreed, because his hand dropped down my side. Without breaking the kiss, he guided me up from the chair. His fingers caught my thigh in their deft grip. He hefted me onto the edge of the table, my legs splaying, his whole torso flush against mine.

My hip bumped into a teacup. It toppled to the floor with a crunch of shattering porcelain.

Hatter jerked back just far enough to stare down at the broken cup. He looked dazed, if he didn't recognize what he was seeing. His chest heaved with a ragged breath.

"I'm sorry," I said automatically, though technically it was his fault the cup had fallen. Sitting on the table hadn't been my idea. Even if I was totally on board with it.

Hatter's hand was still on my thigh. His thumb traced a slow arc through the fabric of the dress as he raised his head. Only about a foot of space had opened between us. As he hesitated, his eyes searching mine, I thought I saw the hunger overcoming the uncertainty in his expression. I could have sworn he was about to shift forward and reclaim my lips when footsteps thundered down the stairs behind him.

"Dad!" Doria shouted before she'd rounded the corner, panic crackling through her voice.

Hatter shoved himself away from me and around to face her. I hopped down onto the floor and swiped my dress straight just as his daughter came into view.

"The Knave's here," Doria said in a frantic whisper. "He just went into the shop. I think—"

A heavier set of footsteps rattled the stairs leading up to the apartment.

CHAPTER TWENTY

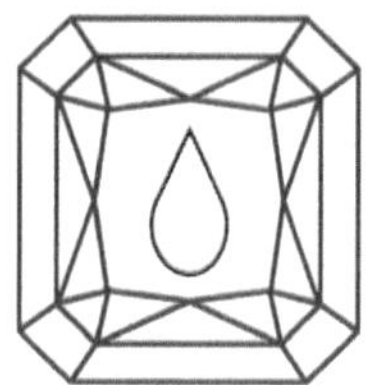

Lyssa

Hatter stiffened at the footsteps. He waved at Doria and me with a jerk of his arm. "Get yourself and Lyssa out of here," he said to his daughter in a low urgent voice. "Onto the roof. Stay out of sight. Go!"

He strode past me with his gaze fixed on the apartment door. I didn't know what to do other than hustle over to Doria. She grabbed my arm and urged me up the stairs.

We kept going past the third floor, up to the fourth I'd never ventured into before. It was set up like a separate apartment of its own. We darted through a little open-concept kitchen and into what looked like a master bedroom, the covers bunched as if two different people had been sleeping under them.

I didn't have much time to think about that. Doria shoved open the window at the other end of the room and motioned for me to follow her.

She clambered out onto the roof, and I followed her. The cyan tiles under my feet felt like rubber, which at least was quiet.

Doria eased the window back down, clicking it into the frame.

"Dad will come get us when it's safe," she whispered, and scooted farther across the slanted surface. We were at the back of the house, looking onto a stumpier one with a top like an inverted vault, the kind of thing skateboarders might have enjoyed taking a spin on.

Doria crept around to the side of the building and peered onto the street. Her shoulders were rigid, her face still pale as the warm wind whipped through her hair. I shoved my own hair back from my face as I sat gingerly on the tiles.

A few strands grazed my lips, still tender from kissing Hatter. I was pretty sure Doria had been so distracted by her panic that she'd missed any shift in the dynamic between me and her dad.

What was going on in the rooms beneath us now? Was Hatter going to be okay? Doria hadn't seemed like the type to be easily fazed.

"Who is this Knave guy?" I murmured.

She sat back on her heels, keeping her body low. "He's the leader of the Hearts' Guard," she said. "He doesn't usually come into town unless he's investigating the Spades—or he's got orders to take somebody's head."

My mouth went dry. "But Hatter's not— He hasn't done anything."

"No," Doria said quietly. "Not in a long time, anyway. But I've done plenty."

Oh. I groped for something to say and reached over to squeeze her shoulder. "He'll know what to do, right? He's gotten by all this time. He'll be okay, and I'm sure he'll make sure you're okay too."

I suspected Hatter would have confessed to the highest crime in the land before he let the Queen's guards pin Doria with it, but saying that wasn't going to comfort her.

"Yeah," she said. "It might not be anything serious at all. The Knave didn't look angry or anything… I don't know. It's hard to tell. He has this face… You'll see."

After what I'd heard about the guy so far, I kind of hoped I didn't.

"So, your dad used to be involved with the Spades?" I said, partly to distract her from the possible catastrophe below, but partly because I just wanted to know. "He's not very interested in filling me in."

"He wouldn't be," Doria said. "He won't tell me anything about what-all he used to do either. But I *know* he did things. I've heard the way he talks with Chess or the other guys sometimes." She scowled. "He gets all worked up about me taking on the smallest errand for them when he was running around helping destabilize the Hearts for *years* longer than I've even been alive."

"He's worried about you," I suggested. "He doesn't want you to put yourself in danger. I think that's pretty normal parental stuff." When you had parents who were functioning reasonably normally.

"Yeah, well, he got to make that decision for himself, so I don't see why I shouldn't be able to make my own decisions too. We're not going to take down the Queen if we're playing it *safe*." She cupped her hands together, massaging one thumb over the other. "They killed my mom and my other dad, you know. My birth parents. The guards came and grabbed them one night, dragged them out into the street, and—"

Her voice broke. I'd momentarily lost mine. The bed downstairs with the empty hollows under the covers made a sudden sick sort of sense. It must reset every night as if the figures who'd used to sleep there would reappear even after death.

"I'm sorry," I managed finally.

Doria grimaced at her hands. "He doesn't like to talk about that either. It's only a warning, telling me I don't want to end up like they did. But I think… I think I'm a lot more likely to lose my heart while the Hearts are still in charge than if we can topple them. They deserve to fall after everything they've done, and if I can make that happen faster, of course I'm going to."

Funny how the exact same tragedy could make Hatter and his daughter veer in completely different directions. Other than that it wasn't funny at all.

Doria edged forward to survey the street. Her head cocked. "Interesting," she said under her breath.

"What?"

She motioned to a woman who was walking by on the street, briefly visible to me in the gap between Hatter's house and the next.

I would have known the woman was one of the courtiers Chess had called "Diamonds" even if I hadn't caught the glitter of the diamond brooch on her chest. She held her head at a haughty angle, more diamonds dripping from her coiled blond hair and the rims of her ears. The lavender fabric of her sleek fur-trimmed coat rippled around her with her sharply elegant strides. Her lips were pursed as if with distaste at her surroundings.

"That's the Duchess," Doria whispered, tracking the woman's path. "I've never seen her in the city at all before. I wonder where she's going..."

A wild glint lit in her eyes. She glanced at me. "What do you say we find out? We're safer being somewhere else as long as the Knave's here at home anyway."

My body balked automatically. Staying put felt a hell of a lot safer to me, but her logic made sense too. And there was something a little desperate about the gleam in Doria's eyes. Maybe she needed a better distraction than I could give her on my own.

"All right," I said. "But I don't think we should go down there. We don't want her seeing us, right?"

"Of course not," Doria said. "No problem." She scooted down to the edge of the roof, poised, and sprang across the two-foot gap to the neighbor's, which was flat other than several protrusions that might have been chimneys bent at right angles.

Gathering my courage, I crept after her. The jump wasn't all that hard, really, just a thump of shock through my knees. Doria had already dashed to the other side of the roof. She sprang from there onto the next and peeked over one of its many dormers to check the road.

"Still walking!" she called back to me in a hushed voice as I reached the gap.

We went on like that across several buildings. As luck would have it, the Duchess turned in our direction at the next corner. We followed her around the bend. I eyed the next street up ahead, knowing there was no way we could keep up our amateur surveillance operation across the rooftops, unless Doria had some trick up her sleeve for leaping ten or more feet at a time.

Doria snatched another glance below and hesitated, braced against a slice of metal-lined roof that appeared to have been tipped on its side. "She stopped," she said when I came up beside her.

The Duchess certainly had. She swiveled in a slow circle, taking in the shops around her, her hand propped against her chin in a dainty gesture. With a sigh loud enough that I heard it from the rooftop, she shifted her weight from one foot to the other. She looked for all the world as if she were waiting for someone. Who would she have come *here* to meet?

"This is really weird, right?" I murmured. "Her being here at all—even by Wonderland standards?"

"Especially by Wonderland standards." Doria made a face. "The only time I've ever crossed paths with a Diamond in the city, he looked at me like he thought I might stab him just for the fun of it. That was when I was ten. They don't think much of Clubbers or Spades, and that's about all you get in the city."

"Chess said something about the Queen blaming the Spades for her son dying," I said. "Was he really murdered?" If the Diamonds bought into the story about the Spades having killed him, that could explain the kind of reaction Doria had gotten.

"Yep," Doria said. "It was way before I was born, but what I've heard from sources I trust is it looked like some thief broke into the palace, and the prince caught them in the middle of the heist. Whoever it was cut his head right off. Apparently the Queen found him—his head, lying there in a pool of blood, with broken pieces of pottery from the vase the thief had been going to take all around."

She shuddered as I cringed at the image. "Because beheading is the way she kills 'traitors,' she assumed it had to be a rebel who did it," she went on. "But it wasn't us. No one in the Spades would have done it. I'm *sure* of that. He was younger than me, you know? Thirteen and murdered over a vase they didn't even get to take."

I might have questioned Doria's certainty that it couldn't have been anyone associated with the Spades, but Chess *had* been around back then, and he'd sounded certain the Spades hadn't been involved too. Whatever I thought about the Queen of Hearts, losing a kid like that had to be awful. And that murderer must still be on the loose. Wonderful.

Doria's gaze jerked up. "She's on the move again."

The Duchess strolled farther down the street at a more leisurely pace. I got the impression she was lingering as if still waiting for someone to catch up with her. She meandered past the next cross-street and started to travel out of reach. Doria was scanning the side of the building as if she were considering climbing down to the street after all when a figure shimmered into view just in front of the Duchess. My heart stopped.

It was Chess. I knew it before the sun even caught on his auburn hair and brawny shoulders, because who else could step out of the air like that?

Doria went still, staring. She obviously found the sight as unexpected as I did. Why would Chess go speak to a Diamond?

The Duchess didn't look at all startled. She tucked her hand under her chin again and smiled coyly, grazing her other hand down his shirt at the same time in a *very* familiar way. Chess said something and batted her hand to the side, but he stayed there, tense yet ready to talk. The Duchess commented on something, and he nodded. They were too far away for us to make out even a hint of their voices.

The realization settled over me: She'd been looking for him. Waiting for him. Knowing somehow that he'd find out she was there and come to her? He'd said he'd mingled with the Diamonds at the palace in the past, but he'd also sounded disgusted with them now. Yet here he was, gabbing away with one of them. Showing up as if he'd allowed her to summon him.

My stomach knotted. He had to be up to something that the others didn't know about. He couldn't be helping the Diamonds somehow, double-crossing the Spades, could he?

My legs wobbled under me. I dragged in a breath and sank down on a glossy black bubble that protruded from the roof. Even when I tipped my head into my hands, my thoughts swam around like too many fish crammed into a bowl, slippery and colliding.

The head of the Hearts' Guard was coming calling at Hatter's house. Chess was chatting with Diamonds. Theo had made it sound as if I just needed to step in for one simple mission and everything would be fixed, but how could it be simple when their enemies were already at our heels and maybe luring in the few people I'd thought I could trust?

How was I supposed to know what the right thing to do here was? This wasn't even my world. Right then, with a knife of longing that cut straight through my chest, all I wanted was to be home in my regular predictable orderly Otherland again.

"Lyssa?" Doria said, with a note of concern. I swallowed hard and shook off the wave of dread that had nearly overwhelmed me. I didn't want to freak her out. I was responsible for her now too, wasn't I?

That thought made me choke up all over again, but I pushed myself to my feet and managed a shaky smile. "I'm okay."

"They left," Doria said. "The Duchess started walking again, and Chess disappeared. I have no idea what that was about."

I glanced back the way we'd come. "I guess we should get back to the house, then."

Doria rubbed her arms. "I don't know. The Knave might not be done there yet. And I'm feeling kind of hungry." She caught my eye with that sly glint I was quickly becoming familiar with. "What do you say we grab some brunch before we head back? There's nothing suspicious about that."

"I think we should get back there now," I said. "Your father will freak out if—"

"Pops needs to loosen up," Doria declared, the glimmer in her eyes turning manic. Without bothering to argue any further, she sprang to the next rooftop and then swung onto a fire escape of sorts that zigzagged down into the narrow alley she'd just leapt.

I stood frozen for a second. Hatter wasn't going to be any more happy if I came back without his daughter. Fuck. At least if I was with her, *I'd* know she was okay.

"Wait up!" I called as loudly as I dared, and dashed after her.

CHAPTER TWENTY-ONE

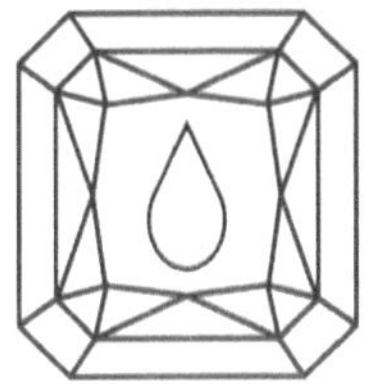

Hatter

It hardly seemed fair that in the space of a few breaths, I'd gone from gazing into one of the prettiest faces I'd ever seen to bracing under the scrutiny of one of the most foul. Not that I had much belief in fairness left.

"When was the last time you went by the bakery?" the Knave was saying, his voice like the hiss of a knife scraped over a whetting stone. It fit his sharkish features. His whole head appeared to have been built to angle toward his bulging pointed jaw. His small wide-set eyes and the blue-gray sheen to his skin only added to the impression.

He wore the same pleated red-and-pink uniform the rest of the Hearts' Guard did, but with a thick crimson over-jacket trimmed with gold, and his heart-shaped helm stood half again as tall as that of any of his underlings.

I'd had the occasion of being under the scrutiny of those cold little eyes a few times before. It never got any more pleasant.

"I was there yesterday morning," I said steadily from where I was leaning against the back of the wingchair. The most important thing with the Knave was to keep your cool. He clamped on to fear like a shark scenting blood in the water. So far his questions hadn't given any hint that he was aware of Lyssa's presence or that Doria had treaded too carelessly.

"And what did you do while you were there?"

"I bought some scones," I said. "As I do most mornings. Baker could have told you that."

"She did," the Knave said. "She said you picked up more than usual yesterday."

I shrugged. "I was expecting company for tea. I'm not sure why the Guard is concerned with my breakfast habits?"

"We are concerned that someone has been skimming from Baker's supplies." The Knave studied me as if waiting to see if I'd show some guilt.

I didn't even have any to hide. "Skimming supplies?" I repeated with genuine confusion. "Why in the lands would anyone do that?"

"I couldn't begin to guess," the Knave said darkly. "But Butcher and Cheesemaker have been trifled with too. You don't mind if I have a look around?"

His tone didn't offer any room for argument. I held up my hands. "Be my guest."

He slunk through my kitchen, peering into the fridge, searching the cupboards. I might have found the whole process absurd if a prickle of understanding hadn't run up my back.

I'd been buying food that Lyssa had eaten over the past few days. From the bakery mostly, but cheese and meat for the meals beyond breakfast as well. A few pieces of fruit, too, but either Fruitsman hadn't noticed or the Knave hadn't mentioned that loss.

Since the freeze, what any of us had eaten had made no impact on the shops' stockpiles, any more than my sending someone off with a hat prevented me from offering that same hat to a different customer the next day. The flour and butter and whatever else Baker put into her wares would have reappeared in her pantry overnight.

Other than what Lyssa had partaken of. The food she'd eaten would stay consumed just as her cup that first morning had stayed ringed with tea. After innumerable years of finding her ingredients in the exact same state, it couldn't have taken much of a difference for Baker to notice their sudden depletion.

The Knave couldn't possibly suspect the truth of the matter, could he? There'd never been an Otherlander in Wonderland during the freeze before. Not that I'd heard of, at least. The effect of Lyssa's presence had seemed as much a surprise to Chess and Theo as it had been to me.

The Knave came around the other side of the table, and his narrow gaze fell on the cup that I supposed I had to accept was irrevocably broken. His eyebrows rose just a smidgen. "Got rather violent with your tea today, did you, Hatter?"

Violent was not really the word for it. Even under his stare, my pulse kicked up a notch with the giddy delight of the memory. Watching Lyssa fumble her way through telling me everything she admired about me, reveling in the dawning realization that maybe what I'd been telling myself I could never have wasn't so out of reach after all, and then her soft hair tangling around my fingers, her mouth hot and sweet against mine, the little noise she'd made when I'd kissed her harder—

Fuck. My nerves were still crackling with contained electricity from that moment. A flush rose over my skin despite the Knave's chilly scrutiny.

He was waiting for my answer. I offered a sheepish smile. "I stumbled clearing the table. Nothing a new day won't fix."

"Indeed." He sidestepped the small puddle of tea and peered around the rest of the room, but he didn't make any move toward the upper floors. Doria would have gotten herself and Lyssa out of view by now, but I didn't want to test the limits of her skills of concealment if we didn't have to. It was one thing for Chess to say he'd brought a Dreamer to the club; something else altogether for me to claim I'd been hosting one for days on end. The Knave would have a lot more questions than Caterpillar had.

"Is there any other way I can assist?" I asked, bringing all my attention back to the intruder.

"You can pass on the word of any murmurs you hear, if you know what's good for you," the Knave said. "We've been very easy on you considering the company you kept."

His vague gesture toward the ceiling brought back an utterly different and not at all pleasant memory. Only the most awful night of my life.

The sensations washed over me in the space of a choked breath: the thunder of the guards' footsteps as they'd barged into the apartment. My heart thumping almost as loudly as I'd stumbled out of my bedroom, only to realize it wasn't me they'd come for. It'd leapt to my throat as they'd dragged March and May by, and I'd been about to jump in, to argue, to throw myself in front of the sword, but March had clutched my arm hard enough to bruise.

Take care of her. Please.

In the whites of his eyes, I'd seen our future if I took a stand. We'd all be executed, and little toddling Doria would be left alone. March and May were already implicated; it was too late for anything to save them. The guards clearly didn't have anything on me—yet.

So I stood down.

Now, anger balled at the back of my mouth. *They were better company than you could be to anyone.*

I held my tongue with a slow inhalation. A sharp retort wasn't the best way to defend my old friends' interests either.

"I serve the Queen as I am able," I said.

I might not have been able to entirely smooth the bite from that comment. The Knave's mouth pressed flat, but he turned on his heel and stalked out of the apartment without another word.

I stood there for a long moment after he'd left, attempting to recover my equilibrium. When I was sure he'd moved on, I'd have to go retrieve Doria and Lyssa. I'd have to—I'd have to—

I could feel the kiss when I wet my lips. The electricity thrumming through me had taken on a painful edge. What the fuck had I been thinking? I should know better than to get caught up in a little affection in a pretty girl's eyes. Especially an Otherlander's.

She'd left her mark. These lips would never not have been kissed by her, the fingers that curled into my palms now would never not have gripped the smooth curve of her thigh. Nowhere she'd touched me could ever be reset, no matter what I did next.

It was too late to change that. I'd already let her too far in. How could I feel both so thrilled and so terrified by that fact at the same time?

The patter of my pulse as I headed upstairs crept toward the thrilled end of the spectrum. I'd talk to Lyssa about what I'd gleaned from the Knave, and we'd work out the safest course of action together. She'd *want* that. She'd proven with every action and word so far that she cared what happened to us here. That she could be the answer to the problem even the White Knights had never been able to solve.

We might really be on the verge of freedom, thanks to her.

And after we talked, perhaps…

A shiver of heat ran through me. I caught myself on the verge of a grin as I nudged open the fourth floor window in what had once been March and May's bedroom.

No one came to scramble back through the window. I eased my head out, peering across the rooftop in one direction and then the other. My heart started to beat even faster, with a jab of panic that speared through my gut.

No one was out there. Lyssa and my daughter had vanished.

Footsteps padded across the roof's tiles. With a flash of relief, I pushed myself off the edge of the bed that still held the shapes of March and May's bodies.

The relief didn't manage to dislodge the choked feeling that had gripped me the entire time I'd been sitting there, grappling with the question of whether I was more likely to help my daughter by going out in search of her or staying put in case she needed me here. Apparently I'd made the right choice. That fact wasn't much of a balm either.

I'd left the window a couple inches ajar. Doria tugged it higher and slipped in first with a swish of her partly braided hair. She stiffened when she saw me waiting there and then sauntered a few steps to the side to make room for Lyssa to clamber in. There wasn't a scratch on Doria, only a smudge of icing sugar on her black dress that told me she'd been to the café that served her favorite currant-jelly donuts.

"Hey, Pops," she said.

Lyssa caught my expression and winced. "I'm sorry," she said. "We saw a Diamond on the street, and it seemed like it might be a good idea to find out what she was doing here—"

"You followed a *Diamond* while the Knave was on the hunt?" I snapped.

"We were fine," Doria said. "She never even saw us. It's not like we were in danger."

"You had no way of knowing that when you had no idea what the Knave showed up here for," I said. My gaze jerked back to Lyssa. Lyssa with those big blue dangerously naïve eyes. "And then you went for donuts?"

Lyssa's eyes flicked to Doria and back to me. "We—I wasn't sure if it might be better for us to be away from the house while he was there. I lost track of the time."

"Lost track of—"

"*Dad*," Doria said, raking her hand through her hair. "It was—"

I'd been wrong. She did have a scratch—a raw pink scrape beaded with scarlet just below the inside of her wrist. My pulse stuttered. "You're bleeding. Are you all right?"

"I told you I'm fine," she said. "I just bumped it on a rough spot on the ladder. It was no big deal. Look—"

"No," I said. "Go clean it. Bandage it up. I need to talk to Lyssa."

"But I—"

"Doria," I said through gritted teeth. "*Go*. You and I will have lots of time to talk later."

She stomped out of the room.

"I really am sorry," Lyssa said, her hands twisting together in front of her. "I didn't want you to be worried."

"I was fucking worried all right," I said. I managed not to yell, keeping in mind Doria's keen ears, but my voice came out sharp enough to cut. "For good reason. How could you think it was a good idea to take off around the city like that?"

She had no idea. I'd thought she was better than that, but maybe Otherlanders just couldn't help charging recklessly into situations they didn't fully understand. The second I'd let myself trust her—

"We were careful," she was saying now. "I swear nothing happened that would raise any suspicions. I didn't even touch anything."

"It doesn't matter. You should have stayed on the fucking roof!"

"Okay. I'll know that next time—if there is a next time."

"There won't be," I said. "I'd sooner deliver her to the palace than send her anywhere with you again."

Lyssa opened her mouth and hesitated. It was too damned hard not to see the pain on her face, not to remember the feel of those full lips on mine just a couple hours ago. The rage inside me clenched tighter.

"Did something happen with the Knave?" she asked. "Is that why — You're obviously really upset. If there's something else going on—if this is about earlier too—"

"It's about you going off with my daughter and putting her and you and all of Wonderland in harm's way without even realizing what you're doing," I broke in. "Don't tell me how upset I'm allowed to be. I know the second you slip up, the second things actually get tough for *you*, you'll be running off through that looking-glass back to your calm, peaceful home, looking-glass girl. You'll vanish and leave us to pick up the pieces."

Lyssa's jaw tensed. "What are you talking about? I'm here. You have no idea—if there's *anything* I'm good at, it's sticking around for other people no matter how awful things get."

A scoffing sound tumbled out of me. Her whole body went rigid at that. "I don't have to prove anything to you," she said, her own voice rising.

"As a person would say when they know they can't prove anything anyway," I shot back.

Her hands balled at her sides. "Fine. Fine. I'll stop being such a huge problem for you then."

She marched out of the room. My heart tore as she disappeared from view. My legs screamed to run after her, but I kept my feet planted firmly on the floor and squeezed my eyes shut.

A door thudded somewhere downstairs. I rubbed my hands over my face. The choked feeling had spread through my entire chest and abdomen.

"I'm sorry, March," I muttered. "You asked me for one thing…" And I fucked it up the second a girl like that looked at me the right way.

I didn't exactly feel as if I'd un-fucked anything yet. After a minute, I pulled myself together and went out to check on my daughter.

Doria barged into the hall to meet me when I reached the third floor. "Why did Lyssa leave?" she demanded with a wave of her arm, the white bandage she'd pasted over her scrape flashing. "What did you say to her?"

"Only what needed to be said. She put you in danger. She—"

"She didn't put me in any danger. We were perfectly safe."

"You weren't," I said. "I told you to go on the roof."

"And we did. We just went farther than that too. You can't be angry at Lyssa. If you even stopped to listen for two seconds—"

I reined in as much of my frustration as I could, but I could hear it vibrating through my voice anyway. "Listen to *you*? I'm your father, and—"

"No, you're not," she spat out. "My father's dead."

She might as well have punched the air from my lungs. I stared at her, a sharper ache spreading through my center.

Doria's face blanched with horror. "I'm sorry," she said shakily. "I didn't mean it. I really didn't."

My anger seemed to have deflated too. All that was left was the lump in my throat and that awful ache.

I reached out, and Doria darted into my arms. For a second I just held her, reminding myself that she was still here. That I'd managed to keep her alive for twelve years, at least, even if sometimes she seemed hellbent on ending that record as soon as possible.

"I know, Mouse," I said roughly. "But I also know it's true. I—

You know I've never been anything but glad to have you in my life, don't you?"

She let out a choked-sounding laugh. "I'd have to be pretty stupid not to, with all the trouble you go to trying to make sure I stay in it."

My lips twitched. I hugged her closer, and she leaned her head against my shoulder. It'd been a while since she'd grown out of the really huggy stage of her childhood. I hadn't realized how much I'd missed it.

After a little while, when the tension had seeped out of the air around us, Doria eased back with a quick swipe at her eyes.

"It really wasn't Lyssa's fault, you know," she said. "She just didn't want to put the blame on me, I guess. Following the Diamond, and then going off into the city—those were my ideas. She tried to *stop* me. I think she only came along because she wanted to look out for me."

I found, now that the fiercest flare of fear and anger had faded, that Doria's admission didn't surprise me. I swallowed hard. That didn't mean I should have let myself get caught up in that moment in the kitchen earlier, necessarily… but, Hearts take me, remembering some of the things I'd said to Lyssa made me cringe inwardly. That hadn't been right of me either.

I was supposed to be protecting *her*—I'd given the White Knight my damned word.

Even if I hadn't, even if I never touched her again, I'd still have hated the thought of Lyssa getting hurt. More hurt than she'd already been by my words.

"I should go look for her," I said. If she even wanted to see me right now. *Someone* should be looking out for her.

I could chase down Chess first, tell him to keep an eye out. She wouldn't have any reason to avoid him.

"Yeah, you probably should," Doria said. "And—I think you should know, because I don't like sneaking around on you… I'm going to the big meeting near the Tower this afternoon. There's no way the White Knight is going to let me in on the run to the palace for the watch tomorrow, but if I can help somehow from the sidelines, I'll take whatever role the Spades will give me."

She braced herself as if she expected further argument. And a protest did instinctively spring into my throat. The wrenching of my resistance to the idea echoed the emotions that had gripped me when I'd lashed out at Lyssa. I stopped myself, absorbing the shape of that discomfort.

Maybe I shouldn't be accusing other people of running from the fight when that was all I'd been doing for the past twelve years. This wasn't even Lyssa's world. It was mine. What had I done in all that time to help us toward freedom?

How could I ask more of her than I was willing to ask of myself?

"Where is that meeting?" I asked, the question dragging on the way out. "And when?"

Doria eyed me suspiciously. "I don't need a babysitter, Dad."

"I wouldn't go to chaperone you," I said. "I was simply thinking… I might want to find out how *I* can pitch in."

CHAPTER TWENTY-TWO

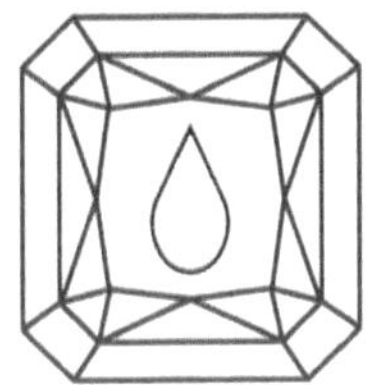

Lyssa

The betrayal in Hatter's eyes and the accusations he'd made dogged me through the city. I couldn't walk quite fast enough to leave them behind.

I rambled beyond the buildings and out to the pond, peered into its salty depths until the restless tangle of my emotions urged me on again, and wandered farther until I reached the forest of giant mushrooms. The murmurs and laughter of the workers somewhere beyond my view made my skin prickle. I might be able to blend in while I was in the city, but no one else was walking this road. And even if Theo hadn't warned me, I wouldn't have wanted to venture all the way out to the bizarre hills where that jabberwock thing had come charging by.

I retraced my steps to the city and set off on a meandering path through the streets. Without any conscious direction, my feet carried me to the place in Wonderland I'd come closest to pure joy. I looked up and found myself staring at the whirling walls of the Caterpillar's Club.

It was only mid-afternoon, the sun still beaming over the city, and the club gleamed with swirls of silver and gold. Too early for dancing, I thought, but as I was about to turn away, a couple of women—one an upright goat in a sundress and the other human-shaped other than her mink-like head—walked right up to the spinning building and blinked out of view into its depths.

The responsible thing would be… would be… I didn't really know. Hatter hadn't wanted my apologies. Theo didn't need me for his plan until tomorrow. He'd told me to enjoy Wonderland as much as I could until then.

Fuck responsible, Melody would have said.

I hesitated for only a second, and then I strode in after the Wonderlanders, picturing the doorway that had opened up for me before.

As my feet hit the club's uneven floor, a wave of calm swept over me. The vast room was hazily lit with softly pulsing lights that filled the space with a turquoise glow, as if I'd stepped into a vast tropical aquarium.

Clusters of Wonderlanders lolled together in the dips in the floor. Some of them chattered in soft yet bright voices. Others blew streams of colored smoke into the air from slender pipes. Over near the wall, a young man had draped himself against the side of a rise while his two companions, a woman and another man, kissed their way down either side of his naked chest.

I guessed Caterpillar's club operated all through the day too.

One of the clusters of smokers had noted my arrival. "A Dreamer!" one woman murmured to the others in a delighted tone.

The man next to her waved me over. "Come join us, Dreamer. Have a pipe and savor Wonderland."

They beamed at me so welcomingly that I let myself walk over. They didn't look remotely suspicious about my being here. As long as I kept my mouth shut about how exactly I'd found myself in Wonderland, why shouldn't I hang out with them while I figured out what to do next?

I hunkered down on the slope near them. One of the Wonderlanders made a beckoning gesture in the air, and a server appeared with one of those narrow pipes on a platter. He bent down to offer it to me.

"Um, I don't know," I said.

"Go on, go on," the woman who'd identified me as a Dreamer said with a languid motion of her hand. "It'll just make you dream a little more."

Chess had warned me about the mushrooms. He hasn't said anything about pipes being a problem. I took it off the platter, my fingers slipping over the warm clay surface. Tentatively, I raised the end to my lips.

The smoke tickled into my lungs and through my nerves like a drift of the softest snow, fluffy and sparkling, with just a slight nip of cold. It numbed the sharp edges of the memories that had been hounding me.

"That—that's nice," I said, and the whole group twittered. Their laughter sounded pleased rather than mocking. I inhaled another gulp of pipe-smoke and relaxed against the floor with a smile.

Their conversation, nothingness about the lights overhead and the shapes they could see in the smoke, flowed around me. Another server ambled by with little twinkling glasses, and I took one of those because everyone else did. The glittering liquid streamed down my throat with a sweet burn and filled my chest with giddy bubbles to dance amid the snow.

I wanted another one of those. I wanted to just lie here forever. There was nothing inside me or out right now that could possibly hurt me.

A new woman joined our pocket with a tray of paints and brushes. My companions oohed and ahhed. Soon the whole dip in the floor was dappled with looping vines and bushy ferns. I painted a ring of blooming flowers with delicate strokes. The man who'd invited me over in the first place dabbed petals along my arm.

The lights started to dim. Music drifted through the room, quietly at first and then rising as more people streamed into the club. A woman with a fox's head tugged me to my feet and spun around with me.

The bubbles from the drink coursed up from my chest into my head. I laughed and whirled away into the growing crowd of dancers.

The music caught me like it had before. I swayed and bobbed across the undulating floor under the strobe lights. Just a speck tossed on a vast sea, no one to answer to but myself.

A server walked by with a platter of mushroom slices. My hand reached out to pluck one up. Chess had warned against them on the night I'd needed to make my way home. I wasn't going anywhere tonight. It didn't matter whether I kept my head clear.

I popped the slice into my mouth and bit down.

The cloying earthy flavor burst over my tongue. I swallowed automatically. A quivering shot through my limbs, my stomach lurched, and I was abruptly sure I'd made a bad decision. My spine was twanging and my head—my head was coming right up off of my body, peering down over the dancers I'd been in the midst of a moment ago. I groped at my neck—my neck that was stretching already twice its previous length, and—

"*Lyssa*." Solid hands yanked me down. Chess grasped my shoulders, holding me beneath the heads of the crowd, his blue eyes wide. "What did you eat?" he asked in the most serious and urgent voice I'd ever heard him use.

I coughed and spat out the bits I hadn't swallowed. "Mushroom," I mumbled. The words had to travel so far up my still lengthening throat to my mouth.

Chess muttered something that sounded like a curse and tugged me through the crowd, keeping me low and close to his broad body. He sat me against the wall. My head listed to the side on my extended neck. My legs splayed out on either side of me as ungainly as a giraffe's.

"Wait here," Chess said. "And try to look small."

I might have laughed if I hadn't felt so bewildered and out of control. I tucked myself as close to the wall as I could get and arched my neck to hold my head in my hands, willing the shadows to hide me. My eyes closed. The strobe lights flashed against my eyelids.

Then Chess was back, a warm presence at my side and a hand on my shoulder, slipping what felt like another sliver of mushroom into my hand.

"Eat that," he said by my ear. "A bit at a time. We don't want to go too far in the opposite direction."

I was too full of bright snow, giddy bubbles, and terror to totally make sense of that, but he sounded like he knew what he was talking about, so I did what he said. The moment I'd gulped the first chunk, my legs and my neck began to contract. I stiffened, waiting out the sensation, and then nibbled some more when my body hadn't quite returned to its usual state. After a couple more tiny bites, everything seemed to be where it should be.

"Can you walk?" Chess asked.

I thought I could, but when I tried to get to my feet, my legs wobbled under me. My head was spinning. Chess made an apprehensive sound and scooped me right into his well-muscled arms.

He tipped me against his chest and strode around the edge of the room to the exit. I grasped the smooth fabric of his shirt, inhaling the heady scent that rose off his skin, like licorice and red wine. So delicious my tipsy mind started wondering what he tasted like.

We slipped out of the club. Chess stopped somewhere dark and quiet amid the trees. He set me down on a log and sat next to me, close enough that I could lean on him if I needed to. I tried not to.

"What was that?" I said, rubbing my forehead, which thankfully was now no farther away from the rest of me than usual. "What happened to me?"

Chess's grin was tight. "The mushrooms make us feel as if we're growing larger or smaller. It appears that they affect Otherlanders in a more literal way. At least the Otherlanders who are fully here and not just dreaming their way in." He gave my hair a playful tug. "It's a good thing you grabbed the larger kind and not the smaller kind, or I might not have spotted you at all. Trampled by Clubbers—not the way I'd want to go."

"No," I said, and swayed.

Chess caught me with his arm around my back. He studied my face. "What else did you have, before the mushroom?"

"A very nice pipe," I informed him. "And a sparkly drink. That was also very nice. Maybe I had two of those. I don't totally remember." I cocked my head in thought and got dizzy all over again.

"I think you'd better have some of this, then." He produced a brass flask from his pocket, unscrewed the lid, and offered it to me.

I took a gulp and then another. The cool liquid inside coated my throat and stomach, and the snowy bubbly feeling eased off just a little. I peered at Chess over the top of the flask.

"Why are you so nice to me?"

He arched an eyebrow, his grin loosening a little. "Why shouldn't I be? Don't you think you deserve nice things, lovely?"

"Hatter doesn't think I do," I muttered, and tipped the flask to my lips again.

Chess chuckled. "I'd imagine the problem is likely more that Hatter doesn't believe *he* deserves nice things. Perhaps it's the pressure of all those hats weighing down on him over time."

"What about you?" I asked. As the fog in my head retreated, it occurred to me that I'd had reasons to believe Chess might not be so nice after all. "You like the Diamonds."

Chess's jaw tensed. "What?"

"You were talking to that Diamond today. Doria said she was… the Duchess." I waggled the flask at him accusingly. "You said you didn't like them anymore."

"Oh, Lyssa." He nudged the flask back toward my mouth. "Finish that, and I'll explain."

I might not have accepted that answer, except whatever he'd given me, it was easing me down from the high I'd barely realized I was on with each passing second. When I'd drained the flask and handed it back to him, my thoughts were still a bit jumbled, but I could connect one to the next without much trouble.

The gnawing in my chest had come back too. I guessed I'd just have to live with that.

"The Duchess?" I prompted.

Chess tucked the flask away and leaned his elbows onto his knees, gazing into the night. "I told you I used to visit the Diamonds in the palace. I know her from then. The Queen's people have noticed a few minor oddities around town, and she thought that I might have an idea why. That she might be able to coax something out of me more easily than the guards with their rods and their swords. She was wrong."

"Why did you talk to her at all?" I asked, remembering how he'd stepped out of the air to meet her on the street. "You could have just avoided her."

"The Duchess can be very tenacious when it comes to getting her way," he said. "I thought it better to give her enough of an appearance to satisfy her and see her on her way than to leave her wandering our city all day."

His tone was casual, but there was still something defensive in his stance. Because I'd implicitly questioned his loyalty? If he'd wanted to hurt the Spades' cause somehow, all he'd have needed to do was not step in just now in the club and let my odd presence be discovered. Instead he'd done everything he could to shield me. I couldn't see how I could ask for better proof of his allegiances than that.

"That makes sense," I said. "You'd know what's smartest better than I do." I touched his arm, leaning in enough to breathe in his licorice-and-wine scent. "Thank you. For looking out for me."

"Of course, lovely," he said, his eyes glinting bright in the darkness. I could have sworn I saw a flicker of desire in them, that he eased a little closer to me with a wash of heat. But then he was jerking his gaze away and standing up.

He'd never answered my question about what he thought he deserved, had he?

"I should get you back to Hatter's," he said. "Whatever he said to you, I expect he regrets it now. He's been looking for you, you know, with rather a lot of urgency."

Because Hatter was worried I was off causing some catastrophe, probably. That didn't mean he hadn't meant what he'd said to me.

The thought of going back to the apartment and facing his caustic tongue again made me want to curl up into a ball and go to sleep right here next to this log.

That wasn't my only alternative, though. My pulse skipped in my chest with an eager flutter as I remembered an open invitation.

"No," I said, pushing myself to my feet. "I think Hatter needs a break from me. I told Theo I'd come by today—I never ended up doing that. Walk me to the Tower?"

Chess hesitated for a second—out of a friend's loyalty to Hatter, I guessed. Then he produced his familiar carefree grin and offered me his elbow. "Of course. Lands know our White Knight will take care of you."

CHAPTER TWENTY-THREE

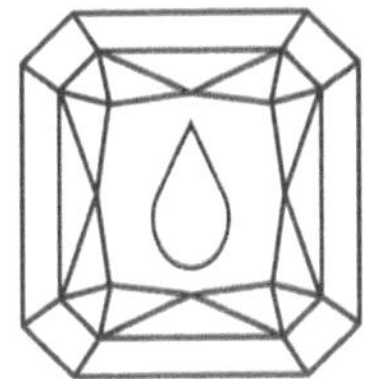

Lyssa

Chess picked his way through the city so craftily we didn't encounter another Wonderlander, even though I heard distant whoops and laughter—and once an eager moan that sent heat prickling through my chest. The Tower stood like a brilliant spire painted against the night sky, light streaming down over its silver walls from its peak.

Even though I could have operated the elevator myself, Chess came up with me, his hand resting protectively on the small of my back. As if he couldn't feel quite secure until he saw me deposited directly into the White Knight's care.

I couldn't say I really minded his attentiveness.

Theo stepped out of one of the office's side rooms just as we came in. "Here you are," he said, with a slow warm smile for me. His gaze slid to Chess. "There wasn't any trouble?"

"I believe I satisfactorily saved our Otherlander from herself," Chess said, winking at me.

"I'm sorry it's so late," I said. "I got distracted…"

Theo waved off my concern. "Now is fine. You're doing *me* a favor, not the other way around."

I ducked my head. "I was kind of hoping you could do me a favor too. I think it'd be better if I stayed here in the Tower tonight, like you said I could if I needed to. If that's still all right."

"Of course," he said, his tone softening. "It's no problem at all. I'm not in the habit of extending offers I wouldn't see through."

Chess gave my shoulder a light squeeze. "Good night then, lovely. Until tomorrow's adventure."

"Is everything ready for tomorrow?" I asked Theo with a stutter of my pulse as Chess vanished into the elevator. I'd gotten so carried away I'd forgotten how much he and his people might need me for the preparations. The tangled bramble of my emotions dug its thorns in deeper.

"There's one thing I'd have you do now," Theo said, "and you've come at the perfect time to see that through." He motioned me over to one of his worktables, striding to meet me there with his unflappable air of assurance. Watching him, it was hard to imagine him ever doubting himself.

I recognized the pocket-watch retriever sitting on the table from yesterday's visit, although the current version had a few more wires running through it and other bits I didn't think had been on it before. Theo set his hand on it with a fond smile. He liked making his contraptions for more than just being able to use them, I could tell.

"This is finished," he said. "With the best possible materials I've been able to track down. I've tested it, and I'm sure it'll do what we need it to do—as long as we keep it with us in its current form when the day flips over tomorrow. Just picking it up like you did yesterday should be enough."

I eased my hands under it and lifted it. The retriever was awfully light for that much metal. I held it up for a few seconds, just in case the effect needed a little while to take hold, and then replaced it on the table with a questioning look toward Theo. He nodded, his brown eyes bright, as if he were picturing how that device with my magical Otherlander touch would bring him the victory his people needed.

So much of his rebellion's success rested on my supposed power.

A wave of dizziness washed over me, knotting my stomach and rocking my balance. I braced my hand against the edge of the table.

Theo's smile disappeared in a blink. "Are you all right?" he asked, stepping closer.

I shook off the dizziness and managed a smile. My stomach stayed clenched. "I—I actually haven't eaten anything since this morning. I guess that wasn't the wisest choice ever."

"Let me remedy that. I have a few things around that could serve as a late dinner. Here, you should sit down."

He ushered me into the lounge room where we'd talked about my grand-aunt the other day. I sank onto a peach-colored sofa, digging my feet into the shag rug. "Any requests?" Theo asked, half of his smile returning.

"No mushrooms," I said. "Otherwise whatever you have around is great."

He chuckled and vanished into another room. How big was this office-slash-apartment, anyway? The base of the Tower took up an entire city block, but it narrowed on the way up.

Theo emerged with an individual-sized pie on a china plate. "Pheasant and blueberry tart," he said, offering it to me along with a fork. "The most dinner-like option I had on hand. Absolutely no mushrooms, I promise."

The savory smell rising off the pie made my stomach gurgle impatiently. I grabbed the fork and dug in.

The tart tasted just as good as it smelled, the crust thick and buttery, the bits of meat and berry mixing together in a rich sweet gravy. I plowed through half of it before the gnawing of hunger inside eased off enough to let me come up for air.

"What is it with Wonderlanders and pastry?" I asked, forcing myself to take my next bite in a more restrained way. Hatter and his scones, Doria and those powdered donuts she'd shared with me this morning. "You all seem hooked on the stuff."

Theo chuckled. "Every society has its tastes. Is that a complaint or just an observation?"

From the speed with which I'd devoured the tart, I was pretty sure he knew I wasn't complaining. "Observation," I said. "By all means continue feeding me sugary baked goods." Then I dug back in.

Theo got up again and returned with a tea set and a couple of cups. I hesitated over my last bite of tart as he poured the amber liquid from the pot.

"To wash your dinner down," he said. "I never used to enjoy tea, but I acquired a taste thanks to Hatter."

My gut twisted in a way that had nothing to do with hunger. Theo glanced up at my silence. He must have read something in my expression, because he slid my cup across the low table in front of the sofa and leaned back against the opposite arm with his gaze lingering on my face.

"Do you want to talk about why you're here and not at Hatter's?" he asked, so gently I believed he'd accept "No" as my answer.

I owed him more than that, though, didn't I, showing up on his doorstep this late without warning? I bit my lip as I tried to decide what to say.

"Hatter made it very clear that he doesn't want me around."

"Did he?" Theo said in the same even voice, but there was no mistaking the edge in those two words.

It was difficult to convey the depth of Hatter's anger without feeling as if I were tattling on him like a schoolgirl. "There was yelling," I said finally.

"What exactly did he yell at you about?"

"He…" I set down my plate and curled up my legs on the sofa as if they could shield me from the memory. "The Knave came by, and I went to hide with Doria, except she wanted to take off, and I figured I had to go with her, so… We came back way too late. He thought something had happened to her. He said he shouldn't have left me alone with her, that he couldn't trust me, that I—that if things get hard, I'm going to run back to the Otherland and abandon all of you."

I hadn't noticed Theo's stance had tensed, it'd been so subtle a shift, until now as his shoulders came down a smidgen. "Hatter is very… sensitive about his daughter's safety," he said. "I've been at the receiving end of his temper often enough to know that. I'm sure now that he'll have cooled off, he knows you didn't mean any harm and that he overreacted."

Remembering Hatter's tone, the way he'd looked at me, brought a lump into my throat. "I don't think it was just about Doria. There was more to it, I could tell. And…"

"And?" Theo prompted quietly when I didn't go on.

I swallowed hard. I didn't want to tell Wonderland's White Knight this, but maybe he deserved to know what he was staking so many of his hopes on.

"And he was right," I said in a small voice. "I came back to Wonderland because I wanted to have somewhere no one expected or needed anything from me. I've spent almost my whole life trying to make everyone around me happy or at least okay, and I thought… I thought I'd found someplace where I didn't have to worry about anything except what would make *me* happy. But then I found out what's really going on, and how much is riding on me making the right choices, and it was feeling like too much. I *did* want to run home and leave behind the responsibility."

The shame prickled across my face and through my chest. I had to look away. Theo set down his tea and eased closer to me on the sofa. He took my hand where it was resting on my knee.

"Lyssa," he said, and waited until I met his eyes. His gaze held mine steadily, not judging or angry, but maybe a little… sad? "I understand that feeling," he said. "More than I can tell you. You've been carrying heavy burdens for a long time—burdens that aren't even your own. Why wouldn't you want an escape from that? You *should* have an escape. I'm sorry Wonderland gave you false hope and then added to the weight you're carrying. If I'd known…"

"What?" I said. "You'd have switched off the Queen and her awful guards and all the rest while I was here? It's not like you're having this rebellion for fun. You don't have a choice what you're fighting against or when."

The corner of his mouth quirked, but he still looked sad. "I suppose not."

"*I* had a choice," I said. "I decided to stay and find out what was happening."

"Yes," Theo said. "Because you saw the need and your first instinct was to try to help. Because you're a good person. Having doubts doesn't change that."

He glanced away for a second with a slow exhalation and then returned his gaze to me. "I can promise you that all we need from you tomorrow night is for you to be there with my people when the day switches over. The larger risks won't be on you at all. And you don't even have to do that. You can still change your mind—we can get you home. If that's what you want."

"No," I said automatically. "Of course I'm staying. You're not even asking for that much. I was just being selfish."

His hand rose to brush his thumb over my cheek. "You were briefly uncertain whether you wanted to continue being so selfless. That's a very different thing from being selfish, and having known many selfish people in my life, I'm in a position to know. Nothing you've said tonight has diminished my admiration of your courage and generosity, Lyssa."

The conviction of his words soothed the lingering prickles of shame. If my throat was still choked up, it was more from relief than anything else. "Thank you," I said.

Theo shook his head at me. "I should be thanking *you*, a thousand times over." A slow smile crossed his handsome face. "You know, I think I have the perfect way to make a start of that. Come with me?"

Who was I to say no to this man?

He led me down a narrow white hallway and nudged open a door partway down. "I use this space to experiment with possible inventions sometimes. It can be useful for working out all the possibilities."

We stepped into a room about the size of my apartment's living room but with a ceiling twice as high. A layer of soft dove-gray cushioning covered the floor and walls—and as far as I could tell the ceiling too, light fixtures glowing softly through the fabric. Even the inside of the door was padded.

I raised an eyebrow at Theo as he closed it. He grinned at me and flicked a second switch beside the door. And all at once my body turned weightless.

A squeak of surprise slipped from my lips as I floated up off the floor, my hair fanning out around me. Theo started to drift up and caught a loop of fabric on the wall to hold himself in place. His eyes sparkled with amusement.

"Did you—did you just switch off *gravity*?" I said, and swallowed a gasp as I tipped forward. I was hovering several feet off the ground now. The skirt of my borrowed dress swirled around my thighs, but it was hard to worry much about modesty when I was literally flying.

"This room has been here longer than I have," Theo said, still grinning. "Wonderland is full of wondrous things, no matter what else we face." He let himself glide higher, keeping his hand against the wall. "You'll get the hang of it quickly. It's easier if you start with a jumping off point."

He held out his hand to me and, when I clasped it, tugged me over to the wall next to him. I braced myself against the padded surface. My heart beat with a heady thump.

When was I ever going to experience anything like this again?

I pushed off and soared across the room to the opposite wall. With a twist of my waist, I managed to land with my feet against the padding. I sprang up toward the ceiling, exhilaration racing through me with the burst of speed.

Theo had been right. Every leap I made, my confidence grew. I drifted along on my back, flipped onto my stomach to dive down, and then whipped into a somersault. Laughter tickled up my throat.

Flying was a way more satisfying high than the one the pipe and the glittering drinks had given me. Weightless, I could do anything.

Theo had stayed by the wall, watching me. The warmth in his expression sent a rush of affection through me. He *had* understood, enough to give me the perfect, if temporary, antidote to all those tangled emotions that had been dragging at me.

He walked around carrying the weight of an entire rebellion on his shoulders. Shouldn't he get to let loose too?

I swooped toward him, and he let go of the steadying loop to catch me if I needed it. Perfect. I veered at the last second, tucking my arm around his elbow and pulling him off into the air with me. Theo let out a hitch of breath that morphed into a laugh.

We tumbled together, bounced lightly off the ceiling, and started to drift apart. Theo grasped my hand, and we spun in a slow circle in the middle of the room. "Decided I wasn't having enough fun, did you?" he said.

"You *definitely* weren't," I informed him, and kicked off the wall at an angle that accidentally sent us spiraling head over heels.

Theo wrapped his arm around my back and turned us so he took all of the impact when we bumped against the cushioned floor. I collided with the solid heat of his chest.

My fingers curled into his crisp white shirt before the momentum could lift me away from him as we drifted back upward. My face tipped against his shoulder. He smelled even better than the pie had, like the raspberry rose jam I'd gotten at a farmer's market once mingled with masculine musk.

Theo's hand slid up to brush over my hair. My pulse skipped, and it occurred to me that I could make this moment even better if I brought his mouth to mine.

I'd already made that gamble once today, and I couldn't say it'd turned out very well. But Theo seemed like the kind of guy who'd be used to women throwing themselves at him, the kind of guy who had practice at letting them down gracefully if he wasn't interested. I didn't think he was going to start yelling at me, anyway.

This was still Wonderland. I could still go for what I wanted, even if there was a hell of a lot I didn't.

Before I could argue myself out of the impulse, I eased my head up and pressed my lips to his.

The muscles in Theo's chest tensed, but he kissed me back without hesitation, softly and intently. Then he pulled a few inches back, sliding his fingers up my jaw as he gazed into my eyes.

"Lyssa?" he said, in a way that sounded like several questions balled into one.

"I just—I wanted to kiss you," I said. "Is that okay?"

The corners of his mouth twitched up. "It's completely okay. I only want to make sure— I don't expect anything from you. You don't owe me anything for letting you stay here. If this is out of any sense of obligation…"

"No," I said quickly. "Not at all. I know you wouldn't think like that. And I know… I mean, it's not like this can be anything serious, right? I'm not even from this world. I'd just like to enjoy tonight as much as I can. As much as you want to too."

"I can't argue with that," he murmured.

My lips tingled with the desire to find his again, but maybe there was something else I should admit before we took this any farther. I hesitated and made myself say, "I kissed Hatter this morning."

I'd been a tad afraid of Theo's reaction. He simply tipped his head back with a laugh. "Was that before or after the yelling?" he asked, sounding so relaxed about it that my hesitation seemed silly.

"Before." I grimaced. "Just so you know, I'm not normally like this. It's something about this place. I've never been bouncing between three guys at the same time before."

"Three?" Theo repeated with an arch of his eyebrows.

Oh. Oops. I probably hadn't needed to mention *that*. "I, er, might have kind of a crush on Chess," I said, a blush spreading across my cheeks.

Theo bumped his slightly crooked nose against mine with a fond grin. "And have you been kissing him too?"

"No," I muttered. "I've just wanted to."

"I could call him back, you know. We could all enjoy each other. I suspect he'd be all for the idea."

A thrill shot through me at the thought, even though I'd never done that before either. But after the tentative way Chess had handled me tonight, I wasn't sure I agreed with Theo's assessment of his enthusiasm. It'd be kind of pressuring, a request like that coming from the guy who was sort of his boss, wouldn't it?

No, if anything was going to spark between me and Chess, I wanted it to be because the moment was right. Besides, I was feeling a little overwhelmed with just Theo's taste on my lips, his body aligned with mine.

"Not tonight," I said. "I've already got exactly the man I want to be with right now."

He leaned in. "Then let's make sure you get a night to remember," he murmured.

Instead of kissing me right away, he grazed his thumb over my lips, the touch so teasing it sensitized every nerve. Longing trembled through me. By the time he captured my mouth, I was almost dying for it.

I looped my arm around the back of his neck and kissed him harder. His fingers trailed down my neck and up again to tilt my head at just the perfect angle to deepen the kiss. He held me there, encouraging my lips to part and teasing out my tongue with the hot slide of his, commanding a pleased shiver out of me. Controlled power radiated from his every touch.

If he wanted to rule over me tonight like he ruled over the underside of Wonderland, I was more than happy to let him. There wasn't anyone I'd rather let take me over.

We came to rest against the wall. Theo caught one of the loops and pulled himself closer against me, flooding me with heat. My hand slipped into his thick chestnut curls as he tasted every inch of my mouth. A whimper worked its way from my throat.

My hips arched against his instinctively, and the bulge of his cock brushed my core through our clothes. His stutter of breath told me this encounter wasn't just about indulging my desire. He wanted me. He wanted this.

I wanted *more*. I reached for his shirt and fumbled with the buttons. I'd managed to undo two when Theo drew back with a gaze so darkly heated it nearly melted me. He tugged his shirt right off and tossed it away.

We drifted as he returned his attentions to my mouth. Every nerve in my lips was tingling. Hell, most of me was tingling, everywhere his body touched mine.

He palmed my breast, teasing the heel of his hand over my nipple, and pressed his lips to the crook of my neck at the same time. I gasped at the flash of pleasure. When I closed my eyes, floating there, it was as if nothing existed in the universe except this man and the reactions he seemed to know exactly how to provoke.

My fingers traveled over his sculpted chest and shoulders, charting all that solid muscle, clutching him when Theo rolled my nipple into an even stiffer peak. He caressed my thigh with his other hand, easing my dress up and up until his thumb traced the hem of my panties. I let out a needy sound, twisting my hips toward him, and without a second's hesitation he found the exact spot where I'd been aching most.

My breath hitched as he teased my clit through the already dampened panties with an approving hum. At his nudge and my yank, my dress flowed up over me and floated off into the gravity-less space. Somehow Theo managed to unclasp my bra in the same movement. Aunt Alicia's key drifted on its chain as he tucked it behind me.

He brought his mouth to the tip of my breast with a swirl of his tongue and swiveled his fingers against my clit at the same time. I arched into the air, free and held all at the same time, my body thrumming with pleasure.

It still wasn't enough. When Theo rose up to claim my lips again, I grasped the waist of his slacks. My fingers brushed over his straining erection, and he made a hungry sound that was almost a growl. With a flick of his thumb and a kick of his legs, he'd cast his pants aside. We wrenched my panties down in turn.

"Lyssa," Theo murmured as the head of his cock grazed my core. For one fleeting second, all the concerns I would have had about this kind of encounter back in the real world raced through my head. But I had my implant and Wonderland was one big disease-free safe zone, so fuck normal precautions.

I raised my hips, and he plunged into me with one smooth motion. A moan reverberated out of me. He was so thick and so hard, and he fit my body against his at just the perfect angle as he slid almost all the way out and back in again with a deeper thrust. We were flying together, inside and out. I'd never been with anyone who could summon so much bliss from my body.

I rocked to meet Theo, urging him deeper, faster. Pleasure trembled and spiked through my core. I could feel my release building and building, so high and so quickly I lost my breath.

Theo kissed me, his lips firm and certain. His hand was hot as a brand on my hip as he filled me over and over. "Let it out, Lyssa," he said, his voice ragged. "Let me hear you."

The command opened my throat. "Oh, God," I mumbled. "Oh, fuck. Oh, please. Please." Then my voice blurred into a wordless sound of ecstasy as he plunged into me even more completely and my orgasm shattered through me.

My core and my thighs clenched around him, and he groaned. With a shudder and another searing kiss, he spilled his own release into me. In that moment, with bliss still ringing through my nerves and my body tucked against Theo's as if it'd never been meant to exist anywhere else, every doubt and every fear washed out of me.

This was my Wonderland right here, and I was sure as hell willing to fight for it.

I woke up nestled against Theo on the anti-gravity room's cushioned floor. At some point he'd flipped the gravity back on, but my body kept a faint sense of that weightlessness. I snuggled closer to him, and he rolled toward me, brushing one soft kiss to my lips.

"Well," he murmured with a smile, "now we know for sure that you can keep a person with you through the night, despite the reset."

"Let's just hope I don't have to be naked to accomplish that," I said.

He laughed. "No regrets?" he said, searching my eyes as if he really thought I might have some.

"Exactly zero," I said, and he smiled again, a little more easily.

We'd found our way back into our clothes when a little automated voice carried through the room. "Chess is arriving alone," it intoned. Theo motioned for me to follow him.

We reached the main office just as the elevator dropped Chess off. He took in the two of us with his bright gaze—Theo's collar askew and his normally slicked-back curls disheveled, my hair probably even more of a mess—and the grin he gave us looked knowing.

"I thought breakfast might be in order," he said, producing a paper bag.

"Bring it over here," Theo said, heading to the table with his retriever device. Nothing about it had changed since I'd seen it last night, I realized with a lift of my spirits. I'd really done it. Just by touching it, I'd kept it whole—and ready to use tonight.

"Perfect," Theo murmured. He turned to his shelves and picked up a box of parts. "I'll put together a few more basics for the mission—it shouldn't take more than a couple hours. Then you'll have—"

"The Knave of Hearts," the automated voice announced, with the hiss of the elevator door opening.

Chess leapt forward with more speed than I'd have guessed that brawny body was capable of. He caught me around the waist and dove behind the solid base of the worktable, pulling me with him.

I flinched as my ass hit the floor and then stiffened. Chess braced himself beside me. We held there, still and silent, as heavy footsteps thumped across the room.

"Inventor," the Knave said in a harsh voice that made my nerves wobble. "I'd like to have a word."

He must have done something to the elevator to stop it from announcing him earlier. Fuck. My pulse thudded past my ears, so loud I was afraid he'd hear it. I inhaled shallowly, my palms sweating on the tiled floor, pressing myself as flat as I could against the worktable's base.

"Feel free," Theo said, smooth and confident as ever. "What's this about?"

The Knave's feet kept up a steady rhythm as he must have been pacing the room. "A number of anomalies have come to our attention in the past few days," he said. "I don't suppose you've been trying out some strange new device? Something to produce a little time, despite the Queen's decry?"

Time. A chill crawled down my spine. He knew that much—someone had noticed. I must have screwed up somewhere.

"I wouldn't defy the Queen's sanctions," Theo said. "And as far as I know, such a device would be impossible."

The Knave stopped with a snap of his heel. "Then perhaps you could tell me what *you* think might be leaching food from our shops and painting flowers on the floor of Caterpillar's Club."

I winced, clamping down on a groan. The paint at the club yesterday—I'd been so out of it I hadn't even thought about the consequences. I tucked myself even smaller against the table. Chess's hand slipped across the space between us and touched my ankle with a reassuring pressure.

"I can't say I know anything about that," Theo replied. "My apologies." He stepped to the side where his body would block view of us if the Knave walked closer on that end of the table.

"I don't know about that," the leader of the Hearts' Guard said. "You keep track of everything that happens in the city. I can't believe something so unsettling could slip your attention. Or some*one* so unsettling. The Queen begins to suspect an Otherlander is involved, and I have to say the evidence adds up."

And what would he do if he found the Otherlander who was very much right here? I swallowed thickly, struggling to keep my breaths even.

"A Dreamer?" Theo said. "I spoke to one briefly the other day, but as far as I know they've never had any effect on Wonderland."

"Not a Dreamer. The other kind."

"I'm afraid I can't help you there. If I do hear anything—"

There was a rasping sound, and the box of mechanical parts that Theo had set on the neighboring worktable flew over the edge and crashed to the floor. Metal bits clattered across the tiles. I bit my tongue, holding in my flinch.

"Oh, dear," the Knave said in a cutting tone. "I hope you hadn't put anything together in there that you need all that much today. Of course, if you give me what *I* need…"

"I can't give you what I don't have," Theo said, quiet but firm. "Knave, I give you my word, I—"

He cut himself off with a sharp little breath. Panic jolted through me before the impact even came.

The retriever skidded off the edge of the table above Chess and me and hit the floor just inches from my feet. The joints shuddered and snapped apart; porcelain fixtures shattered. The crystal sphere in the center burst into shards. The spray battered my legs and my arms where they were hugged around my knees. A cry snagged in my throat.

They'd touched me. The broken pieces of Theo's device—the crystal he'd said it'd taken him so long to find—and the Knave's boots were thumping across the floor again.

Any second, he was going to stride around this table and see us. Then it'd be my head rolling across the floor.

CHAPTER TWENTY-FOUR

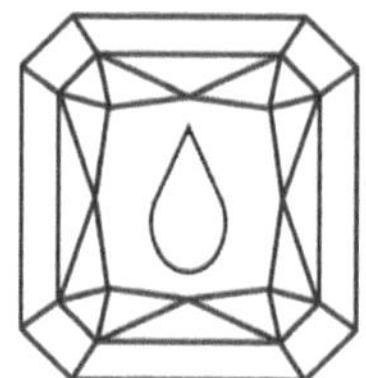

Chess

Lyssa's fear spiked the air, sharp as the chunks of metal and crystal scattered around us. Her face had gone sallow, her shoulders rigid as she clutched her knees. My jaw clenched, seeing her that shaken. Even an iron will could tremble when it was pushed to the brink of disaster.

Why hadn't the White Knight been better prepared? The Knave was stalking closer, and I didn't see how he could be talked down. There was nowhere else for our Otherlander to hide, nowhere she could run to.

Unless…

Resolve wound through my chest. The White Knight had brought Lyssa into the path of danger. Perhaps it came down to me of all people to get her out. I couldn't let her fall into the Queen's hands because of a plan that had been all for our benefit and not for hers.

The Knave's steps thudded closer. I shifted my weight onto my feet, grasping Lyssa's wrist. When she looked at me, I jabbed my thumb toward the door and then held up a finger. Just one minute. Probably less. That was all I needed.

She stared at me, wide-eyed, but I couldn't talk to explain any better than that. The girl had a good head on her shoulders, which was where I intended to see it stay. She'd figure it out once I set the ball rolling.

With a slow inhalation, I willed myself into the space between the particles of air. The voices around us dulled. The edges of shapes came into sharper focus. I stood up and strode toward the hall door the White Knight had left open, not the slightest current grazing my skin as I moved beyond sight and sound.

Normally I took a certain comfort in that numbed space. Now, my heart pounded adrenaline through my veins. It had been a long time since I'd been able to contribute anything to the cause that would make a significant difference. That came anywhere near to a matter of life and death.

I slipped past the door and in its shadow flicked my hand out of the invisible space. My fingernails twinged as I scratched them against the wall.

"What was that?" the Knave barked, thundering over. I yanked my hand back out of view and darted farther down the hall. Here, around the corner, I let one foot fall on the floor, gave another scratch. The Knave bellowed and hurtled onward.

Onward out of the room where Lyssa was crouched.

I'd caught his attention enough. I whirled around, moving completely into the space in-between, and then bolted down the hall. The Knave charged past me unseeing, his teeth bared and a purple flush spreading under the blue-gray sheen of his blunt cheeks. I barreled back into the office just in time to see the flash of Lyssa's white-blond hair swallowed up by the elevator shaft.

I dashed after her. It wouldn't do the White Knight any good for me to stick around now. If the Knave was on a rampage, if the Queen already suspected the truth about Lyssa's presence, Lyssa might need me still, far more than he did.

The elevator caught me and shot me down toward the base of the Tower just behind her. When I made it to the ground, Lyssa was already loping down the street, looking around her as if she wasn't sure which way to go. Which maybe she wasn't. She really hadn't sounded keen about seeing Hatter again, and she didn't have anyone else here to go to.

I hustled after her. "Stick with me, lovely," I said, pitching my voice to travel out from the in-between space. Lyssa turned toward me, and a pair of palace guards marched out of a cross-street just ahead of us.

They stiffened when they saw her. "Hey!" one shouted. "You there —stop!"

I grabbed Lyssa's elbow with my invisible hand. She whirled toward the nearest alley before I even had to guide her. I ran with her, urging her faster, keeping my grip loose but steady so she'd know I was with her.

A louder shout rang out, with several more echoing it in answer. By the lands, how many of those helmet-heads had swarmed the city today?

I tugged Lyssa to the right, down a flight of stairs, under a bridge, and up into another alley. Her head jerked at the sound of more hollering, somewhere on the other side of the buildings around us. Her face was still pale, her hair wisping even wilder around her face than it'd been when I'd walked in on what had looked very much like post-coital disarray.

Happy post-coital disarray, at least. I didn't know what the White Knight thought he was doing exactly, but I hadn't seen a shine like that in Lyssa's eyes since her first night in Wonderland, so I supposed I couldn't criticize him for eliciting it.

"Chess?" she said now, with a quaver in her voice.

I moved around her, letting my arm slide up to hug her shoulders. She leaned into me for a second, and a pang of regret ran through me.

If I'd had a place to take her, if I'd been more than a rambling, aimless creature, I might have been the one she'd turned to last night for that other more intimate dance. I might have put that shine in her eyes. I'd felt attraction crackle between us, but I'd shied away from it.

What if I couldn't? What if I wasn't capable of giving what she needed at all?

I embraced the visible world again, so she could at least have the comfort of seeing me beside her, as much of a comfort as that might be.

"You're all right," I told her in a low voice. "You got away from the Knave. We won't let his lackeys find out."

"Where do I go?" she asked. "I can't even— The Knave is suspicious of Hatter already. I can't bring even more trouble down on him." She gnawed at her lower lip. "The guards seemed to know I was the one they were looking for the second they saw me."

"The Knave said something about a painting in the club," I said. "You did something there last night—something that left a mark?"

She nodded with a grimace. "The Wonderlanders I was sitting with thought I was a Dreamer."

"The Guard must have questioned people who were there, gotten a description." My stomach balled into a knot. That meant every guard in the land might know Lyssa on sight. We couldn't pass her off as a Dreamer any longer.

Another shout rang out, even closer than before. My pulse hiccupped. "Come on," I said, without entirely knowing where I was leading her. "Let's go."

As we veered down another alley where the buildings leaned together so closely they almost touched overhead, a sinking certainty filled my chest. The answer that had come to me wasn't what the White Knight would want—but he wouldn't get to see his plan through if we lost Lyssa anyway. He wasn't here to adjust course. Someone had to think outside the lines he'd drawn.

We dashed across a street and ducked into an alcove between two houses. Lyssa leaned against the wall, panting. The yells of the searching soldiers careened by us.

I touched her cheek, drawing her gaze to mine. The only shine in those bright blue eyes now was one of panic. I had plenty of reasons to wish the Knave dead, but seeing that, I'd happily have gutted him myself.

"Lyssa," I said. "You can't stay here. I have to find a way to get you to Caterpillar's looking-glass."

Lyssa stared at me. "But Theo's plan—tonight—I'm supposed to—"

I shook my head to cut her off. "After the Knave is done with the White Knight's workshop, I'm not sure we'll have the tools to carry out that plan tonight anyway. We'll certainly lose any chance if you lose your head to the guards. There's nowhere here you'll be safe. Maybe in a day or two, if nothing else happens, they'll decide the anomalies were a fluke and ease off, and then we could talk about our next moves. I can't leave you in this much danger waiting for that."

"A day or two," Lyssa repeated. "I'd go home and then come back?"

I didn't let my gaze waver. "If that's what you wanted. If it isn't, if you simply stay there… No one should fault you for being where you're meant to be. I certainly wouldn't."

Her jaw tightened, but she nodded. "How do I get to the looking-glass? If they know I was in the club, they have to have that place guarded."

"Leave that to me."

We slunk and darted through the streets, with me occasionally slipping ahead through the in-between to scout out our route. Twice we had to stop, crouched behind a bit of shelter, waiting for a squad of guards to pass. When we finally reached the edge of the city near the club, my heart sank.

A dozen guards were stationed outside. My powers of trickery and distraction might be extensive, but the palace folk knew me. I wasn't going to be able to divert all of them with my ploys, not when they knew *their* heads would be on the chopping block if they failed the Knave.

They'd only leave their post if they saw something they couldn't explain, which might therefore be part of the anomalies they were pursuing. Something they had no reason to expect.

My throat constricted. I shook myself, trying to shed the sensation of hairs rising all down my back.

"There are too many of them, aren't there?" Lyssa murmured. "Chess, it's okay. It's my fault for making that stupid painting. I'll just hide as well as I can, and they'll never know you or Theo or Hatter helped me. If they find me, I swear I won't say anything about the Spades or the rest of it."

Oh, this Otherlander was something, wasn't she? Lovely indeed. Her life on the line, and her first worry was how she was risking *me* and the others who'd dragged her into this mess.

I'd sworn to myself I'd do right where I could. If this wasn't a moment for that, then when was?

Besides, what did it matter anyway if this one more person found out? If she knew what was good for her, she'd stay on the other side of that looking-glass and never set foot here again.

I traced my thumb across Lyssa's cheek, stopping at the corner of her mouth. Her lips parted. The beautiful lips that the White Knight had recently been kissing.

He had brought her pleasure. I would bring her home. In some ways, this actually came easier.

"I'll get them away from the club long enough for you to slip inside," I said. "As soon as you have the chance, run for it. What you're about to see—I never want you to talk about it, not with me or with anyone else. Can you do that for me?"

She knit her brow. "Of course. But Chess—"

I tapped my thumb to the middle of her lips to quiet her. "You're getting my secret because you're special, lovely. Be ready."

I turned away from her with a roll of my shoulders. My breath came out shaky. It had been a long time. Even the thought of the shift came with a stale twinge of shame.

This time I was using it for something worthwhile. For something deserving.

I hunched over and sank my fangs into the inside of my cheeks.

The pain crackled through my flesh from my head down to my toes. My skin contracted with it, bones shrinking and realigning, fur sprouting up. A puffy tail sprang from the base of my spine and snapped from side to side.

When a cat wags his tail, you know he's mad.

On broad furred paws, I leapt into the street and dashed toward the guards. As I streaked past them, swaying my rounded body and waving my tail like a signal flag, I slipped into the in-between, and out, and in, and out. Now just my tail showing. Now just my head. A bizarre beast made of jumbled parts. An anomaly.

The guards let out a cry. I dodged one and bolted between another's legs, sprang over a third's snatching hands. Out of sight, back into it.

This could be your lead, lackeys. Come and get me. Make your Knave proud.

The thumping of feet behind me sounded promising. I veered into the forest, making sure I stayed where the streams of sunlight caught on my amber-and-brown striped fur. The guards chased after. I clambered up a tree and spun for just long enough to catch a glimpse of Lyssa flinging herself over the club's threshold. With a grin that prickled the muscles of my face, I blinked out of sight for good.

When I entered the White Knight's office for the second time that morning, he was sitting on the floor, his expression tight, picking through the pieces of his smashed device.

"Lyssa?" he said without looking up.

"She's safe," I said. As far as I could tell from my observations at the club. I could save the explaining of exactly how I'd ensured her safety for another moment. "Your invention?"

"I don't know." He let out a ragged breath. "Some of the pieces touched her when it broke, didn't they?"

I nodded. He rubbed his hand jerkily past his mouth and then swiped it through his dark hair.

"Some of the materials…" He held up a fragment of crystal. "I don't know how long it'll take me to find a functional replacement if the pieces remain in this state tomorrow."

"And we can't get the watch without it?"

"It doesn't do us any good getting to the palace if we can't retrieve the damned thing from its holding cell." He sighed and tipped his head back against the wall. "We were so close, Chess. So fucking close."

I hunkered down beside him. "Maybe that bit didn't touch her," I said. "Maybe we just need one more day." If Lyssa was foolhardy enough to return.

"She was already hesitant about staying this long. With the Knave on her heels… If he catches her…"

Was he more worried about her or his plan? Perhaps this was the right moment after all. I cleared my throat.

"About that…"

CHAPTER TWENTY-FIVE

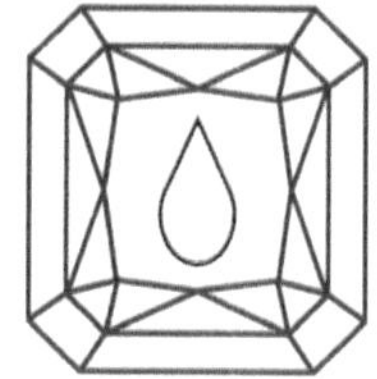

Lyssa

I burst into the club so fast I nearly tripped down the floor's slopes. The first thing I registered through the thundering of my pulse and my whirling thoughts—Chess had transformed into a *cat*?—was that not even the lounging smokers hung out here this early in the day. No one occupied the vast dance floor other than me and the two guards who'd startled by the basement door.

They were Caterpillar's guards, in the uniforms I'd seen my first night here, not the Queen's red-and-pink stripes. They looked more confused than fierce. My heart felt as if it were about to batter its way right out of my chest, but I made myself hustle over to them.

"The Otherlander has already gone down!" I said in the most urgent voice I could manage. "The Queen is furious. You have to catch her!"

I must have been convincing enough, or else they were just that scared of the Queen of Hearts' possible anger. The guards whipped around and yanked open the door. I hurried after them as they barged into the dim hallway on the other side. As long as I kept talking and reminding them of the Queen's supposed wrath, maybe they wouldn't question me.

"The Otherlander doesn't know where she's going. There's still a chance to catch her before she finds her way out. The Queen is on her way here right now. If she finds out you let the girl get past you—There she is!"

I jabbed my hand forward as if I'd caught a glimpse of a figure farther down the hall. The guards dashed faster.

I ducked into the thinner hall that had just appeared at my left. Theo's instructions from several nights ago were burned into my mind. *Back up into it and then go forward.*

The second the sliver of the other passageway opened across from me, I darted down it. The guards' footsteps were still pounding away from me, but I didn't know how long it would take them to figure out they'd been tricked. The dry air scratched at my throat as I hurtled up the stairs.

When the steps flipped over, my momentum threw me forward even harder than before. My bare knees banged on the rough floor with a sting that told me I'd scraped the skin raw. Even as I winced, I scrambled onto my feet and ran into the tunnel ahead as fast as I could, hunching beneath the low ceiling.

A shout carried down the stairs behind me. Fuck. I pushed myself faster, the earthy smell of the dark tunnel clogging my nose. Left. I had to go left. Around and back to where I'd begun.

Unfortunately, where I'd begun was exactly where the guards were headed. I came around the loop and bolted past the stairs a second before they reached the lower level.

The guard in front lunged forward and grabbed my wrist. My tendons yanked. The only thing that saved me was the self-defence course Mom had insisted we take together when I started university. I'd practiced a few of those moves enough that my body reacted on muscle memory.

I spun around and kneed the guy in thc groin.

He doubled over with a gasp, his grip on my wrist loosening, but at the same time he slashed at me with the dagger in his other hand.

The blade sliced a burning line across my forearm. A yelp broke from my lips as I shoved myself away from him.

The tunnel's cool air chilled the blood seeping over my skin. I didn't have time to do anything about the wound now. I'd lose a lot more than blood if I didn't make it to the mirror.

Clutching my arm to my chest, I careened the last several feet to the little earthen room with its gold-framed mirror. Without a glance backward, I jumped straight into the glass.

Cold rushed over me, and then I sprawled on the floor of Aunt Alicia's attic. My shoulder jarred. A fresh jab of pain shot through my arm. Gritting my teeth, I rolled onto my back.

It was dark outside the narrow window. I'd definitely come back a while later than I'd left. Lying there amid the familiar *normal* smells of the world I belonged in and the furniture with its duller colors, my mind jarred too.

I was back. This, *this* was my home. No one stabbing daggers at me. No one looking to chop off my head.

The adrenaline coursing through me started to ease off, and the pain in my arm dug deeper. I glanced down at myself and winced at the blotch of scarlet smeared across the front of the borrowed dress. I guessed I wasn't returning this to Hatter.

The cut ran from the side of my wrist nearly to my elbow, narrow but deep. Looking at it, my stomach roiled. That guard really would have killed me if I'd given him the chance.

I could have died there. The cold fact of it hit me like it hadn't even when I'd watched the guards beating up the woman in the club the other night.

I could have died, and no one here would ever have known what happened to me.

Oh, shit. Melody. Was it even the same day? Was she freaking out about me disappearing after my supposed booty call?

Pressing the side of my arm against my belly, I stumbled to the toy chest and grabbed my phone. A quick tap showed me it was still the same day as when I'd left, just several hours later. I exhaled in a rush of relief and typed out a text as quickly as I could one-handed.

Back at the house safe. Good times!

Melody texted back almost instantly. *You go, girl!*

My smile turned into another wince. I had to take care of my arm before the whole dress was dyed red with my blood.

I gripped the railing tightly as I descended the spiral staircase. In the bathroom, I flicked on the light and pawed through the cabinets. Aunt Alicia had band-aids and antiseptic cream, but nothing that'd treat more than a scratch. I just needed to stop the damned bleeding.

My head was feeling a little woozy by the time I made it down to the kitchen. I grabbed a dish towel from the drawer of clean ones and wrapped it around my forearm. A streak of red started seeping through the layers of fabric almost immediately.

Okay, maybe this injury was a little more than I could handle on my own. I fumbled with my phone and found the nearest hospital on the map. A half hour drive.

I stood still and turned my head from one side to the other. I wasn't *that* dizzy. If I just wrapped one more towel around my arm even tighter, I should be able to make it on my own, right? It was just a cut. Calling an ambulance seemed ridiculous.

I was still wavering between my options when an enthusiastic rapping reverberated through the front door. Had I psychically summoned medical attention? I went to the door in the daze and opened it to find my best friend grinning at me.

"Lyss!" Melody said. "I wanted to get the full scoop in person. I —" Her gaze snagged on my blood-smeared dress and towel-wrapped arm, and her voice cut off with a choked sound. "Oh my God. What the hell happened to you?"

"I, um," I said, which was about all I could manage as a thicker rush of dizziness raced through me. I hadn't thought up a story. I hadn't known I was going to need one. The most obvious possible lie fell out of my mouth. "I fell."

"Uh huh. We're talking about this more later. Come on, we've got to get you to the hospital."

Well, at least that solved my most immediate problem. I let Melody haul me out to her car, just barely keeping my balance on my wobbly legs.

Had I ever felt as content as I did sitting in Melody's studio apartment with the sunlight streaming through the skylights and hazelnut coffee warming my stomach? I couldn't think of when. I tucked my legs up on the armchair and took another sip from my mug.

My best friend started her dishwasher running with a thrum and flopped into the chair across from me. Totally normal chairs that matched the totally normal coffee table.

With each hour that passed since I'd last been in Wonderland, it was harder to believe my time there hadn't been a crazy, thrilling, horrible dream. That the story I'd made up about slipping with a butcher knife while I was making dinner hadn't been the truth.

I could call a moving company and have all the furniture, including that mirror, packed up by the end of the day. Then it wouldn't matter what was true, whether there really was some bizarre world alongside ours where trees could grow upside down and queens could lock time away in a pocket watch. It wouldn't matter whether the Spades' rebellion succeeded.

Hatter hadn't believed I'd see things through anyway. Chess had *told* me to go home, to escape. I had no way of knowing when the Queen's efforts to find me would taper off. If I went back, I might tumble into the pond only to meet another dagger, this one at my throat.

The thought sent an icy shudder through me despite the warmth of the sun.

I'd caused almost as much harm as good in Wonderland, hadn't I? Theo's device was irrevocably broken because of my presence. I'd only been a shortcut to seeing his plan through. He'd figure out another approach. And there were people *here* who needed me—who needed me with my neck intact.

When I wet my lips, the pressure of my tongue and the lingering sweetness from the sugar in the coffee brought back a flicker of memory: his mouth against mine as we glided through the air.

Melody cleared her throat. "You're going spacey again. Come back to earth!"

I jerked my thoughts back to the present with a crooked smile. "Sorry. Just thinking."

She made a skeptical sound. "Not about that jerk of a neighbor, I hope." She hadn't really bought my butcher knife story—I was pretty sure she figured my supposed paramour had something to do with my cut and my scraped knees. "It's not like you to zone out so much, Lyssa. Are you sure you don't want to go back to the hospital and ask them to check you out again?"

"I messed up my arm, not my head," I reminded her. My fingers traveled over the stitches that dappled the side of my arm. Twenty-four of them. The doctor had announced the number like it was some kind of record. "It's just the painkillers."

The truth was I hadn't taken any more of the Vicodin I'd been prescribed after the first night. The wooziness had reminded me too much of that moment in the Caterpillar's Club when my head had stretched up toward the ceiling. I'd rather deal with the now dull ache in my arm than relive that sensation.

"I have to be at the shoot this afternoon," Melody said. "Do you want to come along? Or you can just hang out here."

I hesitated, my hand drifting from the cut to the key dangling from its chain beneath my shirt. The dagger wound wasn't the only thing I'd brought back from Wonderland. As much as the last few days with Melody doting on me had been comforting distraction, I couldn't run away from everything I'd learned. Aunt Alicia was part of this world. She'd had something to give me.

It couldn't hurt to find out what. I owed it to her. I owed it to myself to understand what I'd been through better.

"I thought I'd go back out to the house," I said cautiously. Melody and I had driven out there the day after the hospital to get my car, but she hadn't left my side for a second. The woman who'd been looking after the cats when Aunt Alicia was in the hospital had taken over while I was gone, but otherwise no one had been in the place since I'd left it three nights ago.

"Lyss," Melody started.

I waved off her protest. "I'll be fine. I promise you, there's nothing to worry about there. I've been sponging off you long enough. I've got to finish going through the furniture and figuring out what to do with it all, and it was kind of nice having some time in a completely new space. I won't go see my neighbor again." Not the fictitious one, at least.

Melody sighed. "Look, I just…" She made a face at her hands and looked at me again. "I'm really worried about you, Lyssa. I've seen a lot of people I've worked with crash and burn; I know how quickly things can spiral. I've taken it for granted that you'll always have it together, so maybe I missed things I shouldn't have. That's on me. If there's something else going on, if you need *help*, please don't shut me out."

My stomach knotted. Oh, Melody. There was no way she could help with this dilemma or the potential dangers on the other side of it. "You encouraged me to take some risks," I reminded her. "I'm okay. No permanent harm done. These things happen when you let loose, right?"

"But you're *you*," Melody said. She motioned to my arm. "If you're going this far… Something's got to be wrong."

An emotion more like frustration prickled up through my chest. I'd taken the risks I had with my eyes wide open. I'd just wanted something *different*, something weird and wonderful. How could I ever really let loose or strike out in a new direction if everyone in my life was going to step in my way because of the expectations they had of me. Even Melody wanted me to stay the same old careful practical Lyssa.

Maybe she was right. Maybe I'd already gone too far over my head. I kind of wanted her to order me to stay put so the decision would be made for me. But even more than that, the limits she was trying to set on what I could do, who I could *be*, made me bristle. She had no idea just how much I'd experienced and survived in the last few days.

I kept my voice calm. "I promise, nothing's wrong, Mel. I'm a big girl. A couple more days puttering around a big old house isn't going to hurt me. I'll stay away from the kitchen knives."

Melody couldn't help a crooked smile at that. My eleven years of being the responsible one in our friendship could pay off in other ways. She sank back in her chair, giving in.

"All right," she grumbled. "But if you somehow manage to open any more gaping wounds, please let me know? After you've called an ambulance? I'll text you when the shoot is finished. It shouldn't go any later than eight or nine. And you're mine for the rest of this morning."

She fixed me with a steely look there was no arguing with. I held up my hands and managed to laugh.

After Melody's version of Lyssa rehabilitation therapy, which involved a meander around a new art exhibition downtown followed by dim sum, she grudgingly released me from her care. My heartbeat picked up speed the second I started the engine on my car, and by the time I was pulling up in front of the Victorian mini-castle Aunt Alicia had called home, it was drumming at the base of my throat.

I couldn't lie to myself. The thought of traveling back to Wonderland terrified me, but the mirror called to me at the same time.

I made myself ignore the spiral staircase, heading straight to the library instead. The box and Aunt Alicia's note were sitting exactly where I'd left them. I unclasped the chain from around my neck and slid the key off before fitting it into the lock.

It turned with a click and a tingling quiver over my skin that made me wonder if any locksmith *could* have forced the thing open. With that symbol on it, this box might have come from Wonderland. Who knew what magic it had on it—or in it?

I eased the lid open. On the crimson velvet lining, several folded papers and a sphere of gold filigree rested. I recognized Aunt Alicia's fluid handwriting as I picked the papers up.

It was a letter, addressed to me. A much longer one this time. The quiet of the house closed in around me as I leaned against the leather-padded back of the chair and started reading.

My dear Lyssa,

. . .

If you're reading this, then you've been to Wonderland. I'm sorry I couldn't explain things earlier. Maybe if I'd made this decision while I was still well enough to attempt the trip myself… But I didn't, and here we are. I knew you'd find your way to the mirror. Whether a blessing or a curse, that tie runs through the blood in our veins.

I don't know what you'll have found there. It's difficult for me to imagine how much that place might have changed—or on the other hand, how much it may have stayed exactly the same—since I last set foot there. You can trust the Spades. If you have the key, you must have connected with at least one of them.

There are two things I need to pass on to you: a token and some insight from one who's gone and come back and then lived the rest of her life as if she's never heard of a place called Wonderland.

I did not treat Wonderland well, Lyssa. I fell through the mirror and got caught up in that wild wicked place: in the thrill of joining a growing rebellion and spurring it on toward victory. I threw myself into their turmoil as if it were an exciting new game, not a struggle where real people might live or die by the outcome.

I didn't really know or understand how I fit in there or what my true purpose was. When the pieces all collided, I panicked. I ran away and I shut up that attic room. I kept you away, and I made a hash of things with your mother, all in the name of what I thought was protecting you.

I was wrong.

Only you can decide what you do there or whether you return at all. But the truth is that, for me, abandoning Wonderland is my greatest regret. I left behind friends. I broke promises. They were counting on me, on the things I said I'd bring back from this world, and I simply never arrived. Maybe they overcame the Queen of Hearts without me. I'd like to think so. But I can't comfort myself assuming it.

I can't tell you how ashamed I am that I let them down, even after all the decades I tried to bury those memories. It may be I let myself down too. I never got to find out who I could have been, other than a coward. If you see any of them who might remember me—the White Knight, March and May, Hatter, Carpenter—it would mean a lot to me if you told them how sorry I am, and that I realize those words don't come close to making up for my lack of faith.

Let me be clear, Lyssa: My mistakes are not yours to fix. I place no load on your shoulders. Even when I knew you, you'd had enough of that. I only want you to be aware of one way a choice can play out. I hope knowing will help guide you as you go forward.

I wish I could explain more about you and me and the Tenniel family's connection to the mirror upstairs, but whatever magic runs through our bloodline has strict ideas about what we must discover for ourselves. I can give you the ring. I can warn you that the way won't be easy. And I can tell you that I wish I'd picked Wonderland.

If you've remained like the little girl it was my greatest pleasure to help raise, I know you will be strong enough.

Regards and my love, always,
Alicia

I sat there staring at the last page for several minutes, letting my grand-aunt's words sink in. Suddenly Hatter's anger and accusations made a lot more sense. He'd said Aunt Alicia had left not long before the Queen had trapped time. God, was it *her* fault that Wonderland had ended up trapped in that awful loop?

Why would he trust me after the last Otherlander he'd known had gone back on her promises?

Not everything Aunt Alicia had said totally made sense, though. What had she found out that had scared her off? It sounded like she meant more than just the violence that had shaken me. Something to do with our family's connection to the mirror and Wonderland…

Had there been *other* relatives of ours who'd gone through? My gaze drifted to the framed family tree on the wall beyond the nearest bookcase, but it couldn't tell me anything on that subject.

I picked up the ball of filigree and found it encircled the top of a gold band. The ring her letter had mentioned. When I found the catch, the sphere snapped open to reveal a large ruby setting. The brilliant gem had the same shape as the symbol on the box and on that ruin near the Topsy Turvy Woods.

Almost the same. A little point rose up in the middle of the stone. I ran my thumb over it instinctively to test it and let out a yelp at the prick of pain.

A drop of blood welled from my skin and slid across the ruby's surface. In that second, a glow rose up through the gem as if from within. A warm shiver shot through my nerves, so potent I almost dropped the ring.

Then the light faded, the blood vanished, and the stone looked perfectly ordinary. Well, still gorgeous, but hardly magical.

Okay, then. Aunt Alicia *really* couldn't have explained even a little more about that? I glowered at her letter.

She was right, though. I'd known before I even arrived at the house that I'd be making a choice—if not today, then soon. Because the longer I put off deciding, the more that evasion became a decision in itself, avoiding the fact that Wonderland existed at all.

I set the key on the desk beside the box and fit the filigree back around the ruby. Then I strung the ring on the chain I'd used to hold the key before. Wearing jewelry that might slice me open if my hands slipped seemed unwise, but I wasn't going to leave some magical artifact just lying around either.

If I went back, maybe Theo or one of the others would know what it meant.

That was the choice right there, wasn't it? If I went back.

My body balked. There were so many reasons to say no. The Hearts' Guard was out for my head. I still didn't understand much about the world I'd wanted to help. If I went, I didn't know how easily I could get back again. There might be a hundred guards between me and the Caterpillar's mirror next time.

And if I was stuck there too long—God, Mom would get into such a panic. It'd break her heart, thinking something horrific must have happened to me. Melody would freak out too. How could I risk it?

Even as those worries passed through my head, I was remembering Hatter's rare smile, the scones and tea left on a bedside table, the intensity in his eyes right after we kissed. Chess's glib remarks and effervescent grin, the swiftness with which he'd come to my defense over and over again. Theo's unshakeable certainty that I could be everything he saw in me, the ease with which he'd offered me the freedom I'd needed the other night.

They'd risked so much for me. How could I *not* take on a little more in return, when just being there might free them?

Was I really going to help them, though, when my special powers appeared to be allowing built things to stay built and causing broken things to stay broken, and I'd already broken the wrong thing? Well, and growing and shrinking with the bite of a mushroom, so *incredibly* useful—

I paused with my hand braced against the edge of the desk as an idea lit like a spark in my head. Oh. *Oh.*

Maybe Theo's plan to retrieve the pocket watch wasn't broken after all.

A rush of resolve coursed through me with my next breath. I let it carry me onto my feet. I didn't know if the sensation would last, but right then, what I could offer didn't feel like a burden at all. It felt like a gift.

This wasn't about me trying to prop up a floundering family or a failing relationship. This was all of us coming together to set something right that had been horribly wrong for too long. I could see the plan through with Hatter, Chess, and Theo, because that was who I wanted to be, not a woman who'd be writing letters of regret to her grand-niece fifty years from now.

I paused for just long enough to type out a quick text to Melody to buy me the night—*Going to bed early, kind of wiped, didn't want you to worry if I don't answer right away!*—and then I dashed for the spiral staircase.

CHAPTER TWENTY-SIX

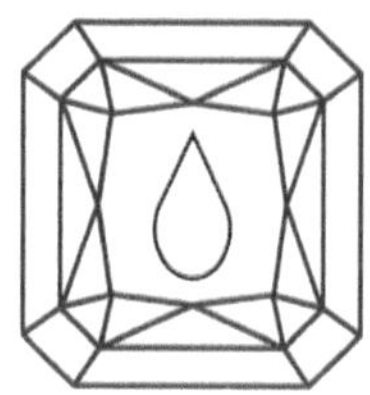

Lyssa

The first two times I'd swum up through the pond, I'd been aiming for speed. This third time, I spread my arms through the cool water to slow my ascent. The current tickled around me as I floated up toward the rippling surface.

I didn't know how safe it was going to be out there, and even if this was the craziest decision I ever made in my life, I intended to hold on to my head, thank you very much.

Only a thin light danced across the surface of the pond. The still-healing wound on my arm twinged. It'd been more than forty-eight hours since I'd gotten the stitches, but somehow I suspected the doctor hadn't anticipated me taking a swim in a big salty pond when he'd given his instructions. Oh well.

When I eased my head above the level of the water with the softest breath I could manage, I saw why. The sky was turning purple with the coming evening. It was later in the day here than it'd been back home. Whatever day this was.

I swam quietly to the side of the pond rather than heading for the end by the path. My caution paid off a second after I'd slipped out onto the rocks. Just as I ducked into the shelter of the ferns, a couple of guards in red-and-pink uniforms stalked into view over there. One of them scowled.

"Why does this pond even matter?" he muttered to his companion.

"The Queen says we guard it, so we guard it," the other replied.

They trudged back out of sight along the path. I crouched among the ferns for another minute, watching and listening. My hand came to rest on my chest to check the lump of the ring beneath my shirt and confirm I hadn't lost it in the fall or the water.

When the coast seemed reasonably clear, I slunk off through the vegetation with careful steps. I aimed myself on a diagonal to reach the road.

As the ferns started to thin ahead of me, I slowed and peered between their fronds. Another guard was striding along the blue-and-yellow cobblestones, a baton dangling at one hip and a sword at the other. The skin around my neck quivered.

I drew back a few paces and set off toward the city parallel to the road. The way had been pretty straight from what I remembered. How I was going to keep out of view once I reached the city, I could figure out there. Clearly the Queen's search hadn't been called off completely, however long it'd been since my escape.

My damp clothes clung to my body, cooling with the evening air. I fought off a shiver. The khakis and baby-blue tank top weren't bright enough to fit in with Wonderland wear, but I didn't want to stand out right now anyway. At least they were easy to move in.

The forest of ferns gave way to a narrow field before the city's buildings rose up. There was no sign of any guards. I darted through the hissing grass and ducked into the thicker shadow under the awning of a now closed shop.

Keeping close to the buildings and staying in the shadows as much as I could, I crept through the streets toward the Tower. Whenever any of the locals came into view, I froze until they were out of it again. Thankfully, there weren't many out on the streets at this hour. I guessed most of the Wonderlanders in the city would have headed to the club already.

A few members of the Hearts' Guard marched by, but the city wasn't flooded with them or anything. They'd loosened up their patrols since my dash out of here.

I held my breath as I sprinted the last several paces to the base of the Tower, only letting it out when I was safe behind its silvery door. "Twenty-seventh floor, Lyssa coming calling," I told the elevator.

The air beneath my feet didn't budge. "The Inventor is not in," an automated voice murmured.

Shit. Where could Theo be? Had they gone out to the palace to make an attempt of some kind without me? Had the Knave realized he'd been sheltering me and brought him to the Queen?

I hesitated and then tried the only other inhabitant in the building I knew. "Twenty-eighth floor, Lyssa coming calling."

The air beneath my feet propelled me upward. I guessed Mirabel *was* in. I hoped she wouldn't be disturbed by my unexpected visit.

When the elevator deposited me at the White Queen's apartment, I gave the door a couple of careful knocks. "Mirabel? It's Lyssa. I—"

Mirabel whipped the door open. She was wearing a silvery dress that looked as if it'd been made out of heaps of tinsel, her hair piled high on her head like before, her eyes wide. "Of course, I wouldn't delay you," she said. "I could tell it had to be a short visit."

Was she looking backwards through time now? I fumbled for the right thing to say. "I'm looking for Theo. He isn't in his office. Do you know—?"

She was already nodding. "That's right. I'm not sure the exact building, but I know he has his meetings somewhere nearby. I wish I could be of more help."

"He's at a meeting with the Spades?" I said. Thank God—that meant the Knave hadn't arrested him.

Mirabel cocked her head with a dreamy smile. "You found the key and brought it with you. Such a good thing you had it on hand."

The key? How far into the future—or past—was she looking now?

"I think I'd better go," I said. Before Theo launched a plan that might not work without my help. "Thank you so much."

"Don't worry," Mirabel said, patting my cheek. "I'm sure we can sort this out."

I guessed you just didn't have straight conversations with the White Queen. What did the Queen's guards make of her?

I descended the Tower and stepped out just as a guard came around a corner down the street. With a lurch of my heart, I threw myself around the side of the building and flattened myself against the cold metal wall.

No shout came. I exhaled slowly. When the guard had strode out of sight, I ventured into the street again.

A meeting place in a building somewhere nearby. None of the stores or houses around me looked particularly more promising than any of the others. I treaded softly down the street, peering through windows.

I'd only made it past a few when the door of one of the shops ahead of me opened as if by some invisible force.

Chess? I hurried over as the door tapped shut. At my tug, it opened to a small foyer. The inner door in front of me didn't budge.

I paused and looked around. Very little in Wonderland was exactly as it seemed. I traced my hands down the wall to my right, testing it here and there, and then switched to my left.

My finger hooked into a notch my eyes hadn't made out. I pressed on it, and a flap opened in the wall by my waist. I crouched down and clambered through.

The space on the other side was so dim I almost fell down the steps before I realized I'd come out at the top of a staircase. As I eased my way down, voices carried to me from the room below.

"Is there no plan we can initiate without this Otherlander?" a woman was saying. "We were on the verge of action."

"Action doesn't serve us well if we have no chance of winning," Theo replied in his smooth baritone. I'd found him—and a meeting of the Spades, it sounded like.

"We have to do something," another man said. "The Otherlander obviously isn't coming back."

A fourth voice spoke up in a familiar tenor with a bit of bite to it. "We don't know that yet."

Was that *Hatter*? Meeting with the Spades? Defending my absence?

"I told her it might not be safe for her to return for a few days." That was definitely Chess's light and languid voice. "Time moves differently between the lands. I agree that we shouldn't count her out yet—but we need a revised plan either way."

My feet hit the floor at the bottom of the steps and sent a stray pebble rattling. "Hey!" someone snapped, just as I came around from the stairwell into the wide low-ceilinged room.

"Maybe I can make a few suggestions," I said to the twelve Wonderlanders now gaping at me from where they stood around a big wooden table under jaundiced light.

Chess was there, and that *was* Hatter, blinking at me from beneath the shade of his derby hat. Doria bobbed on her toes to catch a glimpse of me over the shoulders of the taller women she was standing near. The stout red-haired guy I'd seen her greet the other day stood near Theo with another young man whose face and hair were identical but the colors on his clothes inverted.

Theo recovered first, of course. A smile spread across his face, as if he'd never doubted I'd appear and I couldn't have come at a better time.

"Lyssa," he said. "I'm glad you could join us."

From what I knew about his device's crystal and all this talk about revising plans, it didn't seem like a stretch to say, "Your pocket-watch retriever is out of commission?"

"I'm afraid so. And it was a rather essential component of our original plan."

"That's okay," I said, ambling over with my arms crossed loosely over my chest. "I've got another idea."

Theo emptied the pouch that had been hanging at his hip onto a small table in the corner of the room. "Just touch all of these and work your Otherlander magic on them," he said with an affectionate squeeze of my arm. Then he was swiveling to face the others, his voice turning commanding in an instant.

He motioned to the redheaded twins. "Dee, Dum, swing by the

club and pick up the rest of the supplies we need. Meet us by the wall. Everyone else, make sure you're clear on your part in the plan and you have whatever you need. We move out in ten minutes."

The twins dashed up the stairs. I eyed the devices Theo had laid out: five of them like little eggs with a crinkled metallic surface, a couple of wire-woven cubes, a coil of metallic string, a disc of overlapping steel plates, and a folded cloth that was surprisingly heavy in my grasp.

I wasn't sure how any of these were going to come into play, but I trusted that Theo knew what he was doing. I snatched up each of them in turn, holding them for as little time as I figured it'd take for my presence to affect them.

I was just setting down the last one when Chess sauntered by. "Hey," I said, darting around the table to catch his arm. I hadn't gotten a chance to really talk to anyone in the middle of all the planning. Before I thought about what I was doing, I'd pulled him into a hug.

Chess hugged me back, his mouth curling into its habitual grin where it brushed my temple. "You know," he murmured in his breezy way, "a small part of me was hoping you'd be smart enough to keep your distance from this mad place. But the rest of me couldn't be happier to see you, lovely."

My throat tightened at those words. I hugged his brawny form harder, remembering the lengths he'd gone to so I could get home. My last memory of him involved a burly ginger tabby cat blinking in and out of sight as it wove all through the line of guards outside the club.

He'd asked me not to talk about it. Did *anyone* else here know what he could do? I guessed it didn't matter. If the passage to the pocket watch wasn't wide enough to fit an arm through, his cat form would never have made it either.

"Just so you know, your secret is safe with me," I said under my breath.

Chess pulled back, still grinning, and cocked his head. "I have no idea what you're talking about."

Fair enough.

He touched the side of my face, his gaze turning serious in a way

I'd never seen before. "Are you sure about this, Lyssa? All the way into the palace? I liked our White Knight's plan with its half measures for you a lot better."

"Theo's plan won't work anymore," I pointed out. "This one will. It's the whole reason I came back, Chess." I hesitated, letting my cheek rest against his hand. "Well, one of the main reasons, anyway."

Something in his expression shifted as our eyes stayed locked together. Something hopeful and maybe a little hungry. He stroked his fingers over my hair, and my heart skipped a beat—and then he pulled back completely, nudging me around.

"And I expect here's one of the other reasons heading over to say his piece."

Hatter had taken a step toward us, leaving the cluster of Spades he'd been talking with. When I met his gaze, his jaw twitched. He kept walking, lifting his hat off his head and holding it to his chest as he came. He looked as scruffily handsome as ever, and a little naked with the spikes of his dark blond hair completely on display for the first time I could remember.

I tensed as he came to a stop a couple paces from me, not totally sure what to expect. The last time I'd seen *him*, after all, he'd been yelling at me about how careless and selfish I supposedly was. He looked down at his hat and then back up at me, so obviously apprehensive himself that I started to relax. I felt more than saw Chess slip away from us.

"I'm sorry," Hatter said. "Not that an apology seems enough to cover it. I was unfair and unkind to you, and I've felt like an ass about it since pretty much the moment after. I can't make any excuses, so I won't." His gaze dropped to my arm and widened. "Is that from—?"

The line of the cut prickled as if his attention had grazed the broken skin. "When I was making my dash for Caterpillar's mirror," I said. "One of his guards was a little too eager with his dagger, in my humble opinion."

He looked up at me again. "And you still came back."

His expression turned that prickling into a tingling that seeped right through to my chest. "I had things to do. People to see." What was I even saying? "I wouldn't have expected to see you here," I ventured.

A faint smile tugged at Hatter's lips. "No, I suppose not. It occurred to me that if I was going to yell at people for running away, the person I really should start with was myself." He shifted his hat in his hands. "I looked for you, after you ran off. I was worried about you. I didn't mean…" He exhaled roughly and grimaced as if he couldn't quite put the words he wanted together.

"I think you did," I said, to spare him his obvious discomfort. I could meet him halfway. "I don't completely blame you. The only other looking-glass girl you've known ran away—at the worst possible time—didn't she?"

Hatter's eyebrows rose. "And you know that now because…?"

I patted the lump of the ruby ring where the key had once hung. "I opened up the box Aunt Alicia left for me. There was a letter—she explained some things. Not that I'd guess it helps much, but she felt really guilty that she abandoned Wonderland. That's the whole reason she left the house to me, so I'd have a chance to come through and… make my own choices. She wanted me to apologize, to you and any of the other Spades she knew."

"I'm not sure there's anyone else left who knew her more than in passing," Hatter said quietly. "The Queen has taken a lot of heads since then."

I studied him, thinking of all the reactions I'd observed when the topic of my grand-aunt came up, and decided I had to ask. "You yelled at me because you were angry with Aunt Alicia. Did you kiss me because you're in love with her?"

Hatter stiffened. "Did she say *that* in her letter?"

"No," I said. "I'm just making a not-so-wild guess."

"Well, that isn't— It's hardly—" He sighed and set his hat back on his head where it belonged. "I wasn't in love with her," he said. "I didn't know her well enough to be. If it was anything, it was a boy's infatuation with the girl I wanted her to be. A girl who didn't really exist. And that has nothing to do with *you*."

"No?" I said. The tingling came back, a fizzy sensation that filled my lungs as he aimed his intense bright green gaze at me.

"You're different," he said simply. "You're real, not just a hopeful figment I've attached to someone who'll never live up to it. All the courage and compassion and fire I wanted to believe in—you're it. You're *here*."

Guilt clogged my throat even as my pulse fluttered. "I wasn't sure. I hesitated. I could have ended up staying back at home."

Hatter made an incredulous sound. "Are you saying I should judge you based on what you could have done but didn't, rather than by what you didn't have to do but did? We're the choices we make, not the options we had. I should know that as well as anyone." He paused. "Not that my estimation of you revolves around the fact that you came back. Even with what I said before… I'd have understood, Lyssa. You never asked to be part of this. You never acted like anyone other than who you are. I liked you already."

The guilt faded; the fluttering stayed. I suddenly wasn't sure what to do with any part of my body.

Maybe he wouldn't be saying any of this if he realized everything that had happened after the last time we'd spoken.

"Hatter," I said, forcing the words out, "that night, I went to see Theo. I—We—"

When I faltered, the corner of Hatter's mouth curved up at a crooked angle. Maybe he'd already put those pieces together. Chess had seemed to guess in an instant.

"You know," he said conversationally, "monogamy is a pretty rare concept in Wonderland. As you may have been able to guess from everything you've seen here. I don't think any of us are likely to judge a person on *that* basis. I'm saying what I wanted to say. What you make of it is up to you."

Oh. A surge of affection stole my voice. I opened my mouth and closed it again, and noticed the other Spades were moving toward the stairs. It was time to go.

If *I* was going to say anything that mattered, I'd better spit it out now.

The words tumbled off my tongue. "Is there any chance you'd like to kiss me again? I hear that's a thing people do before risky situations, for, er, luck or whatever."

Hatter gave me one of those brilliant smiles that crinkled the corners of his eyes. With a nimble flick of his wrist, he caught my hand and lifted it to spin me around like he had on the dance floor my first night in Wonderland. Only this time he spun me right up against him and then lowered his mouth to mine.

He kissed me with all the intensity of that morning at the breakfast table, if not the same urgency. My fingers curled around the lapel of his jacket and clung on while I lost myself in the firm heat of his lips. Yes, this was a reason to have come back. Too bad it couldn't be the main one.

"Show-off," I murmured when he drew back.

Hatter kept smiling. We fell into step behind the other Spades, and he leaned in to speak by my ear in a low voice. "Just for the record, I'd like to do a lot more than kiss you."

A spike of desire shot through me. "Noted on the record," I said with a grin that was probably giddy, and noticed Theo bringing up the rear of our procession. He scooped his devices off the table and caught my eye with an amused expression. Not a hint of disapproval or jealousy or anything other than pleasure at seeing the two of us together.

Three cheers for Wonderlandian open-mindedness!

Now all I had to do was pull off a feat the Spades hadn't managed to accomplish in fifty years of trying.

CHAPTER TWENTY-SEVEN

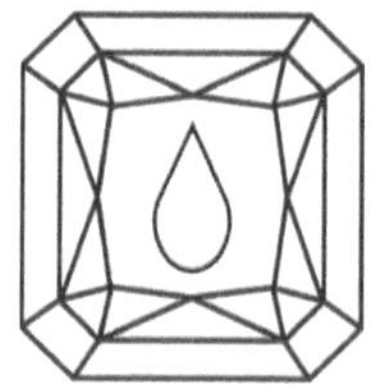

Lyssa

Theo had brought a watch of his own on the mission, one that as far as I could tell had no magical qualities. He checked the hands by the moonlight that streaked between the leaves of the tree the six of us were perched in, just a short leap from the wall to the palace gardens. The thickest branches stretched out like spokes of a wheel from the center-point I'd settled into. Each of the others was braced against one of the branches.

The rest of the Spades, including Doria, had dispersed before we'd reached this spot on their own supporting missions. Now only Theo, Chess, Hatter, the red-haired twin named Dee, a sinewy woman whose name I'd gathered was Sally, and I remained for the main event.

Ten minutes to cross the gardens. Ten more to get to the room from which we could reach the Queen's pocket watch. Five to retrieve it, and five more to get the hell out of there before the guards caught on. The second the day flipped over, we had to be moving.

"Ten to midnight," Theo reported with reined-in impatience. It was the fourth time he'd checked the watch this hour. Now he didn't even bother tucking it back in his pouch.

"Put a little butter in it," Hatter murmured. "Maybe it'll run faster."

A flicker of a smile passed over Theo's face. "You and March," he said with a fond shake of his head.

Hatter's expression stiffened, but only for a second. I guessed it was some kind of inside joke. Hatter had worked with Theo before, clearly. How long *had* he associated with the Spades before he'd cut off that part of his life? From the way Doria had talked and the familiarity I could see between him and the others, I was starting to think he'd been a Spade a lot longer than he hadn't.

This wasn't exactly the best time or place for an in-depth conversation on that subject, though.

Resting the watch on his knee, Theo reached into his pouch and pulled out the heavy cloth I'd worked my powers on earlier. He unfolded it and attached it around his face, and I realized it was a sort of mask. It covered the base of his nose all the way down to his chin with fabric darker than his hair. "There, ready to go," he said through it, with a faint rasp to his voice.

Sally gave him a startled look. "Are you coming through to the palace?"

"I know the way best. You might need my guidance on the ground." Theo set his hand on my shoulder. "And I'm not sending our Otherlander in there while I hang back here. This mask will filter out the scent." He added in an explanation I assumed was for my benefit, "I'm allergic to roses. A rather inconvenient weakness in our current situation."

No kidding. But he'd found a way to work around that weakness so he could stay at our sides—at *my* side. A tendril of warmth unfurled in the pit of my stomach.

It didn't quite chase away my nerves, but it made me even more determined to master them. These people had been building their rebellion for decades. Giving them one night of my life was barely anything.

It was a new feeling, preparing for a struggle with allies just as determined to fight as I was. Matching strength with strength instead of holding together everything as well as I could on my own. I wanted to remember this feeling, no matter what happened or where I ended up afterward. I wanted to find it again.

"Five minutes," Theo said. "Lean in."

I held out my hands, and the other five of them eased off their branch seats to clasp their fingers around mine, Dee snagging only a thumb, Chess catching my ring and baby finger with a hint of a caress. They all shifted closer at the same time, a shin or a thigh or an arm coming to rest against my body. It was a little suffocating, but we had to be sure there was enough contact between me and them to keep them here with me when the day flipped over.

"The moment I give the word," Theo said, and we all nodded. His hand, tucked around two of my fingers, gave them a gentle squeeze. I braced myself, wondering what the flip would feel like.

The breeze rustled through the leaves overhead. The lights beyond the palace wall blinked and swirled. Then all five of the figures around me winced. I didn't feel anything at all.

Hatter sucked out a breath hoarse with awe. Theo was already springing to his feet. "Let's go, let's go!"

We leapt after him. He bent for just an instant to attach one of his devices to a knob on the branch. With a jerk of his wrist, he sent the steel plates unfurling out across the space between the branch and the wall to form a narrow bridge.

It wobbled but held as Theo dashed across it. He turned and held out his hand to me, and I bolted after him with my heart thudding in my ears. It only took three steps, and then he was helping me down the side of the wall.

The others leapt down around me. Chess and Sally darted off through the gardens in opposite directions. Their job was to divert the few guards who were brought back into the gardens by the flip of the day—the ones who'd been patrolling the night the Queen trapped time. The rest of us ran for the palace.

Theo led the way. We skirted a cluster of benches and veered away from one path through the hedges and down another. His shoulders tensed as we sprinted beneath the arch of the Queen's massive rose bush, but his steps didn't falter. The cloyingly sweet perfume flooded my nose and stuck in my throat with my ragged breaths.

When we broke from the shadows, the scarlet palace loomed right in front of us. Theo motioned us to the left, around it. Dee, hustling as fast as his short legs could carry his stout body, came up beside him. The White Knight pointed to a wide balcony on the second floor, and the young redhead positioned himself beneath it with his arms outstretched.

Hatter appeared to know exactly what to do. He hopped onto Dee's arms, and Dee launched him into the air as if those arms were a springboard. My jaw dropped.

"We all have our talents," Dee said with a grin. "Up you go!"

No hesitating now. I inhaled deeply and leapt. Dee flung me after Hatter.

I caught the balcony's marble railing with a jolt that knocked the wind from me and managed to scramble over. Hatter was already crouched by a door at one end of the terrace. His deft fingers were wriggling two bits of metal in the lock.

As Theo sprang onto the balcony, managing to land on his feet like he leapt buildings on a regular basis, the door popped open. Hatter waved the hatpins he'd been using, a triumphant gleam in his eyes. "We're in."

I guessed no one would think it all that odd if they found him carrying those things. "I didn't realize your skills included breaking and entering," I murmured to him as we hurried into the dark room on the other side, Theo taking the lead again.

Hatter let out a soft chuckle. "It doesn't come up very often in my usual line of work. There are many uses a nimble set of fingers can be put to."

Oh. Um. Maybe if we got past kissing, I could discover new ones for myself. Add another item to my list of reasons for coming back to Wonderland.

Hatter had still seemed a little hesitant while we were waiting in the tree, but now that we were in motion, the mission had energized him in an unfamiliar but exhilarating way. What must he have been like when he did this kind of thing all the time, before the Queen's brutality had battered him down?

How could Aunt Alicia have seen him as nothing more than one in a list of several names?

Theo held up his hand to halt us when we reached the hall. He peered through the doorway and then beckoned us onward. *He* moved for all the world as if breaking into palaces was his main line of work, striding across the thick carpet that muffled our footsteps as if he belonged here even more than in that shiny white office of his.

A row of chandeliers overhead, their crystal fixtures shaped into hearts and roses, lit the long empty hall. Gold leaf gleamed all through the flowery wallpaper, the thorns drawn around the roses so pointed I wondered if they'd prick my fingertips if I touched them. The smell of the garden's roses lingered even here inside.

We passed a few paintings with heavy gold frames: a man with a doughy face, a red robe, and a plump crown on his white hair; a skeletal old woman with fierce eyes and an even bigger crown, and then a sort of family portrait.

Somehow I knew at a glance that the woman sitting in the throne there was the current Queen of Hearts. Her coppery hair looped in coils from her face to beneath her crown; a smile that looked sharp enough to cut stone curved above her square jaw. Her wide-set eyes, which shone with an eerie golden sheen that matched the frame, bored into me in an instant.

A man with pasty skin and a matching crown stood beside her throne, his shoulders stooped as he rested one hand on its side. And at the woman's feet, his head tipped against the satin draped over her knees, a little boy sat with a gold circlet of his own, only a little brighter than his tawny brown curls.

Was that the prince who'd been murdered? He'd already been a boy, then, when this painting had been hung before time had frozen. Doria had said he'd been thirteen when he was murdered, but I couldn't stop my mind from picturing that toddler's head lying in a pool of blood. My stomach lurched, and I yanked my gaze away.

Theo pointed to a door. Hatter dropped down in front of it, the hairpins spinning in his fingers. With a jiggle and a click, he'd popped the deadbolt.

The door swung open into a room like an over-crowded gallery, mahogany frames pressed together all across the walls. As we stepped inside, I realized they weren't any kind of artwork. They were doors themselves, dozens of them in every shade of wood, fit up against each other from floor to ceiling. Most of them I could have fit through by crawling, a few by standing, but the smaller ones scattered the spaces between those, a child would have struggled to fit through.

Theo tapped his foot against the smallest, a tiny oak door barely the size of my hand, with an even tinier lock. Hatter had to hunker down on the floor to prod its keyhole. Theo turned to me.

"You'd better prepare. He'll have it open quick."

I nodded, my mouth gone dry. I urged a little saliva onto my tongue as I reached for the pieces of mushroom Dee and Dum had brought us.

Right pocket smaller, left pocket larger, I reminded myself. Dear God, this had better work again. All the Spades, all of Wonderland, was counting on my spark of untested inspiration.

I placed one slice from my right pocket into my mouth and chewed. A prickling sour flavor coated my tongue. I swallowed the whole thing, clutching a second piece in case I needed it. A jolt ran through my body.

I blinked and found my gaze at the height of Theo's chest and falling. My legs were dwindling under me, my chest contracting. I gasped a breath, and dropped to the height of his hip. My pulse raced frantically through my shrinking veins. I held on to my composure with an iron grip.

This had all been part of the plan. *My* plan. I could do this, for all the heads that had rolled, for the Caterpillar's leers and the cut on my arm, for the freedom I'd thought I'd found here that should have belonged to everyone.

My descent halted around the level of Theo's knees. Hatter muttered to himself as he worked at the lock. I still wasn't going to fit through that passage once he got it open. I popped another half a slice into my mouth, hoping that wasn't too much.

My body plummeted in on itself with a lurch. The floor came into sharper view, the bits of dust clinging to the thick red carpet suddenly large as pebbles.

With a squeak, the little door swung open. I didn't wait for any command. The way was clear. With my hands clenched tight, I dashed through the doorway.

The red-walled passage on the other side was even narrower than the door. I hurried along it, feeling as if I were racing down an artery churning blood. My stomach was certainly churning.

Then I stumbled out into a bare red room. The space looked enormous to me at my current size, but judging from the size of the passage, it was probably only a few feet high and around. It held nothing but a wooden platform a little taller than I was, on which loomed a curved glass case that contained a closed brass pocket watch.

"I found it!" I called back, not sure how well my equally tiny voice would carry. Now I just had to get the watch out. The case wouldn't fit through the narrow passage, and I sure as hell couldn't break it while I couldn't even reach the top of the platform it was perched on.

I grabbed a piece of mushroom from my left pocket and ate half, and then another quarter, until I'd shot up to the low ceiling. I aimed one foot at the case and gave it a solid kick.

The case smacked against the wall with a thump but not a single crack in the glass. Frowning, I grabbed it and bashed it against the floor, against the side of the platform. The cut on my arm throbbed with the effort, and the watch jostled around inside, but the thick glinting surface held.

"Lyssa?" Theo said, and at the same time another sound reached me. A distant shout that couldn't possibly be one of our people. My pulse hiccupped.

"I just have to break the case," I said, fighting to keep my voice steady. I slammed the glass structure into the wall with all the strength I had. It bounced off and rolled on the floor, solid as ever.

A door in the other room rattled as someone tried the knob. Panic shot through me. I snatched up the case again, and my thumb caught on the corner, right on the spot where the ring's ruby had pierced it this afternoon.

Mirabel's voice echoed through my head. *You found the key and brought it with you.* Could she have actually meant…?

I dug the ruby ring out from under my shirt. Maybe this was a ridiculous idea, but it was the only one I had left. I popped open the filigree shell and pressed the gem to the side of the glass case, scraping it as hard as I could down the whole length.

The stone sliced into the smooth surface. Not all the way through, but with a crack that spidered around the edges as I dug the ruby in even harder. A victory cry catching in my throat, I hurled the case at the floor one more time.

It shattered apart. The watch tumbled amid the shards. Someone was banging on that outer door now, and beyond the thud of that fist and the muffled hollering, a raw throaty voice cut through the air like a machete, with all the authority of a queen.

"Break it! Break it *now*!"

A cold sweat broke out on my back. I snatched up the pocket watch and pushed at the clasp on the cover. It was made of several tiny bits of metal, and none of them shifted.

Theo had said it might not open easily—that he'd handle it if that was the case. With a shaky breath, I tossed the watch down the passage toward the other room as far as I could fling it. Then I stuffed one of the shrinking mushrooms into my mouth.

My body shot back to the floor so fast my head reeled. I threw myself past the suddenly boulder-like chunks of glass toward the little hallway.

Theo's hand swept down to meet me. I clung to his thumb as he caught me up. "Get down," he ordered, tucking me into his shirt pocket. Then he wrenched the shuddering door open and tossed one of those egg-like devices at the guards on the other side.

It burst open with a billow of black smoke. He ran into the haze, Hatter right behind us. As I ducked down within the white linen fabric, a shriek pierced my ears, vibrating with shock and rage.

CHAPTER TWENTY-EIGHT

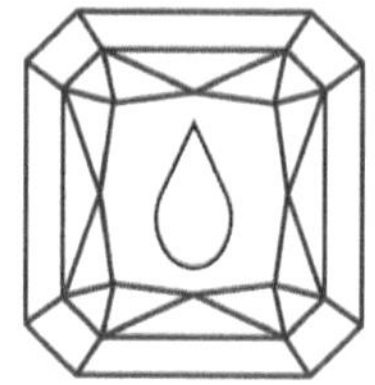

Theo

The Queen's scream sliced through my nerves as painfully as the smell of the roses would have without my mask. My stomach turned over with a queasy shudder, but determination kept my feet steady.

Her guards had fallen back in the wake of the smoke bomb. I tossed another and grabbed the sleeve of Hatter's jacket, yanking him with me through the doorway across the hall. Lands willing, it would still be a guest bedroom and unoccupied.

The guards charged after us with a roar, just a few steps behind us. Lyssa, in her tiny state, had curled into a ball in my shirt pocket, her body a spot of warmth on my chest. The pocket watch bumped against my thigh as my carry pouch jostled. I intended to get both out of the palace and off its grounds safely.

Just before we reached the window at the other end of the room, I flung a skitter cube behind me. It crackled into a hundred slippery slivers scattering the floor. Bodies thumped as the guards skidded and toppled.

Letting them get this close hadn't been in the plan. But then, my plan had needed a lot of reworking in the last couple days.

I snapped the hooks out from my steel-wound rope and snagged them on the window ledge. "Come right after me," I said to Hatter as I scrambled out the window. "It'll hold us both." Then I tossed one more smoke bomb into the room for good measure.

Hatter coughed as he clambered down. The string sped through my fingers. I leaned to the side away from my shirt pocket to make sure I didn't bump the wall at the wrong angle.

The second Hatter's feet hit the ground next to mine, I detached the rope with a jerk of my hands.

"Still okay, Lyssa?" I asked. She nodded, a whisper of movement against my chest.

Dee caught up with us as we raced through the gardens. A ripple of leaves along the side of a hedge told me Chess had rejoined us too, invisibly. "Sally?" I said.

"I don't know," Chess said without reappearing. "I heard a little yelling from that end of the garden. She'll find her way out if she's able."

"She wouldn't want us hanging back waiting for her," Dee added, his breath coming rough.

The garden's lights had brightened into spotlights that swept across the bushes and benches. We ducked low to dodge one, my hand coming up to protect Lyssa's hiding place. Shouts were echoing all across the grounds now.

The wall came into view. Dee pushed ahead with a fresh burst of speed and readied his arms to vault us over. I motioned the other three past me and spun to take in the grounds.

Footsteps thundered somewhere near us, but the Queen's prized rosebush shielded us from sight. For now.

"White Knight," Dee called. The others were already over. I bounded off his arms onto the top of the wall and hooked the rope there for him to climb after us.

Compared to the lights washing over the garden, the forest was pitch black. We hustled over the hill and across its downward slope to the stand of chittering trees. With the rose bushes far behind us now, I tugged down my mask to drink in the fresh night air.

A few of our fellow Spades were waiting there in a pool of moonlight, their expressions tight. Relief washed over their faces when we dashed into their midst.

"You got it?" Dum asked.

I nodded. "Let's end this." But first I slid my hand into my pocket so Lyssa could cling on. I set her carefully on the ground. "I'm sure you'd like to get back to regular size."

"Thank you," she said in a wisp of a voice. She must have had a slice of mushroom at the ready, because an instant later her body started shooting up among us.

I tugged the pocket watch from my pouch. Power thrummed through it, tingling against my palm. For a second, I could only stare at its tarnished brass surface.

My entire life, I'd gone without Time. I was about to experience its proper passage as I never had before.

The latch that held the cover shut was a multilayered one, but I'd seen enough of the Queen's toys to find the pattern. My thumb slid and pressed against the notches. A hush fell over our little group as my companions watched.

The latch clicked apart. I held the watch out into the space between us. "We will be bound no longer," I announced, and flipped the cover open.

A whistling rushing sound louder than the chittering leaves whirled around us. The wave of contained power whipped past our faces, licked over our clothes and hair, and streamed out across the landscape. The second hand on the watch started to tick along.

Time had returned to Wonderland.

My people caught their breaths with a collective gasp. We couldn't feel the change in any major way yet, but a glitter of hope had come into their eyes—more hope than I'd seen in the entire time I'd moved among the Spades and Clubbers before now. The twins beamed at me. Even Hatter looked delighted.

I'd done what I'd come here to do. I'd put this one very wrong thing right. It wasn't enough, and I still had a lot of work ahead of me, but it made every hard choice I'd been faced with undeniably worth it.

My gaze found Lyssa, who was just taking a tiny nibble of mushroom to shrink her a couple inches back to exactly her regular height. She tossed the rest of the slice away and turned to me, her face so bright with joy that my heart stuttered.

I hadn't known how much her smile would mean to me. When she'd come to me a couple nights ago, I'd been glad to hear that she was playing the field, that I wasn't the only man on her mind. We'd indulged in what had felt like simple mutual attraction and admiration without my having to worry that I was taking advantage of her in a much more cruel fashion than I'd ever wanted to. Not to mention that multiple points of attraction meant more ties to draw her back here.

And yet right now, I found myself wishing she'd save that smile only for me.

"You were amazing," I said honestly. "We couldn't have done it without you." I turned to the others. "We should get moving before the guards extend their search this far. As soon as we're back in the city, they'll have no proof we had anything to do with that theft."

As we all started walking, I fell into step beside Lyssa. Her fine pale hair was mussed from all the shrinking and growing and running around. I couldn't stop myself from brushing a stray lock back behind her ear. She eased a little closer to me at my touch, aiming a small but equally bright smile at me. It set off a glow in my chest.

This woman was something special, wasn't she? In more than one way. In the back of my mind, my Inventor's instincts were already spinning through the possibilities of how we could use her presence and her Otherlander quirks to serve the rebellion in other ways.

I didn't think persuading her to stay with us would even be that hard. Lay on the admiration and the awe, let her absorb the exhilaration of being a hero, and I wouldn't need more than a nudge.

Perhaps that was the right thing to do if we were judging right by the greatest good to the greatest number of people, regardless of what it meant for Lyssa. But, Hearts take me, the thought of continuing down that road made me queasy. As if she'd taken a piece of my heart as her own.

I had missed her, those days when she'd been gone. I'd missed that smile and her easy candidness and the sense that she might have understood a lot more of who I was than anyone else around me if I'd been able to let her in.

If I pushed her too far and the horrors of this place broke her, I wasn't sure the knowledge of what I'd done wouldn't break me too.

"You saw us through our mission," I said. "Your mission, I should probably say. What do you want to do now?"

"What are my options?" Lyssa asked. "The guards were still searching the city for me. Is there any chance I *could* get home right now?"

If I delayed her even an hour, most likely not. The words wavered on my tongue. I worked my jaw and forced them out.

"Everyone in the city was reset back to their starting points a half hour ago. If we head for the club right now, I'd imagine we can get you through."

"Really? I think…" She exhaled shakily. "I'm not saying I wouldn't want to come back. There's a lot in this place I'd miss. But I've already caused kind of a commotion in the Otherland *and* here, so maybe it's better if I go back home and let things calm down in both lands before I make the trip again."

I traced my fingers down her forearm to twine with hers. "I do hope you make it again." I meant that honestly too, and not just for the cause.

"As you should be able to tell by now, it'll take more than a mad queen and her army of guards to stop me."

"Then to the club it is."

Her smile came back, wider than before. I might have righted two wrongs tonight.

When we reached the edge of the city, I waved my companions off. "Get home, get to bed like you're meant to be. I'm taking Lyssa to *her* path home, and then I'll be making my way to mine."

Hatter's head snapped around. "You're leaving?" he asked Lyssa, with a hint of hesitation.

"Just for a little while," she said. "I'm planning on coming back. There's still an awful lot I'd like to do here."

A faint flush colored his neck as he grinned back at her. I'd never seen Hatter smitten before. It was rather extraordinary. No doubt we had to thank Lyssa for his assistance tonight too.

"If you don't mind the company," Chess said to me in his languid voice, "it seems to me that three might be better than two should any obstacles present themselves."

"And one more even better?" Hatter suggested.

A chuckle slipped out of me. "Come on, then, before those obstacles multiply beyond even the capabilities of four."

The streets were always quiet at this time with so many Wonderlanders tossed back into sleep no matter what they'd been doing. Dum was woken by a falling branch shortly after midnight every night, so he'd been able to rouse those few Spades to be ready if we needed additional help, but everyone else slumbered. For this last time.

Tomorrow, they'd get to decide where they slept and where they woke, because of me. Because of us.

A movement near the club caught my eye. I held out my hands to stop the others. A figure loped away from the club—a palace guard by his uniform, the moonlight catching on the pleated stripes. Where was he going?

"There might be more inside," I murmured to the others. "Chess, can you check what we're up against?"

He tipped his head to me and vanished. When he returned a few moments later, his expression was pleased but puzzled. "The place is empty. I could hear Caterpillar snoring in the upper rooms. Let's dance by right under him, shall we?"

The dance floor was indeed vacant, only a dim purple light drifting over us from a single fixture still lit on the ceiling. At the basement door, I glanced at the others. "Wait here. Shout if anyone comes."

Hatter's mouth slanted as if he wanted to argue, but he just grasped Lyssa's hand. "Safe travels, until next time."

"I'm already looking forward to it," she said, and the corners of his lips twitched upward to answer her smile.

Chess claimed her hand next and pressed a kiss to her knuckles with a sweeping bow. "May the journey be smooth both there and back, lovely."

I pushed open the door and slipped into the hall right behind her. Lyssa followed the path with practiced steps, to one side and the other, up the stairs and catching herself just before she tumbled down off them, through the thicker darkness of a low tunnel that made my back start to cramp. Her steps sped up as we passed the stairs again. I knew with a sudden shiver of awareness that we were almost there.

Before I'd quite thought through what I was doing, I caught her elbow. With one swift step, I'd pressed her up against the wall and lowered my mouth to hers.

Lyssa leaned into the kiss with an eager sound that sparked through every nerve in my body. Her lips were soft and pliant, a faintly sweet flavor lingering on them that I could have enjoyed for hours, if we'd had that long.

I might not mind if she enjoyed the company of other men, but I could admit I had a competitive streak. Perhaps it was genetic. When she thought about Wonderland, when she dwelled in the memories that called her back, I wanted my touch to be the one she missed most.

Her fingertips teased up my neck to graze my jaw, and I coaxed another pleased murmur from her throat. When I eased back, her hand fell to my chest.

"If you're trying to convince me to stay, you make a very good argument," she said teasingly.

"I'll make plenty more the next time you're here."

"Good. I'm starting to think I'm not going to be able to hang back for very long at all." She slipped ahead of me again, down the second tunnel. "You had perfect timing. The mirror is right—"

She cut herself off with a little cry. I stopped in my tracks at the edge of the little room.

The looking-glass was there waiting for us still. Only it waited in broken shards on the floor. Someone had smashed the mirror right out of its golden frame.

As a chill washed over my skin, my mind darted back to the guard hustling away. To the Queen's harsh shout while the other guards had battered at the door. *Break it! Break it now!*

She hadn't been talking about the door.

Lyssa recoiled from the pieces as if afraid of stepping on them, and then froze. A pained laugh spilled out of her.

"It doesn't matter if I touch them," she said. "Time is freed. The mirror will never reset. It's just broken."

That was true. My throat constricted, but underneath my dismay, a tendril of relief unfurled.

I got to keep her, without the guilt—other than the guilt that thought sent prickling through me.

I shoved those conflicting emotions away as I moved to her side and touched her arm.

"Lyssa, there are other looking-glasses."

"Any we have any chance of reaching tonight?"

"No," I had to admit.

"Okay. It's okay." She rubbed her hands over her face. A breath trembled out of her. Then she drew herself up as determined and regal as a queen—the kind of queen we should have had. She even managed a wry smile. "I guess my next time here is happening right now."

CHAPTER TWENTY-NINE

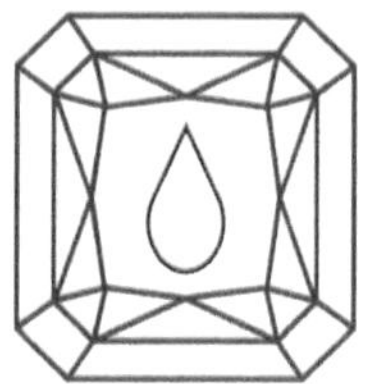

Lyssa

Somehow or other, we all ended up in a little rooftop garden I hadn't known existed at the top of the Tower. The city's lights created a cloud-like haze beneath us, and stars I'd never seen before glittered across the vast expanse of the sky over our heads. No sound rose that high except the whisper of the breeze through the plots of flowers.

I sprawled on the soft grass, leaning against Theo's side with his arm tucked around my waist, absorbing his warmth. Hatter sat nearby, stripping the leaves from a daffodil he'd plucked, his expression pensive. Chess lolled on his back as he gazed up at the night sky.

"One more predictable day," he said. "After that, we won't be able to count on sunny blue skies anymore. We might even get seasons again. I believe we used to have seasons. Maybe it'll *rain*—I can't wait."

A giggle tickled out of my throat. "You'll probably get tired of clouds and rain pretty quickly."

Chess shook his head. "Not a chance. I will savor every shadow and every drop. Especially the ones that dampen the helms of the Hearts' Guard." He grinned.

That remark made me shiver. "The Queen of Hearts couldn't capture time all over again, could she?"

Theo's thumb stroked over my hip with a reassuring pressure. "Definitely not. It won't be tricked like that more than once."

"Lands only know what new act of tyranny she'll come up with next," Hatter muttered.

I nudged him with my foot. "Let's not talk about that *right* now, okay?"

He glanced up, regret stark in his gaze. "I'm sorry."

He wasn't just talking about the comment. He meant that I was stuck here at all. I swallowed hard. But the truth was, when I'd seen the shattered mess of the mirror, something in me had been a little… glad.

The choice had been taken away from me. And maybe this was the choice I'd have wanted to make after all, if I'd let myself think just about what would make *me* happy and not how everyone back home might react. Based on how time had passed during my last two visits, I'd have a couple weeks here before Melody expected to hear from me.

A little more time to see how wonderful this land could be as we pushed back against the Queen. A little more time to explore the weird but exhilarating emotions these three guys had stirred up in me.

Which meant it might be a good thing to make sure we were all on the same page.

I lifted my head, reaching to tilt Theo's mouth toward me. Without a second's hesitation, he claimed my lips. His kiss flooded me with warmth, and a quiver of excitement raced through my chest, knowing the other two were watching us. Knowing that if I had my way, next it'd be Theo watching me with them.

As I drew back from the White Knight, Hatter swallowed audibly. I shifted onto my knees and reached for him. A flicker of surprise passed through his eyes, and then he was moving to meet me, tugging me even closer as his mouth found mine.

Theo's hand trailed up my back as Hatter parted my lips with his tongue, and it was a miracle I didn't melt into a puddle of goo right then. Ecstatic goo.

When Hatter released me, my cheeks were flushed, my pulse thrumming through my body. I turned to face Chess. He was still stretched casually on his back, his head propped on one arm as he took in our PDA. I still couldn't read his expression well enough to know for sure whether he wanted to be part of it. But his gaze didn't leave mine as I scooted closer, stopping just shy of touching his side.

Maybe I shouldn't be trying to decipher his reaction. I could simply own mine, and let him do with it what he would.

"Chess… I want you too," I said, my cheeks flaring as the words came out.

Chess hesitated for the space of a heartbeat, long enough that I was already bracing against my disappointment when that beautiful grin stretched across his face.

"Then come have me, lovely," he said in his lilting voice.

My pulse skipped a beat. I leaned over him, and he pushed himself up a little higher, sliding his fingers into my hair as our lips met. His kiss was gentle yet intoxicating, as if I were drinking down a glass of sweet liqueur. When I eased back, I'd lost my breath.

They were all mine, if only just for this moment. I didn't know how I'd gotten so freaking lucky.

I settled down onto the grass between them, not wanting or needing anything more than those kisses right now. My head was getting fuzzy with exhaustion. Just lounging there surrounded by the three most fascinating men I'd ever met was a thrill in itself.

I should have been content to leave things there for the night, but I was still Lyssa Tenniel, Miss Organized and Prepared. When the question started niggling at me, I knew it wasn't going to back down until I got an answer. So I had to glance over at Theo and ask, "Where exactly are these other looking-glasses, and how hard is it going to be for me to get to one?"

Theo grimaced. "I actually only know of one with any certainty," he said. "And the last I knew of it, the Queen was keeping it in her private chambers, which are always tightly guarded."

His words sank in slowly. “The Queen of *Hearts*?” I said.

“That would be the one.”

Oh, fuck.

WICKED WONDERLAND - BONUS SCENE

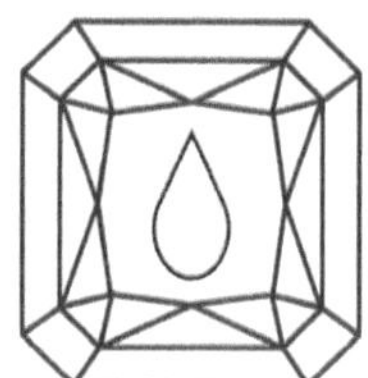

Did you wonder how Hatter's return to the Spades might have gone? This bonus scene from his point of view is set after Chapter 21, showing what happened after he told Doria he'd join her at the next meeting.

Hatter

Doria shot me a wary look before she tipped her head toward the slanted building that was apparently our destination. She still wasn't convinced my motives for joining her were entirely pure. Fair enough.

"You can't treat me like a kid in there," she reminded me.

I resisted the urge to ruffle her hair. That definitely wouldn't go over well. "Consider me on my best behavior."

I needed to be, and not just for her. If I was going to step up from the sidelines, I had a lot of trust to regain. It'd been twelve years since I'd attended one of these meetings, but it felt like several lifetimes. Ages ago when I'd earned the "Mad" my fellow Spades used to add to my name, when March and May would have stood beside me in eager anticipation of whatever new mission we were planning.

Eons since I'd watched their lives ripped apart without any way of defending them that wouldn't have made the tragedy even worse.

Stepping into the dim basement room behind my daughter felt both unnervingly familiar and yet like an intrusion. Half of the faces that turned toward us, I didn't recognize except from glimpses on the streets. There'd been a lot of turnover in the rebellion over the years. Of the half I did know from my past involvement, most either tensed or darkened or both at the sight of me.

Retreating from the rebellion hadn't endeared me much to my former colleagues. Some of them might blame me for March and May's fate. Why not, when I did too?

A cowardly part of me wanted to relive my previous retreat right now—up the stairs, past the trick door, down the street, and back to my shop where I could focus on protecting the things that mattered most to me. Except, of course, that what mattered most to me was Doria, and I had no illusions about convincing *her* to leave.

I'd joined the Spades for a reason. That reason hadn't gone away. The Queen of Hearts was even more a terror than she'd ever been. I wanted a better life than this for my daughter—and for every other Wonderlander, really.

I wanted to be better than a sour shut-in who accused other people of his own failings.

The thought of Lyssa offering herself to this cause that was barely even hers, of the stubborn compassion I'd seen so often amplify her beauty, gave me the last kick of courage to walk up to the table. We had a chance of winning now—even I couldn't deny that. If I could make some small bit of difference toward that victory, I might as well be a traitor not to try.

"Hatter," one of the old-timers said with undisguised skepticism. "I didn't expect to see you here again. Have you come to tell us we should all just give up like you did?"

My instinct was to bristle, but I held that impulse down. These people had a right to be irritated that I'd backed off while they'd kept sticking their necks out for all these years. I'd told myself it was for

Doria's sake, but it's also been to protect myself from more heartbreak, more shame.

"I came because I'm not ready to give up," I said. "I've hung back for too long. If there's some way I can pitch in and help see whatever the White Knight's new plan is through, I want to hear it."

"Hear it and then turn tail to run for the hills again," someone at the back of the gathering muttered.

"Hey!" Doria raised her chin and set her hands on her hips. "That's my dad you're talking about. I've heard enough stories to know that when he was with the Spades before, he took a ton more chances than most of the rest of you have. He stopped because he was worried about looking after *me*. And maybe lately I've been pissed off about his over-protective tendencies, but I'm not going to say I wish he'd been hauling me along on missions when I was a little kid. So… shut up. He's here now, and we're lucky he is."

She shot me a quick smile, warm enough to offset the chill of the others' welcome. Pride and gratitude swelled inside me. While my withdrawal from the Spades had been a lot more complicated than that, a lot of it *had* been for her, and I'd never heard her acknowledge it quite that way before. Coming here was worth it if only just to hear her defend me so vehemently when these days I was normally the one she was telling off.

No one made any more snarky remarks after that. The couple dozen rebels gathered in the basement room shifted on their feet uncomfortably and then fell back into the murmured conversations they'd been having before. Doria ambled over to join the one twin—I hadn't gotten to know them well enough to tell them apart, but from the way she smiled at him, I probably should start paying more attention—and the other younger Spades he was chatting with. No one seemed to be in charge of the present gathering.

Of course not. The figure who'd claimed that role had yet to arrive.

It didn't really matter what any of these people thought of my return. The only person in the Spades who had any real say over who stayed and how involved they became was the man everyone here was waiting for.

The man who strode into the room as that though passed through my mind.

Even though the sight of the White Knight sent a prickle of that old irritation through me, thinking of how easily he'd taken over from his mentor and swept up so many Wonderlanders—including my daughter—into his dangerous schemes, I had to admit he had a presence. A hush fell over the crowd the second his footsteps sounded in the room. All eyes turned toward him. He held himself with an easy yet authoritative confidence I couldn't help envying. There was no doubting who held the power in this room.

The other twin came in a few seconds behind him. No sign of Chess, which I supposed meant he was still roaming the city in search of Lyssa. He'd said he'd scour every street for her, looking about as serious as you could expect to get from Chess. I could hope he'd already found her.

Hearts take me, if something had happened to her because of my outburst… If there wasn't any sign of her after this meeting, I'd take up the search again myself.

The White Knight's gaze skimmed over the gathering with a tip of his head here and a flash of a smile there before his attention settled on me. If he was surprised to see me, he didn't show it, as if he'd always known it'd just be a matter of time before I turned up again. Somehow that irritated me even more. Had he ever really considered any of the criticisms I'd made of him and his approach to the rebellion?

"Hatter," he said, all benevolence, and offered his hand to shake mine. "I'm glad you could join us. We may be on the verge of finally achieving the freedom we've been denied for so long, and I'm sure any assistance you're willing to offer will only speed our plans along."

I bit down on the desire to make some dryly sarcastic remark and accepted his hand. I hadn't come here to spit that peace offering back in his face.

"I thought it was about time," I said. "Whatever disagreements I've had with you over the years, it's nothing compared to my desire to take down our common enemy. What do you have up your sleeve now?"

"I'm not sure you'll fully approve, but I can promise I've given these plans all the careful contemplation they're due."

He stepped up to the table and unfurled a roll of paper across it. Everyone stepped closer to study the drawing on it. It was a blueprint for some large building—or part of one, anyway. The shape of it sent a twinge of nervous familiarity through my chest, but I couldn't quite place it.

Theo ran his hand over the lines on the paper and gave me another thoughtful look. "Your skills may be particularly useful for this operation, if you're willing to dive all the way in on your first outing back. I assume you still know your way around a lock with those hatpins of yours?"

My fingers itched to grip one just thinking about it. A small grin crossed my lips as I remembered all the doors I'd opened for the Spades, each with practiced ease. "My hands remain as nimble as ever. Where are these locks you want opened?"

Everyone glanced toward *me* at that question, watching for my response to his answer. Clearly they already knew. A prickling ran down my spine.

The corners of the White Knight's lips curled slightly upward. "If we're going to win this war, we need to take it straight to the Palace of Hearts."

Ah. That was the shape I'd recognized in the blueprint. The breath rushed out of me. For a second, I could only stare at him as the words sank in. The prickling shot straight down to my gut.

The palace—the center of the Queen's power. By the lands, that was diving all the way in.

But from beneath the prickling, a quiver of something giddier raced through me. A twinge of adrenaline that hearkened back to the mad capers I'd told myself I'd left behind me, more eagerly than I'd ever have expected. Despite my hesitations, my grin widened.

"In that case, I think you'd better have the best lock picker in Wonderland on the job. Count me in."

HATTER'S FAVORITE HONEY-PINEAPPLE-CORIANDER SCONES

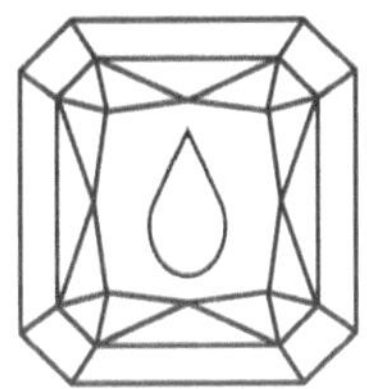

(Recipe makes approximately 8 scones)

Ingredients:

2 cups flour
2 teaspoons baking powder
1/2 cup butter, cubed
3/4 cup crushed pineapple (for lighter scones, use 1/2 cup)
2 tablespoons fresh cilantro, chopped
1/2 teaspoon ground coriander
2 tablespoons honey
3/4 teaspoon salt
1/2 cup milk, plus more for brushing on top

1. Preheat the oven to 425° F. Line a baking sheet with parchment paper.
2. Combine flour and baking powder in a mixing bowl.

Using your fingers, massage in the butter until the mixture looks like fine crumbs.

3. Stir in the pineapple, cilantro, coriander, honey, and salt. Add the milk a little at a time, stirring until the dough is soft. You might not need all of the milk.
4. Shape the dough into balls about 2 inches thick and roll them on a floured surface. Place on the baking sheet and flatten to about 1 inch. Brush the tops lightly with milk.
5. Bake for 15 to 20 minutes until golden brown. Let sit 10 minutes before serving.

Wrathful Wonderland

The Looking-Glass Curse
Book 2

CHAPTER ONE

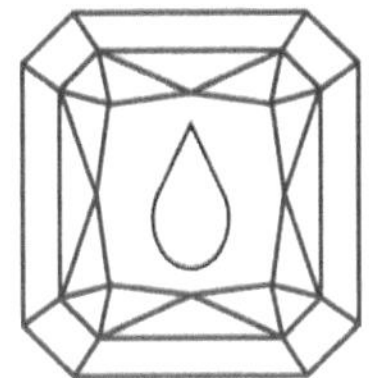

Lyssa

You know you're in Wonderland when you wake up in the morning and the first thing you feel is gratitude that your head is still attached to your body.

I rolled over in Hatter's guest room bed, rubbing my neck as if some part of me needed extra confirmation. Bright mid-morning sun streamed through the window, but my definitely-connected head was still bleary. We'd been up pretty late last night.

We'd taken on the Queen of Hearts and won—maybe not a full victory, but a big one.

A smile curved my lips. I pressed my face into the plump feather pillow, its chamomile tea scent filling my nose. Say whatever you wanted about Wonderland's downsides—tyrant queen, regular beatings and beheadings, weird monsters lurking around the fringes—no one could deny the beds were freaking comfortable.

Part of me wanted to drift off into another hour or so of sleep. But because I was responsible, practical Lyssa Tenniel, a larger part of me was pointing out that I was lucky I'd gotten to sleep at all. The White Knight had given us a device to provide a warning if the Queen's guards came charging up the stairs to Hatter's apartment. It might not have gone off overnight, but it still could at any moment.

We had an awful lot to do before I could feel safe here. Or before I could get back to my real home, where beheadings weren't even a thing.

With a grumble at myself, I pushed back the covers and hopped out of bed. Pain prickled up my forearm along the stitched-up cut I'd gotten when under attack by a guard a few days ago.

I'd slept in the tank top and khakis I'd been wearing when I'd arrived in Wonderland yesterday evening, and the thought of leaving them on any longer made me cringe. I eyed the borrowed dresses in the wardrobe in their bright colors and bold patterns that my best friend Melody would have swooned over, picked one of the less flashy ones, and headed to the bathroom.

We didn't even know yet whether everyone who'd been part of last night's mission had made it back. Sally, the woman who'd come with us into the palace gardens and run off to distract the guards, hadn't met up with us at the wall during our escape. If *she'd* made it home, it'd been alone. Theo was probably already checking on her.

Across the hall from the bathroom, Hatter's bedroom door stood a few inches ajar. I hesitated, hanging the dress on the hook beside the sink. Every other morning I'd been here, Hatter's door had either been firmly closed, because he was up and marking that room off limits, or wide open, because he was still sleeping and that was how it always reset, like the fateful night ages ago just before the Queen had trapped Time to quell the growing rebellion, when he'd fallen asleep in his armchair waiting for bad news.

We'd freed Time in the wee hours of the morning. This might as well be his first brand new day in Wonderland in decades.

I couldn't resist. I padded across the hardwood floor and eased the door farther open.

The only other time I'd looked in on Hatter sleeping, he'd been slumped in that chair beside the bed, fully dressed, as apparently he'd woken up every morning across all those decades Wonderland remained stuck repeating the same day. The position hadn't looked all that comfortable.

Last night, he'd made it to the bed. He lay on his back, the covers bunched across his chest, his angular face tipped into the pillow and the spikes of his dark blond hair veering this way and that in even greater disarray than usual. He'd bothered to take off his hat and his suit jacket, at least, but his maroon tie still hung loose beneath the rumpled collar of his dress shirt. Old habits were hard to break?

The sight of him brought a flutter of warmth into my chest. Well, the sight of him and the thought of what he might or might not be wearing under the covers. It was hard not to think of his smile last night when I'd asked him to kiss me and the intensity of his mouth claiming mine.

I wavered, torn between the urge to climb right into that bed with him and the uncertainty about how he'd respond. We hadn't done anything more than kiss yet. And the last time I'd been in his bedroom, he'd ushered me out very quickly.

Hatter was obviously a light sleeper. I didn't think I'd made a sound more than taking a breath, and he stirred. Raising his head, he stared at the bed around him, totally bewildered. Then the light of understanding dawned on his face, taking him from scruffily good-looking to pulse-thumpingly hot in an instant.

His gaze darted up to find me, and his expression turned wary but not unwelcoming. I guessed I couldn't blame him for being a little uncertain too. We'd had a chaotic time together.

"Um," I said. "Good morning."

"It is, isn't it?" he said, pushing himself higher on the bed. He considered the covers with an awed chuckle. His shoulders had relaxed when he looked up at me again. "We really did it."

I had to grin. "We did."

"I suppose this is going to take some getting used to."

His tone was warm enough that I decided to just go for it. I walked over and sat on the edge of the bed just a foot away from him. My heart beat faster, but the spark of desire in his green eyes encouraged me. I curled my fingers around his loosened tie.

"Just as a tip," I said. "Generally people take these off when they go to bed."

"Hmm," Hatter said. "It's a good thing I have you here to advise me on these matters. I seem to be out of practice."

"Happy to help in any way I can." I tugged the tie looser, and Hatter leaned toward me. He smelled amazing, like lime and wood smoke, bright and dark at the same time. Like Wonderland.

"Amazing that I ever managed without you, looking-glass girl," he murmured, his dry tenor dropping low enough to send an eager shiver down my spine.

"It really is," I said, a little breathless, and then our lips collided.

Hatter tucked his arm around my waist to pull me even closer. His mouth was so hot and sure I nearly drowned in the wave of need that swept through me. All I could do was hang onto his tie like my life depended on it.

He kissed me again, more deeply, my lips parting with a pleased sound to let his tongue sweep over mine. His deft fingers trailed up my side. They teased over the side of my breast, edging closer until my nipple was aching for contact. His thumb flicked over the peak, and I whimpered into his mouth. Heat pooled between my thighs.

I slid my hand down over the taut muscles of Hatter's broad shoulders and his contrastingly lean chest. I was just a moment or two from discovering whether he wore boxers or briefs when a joyful shout pealed down the hall.

"New day, here I come! New dresses. New shoes. Lands, I can change the furniture in my fucking room now!"

Hatter and I had jerked apart at the sound of his daughter's voice. Her bounding footsteps thumped down the hall past the door I'd thankfully nudged shut behind me when I'd come in. My lips twitched in amusement at her solo celebration.

Doria had joined in on the mission last night, but only on the sidelines and at the beginning. Hatter had woken her when we'd gotten back to the house so she'd know we'd returned safely and victorious. She sounded even happier now that the news had sunk in.

"Pops!" she called from downstairs. "There's no breakfast. We need something special for today."

Hatter rolled his eyes at the nickname and gave me one last quick kiss that tasted like an apology to both of us. I got up as he scooted off the bed and was a tad disappointed to discover he'd slept with his pants on. He leaned out into the hall. "Give me five minutes!"

"Fine, but I'm only cutting you slack because you were out saving the world yesterday."

"Teenagers," he muttered fondly, turning to his wardrobe.

If Hatter had actually been as young as he looked, he wouldn't have been more than a teen himself when he'd become a father. He'd told me he'd adopted Doria when she was two, twelve years ago. But he wasn't actually as young as he looked, thanks to Wonderlandian weirdness. I still wasn't totally clear on the timelines, but I wasn't sure how much it mattered.

Definitely not as much as the fact that Hatter appeared to be going to change his clothes without asking me to leave the room. Maybe I'd get the answer to that boxers vs. briefs question after all. I dropped into the armchair next to the bed, and my eyebrows jumped in surprise. The padded velour upholstery was so cozy I wanted to tuck myself right into it.

"This chair is actually pretty comfy," I said. Still not an ideal sleeping spot, but better than I'd expected.

"You can have it," Hatter tossed over his shoulder. He pulled a suit out of the wardrobe—the dark violet one he'd been wearing the first time I saw him—and set it on the bed. "I never want to sit in that thing again."

Fair enough. I *could* move it to the guest bedroom if I wanted to. Either of us could, with time moving properly again.

"I guess you can get rid of things now," I said. "And not have them pop back to where they used to be overnight."

"A feature of our new reality that I'm very much looking forward to," Hatter remarked.

My gaze traveled automatically to the folded paper sitting on one of the bookcases across the room. A folded paper with a charcoal sketch of the house I'd inherited less than two weeks ago from my grand-aunt Alicia.

Aunt Alicia had drawn that sketch for Hatter after she'd fallen through the same mirror I had into Wonderland, some fifty years ago. From the vague letter she'd left for me, I'd gathered our family had a strange tie to this place. I touched the ruby ring she'd also left for me, confirming it was still hanging from its chain under my shirt.

Aunt Alicia hadn't left Wonderland in the best state. Apparently she'd made promises about helping with the rebellion against the Queen of Hearts and then chickened out at the last moment, leaving the rebel group that called themselves the Spades in the lurch. Hatter had commented the other day that he'd have thrown out her sketch if his room, like the rest of Wonderland, hadn't been stuck in time.

Hatter followed my glance, and his hands paused around the tie he'd finally taken off.

"You could get rid of that if you wanted," I said tentatively. I knew he'd been harboring a lot of resentment over Aunt Alicia's betrayal of Wonderland. I also knew he'd had something of a crush on her back then. It was a little weird, thinking that, even though nothing had ever happened between them.

"I could," Hatter said slowly, and paused in a way that sent an uncomfortable twinge through my stomach. He'd probably had feelings for dozens of people before me. *I* had feelings for at least two other men in Wonderland right now, and he didn't see anything weird about that. It shouldn't have mattered.

But I didn't have those Wonderlandian sensibilities by nature, and an irrational little piece of me wanted him all to myself.

"The thing is," Hatter went on, catching my eye, "it isn't Alicia's house anymore. It's yours now. It's where you are when you're not here. When you were gone, the last time…" He hesitated again as if struggling to decide on the right words. "It made the wait easier, being able to look at that picture and know you were safe there."

Oh. My throat felt suddenly tight. He hadn't even known if I'd come back, the last time. He'd yelled at me about the probability that I wouldn't. But even then, it'd mattered more to him that I'd gotten out of danger.

"Better to keep it, then?" I ventured.

A smile touched Hatter's face—small, but enough to crinkle the corners of his eyes the way I loved. "I think so."

I had the impulse to drag him right back into the bed, breakfast be damned, but before I could act on it, Doria let out another shout. A frightened one.

"Dad!"

At the panic in her voice, Hatter blanched. He dashed for the hall, snatching up the top hat sitting on the dresser as he went, as if he'd need it to face whatever trouble awaited. I hurried after him.

Doria was standing by an open window in the living area, peering out. Her fingers gripped the ledge tightly as if she needed it for balance. Her face had paled beneath the fall of her dark brown hair.

Hatter rushed to her side. "What?"

She pointed mutely toward the street outside. He looked, and his expression stiffened.

As I came up behind them, a resonant thudding reached my ears. A voice was hollering something in the distance, too far away from me to make out the words, but something about the harsh tones of it sent a prickle of uneasy recognition down my spine.

I moved toward the other window to get a better view, and Hatter caught my arm.

"Stay back," he said, worry crackling through his words. "We can't let anyone see you. The guards are still looking— You need to put that powder Theo gave you in your hair."

I'd meant to do that during the shower I'd almost forgotten about taking. My gut balled tight. I edged a little to the side but no closer toward the window. From that angle, I could make out a sliver of the street.

Rows upon rows of guards in the palace's red-and-pink pleated tunics and bulging red helmets were marching by along the cobblestone road. As I watched, one came into view in the midst of the procession with a long pole thrust up in the air.

Doria clapped her hand over her mouth with a squeak of horror. Hatter flinched.

I risked easing half a step forward, and my stomach flipped over. Oh, God.

It wasn't a pole—it was a pike. And I could now say with total certainty that Sally hadn't made it home from last night's mission.

With each bob of that pike, her braid swung from her decapitated head.

CHAPTER TWO

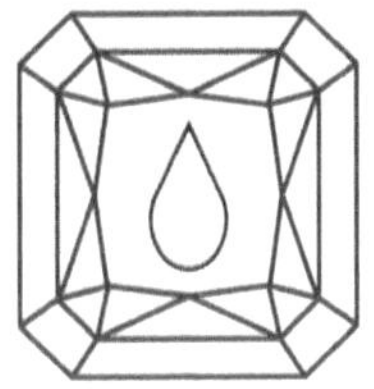

Lyssa

I stumbled backward, bile rising up my throat. The image of Sally's severed head stayed imprinted in my mind: eyes glazed and staring, skin grayed, neck rimmed with raw red flesh.

This was Wonderland, where people cavorted and laughed… and died.

"Lyssa," Hatter said. My legs wobbled, and he grasped my shoulder. I turned, pressing my face to his chest. Drinking in the bright-and-dark smell of him. His arms came around me and tightened when I shivered.

"That's what they do to Spades," Doria muttered, her voice rough. "To anyone who doesn't fall in line."

"They only parade them around when it's a Spade," Hatter said. "And not usually with the entire damned Hearts' Guard in attendance."

The spectacle was horrifying enough when I'd barely known Sally. It could have been Doria's head up there, or Hatter's. It could have been mine if I'd been a smidge slower when the guards had chased me the other day.

"It's not just the Guard," Doria said, with a hitch in her breath that made me raise my head. I still couldn't see much of anything through the window, but the voice from outside carried to us more clearly now. And I did recognize it. Its throaty, commanding tone cut through the stomp of the guards' marching feet.

"People of Wonderland," the Queen of Hearts proclaimed. "This poison calling itself 'the Spades' has seeped around us for too long. They break the peace I have prescribed and force you all to suffer. It is time to stamp them out once and for all! We cannot tolerate it. We must not tolerate it! They will not dare trifle with me again."

"I wouldn't count on that," Doria murmured, but she'd drawn back from the window ledge as if afraid the Queen might reach her even there.

I needed to see the Queen, this villain who'd kept Wonderland's people trapped in the space of a day for nearly fifty years, whose shrieks of dismay had pierced my ears last night. I eased out of Hatter's embrace and crept closer to the window. Hatter made a warning sound, but he didn't stop me.

The Queen of Hearts sat in a golden throne with a heart-shaped back, borne by several of her guards. The immense skirt of her salmon-pink dress billowed out over the narrow platform. Her hair was styled in the same coppery loops I'd seen in a painting of her in the palace, coiled toward the base of her tall gold crown. Her scarlet lips were pursed, and her wide-set eyes gleamed with a metallic shimmer that apparently hadn't been just the painter's artistic license. Her gaze roved over the street as if it could have sliced through the walls around her just by looking at them.

When her gaze swept toward the higher floors of the buildings, I backed up with a shudder. Her voice heaved from her lungs again, so loud I'd have thought she was using a loudspeaker if I hadn't seen her hands were empty.

"You bring this on yourselves," she said. "You harbor these criminals; you look the other way. These beasts killed my *son.* They claim they fight for you. Well, let us see how true that is. Are they willing to give up their own lives when it's merely yours on the line?"

At a jerk of her hand, one of the guards broke from their

formation and slammed open the door of the nearest shop. There was a cry, and he emerged dragging a young woman—a girl, really, not much older than Doria's fourteen.

An older woman appeared in the doorway—the girl's mother? She stared white-faced and tight-lipped but unmoving as the guard lashed a metal cord around the girl's wrists. He tossed the prisoner onto the back of the throne's platform with an audible thump. The girl let out a pained gasp.

The Queen smiled.

"I will collect more of you each day until the Spades come forward to take your place—or until our dungeon is full," she said, sounding almost gleeful now. "If there's no sign of them by then, you will face the punishment for their crimes and cowardice in their place. Do *not* try my patience. If you know anything of these miscreants or the new Alice Otherlander, bring word to the palace, and you will be rewarded for your loyalty."

The procession marched on. The Queen's last words echoed through me, confusion dulling my horror.

"The new Alice Otherlander," I repeated. "Does that mean me? Why would she call me 'Alice'? Why *new*?"

Hatter's jaw worked. One look at his face was enough to tell me he knew the answer.

"We didn't tell you before," he said. "We already had so much to explain, and that part wasn't really relevant—it's all the Queen's paranoia. In some ways you know more about it than I did."

"I think I still need you to tell me the parts *you* know," I said.

He drew in a ragged breath. "Before your grand-aunt, there were two other women who came through a looking-glass into the Pond of Tears. Both of them were named Alice. Alice, Alice, Alicia, Lyssa… The Queen might not even know what your name is yet, but she's gathered enough to assume you're the next in that line. And for whatever reason, she thinks the pattern is part of a plot to overthrow her."

"For the same reason she decided the Spades must have killed the Prince way back when," Doria said, hugging herself. "For the reason that she's *totally fucking insane*."

I wouldn't mind seeing the Queen of Hearts overthrown now, but it wasn't like I'd come here to do that. I hadn't even meant to come here at all the first time. But Aunt Alicia had suggested our family was tied up with the mirror and Wonderland. How far back did that connection go? There had been Alices farther back in the family tree she had hanging in the library. Were they all Tenniels from longer ago?

Mom had said something about that, hadn't she? That my grand-aunt hadn't wanted her and Dad to name me after her. Was the name somehow part of the connection?

Too bad I couldn't really investigate the family side of things while I was stranded here in Wonderland.

"Okay," I said. "So basically, my name just makes her want to chop my head off even more. I guess you're right—it doesn't make that much difference. I'm still in a lot less danger than that girl she grabbed."

Doria sidled closer to her father's side. "Do you think she'll really do it? She'll fill the dungeon with regular Clubbers and then kill them all if we don't turn ourselves in?"

"Hey." Hatter turned to her and touched the side of her face, giving her a look filled with so much fatherly firmness and caring that it turned my heart into mush, watching them. "She's not getting you, Mouse. The White Knight will hear about this. He'll dream up one of his grand plans, and we'll stop as many heads from rolling as we can. Yours is *definitely* staying right where it belongs."

Doria still looked nervous, but a sly glint lit in her eyes at the same time. "*We'll* stop? Does that mean you're officially back with the Spades?"

Hatter gave her a grim smile. From what I'd seen and gathered, he'd been doing everything possible to keep himself and her apart from the rebel group since he'd become her father—until last night. As he'd sprinted across the gardens and prodded the palace's locks open with his hatpins, it'd been clear he was in his element. But that didn't mean he'd changed his mind completely.

"We freed Time," he said to Doria. "We have a real chance now. And I'd rather run those risks than watch you do it. *You* are going to be even more careful than usual while the Queen's on a rampage."

"I'm not promising anything," she said.

He sighed. "I didn't figure you would."

"Maybe I can help somehow, because of that whole Alice thing," I said. "If the Queen feels threatened by me being here... even if I'm not really the threat she thinks I am... there's got to be a way to use that. And I've got this too." I fished the ring out from under my shirt and popped off the gold filigree case around the ruby to show it to Hatter. "This is what Aunt Alicia left me along with the letter. She seemed to think it was important."

Hatter cocked his head as he studied it. "The gem is a match for that symbol you found on the ruin out by the Topsy Turvy Woods."

"I know," I said. "When I asked Chess about the symbol there, he said the Queen freaks out about ruins like that—she orders them destroyed if she hears about them. She's afraid of something to do with them too. It could all be connected. Aunt Alicia never said anything to you about the ring?"

"Unfortunately, no. I didn't even realize she had it." He frowned. "Theo might be able to tell you more."

His tone was a little reluctant. Hatter and the current White Knight had something of a contentious relationship, partly because Theo continued to let Doria pitch in with the Spades and partly, I suspected, because of the circumstances around Hatter's abandoning the group years ago. But Theo did seem to be the most knowledgeable person in Wonderland, maybe because in his public role as Inventor, he had a license to dig into any matter that came up.

I'd already meant to ask Theo about the ring. I'd forgotten about it during the rush of our mission and our victory afterward, but there was no other urgent task to get in the way now.

"I'll head over to the Tower then," I said.

"First get that powder in your hair, and get yourself into proper Wonderlander clothes," Hatter said. "I'm not letting the Queen get a hold of *your* head either."

The dyeing powder Theo had given me darkened my pale blond waves to a light ash brown. Definitely a different look. I stuck the rest of the package on the bathroom shelf—he'd said I'd need to re-dye it every couple days to make sure the color didn't fade too much. Then I pulled my hair back into a bun so it wouldn't be obvious how long it was. No one was going to identify me at a glance as the Otherlander the guards had been looking for.

When I came down in the borrowed dress with its pattern of rich greens and pinks, Hatter and Doria were sitting at the dining table with a platter of scones, and they had company.

"Chess!" I said, a smile springing to my face. Of the three men I'd found myself drawn to since I'd arrived in Wonderland, Chess was both the most enigmatic and the most likely to raise my spirits.

He gave me his characteristic playful grin that showed just a hint of his fang-like teeth. His whole face had a feline look to it, from the shape of his eyes to his prominent cheekbones, features that made even more sense now that I'd discovered he could literally shift into the shape of a large tabby cat when he wanted to. He'd sworn me to secrecy about that talent.

"Glad to see you too, lovely," he said in a light voice. "After the commotion, I felt the need to stop by and confirm all was as well as well can be."

"She's heading to the Tower," Hatter said. "Maybe you can make sure she doesn't get into any trouble along the way."

I wanted to say that I didn't generally get into trouble just walking down the street, but the truth was, I had screwed up a couple times during my last trip here, and with the Queen of Hearts gunning specifically for me, I didn't exactly mind the idea of having a guard of my own. Especially one as built as Chess was. Even with the loud yellow shirt he was wearing covering most of his torso, you could tell the guy had muscles upon muscles.

"If you were thinking of going that way anyway," I said, and swooped in on the scone platter. Hatter had gotten a couple of my favorite flavor: vanilla-cranberry-pine. He caught my eye with a pleased glint in his as I scooped them up, the sweetly tart scent already making my mouth water. "And I'll take breakfast with me. Thank you!"

Chess made an elaborate gesture with his hand as he dipped his head. "I promise to return her to you with all pieces intact."

"You'd better," Hatter grumbled.

"You'd better make sure you both stay in one piece too," I shot back before I followed Chess out the door.

Chess sauntered through the city as if he didn't have a care in the world, but he managed to be stealthy at the same time. We rambled down winding alleys that took us on a more direct route toward the silver spire that shone against the clear blue sky up ahead. Theo's office and apartment were up near the top of that tower.

"I do believe every time I see the Queen, her skirts have added another layer," Chess murmured to me. "Perhaps soon they'll swallow her up and save us the trouble."

As much as the sight of the Queen had chilled me, my lips twitched at the image he'd drawn. "I guess you saw her pretty regularly when you used to hang out with the Diamonds?" I said. He'd told me he used to visit regularly with the diamond-brooch-wearing courtiers who lived alongside the royal family in and around the palace.

"Ah, I preferred to steer clear of her even then. She does put you off your whatever-you-happen-to-be-having. And the only point in going to the palace is to have quite a lot."

"Hatter said she thinks I'm here to overthrow her," I said.

"It's an easy thing for her to predict," Chess said. "Nearly everyone wants to. The issue isn't the motive but rather the means."

He looked down at me as we walked into the Tower. The dimmer light inside didn't dull his bright auburn hair. "You needn't worry, Lyssa," he said. "A Spade dug in is there to stay. We've danced around her for ages."

"She caught Sally."

His glib demeanor faded for a second. "Sally was on her own," he said. "We'll see that you always have company, wanted or not." He punctuated that last comment with a wink.

We came to a stop in the tight but tall elevator shaft that appeared to run up the height of the entire building. My arm brushed Chess's, and my mind darted back to last night, after our victory, when I'd told him I wanted him too and he'd offered himself for a kiss.

He hadn't touched me in any purposeful way the whole walk here. Chess never seemed to worry much about anything, but it was hard to tell what was going on beneath his jokes and wordplay. Had he enjoyed that kiss as much as I had? Or was he regretting it now that the moment and the victory high had faded?

I wasn't used to being this flustered by three guys at once. But there was something so compelling about all of them in their different ways.

"About last night," I said, willing my tongue not to tangle. "The part at the end… I didn't mean for you to feel at all pressured. If you're not sure it's really such a good idea or whatever—I won't be offended."

Chess blinked at me. Then his eyebrows lifted as he must have made sense of my rambling. "You're talking about the kissing part. You're worried I might have decided I object?"

My cheeks heated. "Um, yeah, basically. I don't expect that you *have* to be into me that way. I only want that kind of company if you really want it too, you know?"

The smile he gave me then was a softer version of his usual grin, his expression so tender it sent a giddy quiver through me.

"I think this once I can produce an answer as straight-forward as you could ask for." He raised his head to speak to the elevator. "Twenty-seventh floor. Chess coming calling with Lyssa."

With a lurch, the cushion of air beneath us hurtled us upward. In the same moment, Chess traced his fingers over my cheek and lowered his mouth to mine. His kiss was as sweet as it had been last night, as tender as his smile. My heart leapt with it and with the rush of the air moving past. When he eased back as the elevator slowed, my head spun for a moment as I recovered my balance.

Yep, that was all the answer I needed right there.

"All right then," I said. "I'm glad we got that sorted out."

Chess let out a laugh that practically sparkled and nudged open one of the doors to Theo's office.

And here was the third man I'd been kissing last night.

The White Knight had the kind of presence that filled a room, no matter how many other people were around him. As we came in, Theo looked up from where he was standing by his sleek white desk in the stark white room, where he'd been talking with the redheaded twins who'd helped yesterday's mission. His stance was casual, the motion of his head subdued, but even if you'd never met him before, you'd have been able to tell he was calling the shots. Clothed in his usual white collared shirt and gray slacks, his tall muscular frame wasn't as brawny as Chess's, but it exuded confidence and power.

"I was hoping you'd make your way here this morning, Lyssa," he said in his smooth baritone, with a smile that felt just for me. His dark brown gaze swept from me to Chess. "And Chess, you've got perfect timing. Can you scout out a secure location for a meeting this afternoon? Dee and Dum will round up as many of us as they can."

"As your Knightliness commands," Chess said with an extravagant flourish that ended in a salute. He blinked out of sight as his hand dropped to his side, leaving behind only the flash of his grin for a second before it vanished too.

Chess could turn invisible at will. A man of many talents.

The twins ambled to the elevator, presumably to follow him. The one wearing an orange polo shirt with blue slacks and bowtie shot me a quick smile. The one with a blue shirt and orange slacks and bowtie glanced at me and then away. I wasn't sure which was which, but they weren't identical in friendliness.

Theo came over to join me. He took in my expression, one of his chestnut curls falling across his forehead as his eyes searched mine. His face wasn't perfect, his Roman nose slightly crooked, but that imperfection only made his handsome face more striking.

"The procession came past Hatter's house," he said, not bothering to make it a question.

The memory of the parade of guards and Sally's head bobbing in their midst made my throat constrict. I nodded.

Theo's mouth twisted. "I wish you hadn't needed to see just how vicious Wonderland can be. As you can probably imagine, the Queen's declaration has to put a temporary hold on our plans to get you home. We need to decide how to respond to her threat quickly."

"Of course," I said. It hadn't even occurred to me that he'd be worrying about how to get me to the one remaining mirror he knew of, the one deep within the palace of the Hearts, not with this menace looming over the people he'd dedicated himself to leading.

Now that he'd mentioned it, a pang filled my chest. Melody had been so worried about me when I'd returned home bleeding a few days ago. My mom fretted about me even when I wasn't facing down swords and daggers. If they realized I was missing, completely vanished from the only world they knew of…

But while I was here in Wonderland, time seemed to pass much more slowly in the Otherland where I belonged. I shouldn't be gone for long enough for anyone to worry back home until a couple weeks had passed here. If getting to the mirror took longer than that... I'd tackle that problem when I got to it.

"I do have something for you." Theo retrieved a container about the size and shape of a toothpaste tube from his pocket. "This salve should heal most of your wound so it won't cause you as much pain—and it'll be less noticeable to searching eyes."

I shouldn't have been surprised he'd have taken the time to take care of that with everything else going on. Part of the Inventor's job was coming up with plans, and Theo seemed to have a plan for everything.

"Thank you," I said.

He motioned for me to hold out my arm. The stitches stood out against the angry red line that ran from my wrist almost all the way to my elbow. Theo squeezed out a dollop of a swirling green-and-white gel that even looked like toothpaste.

A cool tingle spread through my skin and down into my muscles as he gently rubbed the gel down the length of the wound. The stitches and the redness faded. By the time he reached my elbow, the cut that had been gushing blood four days ago was little more than a thin pink line across my pale skin. Nothing visible from a distance; nothing noteworthy.

Theo's hand lingered on my arm. He was standing just a foot away, close enough that the warmth of his body tingled over me too. I had an awful lot of tantalizing memories of him—when he'd pushed me up against the tunnel wall for an incredible kiss last night, when we'd had the best sex of my life floating beyond gravity in one of his Inventor rooms here.

But as much as I enjoyed those memories, I wasn't here to get distracted all over again.

"I actually came because I might be able to help you deal with the Queen," I said. "When I went home the second time, I opened the box my grand-aunt left me. There was a ring in it that I think is important somehow, in a way the Queen wouldn't like."

Theo's thumb paused where it had been brushing over my arm in a comforting caress. "A ring?" he said.

"I'll show you." I fished it out from under my shirt. "It appears to have some kind of Wonderland magic."

CHAPTER THREE

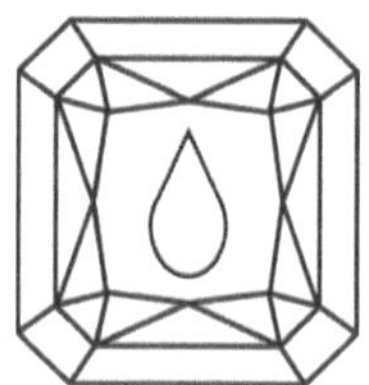

Theo

It took every ounce of control I had to keep my expression relaxed while Lyssa undid the clasp on the chain around her neck so she could slide off the ring. Could it really be what I thought?

And if it was, how could we use it?

She clicked open the golden shell that guarded the stone. My bright office lights reflected through the square ruby setting, flashing crimson as she handed the ring to me. A tiny point protruded from the otherwise smooth surface of its face.

My fingers tightened around the gold band. It hadn't been lost at all—or not completely, in any case.

"You said your grand-aunt left this for you?" I said, my voice sounding far away to my own ears.

"Yeah, just the ring and a letter that didn't explain much." Lyssa grimaced and tucked a stray strand of hair behind her ear. "But I know it has to do with Wonderland—I saw a symbol just like that gem on a ruined wall out near the Topsy Turvy Woods. It was on Aunt Alicia's box too. Well, the symbol also had what I thought was a teardrop in the middle of the gem, but I think that's because—if you prick your finger on that point—"

She reached out as if she meant to demonstrate herself, but I couldn't resist the urge to tap my own thumb to the ruby's surface. The sharp protrusion nicked my skin with a pinch of pain, and a drop of blood fell on the stone. It lay there dully for a second before leaching away into the gem.

What else could I have expected? This ring wasn't meant for me. It wasn't meant for anyone still living.

"Oh," Lyssa said, sounding surprised, as if *she'd* expected something different. "Maybe my eyes were just playing tricks on me before. Can I…?"

I handed the ring over, wondering what she meant. She touched her own thumb to the point. Blood welled from her skin onto the gem—and the ruby lit up from the inside as if someone had sparked a torch within it.

Every muscle in my body went rigid. No. No, it couldn't be. That was impossible.

I hadn't bitten my tongue, but a coppery flavor crept across it as if the blood had fallen into my mouth instead of onto the stone. My stomach listed. I found myself staring at Lyssa's face as if I'd find an answer written there. The trouble was, I didn't even know what to look for. How could I when… when…

"I don't know why it did that for me and not for you," Lyssa said. "So weird." She looked up, and her blue eyes widened. "Is something wrong? Is that a bad sign or something?"

Damn. So much for control. I sucked in a breath with the most blasé chuckle I could summon, forcing the clash of emotions inside me as far down as I could shove them.

She didn't know. She didn't know anything, and that meant I could still decide how this discovery played out. I could make sure it did help us rather than hurt us, as much as possible—all of us, including Lyssa.

"I certainly hope not," I said. "I'm not sure what to make of it. What did your grand-aunt say about the ring?"

"Just that she wanted me to have it. And she said some vague things about how our family was tied to Wonderland and some purpose that she realized she had. I'm not even sure how much that has to do with the ring specifically."

My body relaxed a little more. My thoughts were still spinning. "Quite the mystery, then. Did she say where it came from?"

Lyssa shook her head. "After seeing the same symbol on that ruin, I have to think she got it in Wonderland … That wall looked like it'd been around since way before her time. Although I guess if there were other Alices from our family before her, who knows?"

Hatter or Chess must have finally filled her in on the pattern of Otherlander women who came through the looking-glass. A pattern that apparently wasn't a coincidence after all. I reached for the easy composure that would have had the right words to say next slipping off my tongue, but I couldn't quite find it. Nothing I'd heard or been told lined up with the spark of that ruby as it drank Lyssa's blood.

Lyssa snapped the protective casing back into place around the gem and restrung the ring on her chain. "You don't know anything about the ring or that symbol in general, then?" she said, sounding disappointed.

She'd been counting on me to have answers. That was what nearly everyone in Wonderland counted on me for, one way or another. I'd encouraged that reliance, but suddenly it felt like a weight on my spine.

I needed to think, but I couldn't with her right here waiting. If I was going to tell her anything, I had to do it now.

Without any definite intention, my hand rose to stroke over Lyssa's hair. She leaned into my touch automatically, her expression softening. This woman was made of courage and honesty, and she trusted me. I'd been willing to give her up, to see her home last night, despite all the good I'd thought she might be able to do for Wonderland. She deserved to be able to make her own choices.

But if the ruby shone true, then she might be our key to saving everything.

One small kernel of certainty rose up through my confusion. It wouldn't help any of us if I laid the full truth on her right now. We weren't ready to challenge the Queen on that scale yet either way.

Lyssa had to spend more time with us here before she could make a real choice anyway—before she even had the option of going home. I'd spent my entire life trapped. I didn't want to inflict the same sensation on her.

Let her settle in here, let her see what this land could be, let *me* have time to work out the matter for myself, and then perhaps she could hear it without panicking. Once word got out, if she took a wrong step, she might be dead before she had the chance to make any choice at all.

If we were to challenge the Queen, this discovery opened up new avenues nonetheless. Even as I grappled with the idea at all, part of my mind was already spinning plans. I'd proven myself in the job of Inventor honestly, at least.

"I've heard legends about the blood-marked ruby," I said, picking my words carefully. "It's been said that there are tools of battle marked with the symbol that contain some sort of magic. It could be that ring activates their power? From what I understand, the Queen of Hearts wasn't able to destroy those artifacts, so she disposed of them in the distant parts of Wonderland, as well as she could hide them. If that *is* more than legend."

Lyssa's face brightened so quickly that guilt twisted my gut. "Tools of battle," she said. "Something we could use to push back against the Queen—to stop her from going through with the awful plan she announced?"

"There's a chance," I said. "It would take time to find the artifacts, though, assuming they exist at all, and we'd need to determine where to search. There's much more to Wonderland than you've had the opportunity to see. I'll need to investigate further."

"What about Mirabel?" Lyssa asked. "She's told me things about the past—and the future—that ended up making sense. She might be able to see something about the ring or those tools, right?"

I'd have preferred to speak to our White Queen on my own, but now that Lyssa had mentioned it, I'd rather have her feel involved than put her off. "She very well might," I said. "We could stop by right now."

It was a short hop in the elevator to the next floor. Mirabel called out a cheerful, "Come in," at my knock. We found her in her room of many chairs, curled up on her favorite sofa with her knitting. Her needles worked at a languid pace on what looked like a shawl-in-progress. It didn't appear any recent dreams or memories had stirred up to agitate her.

She sat straighter as we approached with a welcoming smile. She'd left her hair down today, and the golden-brown curls spilled over the broad neck of a white woolen dress she must have knitted too. A faint sound like softly tinkling chimes drifted through the room with its various pastel shades.

"You found him," she said to Lyssa, looking pleased.

Lyssa glanced at me. "I came asking about you yesterday before I found the meeting." Her gaze slid back to Mirabel. "I mean, if that's what you're talking about."

It was often difficult to tell. I wasn't sure Mirabel generally knew herself. She tipped her head vaguely and motioned for us to sit down. "It's the best I can do to help," she said.

With the way her mind worked, dislodged from time and catching glimpses of past and future, she might very well be more prepared for our conversation than we were. Unfortunately, she didn't have much sway over where her thoughts wandered. A result, at least in part, of the blow she'd taken to her head years before my time. The rippled pink skin of the scar peeked from her hairline at her temple.

She could moderate how many of her thoughts she shared, though. I made a small downward gesture with my hand as Lyssa and I sat in neighboring chairs. *Keep any remarks limited.* Mirabel caught my eye and gave me a tiny nod.

"I don't know how much you already know about why we're here," Lyssa said. "But Theo's told me that there are tools we might be able to use to take on the Hearts—ones that have a symbol of a 'blood-marked ruby' on them? They could be hidden somewhere in Wonderland. I thought you might have some idea where we should look." She showed Mirabel the ring. "I have this too. It seems to be connected somehow."

"When Lyssa pricks her finger on its surface, the ruby glows," I said in a measured voice.

Mirabel's eyes flickered, and she knit her brow. "Ah," she said with a rough laugh. "I see."

Lyssa leaned forward. "You do?"

"That is—" The White Queen stopped and collected herself, setting her knitting in her lap. "Let me see what I can remember."

"Anything about the tools would be especially helpful," I said.

"Yes. Yes." Her eyelids drifted down until they were nearly shut. She swayed a bit to the side, her fingers smoothing over the skirt of her dress, her lips tensing.

"They have been found too," she said after a moment in a wisp of a voice. "The sword, the scepter, and the shield. I don't think they offered the strength you were hoping for. But they led you to the truth of your heart."

"The sword, the scepter, and the shield," Lyssa repeated. "Do you know where I'll find—where I found them?"

"Where she searched before, before she'll flee," Mirabel murmured. "The one who came after, who'll leave the ring. She could have—but she ran. The course was clear ahead. He'll wait for her."

She winced and opened her eyes. "Thank you," Lyssa said quickly. "That's a lot. That's—I think that's somewhere to start. You must mean my grand-aunt Alicia, I think? She's the one who left the ring for me. She ran away from Wonderland." She turned to me. "Aunt Alicia didn't tell me anything in her letter about searching for something here, but I can ask Hatter. He might know if she went farther out into Wonderland and where."

Perfect. A clear lead—and a reason for her to leave so I could sort myself out. I got up with her and walked her to the door. But watching her smile, so pleased to have a way to help *us*, every bone balked at the idea of letting her simply walk out.

She hadn't asked for a part in any of the troubles we'd ended up laying on her, but she'd jumped in feet-first. So sweet yet determined that my heart squeezed, looking at her.

I wouldn't let any harm come to her.

"Keep that ring out of sight," I said, setting my hand on her shoulder. "If the Queen of Hearts has reason to fear it, it'll only make you a greater target. Do you want me to escort you back to Hatter's?"

"I think I'll be okay," Lyssa said. "I'm learning all the sneaky routes from Chess. You've got a ton of other things to deal with without babysitting me. I'll be careful."

It was the answer I'd wanted, but I still found it hard to let her go. No matter who else she might be, she was still Lyssa, the woman who'd shared her struggles with me so openly, the woman who'd come apart with pleasure in my arms just a few nights ago.

I couldn't help myself. I didn't just care for her—I wanted her, too.

I brought my fingers to her jaw to lift her chin, and she bobbed up on her toes to meet the kiss I'd been about to offer. The fresh smell of her, like a spring breeze, filled my lungs. Her mouth tasted like tart vanilla, and her lips moved against mine so pliantly it took another gargantuan effort of self-control to ease back.

She beamed at me, her cheeks flushed and her eyes sparkling. Another jab of guilt bit into my gut.

The moment Lyssa had descended the elevator, I poked my head out into the tunnel and said, "Third floor, follow." A second later, Griffon slipped out of the apartment there with a nod of acknowledgment to me. He'd make sure she stayed safe until I could join her again.

When I turned back to Mirabel, she'd gotten up from the sofa, her knitting left behind. "The ring," she said. She didn't really need to say more than that.

My mouth tightened. "Yes."

"So it finally came back."

She didn't sound surprised. She hadn't looked surprised until I'd mentioned the glow, and then only briefly.

"Did you know?" I had to ask, even though I realized I might not get a straight answer.

"I… I might have and then forgotten. It can all be so hazy." She looked me up and down, and I suspected her gaze caught more than the surface of me. Her voice came out gentle. "You must have heard the stories, baby brother. You knew."

My hands clenched at my sides. "I believed it was over, far back in the past, before any of us. It's different hearing it in that distant way and then seeing right in front of you the proof that the tragedy hasn't actually ended. How can I— I hardly know where to start."

"Does it matter that much to you what she signifies?"

"It means I have more wrongs to right than I realized," I said. "And the worst of them may stand in conflict with each other."

"No one can fix everything," Mirabel said. "They weren't your wrongs."

"But they are, too. If I ever want to really lead…"

That was the deepest truth of it, wasn't it? I hadn't let myself dream often of the future time when we might have displaced the Queen of Hearts entirely, when I might steer Wonderland from a throne rather than from the shadows. I would be the obvious choice when the Hearts in the palace fell. I shouldn't have cared about that, but I did.

Of course, nothing I'd learned today had to change that if I laid my plans right.

I swallowed hard. *That* one answer was clear. We needed Lyssa to stay. It was best for Wonderland, and best for everything I might have wanted for myself. And yet I couldn't commit to it.

It was the best possible outcome anyone here could have asked for —anyone except, perhaps, for Lyssa.

CHAPTER FOUR

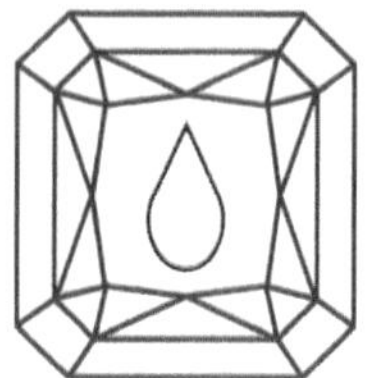

Lyssa

"Magical artifacts?" Hatter said. "Blood-marked ruby? I've never heard legends about any of that."

I leaned onto the table across from him. He was nimbly attaching a twinkling veil to a wide-brimmed sunhat in the back workroom of his shop. The small space had a dry velvety smell to it. I could practically taste the felt on the shelves—as well as Hatter's skepticism.

"That's the whole reason you suggested I talk to Theo, isn't it?" I pointed out. "Because as Inventor, he's heard all kinds of things not everyone has?"

Hatter made a disgruntled sound that I took to mean he accepted my point but wished he didn't have to. I hesitated, torn between memories of the way he'd clammed up when I'd asked him about his history before and the itch of curiosity.

We'd cleared the air between us, hadn't we? If I could make out with a guy, be perfectly prepared to sleep with him, I should be able to ask a simple question. How many times had Melody gotten on my case about trying too hard to be the "cool girlfriend" who never brought up anything uncomfortable? *A good guy will want to talk things through. A not-good guy doesn't deserve you, Lyss.*

I braced myself for his reaction. "I know you have issues with the way Theo has let Doria help out the Spades," I said. "But you used to work together, didn't you? Back when you were a regular part of the group. Is there some other bad blood between you—did something else happen?"

Hatter glanced up, the surprise in his eyes reassuring me. "No," he said. "Well, nothing he did, exactly. My priorities changed. It made me start wondering exactly where his priorities are. But I can't say he's done anything *wrong*. He certainly knows how to draw up a plan. I can recognize that he's on Wonderland's side as much as anyone is."

He gave me a crooked smile. "You know I've been doing some re-evaluating lately. I suppose I should ease off on him while I decide whether he really has been incautious or it's all been over-caution on my side of things."

"That's very generous of you," I said in a teasing voice, and Hatter fixed me with one of his glowers, with enough warmth behind it that it made me a little tingly. Focus, Lyssa.

"It seems like Aunt Alicia might have gone looking for the artifacts," I said. "She did find the ring, anyway. Did she ever mention going farther out into Wonderland?"

"Not that I remember." Hatter gave the veil one last tuck and moved on to an arrangement of flowers on a fascinator. "But she could have traveled around without me knowing about it. I only saw her through her involvement with the Spades."

I frowned. "And no one else from those days is still around. Theo made it sound like it'd be pretty hard to track these things down without a starting point. I wish she'd left instructions or something."

Hatter paused, twirling a peacock feather between his thumb and forefinger. "There is actually one other person she often ran with back then who's managed to keep his head," he said slowly.

"What?" I straightened up with my fingers splayed on the table. "Why didn't you tell me before? You said everyone else was gone."

"Well, he…" Hatter grimaced. "Carpenter has changed a lot since those days. I'd imagine the main reason he's kept his head is he's put it and the rest of him in service of the Queen. The work he does these days… I don't know how he stomachs it. He'd probably turn a Spade in sooner than lend them a hand. We can't trust him. But he might have some idea of Alicia's travels that I don't."

"We have to go talk to him then," I said. "We don't have to tell him it's anything to do with the Spades. Tell him we want to help the Queen too or whatever. It's not like you've been part of the rebellion for a while anyway."

"*We* are not doing anything," Hatter said firmly, pressing another feather into place without even needing to look at his hands. "If he gets even the slightest suspicion that you're related to Alicia, he'll be carting you off to the Queen. I don't want you getting within a mile of Carpenter."

My stomach dropped. "But if I could find the artifacts—"

"I'll go," Hatter said. "On my own. He knows me. He won't be as suspicious. I should be able to approach it in a way that won't clue him in to our purpose." He attached the last of the feathers and considered the spread with an approving eye. Then he raised his head again. "I can go today. We're in a bit of a bind for time, aren't we?"

Gratitude swept through me so quickly it clogged my throat for a second. "I— Thank you. Are you sure you'll be all right going by yourself? If this guy is on the Queen's side now as much as you said… You didn't want to be part of anything to do with the Spades at all just a couple days ago."

It was my idea he was following up on. He shouldn't have to take on all the risks.

"Hey." Hatter came around the table and took my hand. His bright green eyes held mine. "I trust that if you think this is a lead we should pursue, there really is something there. I convinced myself for a long time that keeping out of the rebellion was the best thing for the people I cared about, but it didn't get us any closer to freedom. That mission last night did. Honestly, it felt good to dive back into the action."

I'd been able to see that in the eagerness that had energized him as we'd made our way through the palace. His words didn't completely erase my guilt, though.

"I'd just feel horrible if anything happened to you because of me," I said quietly.

"You don't need to worry, looking-glass girl," Hatter said with a wry smile. "I'll be fine. Believe me, I survived many exploits far more dangerous when I lived and breathed the Spades. I might be dipping my toes back in, but I'm not going to tempt danger unnecessarily. My days of being Mad Hatter are long over."

Mad Hatter. That was a side of him I definitely hadn't seen yet. He sounded so sure of himself that I let myself nod. I'd only be putting him in more danger if I insisted on coming along, wouldn't I?

"Well then," I said, "for luck." I slipped my hand behind his neck and kissed him.

Hatter kissed me back with a restrained hunger that left me giddy. When he drew back, his eyes were sparkling.

When we passed through the shop, Doria was sitting on the counter, peering at herself in a layered confection of a hat draped with silk. The mint-green shade didn't totally fit with her ruffled black dress, as she apparently decided for herself. She tossed the hat back onto the shelf and hopped off the counter.

"I have to run an errand," Hatter told her. "Stick with Lyssa? I don't really want either of you wandering around on your own with the Queen in her current mood."

"Whatever you say, Pops," Doria said.

He ruffled her hair in response to the nickname. "I'll be back tonight, hopefully not too late. Why don't you talk with Lyssa about the thing we were discussing earlier?" He glanced at me. "I'll see you soon with whatever answers I can pry out of him."

He set off with a tip of his hat and a swish of his suit jacket.

"The thing?" I asked Doria.

"Come on," she said, motioning to the stairs.

In the apartment, she led me on up to the fourth floor where she slept. The top level of the building was set up like another apartment in itself, with an open concept kitchen-living area about half the size of Hatter's main one and two bedrooms down the hall. Doria went into the master bedroom at the end, where an unscreened window looked out over a bit of roof and the back alley. The bedspread on the queen-sized mattress was rumpled, but I knew no one had slept here in years.

Doria set her hands on her hips. "This was my parents' bedroom," she said. "My birth parents, I mean. Dad was thinking you should sleep in here instead of the guest room downstairs, so you can hop out the window onto the roof right away if the Knave or whoever comes by again. We can clean things up now that Time isn't stuck anymore."

My pulse hiccupped as I looked at her. Doria's birth parents had been killed when she was a toddler by the order of the Queen of Hearts—because of their involvement with the Spades, from what I'd gathered. When we'd escaped onto the roof to hide before, I'd seen the shapes of their long-absent bodies left under that bedspread, frozen in time like the rest of Wonderland. They were gone, but this room had remained as if they'd never left.

"Are you okay with that?" I asked.

Doria shrugged. "That's what Dad asked me too. It's really not that big a deal. I don't even remember them, you know? This is all just… stuff. Anything I want to keep, I'll stick in my room. I can do that now." She grinned and then reached for the bed covers. "For starters, these haven't been washed in about fifty years."

Thanks to the resetting of time over those years, no dust stirred up as we stripped the bed and remade it with fresh sheets or when we moved to the desk in the corner and the wardrobe beside it. We picked up the few pieces of worn clothing that had been left draped on a chair or a knob. I brought a glass ringed with wine and a plate dappled with crumbs over to the kitchen.

Doria grabbed what must have been her mother's jewelry box and all the darker dresses out of the wardrobe. I hauled the ones she'd picked out for me to borrow back upstairs from the guest bedroom. We shook out the rug over the edge of the roof and left the window open so the warm breeze could drift through. It carried a faintly buttery smell from the bakery down the street where Hatter bought his scones.

Doria studied the stacks of folded shirts and slacks that had been her birth father's with a cock of her head. "I guess I'll ask Dad if he wants any of these, and otherwise we'll take them to the clothing shop," she said. "They're not really his style." She hesitated. "Maybe I'll just keep one shirt. To hang on to it."

"Of course," I said. "I think it's good to hold onto a few things, for when you want to remember—or at least think about them." I sank down on the edge of the bed. "I—I lost my dad too, when I was eight. I've still got a pair of his old gloves tucked away in one of my drawers back home." Big sheepskin ones, so soft when my dad had picked me up and spun me around when I'd been little. Whenever I smelled them, I remembered those first winters—the couple I could remember from before his illness—perfectly.

Doria sat down on the other end of the bed, leaning against one of the wooden posts with her legs drawn up in front of her. "What happened to your dad?" she asked.

"He got sick," I said. "Cancer. I guess that's not really a thing here." Chess had told me there were no illnesses in Wonderland. I groped for a way to explain it. "It's basically—this thing starts growing inside you, crowding in on all the parts of you that you need to breathe and process the food you eat and… everything. We have treatments in the Otherland, but they don't always work. And when they do, sometimes it's just for a little while, and then the cancer comes back."

I didn't like thinking back to those memories—of Dad slumped so sallow and frail on the sofa or in his bed.

Doria grimaced. "That sounds awful."

"Yeah," I had to say. "It really is. He was sick for almost three years before he passed on, and he was really weak and in pain a lot of that time."

"You still had your mom, though?"

More than Doria had hers. "It was hard on her," I said. "For a while she went kind of… vacant. But she was *there*, and she got better, over time." Until then, I'd been the one who held the family together through her listlessness and my older brother Cameron's rages.

Kind of funny that here in Wonderland, where I literally had powers no one else did and a tyrant queen had spent decades crushing everyone's spirits, I had way more support than I'd been able to count on back then.

I couldn't let these people down. There had to be something more I could do to free them completely.

Doria hugged her knees. "Sometimes it pisses me off that I don't remember them at all," she said. "But sometimes I'm kind of glad. It would probably hurt more if I had a clearer idea what I was missing. Which doesn't mean I'm not still *really* pissed off at the Queen."

The corner of my mouth twitched upward. "Obviously. I guess there are upsides and downsides either way. At least you do have one really good dad, even if he hasn't been keen on everything you want to do." No one could see Hatter with Doria and fail to notice how much he loved her.

Doria smiled too. "Yeah," she said. "Parents are supposed to be annoying, right?" A spark of mischief lit in her eyes. "Speaking of which…"

"Uh huh?" I prompted with a raise of my eyebrows when she trailed off.

She twisted the corner of the bedspread in her hand. "Dee came by the shop and told me there's a meeting for all the Spades happening in a bit. I was planning on going."

Which meant either I convinced her not to or I went with her, if I was going to stay with her like Hatter had asked. From past experience, I didn't think the former option was going to pan out.

"I don't think he'll get angry at you for coming with me like he did last time," she added quickly. "He knows I'd go anyway. He even started coming to the meetings with me."

That was true. "I guess he didn't actually say we shouldn't go out anywhere," I said. "Only that we should stick together. And… if the Spades are making plans, I'd like to be in on them too."

Doria's face lit up. "Then it's settled," she declared, jumping up. "We'd better get going. It's almost time for the meeting to start."

CHAPTER FIVE

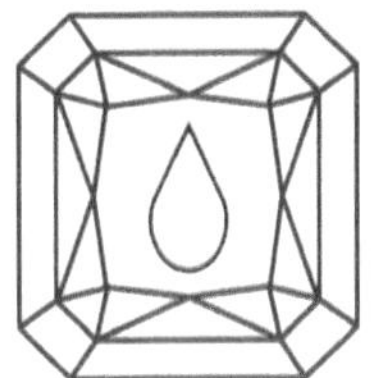

Lyssa

It was kind of a shame that Hatter was missing the current meeting of the Spades, because Doria and I headed up the steps at the back entrance of a costume shop and found ourselves joining what looked like a giant tea party. A bright red table stretched the length of the room, set out with plates of cakes and cookies and pots of tea. I watched one of those pots lift up of its own accord to fill a cup it deemed had gotten too low.

Tall stools with low backs stood all around the table. The refreshments circulated a lot like the rotating conveyor belt at Melody's favorite sushi place, but instead of the food traveling around while the diners waited, the food stayed put and the chairs glided from spot to spot.

Actually, "hitched" was a more accurate word than "glided." The rotation stopped and started at an unpredictable pattern and with a grinding whir that gave me the impression the inner workings were starting to fail. Yellow sheets papered over the place's broad front window, and dust bunnies had gathered in the corners. The sugary smell that laced the air was a little stale. But then, a happening café wouldn't have made a very good secret meeting spot.

Theo stood by the head of the table where the stools shot straight around to the other side. He was the only figure in the room not in motion. Twenty or so others perched on the stools. Chess gave me a wave, and Doria bounded over to the empty stool next to the redheaded twins.

There were a *lot* of empty stools. Something like half of them were unoccupied. My heart sank as I hopped onto one between Chess and a burly guy I recognized from the pre-mission meeting yesterday evening.

No wonder the Spades were having such a hard time taking on the Queen of Hearts. The memory of this morning's procession lingered in my mind—all those rows of marching soldiers. Even if only half of the people Theo might have counted on had shown up today, they couldn't have risen up against the Hearts and won, not on their own.

Looking at the faces around me, most of them drawn and grim, I could tell they were well aware of that fact too.

I hooked my feet behind the rung on the stool's base to help me keep my balance as my seat lurched to the right. There had to be some reason for hope. We'd just ended one of the Queen's most awful acts of oppression. The Spades could make plans that spanned more than one day, build up more resources…

But the Queen's parade and proclamation probably felt much more real to them than our victory. They hadn't even gotten to experience one completely new day yet.

A couple more people trickled in, and then Theo cleared his throat. His warmly commanding baritone carried over the rasp of the mechanical chairs.

"You all know why we're meeting again so soon, and why I wanted as many of you here as possible, so let's not waste time rehashing this morning's events," he said. "Chess, you had a look around the palace grounds?"

"A look and a listen," Chess piped up from his seat beside me. Even *his* grin looked a bit strained. "From what I heard, the Queen has stayed true to her word and locked her current prisoner in the palace dungeon. That is, four floors beneath the ground level, with guards at every level in between."

"Attempting to break anyone out of there would be a suicide mission," the man at my other side said.

The pained set of Theo's mouth suggested he agreed. "Dee and Dum, your observations of the Hearts' Guard in the city?"

One of the twins sat up a shade straighter. "They've cut back on the patrols. Just ten guards that we saw making the rounds—talking to the Clubbers, making friendly." He wrinkled his nose. "They aren't so much trying to catch us outright as trying to make a point about why the rest of the city shouldn't count on us."

"Turning the Clubbers against us right when we might have had a real chance of convincing them to rise up," a woman across the table from me muttered around a mouthful of cookie.

"We can't forget that we struck a major blow against the Queen's rule last night," Theo said. "As difficult a problem as she's presented us with, we've *gained* ground. All this gambit means is that we need to rally our forces and gather more power to our side as quickly as possible."

His gaze found mine for an instant before my stool yanked me past him around the table. More power—like the artifacts he'd talked about. If one of them was a weapon—if Aunt Alicia's ring would allow us to use it—we *had* to find them. The Spades needed an advantage the Queen couldn't match. And we needed it before her dungeon filled up with innocent civilians.

With another jolt of the stool, I found myself facing a woman with a pointed face and beady eyes like a ferret. She stared straight at me, frowning.

"Why is the Otherlander still here?" she demanded. "The Queen is cracking down on us even harder because of her. We've got enough to worry about without that hassle too."

My fingers curled tighter around the edges of my seat. It hadn't occurred to me that I might be unwelcome here.

"I came back because I thought of a way I could help reach the watch," I said.

"And Lyssa did help us," Theo said, a stern note entering his voice.

"We couldn't have freed Time without her. *Because* she was generous enough to put herself at risk so that we could break free of the cycle we'd been stuck in, she's now stuck here with us until we can see her to another looking-glass doorway."

"I'm doing everything I can to make sure I don't draw attention," I added, and motioned to my dyed hair, my clothes. "The Queen won't even know I *am* still here."

A mutter carried from farther down my current side of the table. "If the Otherlander really wants to help us, she should turn herself over. That would satisfy the Queen for a little while—or at least distract her."

My head jerked around, a chill seeping through my skin all the way to my gut. I couldn't tell who had spoken, but none of the faces I could see in that direction looked disturbed by the suggestion.

Chess caught my elbow, his grasp both steadying and protective. When I looked at him, he wasn't so much grinning as baring his sharpest teeth.

Theo's jaw had clenched with a flash of his dark brown eyes. His voice came out low but with a clear warning, so potent it sent a warm shiver under my skin despite my discomfort. "I sincerely hope we aren't turning to the same tactics as the Queen, volunteering others to make their sacrifices for us," he said.

"Of course not, White Knight," several of the Spades hurried to say. Flickers of horror passed through some of their expressions. But there were others who still looked tense, as if they weren't willing to speak up but didn't exactly have a problem with that one speaker's suggestion.

Chess's hand stayed on my arm. I swallowed hard, but my stomach was full of ice.

These people had been working together for years—for decades. I'd dropped into Wonderland for the first time ten days ago. Just with my name and where I was from, I'd provoked the Queen's paranoia and maybe driven her toward the measures she was taking. I couldn't really blame them for feeling uneasy about my presence, could I?

If I did turn myself in to the Queen, would that fix anything? A prickle ran along my neck at the thought. I'd be giving myself over to the same fate Sally had met. It *would* be my head on a pike paraded through the city.

And then what? She'd be happy for a few days before going back to crushing the rest of Wonderland? No. As sick as I'd felt hearing her call out for my capture this morning, I couldn't believe that sacrifice would be the right move in the long run, if I even had the spine to make it. Not now. Not while we still had other reasons to hope.

"There's another plan I'm working on," I said, with a glance toward Theo, looking for guidance. How much would he want me to say about the ring and the artifacts before we had anything more specific to offer? "I'm going to leave the city looking for something to give the Queen a good reason to be scared of me. So, I won't be here to get you in trouble, and if it works, I'll come back with a way to turn the tide in the Spades' favor."

"I'm assisting Lyssa in this venture," Theo put in. "I believe it's the best chance we have to overcome the Queen's rule completely."

"But that doesn't solve any of our problems today, does it?" a rough voice said. A man with a horse-like mane, coarse and strung through with gray, bowed his head where his seat was approaching Theo. "Tomorrow the Queen is going to take more Wonderlanders for her prison. Can you say you'll have this plan ready to see through before her prison is full and she takes all those people to the chopping block?"

"Every day we stand back, the Clubbers will turn more against us," the ferret-eyed woman said. "How many of them might have looked the other way before but could point the finger at us now?"

Theo exhaled. "I won't lie to you. The results are still uncertain, and it will take time for us to discover how far we can take them. Which is why we are meeting here today—so we can decide together how we go forward."

A momentary hush fell over the table, leaving behind only the whir of the stools and the clink as someone set down a teacup.

"Could we bring more Clubbers over to our side now?" I asked tentatively. "They have to see how horrible the Queen is being, that she's the villain here. If all of the people who show up at Caterpillar's Club every night march on the palace, we'd have a chance."

"We've tried to inspire them to the cause," the man beside me said. "As more heads have rolled, fewer new ones have been swayed to our side. It's not that they don't see who the villain is, it's that they dislike the consequences of standing up to her."

The Clubbers needed a sign—like an artifact. Like magic. But we needed to give them that *now*.

"I'll go," the gray-haired man said. He set his gnarled hands on the tabletop, letting them slide when the stools shifted again. "I'll turn myself in to the palace in exchange for that girl. We can end this ridiculous challenge right now."

The ferret-eyed woman stared at him. "Smith…"

"I've only ever contributed bodily strength to the rebellion," Smith said, his voice weary but firm. "And my supply of that is dwindling. I've had a life longer than so many who've fallen to the Hearts' blades. We can prove that we won't let innocents die in our place and stop this horrible scheme of hers in its tracks before she can demand more than one of us. That will buy us time. It may convince a few of the Clubbers to find a little courage in themselves."

Every particle in my body balked at the idea of this man giving himself over to be killed. "This group is so small already," I said. "Can we really afford to lose anyone?"

He gave me a pained smile that he then turned on the rest of his comrades. "If we wait even until tomorrow, she'll demand more of us as a 'fair' trade. I've seen this moment on the horizon for years. I didn't know it would come this way, but at least it'll serve Wonderland more than if I was simply caught by a guard over the wrong comment overheard."

There had to be a better answer than that… didn't there? My gaze darted over the faces around me, but an air of resignation had come over the gathering. Theo left his spot at the head of the table to grip Smith's shoulder.

"If that is the choice you wish to make," he said, "it *is* yours to make. We'll make sure you're remembered often and well."

Even he couldn't see a way around this? I opened my mouth, wanting to protest more, but no real arguments came to me.

Who was I to argue anyway? The actual Spades were accepting this solution as if there was nothing so strange about it. Suddenly I could see why Hatter might have had qualms about the group's guiding philosophy.

They could be cutthroat in their own way when they wanted to be. They were willing to give up a life if it seemed to benefit more people than it hurt.

Doria had said there was no way the Spades could have killed the young prince, but watching this scene play out, I wasn't so sure she was right. If they were willing to send one of their friends to the slaughter, why would they balk at killing one of the Queen's children?

Smith stood up, and the rest of the Spades slid off their stools to gather around him, offering fond words and grateful gestures. I'd just gotten up awkwardly, not sure whether I had any place joining in, when a man with a lizard's head spun around where he'd been peering past a gap in the window's papering.

"There's a guard heading toward the building. Scatter!"

At those words, the group broke apart in an instant, everyone rushing toward the stairwell. My heartbeat stuttered as I caught up with Doria. Theo reached us a second later, his hand coming to rest on my back, his expression tense.

"The Tower is closer than Hatter's house," he said. "Come with me."

He motioned to the twins too. All of us hustled down the stairs and into the alley behind the shop.

The other Spades scattered in various directions, slowing their pace and taking on a casual demeanor as they spread out. Theo led the four of us through a gap between two buildings so narrow I had to walk sideways to fit, across the street to another alley, and then out onto the cobblestone road just a short jog from the silver spire the White Knight called home.

He knew his way around the city like Chess did. I guessed that shouldn't surprise me. The thought of Chess made me glance around, but the other man hadn't come with us.

Chess should be safe. He could simply blink out of view if a guard came too close.

Somber silence filled the elevator shaft as it propelled us up to the twenty-seventh floor. When we reached Theo's level with its doors on every side, Doria rubbed her hand over her face and glanced at the twins.

"Since we're here anyway… It's been a long time since I got to challenge you guys in the games room. Who's up for blowing off some steam?"

"Sounds extremely satisfying to me," the more smiley twin said. His brother didn't look as enthusiastic, but he glanced at Theo as if for permission.

"Be my guest," Theo said. "You *are* my guests for the moment. I'll rouse you when it's safe to leave."

Doria stopped long enough to inform me, "I'll be fine. The worst thing that'll happen is the evil eye from these guys when I whoop their asses." Then she pushed open the silver door as if she knew exactly where she was going. The twins tagged along behind her, one of them laughing as he challenged her prediction of whose ass would be whooped.

Theo eased open the gold door. It opened into the hallway outside his office. I glanced around, disoriented—I'd gotten into the habit of choosing the bronze door, and it always took me right into the office-slash-workroom—and Theo's arm came back around me.

"You look like you need to sit down," he said gently.

I let him usher me into the lounge room we'd relaxed in before. My spine stayed stiff as I sat down on one of the cozy sofas. Theo sat at the other end, studying me.

"I'm sorry you had to hear some of those things," he said. "No one there would really try to send you off to the Queen. They're just frustrated, hardly thinking straight. We barely had a few hours to feel we'd accomplished anything before she found a new way to box us in."

Could he really say with so much certainty that they hadn't meant it? He might never consider lowering himself to those tactics, but I'd felt the hostility in that room, even if it'd been brief. I had the urge to ask him about the prince's murder and the responsibility the Spades shrugged off, but showing I doubted him felt like an insult. He'd indicated before that he didn't believe the Spades had anything to do with that death either.

It didn't matter anyway. By all accounts and all evidence, the Queen had been awful before her son died, and no one death could justify the torture she'd put all of Wonderland through.

"I know," I said. "Is there really nothing else we can do except let Smith get himself *killed*?"

Theo's mouth twisted. He didn't need to tell me how much he hated the solution he'd accepted. *He* would never have agreed to killing anyone in retribution, especially a kid.

"Sometimes the best we can do is make a small concession to prevent a larger tragedy," he said. "I don't like it, and if no one had offered themselves, I'd have gambled on us retrieving the artifacts in time—on them making enough of a difference. But I won't stop someone willing."

A lump rose in my throat. I didn't want to die, but the situation we were in was a lot more my fault than Smith's.

"I feel so useless," I said. "The Queen is angry about me, and I'm not doing anything to change that."

"You're doing everything you can," Theo said. "What did you find out from Hatter?"

"He's gone to talk to Carpenter," I said. "He isn't sure whether he'll know anything—or tell Hatter anything—though."

"But he might." Theo eased forward so that his knees rested against mine and took my hand. "I know Hatter. He wouldn't go trekking across the land on too slim a chance. So you wait, and when he comes back, then you can move forward."

"What if it's still not enough?"

"You've already done more than anyone in Wonderland has managed to accomplish in nearly fifty years," he said. "Don't you dare beat yourself up for not having even more answers than the rest of us do."

So much passion rang through those words that most of my doubts disintegrated. I was doing it again—feeling like I had to take on the responsibilities for everyone around me. For an entire country, now, instead of just my family. I dragged in my breath and managed a smile. "Okay. I'll work on that."

Theo's thumb traced a line across the back of my hand. The warm contact brought back the memories of all the even more enjoyable ways he'd touched me just a few days ago. But his gaze was still fixed on my face, his eyes dark with concern. "I know you have plenty of other reasons to be unsettled. What do you need right now, Lyssa?"

With him touching me like that, looking at me with so much determination and affection, the answer rose straight from the core of me.

"I need you," I said.

Something shifted in Theo's eyes, almost as if I'd surprised him. Then he moved forward, his hand sliding to my waist, the other rising to tease along my jaw. When his mouth finally met mine, I was starving for him.

I could have this. For now, while I waited to find out what else I could give, I'd have whatever he would give me.

CHAPTER SIX

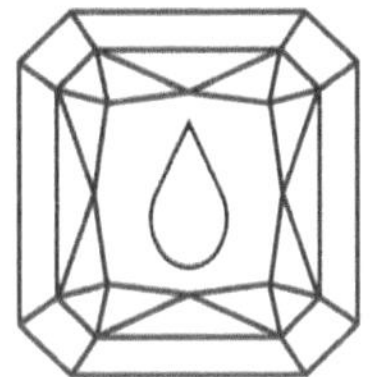

Hatter

I smelled Carpenter's workplace before I saw it. A ring of tall craggy rocks sheltered the Oyster Cove, but the mingling odors of salt, seaweed, and raw flesh drifted along the paved path that led out there. I breathed through my mouth, more and more shallowly the closer I got.

If it hadn't been for the smell, the cove would have looked appealing enough at a glance. The blue-gray water lapped the shore along its crescent of pink sand. In the distance, across the larger endless expanse of sea, a few scattered clouds were turning purple as the sun sank toward the horizon. The wind made a cheerful whistling sound as it passed through the gaps in the rocks.

All perfectly pleasant until you noticed the wooden cart pulled off to the side with a headless body lying prone within it.

Carpenter was down at the edge of the water next to a dimpled metal track that stretched from halfway up the beach to deep within the water. He'd put on more bulk since I'd last seen him, years ago, but his legs were still just as short. His rounded gut pressed into his knees as he crouched down. I didn't know how he could bear to eat at all, let alone in excess, carrying the memories of his time here.

Another form moved in the water. Walrus surfaced, his coarse gray skin dotted with liver marks, the wet collar of his shirt clinging to his wide neck.

"This one's ready!" he announced in his guttural voice. "Sending 'im up."

He gave a heave, and the water rippled as a marble platform surged along the track to the shore. Carpenter spread his meaty hands to catch the end. A greenish-black casing, which in my humble opinion more closely resembled an immense seedpod than an oyster's shell, sprawled across the entire length of the platform, water trickling off its ridged surface. Carpenter hauled the platform all the way up the sand and then stepped around to the side.

I cleared my throat, walking out of the shade by the ring of rock. "Carpenter. I heard I'd find you out here this afternoon."

Carpenter's egg-shaped head came up. He still had the same short brown beard, grizzled now with flecks of silver. His hazy blue eyes, like a pale reflection of the water, widened at the sight of me. The grin that crossed his face looked more amused than anything. That seemed to bode well for this visit.

"Hatter!" he said. "It's been a long time. What in the lands brings you all the way out here, far from your city comforts?"

The ribbing note in that question wasn't entirely friendly. A reminder to keep my guard well up, even if I saw reason for optimism.

"I realized what a long time it had been," I said. "And I thought you might be missing some of those comforts. When was the last time you got your hands on one of Baker's mince pies?" I held up the box tied with cloth that I'd picked up from the bakery before heading out here.

Carpenter's face brightened just as I'd hoped it would. When we'd been friends, I'd seen him down as many as five of those pies in the course of a meal. It was both a gesture of good will and a callback to the past times I wanted to get him talking about.

"Let me finish up here," he said. "I've got an oyster to hatch and another to plant. Do you want to help?"

The question felt like a test. I didn't want to, in the strongest possible terms, but I needed to win points with my former comrade, not lose them.

"Why not?" I said, as if I found nothing about his work unsettling. I set down the boxed pie and then my suit jacket on top of it, rolled up my sleeves, and forced myself to walk right up to the pod-shell-thing across from him.

"Grip it right here," Carpenter said, tracing a seam that ran along the ridge at the top of the casing. He dug his fingers into that narrow gap. I followed suit farther down, restraining a cringe at the cool slimy texture. "Now pull!"

He yanked the one side of the casing toward him, and I tugged on the other side at the same time. The thing split down the middle with a sputter of gas and a thicker stench like fermented seaweed. I dodged to the side as it crumpled by my feet.

A pale body with pearly skin lay in the slick remains of the casing: a young man, black-haired and slim, his eyes closed. Carpenter knelt down.

"It always takes the pearl-heads a while to come to," he said casually, and smacked the man's cheek a few times with the back of his hand.

The man's head listed to the side. Then his eyes fluttered open. He stared vaguely forward with a few slow blinks. His body twitched, and he turned to look at me. His dazed expression made my stomach clench. Whoever this man had been before, nothing remained of him now except a blank slate ready to receive orders.

"You, pay attention over here," Carpenter said with a loud clap. "I'm your boss until you get to the palace. Listen up."

The pearl-head's face swiveled toward him. Carpenter motioned him up, and the man pulled himself off the casing onto wobbly legs. Carpenter tossed him a burlap tunic. "Put that on. Then get yourself into the cart and sit down. The palace folks will give you a proper uniform when they decide what to do with you."

As the man absently pulled on the tunic, Carpenter strode to the cart where the headless body was lying. "Give me a hand?" he said to me.

My stomach balled tighter as I joined him. I could guess from the body's overall shape and the timing that I was looking at the part of Sally that the Queen hadn't put on display.

It wouldn't be her when Carpenter and Walrus were finished with her, just a dull-minded drone. The woman I'd bantered with before I'd left the Spades, who'd charged into the palace gardens last night ready to take on every Heart, had already left this body. The head that regrew in the watery chamber wouldn't be more than a facsimile of her looks, nothing of her spirit.

That knowledge didn't make me feel any less sick about grasping her shoulders to carry her with Carpenter to the platform.

He tucked the folds of the deflated casing around her until her body was completely hidden. Then he nudged the platform back into the sea. Walrus shifted into place to receive the casing and fix it to the equipment beneath the surface.

A bit of grit had stuck to my hands from Sally's body. I'd have given anything to wash them, but the cove's water hardly seemed any cleaner. At least I'd won those points with Carpenter. He brushed his own hands together and gave me a warm smile.

"Let's have that tart," he said.

"How long does the new head take to grow?" I asked as we headed to the back of the beach by the rocks, pretending an approving interest in his work.

"Depends on the body," Carpenter said. "If it's a weak one, or too young or too old, we don't bother at all. With the decent ones, it could be a week, maybe two, or anywhere in between. We've usually got a few down there at any given time. Can't always replace 'em as quickly as she removes 'em."

He snapped his mouth shut after that last word and glanced toward the water as if checking to see if Walrus might have heard that almost-criticism of the Queen. His co-worker hadn't yet resurfaced. Carpenter let out a chuckle as if it'd been a joke all in good fun. As if even jokes couldn't cost you your head these days.

The palace needed servants, and the Queen had the disturbing habit of running through them—and running them through—a lot more quickly than their natural lifespan should have been. Waste not, want not. Even the pearl-heads could be re-pearled if their bodies had held up, from what I'd heard.

"I'm glad to see you're well," I said carefully. I'd have had to take care with this subject even if I had really been here as a friend. "I have to admit one of the reasons I thought to come out here was, ah, concerns prompted by recent events. No ground feels completely secure when the atmosphere is constantly shifting, does it?"

I wasn't sure how much Carpenter knew about the Queen's proclamation this morning, but the tightening of his mouth told me he understood what I meant well enough. He gulped a bite of the pie, crumbs sprinkling his beard. "I make myself of use," he said, by which I figured he meant, there weren't many willing to do this job, so the Queen might not be in too huge a rush to displace him.

"You do indeed," I said, managing to hold back the dryness that wanted to creep into my voice. "I admire your ambition. It's only…" I glanced toward the water as he had. Still no sign of Walrus. I lowered my voice anyway. "I've heard a little talk about the previous Alice, saying she came out near this cove. That would have had to be before you had anything to do with this place, of course, but I'm not sure, when emotions are running high, all those details would be considered."

Carpenter paused in mid-chew. He swallowed, but he'd turned a bit sallow. "No questions have come my way," he said, seeming to gather his confidence. "Perhaps the suggestion has already been dismissed."

"Perhaps," I said, about to lead into my real gambit.

A faint splash brought both our gazes up. Walrus's gray head had broken through the water's surface. "Is he still here?" he asked in his ponderous voice, presumably meaning me.

"An old friend," Carpenter said. "The work's done, isn't it?"

Walrus let out a huff of breath. My skin prickled. I couldn't prod Carpenter with him listening. Especially when he was studying me with shadowed eyes.

"What's his business anyway?" Walrus muttered.

I gave him a smile and raised my hat. "Hatter. I do have a few that can work in the water, if you're ever so inclined."

He grimaced as if the thought disgusted him, but to my relief, he pushed away from the cove. He swam for a few strokes above water and then dove back down.

"He isn't a bad sort," Carpenter said after a moment. "Just not very interested in being company."

"Fair enough." I hesitated, waiting until I was sure Walrus wouldn't re-emerge, and then shook my head, making my tone as rueful as I could. "That story about Alicia is crazy anyway, isn't it? I expect I knew just about everything that went on back then, and she never left the city."

Hope lit inside me the second Carpenter's chest started to puff up. Even when he'd been a Spade, he'd never passed by the chance to one-up someone else if he could. I'd purposely exaggerated my confidence to provoke his self-importance—and apparently there'd been something on that subject to provoke.

"You didn't know so much as you think," he said with a smirk. "That last time she came through, she snuck out to the Checkerboard Plains. Asked *me* to show her the way to the train."

"The Checkerboard Plains?" I said incredulously, tamping down on my eagerness so it wouldn't show. "What would she have wanted out there?"

Carpenter shrugged, leaning back against the jagged rock and devouring another chunk of pie. "She was all mysterious about it, like she liked to be. I got the impression the idea came from something she saw or heard while she was in the Otherland, but she didn't say what. Not that it matters now, does it?"

His tone darkened on that last question. I laughed as casually as I could. "If it didn't back then, I'm sure it doesn't now."

Something she'd seen in the Otherland—something from one of the previous Alices who'd traveled to Wonderland, the same way Alicia's notes had directed Lyssa? The information was a start. At least we'd narrowed down the scope of any investigations we took on.

I had enough wits not to leave the moment I'd gotten that answer. "Is it true the orangeberries grow better out here?" I asked, and let us ramble through another half hour of meaningless conversation.

The sun brushed the surface of the sea, and Carpenter stood up.

"It's getting late," he said. "A long walk back to the city. I could give you a ride as far as the edge of the palace grounds if you don't mind joining me and my pearly friend in the cart."

The cart where the body of a friend had been lying just an hour ago. A creeping sensation ran through my nerves. But it would be ridiculous to turn an offer like that down if I wanted him to believe I was at ease with his current line of work.

"Perfect," I said, girding myself. "Thank you for the lift."

The sky was stark black with a scattering of stars by the time I reached the hat shop. I hustled up the stairs to the apartment, trying to be both quick and quiet. It turned out neither mattered that much.

Doria was curled up in the wing chair by the table, her hands circling a cup of tea. The smile she gave me managed to look accusing—and a little bleary.

"You said you wouldn't be home too late," she said, waving the half-full cup at me. The milky liquid nearly sloshed out.

"I believe I said I *hoped* I wouldn't be back too late," I said, coming over to lean on the back of the chair. I tugged one of the braids mixed in with her hair, and she made a face at me. "You didn't have to wait up."

"I missed the main excitement yesterday. I wanted to have a front row seat if anything interesting happened tonight." She cocked her head at me. "Did you get some answers?"

"I think so," I said. "But nothing all that exciting. Sorry to disappoint you."

She sighed and motioned to the dish rack, where another teacup was drying. "Lyssa meant to wait up too, but I had to order her to go upstairs after she almost fell asleep on the stool."

Of course our looking-glass girl would have insisted on washing her dishes even then. "She's been through a lot in the last day and a half," I said. "I'll give her the news, such as it is, tomorrow. Now I'm ordering *you* to bed. Off with you!"

"Yeah, yeah," she muttered around a yawn.

As she headed up, I turned on the alarm device Theo had given us and pointed it at the apartment's front door. Then I ordered myself to my own bed. It'd been a couple of long days for me too.

After all those years, it was hard to imagine I'd once slept in this bed every night. Remembering Lyssa's morning greeting with a grin and a flicker of heat, I pulled off my tie. I did have actual pajamas around here somewhere, didn't I? I hadn't bothered with them in years since I'd always been reset back into that damned suit anyway.

There, folded in the drawer in the base of the wardrobe. They were nicer than I remembered, a silky fabric with purple and green stripes.

I burrowed my head into the pillow and let the memory of Lyssa's presence sitting next to me on the bed paint over the images of the Oyster Cove and Carpenter and the cart ride partway home. The taste of her lips. The heat of her hand moving down my—

I jerked awake without any sense of having fallen asleep. The sheets had tangled around my legs. A voice was hollering loud enough to carry from the street outside…

That was the Queen's voice.

My pulse hitched, and I scrambled out of bed in an instant. The light drifting into the hall was only a touch brighter than dawn's pallor. I hurried down to the living area with its large windows.

Looking outside, all my nerves jolted with the thought that our world had been reset after all. The rows of guards, the Queen on her throne, it was all as it had been yesterday morning.

Except not. As my heartbeat thudded on in my ears, I remembered that the sun had been higher when I'd watched this horrible spectacle with Lyssa and Doria. The sky had been unclouded.

And the head on the pike brandished in the midst of the parade had been Sally's, not this one with the mane of faded hair I recognized as Smith's.

Oh, no. He must have offered—and of course our White Knight had accepted.

The Queen didn't sound anywhere close to appeased by the fact that the Spades had answered her challenge. "This is barely a start," she was ranting, waving her hands from her ported throne, her face flushed ruddy. "Where are the rest of the Spades? How will they atone for the crimes they've committed against all of us? Yesterday I took one. Today I take two. The deal remains the same. Let's see how long they can pretend to be heroes."

Even as she spoke, one of the guards was grabbing a man who'd been watching the parade with his door cracked ajar. An elderly woman already lay bound behind the throne.

"Oh, God," Lyssa murmured.

I startled. I'd been so focused on the Queen that I hadn't heard our Otherlander coming downstairs. She stood a couple steps back from the window, a caution I appreciated even as I wanted her all the way on the other side of the room. The color had drained from her face. Horror shimmered in her eyes as her gaze shifted to meet mine.

"Everyone thought she'd stop with this tactic if she got what she wanted yesterday—if the Spades proved they wouldn't let other people die in their place," she said in a thin voice. "Smith gave himself up to buy us some time. But she doesn't care. She's going to keep at it anyway. He didn't change anything, and we're still in the same awful position we were before."

I rubbed my mouth as if that would draw the right words out of it to set Lyssa's mind at ease. But *my* mind wasn't remotely at ease. My spirits were sinking.

What I'd done yesterday hadn't been enough either. There were too many people I didn't know how to protect.

"Yes," I said. "It appears we are. Let's see what we can do about it."

CHAPTER SEVEN

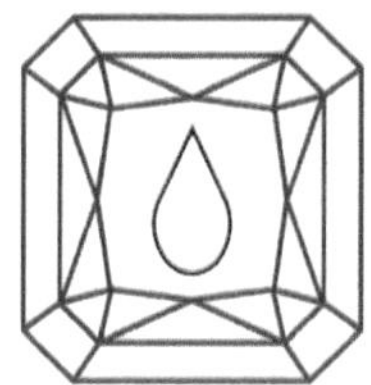

Lyssa

I walked into Theo's office and nearly ran right into him as I pushed past the door.

"Lyssa," he said, touching my shoulder to steady me and then nodding to acknowledge Hatter, who'd come in right behind me. With the sleeves of his white button-up pulled straight over his muscular forearms and his dark curls slicked back from his face more forcefully than usual, he looked like he meant business about whatever he was preparing to do.

He gave my shoulder a light caress before letting me go. "I was about to summon another meeting. You can come with me."

"No," I said, the words spilling out in a rush. "We don't need a meeting. There's only one thing to do that makes any sense."

"All right," Theo said, calmly enough, taking a step back to give us room to really come in. "And what's that?"

I sucked in a breath. "Smith turning himself in didn't stop the Queen's plan. She's obviously going to keep grabbing random people until she's convinced she's gotten all of the Spades, or at least most of you. And maybe me too." That last bit made my throat constrict. I forced my voice out. "Sacrificing someone else isn't going to help, and you said yourself that you're not in a position to take her on head-to-head yet. Hatter got a lead—we know where my grand-aunt went exploring outside the city. I'm going to track down those artifacts, and then we'll stop the Queen from killing anyone else."

I couldn't see another head waved on a pike. I couldn't watch her slaughter Wonderland's citizens to prove her warped and vicious point. Not when there was a chance the tools to defeat her were right here, waiting to be uncovered.

Theo's gaze snapped to Hatter. "You found out something about Alicia's travels?"

Hatter's mouth twisted. He hadn't been quite as committed to this plan as I was. I got the sense he'd come to the Tower with me at least as much to keep an eye on me as to provide support.

"Carpenter said the last time she came to Wonderland, she went out to the Checkerboard Plains," he said. "I've got no reason to doubt him—he said she asked him to help her get on the train. That's all he knew, though. It's a still a lot of terrain to cover, without a very clear idea what we're looking for."

"But there's got to be something important out there," I put in. "Either she found the ring there, or something to do with the ring… Whatever she found, it made her feel like too much was riding on her —that's why she ran back home and never came back."

I wouldn't falter like that. If my childhood had taught me anything, it was how to stand steady even while everything around me was falling apart. And this was about saving dozens, maybe hundreds, of lives.

"The Checkerboard Plains would make sense," Theo said. "It's a confusing place, often difficult to keep your sense of direction—ideal for hiding things the Queen would hope no one ever discovered."

"Ideal for us ending up lost and without anything more than we started with," Hatter said, but he didn't sound too set in his pessimism. He *had* come with me rather than trying to argue me out of my plan.

"We have to try," I said. "If there's something in the Checkerboard Plains that the Queen is afraid of, we *need* it. Once we're out there, maybe I'll be able to figure out more as we go—maybe I can connect the dots from things Aunt Alicia said that I didn't realize the full meaning of at the time. It's not as if I can head home and look for more clues there instead."

Even as I laid out my case, my heart thumped faster. I didn't actually like the idea of rushing out onto unfamiliar terrain—terrain Theo had just admitted was difficult and confusing—with only that vague plan. This was Wonderland. Almost *anything* could be waiting for us out there.

But *because* this was Wonderland, I also had people here on my side. Knowing that helped balance out my uncertainties.

As if he'd read my mind, Theo's next words were, "You can't go on your own. I'll go with you—the legends I've heard may help guide us too. And we might need more help than that. I'll gather a small team, assemble a few devices that may be useful along the way, and we'll set off."

I exhaled in relief. "All right. Good. We should leave as soon as possible, right? How long do we have before the Queen fills her dungeon if she keeps taking more people each day?"

Theo frowned. "I don't know its exact capacity—and she may decide 'full' is a subjective term. I wouldn't count on more than a week."

Seven days to save Wonderland. Great. But it was a heck of a lot better than no chance at all. "Is there anything I should pack to bring along?" I asked. "I don't know what to expect out there."

"We can pack together," Hatter said. "I'm coming."

I glanced at him, startled. He crossed his arms over his chest in a defiant pose that I guessed was aimed at Theo, because a faint smile crossed his lips when he met my eyes. "I'm not sticking around here while you do all the work."

He turned to Theo. "And we'll bring Doria too. The way things are going, it'll likely be safer out on the Checkerboard Plains than it will be here in the city the next few days. The Knave already dislikes me. I wouldn't put it past him to 'randomly' choose her for the dungeon next."

If he'd expected an argument from the White Knight, he didn't get one. Theo just smiled in return.

"It's settled, then. Meet the rest of us on the road at the Plainsward end of town as soon as you're ready."

The road Hatter, Doria, and I took out of the city didn't look quite as pristine as the one that went by the pond and the mushroom farm. By the time we reached the last few buildings, the orange paint on the cobblestones was worn down and dull. I sidestepped a couple of gaps where old stones had been dislodged and not yet replaced.

"I thought you said people walked everywhere in Wonderland," I said to Hatter. "Now there's a train?"

"The train only circles through the Checkerboard Plains," Hatter said. "Not many have any reason to go out that way these days. Some Clubbers used to take day trips for a little novel excitement, but the dip where the tracks veer closest to the city is still an hour's hike from here. Even those who could be bothered to make the trip got bored after we found ourselves stuck in that one day."

"*I've* never been out there before," Doria said. "Dad wouldn't let me."

Hatter gave her a narrow look. "You get into enough trouble in the city. Anyway, I'm taking you now, aren't I?"

"True, true. I shouldn't complain." She grinned at me. "And I'm getting to go as part of a special secret quest." Her voice lowered. "Do you really think we're going to find some kind of weapon out there that'll take down the Queen?"

I wished I could answer that question a little more confidently. "I hope so," I said. "If it's out there, I'll do whatever I can to find it."

That reply seemed to satisfy her more than it satisfied me. She bounded on ahead, faster when a group of four figures came into view under the shade of a tree with leaves so vibrant they might as well have been carved out of jade.

"Chess!" I said, a smile springing to my face despite my nerves at the sight of the brawny guy. Theo hadn't said who he wanted to bring for this mission-of-sorts, but I couldn't have asked for any additional company I'd have wanted more.

Chess gave me a broad smile in return. "I wouldn't miss an adventure like this for anything, lovely."

Doria had planted herself between our two other comrades: the redheaded twins. "You guys are coming too? This is going to be amazing!"

"It's still a covert operation," Theo said, his eyes amused but his tone serious. "Let's move out before our gathering can draw any attention. Just a group of friends off to have a mid-day picnic." His eyebrow quirked upward.

I did actually have food packed in the canvas bag that I'd slung over my shoulders like a knapsack. Hatter had bundled up bread and cheese and meat—and of course a few scones—in sheets of waxy paper he'd told me would keep them cool and fresh. I was going to assume he knew what he was talking about, or all of Wonderland would have died from food poisoning by now. He obviously hadn't thought it was likely we'd come across any restaurants or grocery stores out on these plains.

Other than that and a couple changes of clothes, I hadn't brought much. The ruby ring weighed against my breastbone as we set off along the road. It was the most important thing I carried.

"How often does the train come by the city?" I asked. "And how big are the Checkerboard Plains anyway?"

"The squares are always shifting," Theo said. "It could take anywhere from hours to a day to circumnavigate the entire area. But the train has a habit of arriving when passengers are waiting to board."

That made about as much sense as anything in Wonderland did.

After a while, we veered off the main road onto a narrower dirt one that wound through a stretch of scattered trees. Theo motioned us deeper into the sparse woods to avoid a stand of enormous flowers like the ones I'd chatted with before near the pond. The fewer witnesses, the better.

We came out onto a flat stretch of land with shimmering neon-green grass. A dark haze hung over the landscape in the distance like a thundershower, which maybe explained the ozone-y scent that laced the crisp breeze. And just a short walk ahead of us curved an arc of train tracks, gleaming with a coppery tint over black mica-laced pebbles.

There was no sign of anything like a platform or a station. I squinted along the line of the tracks. "Where does it stop?"

Chess chuckled. "It doesn't. Ever. If you want to ride the Plains train, you'd better be ready to hop right on."

Oh. This was going to be… interesting.

One of the twins pointed to a streak of violet smoke that was streaming across the sky in the distance. "Looks like it's on its way."

I adjusted the straps of my bag on my shoulders, making sure my cargo was secure. Doria bobbed eagerly on her feet as she peered off in the direction the train was arriving from. The other twin pulled a dumpling out of his vest pocket and ate it in a few quick bites.

The rumble of an engine and the rattle of wheels moving over the tracks reached my ears. A dark brown shape came into view, speeding toward us. The engine looked as if it'd been carved out of mahogany and then polished. The cars behind it, all four of them, were made out of the same material, I realized as it barrelled toward us.

It was coming awfully fast. A nervous shiver ran over my arms. The most dangerous part of this journey might be setting off on the journey in the first place.

"Get ready," Theo said. "Dee and Dum, you can handle yourselves —and make sure you catch up Doria along the way. Hatter, you're the fastest. You and I can make our way on first, and then—"

"Look what we have here," a sharp hiss of a voice interrupted.

The seven of us spun around. My heart lurched against my ribs.

The Knave of Hearts, with his blunt shark-like face and heart-shaped helm, was emerging from the forest with three of the Queen's guards behind him. All of them carried swords or daggers. My arm twinged in memory of a blade like that slicing through my flesh.

The Knave sneered at us, revealing several jagged teeth. "I heard Hatter was interested in the Checkerboard Plains. And how much company you've brought with you!"

Hatter muttered a curse in which I thought I caught the name "Carpenter." His former friend must have reported their conversation to the palace. I braced myself, not sure what to do. I wasn't equipped to fight, but there wasn't anywhere to run to.

At least we could be glad the Knave hadn't anticipated running into a group this large, or he might have brought even more guards with him.

"I wasn't aware it was a crime to take a ride on a train," Theo said, stepping forward with an air of total authority. "Or were you simply meaning to see us off?"

The Knave waggled his sword at Theo. "I knew I'd catch you at something eventually, Inventor. You think we can't suss out there's treason afoot?" His gaze shifted to me, chilling my skin. "And who is this? Not a face I recognize. She wouldn't be an Otherlander, would she? The one the Queen has expressly demanded be turned over to her care?"

A whistle shrieked, almost right behind me. I flinched. The train roared toward us, and Theo shouted over its racket.

"Dee, Dum, Chess!"

The three of them sprang forward without a second's hesitation. Chess blinked out of view and back into it right behind one of the guards, knocking the blade from his hand with a powerful blow. Dee lunged for another and hurled him with his elastic arms, sending the man tumbling head over heels into the forest. Dum aimed a kick at the third soldier that propelled him up into the branches of a tree.

Hatter tugged me toward the train, waving to Doria too. "I'll get you on," he said, and dashed ahead, down the length of the train.

Apparently he was as quick on his feet as he was with his hands. In a few swift strides, he'd reached the car second from the end, which had an open walkway along its side. He caught a hold of a rung, swung himself up, and leaned over the railing with his arms outstretched.

The Knave was letting out a furious shout behind me, and someone else yelped in pain, but I couldn't risk looking back. Doria reached Hatter first as the train propelled him past us. He grasped her hand and heaved her onto the walkway beside him. I threw myself forward just in time to snatch hold of his reaching fingers.

My grasp wasn't solid. Hatter yanked me up, but my feet only landed on the walkway's edge. I teetered for an instant, and then a hook snagged the railing beside me.

Theo had tossed an odd jointed rope at the train. At a jerk of his arms, it contracted, launching him toward the train with the same elastic spring as Dee's arms. He caught me against his body just before I might have fallen. His momentum carried both of us into safety. With his arm around me, he looked back toward the fight.

The twins were already hurtling toward us. Dum bounced into the air on his flexible legs and landed at Hatter's other side. Dee flipped over and pushed off his arms with a similar effect. He soared right over the railing.

Chess was still flickering in and out of sight. He ducked under the sweep of the Knave's sword and dodged the jab of a knee.

"Chess!" Theo hollered. The train was rushing onward. We were leaving him behind. The other soldiers were scrambling back to help their commander.

Chess glanced back at us with a wild grin. He vanished and reappeared just long enough to slam his fist into the Knave's face. The Knave stumbled backward, and Chess slipped away into the air.

When he popped into view a second later, he was sprinting after the train. He was already a full car-length behind, and the gap was growing with each thud of my pulse.

Theo whipped out the rope he'd used to pull himself on, but the end pattered to the ground just out of Chess's reach. Shit. My hands clenched around the railing, and suddenly the jolting of the walkway beneath my feet and the thick smell of polished wood and metal flooded my senses. I clenched harder.

Just slow down. Just for a second. Please, slow down.

Heat flared beneath my shirt. The ring felt as if it were burning my skin. I winced, but I held on—and by some miracle, the engine eased off. The rumble faded.

Chess closed the distance between him and the final car in the space of a breath. He sprang onto the back with a whoop of victory.

The Knave and his men were charging after him. I jerked my hands from the railing, shattering the pressure that had been building inside me. The train lurched forward at its previous speed. And I realized everyone around me was staring at me. Well, at my chest.

I glanced down in time to see a faint reddish light glowing through the fabric of my dress. In a blink, it had dulled, at the same time as the ring had stopped burning. I let out a shaky breath.

Chess strolled out of the car behind us onto the walkway. "That was a bigger trick than I expected you could pull off, Inventor," he said with his unshakeable grin.

"I can't take any credit," Theo said, his gaze still fixed on me. "It was all Lyssa."

CHAPTER EIGHT

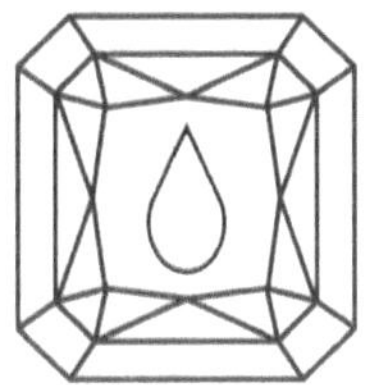

Lyssa

"Dee!" Doria said as we filed off the walkway onto the much less precarious floor inside the train car. "One of them got you."

A thin gash ran across the one twin's bicep just below the short sleeve of his shirt. He shrugged with an easy smile. "Just a nick. Nothing to worry about."

"It's still bleeding," Dum muttered, checking his brother's arm. "Good thing the White Knight asked me to bring the rest of that salve I picked up."

"It's totally fine," Dee said, but Dum ignored him. He produced a tube from his pack and dabbed the cut with the same green-and-white gel Theo had used on my wound. So he'd been the one to find that for me—on Theo's request.

And now I knew how to tell the twins apart even when they weren't using their super-powered limbs. Dee was the friendly one, and Dum was the standoffish one.

The other guys had started to amble through the train car. High-backed seats lined both sides of the space, wide enough to seat two or maybe three very skinny people, although no one was sitting in any of them right now. They were made of the same mahogany as the outside of the train had appeared to be, with padding that looked like moss in both color and texture. The smell of wood polish tickled my nose. The rattling of the rails beneath us sounded ominous in the quiet.

"Is it just us?" I asked. "There won't be any other passengers?"

"No one in the caboose," Chess reported.

"We might as well check the other two cars," Theo said. "But few have much use for the Plains train these days."

That fit what Hatter had said about it. We ventured across the short bridge of wooden slats between our car and the next, passed through another space identical to the one we'd left, and then moved on to the one right behind the engine. I picked up a lacy pink scarf that had been left behind on one of the seats. From before the Queen had trapped time, I had to guess, or it would have vanished back to its original place with the passing of the day. Did the original owner even remember she'd lost it?

Something Theo had said came back to me, about the train arriving when passengers were waiting. "Will the Knave be able to catch up with us?" I asked. "Is there some kind of magic that'll let him hop on this train before we've come all the way around?"

"I don't think he can contrive to end up on this one," Theo said. "But there may be echoes of this train running along the same track—and the palace has other resources for traveling. We'll need to stay on guard. I don't think he's likely to give up the chase."

All at once, the sunlight that had been shining through the windows blinked out, leaving us in darkness. Lights crackled on overhead along the length of the ceiling. Beyond the windows, I couldn't make out anything but black.

"What the hell was that?" I said.

Chess dropped onto one of the seats and stretched out his legs. "We've passed into a new square. They switch between night and day all the way across the plains—like a checkerboard. The way we name things here may not always sound sensible, but there's still plenty of sense to the names."

We were going to keep jumping from light to dark and back again, then? That should be… interesting. I slid onto the seat across from him and peered outside. It was hard to make out anything even up close with the inner lights reflecting off the glass. How was I supposed to tell whether any location out there looked promising?

Well, I guessed Aunt Alicia would have had the exact same problem when she'd come out here, and she'd found the ring anyway.

Dum frowned and leaned his arm against the back of a nearby seat. "Are we going to talk about the way the Otherlander messed with the train? It doesn't normally slow down like that." His eyes settled on me warily.

Oh, right. I guessed I couldn't blame him for wanting answers even if I didn't have any.

"I don't know what I did," I said. "I just wanted it to slow down enough for Chess to catch up, and it… did. It felt like this ring might have helped." I pulled the ruby ring from under my shirt to show him and anyone else who hadn't seen it before. "This ring is the whole reason we're out here—I think my grand-aunt, Alicia, found it out here, and maybe something else. It's obviously got some magic of its own."

"A magic I highly appreciate," Chess said, beaming at me.

"That's so cool!" Doria took the seat beside me. "Can I give it a try?"

"Doria," Hatter said with a warning note.

She rolled her eyes at him. "I won't do anything crazy."

"I think it's better if we don't experiment with the train's speeds any more than we already have, unless it seems necessary," Theo said, gently but firmly. "Especially when we don't know how close the Knave and his men may be at our heels."

"I don't have any idea how it works anyway," I told Doria when she crinkled her face with disappointment. "It might not have done anything if I hadn't been so worried."

"Still pretty amazing," she said.

Hatter opened up his bag. "Why don't we have lunch while we wait for the next daylight square? The way things are going, we may not get many good chances to refresh ourselves."

He passed me and Doria sandwiches he'd put together, and the others dug into their own supplies. My stomach churned around the bites of fresh bread, cheese, and ham.

What if I couldn't figure out where we should go from here even when we were in daylight again? I'd dragged six people off on this uncertain mission, and now we had the most vicious of the Queen's guards after us too.

Chess nudged my calf lightly with his foot. "Cheer up, lovely. Focus on the fun parts of the adventure, and the rest can be an afterthought."

I didn't think my brain was programmed to work like that, but I shot him a small smile anyway.

Not long after I'd finished my sandwich, the view outside the window snapped into full daylight just as quickly as it had turned to night. My chest loosened a little as I studied the landscape outside the window. The "square" we were traveling through was all grassy hills, each with a single tree at their peak. Weird. Beyond the hills lay another dark haze I realized must be a patch of night.

The train jostled us as the tracks veered up one of those slopes, and then I could see across what might have been the entire Checkerboard Plains, all laid out in squares of light and dark. Some of the bright squares held thick forests, some massive lakes, others fields as flat as a pancake. Far off in the distance, several squares away, I spotted a taller hill that curved over on itself like a wave frozen just before it crashed.

The moment my gaze caught on it, my pulse stuttered. There was something so familiar about that odd image…

Aunt Alicia's pictures. She'd hung her framed sketches all around her house. I hadn't known what to make of that shape when I'd noticed it before, but I could picture the delicate charcoal lines where that drawing was mounted in the upstairs hall.

Only the angle had been a little different, hadn't it? As if she were remembering looking up at it from much closer.

"That hill," I said, pointing so energetically that my finger tapped the window. "Is there something special about it?"

Theo leaned over to consider it. "Not that I'm aware of. Why?"

"Aunt Alicia drew it. I saw it in one of her pictures in the house. I think she must have gone all the way out there before, or at least gotten pretty close. And it must have stuck in her memory." Because something important had happened out there? My heartbeat had evened out, but it was still thumping along faster than before with a quiver of hope. "We have to go there. Will the train take us that far?"

"It'll loop around the plains. I'd imagine we can get off fairly close to that spot. It'll just take some waiting." Theo smiled at me, but I thought his shoulders had tensed a little. Was he worried that I was wrong—that I really was leading them on a pointless mission?

The train rumbled across the countryside. We passed through another stretch of night, but this time I could make out stars glittering in the indigo sky overhead. A few of them swayed back and forth as if in some sort of dance. I felt a little proud of myself that I didn't even stare. It'd take more Wonderland weirdness than that to catch me off guard now.

We emerged from the darkness into a sunlit stretch of tall waving grass. The train's rattling intensified as the tracks led it over a bridge across a wide river lined with cattails that… looked like they might be actual cats' tails, striped or spotted fur and all. Okay, I might have stared a little at those. Then my gaze traveled along the rippling blue water to the hump of an island barely visible near the night haze of the next square.

A sudden burst of heat against my chest made me bite my lip. The ring was burning against my skin again. I tore my gaze away from the island, and the sensation faded. The second I looked toward it again, a fresh spot of heat seared my skin.

I'd been sure the wave-like hill was important, but how could I argue with the ring's reaction? The train was already whirring off the bridge and away. If we were going to investigate, we had to go *now*.

"There's something by that river," I said quickly, pushing out of my seat. "We have to get off."

Chess leapt to his feet immediately. On the other side of the aisle, the twins glanced at Theo. When he motioned them up, we all hustled to the car's door. This quest might have been my idea, but some of our companions still saw their White Knight as the leader. That was fine by me. I knew I wasn't exactly an expert on anything Wonderland.

"No hesitating; just jump!" Chess said, and did exactly that an instant later. Doria sprang after him. I took a deep breath and threw myself toward the tall grass.

My momentum slowed as I left the train behind, as if my body were moving from one plane of reality to another. I landed amid the grass with only a faint jolt through my knees. Four more thumps followed me.

"Where to from here, lovely?" Chess asked.

I motioned toward the far end of the square. "There was an island in the middle of the river, pretty far down. The ring reacted when I was looking at it, so I think that's where we need to go."

We fell into step in a loose procession, walking to the bank of the river and then along it. The ground turned moist and sticky beneath our feet, and the cattails at the edge of the water whispered against each other's fur. Within a few minutes, I was wishing I'd brought boots as well as my sneakers.

"Still finding the adventure fun?" Hatter asked Chess from where the two of them had ended up side by side just behind me.

"It's certainly a place full of fascinating sounds," Chess said brightly, with a squelch of his foot into a patch of mud.

The humid air was congealing against my skin. I rubbed the dampness from my arms. "I really hope this ring knows what it's talking about," I said. "This isn't—"

I set my foot down in a shallow silty dip in front of me, and the ground gave way completely.

My body plunged into thick cool muck. I snapped my mouth shut a second before the oozing dirt could have filled it. Then my head was under too, a slimy pressure against my face, my feet still sinking down and down as if I'd fallen into an endless sinkhole. Which maybe I had, it occurred to me with a spark of panic. Or maybe there was something worse than mud waiting for me down here. This was Wonderland, after all.

My arms had shot up as the ground had swallowed me. I groped at the mud around me, searching for something to hold on to, to pull me back up. A prickling burn spread through my lungs as they begged for air.

It might not matter how deep this hole was or what else lurked in it. I might be dead before I had to find out.

My arms flailed again—and my hand connected with something firm. Fingers closed around my palm. I gripped on as tightly as I could, and my rescuer heaved me upward with a sharp yank. My body traveled up through the wet earth with much more resistance than it'd plummeted. But at least I was going up now.

I swept my other hand through the muck and managed to grab hold of my rescuer's wrist. With another lurch, my head broke through the surface of the sinkhole. I spat and sputtered, clutching Hatter's muddy sleeve for dear life.

He was totally drenched in mud, from his spiky blond hair to his dress shoes. Only his hat, which appeared to have fallen to the side as he'd dived after me, remained untouched. As he hauled me the rest of the way out, Chess shifted to the side, his own arms tacky with dirt up to his elbows. The imprint of his fingers remained around Hatter's ankles.

They'd both dived after me, one and then the other. The swift and the strong. A good thing, too, or Hatter and I would both have been lost.

"Are you all right?" Theo said, hovering over us. His expression was taut with concern.

I spat out a little more mud. Hatter produced a handkerchief from his pocket and wiped his face on one side of it, leaving it nearly as muddy as the rest of him. He offered the untouched side to me. I took it gratefully, swiping at the worst of the grit. The mud had saturated my clothes—my hair felt leaden with it—ugh.

But it was hard to mind that too much when a minute ago I hadn't been sure I'd survive to see this minute.

"I'm okay," I said with a shaky breath, and then my arms threw themselves around Hatter of their own accord. I hugged him tight, not really caring that the collar of his jacket was getting my face muddier again.

"I suppose we'd better steer clear of the clear spots," he said in a dry voice, but he hugged me to him just as tightly.

I let go of him to grab Chess in a similar embrace. Chess chuckled and pressed a kiss to my forehead despite my current dirt-infused state. "No more taking side adventures without inviting us along first," he teased.

"Sounds good to me," I muttered.

Theo touched his hand to my head as if he needed that contact to be sure I really was all right. Then he strode ahead, giving the silty dip a wide berth.

"I'll take lead from here on," he said. "And everyone, hold on to this. I intend to make it back to the city with exactly the same number of people we started with."

He passed the end of his stretchy rope to me as I scrambled to my feet, and I passed it back down the line, keeping one hand loosely around it. Walking along in a rope chain felt very kindergarten, but I'd take that over drowning in mud any day, thank you.

My drenched clothes shifted against my body as I started walking. So gross. At least the mud shouldn't have had much time to seep into my bag. And maybe I could clean off my current outfit—and my hair—when we had to swim to the island.

By the time the river widened, the mud caked on me had dried into a crust that cracked and flaked off in bits of dust with every step. At least the sun baking down on us had warmed me up.

We treaded carefully through the thick grass right up to the bank. The cattails had thinned. We had a clear view of the island, floating there like a massive treed barge. It had to be twenty feet across and at least ten times as long.

The ruby ring burned beneath my shirt as if to say, "Good job; here we are!" I stepped forward to dip my foot into the water, deciding I'd rather walk in squishy shoes than take off my sneakers and expose my bare feet to whatever was down there, but Theo held out his arm to block me.

"It's surrounded by razorweed," he said, pointing. When I squinted, I made out dark sinuous lines wriggling just beneath the surface of the water all along the island's rocky shoreline.

"Razorweed?" I asked. Just from the name, I was going to assume that wasn't good.

"It can slice straight through bone," Dum said with a shudder. "I've never seen it myself before, but I know a man who lost all the fingers on one hand to a clump of it."

"Okay," I said. "So swimming isn't a great idea. How do we get over there? Whatever we're looking for is definitely on that island." According to the ring scalding my breastbone, anyway.

Dee cocked his head. "It's not that big a leap," he said. "I can toss you all over easily enough, then stand guard here. I don't know how you'll get back, though."

A smile crossed Theo's face for the first time since we'd set out. "I can handle things from there."

Dee planted himself on the edge of the river and intertwined his fingers to turn his joined arms into a sort of slingshot. "Shout if you see hide or hair of *anyone*," Dum told him, and his brother nodded before launching him into the air. Dum soared in a neat arc and landed at the foot of the island's nearest tree.

One by one, Dee propelled the rest of us over. I had to swallow a yelp as I careened through the air, but I managed to brace myself for a good landing, and Theo caught my arm before I could even wobble.

Closer to the island's edge, a faint sound reached my ears from the water, like hundreds of teeth gnashing. It rose and fell in time with the slithering of the razorweed. I shuddered and turned to peer between the trees.

Nothing stood out, but the ring blazed against my skin even hotter. Restraining a wince and watching the ground carefully, I set off into the pocket of forest.

Tall spindly shrubs had sprouted up around the trees. I brushed past one, and its round leaves twitched toward me, all of them opening to reveal human-looking eyes. Dozens of eyes, staring at me. A thinner leaf parted with the swipe of a tongue.

I nearly bit my own tongue. Holy shit, that was disturbing.

"They won't hurt you," Theo said. "I'd imagine they function like a scarecrow—designed to make you think twice about continuing."

Yeah, I could see how that could work. Even Doria looked a bit green around the gills taking in those plants.

I pushed on, clambering over a fallen log and dodging another sinkhole dip. A few steps later, I emerged in the midst of a thick ring of those staring shrubs. They surrounded a pool of water that was only seven or eight feet across but so deep I couldn't make out the bottom.

I had just enough time to register that, and then the staring shrubs started to shriek.

All around the pool, they leaned their unblinking eyes toward me and vibrated their leafy mouths with a sound that perforated eardrums. I clapped my hands over my ears, my nerves scattering. But while I stood there frozen, the shrubs didn't move, didn't do anything other than stare and shriek.

Like scarecrows, like Theo had said. Trying to frighten me off by giving the impression they were a threat when really there was nothing they could do.

The ring lay against my chest like a molten ball. This was where I was meant to be. I scanned the water for any sign of razorweed and stepped into the shallows by the edge.

The water swirled around my legs, cool but not unpleasantly so. Theo, Chess, and Hatter moved to follow me. Chess made a face as he sank in up to his knees. "By the lands, I do hate getting wet."

The comment struck me as so fitting for a man who could turn into a cat that the tension inside me cracked with a laugh. "Really?" I said. "How strange."

He grinned at me sharply as if he thought I might need reminding that his secret was meant to stay secret.

Hatter shook his head at both of us. "I should be the one complaining. I've got the nicest clothes here, and they're getting ruined twice over." He pulled his hat more securely down on his head.

"Wash them off, then," I said. A tugging sensation ran through my chest as I stared into the pond's depths. "I think I need to go down again. At least the coming back up should be easier here."

"Are you sure you want to be the one to do this?" Theo asked.

My gut clenched, but I nodded. I wasn't sure whatever lay down there would release itself to anyone without the ring, and the thought of handing the ring over made every particle in my body balk.

It was mine. It had lit up for *me.*

Theo didn't argue. "Then, in case the coming back up isn't so easy…" He handed one end of his rope to me. "Tie it around your waist. I'll hold onto the other end. Give it a hard tug if you need help swimming back up."

"Thank you." I tied the jointed rope and tested it to make sure it was secure. Then, dragging in enough air to fill my lungs, I jumped from the shallows into the dark center of the pool.

The water coursed over my dress and hair as I plunged down. When I slowed, I jerked my head and shoulders downward, pulling myself deeper with my arms. There was nothing around me but a haze of murky water, the debris so thick I couldn't see more than a foot in any direction.

Where was the bottom? I kicked and swept my arms again and again, my lungs starting to ache with fresh strain. Then my reaching fingers grazed a powdery surface.

I dragged my hands across the floor of the pond, and my other hand snagged on a hard edge. Even in the cool water, the ruby flared hot where it was floating beneath my shirt. A ruddy light glanced off the murk.

I curled my fingers around the edge of the object and yanked. Whatever it was held and then popped free. Wrapping my arms around the thing I'd retrieved, I righted myself and pushed off the bottom back toward the surface.

The guys were waiting to tug me back into shallower ground. I gasped, refilling my lungs, and held up the thing I'd unearthed to see it.

My lips parted. The shrubs around the pool kept up their shrieking, but I could barely hear it, and not just because my ears were full of water.

I was holding a piece of armor, like a fancy version of a chainmail vest. Strands of a shimmering dark gray metal wove together to form a garment that would have covered me from shoulders to stomach. They bent beneath my testing fingers, but those pliant fibers felt as hard as steel at the same time.

A crescent of rubies glinted across the chest, just above the swell that would accommodate my breasts. This was armor meant specifically for a *woman*.

"Wow," I said, but even as the word slipped out, my awe started to dim.

I'd found one of the artifacts the ruby responded to. It was beautiful and impressively made. But a piece of armor wasn't going to defeat a tyrant queen.

CHAPTER NINE

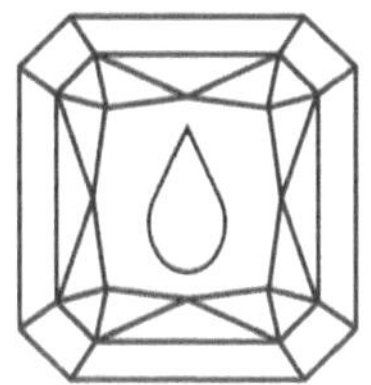

Chess

One of the upsides of traveling through wilderness with the Inventor was getting to sleep in a tent that was really more like a tiny cabin. Somehow our White Knight had been carrying the entire structure I'd just woken up in folded inside his pack along with food and other supplies. The twins had each carried one as well.

The panes of wood-like material that made up the walls were thick enough that no light penetrated them, not that there was much light out there anyway in this square of night. Only the crackle of a fire and the sizzle of what smelled like sausages told me and my stomach that it was morning.

One of the *downsides* of this trip was the variety of terrain we'd already had to deal with, and how much of it was wet. I really shouldn't have complained about stepping into the pool to my thighs. We'd had to outright swim across the awful river to get back to Dee, after the White Knight had cut away a swath of razorweed to clear a safe path with a whirling blade he'd also constructed himself.

I had the urge to shake myself just thinking about it, even though I was perfectly dry beneath my blanket. Perfectly dry and much hungrier than I was still sleepy. I kicked off the blanket and emerged from the cabin-tent-whatever I'd shared with the Hatter.

Lyssa was just emerging from the "girls" cabin where she and Doria had slept. The others were already sitting around the firepit we'd made by the light of the moon, the shining orb which appeared to have slid to one side of the sky and was now yoyoing its way back to the other.

Lyssa's hair shone like moonlight come to earth. When she'd rubbed the rest of the mud out of her pale waves during our swim, the dirt had taken most of the dye with it. She'd have to cover her head when we returned to the city, but I couldn't say I was sorry to see it back to its normal state. It was best when people looked like themselves.

Dum was the one cooking the sausages. Hatter was cutting a few apples into slices with swift flicks of a paring knife. "I'm sure your skills are up to more than that," I said with a grin as I sat down beside him. "Trim out a rosette or a bird like you adorn your many hats."

"If we were going to wear them rather than eat them, maybe I would," Hatter retorted.

Theo passed around halves of rolls toasted over fire, and then Dum the sausages and Hatter the apples. It was as satisfying a breakfast as I'd ever been able to count on. As I licked the mingled grease and apple tartness from my fingers, Lyssa shifted forward on the rock she was using as a seat.

"What do you think is our best route from here?" she asked. Her gaze traveled around the whole circle, but it stopped on the White Knight. He had shown he knew more about this place than the rest of us did. "We could keep walking across the Plains to head directly to that hill I saw, or we could go back to the train and keep going around."

"The Knave might have caught whatever train comes by next," Dum said. "Soon as we left the first one, we gave up the lead."

"But he doesn't know that," Dee said. He chuckled. "Let him chase all around the tracks thinking he's just behind us."

The White Knight slid the frying pan—which also folded, somehow or other—into one of the packs. "Dum raises a valid concern. It will take longer to reach the other end of the Plains on foot, but there's no way for the Knave or his guards to determine where or even if we got off the train. The question is whether we're safer facing him or dealing with the potential dangers the Checkerboard might present."

"Sinkholes and some weeds?" Doria said. "We handled those. I want to see what else this place can throw at us. I vote for walking."

"Of course you do," Hatter said, but he didn't look upset about it. I imagined he'd prefer to keep his daughter as far away from the Knave as possible, no matter what the rest of the Plains might have in store. He sighed and leaned back on his hands. "I'd say we walk too. We'll have more control over our route, more flexibility about how we deal with any problems we run into. Unless you know of some danger up ahead that we wouldn't want to face, White Knight?"

The last question came with a bit of bite, the way Hatter often talked to the leader of the Spades these days. Which side of him was more the real Hatter? This one who prickled at the White Knight's presence or the one who'd used to laugh with him and egg him on when I'd first stumbled into their rebellion?

"Nothing I'm aware of," the White Knight said. "But we should still stay on guard. Wonderland may be stretching itself a bit after so long in stasis."

"I'm happy to go by whatever way will take us to the place we're wanting to go," I said.

Lyssa smiled at me with an amused glint in her eye. "As long as it's over dry land?"

I grinned back. "I'll brave the watery depths again for you, lovely. I just can't say I'll like it."

When we set off, Lyssa had pulled her woven vest of armor over the bodice of her dress. The dusky gray metal gleamed almost as much as the embedded rubies did. She made a face when she saw me looking.

"I know I look a little ridiculous. It's just easier to wear it than to carry it."

"Not ridiculous at all," I said. "If we come across something that wants to stab you rather than drown you, I expect we'll all be glad you've got it on, too."

We didn't come across any trials of either sort as we marched across the moonlight terrain and passed into the next stretch of daylight. A few of the squares were willing to give us some peace. It wasn't the most pleasant going, though. The sun over this square had scorched the sky and the ground dry. Cracked earth gave off puffs of dust under our feet—and sometimes where we didn't step too. Sweat trickled down my back.

We walked at a diagonal to get us back in the row where Lyssa had spotted her special hill, which meant crossing that square took even longer. I think we were all ready to be done with the place by the time we reached the corner where two edges of cool dark haze touched just before another square of daylight. We gulped down a hasty lunch and walked on.

Vines slithered and bats flapped through the jungle beyond. After a few hours' hike, we emerged from at the top of a hill overlooking a wide plain flecked with wildflowers—and a small town.

The White Knight motioned for us to stop where we could stay hidden from view in the shade of a stand of trees. People swarmed around the scattered buildings, far more than could possibly have lived in that place. The sun caught on brilliant glints on their chests and the bright colors of their elegant clothes. Diamonds, I realized. Yes, there were the hunched beetle-like forms of the palace's silver air trolleys parked in a row beyond the buildings.

"What are they all doing there?" Lyssa asked.

As I squinted, two figures broke from the cluster of buildings onto the open plain, both of them wearing scarlet short pants and nothing else. Ah. Unicorn shook his sparkling mane, his glittering horn streaked red and his hooved hands raised to fight. Across from him, Lion let out a roar that shook the air all the way to where we were watching. His teeth flashed, and he lunged forward with a swipe of his massive paw. His claws raked a fresh gash across Unicorn's arm. His own shoulder was seeping blood where the horn had pierced it.

"The Lion and the Unicorn went fighting through the town," I murmured, and turned to Lyssa. "It's one of the many palace spectacles: pitting Lion and Unicorn against each other. The Diamonds never get enough of watching them fight. They must have decided the resumption of Time was as good a time as any for a temporary change in scenery."

"They do this all the time?" Lyssa said. "Don't the two of them mind all the fighting?"

"I suspect they got tired of it a long while ago," Hatter said. "But what the Queen says will be, will be as she said."

I couldn't have put it better myself.

Unicorn landed a punch with one of his hooves that made Lyssa wince. Lion reeled backward. Before the equine figure could even lower his horn, the feline one had sprung up again. He hurtled at Unicorn with another roar, and Unicorn didn't sidestep fast enough. Lion knocked him to the ground. They sprawled, the tawny man pinning the sparkly one beneath his paws.

Lion snapped out a command with a jerk of one hand. I didn't need to be able to hear his voice to know what he'd asked for. My body stiffened as a giddy lady among the Diamonds presented him with the victor's knife. He raised it triumphantly.

I should have looked away, but what can I say? I was stubborn as a cat. My limbs stayed tensed, a metallic flavor creeping through my mouth, as Lion lowered the blade to Unicorn's throat and sliced across it.

Not deep enough to kill. Just enough to mark him with that streak of blood that sprang up in an instant. A jabbing sensation shot through my ribs. Then I yanked my gaze away.

"But if he dies," Lyssa was saying.

"It's only a superficial wound," Theo said with a note of disgust. "A symbolic gesture, though a painful one. They'll seal it up with salve after they've all celebrated the victory."

"I expect Unicorn is used to it by now," I made myself say, my voice steady even if it felt detached from the rest of me. "He's the loser more often than not."

The crowd of Diamonds was milling out of the town around the two fighters, one still prone on the ground, the other standing with paws raised in triumph. Blood had spilled all down Unicorn's pale neck, but at least the knife was out of view.

"Let's leave them to their bloody fun," I said. "We've got better sport ahead of us, don't you think?"

No one seemed inclined to argue. We skirted the edge of the night-bound square until we'd come down the side of the hill. Then we ventured on toward Lyssa's cliff through a shallow grassy valley.

I strolled along at the back of the bunch, drinking in the bright floral air. Other than our company on the other side of the hill, this was my favorite square yet.

Lyssa drifted back to join me. She walked alongside me for a few minutes simply taking in the scenery. Then she said, quietly, "Are you all right?"

I hadn't hidden my reaction as well as I'd hoped. The lingering effects had all vanished now. I could give her a perfectly genuine grin and roll my answer lightly off my tongue.

"The people of the palace are like the food they serve there—so rich they give you indigestion. Nothing a brisk walk and a sweet breeze couldn't cure."

Lyssa nodded even though the slant of her mouth suggested she didn't totally accept my answer. She was getting keen, our Otherlander. I admired that canniness even as I wished she didn't notice quite so much about me.

"You Wonderlanders have quite the violent streak, huh?" she said. "Or maybe just the Hearts and the Diamonds do?"

"I can see how you might draw that conclusion," I said. "And I won't claim it's a false one. Are people in the Otherland so different?"

She grimaced. "Maybe not. Fair point. I guess everything else in this place is so different it's hard not to think the people should be too."

She paused, with a silence that tasted of words on the verge of being spoken. Her steps slowed to let the others gain more ground on us. I eased up on my pace to match hers. A flicker of pleasure passed through my chest at the thought that out of everyone here, she was taking me into her confidence. That she wanted to hear my thoughts on serious matters despite the fact that I so often turned them into a joke.

"Chess," she said finally, her voice low. "Are you *sure* the Spades didn't kill the prince? Maybe just one or two of them off on their own, without Theo's permission? The way they did it—Doria told me they cut off his head, like the Queen does to everyone else… If that's even true."

"It is," I said with a twist of my stomach. "I saw it myself." More years ago than I'd bothered to keep track, but the memory still rose up vividly behind my eyes. All that blood splashed across the gleaming marble floor. Prince Jack's head lying in the midst of it, golden curls stained red so they almost matched his mother's hair, face bruised and battered as if his killer had played a game of kickball with it.

The Queen had barely had time to scream. Barely time to cast about to find the rest of him. It'd been just a few minutes before midnight when I'd darted over to investigate the commotion. With a tick of the clocks and a jolt, we'd all ended up back where we'd started—and the Queen's youngest son had been wiped from this world.

I willed the images away. "All I can tell you with certainty is that I've never heard so much as a murmur suggesting anyone with the Spades knows more about the murder than I do," I said. "And the way it was done—it wasn't set up like an act of rebellion. They pretended they were trying to *steal* something from the palace—that broken vase—as if killing him were an accident, which is ridiculous anyway because it's not as if anyone could have stolen anything for more than a day before it hopped back home. Or a matter of minutes, in this case. It was nearly midnight."

"Maybe they didn't *want* the Queen to think it had anything to do with the rebellion," Lyssa suggested.

"That's possible," I said. "But I wasn't part of the Spades back then, and even I knew she'd blame them no matter what the evidence showed. I've often wondered if it wasn't carried out by a Diamond."

Lyssa's eyebrows shot up. "Why would a Diamond kill him?"

"Oh, the Diamonds have large appetites, and for many things other than food," I said. "Power, for example. If one of them saw a clear enough opening to grasping the crown, they'd take it like that." I snapped my fingers. "I could see them thinking the murder would destabilize the Queen's rule. She did dote on Prince Jack. Before he came, many said she couldn't have another child, you know—her others were all grown by the time he was born. Losing him definitely broke something in her. But possibly not the way they hoped."

Lyssa made a humming sound. She studied the grass for a moment before saying, hesitantly, "You were there, even though it was almost midnight. Did you stay out at the palace all the way into the night very often?"

"At least as often as I didn't," I said glibly.

She glanced up, turning that pensive gaze on me, as if she were trying to read answers to questions she couldn't quite bring herself to ask out loud. I smiled and picked up my pace to catch up with the others. "Let's not get left behind."

If she ever got around to asking those questions, I hoped she made sure she truly wanted the answers.

CHAPTER TEN

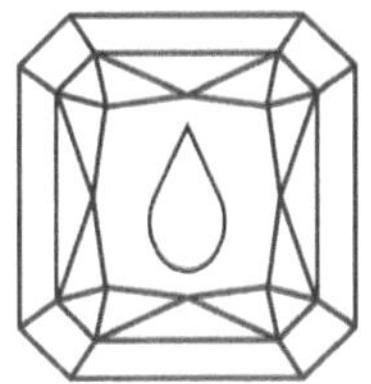

Lyssa

It was amazing how easily I could tell apart the twins now that I'd matched personalities to names. In the moonless, starless square of night we'd been trekking across for a couple hours at least, Dum was obviously the one who'd pulled a lantern out of his pack to help light the way, and Dee was the one making goofy shadow shapes in front of that lantern as they walked.

Theo had kept his place in the lead with a lantern of his own. We'd had to edge across a narrow bridge that connected two sides of a chasm that dropped so far down the lantern-light didn't reach the bottom. After that, we'd needed to circle around a bunch of thorny tumbleweeds that gouged their way across the rocky terrain in an endless ring. At the moment, the walking was pretty easy, comparatively speaking. Especially when I could make out the glow of the next daylight square getting brighter up ahead.

"And then I flung it so hard I'll bet they never found it again," Dee said with a laugh, finishing his recollection of a mission he and his brother had been part of, with shadowy animation to illustrate.

"How long have you two been with the Spades?" I asked. They looked younger than the other guys—I'd have guessed college freshmen age—but Hatter had told me that people in Wonderland didn't age much once they reached adulthood, and then only in fits and starts. You couldn't really judge just by looking.

"Since we were kids, pretty much," Dee said cheerfully. "Our talents showed up young."

"The White Knight didn't have us running missions," Dum put in. "He protected us."

"Yep. Because if the Queen got wind of those talents, we'd have been assigned to the Hearts' Guard in a snap." Dee raised his feet high as if imitating the springy steps his twin could make, his shadow-legs stretching into the distance. "Mom went to the White Knight, and he helped us keep the secret. Started teaching us all the stealthy Spades stuff at the same time."

Dum frowned as if he didn't like his brother telling me so much about their situation. I still got the impression he didn't like me all that much for whatever reason. "Although some of us remember those lessons better than others," he said.

Dee waved him off and shot a smile at me. "Dum thinks it's his job to worry about both of us. *I'm* actually the older twin, you know. Ten whole minutes."

I wasn't sure what Dum would have been worried about. When Dee had gone on the mission into the palace grounds with us a few days ago, he'd taken it seriously enough, as far as I could tell. Chess was proof that you could be a joker around here but still get the job done without losing your head.

"Well, thank you for coming along to help with this—" I started, and a burbling moan echoed through the air.

My mouth snapped shut, all the hairs on my arms standing on end. Our whole procession jerked to a stop, even Dee's eyes widening.

I'd heard that noise before. Hatter had called it a—

"Jabberwock," Chess said behind me in a deadpan voice. "Oh, how very delightful."

Another wavering groan rippled over us. Dum turned toward Theo. "Should we put out the lamps?"

"What direction is it coming from?" Hatter asked, his head swiveling.

The ground shook with a scrabble of claws that was *definitely* just ahead of us. The next moan sounded more like a roar. Theo spun around, his lantern swinging so the light swayed over us. "Run! Back to the spike-wheels."

I guessed those thorny tumbleweeds might give us some cover. We all dashed back the way we'd come, Hatter waving us on with his hand hooked around Doria's elbow, Chess touching my back to urge me faster.

Jaws snapped behind us with an unnerving rasp of scraping teeth. Somehow I didn't think my fancy metal vest was going to do much to protect me if that thing decided to chomp on me. Why couldn't it have been a full body suit of armor?

The monster's moan warbled over us so close it rustled my hair, with a wash of hot breath that stunk like raw meat drenched in vinegar. I coughed and pushed my legs faster. The jostling lantern light caught on the prickly edge of one of the tumbleweeds just ahead—and then on four figures charging toward us.

The Knave and his guards. They must have been tracking us, nearly caught up with us. My heart stuttered at the glimpse I got of that gray sharkish face, yellowed by the lantern's glow.

My feet stumbled over a ridge in the rocky ground, and Chess yanked me to the side, out of reach of one of the guards' swords. Hatter and Doria had veered off in the opposite direction.

The Knave slashed at Dum, who sprang out of the way a second too late. Blood welled along a thin line on his forearm as his lantern slipped from his grasp. It rolled across the ground, the light wheeling like the tumbleweeds did, and a massive form barreled into our midst.

The jabberwock looked like the deformed offspring of a dragon and a macaw. Red and gold feathers shuddered all over its bulky body. Its long sinuous neck reverberated with one of its burbling moans. Even the ends of its wings had glinting talons, but I was more nervous about the claws that cut into the stone beneath each splayed toe on its wide feet.

Theo jumped in front of me with a flash of his lantern. The

jabberwock's rectangular jaw detached from the rest of its snout to yawn open, revealing rows of jagged teeth like broken glass. Its head shot down, and it clamped those jaws shut around the torso of one of the guards.

The guy barely had time to gasp in pain before his voice cut off completely with a crunch of bones. My stomach churned. The jabberwock shook the now-limp body from side to side like a puppy with a toy and then hurled it off into the darkness.

We scrambled backward as it lunged at another of the guards, its nearest target. The man threw himself out of the way, but the creature veered to follow him at the last second. Its claws plunged into his chest with a gush of blood.

Oh, fuck. How the hell were we going to fight off that? I wasn't sure even an avalanche of thorny tumbleweeds would slow it down.

The jabberwock raked its claws through the guard's abdomen, scattering his innards across the ground. As if bored with its catch, it swung around—toward Hatter and Doria.

Every nerve in my body screamed in protest, and the ruby ring turned hot against my chest. The rubies on my vest gleamed with a faint glow. A tingling sensation ran through me, like the sense of certainty and power I'd felt in that brief moment when I'd slowed the train.

No. This monster would not kill my lovers, my friends, my allies. *No*.

Without thinking, I stepped toward it. "Lyssa!" Theo said, grabbing my arm, but I pushed him back.

"Jabberwock!" I called. My voice rang through the scattered light. "*Stop*."

Hatter had produced one of his hatpins that he usually put to work opening locks, holding it like a narrow dagger in front of him, his other arm extended protectively in front of his daughter. His face tightened and paled even more than it already had when the jabberwock paused. The creature's head swiveled around toward me.

Blood dribbled over the jabberwock's feathered jaw and streaked the ground beneath its feet. Its narrow eyes burned with a violet glow. My pulse thudded hard, but I took another step toward it and another, holding out my hand. The ring flared hotter; the rubies glowed brighter. The sense of sureness flooded me, taking the edge off my fear.

"Jabberwock," I said in a quieter voice. "Stand down. We're not your enemy."

The creature turned its whole body toward me with a swish of its tail. Its head dipped down toward my hand, but so slowly I didn't flinch. Theo had come up beside me. From the corner of my eye, I saw him stiffen. Chess sucked in a startled breath. Across from us, Hatter simply stared.

The jabberwock bumped its snout against my fingers. A whiff of that sour meaty smell wafted over me. Swallowing hard, I gave the beast a light scratch just above its nostrils like I might have with a horse. Never mind that this thing was twice as tall as the biggest horse I'd ever seen and outfitted with much sharper appendages. It had responded to something—to the ring? To the vest? To both in combination?—and that was all that mattered.

"Thank you," I said. "Now you go, and leave us—"

A figure barreled out of the darkness, sword raised over his blunt head. I yelped, and the jabberwock wrenched away just in time to prevent the Knave from delivering a killing blow. As it was, his blade cut through the creature's neck with a spray of orange-gold blood.

The jabberwock shrieked and whipped toward its attacker. Its legs wobbled under it. The Knave might kill it after all.

A lump of guilt clogged my throat despite the monster's carnage. It was my fault; he never would have gotten that strike in if I hadn't lulled it. But Theo was yanking me away, and I had to follow him. If the jabberwock won its duel with Knave, I wasn't so sure I could calm the beast again if it turned on us afterward.

And if the Knave won, we definitely didn't want to stick around for him to turn his sword on us.

Footsteps pounded around me. It was hard to make out much except a shaky view of the landscape just ahead as Theo's lantern jostled in his grasp. "Do we have everyone?" I asked, taking a quick glance around. There was Hatter and Doria. Chess was still right behind me.

"Pulling up the rear!" Dee called, with a flash of the lantern he must have scooped up, and I could tell from his buoyant tone that his twin was with him.

All we had to do was put enough distance between us and the two vicious creatures behind us to make sure the victor of the battle didn't find us. Easy peasy. Ha.

The muscles in my calves ached from the mad dash toward the tumbleweeds and now this new marathon. The uneven rocky ground stung the soles of my feet through my sneakers. I pushed myself faster anyway. The glimmer of the next daylight square came into view up ahead, expanding and brightening as we raced toward it.

A groan burbled up in the distance, trailing off with a painful gurgling. A shiver ran through me. I was pretty sure I knew who'd won the fight.

We burst from the darkness and nearly tumbled right over the jagged edge of a gully. Theo caught my hand and Chess my waist as we teetered on the crumbling rock.

A forest covered the landscape all around us, but the trees were so narrow and pointed they only provided streaks of shade from the sun glaring overhead. To our right, the woods stretched out over what appeared to be reasonably flat ground, the vegetation more sparse there. To our left, it dropped away steeply into a valley clotted with those narrow trees and other vibrant greenery.

My head reeled with the abrupt transition from darkness to light, open plain to forestland. The smell of blood lingered in my nose—had it gotten onto my clothes? My gut lurched at the thought. Images of the bodies the jabberwock had mangled darted through my memory.

But I couldn't say it was necessarily a more brutal monster than the Knave who was still on our trail.

"We can move faster on even terrain," Theo said, easing back from the gully.

As my gaze traveled down into the valley, the ring under my shirt heated with fresh energy. I inhaled deeply. Dry piney air filled my lungs.

I could do this. I could keep going.

"I think there's something down there," I said. "Another artifact, maybe. And it'll be harder for the Knave to spot us in the denser forest, won't it?"

I glanced around at my companions. They all hesitated, the three guys I knew best looking back at me with expressions that appeared a little dazed. Theo recovered himself first.

"If you feel there's something down there, then down we'll go. Quickly, everyone."

We hustled along the edge of the gully to a rough path that allowed us to scramble and skid through the brush rather than tumbling right down. After the first several feet, as the trees closed in more densely overhead, the slope evened out a little. We hiked on, needing to hold onto the branches around us less tightly than before. A drone of insect life hummed around us. The sun continued to glint between the tall peaks of the trees.

"There," I said, wiping sweat from my brow. "This isn't so bad."

"What the heck did you do back there?" Doria burst out. "You walked right up to the jabberwock—and it let you *pet* it."

"It was pretty fucking incredible," Dee said.

Oh. Right. *That* was probably why the guys had been looking at me so strangely.

I rubbed my mouth. "I don't know," I said. "It was like with the train. I just… felt I should do it, and the ruby got hot, and so far following it has worked out. There wasn't any other way I could have stopped it from charging at you two." My gaze slid from Doria to Hatter.

"I've never seen anything like it," he said, his tone dry but his eyes warm. "I think you might be able to challenge Chess for the title of maddest one here."

Chess harrumphed. "No one is ever going to top me for madness," he said breezily. He brushed his hand over my hair, and his voice softened. "It was quite a sight."

"Another testament to the ruby's power," Theo said.

Dum let out a sharp breath. "If only it worked on the Knave—or the Queen—too."

I touched the vest where the ring was tucked behind it. "Yeah, I definitely didn't get any impression I could tame *him*."

"Maybe the artifact we unearth down here will lend a hand with that conundrum," Chess said.

"If nothing else, I'm glad to get a breather after all that," I said, skirting a rock that jutted into our path.

And then a giant gnat dive-bombed at my face.

CHAPTER ELEVEN

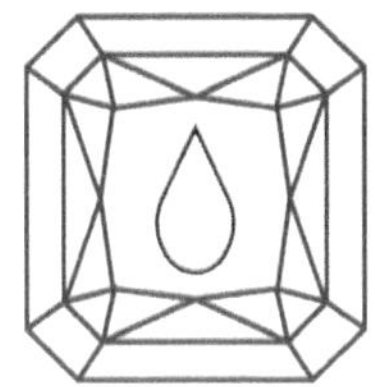

Lyssa

I ducked down, jerking my arms up to protect my head. The rubies on my vest glowed with a tingling heat, but if it was supposed to protect me, it wasn't covering the currently important parts. The gnat's hooked forelegs rasped across my wrist, scraping raw lines into my skin.

I barely had time to register the pain. As the gnat—which was big enough to take on a mid-sized owl—whirred through the air and whipped back around toward us, more massive insects careened out of the foliage. I spotted a few more gnats, creatures with glossy wooden bodies and horse-like heads that I guessed were the Wonderland version of horseflies, dragonflies longer and thicker around than my arm with prickly wings like holly leaves, and butterflies flapping fluffy bread slices on their backs and baring vampiric fangs.

"You're fucking kidding me," Hatter muttered.

I grabbed a fallen branch from the ground and smacked it into a horsefly that was careening toward me. The impact sent it spinning away, but two dragonflies zipped in to take its place, their wings clicking like knives.

Chess leapt up, batting bugs out of the air like a cat swatting at moths. Theo produced a baton that reminded me of the ones I'd seen some of the Queen's guards carrying before, except his gave off an electric sizzle of sparks when it collided with one of the fanged butterflies. The twins spun around, Dee punching and Dum kicking with their elastic limbs. Doria took her cue from me and grabbed a stick of her own. She snapped off the end to form a jagged point.

"Come on," Hatter said, waving us after him as he scrambled nimbly on down the slope. I skidded over the pebbled ground after him. The others followed in an avalanche of feet and rattling stones.

More bugs shrieked through the air. A gnat slammed right into Hatter's bowler hat. He groped after it, but it went spinning off between the trees and disappeared amid the brush. The next dragonfly tried to take his scalp clean off. Doria leapt in with her branch, and Hatter pushed on with a grimace.

"There's a cave up ahead," he said. "We can hope those things won't follow us in there."

We clambered after him down the last steep incline to the bottom of the valley. A leap over a trickle of a stream brought us to the narrow mouth of the cave Hatter had spotted, its outer walls patchy with glowing yellow moss. He leapt in, and the rest of us hurried after him into the cool shadows.

Hatter stopped several paces down the cave, where the passage opened a little wider. Water dripped from the ceiling onto the spikes of his bare hair. He swiped his hand over his head, still grimacing, and peered past us to the entrance.

The bugs hadn't followed. I exhaled in relief. When I peered into the cave's depths beyond Hatter, I couldn't make out anything but darkness, but my ruby flared with renewed heat.

"I think this is where the ring wanted us to go," I said. "I'm thinking a lantern or two would be nice?"

The White Knight fished his back out of his bag and passed it to Dum. Theo kept his electric baton in hand as we eased deeper into the cave. Hatter paused and hopped a gap that had opened in the floor ahead of us. He held out his hand to help me make the same jump.

As we walked on, he reached up instinctively as if to straighten the hat that was no longer there. His fingers curled around the air, and he yanked them back to his side. Going without something on his head clearly irked him.

A low rumbling carried from the darkness ahead. We all froze, our taste for caution finely honed after what we'd been through over the last two days.

The sound didn't get any louder, though. There was a pulsing rhythm to it, like some kind of heavy machinery. The ruby's heat seared through my skin.

I headed toward the sound, ignoring the fresh drips of water off the ceiling and the slick texture of the rock against my fingers when I brushed the wall for balance, but still moving carefully. Dum caught up with the lantern just as the source of the rumbling appeared at the edge of its light.

The floor opened up again in front of us, but not in a chasm like before. This was a pit. And it literally *opened*—and closed, and opened, and closed, the rocky edges knocking against each other in a rough approximation of smacking lips. The floor of the cave seemed to be chewing on something very enthusiastically.

I eased closer. Theo stayed right beside me as the ground beneath our feet quivered. The lantern light fell into the pit, and my breath caught.

At the bottom of the pit, maybe seven or eight feet below us, a sword gleamed. Its grip was wrapped with some sort of pale cloth, but the pommel and the guard had a golden glint, and a large ruby shone at the top of the hilt. I wasn't exactly an expert on olden-time weaponry—okay, or any weaponry—but I didn't need to be to know it was gorgeous. And the sizzling energy of the ruby beneath my shirt insisted it was also *mine*.

As long as that freaking pit mouth didn't chew me up the second I tried to grab it.

I circled the pit, absorbing the rhythm of the chomping rocks and the shape of the sword beneath them.

"If I had something to hook it and pull it up..." Theo said. "The rope I brought wasn't made for this."

"There are swords back in the city," Hatter said. "You don't have to risk your life for one."

I shook my head. "The Queen is scared of *this* sword. She tried to make sure no one ever retrieved it. That means we need it." A sword would get us a lot farther in a battle than the armored vest would.

Hatter shrugged off his suit jacket. "Then I'll go for it," he said, rolling up his sleeves. "I'm the fastest here."

"I could hop down and spring right back up," Dum put in.

"I could hold the rocks open as well as I can," Chess offered.

That suggestion made me think of the sound of crunching bones. The rock was too relentless. And the same sort of prickling was creeping over me as with the jabberwock, as with the train.

"I think I have to do it," I said. "I have the ruby. It might not… *let* anyone else take it. But that also means…"

I breathed in and out, focusing even more intently on the rhythm. My hand came up to the center of my chest over the ring, willing more of its powerful heat through my body. That was magic. While I had it, I had magic too.

"We can do the same thing we did with the pool yesterday," I said, motioning to Theo. "Tie your rope around my waist. I'll jump down and lie down flat under the rocks while I grab the sword. The second they open again, you haul me back up as quickly as you can."

"Lyssa." Theo touched my cheek, turning my gaze toward him. "Are you sure you want to do this?" he asked, his dark eyes holding mine.

"Wouldn't you, if you thought you had the best chance?" I said.

His jaw tightened for a second, but all he said was, "I would."

"Then there you go. Get out the rope."

I stood braced at the lip of the pit for a few seconds after he'd secured the knot. Then I jumped.

My body tucked itself into a crouch instinctively. The second my feet hit the rocky base, I sprawled forward, my hand shooting out to clutch the sword's hilt. The rocks chomped over me even closer than I'd bargained for, catching a bit of my hair and yanking. But the rest of my body stayed uncrushed. The rocks jolted open, and the rope jerked my body upward with a massive heave.

I swung around to push my feet off the pit's wall and bounded back out. As I landed, a laugh tumbled out of me. My fingers clutched tight around the sword. I held it up toward the cave's ceiling, unable to stop myself from grinning like a maniac.

"The sword of the blood-marked ruby. The Queen of Hearts had better watch out."

"You mean you're actually going *hunting*?" Doria said, looking from one twin to the other. "Do you even know what you're doing?"

Dee grinned. "Our mom sometimes gets paranoid about what the butcher shop offers. She taught us a few tricks. It'd be nice to have something extra for dinner to celebrate, don't you think? Why don't you come with us?"

Doria glanced over at Hatter where he was standing with the rest of us contemplating the site we'd picked to spend the night. The hilltop gave us a vantage point all around the square in the starlight from the clear sky. With at least a couple of us standing guard at any given point in the night, the Knave wouldn't have a chance to sneak up on us.

Hatter made a shooing motion at his daughter. "Stay close to them. They've proven they can take care of themselves; I'd imagine they can handle you too." He shot the twins a look that said they'd better or there'd be hell to pay.

Dee saluted him, and they set off down the hill.

Theo grabbed a couple things from his bag. "Chess, why don't you come with me to make sure there's nothing else in the area we need to be worried about. I have a couple deterrents I'd like to set down too. If there's one jabberwock on the prowl, there could be others." He turned to Hatter and me. "Can you two get the cabins set up? Holler if you need anything. This might take some time, but we won't go *too* far."

"Cabin assembly it is," Hatter said with a waggle of his nimble fingers. "Come on, looking-glass girl."

I stripped off the metal vest, which was starting to weigh heavy on my shoulders, set it next to the sword by my bag, and got to work.

The assembly of the tiny but sturdy cabins Theo had brought for us to sleep in happened about three quarters through Hatter's efforts rather than mine. In my defense, it was hard to keep up with him. His deft hands bent the folded structures into shape and snapped this piece and that into place as if he'd spent most of his life making temporary homes and not hats.

I managed to do most of the work on one, though. I stepped back to study it in the amber light of the lantern the others had left behind for us, making sure the roof was straight where it slanted around the height of my shoulders. When I decided it was level enough and glanced toward Hatter, he was watching me, an awed warmth in his gaze.

"What?" I said, abruptly self-conscious.

He shook himself out of his apparent reverie. "Sorry. I was just remembering that moment when you had the jabberwock bowing to you." He let out a rough chuckle. "That was something special all right, even if it was mad."

My cheeks heated. "The ring is special," I said, and grabbed a couple of the blankets and the lantern. "I couldn't have talked it down without that."

Hatter made a dismissive sound as he ducked after me into the first cabin. He spread a blanket at one end while I took care of the other. The spongy floor wasn't as comfortable as a mattress, but it offset the hardness of the actual ground we'd had to sleep on just fine.

"I happen to be pretty familiar with people and their accessories," he said, sitting back on the blanket. "I should know the impact has a lot more to do with how the person wears the item than how the item wears the person."

My gaze leapt to the uneven spikes of his dark blond hair, still uncovered. "Or how the person doesn't wear it? I guess you didn't pack another hat."

Hatter winced. "No. I suppose I'll just have to hope everyone can remember my name without one until I get back."

He said it like he was joking, but I could read genuine discomfort in his expression despite the softness of the lantern's glow. I scooted closer so I could ruffle those spikes. He caught my wrist when my fingers had already grazed his hair. A different sort of heat washed over me, kneeling that close to him, his fingers encircling my arm, his hair unexpectedly silky beneath my own fingertips. I could almost hear Melody egging me on: *Go get him, girl.*

"I didn't expect you to have to sacrifice so much, coming out here with me," I said, half teasing, half serious. "I'm sad that it came to this."

"I suppose I'll survive somehow," Hatter replied. "Better my hat than my head."

His grip on my wrist loosened, and my hand came to rest not-entirely-by-accident on his thigh. It was a little hard to think, but part of me felt the need to be completely serious for a moment.

"Really," I said, looking into his green eyes. "You didn't have to come with me at all. You weren't even sure the artifacts existed. I wouldn't have blamed you if you'd stayed back in the city, and I hope the trip hasn't been too horrifying."

A smile twitched at his lips. "Lyssa," he said, "loss of hat, sinkholes, blood-thirsty monsters, and all, there's nowhere I'd rather have been. What we're doing here is worth some unpleasantness." He paused. "*You're* worth going through some unpleasantness for."

"Oh," I said, a giddy flutter rising in my chest. "Well. I'm sorry about your hatlessness anyway."

His smile curved higher, the corners of his eyes crinkling. "You could always distract me from the agony of the loss."

I couldn't help grinning in return. "And how would you suggest I do that?"

He didn't bother to answer, just lowered his mouth to mine.

If Theo kissed like he was taking command, then Hatter kissed like he was dedicating himself to the cause. His breath mingled hot with mine, and his fingers eased up my side, trailing tingles of warmth in their wake. I leaned into him, my hand sliding behind his neck and then pushing at his suit jacket. He shed it as easily as he had when he'd been volunteering to dive into that chomping pit to retrieve my sword.

His body felt even hotter with only the thin layer of his dress shirt in the way. He kissed me harder as I traced my fingers over the muscles of his shoulders and down his chest. Then he palmed my breast with a quick swivel of motion that raised my nipple to a point with a spark of sensation. I gasped into his mouth.

Hatter tugged the wide neckline of the dress down over my shoulder and dislodged my bra at the same time. His hand slid under the fabric to cup me skin to skin. With one flick of his skilful thumb, my whole body was quivering with desire.

"Perhaps best if we merely rearrange clothes rather than removing them," he murmured. "Seeing as our situation here may turn out to be precarious." He hesitated, his hand stilling. "Unless—if this isn't how —if you'd rather wait—"

For what? A bed we might never actually make it back to if this adventure took a turn for the even worse—a bed where we'd been just as easily interrupted anyway? The others were out around the camp keeping an eye on things, and it'd sounded like they'd be gone a while. And right now I wanted this man with all the determination and tenderness he was capable of more than I'd ever wanted anyone.

"Fuck no," I said.

Hatter beamed at me, so brilliant in his delight that I had to catch the knot of his tie and pull him into another kiss.

He tipped me over on the blanket, one of his knees settling between my legs. As we kissed and caressed, my hands yanking his shirt from his slacks and traveling up over the bare skin beneath, I couldn't help arching toward him. My core ached for attention. My thigh brushed the bulge beneath his fly, and his breath stuttered before he re-captured my mouth.

That contact appeared to be all the cue he'd needed. Hatter reached down to draw the skirt of my dress up, his fingers tracing an electric path across my skin to the hem of my panties. His thumb grazed over the fabric in a teasing circle and then pressed down right on the spot where I needed it most.

My hips bucked up with the bolt of pleasure. I sucked back a cry. If Theo and Chess were close enough to pick up a holler, I didn't want to test the limits of their hearing.

I felt more than saw Hatter's smile. He worked my panties down just a couple inches and cupped me completely, his mouth marking a scorching path across my jaw and down the side of my neck at the same time. Another gasp escaped me as he dipped two fingers into the slick needy center of me. With a few swift strokes, he found the perfect point of pleasure. I bit my lip against a moan, bucking into his touch.

There are many uses a nimble set of fingers can be put to, he'd told me once. No fucking kidding.

I reached for his slacks, but Hatter nudged my hand to the side. "Not yet," he said by my ear, his voice rough but steady. "I want to watch you find your bliss, and then I want to hear you, and then I want to feel you."

My mind was already too hazed with the bliss he was generating to totally make sense of that, but as his fingers pulsed inside me and his thumb whirled over my clit, I was in full agreement with whatever he wanted to do with me.

His mouth came back to mine, our tongues twining together until my breath broke into panting. Hatter gazed at my face with so much hunger that his expression as much as the deft twist of his fingers tipped me over the edge. My eyes rolled back with the wave of pleasure that radiated through me. In an instant, my limbs turned into ecstatic jelly.

"Beautiful," Hatter said in a ragged voice that turned me on even more. He brushed his lips against mine once more and dipped his head to my chest. As he caught one nipple in his mouth through the dress's delicate fabric, a fresh knot of need formed down below, as quickly as the last one had shattered.

He worked over one breast and then the other until I was whimpering, my fingers tangled in his hair. Tugging my dress higher, he eased his way down. His lips grazed my sternum, my belly, the dip just beneath. Then he swept his tongue across my clit, and a fresh rush of pleasure raced through me.

All I could do was clutch on to his hair, trying not to pull too hard, as his mouth provoked a whole new range of sensations from my sex. Lips and tongue and teeth as skillful as his fingers had been, and oh God that surge of bliss was building all over again, so swiftly I could hardly breathe.

He'd said he wanted to hear me. I let more of the whimpers I'd been trying to contain slip out, followed by a moan as he gently nipped my clit. "Hatter," I mumbled. "So fucking good." And then something inarticulate that hopefully got the idea across all the same as his tongue curved right up into my slit. My body shuddered with the force of my second orgasm.

I still hadn't gotten what I wanted most, though. Hatter raised his body so he could kiss my collarbone, my neck, before making his way back to my mouth, and I found the wherewithal through my jellified state to grasp the zipper of his slacks. This time he didn't stop me. My fingers grazed his straining erection through the silky material of his boxers—question finally answered!—and he groaned with a shaky inhalation.

Together, we tugged his slacks down, and he yanked my panties completely off. I raised my hips, and he bowed his head over me as he slid inside. I was so wet and ready his cock practically glided through me, hard and hot and exactly what I'd been waiting for.

The deeper sense of bodily connection brought a rush of emotion into my chest. I hugged him tightly where I'd slipped my arms back up under his shirt and lifted my head. Hatter met me for the kiss I'd been seeking, drawing it out as he started to move inside me.

After all that build-up, I'd expected our final coming together to be frantic. Hatter rocked into me, sinking a little deeper still with each pump of his hips, intense but deliberately drawing every ounce of pleasure he could out of our joining. It was the most delicious torture. My body quivered with the heady sensation expanding from my core. I wanted him to hurry up already, and I wanted this never to end.

I raised my legs to brace against his thighs, letting him plunge so far his body brushed my clit. I gasped, and the control Hatter had been holding onto broke. He thrust into me harder, faster. "Lyssa," he muttered into my hair, gripping my hip and urging me higher to meet him. "Fuck. You drive me mad, but in the best possible way."

A giggle slipped out of me. "You make me pretty bonkers too," I managed to say before I was whimpering again, rocking into his thrusts, chasing one more ecstatic release. His cock pressed against that sweet spot inside me as it filled me in a way his fingers hadn't managed. The bliss of it swelled from my core through my entire body. Then it hit me like a tidal wave, crashing through my body.

I clenched around him, and Hatter made a strangled sound of pleasure. His hips jerked faster. As I clung to him, he came in a searing liquid gush inside me.

We stayed like that for a moment, him braced over me, our bodies joined, both our chests heaving. Then he eased himself down beside me, rolling me to face him. With his hand on my cheek, he kissed me as thoroughly as he'd just made love to me.

"We should probably finish getting the camp set up," he said under his breath when he drew back. "But… maybe not quite yet?"

"Definitely not quite yet." I squirmed closer to him and tucked my head against his chest. The citrusy smoky smell of him filled my nose, and a pang formed in my chest.

All of this was only temporary, only until I could find my way back to the Otherland. I didn't belong here in Wonderland. I didn't *want* to abandon my life back home. But in that moment all I wanted was to pretend this brief bliss could last forever.

CHAPTER TWELVE

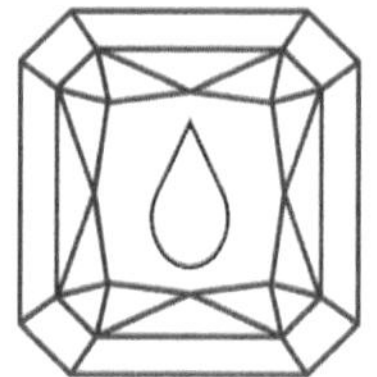

Theo

Lyssa was already starting to bloom into her role. I could see it in her posture, in the ease with which she pulled the woven metal vest back on after she'd eaten a brief breakfast. She didn't even know what she was meant for yet, and still she was moving toward it at full speed.

The observation sat strangely in my stomach, admiration and irritation mingling together. The former she'd earned; the latter had nothing, really, to do with her. Maybe when we were back in the city, where I had my office and my materials at my fingertips, all my people to call on, it would fade completely.

I certainly hoped so. It didn't befit the man I was meant to be at all.

The twins shuffled around the fire pit, dousing the flames and packing up the few dishes we'd used. Hatter and Doria were folding up the cabins. Chess stood poised at the edge of the hilltop, gazing toward the square of daylight we'd recently left as he kept watch for the enemy who might emerge at any moment.

I stood up and turned toward Lyssa. "I think we've found enough.

With the Knave potentially so close at our heels, we should head back to the city now."

We'd have to deal with the Knave and his remaining guard along the way, if the jabberwock hadn't fatally wounded them in the skirmish. We couldn't let him go back and inform the Queen of the company Lyssa had been keeping. But I didn't think that idea would go over well with our Otherlander. Better for her conscience that I arranged it more as if by chance than as a straightforward plan to end a man's life.

Perhaps I could send the twins off on a little side mission when we had a better idea of the commander of the guards' location. He hadn't appeared overnight. I wasn't going to assume anything from that fact, though. He might have only temporarily lost our trail, or he might be hanging back on purpose, wary of our now much greater numbers, waiting for an ideal opportunity to achieve an advantage.

Lyssa frowned, blinking at my suggestion. "Head back? But there's got to be at least one more thing. Mirabel said, 'The sword, the scepter, and the shield.' I guess this must be the 'shield'." She tapped the vest. "So the scepter is still out there. *Something* is at that hill Aunt Alicia drew. I'm sure of it. What if we need it if we're going to stop the Queen?"

That something was what had sent her grand-aunt running, no doubt. I wasn't sure Lyssa finding it would do more good than harm. And the thought of the Knave getting his hands—or his sword—on her made every part of me tense.

I tipped my head toward the sword she'd leaned against her bag. "I expect a sword will be a lot more useful for that purpose," I said honestly.

"We don't know what magic the scepter might have in it, though. We're already out here. The hill can't be that much farther."

True. I didn't think it would take us more than the day to reach the spot we'd seen from afar. Nevertheless…

"We've already escaped death by a hair multiple times since we arrived here," I said. "Sometimes only through luck. I'd rather we return in one piece with what we've gotten so far than die trying for more. You've done enough, Lyssa. You've done more than most people would have believed was possible."

I let all the warmth I felt for her flow into my voice, but the praise didn't soften her expression the way I'd managed in times past. She'd believed in me above anyone else in Wonderland back then.

She was learning to believe in herself here in our land. I wished I could have been nothing but pleased to see it.

"It doesn't feel like enough," she said, and hesitated. Her jaw set. "If anyone wants to head back now, that's all right. I don't want anyone risking their lives just because I said so. But I'm going to that hill. If there's something there, I'm going to find it."

More protests swelled in my throat. My concern about the dangers ahead was perfectly real. And also, she wasn't ready for the full truth of these artifacts yet. I needed more time to ease her into it. But I couldn't tell her that.

What else could I say that she would listen to? I could push on the idea of the Queen beginning her executions, but I'd told Lyssa before we should have at least a week.

The longer we argued without my convincing her, the more my authority diminished in the eyes of everyone watching us. My whole body balked at the thought of backing down, but looking at the determination in her face, I suspected that was the stronger move.

I certainly wasn't leaving her to fend for herself against whatever other horrors the Checkerboard Plains might offer up.

I let out a chuckle, forcing my lips to form a wry smile that I hoped didn't betray the tension inside me. "I should know better than to underestimate you," I said, as if it were only her willingness I'd been concerned about. "If you're ready to adventure onward, then let's see where the Plains take us next."

No one else offered any argument. Doria scooped up one of the lanterns and set off in the lead as soon as we'd packed up. Hatter hurried after her with a wary scan over the landscape. Chess grabbed the other lantern and meandered a little apart from our procession to cast the light over a wider span. Lyssa jogged to catch up with Hatter and his daughter, the ruby-set sword swaying awkwardly in her grasp.

Anyone who knew anything about sword fighting could have seen that Lyssa knew nothing at all. When we'd been making our way through the gully yesterday, she'd tried wedging the weapon into her bag for a while, but the hilt had kept banging into her back, so she'd switched to carrying it by hand. The way she was holding it, an opponent could have knocked it out of her fingers in an instant. And that was when she hadn't switched it to her weaker hand to rest her arm.

When we were back at the city and I could unearth a sword of my own, I'd have to give her a few lessons. It should actually be rather invigorating, in more than one way, watching her take to the weapon. The ten years of training under my belt might as well have some additional use.

My imagination drifted for a moment to the way I might set one hand on her hip and stand against her from behind as I guided her arm, feeling every motion of her muscles tensing and relaxing. At the thump of a stone Dum kicked, I jerked my mind back to the present.

My gaze lifted to Lyssa automatically. My feelings for her were all tangled through the rest of me, too thoroughly to be easily picked apart. By the will of the lands, I wouldn't need to.

"Any idea what specific dangers we might be up against today, White Knight?" Dum asked where he'd fallen into step beside me.

"Of course you'd ask about that and not what wonders we might see," Dee teased at my other side. "It's been a wild ride, that's for sure."

"Thank you for coming along for it," I said. The twins had proven themselves dependable in their different ways as they'd matured, but I hadn't been able to warn them of all the risks we'd face on this particular journey. If I'd known the Knave would wind up chasing us, or that we'd find ourselves walking clear across the Plains…

No, they probably still would have come. I'd earned that loyalty, and they gave it happily. As if I would have turned away their pleading mother and let the Queen's recruiter notice their fledgling abilities. With their rebellious spirits, they'd have been lucky to make it a year before they were sent off to the Oyster Cove to have their heads regrown like dim automations.

They'd always balanced each other out, Dum holding Dee back when his eagerness got away from him, Dee helping Dum loosen up. That was the kind of teamwork you couldn't manufacture.

"You asked, we came," Dum said, as if it really were that simple to him. He shrugged. "It hasn't been *that* bad on the whole." He paused and glanced sideways at me. "Are you sure continuing on was the right idea?"

That argument had sown doubt in the wrong places. I gave a light laugh. "I simply thought it was a good moment to test our Otherlander's resolve for going forward," I said, in a low voice so Lyssa wouldn't overhear. "If she wasn't completely dedicated to continuing, she could falter and get the rest of us into trouble."

"No need to worry about that one wavering, from what I can see," Dee said. "She's got the guts it takes to run with the Spades, no question." He sucked a breath through his teeth with a soft whistle. "Can you imagine how much these artifacts will freak out the Queen? We'll turn the tables on her for sure. I can't wait."

Dum shot him a skeptical look. "I don't think it's going to be *that* easy, even with a pretty sword and all. And the Otherlander..." He studied Lyssa's back. "She's held her own. No one could argue that. But she's shifting things too. She still might get us into a lot of trouble, and does she really know what she's in for then?"

She didn't. Which was exactly why we couldn't drop a huge burden on her head without proper preparation.

"Can she even fight with that thing?" he added, nodding to the sword.

"We can always pass the ring and all on to someone who's a better fighter, right?" Dee said. "Her aunt or whoever might have found it, but it belongs to Wonderland."

It did, and it also belonged to her. The weight of the falsehoods I was juggling pressed down on me for a moment. I squared my shoulders. "Always a possibility," I said. "We'll see how we can best position ourselves and the things we've found once we return to the city."

That answer appeared to satisfy the twins for now. As we walked on through the hazy darkness, the weight sank down to my gut.

How many doubts would they have if they realized how much of the truth I'd held back from them? Was there some way I could make it seem as if I'd only just discovered the full story too?

But then, there were other, deeper lies I'd been telling for much longer, lies I couldn't avoid taking responsibility for when the time came.

No point in building a solution until you see what the problem is, the old White Knight, my mentor, used to say. He might have had some odd ideas about some things, but he'd been wise about that.

I strode on faster. The sooner we made it to Lyssa's hill, the sooner I could be back on familiar ground.

A long hike later, we reached the next daylight square. We stepped out into dry heat beneath a clear sun-soaked sky. Sand shifted beneath our feet. Cacti dotted the desert that sprawled out ahead of us. As we paused to take in the landscape, several of the prickly green forms adjusted their positions, twisting one way, turning an arm up or down. Lyssa stiffened for a second.

There didn't appear to be anything especially threatening about the vegetation. I motioned the others onward, stepping up to the front of the procession.

The sand hissed, and a serpentine body arced up into view, purple spines jutting along its sinewy back. Lyssa let out a squeak, and it dove deeper. In a second, it had vanished.

"Scrapeworm," I told our Otherlander. "It won't hurt you as long as you don't eat it. Highly poisonous."

She sputtered a laugh. "I don't think there's much chance I'll do that."

The sand dragged at our shoes as we marched on. It felt pleasant enough, soft and smooth, but walking over it was twice the strain solid ground was. We weren't going to make great time through this square—but detouring would take even longer.

I focused on finding a rhythm. I'd just settled into one when a skittering noise brought my gaze to the right.

A pack of birds trotted toward us down a dune flecked with gravel. They looked for all the world like overblown basketballs decked out in fluffy blue feathers, tiny heads posed tight against their rounded bodies, each nearly as tall as my waist. My spine went rigid. Jubjub birds.

"Oh my God," Lyssa said. "Those are actually really *cute*. That's a nice change of pace from disturbing and bloodthirsty."

"Ah," I said, and that was all I managed to get out before the couple dozen birds broke into a full-out charge.

The Jubjub birds' heads shot out from their bodies on spindly necks, pulling out the long piercing beaks that had been hidden in their feathers too. Beaks hard and sharp enough to puncture steel. Human flesh was a piece of cake. And unfortunately they did enjoy fresh meat when they could get it.

Hatter whipped out one of his hatpins, and Chess raised his fists. Lyssa swung her sword in front of her, her arms wobbling, and something inside me twisted.

I couldn't stand to see her try to take those things on and lose. I wasn't sure I could stand it if she saved the day all over again either.

"Lyssa!" I said before I could second-guess the impulse. I held out my hand. "The sword. Now!"

I still knew how to make a command. Lyssa startled, but she heaved the sword toward me, aiming the hilt toward my reach. As she ducked back behind the others, I snatched the sword out of the air. In one swift motion, I sprang forward and sliced the blade through the pack of Jubjub birds.

With that one slash, three of their heads burst off their bodies, their fluffy forms collapsing. I gave a shout, stomped my foot, and ran at them with another swipe to cut through a couple more.

The one thing you need to know about Jubjub birds, if you're going to know anything, is they're cowards at heart. The spray of a few of their companions' blood and my yell sent the others scattering. The pack raced back over the hill they'd attempted to ambush us from, leaving a rain of frightened feathers in their wake.

Dee started to clap as I lowered the sword. "Nice one, boss!"

I started to smile, but my sense of accomplishment faded behind a prickle of shame when I remembered why I'd asked for the sword in the first place.

Maybe there hadn't been time to talk Lyssa through what she needed to do. Maybe it'd made the most sense for me to step in. But I could admit that hadn't been the only reason I'd done it.

That didn't matter as long as no one but me ever knew it.

CHAPTER THIRTEEN

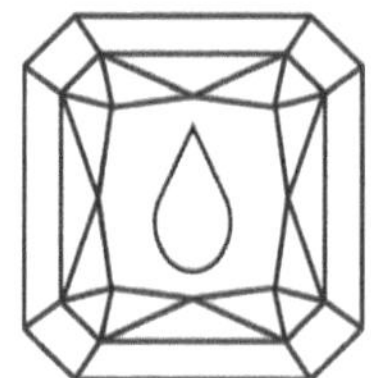

Lyssa

Theo adjusted his grip on the sword, looking every inch the warrior even in his white button-up and gray slacks. It was easier to admire the strength in his form, the speed with which he'd dispatched those freaky killer birds, now that said freaky killer birds weren't stampeding toward us. I'd started to freeze up, and he'd been there, ready to tackle anything in the blink of an eye.

Should I have gone along with his suggestion this morning that we head back to the city immediately? It hadn't *felt* right, and my feelings had seemed to guide me pretty well over the last few days, but I hadn't enjoyed arguing with him. He'd guided me awfully well since I'd arrived in Wonderland too.

But it hadn't been personal. I had more of a connection to the artifacts than he did, thanks to Aunt Alicia's ring—I understood the power coursing through those rubies better than he could. And he must have recognized that, because I hadn't needed to say that much before he'd agreed.

He'd trusted my judgment. That memory made me almost as tingly as watching the flex of his muscles as he lowered the sword.

Theo started to turn toward us, and the ruby flashed red. His fingers jerked apart, dropping the sword as if it had burned him. It thumped on the ground. Theo smacked his hand against his side. From the flinch of pain through his expression, it really had hurt him.

"Are you okay?" I said with a hitch of concern in my chest, stepping toward him.

He waved me off with his other hand as he lowered the possibly wounded one to his side. He kept it angled toward him so I couldn't see the skin on the inside.

"The grip heated up all of a sudden," he said in an even tone. "Took me by surprise. Those rubies do pack a lot of kick, don't they?" He shook his head ruefully.

He bent as if to pick the sword up, and I leapt forward first. I was the one who'd started us on this quest—if it was going to burn anyone, it should be me.

"Thank you," I said. "I revise my earlier statement about those bird-things. Definitely not cute. Definitely not a change of pace."

Theo's chuckle didn't sound particularly strained. But as he let me take the sword, he motioned Dum over. The solemn twin passed him the tube of salve without any spoken request.

I curled my fingers gingerly around the sword's grip. The cloth that bound it felt warm, but not unpleasantly so. Of course, the ruby had gone dull too. I'd felt how searing the ring could become.

It had never physically burned me, though. Did the sword not like to be used for killing monsters? I wasn't sure it would be much use to us then. It would figure if a weapon worked that way in Wonderland.

"Onward?" I said, with a tentative look Theo's way.

"Onward," he said with an easy smile. Maybe it hadn't even hurt him, only startled him. He might have wanted the salve for a blow one of the birds had struck during the fray.

I held the sword a little tighter as we walked on, scanning any slopes we passed for hints of blue feathers. The cacti kept up their periodic vogueing, but no more killer birds appeared. We even passed a pool of faintly sweet water where everyone refilled their canteens. I gulped a little extra with my hand to counter the dryness in the air.

The dark haze of the next night square ahead of us shifted in rippling patterns as we approached. I understood why the second we crossed the threshold. Wind whipped through the darkness, yanking at my hair and swatting my face. The lanterns tossed in the guys' hands.

I braced the sword against my vest so the wind couldn't catch it. How far were we going to have to walk through this?

We formed a tight line, Theo at the head with one lantern and Dum at the back with the other, huddling against the wind as we walked. If Hatter hadn't lost his hat yesterday, I doubted he'd have been able to hang onto it through this place. My gaze settled on the back of his head, the tufts of his hair blown even spikier than usual, with a flutter in my stomach that was both affection and heat in memory of our little interlude yesterday.

The wind fell back, even though it still howled all around us. Had we entered a sort of eye in the storm? Doria eased up beside me as we hurried on through the dark. Maybe she'd noticed my fond glance a moment ago, because she cocked her head and spoke just loud enough for me to hear her over the bluster around us.

"So… you and Pops are having kind of a thing, huh?"

I nearly swallowed my tongue. "Um…"

"It's okay. That's why I'm asking. *He'd* have a conniption before he told me anything like that. But I think it's kind of cool. You're cool." She smirked. "You got him to stop being such a spoilsport all the time."

"I mean, it's not—" I hesitated. It was hard to say whatever I had with Hatter wasn't serious, especially after our intense encounter yesterday. Especially with the way my heart lifted just looking at the back of his freaking head. I groped for the right words. "I'll be going back to the Otherland when we can find another mirror that'll open up the way there. Hopefully after you all take down the Queen of Hearts, but… I'm going back."

Doria shrugged. She'd grown up in Wonderland with all those laissez-faire ideas about relationships and intimacy, after all. I guessed I shouldn't be expecting her to react like the teenage daughter of a guy back home might.

"Most people here don't stick together very long anyway," she said.

"Dad says my birth parents were unusual that way. They had something really special." The corner of her mouth turned up as her gaze traveled to one of the twins—Dee, I thought, from his relaxed expression. "Maybe I'm weird, but I hope I get to have that too someday."

It looked like I wasn't the only one crushing hard. Did Hatter know his daughter was swooning over one of the guys here?

Probably better if he didn't. I didn't know how Wonderlanders felt about age differences, but Dee didn't seem like the type to take advantage where he shouldn't anyway.

"You know," I said, "back in the Otherland, wanting that wouldn't be weird at all. Never settling down is weird to us."

"Hmm. Maybe I should visit sometime."

She laughed, and the sound was caught by the wind as it roared up around us again. Goodbye, eye of the storm. I ducked my head against it, shielding my watering eyes with my arm, and we trudged on without trying to talk any more.

Between the sandy landscape before and the windblown one after, my legs were throbbing by the time the edge of daylight crept into view ahead of us. My knuckles ached where my fingers were clamped tight around the sword's hilt. I pushed myself faster anyway, just wanting to be out of this blistering gale already.

The second we stepped out into the gentle sunlight, my spirits leapt. We'd finally reached the hill I'd spotted from a distance. It looked even more like a wave up close, arcing up over the landscape with its narrow peak pointing almost straight down. All that lay between us and it was a stretch of field scattered with several trees hunched in a similar shape and strands of long grass that also bent over on themselves, as if the whole environment were echoing the hill.

As I gazed at our surroundings, taking a moment to catch my breath, a faint clattering broke through the peaceful murmur of the breeze. The Plains train with its mahogany engine and cars whirred into view at the far end of the square, beyond the hill but near enough that I couldn't imagine it was more than a couple hours' walk farther. A grin sprang across my face.

"We're right by the other end of the loop," I said. "We can check out the hill and then hop back on right away." Maybe we could make it back to the city before even one more day had passed.

"Let's get to it, then," Dee said, bounding forward. I hustled after him with a skip of my pulse. What had been so important here that this specific place had stuck in Aunt Alicia's mind—that she'd drawn it and kept that drawing even long after she'd left Wonderland behind?

We were several steps into the tall grass when the blades around me whipped upward. With an unsettling hiss, they split apart into flayed strands that shot toward my legs, my waist, and my arms.

A squeak of protest slipped from my lips. My sword hand slashed out instinctively. The shining blade sliced through the flayed blades of grass with a snickering sound, but more were already launching themselves at me.

Several strands snagged around my ankle. One licked over my wrist just before I chopped it down, scraping across my skin with a sandpaper texture that left a raw trail in its wake.

Someone swore behind me. I swung the sword again, hacking this way and that, managing to free my ankle. I dodged out of the way of another spray of strands and chopped right through them. The grass all around me lay cut and limp.

The others were still struggling against the grassy bindings. Theo was slicing his way free with a little knife that was making slower work than my sword had, but the others hadn't been carrying any blades they could quickly reach. I hurried to Doria, severing the strands that had yanked her wrists together and then those that were tangled around her legs from thighs to feet. She darted away from that spot with a sputter of relief, and I turned to the guys.

Hatter had fared the best with his full suit. The grass hadn't managed to scratch him up at all. When I'd hacked him free, he produced a hatpin from inside his suit and set to work piercing and ripping the strands that had wound around Dum while I slashed the ones holding Dee. The cheerful twin had managed to snap the strands around his wrists with his flexible arms, but they held him tight around his waist and knees, and the ones he'd broken had left tracks across his bare forearms.

By the time I'd finished with him, Theo was just hewing away the last few bits of grass twined around his ankles. Where the hell was Chess? My heart lurched as I scanned the field. Had he been whisked away somehow in the chaos?

My gaze caught on a heap of grass that appeared to have formed a sort of funnel farther across the field. It twitched slightly as if moved by some presence inside it. An invisible presence.

"Chess?" I said, moved toward it. He might have slipped out of sight to avoid any additional dangers that came at us, but I didn't know why he was staying so still and quiet now. A nervous prickle ran down my back.

He didn't answer. I stopped in front of the heap of grass, more obviously shaped around a brawny torso and legs now, and tentatively reached toward the air above it. My fingers collided with the warm fabric of Chess's shirt over his chest. It rose and fell with a shallow shaky breath.

Had the grass done something else to him while it held him—poisoned him or put him into some kind of fugue state? My pulse thumping harder, I slid my hand up to cup his jaw.

"Chess," I said softly, trying to keep the panic out of my voice. "I need you to make yourself visible again so I can cut the grass off you. I don't want to cut *you* by accident. Can you do that?"

He gave a twitch of a nod. Then he shimmered into view, all of him at once, no floating grin. Because he wasn't grinning at all. His mouth was set in a tight line, his forehead damp with sweat and a glassy look in his eyes.

The grass must have poisoned him or made him sick somehow. Gritting my teeth, I chopped at the strands that held his wrists and then his waist and his legs. When he was free, he stumbled forward, and the edges of him wavered as if he were going to vanish on us again.

"Hey," I said, catching his elbow. "Stay with us. Stay with me." I turned to look toward the others. "Do you have any idea what's wrong? Is there something we can give him?"

Theo shook his head, looking genuinely confused. Hatter's eyes had darkened with what looked like understanding.

"I think he'll recover now that you've gotten him out," he said. "Give him a minute."

What did he know about Chess that I didn't? I turned back to the other man. A bit more color was starting to return to Chess's face, but he still looked sick. My stomach knotted.

On an impulse, I eased closer to him and wrapped my arms right around him. "I've got you," I murmured into his shirt.

Chess's hand came up to rest on the back of my head. After a second, a chuckle escaped him—a little weak, but much closer to his usual self. "So you do, lovely," he said in a light tone. "We did get ourselves into quite a tangle for a moment there, didn't we?"

I looked up at him, not releasing my embrace. "Are you okay?" I asked. "You seemed really... out of it for a minute there." And all the minutes he'd stood there silent while I was helping the others.

"Oh, I go out and in and all around," he said with a wave of his hand. His grin came back, solid as ever. He tucked his arm around my shoulders and turned me toward the hill. "We've almost reached your destination. Let us go and see where it gets us, hmm?"

I didn't totally believe his nonchalant demeanor. Something had really shaken him up. But he obviously didn't want to tell me about it, at least not right now, here, with the others.

The knot inside me expanded to encompass my entire stomach. The men around me put forward a tough front in their various ways, but none of them were invincible. I had the feeling they were putting on that front for *me*, so I wouldn't feel guilty about dragging them on this quest—so I didn't think I needed to worry about them. But they'd been here for me so much. I wanted to be strong for them when they needed it, if they'd let me.

I bobbed up on my toes to brush a quick kiss to Chess's cheek. "If you want to talk about it with me later, whenever, you can," I murmured for just him to hear. "I want you to know that."

He dipped his head to kiss my temple in return. "Sentiment appreciated, but there's nothing to talk about," he said. His hand closed around mine, with a gentle squeeze that felt like a thank you in itself.

That answer didn't really satisfy me, but we did have the end of our quest right in front of us. Keeping my fingers twined with his, I strode forward.

The bowing grass at the edge of the ring I'd cleared hissed as I approached. I waved the sword at it, and to my relief the strands stilled. I'd shown them there was a force to be reckoned with around here.

All seven of us stayed close together as we waded through the subdued field, me staying in the lead this time, sword ready. Nothing jumped at us or grabbed us the rest of the way to the hill. As we came up on the immense shadow beneath the curve of the wave, I made out the raggedly arched entrance to a cave at the base of the hill beneath.

We'd just reached the edge of the shadow when a slim figure stepped out of the cave. I stopped in my tracks, raising the sword higher defensively.

The man gazed at us with a joyful light filling his wizened face. He swiped a hand over his wisps of white hair in an effort that didn't do much to smooth it down and stepped forward with a clink of his plated armor, tarnished metal dappled with patches of worn red paint. With a grand sweep of his arm, he dropped into a bow on his knee in front of me. His voice creaked out of him like a wind-swayed branch.

"It is an honor to finally greet you, your Majesty."

CHAPTER FOURTEEN

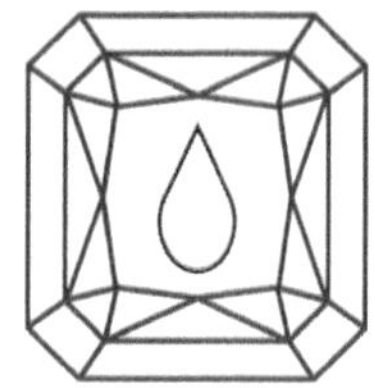

Lyssa

Your Majesty?

I let the sword drop to my side. "Er," I said to the old dude in the armor, who was still crouched in his very committed bow. "There's been some mistake. I don't think any of us here is a majesty of anything. I'm definitely not."

He looked up at me with an expression that was both awed and amused. "You wear the armor of the blood-marked ruby. You carry the sword. I assume you have the ring on you somewhere, for it will have led you to them. You are of the line of Alice, are you not?"

"Well, yeah," I said. "If you mean the Alices who came here from the Otherland. Our family isn't royal."

His pale blue eyes twinkled. "Not in the Otherland, it isn't. Here in Wonderland, you are our rightful ruler. The Red Queen, come to reclaim her throne from the usurping Hearts."

None of this was making a whole lot of sense to me. If there was a Red Queen who could topple the Queen of Hearts, wouldn't someone have mentioned that before?

Beside me, Chess looked bemused. The shocked confusion on

Hatter's face echoed all the emotions rushing through me. I couldn't see the others, but no one had piped up with an, "Oh, right! We forgot to mention that completely vital fact," so I was going to guess this was news to them too.

"I really don't know what you're talking about," I said. "My grand-aunt Alicia left the ring for me. I was using it to help the Spades find the ruby artifacts so they might be able to stop the Queen of Hearts, not so I could turn into some kind of queen."

The man straightened up, his wispy white hair drifting with the cool breeze. "You don't need to turn into a queen," he said. "You already are one. But I know the Hearts family has wiped out every trace they can of their true history. Come here, all of you, and we'll talk." He glanced over my companions. "It's good that you already have allies. Better still that you braved this land's threats to find the sword and the armor. I hope that means you will stay with us where Alicia did not."

He motioned for us to follow him deeper into the shadow of the arced hill. My pulse stuttered as I hurried after him. "Wait, you knew Aunt Alicia?"

"That ring led her to me," he said over his shoulder. "I told her what her true purpose here was, but she didn't want to believe me. Perhaps it is better that the task came down to you, if she wasn't ready to face it."

The words from Aunt Alicia's letter came back to me. *I didn't really know how I fit in there or what my true purpose was. When the pieces all collided, I panicked. I ran away.*

She'd run away from whatever this guy was about to tell us? I swallowed thickly. I'd come into the Checkerboard Plains hoping to find answers, but maybe I was going to get more than I'd bargained for.

Theo's voice carried from behind me, a bit of an edge in his normally smooth baritone. "Who exactly are you, if we can ask that?"

"Ah," the old guy said in his creaky yet resonant voice. "I am the Red Knight, loyal servant to the Red royal family. I have guarded the last of the artifacts until such time as the true rulers of Wonderland could be restored. It has been… a long time."

No kidding. From the looks of him, he might be over a hundred in Otherland years. In Wonderland that could mean way older.

"Do you have a real name?" I asked, thinking of the other man I knew who went by the label Knight. "I mean, one that's not just your role?"

The Red Knight paused at the edge of a firepit ringed with crumbling stumps. "I believe I did," he said, his voice diminishing. "But I can't say I remember what it was. I haven't had much opportunity to introduce myself to anyone out here."

Clearly. I sat down gingerly on one of the stumps near him. The others took seats all around me, Doria sitting on the grass between Hatter and Dee when it turned out there weren't enough stumps. The Red Knight made an apologetic grimace.

Theo was watching him, his gaze considering but his jaw clenched. With the question he'd asked—did he not trust this guy? Had something the Red Knight had said contradicted his understanding of his world?

It was hard to figure what motivation the old man could have had for making this up, though.

"Let me try to tell the story fully," the Red Knight said. "If I ramble some, I apologize in advance. There's much to tell. And if you find yourself confused, do stop me and say so. It's been fifty years since I last needed to explain, and that attempt didn't go particularly well, as I've mentioned."

He shifted forward in his seat with a clink of his armor, the tarnished steel plates covering him from feet to neck with small gaps in between. His gaze skimmed the people I'd brought with me.

"The only Queen you know of is the Queen of Hearts, am I right?" he said. "You believe Wonderland has been ruled by the Hearts for as long as it has been Wonderland."

"Of course," Dum said. "No one's ever talked about any other royal family."

"Because the first Queen of Hearts took the heads of anyone who breathed a word about it," the Red Knight said. "I was there, nearly two centuries ago, when the Hearts family and the followers they'd rallied stormed the palace. We weren't prepared for a sudden assault. It was the middle of the night, and the attackers went straight to the royal chambers—slaughtered the few guards there, the king and the queen and their children in their beds. Claimed the rule as their own, made the property over in their image, smashed or beheaded anything and anyone that might hint at their treachery."

"And Wonderland just *forgot*?" Hatter said.

"I expect some memory of it was carried on for a brief time," the Red Knight said. "But as those who could directly remember the Red Queen and King passed on, there were so few left who'd heard, and the risks for speaking up were so great—and she'd destroyed any proof she could that would prove the story—" He gave us a tight smile. "History is to the victors, is it not?"

"You said the 'first' Queen of Hearts," I said. "Not the same one who's ruling right now?"

He shook his head. "She would be the third, if my understanding is correct. Her mother was a child when the coup took place. From what I hear of her attitudes, I'd imagine *that* experience was passed down: the knowledge that no matter how high you sit, you can always find your neck at the wrong end of an axe in the blink of an eye."

"You haven't connected this story to Lyssa," Theo said quietly. He didn't sound as if he doubted the guy now. "You said the Hearts killed the entire Red family."

"They thought they had." The Red Knight looked down at his hands, his mouth tensing and then releasing. "I had a daughter then," he said. "A year younger than the youngest of the princesses, who'd only just turned sixteen. They didn't look a great deal alike, but their hair was a similar color, and in the night, when the attackers cared more about spilling blood quickly than checking who lay in which bed..."

He let out a ragged breath. "I heard them coming. I understood what I was hearing. I loved my daughter, you understand, but my first duty, the duty I'd sworn to carry out before all else, was to the Red family. Princess Alice had the last bedroom in the row—the most time for me to act. I got her up and had Matilda take her place in bed, and I fled with her, by the best ways I knew."

"Princess Alice," I repeated. My pulse had started to race.

The Red Knight met my eyes. "Yes. But I didn't know where to take her to keep her safe. The murderers realized *I* was gone and took up the search for me. We found ourselves at the edge of a small pond outside the city. The one they call the Pond of Tears now, for all the weeping, even though no one remembers what anyone all that time ago would have been weeping for. Princess Alice looked at her reflection in the water, and she declared it was like a mirror, and that like those other special mirrors, it would carry her to another world where the ones who'd come for her blood couldn't find her."

Chess raised his eyebrows. "And it worked? Lyssa could have gone back through to the Otherland through the pond all this time?"

"No," the Red Knight said. "That is, it did work. She leapt in before I could argue with her, and the water swallowed her up. But as she jumped, she commanded the pond that it should admit no one but her to where it would take her. She didn't want there to be any chance of the villains following her, you understand. Even *I* couldn't, diving in right after her. Although I've come to feel that was for the best—that I've served better on this side of things."

"And you think she made it through to the Otherland," I said. "You think I'm related to her."

"I don't know exactly what transpired on the other side of her slapdash looking-glass. But I know that more than once, young women named Alice or a variation on her name have traveled back through the Pond of Tears as no one else ever has. I know the proof your grand-aunt showed me with the blood-marked ruby. You do have the ring?"

I tugged the chain out from beneath my shirt, cupping the ring in my hand. He motioned for me to take off its protective shell. "Have you pricked your finger on it yet?" he asked.

"Yeah," I said. "It—"

Oh.

"It glowed, yes?" That awed light came back into the Red Knight's face. "Let me see it, if you don't mind?"

My chest tightened, but I touched my thumb to the sharp point in the middle of the ruby anyway. It pinched through my skin. The drop of blood fell, and the ruby shone with that magical light.

"That ring is the marker of the Red royal line," the Red Knight said in a hushed voice. "It will only glow for those who bear royal blood. Not even I…"

He held out his hand to demonstrate. The ruby's glow had already faded. I let him nick his finger against the stone. Like with Theo, the blood simply seeped away into the stone dully.

Aunt Alicia had talked about the magic that ran through our bloodline. That had to be what she'd meant. I still couldn't wrap my head around it.

"There were ruins—part of a wall—out near the Topsy Turvy Woods," I said. "It had the ruby symbol on it."

The Red Knight nodded. "During the reign of the Reds, the royal family had structures all across Wonderland. The people of Wonderland wandered farther abroad much more often. The Red Queen and King served well, with generosity rather than greed. The Hearts destroyed all of that."

"So, Lyssa is really going to be *queen*?" Doria said, her eyes wide.

I didn't know how to answer that question. To my immense gratitude, Theo patted her shoulder and gave me a reassuring smile. "I think we'd better give our Otherlander some time to process this revelation. *All* of us need to rethink a lot of what we believed."

The intent look he fixed on me felt like an offer of help, if I wanted it. I wasn't sure what he could do to make this situation any less complicated.

The Red Knight stood up. "I should bring you to the last artifact," he said. "I only managed to track down and recover the one of them after the Queen of Hearts hid them away. If I could have gathered all of them for you…"

He sounded heartbroken over his supposed failure. I pushed myself to my feet with a twist of my gut.

"It's fine," I said. "I got the other ones anyway. And that was hard enough with company. I can't imagine doing it alone."

"You'll never be on your own again," the Red Knight said with a determination that sounded almost more ominous than comforting to my ears.

This guy had been waiting almost two hundred years for his new queen to show up. No pressure or anything.

He led me into the cave at the base of the hill. Inside, the rocky floor and walls were smooth and dry, almost pleasant as caves went. I caught glimpses of a few rooms near the entrance, one holding a narrow bed, another with shelves of food.

At the end of the tunnel, the Red Knight ran his hand down the wall and pressed a spot that didn't stand out at all to me. A stone slab slid back, revealing another room.

Mirabel had seen right about the three artifacts. A scepter lay on a small stone platform, most of its length a polished cherry wood, its head a massive glittering ruby encased in a chamber of gold shaped like a crown. More gold shimmered at its base.

I picked it up to test its weight. The scepter wasn't half as heavy as the sword, which was a relief. It'd have been nice if my supposed royal ancestors had thought to include a scabbard or some sort of carrying case for their weaponry.

The ring I'd tucked back under my shirt flushed with pleased warmth. "What does it do?" I asked, turning the scepter from side to side.

"I have to admit I'm not sure," the Red Knight said, with the same shamed air he'd had when he'd talked about not retrieving the other artifacts. "I saw the Red Queen—my first Red Queen, begging your pardon, your Majesty—command a herd of borogoves with it once. But the royal family didn't use the artifacts often. I hadn't much chance to witness their powers. I'm sure now that they're in your grasp, your instincts will aid you in discovering all they can offer."

Because I was on my own in this. If I believed everything he'd said, I was the only surviving descendant of Wonderland's Red Queen—and as much as I'd have liked to argue his story away, I didn't know how to dismiss the proof of it. The ring. The way the train had slowed for me—the way the jabberwock had gentled.

Hatter had been right. It wasn't just the ring I was wearing. It was because it was me, wearing that ring.

Everything and everyone in Wonderland depended on me.

My lungs constricted for a second, with a flash of memory that shot me back to my eight-year-old self, watching my mother sob and sway over Dad's old clothes. Pushing her toward the door to get to work, grabbing the money she left out before my brother could and buying the cheapest dinner fixings I could find after school, reading the bills, writing checks for Mom to sign, and on and on.

I'd survived that. I'd held my family together and made it through. But an entire land was a lot more than our tiny family.

I hadn't signed up for this. Not at all.

"I don't know if I can even do this," I said to the Red Knight. "I don't have any idea what it takes to be a queen. I don't have any… training, or whatever queens usually get."

"You'll find your way," the knight said confidently. We stepped back into the cave's main hallway. "It's your heritage. You're meant for this."

I could have had a hundred doctors in my family tree, and I still wouldn't have known how to do a heart transplant just by being "meant for it." Somehow I had the feeling ruling a country was at least as complicated.

And a task that took quite a bit longer. A task that never really ended.

"I have a life back home," I said. God, what would Melody say if I tried to tell her about any of this? Wonderland had been crazy enough before I'd been a supposed *queen*. "I know you think this is what I'm supposed to be doing, but I'd never even heard of Wonderland until a couple weeks ago. I have a family back there, I have friends—"

"They will understand that you must rise to your new role. How could they deny you an honor such as this?"

Well, for starters, if I told them they'd probably deny that I was sane. And that answer ignored how *I* felt about this new role. "That's not really…"

I trailed off. What could I say to him that he'd understand? Even after Aunt Alicia had taken off on him, he still believed in me, in the rightness of me picking up where the queen he'd served had left off, as if it were entirely inevitable.

"Red Knight," I said, still figuring out what I wanted to ask.

A frightened shriek pierced through the air from outside.

CHAPTER FIFTEEN

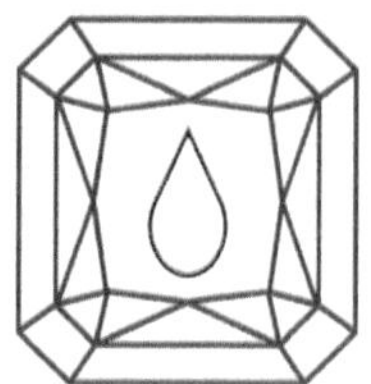

Hatter

"This is amazing," Doria was saying as she hopped from one stump to another around the shadowed firepit. "We've got the real queen right here with us! Bye-bye, Hearts!"

Dee rubbed his hands together. "Can you imagine the look on their faces when they find out we know their claim on the throne is a bunch of bull? It's going to be epic."

"Completely epic!"

I watched them, wishing I could absorb their enthusiasm. My thoughts were racing around in my head as if they'd been sucked into a whirlpool that had no bottom. My balance felt rather unsteady too. I glanced toward the cave Lyssa had disappeared into with the Red Knight, torn between wanting to see her coming back to us right now and wanting to have the right words to say to her before she did.

I couldn't say I didn't see it. What quality would I want in a queen that Lyssa hadn't proven she possessed in the past several days? Courage, compassion, determination, patience, smarts… The very fact that we'd made it here with the two artifacts no one before her had been able to retrieve showed she was meant for this role. I could picture her so easily standing with chin raised and eyes bright like she had when she'd insisted we set off on this quest, only with a crown resting on her head.

She hadn't come here looking to wear a crown, though. She hadn't meant to stay more than a couple of weeks. She wouldn't be the Lyssa who lingered in my mind even while she was gone if she hadn't cared so deeply for her loved ones in the Otherland.

And perhaps some selfish piece of me was niggling at me about where *I* could possibly fit into the life of a queen, if somehow she stayed.

Chess sidled closer to me, rubbing his hand over his auburn hair. He appeared to have fully recovered from his lapse in that field of vicious grass, but then, I suspected this was the sort of revelation that would shock any other emotion right out of your system. His gaze kept creeping back to the cave entrance too.

"Well, now we know why the Queen of Hearts was so obsessed with the idea that the Otherlanders named Alice were after her throne," I remarked. "Even if she thought the princess was dead, it'd be hard to see that name as a coincidence. Especially when you're a raging lunatic."

"But not a lunatic on that score," Chess said glibly. "She wasn't being paranoid. They really *were* the echoes of her past come to haunt her."

"Not on purpose," I couldn't help pointing out. I'd thought we were putting a lot on Lyssa just telling her about the Queen and the rebellion against her. This… She'd simply looked stunned as she'd followed the Red Knight to retrieve whatever he'd been keeping in that cave.

Theo's arms were crossed over his chest in a pose that looked uncharacteristically defensive, but when he spoke, his voice was as steady and assured as always. "Accepting this new role is a lot for Lyssa to deal with. We need to rally behind her, show her that she has all our support."

"White Knight?" Dum took a step back from where he'd been gazing across the field beyond the curved hill. "We might need to rally right now, for other reasons."

The ground shuddered as we spun around. A burbling cry carried across the field as not one but two jabberwocks charged across the thick grass toward us. Their eyes blazed with a white-hot fire, and smoke gushed from their maws like a rapid dog's drool. Their huge feathered bodies shook with fury.

We hadn't provoked that fury. The Knave and his remaining guard rushed from the square of night after them, the Knave cracking a whip across one jabberwock's tail and then the other. I didn't know where he'd found the creatures or how he'd gained control, but he was driving them now as surely as the wind in that patch of darkness had driven us.

At the next lash, flames belched from the jabberwocks' jaws, charring the grass in front of them in an instant. The acrid stink of the smoke clogged my nose. Doria let out a shriek, more terrified than I'd ever heard her. With the thump of racing footsteps and the clank of aged armor, Lyssa and the Red Knight burst from the cave.

My body went rigid. Two monsters—four if you counted the Knave and his man, which I would—were barreling toward every person in this world I still gave a damn about. My daughter, my lover, my friends…

A dizzying surge of emotion crackled through my nerves right into my head, hazing my vision, jolting me into action in a way I hadn't felt since I'd left the Spades, probably not since that last night—

I threw myself away from the memory and out of the shadows under the hill. My fingers closed around the base of one of the hair pins tucked into my jacket and yanked it free. The hard thin length felt good in my hand, but it wasn't going to stop a jabberwock.

My legs carried me on instinct, close enough to one jabberwock to wave the hair pin almost under its snout, leaping out of the way when it snorted another sputter of fire. "Dad!" Doria yelled, but her horrified voice only propelled me onward.

Now the jabberwock was pissed off at me. It thundered after me with a hissing rustle of its wings and another burbling moan. I was counting on the story I'd heard that those wings were only for show, that they couldn't actually hold the creature's massive body up. If that was wrong, well, in a minute I'd be cinders and jabberwock chow.

I veered around the far side of the hill and scrambled up its slope. The jabberwock hurtled after me over the thinner grass. My feet slipped on the steepest section, sending me to my knees. I scrambled up and hurled myself onward as flames singed my heels. Up, up, and then skidding down past the crest of the wave toward the sudden drop…

I almost misjudged my speed and toppled right over myself. At the last second, I tossed myself sideways and managed to grab hold of a ridge of rock protruding through the soil.

The jabberwock was too blinded by rage to notice the hill ended. It careened on over the edge—and plummeted down.

Its wings flapped frantically but barely caught the air. It tumbled head first and hit the ground below with a skull-cracking thump. Its body sprawled, the smoke dissipating around its crumpled snout.

Adrenaline from the dash coursed through me. I heaved myself to my feet. Down below, the others had scattered in the wake of the other jabberwock—and the Knave and his man were taking advantage of the chaos. Doria had ended up at the edge of the hill's shadow, and the guard was racing toward her with sword drawn.

Fuck, no. "Dee!" I shouted with all the air in my lungs. "Catch me."

His redhaired form appeared just beneath me. I sucked in a breath and jumped without a second thought.

We might not have pulled off this specific move in over ten years, but it seemed our bodies hadn't forgotten. My feet hit his arms in just the right spot, and he catapulted me toward Doria. I braced myself as I landed on the earth and whipped around.

The guard had diverted to another target, but the Knave was lunging at us now, dagger clutched in his hand and a killing glint in his beady eyes. I only had an instant to react. In that instant, my arms shot up. I slammed the hair pin into the vulnerable flesh just above his collarbone.

The Knave still managed to hack at me with his dagger. It raked across my sleeve as I jerked out of the way. Blood welled up through the cut he'd landed, but a lot more blood was bubbling from his throat.

A gurgle escaped his bulging neck. His face turned even grayer. He tried to sputter something over his jagged teeth, but the words didn't come. With a shudder, he slumped at my feet.

"For the honor of the Reds!" the Red Knight was hollering. He stabbed his sword into the guard's gut, and the other man keeled over. Lyssa had leapt in front of the jabberwock. Its head was weaving from side to side, that manic flame still dancing in its eyes, but she'd brought it to a halt.

"Go!" she said, waving a large wand with a ruby at its end. The last artifact, I supposed. "Go back to wherever you came from. We don't want to hurt you, but I can't let you hurt any of us either. Go on!"

I tensed as the jabberwock lurched toward her, but it was only heaving itself into a turn. It wheeled around and loped back across the field.

Dum was lying on the ground, clutching a burnt spot on his side, but his gaze was clear, his breaths coming steady. From the bruise forming on Theo's jaw, he'd taken a blow or two. Nothing too serious, though.

We were all alive. We'd survived.

Everyone on my side, anyway. My gaze fell to the blood-soaked grass around the Knave's limp body, and my stomach flipped over. The adrenaline high that had carried me through the fight was fading, and queasiness churned beneath it.

"Well, now," Chess said with a grin, clapping me on the shoulder. "There's the Mad Hatter we all loved. I knew you couldn't have lost your grip on insanity completely."

Doria was staring at me. At the bloodstained hair pin still clutched in my hand. I dropped it. I had another one in my jacket.

Resolve formed around my nausea. I hadn't had a real choice. I'd protected her—I'd protected Lyssa, and all the others too. I had to keep doing that until nothing in this land still threatened them.

If someone had to fall, better it was me than them.

Theo had knelt to see to Dum, who was smearing salve on his burnt flesh now. The White Knight straightened up now. He took in our fallen enemies.

"We've bought ourselves a little time," he said. "But there'll be a new Knave risen; there'll be more guards. If we want to make the most of this advantage, we'd better get on that train and back to the city while there's still a chance no one there has put two and two together."

Night had fallen long before we made it back to the city. The clouds congealing in the sky overhead turned the landscape even darker. A faint drizzle came down through the damp air as we waited for Dee to return with the ally the White Knight had sent him to collect.

Doria stepped closer to me, tugging nervously on her dark hair. This was her first rainfall.

The twin came into view with a woman at his side whom I recognized from the recent Spades meetings. She studied our group with curious eyes where we stood amid the trees near the road outside town.

"What's the word since I've been gone?" Theo asked.

The woman's lips pursed. "The Queen has taken more people from the city each day, as she promised. Three yesterday, five today." Her gaze slid to Chess. "The guards are out looking for Cheshire now too."

Theo grimaced. "The Knave sent word back one way or another, then. They'll be waiting to haul all of us in. All right, we'll simply—"

"No," the woman broke in. "It's just Chess. The call went out just this afternoon. They're saying the Duchess made a claim that he's a traitor."

I only caught Chess's brief stiffening because I was already looking at him. A second later, it was gone. "Well," he said, "if it was going to be anyone, it may as well be me, seeing as I'm the only one here who can vanish quite literally."

The drizzle picked up speed, droplets flecking my face. I adjusted my suit jacket. Chess's shoulders hunched slightly under the rain, the only sign that it bothered him.

"You could come back to my place for the night," I said. "I have room. We have the White Knight's alarm system in place. You still get wet even if you're out of sight, don't you?"

Chess shrugged. "Not if I remove myself from the source of the wetness. Offer appreciated but unneeded, Hatter. I think I'll go take a closer lay of the land."

He brushed Lyssa's arm in a farewell gesture and faded away.

"You would not believe what we found out on that trip," Dee started saying to the woman, excitement dancing in his eyes. "The—"

"Dee," Lyssa said quickly. "I think I'd like some more time to figure out how I'm going to handle this situation before we tell anyone else. There'll be a lot of questions… I want to be able to answer them."

Dee glanced at Theo, as if he needed the White Knight's approval to follow Lyssa's request. The request of his probable future *queen*.

And Theo gave it, as if he had that authority. He dipped his head. "We'll meet tomorrow. For now, I'm sure we all need our rest, in proper beds." He turned to Lyssa. "You could stay in the Tower tonight if you'd like."

Lyssa's arms came up to hug herself. "The Knave almost caught me there before," she said. "At Hatter's, I have an easy escape route. I think I'll stick with that for now."

He nodded and leaned in to kiss her, clearly suffering from no doubts himself about how he fit into her life now. In fact, something in his stance gave me the impression he was staking a claim. I swallowed a prickle of jealousy.

"Let's go then," I said. "Before anyone notices us standing around out here."

"Where Lyssa goes, I go too," the Red Knight announced, clicking his visor up. He'd grabbed a helmet to match his worn armor before we'd caught the train. "She is my purpose."

Wonderful. "Fine," I said, waving for him to come along too.

When we reached my building, he eyed the shop and then the main floor of the apartment grimly.

"There's a guest bedroom free on the third floor," I said.

"No," the Red Knight said. "I will stand guard through the night."

"You've got to sleep sometime," Lyssa pointed out. "Theo gave us a device that'll wake us all up if anyone comes up the stairs."

The Red Knight hesitated. "I will rest on the sofa," he said, pointing across the room. "So that I may be the first line of defense for your Majesty if the occasion arises."

Lyssa winced at the "your Majesty." Doria hurried on up to her fourth-floor bedroom ahead of us, but Lyssa paused by the bathroom door. She looked tired, and I didn't think it was just from the long days of travel behind us.

I stopped outside my bedroom door. "Do you want to talk?"

She opened her mouth and closed it again. For a second, her expression turned so haunted it made my gut clench. She tugged her gaze up to meet mine with a smile that looked forced.

"Does it change a lot, this whole thing about me being queen?" she asked.

Between us? Hearts take me, was that what she was worrying about? The corners of my lips quirked upward. "It hasn't lowered my opinion of you in the slightest, I promise," I said.

Lyssa's smile relaxed a little. She stepped toward me, and I met her for a kiss that sent a thrill through me even though I could tell she wasn't looking for more in this moment. It had been an honor to make this woman tremble with delight little more than a day ago.

She walked up the stairs with more lightness in her steps than before, but my heart still squeezed as I watched her go. I'd helped some, but was it enough? I couldn't shake the sense that I was failing her. Maybe failing her and Doria both. I might have already failed them by stepping back from so much of who I'd been before either of them had really needed me.

No more hanging back. No more shying from danger. From now on, I ran straight toward it.

CHAPTER SIXTEEN

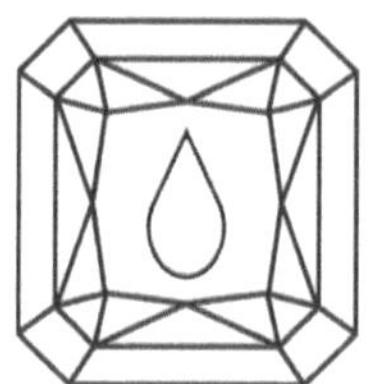

Lyssa

I'd had plenty of restless nights in Wonderland, but none of them half as bad as this one. The rain drummed against the window like the thoughts that wouldn't stop nagging at me even as I buried my face in my pillow. The warm metal of the ring pressed against my breastbone under the blouse I was wearing as a nightshirt.

I was something like the great-great-great-great-great-granddaughter of Wonderland's rightful queen. The land fucking *recognized* me as its ruler, responded to me like it did no one else. There was a man resting downstairs who expected me to challenge the Queen of Hearts and then take back my family's place on the throne. Possibly some of the people who'd been with me for that revelation expected the same thing.

Back home, I couldn't even convince my mom not to fret about me constantly. How the hell was I going to command an entire country?

Could I just run away from all this like Aunt Alicia had? My stomach knotted at the thought. Ten innocent people were sitting in the Queen's dungeon right now waiting to have their heads chopped off. Hatter, Chess, Theo, and the others could have lost theirs just for helping me in my quest, which they'd done before they'd had a clue I was anything other than a wayward Otherlander. What kind of person would I be if I let them keep suffering when I had the ability to change that?

Also, there was the slight complication of having no available means to get home at the moment.

Stewing over it wasn't making my mind any clearer. If I could just get to sleep, maybe I'd feel less confused in the morning.

I tipped from my front onto my side, and a sharper rapping joined the patter of the rain against the window. My heart stuttered. I jerked upright, my hand shooting toward the ruby-set sword I'd left on top of the covers next to me.

Thunder rumbled, and a flash of lightning caught on auburn hair and high cheekbones as the figure outside leaned close to the glass. It was only Chess.

A short laugh sputtered out of me. I scrambled off the bed and unlatched the window to push it open.

Chess slipped inside, his wet clothes plastered to his brawny form, his darkened hair sending droplets over his pale face. When I grasped his elbow to help him in, the fabric chilled my fingers. A puddle of rainwater formed on the floor beneath him in an instant. He held his body tight, but a shiver he couldn't restrain rippled through him.

"I rethought Hatter's offer," he said, with a click of his teeth as if he'd snapped them shut to stop them from chattering.

"Stay right there," I ordered him. I switched on the bedside lamp and hustled down the hall as quietly as I could. No need to wake up the whole apartment.

I grabbed a couple of towels from the stack in the fourth-floor bathroom and carried them back to the bedroom. Chess tugged one tight around his torso and rubbed the other over his hair. A little color came into his cheeks as he started to warm up.

"You know, there are these things called doors," I said.

He gave me a crooked grin. "I figured it was better to come in the back way rather than set off the White Knight's alarm downstairs and throw you all into a panic."

Okay, he had a point there. "You couldn't find anywhere to get out of the rain?" I asked. He'd never actually mentioned any kind of a home. Where did he usually spend his nights?

Chess shrugged. "Nowhere with company I wanted to keep. I have to admit, rain is not quite as delightful as I recalled. Maybe there's a better sort, but this kind is entirely too wet." He made a face at his still-drenched clothes. Another shiver ran through his body. I touched his hand and winced at how cold his skin felt.

"Come on," I said, deciding this wasn't the time to be worrying about modesty or people getting the wrong idea. "Take those wet clothes off and get under the covers before you catch hypothermia."

Despite his shivering, Chess raised his eyebrows, mischief glinting in his bright blue eyes. "You're asking me to strip and hop in bed?"

"So you can *warm up*," I said emphatically, although let's be real, my mind had already gone to all sorts of other places.

Chess chuckled to himself, but he complied. He peeled off his shirt and kicked off his sodden shoes. Rather than ogle him as he tugged down his pants, I slipped back into bed to warm up the space beneath the blanket, scooting over to leave room for him. And then, okay, I ogled him a little as he tucked that well-muscled body—still with a pair of boxer-briefs on for a tiny bit of modesty—under the covers next to me.

I let my hand ease over to rest on his bicep, not wanting to assume he'd want more contact than that. Chess had indicated he was attracted to me, but he'd been pretty restrained with any physical overtures so far. Right now he was probably too busy thawing out to be thinking about any more, er, intimate ways of warming up.

"Sorry I woke you," he murmured.

"You didn't," I said. "I hadn't managed to get to sleep yet."

He rolled onto his side to face me. There was still a foot of space between us, but I could feel the spreading warmth of his body gathering in the cocoon under the covers. "Too many thoughts whirling around in that lovely head of yours?"

"It's not every day you find out you're the heir to a long lost royal family."

"Indeed. And being asked to rule over the lot of us—not the most appealing offer I can imagine." He winked.

"That's not really the problem. I wasn't looking to rule over *anyone*." I paused, considering. "It would be the Diamonds too, wouldn't it? Even if a lot of them hate the Queen of Hearts, would they really want some Otherlander taking over the throne?"

"Difficult to determine how those minds work behind the sparkliness," Chess said. "I suppose they'd have to learn to like it."

That didn't sound very promising. My stomach clenched with an ache of uncertainty. "Maybe it's better if I don't think about it anymore for a while. I'm just tying myself in knots without getting anywhere useful."

It occurred to me that I wasn't the only one with a quandary. "Chess, what are you going to do now that the Hearts' Guard will be searching specifically for you? You can't just stay invisible all the time."

"Technically I could," Chess said in his playful way. "It would keep everyone on their toes on a permanent basis."

"Seriously," I said. "Even if we can stop the Queen from taking new prisoners, she'll still want you now that that Duchess woman has accused you."

I'd seen Chess talking to the Duchess once—an elegant young woman covered in gems and layers of silk. She'd come looking for him specifically. He'd said they'd been… friends, or something, when he'd used to visit the palace and hobnob with the Diamonds.

"Do you know why she'd have done that?" I added. "I thought—she knew you before. She thought you'd *help* the Diamonds by giving her information. Why would she suddenly tell everyone you're with the Spades?"

Chess's gaze slid away from me. "She and I had a… rather fraught affiliation. And I believe she has even less grasp on sanity than the rest of us lunatics. Her reasons seem reasonable to her, no doubt."

There had to be more to it than that. "Chess," I prodded.

His mouth tightened as his eyes met mine again. "There's little else I could say that's fit for a queen's ears."

The tension in his expression made the ache in my gut dig deeper. "I'm not a queen right now," I said. "And I don't know if I'm ever going to be one. And… And even if I become one, I'm not going to be like the queen you've got now. I'd still be *me*. I'd want to know what people are really going through, what's upset them, everything. I wouldn't go around using people's vulnerabilities as weapons against them either."

For a long moment, silence hung over us. I dared to raise my hand to stroke the backs of my fingers over his cheek. "I know *something* has been bothering you. The way you froze up when the grass caught you, this thing with the Duchess, secret powers you don't want anyone to know about… If you'd just rather not talk about it, that's fine. But you have to believe me that I *want* to know. I want to know *you*. Okay?"

I meant those words so much my voice thickened with the emotion that had filled my throat. Chess stared at me. Something shifted in his face. Then he took my hand and kissed my knuckles the way he had when he first helped me find my way back home.

"Okay," he said, his own voice rough. "Ask, and I'll tell you."

Now that he'd given me the opening, I wasn't sure where to start. The thought of the Duchess itched at me, but I didn't want to sound like a jealous girlfriend interrogating her guy about every woman he'd interacted with. So I started with, "Why did getting trapped in the grass shake you up so much?"

That couldn't be too intrusive a question, right? Hatter had seemed to have an idea, and he and Chess weren't exactly BFFs.

Chess's raw chuckle told me I'd estimated wrong. "That's the whole story right there," he said.

"All right," I said. "However much you're ready to tell me."

He eased over onto his back again. An uncharacteristic furrow creased his brow as he contemplated the ceiling. Then he started speaking, in a lilting tone that somehow managed to sound flippant and ominous at the same time.

"I told you before that there was a while when I passed time with the Diamonds. I got bored, and they were different, and treading that close to the Queen and her temper was a little thrilling. I thought if things turned dangerous, I could simply vanish. I thought the only thing I had to worry about was keeping my head attached."

I scooted a little closer, tucking my hand loosely around his arm and tipping my head toward his bare shoulder to indicate he had my full attention.

"At first," Chess went on, "I played around with different people there. Mostly women, but occasionally the men too. But pretty soon the Duchess got her eye on me, and I discovered that was something of a thrill too—being chosen, being coveted. And she… was very different. I never knew what to expect. There was always some new element to explore. So we made an arrangement. When I came to the palace, I belonged to her, and we would try everything."

"When you say you 'played' with people…" I said, pretty sure I already knew the answer.

"Indulging ourselves," Chess said. "With food, with leisure, and very frequently with sex. The appetites of the Diamonds aren't so different from those of the Clubbers."

"Except for the Duchess?"

"The Duchess simply…" He sighed. "We experimented with the line between pleasure and pain. It was during the freeze, so nothing was permanent. She would… cut me, or burn me, or whatever else she'd come up with that day, and I ate it up." He wet his lips and glanced at me. "If you'd rather I didn't keep going—"

I brushed a kiss to his shoulder. "I'm listening." Did he think I was going to be horrified by what he'd told me? Even in a world where you *weren't* being driven around the bend living the same day over and over again, S&M wasn't so weird. Melody had a boyfriend a couple years ago who'd wanted her to put clamps on his nipples and things like that.

For a second I thought Chess was going to stop for his own comfort. He swallowed audibly.

"All in good fun," he said, with a self-deprecating edge. "She liked to up the ante, and she became more and more controlling about the ways I could speak to or even look at anyone else in the palace. I started to develop the sense she saw me as a toy rather than a person. But I was getting off, and that's what we Wonderlanders care about most, isn't it? I thought, if I ever got uncomfortable, I could simply leave…"

A quiver ran through his muscles, but this time it wasn't from the cold. I hugged his arm a little harder to say I was here, I was with him. What could have happened back then to leave this strong, gleeful man so shaken?

A faint rasp came into his voice. "I came one day, and she was in more of a mood than I'd ever seen her. She wanted to tie me up, and she tied me hard. And then she started to cut. Not just a little, here and there, but deep. I told her it was too much, but she just laughed. After a while I couldn't talk at all. I couldn't shift to slip out of the bonds—when pain is rushing through me, I can't focus enough to use my deepest talents."

So he'd been trapped there like he'd been in the grass. My throat constricted.

"She strung me up over her bed, upside down, and carved away at me until I didn't have any idea what anything but pain was," Chess went on. "Breathing, swallowing, it all hurt. She worked me to the limit of where I suppose she assumed I wouldn't die, and after that she left. She left me alone, hanging, bleeding all over her *fucking* white satin sheets…"

The last few words came out in a whisper and a snarl. He hesitated, his chest stuttering as he exhaled.

All of me hurt, hearing him describe what the Duchess had done to him. I reached my arm across his chest tentatively, wanting to embrace him properly, not sure if he'd even want that. He caught me and tugged me to him, and I hugged him hard, tears leaking from behind my closed eyelids.

"I thought I was going to die," he said. "I thought she'd gotten bored with me and wanted me gone. Toward the end, I *wanted* to die… I can take a hint. When I woke up where I always did the next morning, I knew I was never going back. But she came looking for me a few days later, as if it hadn't even occurred to her I'd stay away after that, and I realized she hadn't wanted me dead at all. She'd just wanted to watch me hurt, and she'd want to do it again."

"I'm so sorry," I murmured against his chest.

"Ah, well, some good came out of it. Seeing how mad the Diamonds were getting gave me the guts to start helping the Spades. And it wasn't as if I hadn't set myself up to be used."

"You didn't ask for that," I said fiercely. "No one would have. No way in hell can you say it's your fault."

"If a queen decrees it, I suppose it must be so," Chess said. He sounded grateful but not convinced. "In any case, that's the rambling answer to your question. Being tangled up like that reminded me of how she tied me that day… I can't always keep my head straight when the memories leap up. It's also why she's probably made this accusation. She doesn't even know I'm with the Spades. She's just peeved she lost her toy, and it's another way for her to try to control me. And what else was there? Oh, the reasons I keep my transformative skill secret."

"It's all right," I said. "You're *allowed* to have some secrets."

He shifted onto his side and cupped my cheek, gazing into my eyes for the first time since he'd started his story. His eyes were bright again. "Are you saying that for my sake or for yours? If it's too much—"

"No," I said quickly. "I'm just worried about you. I didn't mean to stir up a whole bunch of awful memories."

"Of course you didn't. They're only that—memories. My other form… Being able to shift completely from one thing to another is a rare talent even in Wonderland. If the Queen knew, she'd want me not for my head but for her menagerie. I've generally been circumspect. But more so—when I was more reckless, I let the Duchess see—I had the ridiculous idea of impressing her—and for her it turned into a new type of—"

His mouth pressed flat against something more than he wanted to say. "Since then, I don't shift, even on my own, unless I absolutely have to. It brings back the time with her more sharply. I don't want anyone else to get it into their heads that they could use that part of me. Hatter knows, because I was madder than usual when I found my way to him in the early days, and he helped me arrange that she would forget. So now it's just him and you. Not too shabby."

How exactly had they "arranged" for the Duchess to forget a detail like that? I wanted to ask, but I'd already dragged so much pain out of him. Questions like that could wait.

"Okay," I said. "I'll make sure it stays that way. No one's hearing it from me."

"I know they won't, lovely," he said, a warm smile crossing his face. "And I—" His gaze followed his fingers as they teased over my hair and then down the side of my neck to my shoulder. "I do want you, you know. Very much. But whether you choose to be queen or not, I don't know if I can be all that good for anyone as anything more than the briefest of flings, and you should have more than that."

"Chess."

"It's not just the damage done, you know," he said before I could go on. "Maybe I was already screwed up even before, to let it go on so long, to let it go that far, to have *enjoyed* it until it was almost murder…"

"I don't think that," I said. "It was a screwed-up situation. And you're already more than that. You can make me laugh when I'm terrified, and you've had my back every time I've needed it, even when you had to risk exposing your secret to protect me. I should get to decide what's good for me, shouldn't I?" And God, the brush of his fingertips had felt so good I was already tingling to experience everything else he could offer.

The flash of desire in his eyes turned the tingling into a surge of heat. He leaned in, the tip of his nose grazing mine. His voice dropped even lower.

"I haven't been with anyone on my own since—since then. It's always been with someone else joining in, usually the White Knight… Less pressure when the focus isn't all on my performance. Less intense. I don't know—I don't want to disappoint you."

"I'll take whatever you're ready to give," I said. "And I'll be a lot more disappointed if you *don't* kiss me, as soon as humanly possible."

He gave me a perfect Cheshire grin, and then his mouth captured mine.

Even after that build-up, his kiss was as sweet as the ones before. He tipped his head, teasing my lips apart, and his hand slid down my side to my hip. He left it there, hot as a brand, as we kissed and kissed again, deeper and sweeter until my whole body was trembling giddily with anticipation of what would come next. The tips of his fangs grazed my lip with a sharply thrilling tingle.

I looped my arm around his shoulders, and he rolled us over. The weight of him over me, braced on one elbow as he trailed his fingers up under my nightshirt, and the tangling of our naked legs made me even hungrier than before. I shifted, arching into him, and my back bumped something flat and hard.

The sword. I eased back from Chess and tugged it out from where it had gotten tangled in the covers. "I think maybe we'd better get this out of the way."

Chess laughed. "Now that's a dangerous bed companion."

"Meant to be dangerous to the wrong sort of person coming knocking at my window," I muttered.

"I'll be glad you don't count me among that number." He took the hilt from me gingerly, and it occurred to me that I'd never seen him handle anything with a blade before. Maybe he had bad associations with cutting instruments after what the Duchess had put him through. But he didn't look particularly discomforted by the sword. He just tipped over on his back so he could drop it over his side of the bed. It hit the floor with a thump.

The covers had fallen partly off him, leaving his sculpted chest on full display in the hazy lamplight. On an impulse, I followed him, slipping my knee across his waist to straddle him. Chess smiled up at me with a sound that was almost a purr as I smoothed my splayed hands over those planes of muscle. The burn between my legs urged me to scoot lower, to fit myself against him in the most tantalizing way, but that momentary thought about the sword held me back.

"Is there anything I should make sure to be careful of?" I asked, forcing my hands to still over his pecs. "Anywhere that being touched bothers you?"

I didn't know how to phrase it better than that, but the shadow that passed through Chess's eyes told me he understood. He clasped his hand over one of mine. "Don't worry yourself about that. I've had practice at tuning out that kind of discomfort."

Because he hadn't been with any partner before me he felt comfortable telling about his past. A much more intense emotion than lust squeezed my heart. I squeezed his fingers in turn. “I don’t want you to have to tune any of this out,” I said. “I want you to enjoy all of it. It’ll be easier for me *not* to worry if I know.”

He let out a breath. “It may be best to avoid my neck, and the sides of my ribs, and the backs of my knees.”

The words gave me a flash of an image, the picture he’d drawn with his voice of him hanging there bleeding, the places where she’d dug the wounds deepest. I gripped his fingers a little harder, my throat choking up.

Then he was pushing himself upright to catch my lips again, and everything fell away except the tenderness of his kiss and the intoxicatingly rich scent of his skin.

His hand crept up under my nightshirt again, tracing sparks over my skin, so teasingly slow I squirmed on his lap. His palm finally settled over my bare breast. I barely filled his large hand, but Chess didn’t give any sign of minding. He flicked his thumb over my nipple, and I whimpered into his mouth.

He raised his head to look over my shoulder. A smile that was more a smirk curved his lips. “We appear to have company.”

I glanced over. The bedroom door had opened a few inches; the lamplight caught on Hatter, rumpled and flushed in striped pajamas. He nudged the doorknob farther and then caught it, as if he wasn’t sure whether he should be coming or going.

“I heard a thud,” he said, and I remembered Chess dropping the sword on the floor. “I thought I’d make sure everything was all right. You had a change of heart about my hospitality?”

He was talking as if he hadn’t found us in the middle of anything particularly exciting, but I felt his gaze on us, on me, like a heated caress. It set off a hot flare between my thighs.

“The rain proved too much for me, I’m ashamed to admit,” Chess said, equally casual. He paused. “I believe there’s plenty of room here, if you’d like to join in. If our Lyssa would like that too.” He gave my cheek a gentle nuzzle.

He would like that, wouldn’t he? He’d said he could relax more when someone else was involved. Had he known Hatter’s bedroom was right under this one—had he let the sword fall loudly on purpose?

I wasn't sure it mattered. The idea of Hatter caressing me with his hands as well as his gaze set off a quiver of desire through my nerves. I'd never been with two guys at the same time, but I didn't have a doubt that with *these* two, it would be fucking spectacular. Or spectacular fucking?

Both—definitely both.

"No objections here," I said, extending my hand toward Hatter.

He hesitated a moment longer. Obviously he hadn't joined in with Chess for similar interludes in the past. The thought that this would be new for him too sparked an excitement that radiated through my core as he stepped inside and shut the door.

Chess raised my nightshirt to yank it right off me. As he tossed it aside, Hatter inhaled sharply. He came up beside the bed and tipped my head toward his for a kiss, hot and determined. Chess bent down to slick his tongue over the peak of my breast. My fingers curled around the silky lapel of Hatter's pajama top, around Chess's hair, pleasure spiking through me.

Chess had loosened up, all right. He fondled one breast with his hand while he worked over the other with his mouth so thoroughly I whimpered and rocked in his chest. Hatter was devouring me with a kiss so hard my lips tingled. He stroked his fingertips up and down my back, and Chess gripped my hip to tug me tighter to him, teasing a fang over my nipple. The feel of his rigid cock pressing against me through two thin layers of fabric made me want to explode right there.

I pulled back just far enough to squirm out of my panties. Hatter's fingers trailed over my legs as he offered his assistance. He kissed my neck, my shoulder, as he traced his hand back up my inner thigh. I fumbled with the buttons on his top, losing track of what I was doing when he swiveled his thumb over my clit. A cry broke from my lips.

Chess gave my nipple one last swipe of his talented tongue and wriggled out of his boxer-briefs. He dipped a finger into my wetness as Hatter continued working his magic just above. I sank lower instinctively. "Chess…"

"Right here," he murmured, and guided the straining head of his cock to my slit. Oh, God, it was as big as the rest of him. A burn of pleasure spread out from my core as I eased down onto him. Chess groaned, pressing his mouth to my throat. Hatter kept teasing my clit, his other hand gliding up to tweak the tip of my breast, his breath shaky against my shoulder blade.

Chess caught my mouth as we slid together all the way to the base of his cock. He tucked his hand around to my ass to adjust my position, stroking into me at an angle that made me shudder with bliss. Then he held still, his fingers reaching farther to lightly probe my other entrance. A different but no less eager tingling sparked at his touch.

"You could have us both," he said in a liquid voice. "Double the enjoyment?"

I'd never "had" any guy that way, but the pleasure rushing through me and the promise in Chess's voice made me want to try. My agreement tumbled out. "Yes. I've never—we'll have to take it slow—"

Chess grinned at my stumbling enthusiasm. His gaze shifted to Hatter. "Do you have suitable oil?"

Hatter let out a rough chuckle, looking gloriously disheveled with his hair wild and his top half unbuttoned, his face even more flushed than before. The silk fabric of his pajamas did nothing to hide the erection tenting the bottoms. "I think— Yes, there should be—"

He vanished out the door, walking swiftly but lightly. We definitely didn't want anyone *else* in the apartment waking up. I slung my arms across Chess's shoulders, careful not to set them too close to his neck, and rocked with him through another kiss. Just that subtle movement and the fullness of him inside me took my breath away.

Remembering the fears he'd expressed earlier, I tipped my cheek next to his and murmured, "This is good. This is really good. You can climb in through my window anytime."

Chess laughed and kissed me again, penetrating me with a deeper thrust that had me seeing stars. Then Hatter was back, dashing to the bed. He opened the little jar he was holding and rubbed a slick substance between his fingers.

"Better to warm it up first, I think," he said in a low voice that turned me on even more.

I thought I was ready, but when his hand slipped over my ass to my opening, my nerves jumped and a gasp spilled out of me.

Hatter definitely wasn't new at *this,* whether he'd tried it as part of a threesome before or not. His deft fingers relaxed me as easily as they seemed to do everything. He traced their slick tips around my entrance until I was pushing back toward him, wanting more. One and then another worked inside me. A pleased hum reverberated through my chest, and Chess groaned as I bobbed against him.

When Hatter asked, "Ready?" with that one word so charged with wanting it nearly melted me, I was aching for it.

"Please," I said, and whimpered at the press of his cock, slick as his fingers had been. The two men held me steady between them as Hatter stretched me, filling me twice as much as before. The heady sensation of having them both inside me made my head spin with bliss.

I gripped Chess's hair, my lips brushing his, panting too hard to properly kiss him. Hatter brushed my hair to the side and nipped the back of my neck. His rough breath seared my skin.

We moved together, Chess's hand on my thigh, Hatter's arm around my waist, their lengths pulsing through me in a building rhythm. The stars I'd seen before spiraled before my eyes. One wave of pleasure and another and another rushed through me.

"Fuck," Hatter muttered against my back, jerking a little harder, a little faster, with a shudder that told me he couldn't hold back any longer. The urgency of his release tipped me over the edge right after him. I bucked against Chess, the stars behind my eyelids bursting into fireworks in time with the crackle of ecstasy that swept me away.

"Oh, Lyssa," Chess said, soft as a sigh. As Hatter withdrew, he plunged up into me, pushing my orgasm higher, farther, until his breath broke with the hitch of his own release.

I sagged onto the bed beside Chess, and Hatter settled in at my other side. Tucked there between the two of them, more sated than I'd ever felt in my life and the afterglow still tingling through me, it was hard to imagine ever wanting anything more than this.

"Mmm," Chess murmured. "Now that is what I call paradise. We could teach the Diamonds a thing or three. Not that we'd want to bother."

He said it so breezily that I couldn't help snickering. But as the pleasure of the encounter waned and all the other worries I'd had crept back in, my mind slipped back to other things he'd said about the Diamonds, before tonight.

"Chess," I said quietly. "You mentioned that you thought the Diamonds were unhappy enough with the Queen that someone there might have murdered the prince. Do you think… Are there any of them who'd help us displace her?" Whatever I decided to do, she wasn't going to back down easily.

Chess cocked his head in contemplation. The corners of his lips curled up, and he brushed a kiss to my cheek. "You know what? There just might be."

CHAPTER SEVENTEEN

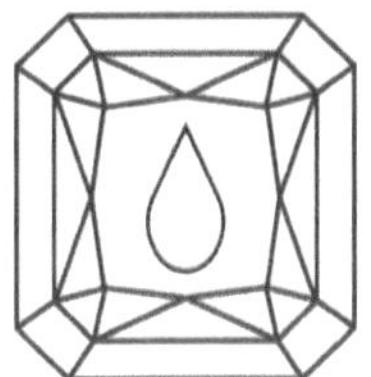

Lyssa

"You're sure he'll be there right now?" Theo asked, glancing over at Chess as we ambled along the road through the city, toward the lane that would take us past the pond of tears. The morning sun glinted off the puddles of rainwater left from last night's storm.

"Unicorn was a creature of habit as long as I knew him," Chess replied. He walked with a spring in his step that I liked to think was as much thanks to our amazing night together as the mission ahead of us. "He always took his run before lunch. The field out past the mushroom stands is a good distance out from everyone. He doesn't like to be watched when he gets down on all fours." He waggled his eyebrows.

He'd told me earlier that he'd followed Unicorn once, invisibly, out of curiosity, and that was how he'd discovered this part of his schedule. Which worked out well for us now, because if things hadn't changed, we should find the palace dweller on his own.

Whether he'd be interested in our proposal was another matter. Chess had seemed pretty certain the equine man could be swayed.

Theo was possibly less certain, as Chess must have picked up on too. "You really don't need to accompany us the entire way, White Knight," he said teasingly. "I'd almost think you don't trust me to spin my words well enough."

Theo smiled, but his eyes stayed grim. "It's not so much how well you spin them but how quickly you can cut to the heart of the matter, friend," he said. "You have to admit you do have a tendency toward obfuscation. Besides, with this much riding on the meeting, I'd like to be on hand even if only to lend authority to the offer of alliance."

The Red Knight, who'd been walking a little behind us, let out a doubtful sounding harrumph. "Can't trust any of the palace folk. No loyalty there."

He'd insisted on coming with us—coming with *me*, mainly—but thankfully we'd managed to talk him into gelling down his wayward hair and shedding his tarnished armor for one of Hatter's suits, which fit his height even if it hung a little loose on his skinny frame. So far he hadn't drawn any unusual attention.

Making sure no one noticed *me* was the bigger concern. I'd darkened my hair with a fresh dose of dye powder and pulled it back into a braid so its length wasn't as obvious. Between that and the bright green Wonderlander dress I was wearing, I felt reasonably disguised, but my skin still prickled whenever we passed anyone.

The streets were pretty quiet, though. The Queen had come through with her procession just a couple hours ago, the guards grabbing six more people, and the city's residents seemed to be hanging back behind closed doors as if worried she might make a second sweep.

That thought brought back the doubts that had been dogging me since the Red Knight had first told his story, along with the more specific ones that had risen up this morning.

"Even if he will join us, even if I wanted to try for the throne, are we in any position to do that right away?" I asked quietly, looking to Theo. "No one else in Wonderland knows about the Red royals—do you think they'll believe that story and take our side if I challenge the Queen of Hearts?"

Theo let out a slow breath. "Unfortunately, no," he said. "To both questions. If you can convince Unicorn, he may turn enough of the palace folk to our side to spur on a rebellion that way. If you can demonstrate the powers of the artifacts, we should be able to sway enough Clubbers to overcome the Hearts' Guard without the Diamonds help at all. But both of those scenarios will require time and care. As soon as the Queen catches wind that you truly are aiming to displace, she'll put all her power into destroying you."

In a weird way, his answer was a relief. It took off a bit of the pressure. If we couldn't try for the throne now, then I didn't have to decide yet.

"Is that what I should ask Unicorn to do first, then? Talk up the cause with the other Diamonds?"

Theo shook his head. "Our first priority has to be getting the prisoners out before she orders their execution. Her dungeon is filling fast. If we lose them, no amount of magic is going to win the city folk over. Unicorn can give us a more in-depth account of the security and perhaps get us access so we can retrieve them."

"Besides, once they're out, it'll be easy to convince more of the Clubbers to join the Spades," Chess said brightly. "Onward toward rebellion."

I tried to ignore the knot in my stomach. "Onward, one step at a time."

That was how I'd approached everything in my life. Get food on the table. Get Mom to work another day. Get this bill paid and then that one.

If you looked too hard at the big picture bearing down on you, it could overwhelm you.

At the edge of the city, just beyond the last of the off-kilter buildings, a woman with wiry gray hair and a slightly stooped back was swaying from side to side as she peered off down the road. She was gripping the shoulders of the boy standing in front of her, who looked to be about ten. His gaze shot toward us at the sound of our feet, and his eyes widened. He shifted backward as if trying to urge her out of view.

Theo frowned. He picked up his pace to pull ahead of us, walking with swift but smooth strides. "What's the matter?" he asked, coming to a stop in front of the pair.

The boy opened and closed his mouth a couple times. "Nothing. Everything's fine."

"We're waiting—" the old woman started, and the boy clenched her hand.

"No, Grandma. We're just—just enjoying the view."

That comment sounded so unlikely that even I knew he had to be lying. Theo's attention shifted to the woman, his expression mild despite the concern in it. "You know me, don't you, Gladey?"

She swayed a little toward him, her eyes twitching before they settled on him. "Inventor," she said. "Why, where are you off to today?"

"To see about solving a problem or two, as I usually am," Theo said. "I'm getting the feeling you might have one."

The boy's eyes had widened even more. "Inventor!" he exclaimed, and bit his lip. "Sorry. I didn't realize..."

"It's all right," Theo said. "I don't believe we've had a chance to meet before. You're Gladey's grandson?"

The boy nodded, suddenly shy. "Winden," he said. "I—I don't know what to do, but I don't think there's any invention that's going to help."

"That's all right." Theo bent forward so their heads were level, as if they were about to conspire. "Sometimes I simply invent plans. What's the trouble here?"

My heart fluttered where the other three of us had hung back. I'd seen Theo leading the Spades as the White Knight, commanding and passionate, but I hadn't had much chance to see him act as Inventor to the Clubbers and other city people. His presence still held its usual air of authority, but softer around the edges, his smile gentle and his stance relaxed, welcoming these people into the opportunity to rely on him.

You couldn't watch and not know how much they mattered to him.

The woman jumped to answer his question. "It's Mallowy," she said. "She's not come back from the mushroom stands yet. I'm going to be here when she comes. I'm going to see her."

"Grandma," the boy said tightly. He looked at Theo and spoke under his breath. "The guards took my mom. Two days ago. Grandma was *there*, but she keeps talking like she thinks she's just got to wait here and Mom will show up. I don't know why. Mom *won't* come, and if the guards see Grandma here acting like this—she was *yelling* for her earlier…"

His voice wobbled. My gut twisted in understanding. If the guards noticed someone standing around talking about wanting to find one of the prisoners, they might see it as an act of defiance. They might take Gladey too.

Theo's jaw tensed. He patted the boy's shoulder, but I could see the pain in his expression. I was feeling it too. We didn't have any real reassurance to offer, any guarantee that the boy's mother would be returned safely. We didn't partly because of my own hesitation.

I braced myself for Theo to glance at me, maybe not even to say anything, but just to catch my gaze and share this moment with me, making sure I knew how much I was needed.

He didn't. He didn't shift his attention off the boy and his grandmother for a second. He simply straightened up and touched Gladey's elbow.

"Gladey," he said kindly, his smile going crooked. "I know where Mallowy is. She's not out at the mushroom stands. You won't find her waiting here. All right?"

"But she must be so lonely, off all on her own," Gladey said. "How will she find her way home?"

"I'm working on a way to bring her back," Theo said firmly. "I promise you, I'll give it everything I have. In the meantime, I know she'll feel so much better if she can be sure you and Winden are at home keeping everything in order for her. Should we go and see if there's anything there I could fix for her before she gets back?"

The old woman lit up, her swaying slowing. "Yes. Yes, there is—that ledge has tipped again. All those years it stayed in place without Time messing with it, and as soon as we're moving again…" She shook her head with a huff.

"Let's get that done right away, then," Theo said. "Let me just give my leave to my friends, and I'll join you."

The boy beamed at him gratefully and clutched his grandmother's hand as she started to shuffle down the road into the city.

Theo came over to us. "It looks like I'm trusting you to pull this off on your own after all," he said to Chess. His gaze slid to me. "You'll be all right, won't you? I'd ask them to wait, but the longer she's out here, the more chance the guards will take offense."

"Of course," I said quickly. "I'm sure we can manage."

He leaned in. "Don't be afraid to show Unicorn how much authority *you* can wield," he said by my ear. He gave me a grateful peck on the lips before pulling away, there and then back to his duty.

An ache of emotion swelled from deep inside me as I watched him go. He took on so much. When did he have time to think about what *he* needed?

I already knew what he'd say to that. He'd say that seeing Wonderland's people safe and free was what he needed more than anything else. And he'd mean it.

He was the one who should be ruling Wonderland, not me. It was an honor that a man like that would even think me capable of it.

I tugged my focus back to the task at hand.

"Come along," Chess said with a careless wave of his hand. "We have time, but not so much we should squander heaps of it."

"I don't recall a Unicorn in my day," the Red Knight muttered as we passed the looming ferns that hid the pond from view.

"From what I heard, here and there, the second Queen of Hearts brought him around to act out that poem with Lion, and the Diamonds simply never tired of it," Chess said. "I've got no idea what he occupied himself with before then. But I'm quite certain *he's* plenty tired of the gig he's got now."

He motioned us off the road into the underbrush when the giant pink-and-purple mushrooms came into view up ahead. "We don't want any of Caterpillar's harvesters spotting us," he murmured. "Follow me, and keep quiet."

We eased between the fluffy fronds of the ferns, a herbal scent tickling my nose, until Chess decided we'd gone far enough. He led us off into a dense evergreen forest where the golden pinecones squirmed and wriggled across the branches like fat bristling worms. I set my feet carefully, avoiding any stray twigs that might crack, pebbles that might rattle.

We heard Unicorn before we saw him. There was a snort, just like a horse, and then the thump of hooved feet against the ground. We crept closer until we could make out the field between the trees without Unicorn noticing us.

The wide clearing was ringed by trees on all sides, which I guessed was why Unicorn had picked it. The grass grew so short it was barely more than moss, reminding me of astroturf with that vivid green shade. Good for running on, presumably. And that was what the equine figure was doing right now. He'd left all his clothes in a pile near the trees except for a sleeveless undershirt and a pair of gray short-pants similar to the red ones I'd seen him in for his fight with Lion, and he was galloping around the clearing on all fours. Muscles rippled in his shoulders and legs beneath the sheen of the coarse, pearly horsehair that covered his body.

"We'll go together and talk to him as we discussed," Chess whispered to me. He raised an eyebrow at the Red Knight. "*You* stay right there, unless it looks certain someone needs running through. Someone other than the two of us."

"Well, you don't need to clarify that," the guardian of the Red royal family muttered.

"It protects me more if he doesn't see you," I reminded the Red Knight. "You're the secret advantage I have in my back pocket."

"Yes," he said, drawing himself up with his narrow chin high. "They will never see me coming."

I didn't know about that, but if we could keep him away from his armor, at least no one would *hear* him coming.

Chess shot me an amused grin as we walked together to the edge of the field. My heart started to thud almost as loud as

Unicorn's hoof beats when we emerged from the shadows that had hidden us.

Unicorn was just loping around the curve in his makeshift racetrack. He jerked to a halt, yanking himself onto his hind legs in an instant, having to wheel his forelegs—arms?—to keep his balance.

"Unicorn!" Chess called, his grin widening. "No judgment here. That's not my style. You remember me, don't you?"

Unicorn strode a few paces closer, his mouth curling into what looked like the horse version of consternation. "*Chess*?" he said, and stiffened. "You're a Spade. A criminal."

Chess rolled his eyes. "When the laws are mad, aren't you mad to accuse by the laws? You *know* me, Unicorn. When have I ever worked all that hard at anything?"

Unicorn took another hesitant step forward. "Why are you here?"

"To introduce you to someone I thought you might like to meet," Chess said. "I saw your battle last night. He got you again, didn't he? How would you like to get them all, hmm?"

Unicorn couldn't suppress the spark of interest that lit in his dark eyes. He turned them toward me. "Who are you?"

I started where Chess had told me too. "I heard you might be tired of the role you've been given," I said. "I think you're worthy of so much more than that. And I can give you a straight path there if you help us open up a path in turn."

The glint of hope didn't die, but Unicorn snorted in frustration. "I can't listen to this," he said to Chess. "You know it's a fool's—"

"You *can* listen," Chess said, crossing his arms over his chest. "And believe me, you want to. You haven't let her answer your question yet."

Unicorn paused. I drew in a breath to steady myself.

It would be okay. I wasn't committing to anything other than helping to take down the Queen of Hearts. What I did after—that was still up to me.

"I'm the thing the Queen fears the most," I said, "and the thing she has the most to fear from. I'm of the line of Alice. I'm the Red Queen, and I will see her off my throne."

The words gained resonance as I forced them from my throat. An unexpected conviction gripped me as I held Unicorn's gaze.

A queen's blood ran through my veins, whether I was prepared to follow it or not. And I was sick and tired of seeing Wonderland's people crushed by that horrible woman.

Unicorn blinked slowly. He snorted again, but it sounded more like awe this time.

"Well," he said. "I think I do want to hear more about this."

CHAPTER EIGHTEEN

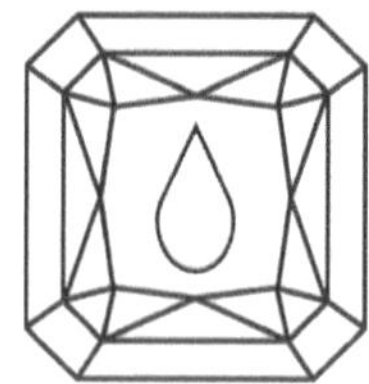

Chess

Insomuch as I was like a cat, I would be one of those types that prowls around getting into scraps and yowling loud enough to wake the whole street. I would definitely *not* be the type to curl up on a warm lap and spend the rest of the evening there. Which was probably why I had the White Knight's entire luxurious apartment to loll around in, and after a few hours the white walls all over the place were starting to feel like a cage.

Thankfully, my mind was as swift as my patience was short.

"You know," I said where I was sprawled on my back on one of the White Knight's sofas, "we should go to Caterpillar's. It'd be good for Lyssa."

The White Knight glanced up at me through the steam rising off the cup of tea he'd just poured. He'd also been doing quite a lot of poring over the map one of the twins had brought him, though all he'd told me about it was that he wasn't sure yet what it would do for him, if anything at all.

"What makes you say that?" he said in the tone indicating that he was open to suggestion but that I'd better start stringing sense into it quickly.

"She's still nervous about the whole queenly bloodline this and that, isn't she?" I said, stretching out one leg and then the other. "Even with Unicorn pitching in to clear her path to our goals. We'll say it's for her to dance out some tension, get back to the joys of Wonderland, which would be good for her too, but it'll also remind her of all those people she could be saving."

"You're a wanted man," he pointed out.

I shrugged. "In that crowd, with that lighting, no one's likely to notice me—or her. They're even less likely to take a mind to tattle if they do. Caterpillar might be another story, but if he comes out onto the floor, we can always scram."

The White Knight ran his thumb across his square jaw, his dark brown eyes turning thoughtful. "That's true. You do raise a good point, Chess—and paying a visit to the club might help with my own end of our plans as well. Caterpillar must still be sending Rabbit through a looking-glass somewhere to get his Otherland ingredient, or the Clubbers would be getting even more restless than they already are. I'd like to know which one and how they're getting to it."

"Perfect!" I sprang up. "Where has our royal Highness gotten to, anyway?"

"She went up to talk to our White Queen-who-is-not-actually-a-queen," the White Knight said with a quirk of his lips. "They must be getting along well. She's stayed quite a while."

He started to get up too, but I motioned him back. "I'll retrieve her. You finish your tea, your Knightliness."

He chuckled, but he let me go. I hustled through the apartment to the elevator with a grin I couldn't have restrained if I'd wanted to. There were many things I enjoyed doing with our Otherlander, some of them very recently discovered, but dancing was up near the top of the list.

When I reached the White Queen's pastel-filled apartment, Lyssa had already come to the door, the White Queen trailing behind her. Lyssa's face was tight with worry.

"What is it, Chess?" she asked. "Is there more trouble?"

My dear lovely woman. The fact that she reacted to my arrival assuming the worst was exactly why we needed to break the stressful cycle we'd dragged her into.

"Not at all," I said, and held out my hand to her with a mock bow. "I wished to request your company at the Caterpillar's Club. You've had a dreadful stay in Wonderland this time, fleeing for your life and trudging through mud and strangling grasses and the rest. Letting loose might help clear your head. The White Knight will be joining us too, with plans of his own."

Lyssa hesitated, but then a small smile crossed her face. "Maybe that would be a nice change of pace," she said. "If Theo thinks we'll be safe enough. Just for a couple hours—to clear my head, like you said." She turned to the White Queen. "Would you like to come?"

The other woman looked startled by the invitation. She curled a strand of her pale hair around her finger, her mouth working. "No," she said in a distant voice. "I don't do that. But thank you."

"Okay, well, maybe another time then," Lyssa said. She slipped her hand into mine so easily my heart skipped a beat. I twined my fingers with hers, relishing just that simple contact as we went down a floor to collect the White Knight.

She knew everything. All the twisted, painful parts of my past I'd tried to forget—and her desire for me, her *caring* for me, hadn't faltered in the slightest. I still wasn't sure I was whole enough to be everything she needed, but I didn't have to be. She had Hatter and the White Knight too.

I could make her laugh. I could make her gasp with pleasure. If that was enough for her, then it'd be enough for me too.

When the White Knight stepped into the elevator, he slipped his arm around Lyssa's waist. "Did you have a good chat with Mirabel?"

"Well, she didn't tell me anything that I'm sure can help us get the prisoners free," Lyssa said. "But it sounded like the Unicorn is trustworthy. If I got the gist of that part right. And then she showed me her knitting—she offered to make me a dress—and we talked a little about Wonderland in general. I asked her if she wanted to come with us to the club, but I guess she wasn't up for it."

Just for a second, the White Knight looked as startled by the idea as the woman herself had been. "That was kind of you," he said warmly. "It isn't any comment on whether she enjoyed your company, you know. Mirabel never leaves the Tower."

Lyssa blinked at him. "*Never*?"

"Not for as long as I've been here, at least. My people bring by food and whatever else she needs. You've seen her scar…" He motioned to his temple. "Her attacker was never brought to justice. She's afraid if she's discovered, the next attack will be worse."

"That's awful." Lyssa winced in sympathy. "I hope someone does catch him so she can feel safe again."

"We've certainly tried," the White Knight said. "You've seen how easily violence can lurk beneath the surface here."

She nodded with a sharp exhalation. "Oh, we'd better bring the Red Knight along too. He'll freak out if he checks in on me and I'm no longer in the building."

When we'd stopped by there, the White Knight had set up his sort-of counterpart in the third floor apartment that various Spades used from time to time. The Red Knight preferred to keep up his "watch" closer to the ground floor. *First line of defense!* he'd declared, without any explanation of how he expected to determine anyone needed defending, but I thought Lyssa had been glad to take a little break from him shadowing her. He couldn't provide any protection the White Knight couldn't offer tenfold.

True to form, when Lyssa told the Red Knight where we were off to, he blustered about crowds and secure settings. But he was also loyal to the core, so he came along, muttering his continued complaints under his breath.

As we came up to the club, *I* was glad when he came to a halt and remarked, "I feel I can be of most service guarding the outside of the building. Should any threatening figures make an appearance, I will reach you and usher you to safety before they can carry out their evil deeds."

"Perfect," Lyssa said. "But if you change your mind, feel free to come in even if there isn't any evil to warn me about."

As soon as we stepped through the spinning walls onto the vast undulating dance floor, most of the tension that had been gripping me fell away. The thump of the bass oscillated through my bones. Red and orange strobe lights flashed over the mass of dancers, making them look like a churning wave of human flame. No one gave us a second glance.

If the Clubbers had even heard about the Queen's call for me, they didn't give a shit. Keep your head low, dance your heart out, and don't let the darkness touch you—that was the way things worked here. These were my people as much as anyone in Wonderland was.

The Duchess could sic however many guards she wanted on me. I wasn't letting her own me again. I could live my life exactly as I had been before.

The White Knight gave Lyssa a quick kiss and turned to me. "I might need you later," he said, just loud enough for me to hear despite the music. For my vanishing skills, no doubt. I tipped my head to him.

My gut pinched at the same time. Finding another looking-glass meant offering Lyssa a way to her home in the Otherland. But she'd found out that *this* was her true home. She'd see that we were better for her than anyone in that dreary place could be, wouldn't she? Once she was on the throne, everything in Wonderland could be joyful.

The White Knight moved off through the crowd to get eyes on Rabbit or Caterpillar. The hulking owner of the club with his turnip-shaped head and segmented, quadruple-armed body was nowhere to be seen in the main room. All the better for us. I grasped Lyssa's hand tighter and spun her around with me, merging with the throng.

Lyssa laughed as her body settled into the rhythm. She let her head fall back and swayed her arms in the air. Her dress, another of May's old ones I thought, swished around her thighs. With her hair darkened and pulled back, she didn't look like quite the free spirit she had when I'd first brought her here, before she'd had any idea there *was* anything to this land other than joyful self-indulgence, but her eyes shone brighter when they met mine again.

Yes, this had been the right idea, for both of us.

The songs bled from one into the other like they always did. Lyssa stayed with me, her fingers brushing over my chest as we swayed together, her body easing even closer when I rested my hand on her hip. I leaned in to kiss the crook of her neck, teasing the tips of my sharpest teeth over her skin to make her breath catch. Her fresh scent filled my nose. Hearts take me, how could I want her this much when I'd just had her last night?

I'd been holding back before, afraid to offer what I couldn't really give. But she wanted me as I was. And I wanted her, every night, over and over again.

Maybe I could have her tonight. I had the feeling the White Knight would be game once we were done here. We'd played together enough times that I wouldn't have to think at all when he was the other one there. Just feel and enjoy.

I wasn't sure how many songs we'd danced through when I spotted the White Knight's pale shirt catching the sporadic lights as he made his way over to us. I slowed down, loosening my hold on Lyssa, mentally preparing for whatever mission he might be able to send me off on.

A hand grabbed my sleeve, jerking me toward the edge of the room. "Here he is!" the guy who'd grabbed me shouted, waving his other arm in the air. "Cheshire's here!"

My pulse hiccupped. As I tried to yank my sleeve from the guy's grasp, two of the queen's guards hustled over around the fringes of the crowd. Had they been lurking at the far end of the room the whole time? Or had our supposed guard outside been even more useless than I'd expected?

The man hauled at my arm, and panic shot through me. I kicked him in the side with everything I had. The second his grasp broke, I slipped away into the in-between, where the music was dulled and the edges of every form around me turned stuttered and sharp. Where no one could see me at all.

They could still feel me. A dancer's foot jammed down on my toes; another's elbow caught my ribs, sparking a fresh wave of panic. I threw myself away from them, out of the crowd, past the cursing informant and the guards rushing to meet him. In the gap of open space near the wall, I spun around.

Lyssa had come after me, maybe without any clear idea what was going on. I hadn't even stopped to warn her. A shamed chill trickled through me as I watched her freeze at the sight of the guards. The White Knight caught up with her, grasping her shoulders from behind.

He'd get her out of here. *He'd* protect her, when I'd been the one who brought her here, when I'd been the one the guards were looking for.

The Duchess had won after all, hadn't she?

Even as my throat tightened with that thought, one of the guards whirled around and snapped at a young guy—a boy, really—who'd accidentally bumped into him. The boy paled under the dappling of the lights. He held up his hands.

"I'm sorry, I really didn't mean—"

"You need to learn proper respect for the Hearts' Guard," the other guard bellowed, and whipped out his baton. He smacked it across the boy's skull so hard the kid reeled.

"No!" another voice shouted—a voice I knew so well my heart stopped before my eyes even registered Lyssa shoving the rest of the way forward. She threw herself between the guard and the cringing boy.

They could see she had a queen's blood running through her veins, couldn't they? She stood straight and steady, her chin raised and her eyes lit with determination.

Oh, lands, what did she think she was doing?

I took a step toward her, wanting to intervene, but if I showed myself, even invisibly, I'd only make things worse for both of us. As soon as they knew she had anything to do with me, they'd take her whether they realized she was the Alice their queen was looking for or not.

"Now look here," one of the guards started to growl, raising his baton threateningly.

Lyssa's gaze twitched. A flicker of fear passed through her expression—but only a flicker, and then her jaw set again.

"He didn't do anything," she said, pointing at the boy, who was still clutching the side of his head. "Aren't you supposed to be catching a criminal here? Why are you beating up on some kid instead of doing your job?"

I could have laughed if I hadn't been so terrified for her. She was turning their loyalty back around on them, acting as if she were even more concerned with the Queen's decrees than they were. A perfect gambit.

Perfect enough to work? One of the guards had stepped back, but the other was still eyeing her, his knuckles white where he was gripping his baton.

Then the White Knight was there, hooking his arm around Lyssa's and giving the guards an apologetic shake of his head.

"My apologies, men of the Hearts," he said in his ever-smooth voice. "I ran into a Dreamer and thought I'd show her the sights, but she hasn't quite figured out the rules of this place yet. I'll see she doesn't interrupt any more of your work."

Lyssa's lips flattened with annoyance, but she was smart enough not to protest in front of the guards. The White Knight ushered her toward the exit.

Where I'd better go too. I hurried after them through the muted space of the in-between, the momentary exhilaration of seeing Lyssa challenge the guards fading as quickly as it had rushed through me. My spirits sank with it.

Queen or not, how could I possibly be worthy of her when my solution to the first sign of trouble was to vanish?

I couldn't blame that on the Duchess, not completely. That was me, through and through.

CHAPTER NINETEEN

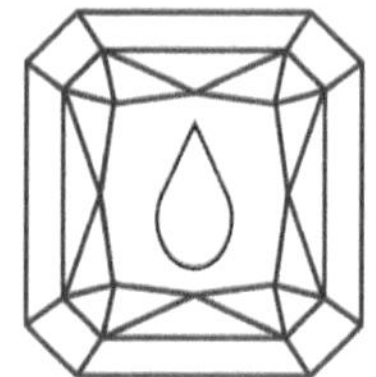

Lyssa

Theo led the way back to the Tower through a series of side streets he must have felt were most likely to keep us out of view. I kept waiting, hoping, for Chess to appear out of thin air beside us with his carefree grin. The shining silver spire came into view up ahead, and he still hadn't turned up.

"Do you think Chess is okay?" I asked in the elevator shaft after we'd let the Red Knight off on the third floor.

"If there's anyone who can keep out of sight, it's our Cheshire," Theo said, but I could still see a little strain in his expression. The confrontation in the club had bothered him more than he was trying to let on. The frustration that had been niggling at me since we'd left chomped down harder.

I held my tongue about that for now. "Did you find out anything about Rabbit?"

"If what I saw indicates what it should, then we're not much closer to finding you a route home than we were before," he said. "I believe I saw the mark of the Queen's seal on his hand, which would suggest she's given him permission to travel via her personal looking-glass."

"The one you already knew about," I said, my heart sinking.

"Yes. I'm sorry, Lyssa. I'll test my suspicions as soon as I can."

I wasn't sure how much I'd really believed there might be another mirror, easier to get to. I definitely still wasn't sure what I'd do if we found one.

When we came into his office, Theo headed straight across the room toward the hallway that led to the more private rooms. I stopped in my tracks halfway there. If I was going to say it, I might as well say it now.

"You didn't have to step in, back there in the club," I said. "I was fine."

Theo turned, his shoulders tensing. "You were challenging the Queen's guards. They have the authority to take your head without thinking twice, Lyssa. The less you talk to them, the less you even *look* at them, the better."

I crossed my arms over my chest, fighting the urge to outright hug myself. "I didn't give anything away. I made it sound like I was on the Queen's side. And I stopped them from hurting that… that *kid*. He hardly looked older than Doria."

"He was already apologizing. They wouldn't have taken it too far."

"How far is too far?" I said. "Even if they just bash him around, he isn't going to reset in perfect health overnight like everyone used to, remember?"

The flicker of Theo's eyes suggested maybe he hadn't quite remembered that. He'd been born into the freeze, after the Queen of Hearts had trapped time, he'd told me. Until the last week, he'd never known anything except a world that reset around him with every midnight.

He raked his hand through his chestnut curls. "He'll be a lot worse off if we lose you," he said. "You're the key to bringing her down, whatever you decide to do after that. Wonderland needs you—with your head attached."

"What kind of queen am I going to be if I stand back and watch while a couple of bullies beat up a kid?" I demanded. "If I'm going to make a decision, I have to know—I have to see—I have to at least *try* to stand up for someone. I have to know how much risk I can handle.

I have to know if I'm willing to do enough. I sure as hell shouldn't be taking any thrones if I can't handle myself even in a little scene like that. Shouldn't a queen be ready to defend her people?"

For possibly the first time since I'd met him, the confidence in Theo's stance faltered. He stared at me. There was something so fraught in his expression that my stomach knotted.

"I get that you want to protect me," I said. "And I appreciate it. You've done so much for me. I just feel like it's time I start to find my own feet here. I want to do the right thing. Can you understand that?"

His chuckle came out ragged. "I understand. Lyssa, you don't have anything to prove."

I swallowed hard, my arms tightening around my chest. "I do. To myself, to find my limits. And…" I thought of him this morning, the way he'd responded so quickly to the plight of that old woman and her grandson. All the times before that I'd watched him devote himself to the cause of helping Wonderland's people. It wasn't just my hesitation about my supposed role here that had pushed me to act. The ache in my heart propelled the words up my throat.

"I want to prove to you that I'm strong enough to at least see this rebellion through. I—I want to prove that I'm worthy of your respect, as an equal, not some stumbling Otherlander."

"You've already proven all of that," Theo said. "And my opinion shouldn't matter that much anyway."

"It does," I said. His dark brown gaze held mine so intently I couldn't look away. I couldn't stop the words from coming out either, even though my voice dropped to a whisper. "It does because I'm falling in love with you."

His whole face shifted then, with a mix of emotions I couldn't track. Somehow his eyes brightened and darkened in the same moment, relief and hope and horror colliding.

"Lyssa..." He didn't seem to know what to say.

"I don't expect anything because of that," I said quickly. "It is what it is."

Theo was shaking his head. He gripped the edge of the worktable beside him. "That's not why— We haven't had much time to get to know each other. I haven't let you get to know certain sides. There are things about me that, if you knew them… I doubt you'd even like me anymore."

Now it was my turn to stare at him. Was he kidding me? "I'm sure there can't possibly be anything that bad," I said.

He gave me a tight smile. "Oh, there is."

I found the courage to take a step toward him and then another. What painful secrets was he holding in, like Chess had, out of masculine pride or whatever?

"Why don't you tell me then, and see if I think this stuff is really so awful?"

Theo let out a halting laugh. "You know, I thought I was holding back because I was putting Wonderland ahead of everything. But more and more I'm not so certain. I'm starting to think it's actually that I'm more selfish than I'd like to admit, and I haven't convinced myself yet that telling all is worth the risk of losing you."

Something like hope fluttered in my chest. What we'd shared together had meant more than just a little enjoyment to him too, then. God, I didn't even know how much longer I was staying here, but faced with him looking at me with all that conflicted passion, it was hard to think of how anything could be more important.

I walked over until I was close enough to rest my hand on his chest. He gazed down at me. I charted every inch of his face, from those warm eyes to his beautifully crooked nose to the full lips set over that square jaw.

"I don't think you could have done anything I wouldn't understand," I said. "Maybe I haven't known you that long, but I've seen you when lives are on the line, when everything depends on the orders you give or how you act. I *know* you. I know how much you care about people. I know how far you're willing to go for them."

Theo set his hand over mine, letting his head bow until his forehead almost touched mine. "You have no idea how much I'd like to be the man you've seen and nothing more—or less."

"You are that man," I said firmly. "I don't think you're perfect. Everyone makes mistakes. But, hell, I'd bet *no one* could meet whatever standards you're trying to hold yourself to."

"I should be able to. I'm the Inventor, and the White Knight, and — I'm the person all of Wonderland needs to turn to."

"Not on your own," I said. "At least for a little while, they can turn to me too."

Theo made a strangled sound, and then he was sweeping his fingers into my hair and tugging me to him. His mouth claimed mine with a deeper hunger than I'd ever felt from him before, so forceful and potent I lost my breath. He *was* claiming me, in every sense of the word, one hand loosening my braid, the other tracing a heated path down the side of my body, his hot tongue delving into my mouth.

His fingers traveled up over my ass and back beneath my dress, hiking it to my waist. He loosened my bra with a yank. I whimpered into his kiss as he fondled the sensitive curves of my breasts, not rough but raptly, as if he meant to work every ounce of pleasure he could into my body. My tongue tangled with his. I quivered with the swivel of his palm.

Theo devoured me with one more searing kiss. Then he pulled back with a sound in his throat as if the brief loss of contact was painful. He wrenched my dress off and tossed it onto one of the worktables. An instant later, he'd captured my mouth again. Without breaking the kiss, he walked me backward until my shoulders hit the wall. His body pressed against me—his still clothed, mine nearly naked—with so much coiled strength my panties dampened at the sensation.

He dipped lower to chart a path across my throat and collarbone before flicking one of my nipples into his mouth. My fingers dug into his hair as he sucked it hard and teased it with the edges of his teeth. A whimper of need broke from my lips. Without missing a beat, he shifted his attentions to my other breast, his thumb massaging over the one he'd just marked. Every swipe of his fingers and his tongue sent shivers of ecstasy through my chest.

I groaned in protest when he released my tender flesh, but my disappointment only lasted a moment. He trailed kisses down my stomach to my panties and pressed his mouth against my core through the thin fabric. I gasped, my hips bucking. Pleasure coursed through me as he worked me over through that delicate barrier and then wrenched them down to taste me skin to skin.

My knees wobbled. I clung to his head as a moan rippled through me. He sucked on my clit, and I nearly burst apart right there. But God, I wanted more than this. His urgency was catching. I wanted all of him, and I wanted him now.

"Theo," I gasped out, my grip tightening. I urged him upward, and he came. His mouth caught mine again, tart with my own musky flavor and his rose-raspberry scent. I arched against the bulge of his erection.

"Lyssa," he rasped, tearing his lips from mine for just a few seconds. "I want you to be my queen. I want to worship you on that fucking throne."

My throat swelled with promises I wanted to give when he was driving me this wild but couldn't quite bring myself to say. Theo didn't wait for an answer. He kissed me hard, the solid length of his cock flush against my clit, and I was ready to be worshiped right now, in every way he felt like offering.

I tugged open his slacks. His breath hitched when I curled my fingers around his straining erection.

He hefted me up against the wall and thrust into me in one smooth movement. I cried out as pleasure shot through my core. He held me there, braced between the wall and his weight, his hand clamped on my thigh.

My legs locked behind him. My world narrowed down to the cool surface against my naked back and the scorching-hot man between my thighs, plunging deeper as I bucked my hips to meet him as well as I could. Bliss spiraled through me, faster and sharper each time he drove into me.

"Yes," I mumbled. "Yes." Not to being queen, just to being fucked this hard. I clasped my hands behind Theo's neck. Our kisses had become so sloppy with our ragged breaths that my teeth nicked his lip. He shuddered against me with a groan.

His hand dipped down, and his fingers swiveled against my clit, jerky but sure. The fresh bolt of pleasure sent me careening over the edge. "Oh, fuck. Oh, yes." My head tipped back against the wall, my body shaking in his hold, and my vision whited out in the blaze of bliss.

Theo thrust even harder, and I came apart a second time right on the heels of the first. As my body clenched around him, he came too, the rush of his stuttered breath as hot as the gush of his release inside me.

My legs were still wobbly when he helped me ease them to the ground. He stayed leaning over me, warming me and holding me in place. I grasped the front of his shirt, suddenly unsure what to say. I'd confessed my feelings. He hadn't actually said anything directly about his. I didn't know how much any of this could mean anyway.

Theo made it simple. He tipped his head close by my ear. "Stay the night?" he asked. "I can send one of the twins to let Hatter know you're okay."

I could do that. And maybe the fact that he'd asked was all I needed to know. I smiled and kissed his cheek.

"Yes."

CHAPTER TWENTY

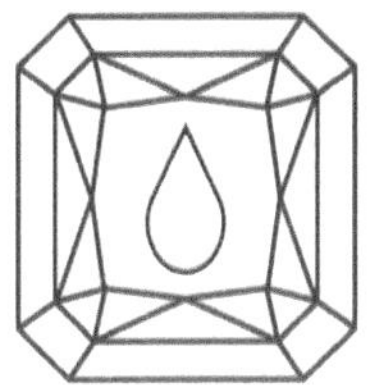

Lyssa

I found the Red Knight sitting with a bemused expression in a boxy armchair in the third floor apartment's living room, watching Dee and Dum play a board game that appeared to involve a lot of cheering and hand-waving. Dee turned one of his waves toward me with a smile. Dum offered me a quick nod.

"I should go by Hatter's and see if Chess has turned up," I said to my recently acquired bodyguard. "And I'm supposed to be meeting Unicorn in a bit. I assumed you'd want to know where I'm going."

"I'll be going where you're going," the Red Knight said with a determined huff, springing to his feet. His gangly body was still pretty limber despite his obvious age.

"Good luck with the horny one!" Dee called after us as we headed to the elevator. Dum snorted at the pun.

Walking down the hall, the Red Knight brushed his hands over his borrowed shirt and trousers. "I would feel more at ease in my customary uniform," he said with a hopeful note in his voice.

"I know," I said. "But no one around here wears armor. If the people here are willing to report Chess, someone's bound to let the guards know if they see you in that get-up. It keeps both of us safer if you blend in."

"That's the only reason I agreed." He tugged at his wispy hair, which was starting to fluff up again, and sighed with a pat of his pocket. "I'm less convinced about trading my sword for this knife. I am trained in the *knightly* arts, not those of pickpockets and scoundrels."

The corners of my mouth twitched with suppressed amusement. "I'm pretty sure honorable people can use knives too. A sword would definitely attract attention. If we plan on getting into a real fight, you can bring it along then."

"And you can bring yours, your Majesty," he said, looking pleased at the thought.

Other than the ruby ring, which I was still wearing on the chain hidden under my shirt, the Red royal artifacts were hidden in a secret compartment Hatter had shown me in the back of my bedroom's wardrobe. I hadn't actually used the sword on anything other than grass so far. The idea of using it on another human being made my stomach twist. I'd do it if I had to, but it wasn't something I'd look forward to.

"Will we be marching on the palace soon?" the Red Knight asked me as we came to a stop at the elevator door. "It will be a blessing to see you take your rightful place at last."

He never seemed to remember that *I* hadn't been waiting for this moment for hundreds of years—that I hadn't even existed to be anyone's heir until a couple decades ago. What would he do if I left for home instead of claiming the throne after the Queen of Hearts was overthrown? Go back to his hilly home and hope I'd have a daughter or granddaughter who'd be more interested in ruling?

The twist in my gut turned into a pang of guilt when he beamed at me. I paused before stepping into the elevator shaft.

"I don't know," I said. "That's a bigger fight than we were prepared to jump right into. First we have to make sure the prisoners she's been taking get out of there safely. And… you know I've told you I'm not sure I actually want to be queen."

Like before, he brushed off the idea with a guffaw. "Once your place is open to you, you'll feel the rightness of it. You were born for this."

Hadn't Aunt Alicia been born for it too? And the two Alices who'd turned up in Wonderland before her? None of them had ended up on that throne. How could I tell if I was the right one when they hadn't been?

"It just doesn't seem fair that you're spending all your time following me all over the place, ready to protect me, when I'm not even sure what I'm doing," I said. "It's not fair to *you*. Isn't there anything else you want to do now that you're in the city? You should get to have a life that's more than just waiting around for me."

The Red Knight caught my eyes with his pale blue ones. Normally they looked a little foggy, but in that moment they gazed back at me perfectly clearly, with a glint of awareness that made me wonder if he'd been hearing me better than he'd let on.

"My dear Princess Lyssa, soon to be Queen Lyssa," he said. "Your family *is* my life. I went into the service when I was but six, running errands in the palace, and it was my greatest honor to rise to the rank of Knight. For a short time, I was a part of the goodness and grandeur that Wonderland used to be—for all its people. I gave up my daughter so your bloodline could live on. Spending these days with you after spending so many waiting on my own across the Plains is no sacrifice at all."

A lump rose in my throat. "I don't know if I'll be as good or as grand as you hope I'll be."

His wizened face shifted with a soft smile. "It's enough to be here to see you try. I had faith the time would come before my own time ended. My faith was rewarded. That's all I need. There's nothing you could offer me that would make me want to miss one moment toward you finding your place here, however that may come to be."

I didn't know how to argue with that. How could his belief in me feel like a gift and a burden at the same time?

But maybe the trying really was all he needed. I *was* going to try my fucking heart out to make things better here, even if better didn't involve me on any thrones. I couldn't run away and leave these people under the Heart family's thumb, not even if I found a mirror that would take me home with a brush of my fingers.

"Okay then," I said. "Let's see what we can do to bring down a tyrant."

I stayed cautious as we moved through the streets toward Hatter's place. There might not be anything about my looks that should catch anyone's eye, but I didn't want to put myself in view of the guards anyway.

My vigilance turned out to be a good thing, because my gaze snagged on a curved red helm through the window of the hat shop when we were still several feet away. My pulse skittered. I grabbed the Red Knight's wrist and tugged him off to the side, closer to the neighboring building.

There were two figures wearing the red helms and red-and-pink pleated tunics of the Hearts' Guard in Hatter's shop. I didn't dare get close enough to make out more than that. What had they come to badger Hatter about now? Had someone pointed the finger at him like the Duchess had at Chess?

He might need our help. I had to find out what was going on in there. I swallowed past the dryness in my mouth and motioned for the Red Knight to follow me.

We slipped down the alley between a couple shops farther down the street and came around to the back of Hatter's. Like the shop's front door, the back was never locked. I eased it open, freezing at the faint squeak of the hinges. When no one came to investigate, I squeezed inside, the Red Knight right behind me, and padded across the workroom floor as quietly as I could manage.

It looked like Hatter had been working in that room when the guards had arrived. A half-finished sunhat lay on one of the tables, the veil only attached on one side. The door that separated the workroom from the main shop stood halfway open. I nudged the Red Knight to a stop near the table and edged closer on my own, flattening myself against the wall.

From there, I could see the back end of the counter and Hatter standing on the other side of it, but not a whole lot else.

"But you *did* go out to the Checkerboard Plains," one of the guards was saying in a voice with a snarly edge. I caught a glimpse of him as he stalked past Hatter to the other side of the shop: a beefy man with a tiger's head. I'd seen him before, I realized—in the club, a couple weeks ago, when he'd beat up a woman until she'd bled all over the dance floor.

He was wearing a taller helm than the guards usually did. Any of the guards other than— Oh. The idea hit me with cold certainty.

He was the new Knave. And he was following up on his predecessor's line of inquiry.

"I did," Hatter said, his light tenor only a little strained. How long had the Knave been interrogating him? "My daughter had never been out there before, but she's been badgering me for ages. Now that we could spend more than a day taking in the sights, it seemed like an ideal time."

The Knave spun around and paced back out of view. I reached toward the shelves behind me and groped along them until my fingers closed around a pair of fabric shears. Not quite a sword, but they'd do in a pinch. I braced them at my side.

"So you admit you were pleased to see Time freed, then?" the Knave said.

"Not at all," Hatter said. Just the slightest hint of dryness crept into his tone. "I feel for the Queen and the violation of her home. But once it was done, it was done."

"The Knave before me went out to the Plains with the intention of speaking with you," the tiger-man said. "He'd gotten word that you might have other intentions there. Did you not see him?"

"I can't say I did," Hatter said. "And I can't think of what other intentions I might have had. Is there something out there I should be interested in?"

The Knave made a dismissive sound and continued his pacing. "As you can determine from my appointment, he did not return. I think you must have some idea what happened to him."

Hatter spread his hands. "I can make a guess, if you want my opinion. The Checkerboard Plains have gone even wilder than I recalled. Plenty of danger if you venture from the train. I nearly lost my daughter in a sinkhole, and we saw a jabberwock from afar. Any number of things could have befallen the man. I have no intention of returning, you can believe that."

"I see." The Knave stopped with a tap of his heel. "I'd like to speak with your daughter, then, so I can verify your story."

Hatter tensed, and a movement behind the counter caught my eye. Doria was crouched there in the shadows, out of sight, where Hatter must have told her to stay when they'd realized the Knave was coming in. If the Knave realized Hatter had been hiding her, that was going to look awfully suspicious.

Doria grabbed a dented hat that had been left behind the counter and started to straighten up, maybe thinking she'd use the hat as an excuse for being down there. My grip on the shears tightened.

At the first faint rustle of Doria's dress, Hatter shot forward like he'd been stung. "Come along then," he said, suddenly talking twice as fast. "Although it seems to me she told me that she was—"

A second after he'd passed out of view, there was a squeal and a crash. The guards toppled into my view under the weight of a shelving unit, hats flying everywhere. The Knave gave an angry shout. My heart lurched. What the hell did Hatter think he was doing?

Doria froze, her head just above the level of the counter. Hatter must have made some gesture, because she turned and fled through the workroom. Her panicked gaze met mine with a flash of surprise, but she kept running, her stockinged feet whispering over the floor, out the back the way we'd come in.

As I wavered between following her for my own safety and staying for Hatter's, the Knave heaved the fallen shelving unit to the side with a sharper thump. His sword hissed from its hilt at his side. "You—"

"I'm so sorry!" Hatter said in a quavering voice that hardly sounded like himself. "I was distracted trying to remember, and my hand slipped—those shelves haven't been stable in so long—I really need to get someone in to fix them up. Are you both all right?"

"I will see your daughter *now*," the Knave said, full-out snarling now.

"That's what I was trying to tell you," Hatter babbled. "We could go check for her, but she told me she was going out with friends an hour or so ago, didn't know where they'd end up. That's a teenager for you." He let out a weak laugh. "I understand I've given grave offense. Should we go to see the Queen? I'd be happy to explain to her everything I did to you. Any questions she has, I'll say everything I know."

My chest clenched. He wasn't seriously volunteering to throw himself on the Queen's mercy, was he? Once she had him there in the palace—

I shifted my weight forward, letting the shears drop open so I had a stabbing point if I needed it, but apparently Hatter's reckless gamble had hit the mark after all. The Knave's lips curled in apparent disgust, revealing the gleam of fangs much more vicious than Chess's.

"That won't be necessary," he snapped. "Clean up this mess—and see that your shop's furniture is in order the next time I come by. The Queen has enough to do without bothering with the likes of you. I'll stop in tomorrow to speak with your daughter. Make sure she's here."

He stalked out, kicking aside a couple of the fallen hats as he went. The other guard hustled after him.

Hatter exhaled in a rush.

"Hatter?" I said tentatively.

A moment later, he was yanking open the workroom door. "What are you doing here?" he demanded, in an aggravated tone and with a wary glint in his eyes that felt much more like his usual self.

"What the hell were *you* doing?" I retorted, keeping my voice low. I gave him a little shove. "Are you crazy? You practically attacked the Knave—if he hadn't bought that it was an accident—"

"But he did," Hatter said. "And Doria got out."

"You almost got taken to see the Queen."

"I would have managed that too," he said, the glint in his eyes turning a touch wild. "There's a reason they called me 'Mad' back then, you know. I've been thinking tapping into that side might not be such a bad thing when I have people to protect."

The way he looked at me when he said that last bit made the sharpest bits of emotion melt inside me. "Okay," I said. "If you're sure he's gone, do you want me to help you clean up?"

Hatter glanced over his shoulder and grimaced. "That does look like more than a one-person job. Thank you."

He seemed calm enough as we picked our way among the scattered hats and shattered glass from the shelves, but the tension squeezing my chest didn't loosen. It *had* been kind of mad, what he'd done. Doria had already been thinking up an excuse to use. That might have worked just as well, without potentially pissing the Knave off so much he'd turned his sword on Hatter.

I wasn't sure being Mad was a good thing for protecting *Hatter*.

CHAPTER TWENTY-ONE

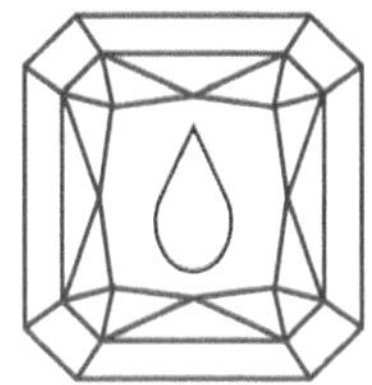

Lyssa

"Do you really think coming with me is worth the risk when the Knave was just questioning you?" I murmured as Hatter pushed through the ferns beside me.

"I wasn't going to leave you to meet Unicorn on your own," he said under his breath, and glanced back at the Red Knight, tailing me as always. "Or near enough to being on your own."

Chess had been supposed to come with me, but Hatter hadn't seen Chess since he'd dropped by the apartment briefly last night. At least I knew the guards hadn't caught him then. Where was he now? Why had he taken off like that?

There didn't seem to be much point in searching for someone who could turn invisible. And if we'd missed the arranged meeting with Unicorn, he wasn't likely to trust us to go forward with any kind of plan. It still gnawed at me, though, not knowing where Chess was or how he was coping.

I followed the same path Chess had that first day, skirting the mushroom farm and then slipping through the dense evergreen forest. Near the edge of the treeline, I stopped Hatter with my hand on the sleeve of his jacket. He looked down at me, his green eyes so intent in his handsome face beneath the brim of today's bowler hat that I lost my words for a second.

"I think you should stay here," I said quietly. "It wasn't really a risk for Chess to come with me—he's already been accused. But if Unicorn turns against us after all, it'll be better if he doesn't know who else is involved. Okay? If it sounds like there's any trouble, you can come rushing in and kick as much horsey butt as you want."

Hatter made a disgruntled face at the suggestion, but he sighed rather than arguing. "I can't deny the logic there," he said. "You'll tread carefully with him?"

"I'm pretty sure out of all of you I'm the *most* careful one," I pointed out.

His lips curled upward. "I suppose I can't deny that either. Though you have had your moments. Maybe madness is catching."

I rolled my eyes at him even though I couldn't help smiling back. Hatter dipped his head to kiss me quickly, the heat of his mouth lingering after he'd pulled back. I took a step away from him with an ache in my chest.

God help me, I was falling for all three of them, wasn't I? Theo and Hatter and Chess. They were all spectacular in their varying ways. Could anyone blame me?

Melody would laugh when I told her. If I got the chance to tell her anything, even a made-up version of what I was going through. If I ever made it back.

That thought sobered me up again. I bobbed my head to Hatter and headed into the field. The Red Knight strode along behind me without comment. I wondered if any of the previous Red Queens had taken multiple partners. Did *that* run through my bloodline too? It didn't seem like the best time to ask.

Unicorn had already arrived. He was strolling around the perimeter of the clearing, his hooved hands tucked behind his back, his equine body fully clothed in a dress shirt, vest, and slacks—yellow, red, and purple, respectively. He stopped and tossed back his sparkling mane at the sight of me.

I hurried over to join him, and he started walking again when I reached him. His restless pace suggested he was still a little nervous of *my* motives too.

"Thank you for coming," I said. "I know it's a lot to ask with the Queen of Hearts as suspicious as she is right now."

Just that acknowledgment brought Unicorn's shoulders down an inch. "It isn't so difficult," he admitted. "I've had a long-standing excuse to come out here and run. It serves just as well for a meeting like this."

"I'm glad to hear that. I want you to know that I realize that even the Diamonds and the other people who stay close to the palace are just trying to survive. I want everyone in Wonderland to have a better life." Except for the Duchess. She could go suck rocks.

"You won't find many who'll argue that this is a *good* life, even if most of them don't have the guts to try to change it," Unicorn said.

"She took eight people from the city this morning," I said, resisting the urge to grit my teeth. "Were you able to find out anything about the timing she's planning for the executions?"

Unicorn slowed his pace, raising one hoof to scratch his white cheek. "The palace dungeon is almost full," he said. "She's already making plans for a spectacle of a trial—all the top Diamonds as the 'jury,' the prisoners cut down one by one and displayed in the city." He winced. "Then she'll send the guards out to call on the city folk to turn in the Spades among them, so they can be punished for the deaths they 'caused'."

After seeing dozens of their own killed without any intervention from the Spades, I wouldn't be surprised if they did. I wouldn't blame them. We had to save those people.

"When you say it's almost full," I said, "how much time do we have?"

"I could see her calling the trial as early as tomorrow," Unicorn said.

My heart sank. Tomorrow. Even if we only focused on saving the prisoners, how the hell were we going to be ready to orchestrate an escape in just one more day?

"Is there anything you can do to delay that?" I asked.

Unicorn sucked his lower lip under his large teeth. "I could make some suggestions for the trial, to increase how impressive it is, that would take more time to arrange. But I doubt I could buy you more than another day." He peered down at me with his big eyes, which were an amber-brown like milky tea. "If you're aiming to break those people out, you'll need to make it through all the guards she has in place. It'll take a lot of manpower. They're so afraid of failing her, most will fight to the death."

The image flashed through my mind of all those figures in their pleated uniforms sprawled in pools of blood. Queasiness pooled in my stomach. Even if I fought for the throne, that wasn't how I wanted to start a new reign in Wonderland—with just as much brutality as the Hearts had used. There had to be other ways.

One day, maybe two. How else could we get to the prisoners? I wet my lips, picturing the palace grounds from memory. We'd managed to make it into the palace before, but under the cover of night, and at a time when no one expected an attack. No doubt the Queen would have her security on high alert around this "trial." We'd have trouble making it past the wall.

At least if we only had the garden wall to deal with, not the palace itself, we'd have a better chance. I glanced at Unicorn. "Do you think there's any other way you could influence the way she sets up the trial? Could you convince her to hold it outside in the gardens instead of in the palace?"

A thoughtful gleam came into my co-conspirator's eyes. His mouth formed a horsey smile. "You know, I think I could. Lion and I will be due for another showdown soon. I can suggest that we begin the trial with that, out on the grounds, like a symbol of the Hearts knocking down the Spades. Properly ironic, since I'm more likely to end up playing the loser, but it'll be the Spades who'll win the day. If you can pull this off."

That was the big if. I ignored the comment. It'd seemed best to pretend I was totally confident in my and the Spades' abilities. Our palace-dwelling ally wasn't someone I wanted to be sharing my doubts with.

"Buy us as much time as you can, and arrange the fight," I said. "Are there any other ways you've thought of that you could help us from the inside? We have our plans, but we'll shift them if you can give us better opportunities."

Unicorn cocked his head. "Well," he said, "if we're already outside and dueling, it shouldn't be too hard for me to create a disturbance near one of the gates. Draw the guards away to give you a clearer opening to burst through. Once I know where the trial will be staged, I can tell you which one to aim for."

"Perfect." A little shiver of excitement ran through me. Maybe I didn't know how we were going to displace the Queen of Hearts completely, but I felt so much closer to saving those prisoners. When I told Theo what Unicorn had offered, he'd have more ideas to build on those plans. We could make this happen.

"Is that all for now?" Unicorn asked. "I would like to get in a bit of a run. On my own, if you don't mind." His tone turned a bit haughty, maybe to cover his embarrassment about how he preferred to run, more animal than man.

There was one piece of the larger scheme I'd been wondering about since seeing the new tiger-ish Knave in the old shark-ish one's place. And I didn't know when I'd see Chess next to ask him. He might not even have the most accurate information, since it'd been quite a while since he'd chummed up to the Diamonds.

"Just a couple more questions," I said. "About the Queen and her claim on the throne. The Queen before her, her mother, she isn't around anymore, is she?"

Unicorn shook his head. "Our current Queen ascended on her death. Unfortunately picking up too many of her practices and adding awful new ones of her own."

"There's a King of Hearts too, isn't there? And they have some children—heirs." When the Spades had talked about the murdered prince, they'd called him the Queen's "youngest" son.

Unicorn let out a snort. "The King is good at standing for portraits and saying encouraging words in commanding tones, and not much else. Sometimes I wonder if she's had him beheaded and pearled, he's so dull. And the children… There seems to be more squabbling between her and them and amongst themselves than there is cohesion. I'd imagine you can divide and conquer easily enough once she's out of the picture."

"They don't have any special powers or weapons or whatever I should know about?" If the Queen had found the magic to capture Time, who knew what else we might face?

"Hmm." Unicorn's brow furrowed in an uncannily humanlike way. "I'd say they're all relatively useless. *She* obviously thinks so—that's why she was so set on having another, and why losing the young prince cracked her up. I don't know that she's even thought of who will succeed her, she's been so busy stewing over that loss. Although it is hard to know for certain, given that she keeps at least one of them locked up."

I blinked at him. "Locked *up*? Her own kids?"

He looked abruptly wary again. His feet sidestepped nervously as we continued our amble around the field. "I'm not sure how many even know about the one. I was simply—if she knew I saw—it was an accident, you know."

What, did he think I was going to tattle on him to the Queen?

"Of course it was," I said in the most soothing tone I could manage. "And she won't find out. What did you see?"

His jaw worked for a few seconds as he worked up to the answer, his gaze shifting straight ahead. His voice dropped so that even the Red Knight at his post on the other side of the field wouldn't have been able to hear him.

"There's an inner courtyard, one I shouldn't have been in. It was a long time ago, just before she trapped Time. She came out with a princess I'd never seen before—it must have been a princess, because she called the Queen 'mother.' A young woman, not much older than yourself. It was the strangest thing. The Queen was fretting about her attempts to get with child—all failed so far—and the princess started talking as if the new prince were already born and partly grown. The Queen told her to stop, and then she said something about the palace walls falling, and…"

He trailed off with a sickly expression. A fresh prickling of nausea was filling my own stomach. *Talking as if the new prince were already born.*

"What?" I said. "Then what happened?"

Unicorn ducked his head. "The Queen struck her, right across the head, back-handed with all those heavy rings, so hard the poor thing fell. There was blood everywhere, and… The Queen hustled her right out of the courtyard, and I never heard another thing about it, never saw that princess again. She must still be locked away in the palace somewhere. If the Queen hasn't killed her since."

The nausea twisted up through my chest. I stopped walking. "Where did the Queen hit her? Exactly?"

Unicorn shuddered, but he raised his hooved hand and tapped me gently on my left temple at the edge of my hairline. Right where Mirabel's scar still marked her pale skin.

CHAPTER TWENTY-TWO

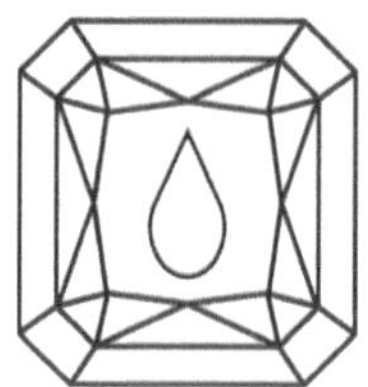

Theo

"You were right," Dee announced as he ambled into my office, his red hair looking even more starkly vivid amid the white walls and furnishings.

Normally I enjoyed being right about things, but I had the feeling this was one of those occasions when I'd have been better off wrong. "About what?" I asked, getting up from behind my desk.

"Rabbit and the looking-glass," Dee said. "Caterpillar must have set up an arrangement with the Queen. Our long-eared friend hops his way over to the palace and comes back with the goods."

Damn. That knowledge didn't help us any. The only way home I knew of for Lyssa still lay deep within the palace walls. Even my inventions weren't likely to get us that far, especially now that the Queen would have her guards extra vigilant after our recent break-in.

Even a few days ago, I might have felt a little happy in the midst of my frustration—that I didn't have to face the possibility of Lyssa leaving just yet. Remembering that, my jaw clenched.

She deserved a real choice. She deserved options. Somehow or other, I was going to give her them.

And if she was given the option to leave and she stayed anyway, then we could both be sure she was where she truly wanted to be.

"Thank you for following up on that lead," I said. "Dum is still gathering intel on the shifts in patrol?"

Dee nodded. "You know my brother. Check everything and then double-check just in case. He'll probably be around in a few hours. Did you need me to handle anything else in the meantime, boss?"

"I could use some more singe-powder, if you know where Dum usually picks that up," I said. "And see if you can't track down Chess in the meantime. I'd like to talk to him." And find out why in the lands he seemed to be making his disappearing act a permanent show. Cheshire had always had some odd quirks, but I wouldn't have expected him to pull a fade when we were on a verge of either the greatest crisis or the greatest victory the Spades had ever been a part of.

"Aye, aye!" Dee gave me a cheeky salute and headed out the door.

I'd barely had time to sit down when the elevator's notification system informed me, "Lyssa is arriving alone."

I sprang back up and walked over to the door to meet her. My heart started to thump off-kilter as I waited for my first glimpse of her beautiful face. It'd only been a few hours since I'd last seen her, right before she'd left this morning. I'd spoken to her dozens of times before that over the days before. But one night had shifted the balance entirely.

The way she'd held her ground in the club even when the guards had started to turn on her. The way she'd stood up to them even then. The way she'd talked to me afterward. *Shouldn't a queen be ready to defend her people?*

I wasn't worthy of her, not as I was now. I wasn't sure I was worthy of much in the face of that devotion. She'd proven in one moment that she was braver than I'd been my entire life. How many sacrifices had I stepped back from and let others take on so I could protect my secrets?

And I still hadn't come up with a solution that I could stomach.

Lyssa hurried in the second the elevator door opened, her eyes wide with an anxious glint and her cheeks flushed as if she'd run at least part of the way. My spirits sank. She'd gone to her meeting with Unicorn, and this was how she'd come back?

"What happened?" I said. "Is Unicorn betraying us? Do I need to warn the rest of the Spades?"

Lyssa came to a halt, her hands clenching and releasing at her sides. She dragged in a breath. "No," she said. "It's not Unicorn. But —maybe we do need to warn people. I don't know. I don't know what to think. He told me something— Theo, how long has Mirabel been here in the Tower?"

Tension prickled through my body. "Since the time of the White Knight before me," I said. "He introduced me to her, already set up in her apartment."

"Do you know where she came from? What did she tell you about how she got that scar?"

Fuck. What could Unicorn have revealed to her? But maybe she didn't actually have the full picture, or even the right one.

"All I need to know is that she wasn't treated well there, and she fled after she was attacked," I said. "Why? Did he say something about her?"

Lyssa shook her head. "Not exactly. But he said he stumbled on the Queen of Hearts once, in part of the palace that was supposed to be private, and he saw her talking to a woman who seemed to be her daughter, who was talking as if she could see the future. And the Queen got angry with her and hit her right here—right where Mirabel's scar is." She touched her temple, her eyes going even wider. "She could be the Queen's daughter, a princess of Hearts. Who else could she be? It's too big a coincidence."

Damn Unicorn. I fought to keep my voice steady. "Perhaps it is. Would it matter that much if that's where she came from? She's here, helping us, not the Queen."

"Do you know that for sure?" Lyssa said. "We have no idea—she knew we were going to the Checkerboard Plains, didn't she? She could have been the one who passed on that information, not the guy Hatter went to see. Maybe the Queen bullied her into acting as some kind of spy. Like I said, I don't know. I don't want to think she'd hurt anyone, but why would she keep it a secret otherwise? We have to at least talk to her about it, find out where she stands."

"Lyssa…" Looking at her, I felt my resolve shift. Here was my moment. Did I really want to delay the inevitable when it would mean telling so many more lies to maneuver around this discovery?

No, I didn't. The lies I'd already told were bad enough.

Before I could decide on the right words to proceed with, Lyssa knit her brow. "You don't seem surprised. Did you already know?"

Well, that was as good a starting point as any. "I did," I said in a measured voice. "I'm the only one who does, as was the White Knight before me. We don't talk about it because she came here to find a safe haven away from the palace, away from the Queen. The Queen would have Mirabel killed if she found out where she is. Only a handful of people other than me even see her, speak with her. She wants to see the Queen of Hearts fall as much as any of us do."

"But…" Lyssa set her hand on the edge of one of the worktables as if she needed it to steady herself. "Why haven't we been asking her for more help, then? Not future stuff, but even—details about the palace, the Queen—anyone who's part of the family must know things even people like Unicorn wouldn't."

My throat tried to lock, but I wouldn't let it. "I don't like to remind her about that time because it distresses her," I said. "And we don't need to get that information from her. I know as much as she could ever tell us."

Lyssa blinked at me. "You can't know *everything*, no matter how closely you keep an eye on things or how many people you talk to."

"I don't know everything," I agreed. "But I know more than probably even Mirabel does, since the Queen kept her locked away. I had free run of the palace for the thirteen years I lived there."

Lyssa was smart. She'd heard enough to put the pieces together just from that. She stared at me for a moment, her mouth falling open.

"Theo, you—"

"Mirabel's my sister," I said, to avoid dragging the revelation out any longer. "I was born a prince of Hearts."

For a moment, she just gaped. "Thirteen years… You're *the* prince? The one everyone thinks was murdered?"

My mouth twisted somewhere between a grimace and a smile. "Yes. Do you want—this is a lot to take in. We could go to the other room, sit down—"

"No," Lyssa said with a sharp shake of her head. She let go of the table to stalk a few paces across the room, then spun to face me again. She peered at my face, her brow furrowed, as if she were looking for answers in the shape of my eyes, the line of my jaw. Did she see a family resemblance now? There wasn't much of one, thanks to my efforts at disguise and my having a different father from my older siblings.

"Tell me now," she said. "All of it. I don't understand. Chess said he was *there*, that he saw the prince's head…"

"Was he?" A raw chuckle worked its way up my throat. "All right. From the beginning." I hesitated, caught by the urge for something to lean on myself. It had been so long since I'd really talked to anyone about this.

"I told you before that I was born into the freeze," I said. "That was true. My mother, the Queen—she managed to shield me from the worst aspects of her rule for a little while, but it didn't take long before I realized how cruel and unjust she could be. I started to sneak off the palace grounds to see what people did in the city and noticed how much hardship they were facing at her hand. She wanted me to be her heir, to be ready to take the throne when her days were over, but her ideas about how to reign… I knew I couldn't be that kind of king, and I knew she'd do so much more harm before I had a chance to change anything from the palace."

"So you ran away," Lyssa filled in. "You managed to convince her you'd been murdered."

A jab of guilt ran through my belly. "I wish there'd been a better way, but I could only work with what I had. Maybe there wasn't any way she could have believed I was dead and not blamed the Spades. I went by the executioner's rooms every day for almost a year, waiting for a corpse to turn up that was close enough. By the time a boy did, I had to take the opportunity. I splashed pig's blood around and bashed the face to hide the differences in features…"

Decades ago, that had been now, and I could still smell the bloody stink of the severed head, still feel its stiffened flesh against my fingers. My stomach turned with the memory.

"I did it late at night," I went on, "so that there wouldn't be time for anyone to notice the head missing from the chambers or any detail that would give away that it wasn't mine before the day reset and the dead disappeared."

"Why didn't *you* reset back to where you were supposed to be?" Lyssa asked.

I smiled stiffly. "The Queen of Hearts has kept many secrets. When she imprisoned Time, she stole a small portion that she tucked away separately for her own use, if she wanted to make a permanent change around the palace. *She* couldn't stand to be stuck, of course. I stole her entire remaining supply when I ran. The vase that was smashed—she kept it in there. I wanted her to think it had been loosed, that it was gone. I used it to escape. I used it to fix myself in this building overnight, once the White Knight had taken me under his wing. I couldn't have managed without it. I thought it was going to be our key to overthrowing her."

"But you didn't use it," Lyssa said, frowning. "When I came—you acted like it was something special that the changes I made and the things I touched stayed that way instead of resetting."

"It was, then. I—I made a miscalculation. I couldn't join the Spades right away. I'd have been recognized. I had to grow older, build my body, change my face… The previous White Knight found me where I was hiding out in the woods. He helped me stay hidden, and he brought supplies like the powder to darken my hair. He broke my nose, as little as he wanted to."

I gestured to my face, the ache of the weeks while that injury had healed coming back to me. "He taught me everything I could have needed to know, and when enough time had passed that we didn't think anyone would notice a resemblance to the supposedly dead prince, he introduced me as his apprentice. He was more a father than my actual father ever was. We were making plans, building our numbers. And then—" My throat constricted.

"And then?" Lyssa prompted quietly.

"A Diamond came, tipsy on something, demanding the Inventor's work," I said, forcing out the rest of the story. "When my mentor told him there wasn't time to finish what he wanted before the day flipped over, he stabbed him and left. I felt his heart stop. He would have disappeared as soon as the clocks hit midnight. I thought there was still a chance, if I could get it beating again—there are ways..."

I'd felt time spilling out around me, fluttering against my skin, as I'd pumped the heels of my hands against the former White Knight's chest, listened for the faintest hint of a pulse, a breath, willing him to come back. That guilt dug so deep I was never going to uproot it.

"I failed," I said simply. "I couldn't revive him. I lost all the time I'd been preserving. I had to work with the same world everyone else did."

"So you took his place, and you kept lying to everyone about who you were." Lyssa's voice was even, but her stance was rigid. She held her arms tightly across her chest. "How many years has it been? Why haven't you *stopped* her?"

"I've been trying," I said, but that answer sounded weak even to me. "I've worked behind the scenes, and I've kept my true role secret, because I can help more this way, Lyssa. If she found out I was alive, do you think I could fight off the horde of guards she'd send to collect me? I have a lot of faith in my abilities, but I'm still just one man."

"You're her son! Wouldn't she listen to you?"

I laughed sharply. "Not for a second. Why do you think *I* was her heir—the youngest, the baby? All my older brothers and sisters managed to disappoint her somehow or other. She wanted to mold me into an echo of herself. I'd have scars too, you know, if she hadn't been careful, if those wounds hadn't reset. She whipped me to bleeding the few times I let slip something that didn't fit her vision of the king I was supposed to become. If she found out what I've done, she's as likely to take my head in an instant as listen to one word out of my mouth."

"You're scared of her," Lyssa said.

"We're *all* scared of her," I said. "She's a fucking terror. And I've got her blood running through my veins just like you've got the Red Queen's. Simply going back there, getting near the palace with the scent of all those roses—it clouds my head. I did the best I could think to do without compromising everything the Spades have worked for."

I saw my mistake in the flicker of Lyssa's gaze. She drew back a step. "You lied to *me*, didn't you? Not just about who you are. About who *I* am. You knew your family had no business ruling at all; you knew they slaughtered the Red royal family like the Red Knight said, that the one princess escaped to the Otherland—you knew about the ring and the artifacts—but you pretended you didn't know that part. I asked you so many questions, and you lied to my face like it was nothing."

I held up my hands. "Lyssa, I swear, I had no idea you had any relation to anyone in Wonderland when I first met you. The Queen of Hearts fully believes my great-grandmother wiped out the Reds. She thinks the Alices are some kind of trick played by someone who remembers, but she doesn't believe they're true heirs—and that's what she taught me to believe too. I didn't know what she thought was wrong until I saw that ring light up with your blood."

"You didn't tell me then either. We went all across the Plains, and you didn't say a word! If we hadn't run into the Red Knight, would you *ever* have told me?" The color seeped from Lyssa's face. "You were using me. The whole time, even before you knew. I was a convenient tool to help you get on the throne *you* want."

My heart wrenched. I started to move toward her, but she flinched, and I halted. "No," I said, but I couldn't look away from the accusation in her eyes.

She wasn't entirely right, but she wasn't entirely wrong either.

"I'm sorry," I said, summoning as much as I could of the princely confidence that normally came so naturally. "I've been fighting for so long to free Wonderland, and I could see how important you were, and I didn't want to jeopardize our progress by scaring you. I didn't want to put *you* in danger by laying all that responsibility on you when you had nowhere else to go. Your grand-aunt found out the truth and immediately fled. I *was* going to tell you—I was going to tell you everything—I was just waiting for the right time—"

"The right time was the first time I asked a question and you lied instead of telling the truth," Lyssa said. Pain vibrated through her voice. "I came back. I've risked my life for this place. Being honest with me was the *least* you could do. Is—Is your name even Theo? It can't be, can it?"

"Theo is the name I picked for myself," I said. "It's been the name I've gone by for more than twice as long as I was anything else. My mother named me Jack."

"Jack of Hearts. That's perfect." Lyssa laughed, but there was no joy in the sound.

"Lyssa—"

"No." She held up her hand to ward me off, backing toward the elevator. "I can't talk to you right now. I can't be around you right now. I don't know if I ever want to see you again."

A cold rush of shame smacked me, but I had to say it anyway. "Please don't tell anyone else what I told you. That's all I ask. It could ruin everything, for all of Wonderland. I've never lied about how much I care about this place or these people." I'd never lied about how much I cared about her, either, but looking at her expression, I didn't think saying that part would go over the way I'd want it to.

Lyssa's mouth tightened. "I won't say anything, for now," she said. "That's the best I can promise."

Then she was gone behind the elevator door, and I was alone again.

CHAPTER TWENTY-THREE

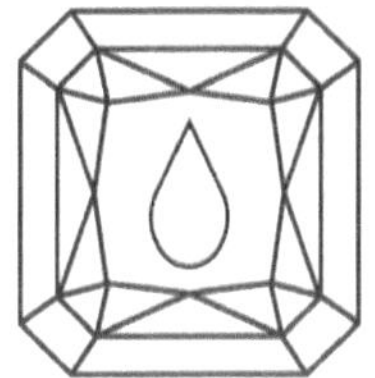

Lyssa

I swung the sword through the air at the angle the Red Knight had shown me, and this time the weight didn't leave all my arm muscles burning. The slice of the shining blade through the air was actually very satisfying. I had plenty of tension to work out.

"Good," the Red Knight said approvingly from where he was standing by the bedroom's wardrobe. "Now try to combine that with the upward thrust I showed you earlier."

An unfortunate choice of words. At the phrase "upward thrust," I was suddenly thinking about Theo—Jack—whatever the hell his name really was—pinning me up against his office wall last night. As furious and confused as I was right now, the memory still set off a flare of heat between my thighs.

I gritted my teeth and swung again, jabbing upward at the end of the arc. I wasn't exactly imagining running our supposed White Knight through, but the idea that I could do it might have been there in the back of my head.

He'd played me so well, hadn't he? Even yesterday, with his almost-confession, he'd acted like he'd wanted to protect me from what he was—and then he'd gone ahead and fucked me after I'd told him I was falling for him, still holding his secret in. Still pretending he hadn't lied to me over and over. If he'd *really* wanted to come clean, he could have done that then.

Well, whatever. I had two other guys I could count on. Okay, one for sure and the other one AWOL. But there was the Red Knight too. And Doria, slipping into the bedroom now with a curious arch of her eyebrows. And all the Spades who were waiting, ready for action.

It didn't matter who the guy at the top of the Tower was. I could still save Wonderland my way.

As soon as I figured out what way that was.

"Are you waging war on the furniture?" Doria asked, plopping down on the end of the bed.

I had to grin. "Nope. Just trying to get the hang of my royal equipment." I waggled the sword. "All of these things are supposed to have special powers that me being… me should activate. If I can get them to."

"So you can use those powers on the Queen of Hearts?" Doria grinned back fiercely.

"That's the idea, one way or another. It'll help me prove my heritage when we're trying to recruit more people to rise up against her. And I'll take any advantage I can get to help us free the prisoners. A little magical boost could make all the difference when we're so outnumbered. I want to know we've got a real chance."

"I guess it's going to be tough crashing the trial even with a few fancy artifacts, isn't it?" Doria said, her grin faltering.

"The Queen has a lot of guards," I said. "But a smaller group can win against a bigger one if they've got the better strategy." At least, I hoped it could.

"Does that sword do anything yet?"

"Well, I think it'll do a decent job of cutting things." I made a face as I swiveled the blade in a slow circle. "The ruby doesn't seem to want to wake up."

"It's all a matter of attuning your energy," the Red Knight said. "They'll respond to you soon enough. No cause for worry."

Soon enough to stop the Queen from chopping off a few dozen heads? I stabbed the sword toward the desk in the corner, willing all my frustration to the surface, but the blade moved and shone just like any other sword would. The ruby on the hilt gleamed with a tiny spark of inner fire at the same time as a wisp of heat trickled from the ring against my breastbone, but a miniature light display wasn't going to topple the Queen or her guards.

Doria watched me for a few more minutes, her expression pensive. Then she hopped off the bed. "Good luck with that! If you can stop a jabberwock, you can take on the Queen. And we'll give you all the help we can."

After she'd gone out, the Red Knight talked me through a few more moves. I practiced them until the burn in my arms expanded into an ache. The sword remained utterly sword-like. With a groan, I set it down on the bed and picked up the scepter.

It hadn't done anything useful in my hands so far either. I guessed I could hope that holding it up and standing in a queen-like pose would impress all the guards into bowing down in fealty? Somehow I didn't think *that* strategy was going to win the day for us.

Maybe if I was wearing the ring on my finger, where it was presumably meant to be? I took it off its chain and slid it into the ring finger of my right hand, which it fit perfectly. As if I'd been born to wear it. The Red Knight gave me a meaningful look as if to say, "I told you so," but we were past the needing to convince me stage already.

I grasped the scepter's handle and held it up. The ring's ruby gleamed, and so did the larger gem at the top of the rod. I whirled it around a bit, pointed it at a bedpost and then at the window, and sighed when nothing happened other than a flicker of warmth over my hand.

"Often these things come to us in the moment of need," the Red Knight said gently.

"That's not very useful for planning ahead," I muttered.

Because I didn't want to go around slicing open people as I walked by, I put the filigree case back on the ring and strung it on the chain again. After I'd tucked the sword and the scepter away in Hatter's secret compartment, I paused and pulled out the woven metal vest.

That armor would be useful even without special powers. I should probably get more used to wearing it even in the city. It was flexible and form fitting enough that I could pull a loose blouse over it. Wonderlanders had such odd senses of fashion, I wasn't sure anyone would notice if I seemed a tad bulky.

I tugged the vest on, adjusting it until it lay against my torso comfortably, and then grabbed a blouse that sort of matched the bottom of the dress I already had on. Clashing was all the rage around here anyway.

Hatter appeared in the doorway, knocking his knuckles against the frame to get my attention. "Have you seen Doria?" he asked.

"She came by… it must have been at least an hour ago now," I said. "Just for a bit. Why?"

His mouth slanted with worry. "She didn't tell me she was going out, but she doesn't seem to be in the apartment. Which isn't entirely unusual, but she tends to tell me where she's going unless she knows it's somewhere or to do something I'm not going to like."

And this was not a great time for Doria to be skirting danger too closely. I thought back to our brief conversation, and a chill tickled over my skin. Something about the way she'd said, *We'll give you all the help we can…*

I'd given her the impression any victory we reached would be hard-won. Had she come up with some scheme to try to give us a leg up, without even talking to me or Hatter about it? Shit.

"She seems to like the twins' company a lot," I said. "Maybe she's gone to hang out with them?" Or get up to some mischief, as the case might be.

Hatter headed back down the hall, adjusting his hat, and I followed him. The Red Knight trailed behind me, of course.

"It's possible," Hatter said. "When you saw the White Knight, he didn't mention anything about a mission before the meeting tonight, did he?"

At the mention of Theo, I stiffened instinctively. "No," I said, in what I thought was a normal voice, but something must have slipped into my tone, because Hatter turned at the top of the stairs to give me a questioning look.

"He didn't say anything about tonight," I added quickly. We hadn't ended up talking about the Spades' plans at all. He didn't know what Unicorn had told me or the suggestions I'd made. Every particle of my body balked at the idea of seeing him again, though.

I'd talked to Hatter about it. We were supposed to meet with as many of the Spades as could make it to discuss strategy later tonight. Probably Theo would show up for that… I just wasn't going to think about it. If anyone asked why I wasn't talking to him directly, he could figure out how to explain it, not me.

I'd said I wasn't going to spill his secret, but that didn't mean I was going to pretend everything was fine.

The street was darkening outside the living area's windows. Hatter peered out into the evening, nervous tension obvious in every twitch of his jaw, every adjustment of his sapphire-blue suit jacket.

"Hatter."

The voice came out of nowhere, and then Chess emerged out of nowhere too, turning visible in the middle of the room. His auburn hair looked scruffier than usual and his face worn as if he hadn't gotten much sleep. My heart panged at the sight.

"I think you should get down to Caterpillar's," he said, looking at Hatter. "A few of the younger Spades, including Doria—you'll have to see it. She's okay, as far as I know, so far, but the Queen is not going to be happy."

Hatter blanched. He dashed for the apartment door.

"I'm coming too," I said, hurried after him. If I'd sounded more hopeful when I'd talked to Doria, maybe she wouldn't have gone off and done… whatever she'd done.

The Red Knight paused just long enough to grab his old sword where Hatter had made him stash it under the sofa. There wasn't time for me to argue with him about it—or to grab my own sword, not that I was going to be much use with it yet. We all hustled down the stairs and through the shop, Chess blinking out of sight as we spilled out onto the street.

Even from this far away, a strange wavering light was visible streaking up toward the darkening sky over to the tops of the buildings between us and the club. Hatter took off at about as brisk a pace as he could walk at without breaking into a run. My heart thudded as I pushed myself to keep up.

Other Wonderlanders closer to the club had clearly caught wind that something was going on. Several people peered from their windows, and a few ducked out onto the street around us. At least that made us stand out a little less.

Hatter stopped at the end of the street so abruptly I had to grip his arm to keep from crashing right into him. Then my gaze caught on the source of the light, and all I could do was stare too.

Someone—the group of Spades that Chess had mentioned, I assumed—had built an effigy I immediately recognized as the ornate gate and wall posts at the main entrance to the palace grounds. It hung from the trees at the edge of the woods beside the club. Flames danced all along the top of the structure, melting the gold-tinted paint on the makeshift bars of the gate and devouring the tops of the stone-like blocks on either side.

Glowing letters across the blocks blazed through the falling dusk. *JOIN US AND WE'LL BURN THE HEARTS DOWN.*

My stomach flipped over. I'd mentioned how outnumbered we were. Doria and her friends had decided to run a little recruitment campaign directed at the Clubbers.

I had no idea if it was going to convince anyone, but it was certainly getting people's attention. A bunch of tonight's early Clubbers had congregated just outside the spinning building to gape at the effigy and its message. The flames flickered, and my gaze caught on a much less welcome sight: the red-and-pink stripes of a palace guard's tunic. Several of them were weaving between the trees beyond the effigy.

If Doria had been here, it looked as though she'd taken off. We stood there at the edge of the street for a few minutes as the flames blazed on. I was about to suggest we head back to the shop and see if Doria had already returned when a shout carried from the woods.

One of the guards strode out, hauling a teenaged boy I'd seen at the Spades meetings by the elbow, baton raised by the cheek he'd already left a red mark across. The flash of panic in my chest eased for just an instant before two more guards hustled out. One of them was dragging Doria by a clump of her dark hair.

"We got a couple of them!" the first guard hollered. "They have spark paste all over their hands."

Doria tried to wrench away from the guard holding her, and he raised his knife to her throat in warning. A wounded sound escaped Hatter's mouth as if he'd been stabbed. Before I could stay anything, he was throwing himself toward them.

If there'd only been one or two, maybe he could have taken them on. But a few more guards were already jogging over to join the three with the captives. Hatter plowed right into the man holding Doria, knocking him to the ground. The next guard grabbed her before she could take a step. Another leapt in and punched Hatter in the face as he spun around. The crack of knuckles to cheekbone propelled me forward.

I didn't know what the hell I was going to do in there, but I wasn't leaving Hatter to fight seven on his own.

The Red Knight charged in with me, letting out a whoop of a battle cry. He slammed his sword right through the gut of one of the guards. I jumped between the one guard and Hatter, and his next punch struck my chest instead of Hatter's head. The impact threw me backward a couple steps, but he'd hit my vest. The guard yanked back his hand, a spasm of pain crossing his face. Then an invisible kick sent him careening toward the growing crowd by the club. Chess had joined us too.

Unfortunately, he wasn't the only one. More guards charged out of the woods and from the other side of the club. My pulse stuttered. I glanced toward the Clubbers, but none of them looked inspired enough by Doria's message to jump in. They just stood there rigid and wide-eyed.

It was their fucking land I was trying to protect. How could they watch and do nothing?

Theo's voice echoed through my head. *We're all scared.*

Hatter hurled himself past me to slam his fist into another guard's jaw. He whipped his hatpin from his jacket. One of the new guards came at me with a baton. I dodged to the side, right into the path of someone else's dagger.

The blade raked across the fabric of my blouse, scraping my vest—and jerked up toward my neck. I tried to fling myself backward out of the way, but hands behind me heaved me forward instead. I gasped, already anticipating the bite of the blade.

"Never!" a creaky voice shouted, and the Red Knight shoved in front of me. His sword clanged against the dagger. He swung it around, his fluffy white hair in disarray and his eyes gleaming defiantly, not quite fast enough to stop the jab of another guard's knife.

A cry of protest ripped from my throat as the guard dug the blade in deep. Red bloomed through the Red Knight's tunic. He staggered to the side.

"I fulfilled my duty to the best of my ability, your—" he rasped out, and the slash of the first guard's dagger cut off his voice and the light from his eyes. He crumpled in a heap on the ground.

My chest constricted. This man had waited so long for me to show up. He'd believed in me so much. And now he'd followed me straight to his death.

The guards didn't offer any time to grieve. They lunged at me and Hatter. Hatter bolted for the one now hauling Doria away, hatpin in his hand. A beefy guy barged into the way, shattering the pin with a smack of his sword. He belted Hatter across the forehead so hard Hatter's hat flew into the air. He skidded backward ten feet across the ground.

They couldn't kill him too. Anguish and desperation seared through me, and the ring beneath my clothes flared. The vest's rubies lit up with a glow that pierced my blouse.

I jerked up my arm to block the blow of a baton, and a wave of energy jolted off me. It slammed into the guards nearby, sending them stumbling backward. What the hell?

I spun and ran to Hatter. Blood was streaking through his spiky hair. I snatched at his shoulder to help him up, but he couldn't seem to lift his head all the way—it kept swaying to the side, his eyes squinting. Oh, fuck, that guard had hit him hard.

And now three more of them were racing toward us, recovered from whatever magic my vest had hit them with. I turned to shield Hatter, willing that magic to activate again, but the rubies' glow had dimmed. The guards didn't even hesitate.

Chess's presence brushed past my side. He hefted Hatter up over what must have been his invisible shoulder and gripped my hand.

"Time to get out of here, lovely," he murmured in a strained voice.

I glanced back toward the Red Knight's fallen body, toward Doria in the guard's grasp—and to the five now rushing toward us. My body protested, but I knew with complete certainty that if we stayed, we were dead meat.

Clamping my jaw against a sob, I spun and fled with Chess.

CHAPTER TWENTY-FOUR

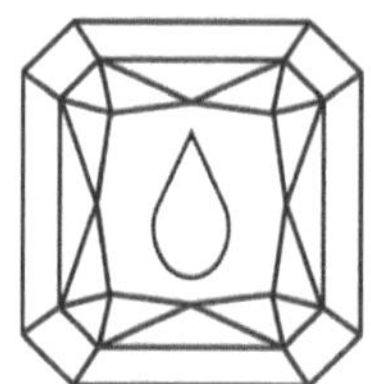

Hatter

I became aware of my surroundings in bits and pieces. First, so loud it drowned out every other sensation for who knew how long, was the blare of pain in my head. It splintered across my scalp and dug through my skull, sparking sharper when someone dabbed a cloth against the wound.

Something was dripping in a halting rhythm, not that far from my ears. A cool earthy smell trickled into my nose. I was lying on a thin padded surface, no weight of a hat on my head. Where was my fucking hat?

Images from before my current situation flashed through my head. The burning replica of the gate. The guards. The guards with their hands clamped around Doria's arms, dragging her off toward the palace, her eyes so round and terrified—

A jolt of horror shot through me. I tried to find my eyes or my mouth through the pain, but I couldn't quite get enough of a grip on either to open them.

"Are you sure the guards won't find this place?" The haze of pain turned Lyssa's voice fuzzy around the edges. She was the one dabbing at my head. A cool prickling started to seep through the wound, dulling the ache.

"This cellar has been a Spades safe house for as long as I've been around and probably a lot longer before that," Chess said. "If they haven't found it before, I doubt they will now. I'd have hidden out here myself the other night if it hadn't proved leaky."

Her hand stilled against my hair. "I don't know what else to do for him."

"It hasn't been too long. Hatter's a resilient fellow." Chess shifted with a rustle of his clothes. "There are people in the Spades with more medical experience than I can offer. I'll check for guards around here and bring someone who'll be able to help if I can. There are food and blankets down here along with the other supplies. Use whatever you need."

"Chess," Lyssa started, but he must have already slipped away. Her voice fell. Her hand came to rest on my arm with a gentle pressure.

I knew the cellar safe house. Lyssa must have put some of the healing gel on my wound. Its chill had eaten away at the worst of the pain, even if my mind was still muggy. I made another effort to blink, and my eyes popped open.

Relief washed across Lyssa's face where she was sitting next to me. Her hand tightened on my arm. "Hatter, are you all right? How do you feel?"

"I can't say this is the most enjoyable sensation I've ever experienced." My voice came out rusty. I cleared my throat. "What happened? Is Doria—"

The distress that flickered through her features was all the answer I needed. I jerked upright instinctively, and Lyssa let out a noise of protest.

I didn't make it very far anyway. The second my head left the bench I was lying on, dizziness hit me so hard my stomach clenched with nausea. It was either lie back down or vomit and then collapse. I let my head fall.

"I'm sorry," Lyssa said. "You're too hurt to go running off anywhere. There was a really big guard, and he hit you hard. Maybe he's got some kind of special physique like the twins do. Until you woke up, I was worried he'd broken your skull."

Tiny shards of pain were still wriggling around the numbed edges of the wound. "Let's not discount that possibility yet. They took Doria? Someone has to go. She can't— They caught her. The Queen might already have ordered—"

"Stop," Lyssa interrupted, squeezing my arm. Her voice trembled for a second. "We're going to get her back. We're going to save everyone. Chess thinks the Queen will hold onto Doria and the other Spades they caught until she holds her big trial, to add to the spectacle. We've got a little time."

Chess couldn't know that. And even if he was right, my daughter was chained up in the Queen's prison now, not knowing if we'd get to her in time, only knowing I hadn't managed to protect her.

Ignoring common sense, I tried to sit up again. This time Lyssa caught me before my shoulders even left the bench. She bent over me, holding me down gently but firmly. I was going to argue with her when I saw her chin wobble. She clamped her mouth into a firm line, but there was no mistaking the watery gleam in her eyes.

"Please," she said, so raggedly my lungs tightened. "I know you want to help her. I want to too. We *will*. But you can't keep— I think you're taking the whole 'Mad' thing a little too far. Pulling crazy stunts doesn't help her if it gets you killed."

"What else was I supposed to do?" I said. "Watch them cart her off and do nothing?"

"No. But if you'd waited a second, you'd have seen how outnumbered we were at the club. Maybe we could have held back and ambushed the ones that took her on the way back to the palace, once they'd split up more. Maybe Chess could have drawn some of them away with his tricks. I don't know. You didn't give us a chance to figure anything out. You just ran right in there."

"They had my *daughter*," I said, but the truth of her words was already sinking in. I closed my eyes. "Fuck."

"If that's how you were back when you worked with the Spades all the time, I'm surprised you didn't get killed back then," Lyssa remarked.

"I probably wouldn't have done anything quite that suicidal," I admitted. "I didn't have anyone I cared about quite that much. And normally there were more of us, working together. I was a wild card—I could turn the tables in ways the Hearts didn't expect if a mission started to go wrong."

But this hadn't been a mission, and I'd made it go wrong. The pain of that realization stabbed deeper than the wound on my head had.

"Maybe you're a little out of practice after all that time staying out of the rebellion." Lyssa drew in a shaky breath. "I care about you, okay? I *need* you. The guards killed the Red Knight. Chess can't seem to stick around for more than five minutes before he vanishes again, and Theo—" She cut herself off, leaving me wondering what in the lands the White Knight had done to her in the last day. "You've been here for me since the start. Maybe it's a lot to ask, but… I don't think I can do it on my own."

My throat squeezed with emotion. I looked up at her, raising my hand to touch the backs of my fingers to her smooth cheek. "You're not on your own. I'm sorry. I was trying to make up for all that time hanging back, and perhaps I let myself go too far in the opposite direction. Moderation may not be my strong point."

A choked laugh spilled out of her. "I'm not sure it's anyone's strong point around here. You do better than most."

She clasped her hand around mine, looking so damned pleased that I hadn't told her to shove off that I could hardly bear it. She had to at least know why—know that I hadn't thrown myself at the guards' fucking swords without a care what happened to her, just off the high of some adrenaline rush.

She had to know what kind of man she was putting her trust in.

"It was my fault," I said.

Her gaze turned puzzled. She must have been able to tell I wasn't talking about the skirmish tonight. "What was?"

"The night when…" I wet my lips, searching for the best way to explain. My thoughts were still scattered, and other sorts of pain wove through me thinking back to that time. I did the best I could.

"March and I grew up together. Friends for as long as I can remember. We joined the Spades together, and he met May there, and they just clicked in a way people here don't very often. We always ran the same missions together. When I took over the shop, I offered them the upper apartment. They were like family."

"Doria was theirs," Lyssa ventured.

I nodded just enough to accidentally wake up the ache in my head. "They cut back on the missions after she came, and even though I loved her too, I was restless. It wasn't the same going out without them. I found out the Diamonds were planning some stupid celebration one night, and I got it in my head that we'd show them if we ruined it. I convinced March and May that we should go for it, just that once, like old times..."

A sharp ache ran straight down my chest. How could I have let myself think—why hadn't I seen—

Lyssa squeezed my hand in silent encouragement. I girded myself and went on.

"It *was* stupid—on my part too. We weren't accomplishing anything other than pissing off the palace folk. March slipped on the way back, must have dropped something, I don't even know how, but the guards figured out the two of them were part of it. They came and grabbed them in the middle of the night."

All that anguish on March's narrow face, not for himself but for Doria. The hoarseness of his voice when he'd asked me to look after her. I couldn't draw that picture for Lyssa, not as sharply as it was still stuck in my head.

"It was my bloody idea," I said. "It should have been me. But—I couldn't even stand up for them that much. They'd have taken all our heads, and Doria would have had no one."

For a long moment, Lyssa didn't speak, and I wasn't sure I wanted to look at her. Then she leaned right over on her stool to rest her head on the bench beside mine, her nose brushing my cheek. She didn't let go of my hand.

"That's when you decided the Spades were too dangerous," she said.

"We weren't accomplishing anything in general, really," I said. "Not since the freeze." I paused and managed to gingerly tilt my face so I could meet her eyes. "Not until you turned up, looking-glass girl."

"So, what you're saying is, our current predicament is really all *my* fault."

My lips twitched upward despite myself. "Perhaps a little."

"Well, if you were expecting me to say you should have gotten yourself killed back then, I'm obviously not going to."

Lyssa eased closer to kiss me, and Hearts take me, the sweetness of her mouth against mine was almost worth the blow to the head. I ran my free hand along her jaw and into her hair. A happy murmur escaped her lips. She deepened the kiss, and I couldn't blame everything about the way my head was spinning on the injury I'd sustained, not anymore.

When our mouths parted, she stayed close enough that our breath mingled between us. "Hatter," she said quietly, "you told me before that monogamy isn't really a common concept here in Wonderland. How about love?"

I swallowed hard, a rush of emotion bubbling up inside me. "It's rare too," I said. "But I think mostly because not many of us want it. March and May had something real. Maybe if we didn't have so much constant threat hanging over us, more people would look for devotion over distraction."

"What have you wanted?"

"Mostly neither, since Doria came along," I said. "I won't lie—I enjoyed plenty of distractions before then. But I can't say I didn't envy what the two of them had. I wouldn't turn it away if I found it." I made myself smile. "And I'd imagine a queen can decide to have whatever she wants."

Lyssa made a dismissive sound. "What about a girl who might not be cut out for being queen at all?"

Did she still doubt her capabilities? I rolled myself onto my side, scooting backward so I could pull her onto the bench against me, my arm around her back.

"Listen to me," I said, with every ounce of certainty I had in me, "I've never known a woman better for that role than you are. If it's not what you *want*, then you follow the path that's right for you. But don't hesitate for a second if all that's holding you back is fear. You go for that throne, and I'll be right there with you, fighting for you however I can."

Whether there was still room for me in the world she inhabited afterward, I was willing to wait and see.

"Hatter," she said roughly. Then she was kissing me again, and if this was what she needed, if *I* was what she needed, then she could have me any way she wanted.

A throat cleared behind her. We pulled apart as Chess shimmered into view, a little hunched beneath the cellar's low ceiling. He gave me an amused look.

"Glad to see you're on the mend, Hatter."

My face warmed, but it wasn't as if we hadn't shared a much more intimate moment with Lyssa together not long ago. "And I'm glad to see you've managed to stay ahead of the Hearts' Guard."

Lyssa sat up, her fingers still twined with mine. "How does it look out there?"

"The palace has made an official announcement that the prisoners taken tonight will be tried alongside the city folk the Queen has already imprisoned," Chess said, with a tip of his head toward me. "And that trial will take place tomorrow morning. So I feel we should make a hasty journey to the meeting of the Spades. I've determined the safest route."

Lyssa's body had tensed, but her jaw set with determination. She turned back toward me and touched my face.

"We're going to get Doria back," she said. "Whatever I have to do. I promise."

I pushed myself upright, managing to make it into a sitting position without keeling over this time. Only a light prickle of pain crept across my scalp. "*We'll* do whatever we have to do," I said. "But I promise to rein the Mad in."

She gave me a crooked smile. "Keep it in your back pocket. The way things are going, we might need it."

CHAPTER TWENTY-FIVE

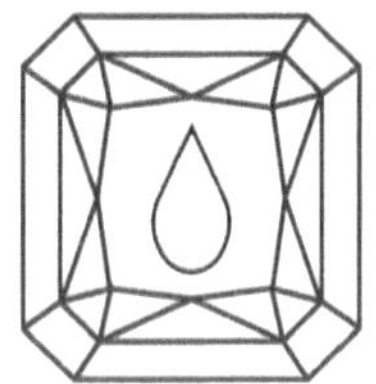

Lyssa

My heart sank as I took in the Spades who'd dared to assemble in the dim basement room. We had even fewer than the last meeting I'd attended. Around the low lacquered table, no one bothering to sit on the cushions that served as seats, stood Hatter and Chess, the woman who'd suggested they should hand me over to the Queen, the burly man I'd been sitting next to on those rotating chairs, and maybe a dozen others.

How many of them had the guards arrested after the stunt at the club, and how many were simply too afraid to risk coming now?

Theo hadn't turned up. Neither had the twins. Had *they* been out with Doria, working on her plan? I'd thought they'd had a little more sense than to go that far, but they were her friends, so it was hard to tell.

"Did you hear where the trial is supposed to be happening?" I asked Chess.

He nodded. "Out in the gardens. I noticed a sparkly bit of horsehair snagged on the wall not far from the eastern gate. I'm guessing that was some sort of message from Unicorn?"

"I think we'll have to take it as one," I said. Our ally inside the palace hadn't been able to delay the trial after all, but he had arranged for it to be outside. I hoped that meant he'd talked the Queen into having him and Lion fight first and that he'd be able to disrupt the guards at the gate. We were clearly going to need every advantage we could get.

My fingers itched for something to hold on to. "I should go by Hatter's and get the other artifacts," I said.

"I don't think that's the wisest idea while we want you to stay on the right side of the prison walls," Chess said. "I slipped by there too. There were guards all through the place, one in every room. Even invisible, I couldn't contrive to retrieve anything that's hidden away."

It wasn't as if I'd figured out how to use either of the other artifacts anyway. But they might have kicked in and given us an edge in the moment, like the vest briefly had. I bit my lip.

Just then, Dee and Dum marched into the room. I stiffened in anticipation of Theo's arrival, but no one followed them. They marched to the middle of the room, hopped up on the table, and swiveled to take in the small crowd.

"We bring word from the White Knight," Dum said. "Lyssa will lead our planning to interrupt the executions."

"So you'd better listen to her!" Dee said with a grin. "She's the one who's been talking with our inside man. She'll find the right course of action."

An anxious murmur carried through the room as they hopped down, Dee bobbing his head to me. My stomach knotted. What was Theo thinking? Most of these people barely knew me.

Maybe that was why he was doing it. If I decided to reach for the throne, I'd have to start ruling sometime.

Or maybe he'd just been wary of having to face me after our conversation this morning.

Dum sidled over to me. From his puzzled expression, I suspected he didn't know what to make of his boss's absence either. "He says, anything you can think of that you need that a person could possibly invent, he'll make it happen," he said. "You just need to let us know, and we'll pass on the word."

"He didn't have any ideas of his own?" I asked under my breath.

"I'm sure he has plans," Dum said. "He's always got plans. But he wants to hear yours first."

Great. No pressure.

I sucked in a breath and climbed onto the table myself. The voices of the gathered Spades hushed as I stepped into the middle of the makeshift platform. The expressions aimed at me were mostly confused or skeptical. We were already off to a wonderful start.

I could have announced everything we'd learned on the Checkerboard Plains. Everything the Red Knight had told us. The memory of his body slumping just a couple hours ago brought bile into my throat.

Your Majesty, he'd always called me. As if I were a queen just by existing. He'd had so much faith that I could find the strength to take on that role, that I was finally the Red Queen he'd waited so long for.

Was I going to tell these people I had some kind of royal magic that would win the day, give them a false confidence I couldn't really back up, and lead them into what would probably be a slaughter? As soon as the Queen of Hearts found out who I really was, she'd have her guards cutting their way through everyone that stood between them and me. It wasn't just about whether I was ready to take on that responsibility. Before I took that step, we all had to be ready for full-out war, and the small group we had here wasn't anything close to an army.

If these were *my* people, if I was going to save them, I had to do it right from the start. Which meant they were going to have to believe in just me, regular Lyssa.

"Here's what we know so far," I said, pitching my voice to carry, willing it not to waver. "The trial will take place tomorrow morning in the palace gardens. First, Unicorn and Lion will be staging one of their usual fights for the spectators. We'll have a chance of entering through the east gate. The prisoners should be out in the gardens too, but we have to assume they'll be restrained somehow. A few of the Spades were taken as well tonight."

"A trial," someone scoffed. "As if there's any question of the outcome."

"I agree," I said. "The Queen is planning on executing them all. It's just a big show to try to turn the rest of Wonderland against the rebellion. Which is why we have to stop her from seeing that plan through."

"I'm all for that," the burly man said. "How do you suggest we do it? For an event like that, she'll have the guards prowling all around the place."

"Honestly," I said, "I'd like to hear what you all would suggest. You've run a lot more missions than I have. What have you found in the past that's worked well when you're dealing with a large number of guards?"

"We don't usually go up against that many if we can help it," a guy near the back said. "The White Knight always says to get out of there fast if the odds turn against us."

Like in the palace, after we'd retrieved the pocket watch where the Queen had trapped Time. When the guards had been breaking down the door, Theo had thrown his devices that had burst into smoke to cover our escape.

Would something like that help us tomorrow? Smoke might confuse the guards and the spectators… but when there were so many of them, I couldn't imagine blanketing the gardens with smoke without getting totally confused ourselves. We still had to make it to the prisoners and get them out.

"I can handle any locks," Hatter said where I'd left him near the end of the table. He had his head cocked a little to the side, probably because his wound was still hurting him. The white patch of the bandage stood out against his dark blond hair. "You won't have to worry about that part."

As if I wasn't going to worry about him running around in the Queen's gardens less than twenty-four hours after one of those guards had nearly put him in a coma.

"Good," I said. "So the main problem is getting to the prisoners and getting them back past the wall."

"Once we're out of the gardens, it won't be too hard to scatter," a woman said. "The Queen won't want to leave herself vulnerable sending too many of the guards after us."

Also good. Unfortunately, it didn't solve the larger problem.

"We've used distractions before," I said. "Can anyone think of something that could draw away most of the guards?"

"From something like this trial she's making such a to-do about?" Dum said doubtfully. He glanced around at the assembled Spades, and I could see him making the same assessment I had.

We were vastly outnumbered, even more than I'd counted on. And the artifacts I'd hoped might make a difference were out of reach thanks to the Queen's guards too.

"At this point, we could probably set fire to the actual palace and most of them would stay with the Queen," someone muttered. "She'd order their heads off if they left."

"What about the mission some of the young ones ran this evening?" the burly guy said. "We might have more support turn up at the wall—that was what they were aiming for, from what I've heard."

"The Clubbers who witnessed the display didn't appear particularly swayed, in my humble opinion," Chess said with an apologetic grimace.

Dee sighed, his normally cheerful expression darkening. "At least they tried. Doria really went big with that display."

His gloom passed over the faces around him, but something in his words made my heart leap.

Went *big*. How big could we go? How big could *I* go?

I had to cover my mouth to contain the slightly hysterical giggle that almost slipped out. Why hadn't I thought about that before? I'd gotten so focused on trying to figure out how to be the queen of Wonderland, how to access the powers of the royal line I'd known nothing about a few days ago, that I'd forgotten who I'd been first.

I was an Otherlander. And Otherlanders could do things Wonderlanders couldn't, as I'd proven when I'd made my dash for the pocket watch.

I could save my people, and I could do it without putting a single one of them at risk. The opposite of what Aunt Alicia had done: I'd run toward the problem and leave everyone else behind where they'd be safe.

That was what they deserved in a queen.

"What are you thinking, lovely?" Chess said, peering up at me with a knowing light in his eyes.

"I know what to do," I said. "I can break the prisoners all free on my own. There are powers I have here as an Otherlander that I can use." It wouldn't have worked when the prisoners were locked away in the dungeons somewhere deep in the palace, but outside in the gardens—it might not even be *hard*. A giddy wave of exhilaration mingled with relief tickled through me.

Hatter was frowning, as if he had anything to complain about after all his mad exploits in the last few days. I swiveled on my feet, taking in the Spades all around me.

"This is the plan," I said. "We'll meet by the road, and you all will wait, hidden, outside the palace walls around the eastern gate. I'll go in alone. You've done so much for this rebellion; I don't want you in any more danger than you need to be. I'll get the prisoners out, and all you'll need to do is help them get away from any guards who pursue them that far. They might need places to hide for a while."

"You're going in alone?" the particularly skeptical woman said. "Are you sure? What's this power you're going to use?"

"You'll see," I said. "I think it's better if as few people as possible know what I'm planning, in case the guards round anyone else up before the trial. I—I'll pass on word to the White Knight, and if he disagrees with my approach, he can direct you differently."

The Spades muttered a little amongst themselves, but they started to disperse. As they moved away from the table, Chess, Hatter, and the twins drew closer.

"What do you need us to tell the White Knight?" Dum asked.

Gears were already spinning in my head. "Chess, the club will still be open, right?"

"It gave every appearance of being so when I moseyed by there," he replied.

Hatter raised his eyebrows at me, and then winced as if the movement had provoked his injury. "*You* need to get off your feet," I told him.

"You're not leaving me behind tomorrow," he said. "Doria's in there. I'm coming."

"You can be right there by the gate waiting for her. All the more reason you'd better rest now." I turned to Dee. "Make sure he gets back to the cellar safe house, will you?"

Hatter grumbled wordlessly, and Dee hesitated, but the more upbeat twin didn't argue. What exactly had Theo said to them about me? As Dee tugged Hatter toward the doorway, I looked at Dum.

"You can tell your boss everything you just heard. He doesn't need to do more than show up to help the prisoners get back to the city either."

Dum crossed his arms over his chest. "I think he's going to want a little more explanation than that."

"Just say I'm taking the opposite tactic to how I handled the pocket watch," I said. "I'll get those people off the palace grounds. He can focus on how to take care of them after."

"You'll be in the cellar tonight if he wants to know more?"

"That's where you'll find me."

He made a face and sauntered off, leaving just me and Chess. The brawny guy hooked his arm around mine. "I take it we're off to the club?"

"Let's go."

"It's probably best if I'm seen as little as possible at the present moment," Chess said as we headed up to the street.

My heart twinged, but I made myself say, "That's fine. As long as you'll still talk to me."

"I doubt anyone will recognize me from my voice, exquisite as it may be." He chuckled and faded into the air beside me. "Still here."

"Good."

We walked in silence through the dark streets for a few minutes, Chess letting his elbow brush against me here and there to confirm he was still with me. I turned the words I wanted to say over in my head several times before I was sure of them.

"*I* haven't seen much of you since last night," I said. "You were supposed to come see Unicorn with me. I've been worried about you. Where have you been?"

I could almost hear Chess's careless shrug. "Here and there. Did you miss me?"

The question was playful, but it made my throat squeeze.

"Yeah," I said. "I did."

His invisible hand found mine, his thumb stroking over my knuckles. "I'm sorry," he said in a more serious tone. "Last night, it hit me that… that I'm still not totally free, in many senses of that word. I wanted to determine the best route for getting to a place where I am without putting you or anyone else in danger along the way."

I wished I could look into his eyes right now. I glanced up at approximately where his face must have been. "You don't have to protect me like that. I want to help you."

"I know. But I feel this is the sort of quest I must complete on my own." The wry note had come into his voice. He paused as we reached a vacant cross-street and tugged me closer to him. The graze of his lips sent a warm flush through me even though I couldn't see the man in front of me.

"If you go down that street, you'll get to the safe house," Chess said quietly. "I think perhaps you should let me take the route ahead of us on my own too, Lyssa. I can slip into and through the club unseen—you can't. Tell me what you need there, and I'll bring it to you."

He might have a point. This part of the plan didn't require both of us.

"All the mushroom pieces you can get," I said. "Especially the kind that makes you feel larger."

All at once, Chess snapped back into sight. He peered down at me. "You mean the kind that would make *you* become larger."

"Go big?" I said with a tight smile.

He brought his hand to the side of my face, bowing his head over me. "No matter how big you grow, you can still be hurt, you know."

"I know," I said. "But no one else will, and that's what's most important."

CHAPTER TWENTY-SIX

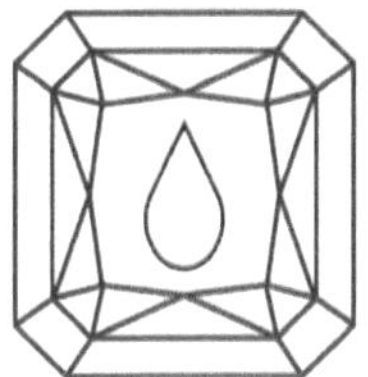

Lyssa

The Queen of Hearts had prepared for the trial as if it were going to be a show at a country fair. From the secret platform among the chittering trees, I could see the stands she'd set up for her "jury" of palace folk, fancier than anything you'd see at a regular fair with the gold railings and red satin ribbons, and the spectator area cordoned off with tasseled ropes. A huge gold throne sat waiting for the Queen's arrival. A glossy podium stood just to the right of it, ready for the supposed witnesses, I guessed. And at the far end of the little meadow between those structures lay a big iron-barred cage.

I'd figured it was wise to keep wearing the armored vest, and the edge of it pressed against my waist where I was sprawled on my belly. I scooted forward. The guards were leading the prisoners out to the cage from the palace now.

My hands clenched as I watched them stumbling along. Doria came in the middle, a bruise blooming purple just below her left eye, and I was abruptly glad that I'd insisted that Hatter stayed on the ground.

The Diamonds started to gather, most of them in the spectator area, but the ones in the fanciest garb settling themselves onto the stands. The Duchess was one of those, primly patting her upswept honey-blond hair. She looked as carefully poised as when Doria and I had spied on her stroll through the city weeks ago.

A fresh rush of anger shot through me with the memory of Chess's story. How she could have tortured *anyone* that way, let alone that sweet, jubilant man…

A few city folk had arrived too—the ones the Queen had under her thumb. Caterpillar's unmistakable jointed body wove through the crowd of spectators. I spotted the long white ears of his lackey, Rabbit, a short distance away.

Trumpets blared. The Queen strolled into view, a blood-red cape draped across her shoulders that would have dragged on the ground if two attendants hadn't been hustling behind her, holding it up. Her massive crown glittered over the whorls of her copper hair. She was smiling the same sharp smile as in the painting I'd seen of her weeks ago, and that eerie gold sheen glinted off her wide-set eyes.

Behind her came a small procession lined by guards on either side. I assumed this was the rest of the Hearts family—the ones who remained in the palace, anyway. The pasty, stoop-shouldered king with his smaller crown followed right behind the Queen's cape, with several men and women I'd have taken to be somewhere in their thirties at his heels. Some had hair matching the queen's coppery shade, some a golden color like Mirabel's. Like the young prince's had been in that painting—like Theo's must be without the dye powder. My throat tightened.

There were no special seats for the rest of the royal family. The Queen sank into her throne, and the rest of the Hearts took spots on the stands at the end closest to her. Everyone, even the princes and princesses, shot wary looks toward their ruler.

We're all scared of her. This was a woman who had kept her own daughter locked away so no one knew the woman existed for decades, who'd hit her hard enough to unmoor her mind even more than it already had been. Who was grinning with a razor edge right now at the prospect of watching dozens of her citizens slaughtered. Nausea pooled in my belly.

The Spades hadn't been wrong about the number of guards. A row of at least fifty of them formed a ring around the section of the garden reserved for the trial, denser by the cage of prisoners. More clustered around each of the gates, including the eastern one I could just make out over the trees to my right.

The Queen clapped her hands, and the chatter that had been flowing through the gathered crowd silenced in an instant. "Where are our champions?" she called, her voice so cutting it carried all the way over the wall to my treetop perch.

"Right here, your Majesty." Unicorn stepped up in front of the throne in the scarlet short pants he'd worn for the previous fight I'd watched. He gave the Queen a quick bow. Lion sauntered over beside him, shaking back the voluminous mass of his mane.

Their duel must be about to start. I'd better get ready. I scrambled down the notches in the tree trunk to rejoin Chess and Hatter.

The other Spades were spread out among the trees. Well, most of the other Spades. When we'd met up, Theo hadn't been among them. Where the hell was he? Even if I didn't want to see him, he was supposed to be here for his people.

I couldn't worry about him right now. "She's there," I said to Hatter immediately. "They haven't beat her up badly or anything like that." But the clock was ticking down on how long Doria would keep her head at all.

My hand dropped to the bag full of mushroom slices hanging from my shoulder. All the growing ones were in there. I'd stuffed the shrinking ones into my pockets.

"I'm going over to the gate," I said. "The fight is about to start. As soon as Unicorn makes his disruption, I'm heading here. You two stay outside the walls with everyone else like we talked about, all right? Just get the prisoners out of here."

"Lyssa," Hatter started with a grimace.

I pointed a finger at him. "You have a head injury." I turned to Chess, whose stance was tense too. "And I don't want to have to worry about accidentally hurting you because I don't see you're there. I can do the inside job on my own. My head will be too far up for them to even think about chopping at it."

Chess grinned at my attempt at a joke, but his voice was tight. "If you need us…"

"I know. I'd better go."

I grasped their arms quickly, bobbing up to give Chess a quick kiss and then Hatter, just enough to leave me a tiny bit warmed as I darted through the trees toward the eastern gate.

The wind whispered through the leaves. I treaded carefully through the brush until I could just make out the gate through the trees. A grunt and a thump of a landed blow reached my ears. The fight had started.

I dug my hand into the bag and pulled out a handful of mushroom slices. My gut clenched, but I forced myself to pop two into my mouth in one go. I had to be ready. I had to be as big as I could make myself if I was going to pull this off alone.

As the tart earthy flavor saturated my mouth, the stretching sensation I'd felt twice before now shuddered through me. My head shot upward, my neck extending, and then my shoulders and chest zoomed after it, the vest expanding around my torso as my body grew.

Wonderlanders only *felt* like their perspective was growing or shrinking when they ate Caterpillar's special mushrooms. It turned out they affected Otherlanders much more literally.

I had to sway to the side as my body loomed up through the trees, my head nearly slamming into a branch. The growth spurt stopped with my head amid the leaves. No, I needed a little more than that.

I gulped down another slice, and my body jerked even taller. A rippling sensation spread through my legs, and I grasped a tree trunk for balance. I topped out with the highest foliage level with my eyes.

Perfect. I could see into the gardens now, but not enough of me was showing for anyone to be likely to notice, especially when they were focused on the fight.

Unicorn and Lion were circling around each other. They'd ended up leaving the meadow of the trial area behind, swiping and dodging on trampled grass closer to the gate. Unicorn must have maneuvered them in that direction.

Lion lashed out with a paw, smacking Unicorn's muzzle with a scrape of his claws. Unicorn shook his head as he yanked himself out of the way. Then he charged, his horn pointed straight at Lion's chest.

Lion started to swerve out of the way, but Unicorn veered with him, driving him toward the gate instead. He dropped to all fours with a sudden burst of speed. Lion wheeled backward, crashing into a guard in his haste to escape that stabbing horn pointed straight at his chest. The other guards by the gate shuffled backward to give them room.

Unicorn hurled himself at Lion, bashing him into the gate with his shoulder. The metal bars clanged, and the door burst open.

Now. I stuffed two more pieces of mushroom into my mouth, ignoring the twisting of my stomach, and pushed forward through the trees.

My body soared up over the treetops as I charged forward. My lungs strained with the heave of air I drew in, trying to fill them. By the time I reached the gate, the once-immense wall only reached my knees. I could have stepped right over it if I'd wanted to.

Several of the Diamonds shrieked and fled at the sight of me. "Monster!" someone cried out. The Queen, looking so small now down there on her throne—barely as tall as my hand—stared up at me, her face flushing nearly as ruddy as her hair. Her eyes flashed.

"Guards!" she screamed. "Destroy this fiend!"

The guards stumbled into one another, gaping, but some of them had the wherewithal to draw their swords or daggers. I strode past them, careful not to step on anyone while they scurried like mice around my feet.

Vicious mice. Pain pierced through my calf as a guard stabbed his sword into the flesh. Another took a slice at my ankle. I winced and bent down to brush them aside with my hands. More blades nicked my fingers, blood streaking across my skin, but I managed to push them aside to clear my way. How many of them even wanted to be here, and how many had been forced like Dee and Dum might have been if Theo hadn't intervened? They didn't deserve to die for trying to save themselves the only way she'd given them.

I *wouldn't* be a monster. I had to be better than that, better than *her*, right from the start.

"I'm not here to hurt anyone," I said, letting my voice ring out of my massive lungs. "Not like her." I pointed at the Queen. "I'm here to set right a horrible crime that's been committed by the ones who rule this place. You think you have power? *I* have power. And I can use it well."

More guards were barreling toward me. I grasped the top of the stands with a light shake to displace the members of the "jury" still seated on it, and smacked down the empty structure in the guards' way to slow them down. Then I curled my fingers around the bars at the top of the prisoners' cage.

I hefted it, gently and then with a little more force. I especially didn't want to hurt anyone in there. The cage wouldn't budge from the ground—it'd been fixed there too fast. Okay, carrying it out of the gardens had only been Plan A. I'd known it might not work.

The guards who'd stood around the cage were slashing at my legs. A steady pulsing of pain was spreading through my calves now. Another heaved a spear at my chest, but it clinked off of my hidden armor.

I brushed the guards away as well as I could and reached down to the chain that held the cage door closed. With one quick yank of my giant fingers, it snapped.

"Go!" I said, jerking the cage door open and motioning toward the gate. "You did nothing wrong. The Spades won't allow the Queen to hold you. I stand with them, and I stand against this pathetic excuse for a queen."

The Queen of Hearts let out an ear-splitting screech. When I turned to cover the prisoners in their dash out of the garden, she'd stood up in front of her throne, waving a scepter with a heart-shaped golden tip in every direction. "Where are my guards? Stop her, stop them, or I'll have all your heads!"

Even with an actual giant in their midst, a lot of the guards were still more scared of their queen than of me. Blades flashing, they sprang at me and at the stream of figures hurrying across the grass beneath me. Ignoring the throbbing in my calves and the stinging cuts across my hands, I pushed them aside whenever they got too close to the escaping prisoners. Fat droplets of blood dribbled from my fingers and splashed on the ground.

This pain was just for now. Just for a few minutes, to save all these people's lives, and then I could get out of here too.

The Queen of Hearts let out another screech of fury. I swept aside another wave of guards and swung toward her. The sudden thought struck me that I could crush her with one squeeze of my hand. My stomach listed queasily with the image of mangled flesh and the crunch of bones, but that would end all the terror, wouldn't it? She'd done so much worse to Wonderland's people.

Even as I tried to convince myself, my gaze slid to her scattered children. This woman wasn't the first Queen of Hearts, or even necessarily the worst. There were plenty of daughters waiting to take her place if she fell. Even if I'd been sure I was ready to commit to taking the throne, I didn't have enough allies for me to hold it. I'd just be starting another reign founded on bloodshed—and they'd spill a lot more blood than just mine.

As if she'd read my initial idea in my expression, the Queen hollered at the guards to surround her. A ring of them ten bodies deep closed in around her protectively.

Fine. That meant fewer harassing the prisoners and me.

A little of the tension gripping my chest fell away at the sight of Doria slipping through the gate. I shoved aside the guards who tried to race after the prisoners, watching as the last in that bunch disappeared amid the trees on the other side. Then I straightened up, just for a moment, to scan the grounds and make sure everyone had gotten out.

From my great height, my gaze swept over the entire royal property and across the forests and fields beyond, all the way to the garish buildings of the city at my left and the Checkerboard Plains ahead of me, a great shimmering sea farther to my right. A weird sense of rightness flooded me from head to toe.

This was Wonderland. This was *my* Wonderland, suppressed by a tyrant's rule but vibrant even so. I'd spilled blood on this ground as nearly my entire family had all those generations ago, and now I was back. I was here, where I was meant to be.

A tremor ran through the ground beneath my feet, as if it were responding to my thoughts. Reaching out to me to tell me it was with me, whatever I'd call on it to do. So much of my life I'd struggled just to hold off the chaos around me, and here the world *wanted* to listen to me.

This place belonged to me, or maybe I belonged to it. Possibly those were the same thing. I *couldn't* go. I couldn't leave Wonderland.

My heart was already in it—in the crazy vegetation and the wild architecture and the bizarre people just trying to be happy. My heart was with Chess and his brilliant grins that could hide so much pain, with Hatter and the fierceness that came from the depths of his caring. Maybe some of it remained with even Theo, with the passionate assurance he'd built on top of his darkest secret.

The certainty radiated through me for one glorious moment, and then my gut lurched.

I doubled over, my vision hazing, my stomach churning as if it meant to toss itself right out of my mouth. My hand clamped over my belly.

Apparently five mushrooms was a little too much for even an Otherlander to handle.

As swords stabbed at my ankles, my gut heaved. A sear of acid raced up my throat. I vomited onto a rose bush, and then wretched again. My legs wobbled, not just with the throb of the wounds but with a pinch of contraction that was an even more unwelcome sensation.

I was shrinking.

CHAPTER TWENTY-SEVEN

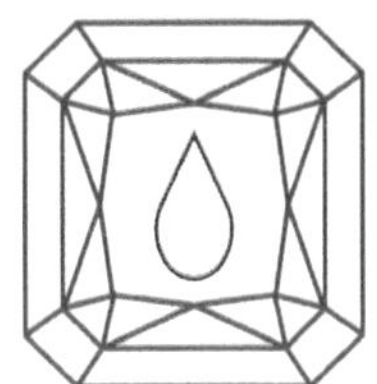

Chess

Lyssa was something to look at in her regular size. The sight of her striding toward the palace gardens at least ten times taller took my breath away. Across the road from me, Hatter's jaw had dropped.

Her dress rippled around her like an immense tapestry, over the mounds of her breasts like small hills, the curve of her waist I could have tucked myself into. She could have fit me in her hand. She could have crushed my bones with a press of her thumb.

Not that I could imagine her ever so much as considering doing anything that horrifying, which was maybe why the thought could awaken that odd flicker of excitement from the same part of me that had enjoyed playing with matches and knives long ago.

But my mind had other places to be. Even within the numbed space of the in-between, my ears picked up the Queen of Hearts screaming out commands. The guards were shouting to each other, and other shrieks carried from farther beyond the wall. This would shake the Diamonds up more than they'd ever been shaken before. They'd wanted thrills, hadn't they?

Lyssa let out a little gasp, and my jaw clenched. Those guards would be hacking away at her, no matter how quickly she displaced them. We should be in there, helping her.

But she'd asked us to be here instead.

Lyssa's voice rang out, clearer and sweeter than anything the Queen of Hearts could have produced. Blood streaked across the backs of her hands as she bent down. There was a snapping sound, and a renewed volley of shouts. Then the first of the prisoners, hair bedraggled and clothes spotted with grime, dashed through the gate.

"This way!" one of the Spades near me called, waving the woman off the road into the woods. More figures raced toward us, sped on by panic. Doria dashed straight to Hatter, wrapping her arms around him with a sob. He hugged her tight, relief and regret twisting together in his expression.

"Go on," he said when he let her go, motioning her after the other escapees. "Hide out, and I'll come when everyone here is safe."

One of the twins waved from deeper in the woods. Doria gave her father one more quick hug and then bolted toward Dee.

A few of the guards gave chase through the gate. Lyssa was whirling this way and that behind the wall, but she couldn't catch all of them. I threw myself forward down the slight slope of the road.

An invisible knee to the gut here. An invisible punch to the chin there. Trip this guard, topple that one. They flailed out with their fists and their swords, trying to fend me off, but the blades barely nicked me as I wove and bobbed through the in-between. It almost felt like cheating.

Hatter leapt into the fray alongside me. He jabbed the dagger he'd brought, only slightly thicker than his hatpins, into the gut of a guard who'd snatched one of the prisoners' shirt hems.

The older man wrenched away, and the guard slumped against the wall. Hatter nodded in my general direction as if to say, *We've got this.*

I wasn't so sure we did in our present position. Beyond the gate, a group of stragglers, limping or shuffling as quickly as their aching legs could carry them, were staring around them with faces white with fear as more guards closed in around them. The Queen of Hearts was squawking about something or other again, and blood splattered the grass near her throne. At least some of it was Lyssa's.

I didn't let myself think any more than that. I hurtled through the gate to knock the legs out from under one of the guards lunging at the escapees. Another guard raced toward Lyssa's ankle with a spear. I clocked him across the side of the head and sent him sprawling, scrambling out of the way just in time as Lyssa's large hands scooped another cluster of guards out of the way. They toppled in a heap like toy soldiers. They must have looked like toys to her.

A few dashed off, unwilling to keep up the fight. The Diamonds were fleeing toward the palace too. More guards were heading our way, though, a bunch of them hauling a cannon.

My stomach dropped. I ran over, my feet thumping over the ground, and slammed the lead guard's head against the iron surface. With a shove that strained the muscles in my shoulders, I heaved the cannon's muzzle to the side to collide with the others' guts.

No one was firing heavy artillery at the woman I intended to see become *my* queen. The woman who for all intents and purposes already was.

I spun around and found myself staring into the last face I'd have wanted to see. The Duchess gazed back at the spot where I was standing, not quite able to meet my eyes in my invisible state, but she'd worked out an approximation of where I was standing. She must have seen my ghost-like combat and put the pieces together.

Her face was as pinched and her lips, painted crimson, as pert as ever. Even hustling away from the chaos, her diamond-laced hair hadn't shifted a strand out of place. Despite the shouts and the cries behind us, her mouth curved into a thin but amused smile. "Hello, Cheshire."

The way she said my name made my skin want to crawl off my body. She said it as if she owned it—as if she owned *me*, as if she believed she merely needed to snap her fingers and I'd be at her feet.

She'd almost been right. Because of her accusation, if I'd been a little slower on *my* feet, I might have ended up in the prison where she could have strolled by and offered her condolences, or maybe a deal to get me out under her conditions.

Every inch of me prickled with the urge to run now. But what I'd told Lyssa last night was true. I wasn't free of my past, not completely, not as long as I had to run or jump because of the hoops this woman set out in front of me.

She'd flayed me nearly inside out, but I'd seen plenty of what lay behind her mask too, hadn't I?

Bracing myself, I strode up to her, letting only my grin flash into view. The Duchess's expression turned as satisfied as the cat who'd gotten the cream. She'd forgotten who the real cat around here was.

I tugged my smile back out of view and stopped beside her, leaning close, crinkling my nose at the bittersweet tang of her favorite perfume. The smell brought back the echo of pain radiating through my ribs, a line of agony across my neck nearly slitting my throat, a searing at the backs of my knees. I squared my shoulders, holding myself steady against the wave of memories.

I was more than those memories. I was more than that creature she'd strung up in her bedroom. And it was time I showed her that.

"Hello, Duchess," I said in a measured, lilting tone. "You've caused me a lot of trouble in the last few days."

She fucking *giggled*. "Poor Chess. And yet you're here. It appears I only told the truth."

"Here's the thing, Duchess," I said, my voice dropping to a murmur. "You don't know why I'm here. You don't know me at all. But I know *all* about you. So consider this your first and only warning. You don't speak my name, you don't say or so much as *think* about me, from this day forward. There is nothing between us. You do not exist to me, so I cannot exist to you."

"A warning?" she said with an arch of her perfectly shaped eyebrows. "And what will you do if I ignore it?"

I let my grin flash again, wide enough to show my fangs, only just holding myself back from gritting my teeth. "I saw and heard all sorts of things your queen and your fellow Diamonds might be *very* interested to learn. I know more than you could even guess. Haven't you ever noticed your memory turns a bit spotty when you think of certain times with me? I stole some of those moments from you, but I still remember everything."

The Duchess went rigid. I didn't actually know if I'd observed any secrets that could truly damage her standing—or perhaps even end her life—but she'd bragged enough about skirting expectations for me to believe she had some that serious. Most of all, though, she thrived on her sense of control. One jab of uncertainty about what I might know from those blanks where I'd wiped the image of my transformations from her mind, and all her confidence unraveled.

"They wouldn't listen to you," she said tartly, but her haughty mask had cracked.

I slipped around to her other side, as if I were all around her. "I think they would. Especially with the details I could provide. You haven't always been quite careful enough in how you cover your tracks. But please, go ahead and test me. I look forward to seeing the Queen raise *your* head on one of those pikes."

She blanched whiter beneath the sheen of pale peach powder covering her face. I'd said all I needed to. Clamping down my queasiness, I let myself dart away the way my legs had been dying to from the moment I'd seen her.

The ground trembled beneath my feet, and as if in echo, a sense of release shivered through me. I'd faced the Duchess, I'd shown her what I really thought of her, and she'd faltered. I—

Up ahead of me, near the gate, Lyssa's enlarged form knifed over so sharply my heart stopped. Her body heaved. With a strangled sound, she vomited in a shower over a cluster of rose bushes. Another wave followed. After each wretch, her figure contracted, a little more, and a little more.

Fuck. I'd worried that so many mushroom pieces would be too much—none of the Clubbers I'd been around had ever taken more than two in an hour without taking the opposite type to balance out the sensations, and even two was extreme. We had to get Lyssa out of here before the guards removed her in a much more permanent fashion.

I hurtled down the garden paths, vaulted over a low hedge, and crashed through the ring of guards that had started to close around Lyssa. She hunched over, sputtering and shaking, only as tall as I was now. Blood trickled from her fingers as she pawed at her belly.

Hatter must have noticed her distress too. He raced into the midst of the guards, jabbing this one and that with his dagger, darting around Lyssa to push them back as quickly as his swift feet could take him. I leapt in behind him to shove and trip whoever I could. Whirling around, I caught up a short sword a guard dropped after I kicked his wrist. The gleam of the blade nauseated me all over again, but that sensation was nothing compared to my terror for the woman behind me.

"Grab her and break a path to the gate," I said to Hatter. If we could just get past the wall, we'd have the forest to fade into.

He started to push at the growing crowd of guards in that direction, but they just swarmed in closer on the other sides. There were certain limitations to trying to fend off this many packed so tightly together when they couldn't see me. I had surprise, but I couldn't rely on feints or intimidation. My lungs tightened.

I'd stood up to the Duchess. I could stand up to these Queen's-asshole-licking lackeys too. For Lyssa. For our real queen, the one we deserved—all of us, even me.

With a crackle in my ears, I emerged from the in-between, plowing over four guards with one thunderous sweep of my arm. My dagger glinted and my fist flew. For a few heartbeats, the guards fell back, startled and wary. I nudged Lyssa after Hatter, and she managed to stumble onward on legs back to their usual size now. Blood dribbled over the grass in her wake.

Right then, I thought we could do it. The gate was less than ten feet away. It was crazy, sure, but we were all mad here, and Hatter and I were madder than anyone.

My knuckles connected with a guard's jaw. My dagger sank into another guard's sword arm. We made it another few steps—and then a mass of them pushed in around us too quickly for me to fend them all off.

One guard caught me with an elbow to the back of my head. As I reeled, another kneed me in the back. I spun around, and two clotheslined me in unison, throwing me right off my feet.

A heavy heel jammed me against the ground. A blade slammed straight through my shoulder, attaching me to the earth with a spear of agony. My nerves jumped with the urge to vanish, to contract into my own smaller form, but my body resisted.

I had to focus to find my way there, and the haze of pain clouded my mind too much. Just like it had back then.

I caught a glimpse of Hatter tackled to the ground, of two of the guards wrenching Lyssa's arms behind her back, too forcefully for her to struggle free. The Queen's voice split the air from far closer to us than I'd ever have preferred. Especially considering what she had to say.

"Their heads. All of them. Now!"

The new Knave stepped through the crowd toward Lyssa, drawing his sword with a hiss. I thrashed against the ground despite the fresh flare through my shoulder, and more feet stomped down on me to pin my limbs.

Forceful footsteps thumped across the ground. Another figure strode through the mob, and for a second, despite my predicament, I found nothing but shock.

Our White Knight was walking up to the Knave, his square jaw lifted, every muscle in his body tensed. Why did his hair look brighter, almost gold? When had he gotten here?

What in the lands was he doing?

His rich baritone reverberated across the gardens as commanding as the Queen's had been, as if he expected even her guards to obey his order.

"Stop."

CHAPTER TWENTY-EIGHT

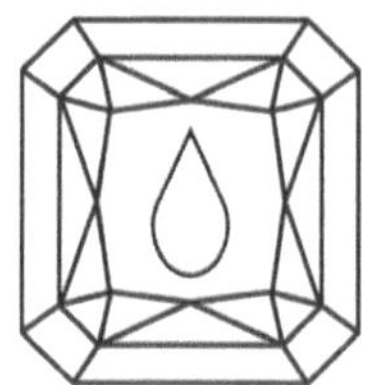

Lyssa

So much authority rang through Theo's voice that the guards holding me actually hesitated, their grip on me loosening enough to ease the pain of their digging fingers, though not to give me enough room to run.

Where the hell could I have run to anyway? There were more guards everywhere I looked—they'd battered Chess and Hatter to the ground. My stomach was still churning, my throat burning with acid, splinters of pain digging through my legs and my hands from all the cuts that had shrunk with my body but not disappeared.

The Knave raised his sword by my head, and Theo grasped his wrist. The sun gleamed golden on his curly hair, no longer slicked back but allowed to fall loose across his forehead. It wasn't quite as bright as Mirabel's, but close. He must have washed the dye out as well as he could.

An ache squeezed around my heart with a sudden understanding —why he'd have done that, why he'd have held back during the fighting. He'd had his plans. One last gambit, in case mine failed.

"I don't answer to you, Inventor," the Knave sneered, yanking his arm back. “Move aside. Or are you officially throwing your lot in with the Spades?”

“No,” Theo said, perfectly calmly, perfectly assured. Like the man I’d thought I was falling in love with. “I’m here to announce that the rebellion is over.” He raised his voice. “Anyone calling themselves a Spade should go back to their homes and set aside these futile conflicts. It’s finished.”

The Queen of Hearts was bustling her way through the crowd of guards, her square jaw jutting out and the eerie sheen in her eyes glowing fiercely. Her vast scarlet skirts flowed around her. “It is not. They must pay for what they’ve done. You must—”

Theo shook his head as he cut her off. “I’ve already settled everything that needs settling, Mother.”

No. Even though I’d criticized him yesterday, even though I’d told him he’d been wrong to keep so much from me, from everyone, every part of my body protested at the admission in that one word.

I’d wanted him to be honest with us, not with *her*.

Even the Knave faltered at his remark. The Queen stopped dead in her tracks at the edge of the ring of guards. She stared at Theo, her rigidly severe expression shifting just for a second. Then it snapped back into place.

“Mother?” she demanded. “What is the meaning of this?”

Theo gave her a pained smile. “It’s me, Mother. It’s Jack. I know I don’t look exactly the same, but you can see it, can’t you?”

Her hand tightened around her scepter, her knuckles blanching. “My son Jack is *dead*. Don’t you dare—”

“That’s what I needed everyone to think,” Theo went on before she could threaten him. It was unsettling how easily *I* could see the similarities now with them standing face to face: the set of their jaws, the confident stance that looked bold on Theo and arrogant on the Queen. The way he could pitch his voice to cut through any others around him.

“What do I need to tell you?” he asked. “How we went through four tutors in a year before you found one who’d teach things right? That my first real lesson was supervising the beheading of the one you liked least? That I once spilled parsnip soup all over your sitting room rug? That the first creature I killed in a hunt was a pheasant I went out and shot with an arrow on my own before presenting it to you?"

The Queen's face had gone as white as her knuckles. Her lips parted and closed and parted again. "It can't be," she said.

Theo was wearing his usual white dress shirt and gray slacks. Without breaking eye contact with his mother, he reached toward his muscled back and drew his forefinger sharply across the linen fabric, first by his waist, then a few inches higher, and then by his shoulders.

"You did it because you wanted me to remember," he said. "Three times. I did remember. This was for bringing scraps from the dinner table to the stable cats. This was for failing to punish the serving girl who brought me the wrong color of wine. And this was for skipping out on a ball to roam in the city instead."

She whipped me to bleeding, he'd told me. She could have without anyone being the wiser. Score him to the bone one night, and the next morning he'd wake up with only the memory of the pain, no evidence of it.

I restrained a shiver. The guards' hands were still clamped around my arms.

"Jack," the Queen said, with so much emotion tangled in that one syllable that I knew he'd convinced her. She gathered herself, needing to maintain her appearance of superiority in front of her guards, I guessed. "You have a lot of explaining to do."

"And I will," Theo said. "The most important part is that you taught me well. I saw that I had to be the prince and the heir that you needed. And that meant ending the one threat that's loomed over our family for so long." He cast his hand toward me. "This is the latest Alice. I deliver her to you."

A sharper chill ran over my skin. He sounded so steady, as if the role he'd taken on really had been one long plan to bring down the Spades and the Red royal line.

"We'll see that she faces the appropriate punishment, but first we must be sure the threat ends with her. I'll bring her to the dungeon while you prepare yourself for the questioning, if it pleases you, Mother."

The Queen's gaze hadn't left her newly recovered son for an instant. When he called her mother, she nodded automatically.

Theo gestured toward Chess and Hatter. "Let them go. Escort them back to their homes. They've all been under her thrall. We must give them the chance to shake off her influence." He grasped my wrist. "Come along now. Don't make your loss any more painful for yourself than it needs to be."

I tried to turn to make sure the guards were really freeing Hatter and Chess, and Theo's fingers clenched tight enough to bruise my skin. A rough pained noise broke from my lips. The Queen smiled as he marched me toward her.

He held up his hand, palm toward her. "I'll need the mark of your seal. Until the guards know me properly again."

Her seal—like she'd given Rabbit, he'd said. The Queen produced a small metal object about the size and shape of a car's cigarette lighter from the folds of her dress. Holding Theo's gaze, she pressed it to his palm. Lines of blood sprang up where the edges cut into his skin, sealing over almost instantly into a stark pink pattern.

"They'll know you properly soon," she said, the shimmer in her eyes almost… joyful. Somehow that was even more unsettling than her rage.

We strode down the path through the garden toward the ruddy walls of the palace, Theo half a step in the lead. His fingers loosened around my wrist as soon as we'd left the Queen and her guards behind, but he didn't let me go.

I didn't know what to say, what I should do. Should I be trying to escape? Or was this a ruse I'd only survive if I played along? I felt like vomiting all over again, and I didn't think the mushrooms were at all to blame this time.

I'd been angry with him, but I had trouble believing even he could have faked the anguish he'd shown me yesterday over his mother's treatment of Wonderland. If his role as the White Knight had been the real ruse, he'd had plenty of opportunities to hand me over to the palace before now. So I stayed quiet, waiting for his cues. He'd earned that much trust.

Whatever his plan was, I was finding it increasingly difficult to follow. He showed the seal mark to the guards at one of the palace's smaller doors and marched past them. Inside, he led me up a flight of stairs, down a hall, and around a corner to another one. A plush red rug cushioned my feet. The smell of dried roses tinged the air.

Yeah, I was going to go out on a limb here and say this wasn't the way to the dungeons. But where the hell *was* he taking me?

My calves were throbbing again. We finally stopped outside a door with an ornately carved wooden frame, where a squad of guards waited. At the flash of the Queen's seal, they stepped aside. As the door thumped shut behind us, Theo's hand slid farther down, brushing the cuts on my hand. I winced, and his gaze jerked to me. He adjusted his hold in an instant.

"I'm sorry," he said, his voice raw.

Those two words dissolved the last of my doubts. He was still on my side, on the Spades' side, as much as he'd ever been.

He ushered me into a sitting room full of fancy old-fashioned furniture, glinting with gold twined into the fabric and glazed over the wood. Fresh roses sat in a vase on the side table and on the buffet at the other end of the room. The smell of them hung so thickly it smacked me in the face.

Theo pressed on into a vast room with a grand piano and more sofas than I could count. Somehow the rose scent was even thicker there. He coughed and swiped at his mouth. His dark brown eyes were starting to haze.

My heart skipped a beat as I remembered what he'd told me about the roses—that the smell of them clouded his mind. I couldn't lose him, not here, not now. I needed him with me if we were both going to get out of this situation alive.

His steps dragged on the floor. I tossed all my hesitations aside, stepped in front of him, and gripped his shirt to pull him into a kiss.

It was as *with me* as I knew how to accomplish. Let him feel me and not the presence of the roses. Something even clearer, even more potent, that he could train his mind on.

Theo's breath hitched, and then he kissed me back hard, his other hand tucking around my waist and pulling me against him. It only lasted a few seconds, long enough for me to notice that it still felt so fucking good being this close to him, and long enough for my fear to creep back in.

He let me go, his hand coming up to the side of my head, his lips almost brushing my hair. "Thank you, Lyssa."

I swallowed thickly. "I don't understand what's going on. Theo—Jack—"

"It's *Theo*," he said. "I'm not hers. I—I'm going to fix this. I'm going to set things right for Wonderland or die trying. There's been so much pain while I watched and I waited… No more of that. Someone has to stand up to her. It ought to be me."

"You didn't have to do it like this," I said.

He gave me a crooked smile. "She was a hair's breadth from taking your head. We need you alive if things are ever going to be completely right. *I* need you alive. You upended my world, but you saved it—and me—too. It's my turn to save you."

"But how…?"

He eased toward me, and I backed up a step automatically. "I'll do whatever it takes to challenge her, to convince her," he said. "I've already used you too much to fix problems that were my responsibility. You'd try to save us all because that's just who you are, but you've done your part more than anyone should have asked. Now I'll do mine. I swear I'll come for you when it's safe, when I've cleared the way, and you can take the place that's meant for you if you want it."

Another fragment of memory came back to me, from after we'd discovered that the mirror in Caterpillar's club had been shattered. When Theo was discussing the other one he knew of. *The Queen was keeping it in her private chambers…*

"No," I said, with a protest that rippled through me from head to toe. I started to turn, but Theo caught my head with his other hand too, holding my face cupped between them. He walked us back another step, gazing into my eyes.

"I love you, Lyssa. I have to do this. I *owe* you this. I promised I'd get you home."

"Theo—"

He nudged me backward another half a step, and my elbow brushed cool glass. "Just think of home," he said softly.

My body recoiled, trying to throw me forward away from the looking-glass—too late. The mirror's pull was already sucking me through. The last thing I saw of Wonderland was Theo's taut expression before I fell away into blackness.

Think of home, he'd said. As I tumbled headlong through the chilly looking-glass void between my world and his, my skin prickled with the certainty that home was not where I was going but the place I was leaving behind.

I groped into the darkness as if I could catch hold of something that would pull me back there. My body flipped heels over head and spun around. A wave of dizziness washed over me, and I stumbled onto hard wet ground.

I hadn't been focused on anywhere in the Otherland while the mirror had heaved me here, so it must have spat me out into my former world somewhat at random. Into a drizzly night with a tarry scent in my nose and a pair of headlights bearing down on me.

A horn blared, I scrambled up and stumbled, and a wallop of pain shocked my senses into an even deeper darkness.

WRATHFUL WONDERLAND - BONUS SCENE #1

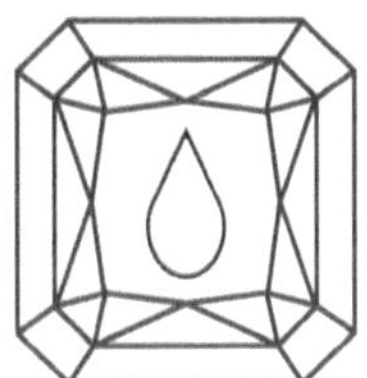

Curious what Chess got up to after he left the others in the rain in chapter 15, before he showed up at Lyssa's window in chapter 16? This bonus scene from his point of view takes you on a little journey around the city and through his conflicted emotions…

Chess

The varied wetness of the Checkerboard Plains—puddles and pools and ponds—had been bad enough. I liked this smattering of water falling from the sky even less. I was already braced against it in the darkness, restraining a wince at the flecks hitting my face, when the Spade the White Knight had called to us said something that dampened my spirits even more.

"The guards are out looking for Cheshire now too."

The White Knight's mouth twisted in dismay. "The Knave sent word back one way or another, then. They'll be waiting to haul all of us in. All right, we'll simply—"

I could already tell from the way the woman had looked at me that her remark had held a more specific menace than that. "No," she said quickly, now averting her gaze. "It's just Chess. The call went out just this afternoon. They're saying the Duchess made a claim that he's a traitor."

Who else? Could I really be surprised? I might have questioned why she'd picked this particular moment, but to tell the truth, I couldn't see how it mattered, so why give her vindictiveness even that much consideration?

"Well," I said, shedding the momentary pinch of discomfort as I wished I could the physical damp, "if it was going to be anyone, it may as well be me, seeing as I'm the only one here who can vanish quite literally." She could call a hunt, but she hadn't a hope in the lands of seeing me brought to ground.

"You could come back to my place for the night," Hatter said, holding my gaze with a steadiness that spoke of various memories he was discreet enough to leave unstated. "I have room. We have the White Knight's alarm system in place. You still get wet even if you're out of sight, don't you?"

I did, and I couldn't say the offer wasn't tempting. But even as I focused on him, the pale-haired figure next to him held more of my attention. Lyssa was watching me too, concern and compassion mingled on her lovely face.

Would she be so sympathetic if she knew what had tangled my life with the Duchess's? If she realized how much of this freakish folly I'd brought down on myself?

She wasn't simply my lovely now. She was a queen—my queen. I shouldn't bring more trouble to her doorstep. Better I did what I could to sidestep it altogether.

I shrugged. "Not if I remove myself from the source of the wetness. Offer appreciated but unneeded, Hatter. I think I'll go take a closer lay of the land."

I shot Lyssa a quick smile I hoped would ease any worries she felt and touched her arm gently before I let myself slip away into that in-between space where I was with them but also alone.

The rain did follow me. If anything, it thickened as I slunk away. I hurried toward the city streets with their sloping and jutting buildings that would offer a little shelter.

If I'd had any idea that I might spy on the Hearts' Guard and learn more about their plans—when it came to me or to the other Spades—I quickly saw I could forget about that. The city folk might have taken some temporary delight in the unfamiliar weather, but the novelty must have worn off fast. The rain-dappled streets lay empty, everyone with a lick of sense tucked away behind their doors. I didn't pass a single guard in my roaming. It appeared they had more sense than I did as well.

There was one place I could nearly guarantee I'd find Wonderlanders still up. Without really thinking about it, I ended up outside the spinning walls of Caterpillar's Club. It couldn't hurt to listen in on whatever gossip was being passed around in there.

For the sake of caution, I stayed in the muted realm of the in-between as I slipped into the club beneath the oscillating lights that colored the dance floor. The thrum of the music didn't fully overwhelm my senses. I bobbed with it, swaying this way and that amid the dancers.

At first, I kept my ears pricked and eyes wide. A couple of guards lingered on the fringes of the crowd, but they spoke to no one, their expressions more bored than anything else. The Clubbers, as I should have expected, let loose no more than calls for drinks and exclamations of revelry. After our time tramping around the Plains, I'd forgotten how little the rest of Wonderland knew of or cared about our questing.

It'd be a relief not to care about it myself for a time, wouldn't it? To lose myself in the whirl and color like I had so often in the past.

I let go of my surveillance, if not my invisibility, and gave myself over to the faded beat. If I brushed against a fellow dancer here or there, what of it? They'd assume it'd been one of the companions they could see.

That thought should have comforted me, but in the grayed space with rain-damp clinging to my clothes, it dulled all the enjoyment I might have felt too. I was nothing to these people, really. They didn't care whether the guards looked for me, took me. While Lyssa and the others rested to prepare for our next steps at saving this land, could I really be so selfish to seek mindless revelry instead?

My stomach clenched. Maybe there was something constructive I could have accomplished in the club, but I couldn't stand to search for it while my skin itched this way. I pulled myself out of the crowd and back into the night outside.

The rain had picked up to a steady patter in my absence. I resisted the urge to shake myself and slunk on through the streets with an eye to finding an unsecured space where I might get some rest of my own. My usual sleeping spot would be more bog than bed in this weather.

The Spades had a safe house I'd made use of on occasion in the cellar beneath a candy café. I slipped down there and immediately wrinkled my nose at the dripping of water that was slicking down the outer walls. Another leak tapped a growing puddle in the middle of the floor. Not the dry escape I'd been looking for. There had to be someplace better.

A few streets farther along, candlelight flickered in a shop window next to a doorframe that had lost its door. The flame blinked out a moment later, but I crept over and ducked inside.

A trio of figures I recognized vaguely from meetings of the Spades had hunkered down among stacks of dresses no one had bothered to hang on the racks. One of them was already snoring. I tucked myself into a corner where the shifting of the silky fabric I lay down on would go unnoticed in the dark and closed my eyes. I'd accepted worse accommodations in times past.

Murmurs carried from the other end of the room, audible in the quiet. "How much longer until the White Knight returns, do you think?"

"He wouldn't leave the city any longer than he felt he had to."

News of our arrival hadn't had the chance to spread far. I was debating showing myself to pass on the word when the first speaker went on.

"Cheshire will be with him, won't he?"

"It's hard to say, the way he vanishes into the air."

"Not well enough to escape the Diamonds' notice, apparently."

"I've heard he used to visit them at the palace ages ago. Can't have been too caught up with them or the White Knight wouldn't trust him, but they may be wise to his tricks."

Not all of them, I thought, but my body stayed rigidly in place, my lips clamped shut.

"Who knows what else he's been up to? He's helped the cause, sure, but he's a difficult one to figure."

"I suppose if there's anything to sort out there, it'll sort out on its own in time."

They lapsed into silence. I stared at the ceiling, hazy in the dark, the knot that had formed in my gut in the club doubling in size.

A difficult one to figure. That was fair, wasn't it? How much of myself had I shown any of my compatriots? By the lands, I couldn't say even Hatter or the White Knight really knew me despite the raw moments they'd witnessed.

And that was my doing, no one else's. I held myself apart. I'd done it again tonight, hadn't I? Choosing to sleep by relative strangers on discarded clothes rather than accept hospitality from the closest figure I had to a friend.

Would I really want to live any differently? I hadn't been thinking only of myself but of avoiding loading more onto them than they could possibly be prepared for. The ragged, wrong pieces inside of me, I couldn't do more than bury deep—I had no reason to believe they'd ever set themselves right. There'd been something off-kilter to my nature to begin with, or I'd never have careened into the situations I had.

The Spades had stopped talking, but a different kind of sounds seeped through my chaotic thoughts. A hitch of a sigh, a rustle of fabric, an encouraging murmur half muffled by a kiss. These two were partners in more than just rebelling.

My mind flitted to moments past: to Lyssa gazing down at me with desire bright in her eyes, telling me she wanted me. To the soft but passionate press of her lips then and as the Tower had whisked us up to the White Knight's apartment the next day. Heat I couldn't suppress unfurled in my chest and flooded down to my cock. Set wrong or not, I was still a man. A man who wished he'd had the opportunity to draw those sounds and more from our Otherlander queen.

The jolt of panic that followed that longing, sharper than any other sensation around me, made me sit up on the scattered clothes. I had the impression of Lyssa's face, etched with horror; of desire vanishing behind pity…

I pressed the heels of my hands to my eyes. She didn't know me either. Not really, not fully. She couldn't.

But right then, damp and disheveled with traces of another couple's pleasure reaching my ears, the instinctive protest felt suddenly absurd. I was running from Lyssa—from the kindest and most compassionate person I'd ever met. A woman who hadn't been fazed by the many horrors this place had already thrown at her. Did I really think so little of her that I expected she'd cast me aside over my past inclinations?

No. I believed in her. I'd once trusted the *Duchess* with that side of myself—how could I say I cared about Lyssa at all if I wouldn't give her even the same chance when she'd earned so much more faith?

I didn't want to stay here. I didn't want to roam aimlessly like a stray tomcat. I might not have a real home, but I had someone who'd welcome me in.

I eased out of the store and through the rain to Hatter's house. My feet moved steadily but restlessly under me. Mindful of the security measures taken, I scrambled up a nearby building and clambered over to the upper bedroom window.

As I perched by the ledge, droplets trickled through my hair and down the neck of my shirt. They turned even colder when I shifted back into the physical realm. A shiver jittered through my body, but still my hand hesitated by the glass.

Lyssa was on the other side. If I could trust I'd get any one thing from her, it was warmth. The rest… I'd take it as it came.

Focusing on the imagined sensation of heat and comfort, I rapped my knuckles against the pane.

WRATHFUL WONDERLAND - BONUS SCENE #2

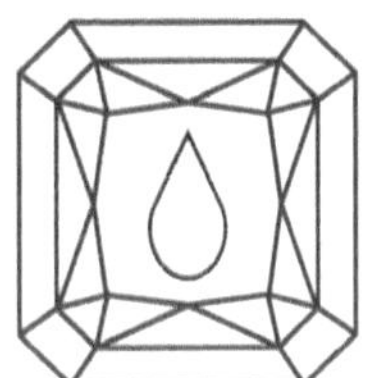

Are you dying to know what happened to Theo after he helped Lyssa escape? Discover the events on the Wonderland side of the story immediately after Wrathful Wonderland's final chapter in this bonus scene from his point of view.

Theo

The mirror's glossy surface swallowed Lyssa in an instant—there and then whisked away, leaving only my tense reflection on the glass. My reflection with the golden curls I'd hidden so long, the features that marked me as one of the Hearts on display in a way that had never felt more obvious.

I closed my eyes, breathing shallowly to limit how much rose scent I took into my lungs, and focused my mind on the image Lyssa landing back at her home, safe from the guards and their swords and my mother's determination to separate this "Alice" from her head. Training every thought on this one good, real thing I'd managed to accomplish.

It was the first in what would need to be a long line, but every journey started somewhere. No matter what happened next, I'd saved Wonderland's true queen and defended everyone who'd turned rebel under my leadership.

My mind slid from the imagined Otherland scene to the embrace Lyssa had offered me just minutes ago. Her sweet flavor lingered on my lips. In some ways she was still here with me, holding me steady against the other influences this palace could work. I'd loved Wonderland and its people for so long, but I'd had no idea my body could contain so much affection and admiration for a single person.

All the more reason I needed to prepare this place for her return as quickly as I could.

Squaring my shoulders, I strode through my mother's rooms to the outer halls. The rose scent faded gradually, but the remembered sensations of a much more welcome intimacy kept me on track. Of course, the real challenge would be addressing the woman who stirred up that scent. As I reached the front of the palace, the tension in my chest gripped my innards.

I'd admitted to Lyssa not long ago that I was afraid of my mother. That was as true now—perhaps even more so—as it'd been then. But if I'd learned anything about a leader's strength from our Otherlander, it was that fear wasn't a good enough excuse to back down or hide away. I had to command the sensation, not let it rule me.

At the end of the hall, a looming window overlooked the front gardens. Bits of the broken stands and cage still littered the grass, and a few of the palace guards roamed between them looking unnerved but determined, but the audience for the Queen's trial had dispersed just as the captive Spades and Clubbers had. I'd put an end to that horrible spectacle—I could take some relief from that.

Before I could decide what my most immediate next step should be, the tapping of hard shoes and the rustle of immense skirts carried from a nearby staircase. My posture stiffened automatically. I turned already knowing who I would see.

My mother swept into the hall with every bit of her usual imperious air, no sign now of how the catastrophe of the "trial" or my unexpected arrival had affected her. Four guards flanked her—

apparently she felt she needed direct protection even inside the palace walls these days. Her eyes settled on me with a coolly metallic gleam, but I caught a momentary hesitation in the set of her face. A hint of motherly concern beneath the queenly façade?

I couldn't count on that, as my own experiences as a child and what I'd observed of my older siblings had proven hundreds of times over.

"Jack," the Queen of Hearts said, her voice all commanding sharpness. The old name I'd cast off decades ago scraped over my nerves, but I kept my expression schooled calm. "Where have you taken the Alice? I've just been to the dungeons, and the guards there haven't seen her."

That question was the one that would tear any trust I'd gained with her to shreds. I swallowed tightly and sidestepped it as deftly as I could.

"I need to speak with you about that and other important matters. Perhaps a private conversation, away from any parties outside the family?"

My mother glanced at her guards. Her chin came up, her lips rigidly pursed. "My guards know better than to gossip about matters that are beyond their station. But we can take a small leave of them." She nodded to the four and strode several steps past me down the hallway, where she could still summon them to her side in an instant but where only raised voices would reach their ears. I supposed that was the most privacy I could hope for given her state of mind.

I followed her to the painting she'd stopped in front of, a scene of minstrels performing in the palace gardens. I might as well be an entertainer about to put on a show now myself. The words lay heavy on my tongue. I had to walk a line even more careful than I ever had in my time balancing the roles as Inventor and White Knight, making my case without wounding a woman so easy to offend. She had to believe I was trying to support her reign, not undermine it.

"I must apologize again for my deception and the long time I've stayed away from the palace," I said. "I never meant to fully abandon my role here—or you. My goal has always been to see Wonderland become the best world it can be with everything we could want for and from our people."

"They have disappointed much lately," the Queen muttered. "I could have used you here beside me to keep the order we need." She peered at me again, her eyes so glittering I couldn't tell whether any real fondness entered her gaze.

"I think I have accomplished better than that," I went on tentatively. "By living among the common people as I have, tending to their more ordinary requests, I've gained a full picture of what tensions we're dealing with. They don't show every side of themselves to those in the palace—out of the due respect and awe, of course." Not to mention fear.

My mother looked skeptical. "Today's events prove that if they need anything, it's a firmer hand and *more* respect enforced. The insolence… The way that girl barged in on *my* home…"

Better to get her off the subject of Lyssa for as long as I could redirect her. My mouth was going dry, my pulse hitching here and there as a thicker rose scent wafted off my mother's dress, but I held my stance and my voice steady.

"I'm afraid we may have gotten ourselves into an unproductive cycle. The commoners act out not because they think they can or should get away with it, but because they feel they have nothing to lose. We ask for a lot from them, but if we did a little more *for* them, gave them more freedom to live their lives as they see fit, they wouldn't see the need to fight. They'd honor you even more."

The queen's eyes narrowed. "That sounds like fanciful talk, not anything based on reality. I know what we're dealing with here. I've seen what these miscreants will do if given any more 'freedom.' Your mind must have gone soft in all the time you've spent among them. Let's have a word with this Alice, and you'll realize exactly how noxious the lot of them are."

I was running out of room to maneuver. All I could do was get out as much of my case as I could and hope some part of the Queen was still capable of listening.

"I have talked to her," I said, "and her only intention today was to save lives. Maybe those lives deserved to be taken in punishment, but

I'm sure you can agree few would accept that judgment for themselves or their loved ones without protest. It's only human nature. Our kingdom will prosper so much more if we work with those impulses instead of punishing people for them. I've given it a great deal of thought. I can lay out a few simple steps we could take that would reduce the rebellious behavior tenfold without you sacrificing a shred of authority. You can place all the responsibility on me. I—"

"You were never against her," my mother interrupted, her face flushing nearly as dark as the crimson on her dress. "All this soft talk—I see it now. She and her 'Spades' have poisoned *your* mind. My son, speaking of freedom and pulling back punishments, excusing the attacks on us as human nature. Where is the Alice, Jack?"

The final question allowed no waffling. I met her gaze unflinching. "Where she should be—home in the Otherland. Where she'll stay until we can—"

"You…" She left off with a strangled sound and snatched my arm, hard enough to bruise the skin. "You will bring her back at once to face the consequences."

"I can't," I said truthfully, bracing myself. "I don't know how to find her there. But she's no threat to you when she isn't even in Wonderland."

"And what's to stop her from returning whenever she sees fit?" Spittle flecked the Queen's lips as her fury grew. "You've turned full traitor—lied to me in front of them all—I will not stand for this. It is their doing, her doing, clearly. We must get the poison out of you and bring you back to your proper self."

Was that perspective better than her understanding I'd taken these actions and said these things of my own free will? I couldn't say, but I knew I didn't want to submit to whatever tactics she intended to use to cure me. If appealing to her rationally wouldn't work, I could turn to my own authority, last-ditch effort though that was.

I tugged my arm from her grasp abruptly enough that her fingers jerked apart and drew myself up even straighter. "I'm the son you raised to be your heir, Mother, and I'm fulfilling my duty to the Hearts with all the skill and devotion I have in me. I'm not a child anymore. Let us sit down and talk this through like the rulers we are—"

"You can rule *nothing* like this," the Queen said, her hand flicking toward the guards. "Take my son into custody. To the medical room, where the doctors can do their work. They must counteract this toxic influence quickly."

"No, Mother, you're not seeing…"

But she wouldn't even look at me now, her face pinched tight. The guards marched over with weapons drawn. I had nothing on me but my wits, which might be considerable, but not enough to escape four armed men.

I couldn't let her take me over again, couldn't succumb to the influences of the palace. I backed up a step with my hands held up in a gesture of peace. "I don't want a fight. You can hear that there's nothing addled about what I'm saying, can't you? Let my mother and me hash this out ourselves."

"Take him!" my mother snapped, and the guards lunged as one being.

I managed to smack the sword from one man's grasp and dodged the swipe of another's foot meant to trip me. My luck ran out there. As I yanked myself to the side, another stepped in with the prick of a blade piercing the fabric of my shirt. It sent a sliver of pain through my side.

Not just pain. A chilly, dizzying sensation trickled through my body from the spot where I'd been cut. My legs swayed under me.

They knew the Queen wanted me alive and relatively uninjured. He'd jabbed me with a dagger coated with some sort of drug. Its effects rolled through me, all the way up to my head, in a matter of seconds. As my mind hazed and my limbs turned to jelly, a single defiant thought stayed with me.

The road ahead of me was going to be longer than I'd hoped. Longer and fraught with peril. But at least the right person was on that road now. I would face the peril, not Lyssa. I would be the man and the prince she deserved.

Then the blackness filled my head completely, and I knew nothing.

LYSSA'S FAVORITE VANILLA-CRANBERRY-PINE SCONES

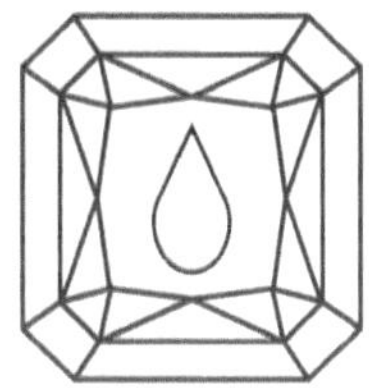

(Recipe makes approximately 8 scones)

Ingredients:

2 cups flour
2 teaspoons baking powder
1/2 cup butter, cubed
1 cup dried cranberries
2 teaspoons ground juniper berries
1/4 cup sugar plus extra for sprinkling
2 teaspoons vanilla extract
3/4 teaspoon salt
3/4 cup milk, plus more for brushing on top

1. Preheat thc oven to 425° F. Line a baking sheet with parchment paper.
2. Combine flour and baking powder in a mixing bowl.

Using your fingers, massage in the butter until the mixture looks like fine crumbs.

3. Stir in the cranberries, ground juniper berries, sugar, vanilla extract, and salt. Add the milk a little at a time, stirring until the dough is soft. You might not need all of the milk.
4. Shape the dough into balls about 2 inches thick and roll them on a floured surface. Place on the baking sheet and flatten to about 1 inch. Brush the tops lightly with milk. Sprinkle with sugar.
5. Bake for 15 to 20 minutes until golden brown. Let sit 10 minutes before serving.

Note: For more of a pine flavor, mix 3 tablespoons ground juniper berries with 1/2 cup of sugar and let sit at least 12 hours. Sprinkle the juniper sugar on top of the scones instead of regular sugar.

Wanton Wonderland

The Looking-Glass Curse
Book 3

CHAPTER ONE

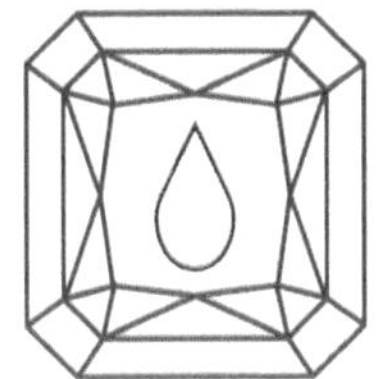

Lyssa

My eyes fluttered open to bright lights and white walls, and my first thought was that I'd somehow fallen asleep in the White Knight's office in his high Tower apartment. The smells weren't right, though: crisp and plastic-y with a hint of chemical cleaner. Neither were the sounds: a steady electronic beeping filtering through a wall and the murmur of the TV set mounted across from me.

I shifted to sit up on the padded surface I'd been lying on, and a thin blanket slipped down my chest. Over the coarse blue fabric of a hospital gown. An IV line slid against my arm. A dull ache spread through my torso and limbs and up the back of my neck to gnaw at my skull.

"Lyssa!" my mother said with a sharp intake of breath. She tipped forward in her chair where she'd been sitting next to my bed to grab my hand. "Honey, are you really awake? Can you answer me?"

"Mom?" I said, bewildered. Her graying blonde hair hung limp around her thin face as if she hadn't washed it in a few days, and her light brown eyes glinted with a liquid shine that was more than just the reflection on her glasses. "Of course I'm awake. What's going on?"

I was in a hospital room, obviously. My pulse stuttered with the memory of the dark wet night I'd fallen into when Theo had sent me through the mirror from Wonderland, the horn and the glare of headlights bearing down on me. I couldn't remember anything after that. How far from my Otherland home had I landed?

"Oh, sweetheart." Mom gave me a careful hug, as if she was afraid the embrace might hurt me. "You were hit by a truck on the highway just a couple miles outside the city. Thankfully the driver called in the accident, and the paramedics rushed you to the hospital right away."

This was my local hospital then. Even though I hadn't been thinking about any specific place in this world when I'd come through the mirror, I'd managed to end up close to familiar ground.

I let out a breath, and my ribs twinged. For being hit by a truck, I didn't feel *that* bad. My arms looked pale but unmarked other than a few pink splotches and the IV. My legs moved beneath the blanket when I tested them. A brace was wrapped around my left wrist, but otherwise I didn't seem to have any bandages. It was actually kind of weird.

"I guess I got really lucky," I said.

"You did," Mom agreed. "Not that I could tell when they first called me in. You were bruised and scraped all over, and they were sure something had to be broken… The doctor said it's incredible you survived. They think that strange shirt you had on must have protected most of the critical areas."

She gestured toward the other side of the room. My vest of armor, made of flexible strands of Wonderland metal woven together with an arc of five rubies beneath the neckline, rested against the bedside table. The impact of the accident hadn't even bent it out of shape or cracked any of the gems. Relief washed over me, followed by a smack of cold as the rest of what Mom had said sunk in.

"When they called you in," I repeated. I couldn't see anything more than a hint of bruises and scrapes on me now. "How long have I been here? I don't remember anything."

"You've been going in and out of consciousness," Mom said, a tremor running through her voice. "And even when you seemed awake before, you were so dazed you couldn't say anything or really do anything. You took a blow to the head—they fixed everything they could, but with the possible brain injury, they weren't completely sure you'd be yourself again—"

She cut herself off with a swallowed sob. "I was so scared for you, Lyssa. I've been here every day, talking to you, trying to help bring you back..."

A lump rose in my throat at her distress. The time she was talking about was a total blank for me. She must have been so freaked out. Even when my life was going well, Mom fussed over the possible catastrophes I might encounter all the time—now she was *never* going to believe me when I told her she didn't have to worry about me.

At the same time, panic dug even deeper. "How many days? How long has it been?"

"Almost four weeks," Mom said hoarsely.

Four weeks. Oh, God. I didn't know how much time had passed in Wonderland while I was laid up here, but that was definitely longer than I'd wanted to be gone.

I hadn't wanted to leave at all. Theo had brought me to the mirror to try to save me, but I'd rather have stayed and kept fighting, however I could. We'd only just freed the Queen of Hearts' prisoners. Who knew what she'd have done to Wonderland's people next?

Theo had revealed himself as her son, Prince Jack, assumed murdered for decades. He'd said he was going to challenge her, force her to change or give up her rule—clear a path for *my* rule as the Red Queen and the rightful heir to the throne. He'd said he would come for me when he succeeded. Maybe he had.

The only way he could have found his way to me here was by using the sketch of Aunt Alicia's house that Hatter had. But I wouldn't have been at the house or anywhere nearby. He'd have had to return to Wonderland empty-handed, not knowing where I'd gone or why.

Either everyone I cared about back in Wonderland was struggling to survive the Queen's fury without me, or they'd been left with an empty throne. They'd think I'd abandoned them. I had to get back soon—now.

"I had a ring," I said tentatively. "I was wearing it like a pendant. Do you know what happened to that?"

Had the vest managed to protect my proof that I was the Red Queen's heir too?

"Oh. Yes. They gave that to me. I think I have it…" Mom dug into her purse with her free hand and produced a plastic baggy that held the chain with the gold ring, its large ruby setting still encased in a shell of filigree. I had to restrain myself from snatching it from her.

"Was it your grand-aunt's?" she asked. "I've never seen it before."

"Yeah," I said. "Aunt Alicia left it for me. Can I…?"

I reached out, and she gave the baggy to me. Her fingers tightened around my other hand. "Do you remember what you were doing out there by the highway, sweetheart?" she asked. "It was an empty stretch —no stores or houses nearby, and it was pretty late at night."

Even if there had been buildings nearby or it'd been earlier in the day, I shouldn't have gone wandering right onto the highway on foot. Clutching my ring, I groped for a reasonable explanation to give her that wouldn't freak her out even more. The ache was still creeping through my head, making it hard to think. Not that I would have had an easy answer ready clear-headed either.

"I stayed up organizing the house and realized I didn't have much food around, so I looked up a late-night place to have dinner and figured I'd walk there," I said, hoping my tone was convincing enough. "It looked closer on the map. Or maybe I got turned around. It was really dark on that stretch, and the rain started—I would have called for a cab, but my phone died on me. Just a really bad situation all around. I must have tripped over something to end up on the road. I don't remember that part."

Mom didn't look any less worried with that explanation, but she must have decided any further questions could wait a little longer. "Oh!" she said. "I have to let the nurses and the doctor know you're awake. And Melody—she'll be so relieved. Your brother, too. He came to see you a few times, you know."

She got up and hustled into the hall, pulling her phone from her purse as she went. My stomach knotted as she went.

How much longer was I going to have to stay here recovering?

More and more days while Wonderland's people—my people—might assume I'd abandoned them like Aunt Alicia had before?

The doctor hustled in, a tall woman in a white lab coat that set off her dark brown skin. She eyed me and the equipment around me, and for a second I thought she looked puzzled. She came over to the side of the bed.

"Miss Tenniel," she said. "I'm glad to see you've rejoined us."

"So am I," I said in a weak attempt at humor.

It did earn me a small smile. "I'm Dr. Nicholson," she said. "How are you feeling?"

"Kind of achy," I said honestly. "But… not really that bad. My mom said I've been here for four *weeks*?"

She couldn't somehow have accidentally said "weeks" when she'd meant "days," right?

"Twenty-six days," Dr. Nicholson said. "But you've proven very resilient." Her gaze twitched toward the metal vest for a second before she caught it. "I'll need to give you a quick exam now that you're back with us."

"Of course."

She shone a light in my eyes and had me test my grip and my range of motion. I was definitely weak from all the lying around I'd been doing. Just lifting my legs up and down a few times was tiring me out. The doctor looked pleased with what she saw, though. Well, pleased and a little puzzled.

"Am I going to be okay?" I asked when she was finished.

"As far as I can tell," she said. "I have to admit, Miss Tenniel, yours has been a rather unusual case. But I see every reason for optimism."

Maybe the vest had protected me with its magic as well as its armor. I wet my lips. "Now that I'm awake, can I go home?"

"With the amount of time you've been unconscious, we'll want to monitor you for at least another day," Dr. Nicholson said. "And even once you're discharged, you'll need to take it easy for a while as you recover your strength. There's also…"

She sank into the chair where Mom had been sitting before and fixed me with a firm but compassionate look. "I haven't mentioned this to your family, but I think it's important I bring it up with you. When you arrived at the hospital, you had a number of small but deep cuts around your lower legs and your hands. They didn't match your injuries from the accident. In fact, I can't think of any sort of accident that could have caused them. Did you want to talk about how you got those?"

Ah, that would be a "No." I'd gotten those cuts freeing the Queen's prisoners and fending off her guards while mushroom-drugged to ten times my regular size. The guards' swords had cut into me like little knives. If I told the doctor that, she'd send me to the psychiatric ward.

"My memory around the accident is pretty fuzzy," I said. "I'm really not sure."

Dr. Nicholson didn't look as if she believed me. "Have you been under a lot of stress recently, Miss Tenniel? We have counsellors here you can speak with if you have any difficult emotions you need to work through in a productive way."

Oh. *Oh.* Understanding hit me like a smack to the head. She thought I'd cut myself out of some kind of self-harming urge. I guessed that wasn't too much of a stretch when by all appearances I'd also walked straight into traffic. Shit.

Hasty denial would probably just make me look even more unstable. I smiled instead. "I really appreciate the offer. I'll let you know if I think I need that. For now I'd just like to rest some more."

"Of course," Dr. Nicholson said. "That'll be good for you."

As she got up, my best friend appeared in the doorway. Melody gave a little cry and rushed over to me. "Lyss! Oh my God. I'm so glad you're okay." She shot the doctor a pointed glance. "She is okay, right?"

"It appears she'll make a full recovery—and a rather speedy one," Dr. Nicholson said. "Go easy on her for now!"

"'Go easy on her'," Melody muttered to herself as the doctor ducked out. She raked a hand through her fine black hair and brandished a patchwork tote bag. "I had stuff packed for as soon as you pulled through. Because I knew of course you were going to pull through. Lyssa Tenniel wasn't going to let some truck get the better of her."

I had to laugh. "What did you pack me?"

"Jeans and one of your favorite T-shirts, all other clothing essentials, and a book I think you'll like in case they aren't ready to let you leave quite yet. *Are* they letting you leave?"

"The doctor said they need to monitor me for a little while longer," I said, my gut tightening all over again. "It sounds like it shouldn't take too long if they think I'm doing that well." If they didn't decide I needed to be carted off to the psychiatric ward after all, for my own protection. "Did you see my mom when you came in?"

"Yeah, she's sorting something out with the nurses about your insurance or I don't know what." Melody sighed and then grinned. She grasped my hand like Mom had. "Do you really feel okay? You know you can tell me if you don't. How you ended up out by the highway—it didn't have anything to do with that asshole, did it?"

"No," I said quickly. I'd given Melody a story about a neighbor I'd been planning to hit up for a booty call as a roundabout way of talking about visiting Wonderland. That lie spiraled a little out of control when she'd found me after my return the last time bleeding all over Aunt Alicia's house. Now she thought some psycho guy lived in the area and might come after me again. "I'm really okay. I mean, not perfect, but if Mom hadn't told me I was hit by a truck, I wouldn't believe it."

Melody kept smiling, but her brow furrowed. When Melody let herself look worried, you knew she was really freaking out. "I want you to know I've got your back, whatever you need, here and once you're back home. I'll grab groceries for the apartment and air everything out, and—"

"The apartment?" I interrupted. "When I get out, I'm going back to the house. I left a bunch of stuff there—I'm still sorting through everything."

Melody's mouth flattened. "Lyss… I don't think that's such a good idea—you being on your own out there after everything. That place seems like it's getting to you somehow. I've never had to visit you at the hospital in the entire ten years I've known you, and within a few days of you inheriting that place, you're in here *twice*?"

Okay, so maybe Wonderland hadn't turned out to be the best for my health, but that was the Queen of Hearts' fault, not anyone else's. And a whole lot more people could be getting hurt because of her right now. If Melody could have understood…

But she wouldn't. No one would. How could I ever explain to anyone what I'd found there, why it was important to me? *I'd* thought I was hallucinating the first few hours I'd spent in Wonderland, with the actual reality of it all around me.

That fact hit me with a punch of queasiness. I cared about Mom—of course I did—and I didn't want to worry her more. I loved Melody like a sister. But I couldn't share anything with either of them about the people and the place I'd fallen in love with.

"Country living comes with unexpected dangers?" I said with an attempt at a wry smile. "It's just a coincidence. You've been through the house—you didn't see anything all that weird there, did you?"

"No. But still. Your mom and I were talking while you were out of it…" Melody looked away and then pulled her gaze back to mine. "We're taking care of it for you, okay, Lyss? It's all still yours; we're just getting it sorted out so you can move on."

I blinked at her. "What do you mean, you're taking care of it?"

She sucked in a breath through her teeth. "We hired movers to come and pack up the place, bring all the furniture and the rest to an auction site. Anything that looked like it was a real heirloom or had sentimental value we already set aside in a storage locker. They should be in there to grab it all today, and then—"

My heart stopped. My voice crackled as it came out, but I couldn't hold it steady. "Mel, that stuff is mine. You can't just—"

"We're looking out for you," Melody said, squeezing my hand. "I promise, you'll be relieved when it's all taken care of. You just have to—"

She kept talking, but I could hardly hear her over the renewed thumping of my heart. It pounded at a panicked rhythm behind my ears. Fuck. Fuck, fuck, fuck. That was about all the coherent thought I was capable for forming for the first few seconds.

Then my practical side, the side that had held me together through Dad's long illness and death, through Mom's depression and my other brother's acting out—the side that had held our whole little family together when I'd been just eight year old—kicked in.

She'd said they were packing up the house today. It was only about an hour's drive from here. I could still catch them before they took away the mirror. If I was fast.

I had to leave. To manage that, I had to get rid of Melody.

"Okay, Mel, maybe you're right," I said when she paused in her explaining. "Sorry. It freaked me out a little, having it sprung on me like that."

"I know," Melody said. "I'm sorry."

"Could you—would you mind—" I touched my belly. "I'm actually feeling kind of hungry. Would you check with the nurse if I'm allowed to eat anything, and if I am, grab me something you know I'll like from a vending machine or whatever? That would be so awesome."

"Of course." My best friend sprang up, not a hint of suspicion on her face. Because even after my various injuries, she couldn't believe responsible, play-by-the-rules Lyssa Tenniel would ever do something as drastic as break out of a hospital against doctor's orders.

She slipped out of the room. I listened to her heels tapping away, and then I tugged the IV free from my arm with a wince, pressing the tape over the puncture point like a Band-aid.

Melody had left her tote bag on the chair. My head spun as I tugged on the clothes, but I didn't have time to take it easy. When I knew where my mirror to Wonderland was—then I'd rest some more.

I fastened the chain around my neck and tucked the ruby ring under my shirt again. My armored vest would look way too weird in here, so I stuffed it in the tote bag for now. Discarding the hospital gown on the bed, I wobbled over to the doorway. A glance outside showed no one I recognized in view—no one who was likely to realize I wasn't supposed to be walking around. I summoned all my strength, and then I set off on my escape.

CHAPTER TWO

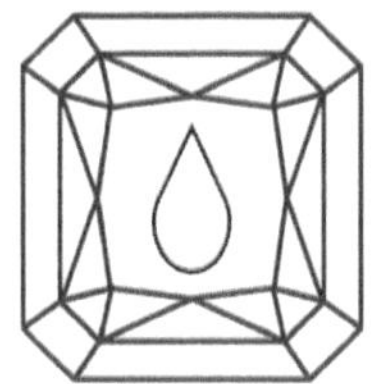

Lyssa

The elevator door stood right ahead of me at the other end of the hall. I walked slowly so I could keep my balance, aiming to look leisurely rather than on the verge of collapsing. When a sharper tremor ran up my legs, I braced myself with my hand against the wall, clutching my tote bag against my side.

Pushing myself onward, I dodged a metal cart and dragged in a ragged breath. Ten more steps. Nine. Eight…

I was at five when a familiar voice carried down the hall. *Two* familiar voices. Mom and Melody were chatting with each other as they came toward me, presumably on their way back to my room.

With a lurch of my heart, I threw myself toward the elevator. My thumb jabbed on the button, that hand holding me upright while my legs trembled. I managed to straighten up just as the car arrived with a *ding!*

A couple of nurses hurried out. I darted past them and jammed my finger on the button for the ground level. The door was just sliding closed when a yell reached my ears.

"Lyssa!"

The elevator was already dropping. I sagged against the wall, gripping the railing. *Come on, muscles. You've had almost four weeks of relaxing. Time to get with the program.*

I had to push my posture a little straighter and paste a smile on my face when a couple who must have just been visiting someone got on at the second floor. Sweat started to trickle down my back. The elevator whirred down one more level. I darted out the instant the door whispered to the side.

The main lobby—I had to find it. I had no idea where my car was, but there'd have to be taxis outside. I had to get out of this building before anyone figured out how far I'd gone. I—

I nearly barreled right into a slouched figure ambling toward the elevator. My shoulder bumped his arm, and his "Whoa!" set every nerve on high alert before he even glanced down and said, "Lyssa?"

My older brother Cameron was staring down at me. I hadn't seen him since our family dinner last Christmas, which he'd showed up late for and left from early after a poke through Mom's wallet.

As kids, we'd had the same white-blond hair, but unlike mine, Cam's had darkened to a shade closer to brown. A new scar flecked his right cheekbone, and his lips automatically curled into a sneer. I wasn't sure his mouth had known how to make any other expression since he was twelve.

"What the hell are you doing down *here*, sis?" he said.

I could have asked him the same thing. Yes, he must be here to see me—Mom must have called him like she'd said she would—but I didn't know why he'd bothered. It wasn't as if he'd cared about anything other than what I could give him in ages. But in that moment my mind latched onto one small but vital fact.

Cam liked cars. He always had a clunker he was driving around while he waited for the funds to "fix it up."

"I'm leaving," I said. "You drove here?"

His sneer wavered. "Uh, yeah. But what—"

I grabbed his elbow and pushed him back the way he'd come. "You're my ride. Let's get going. There's someplace I need to be, fast."

"Are you sure it's a good idea for you to be going anywhere, Lyssa?" he said, peering down at me as I hustled him onward.

Old Lyssa would have tried to appeal to his better nature, or, failing that, to bargain with him. I discovered that Lyssa who was heir to the throne of Wonderland, on the other hand, had exactly zero fucks to give for my brother's shit.

"*I'll* worry about whether it's a good idea or not," I said, my voice coming out with a strident, authoritative tone that was new too. "I need to get somewhere. You wanted to see me. Easy solution for both of us."

Cam's eyebrows jumped up, but to my relief he didn't argue. "All right, all right," he said. "The parking lot is this way. I'll just warn you, you'll have to clear the junk off the passenger seat."

The junk was about a dozen McDonalds food wrappers, a broken pair of headphones, and a crumpled, empty box of cigarettes. I swept everything onto the floor and climbed in, my nose wrinkling at the greasy nicotine smell that permeated the whole car. But beggars couldn't be choosers. I didn't know where my purse was. Now that my whole attention wasn't focused on staying upright, it occurred to me that I didn't have any way of *paying* a taxi for an hour-long ride.

Cam started the engine with a couple of sputters leading into a low growl. I glanced behind us as he pulled out of the parking lot, but I didn't see any sign of pursuit. With luck, Mom and Melody and whatever nurses they alerted would spend a while checking around the hospital before deciding I must have left.

I had the feeling that, especially after my brief outburst when Melody had told me about sending away the house's contents, Aunt Alicia's property was the first place they'd check when they realized I'd fled the coop.

"Take a left," I said. "We're going to want to get on the highway heading north. I'll tell you when we need to get off again."

Cam looked at me sideways. "You're heading back to her house—Aunt Alicia's."

"Yep."

I didn't figure I owed him more answer than that. As he drove, cursing at a pedestrian who was taking too long to cross the street, I fiddled with the brace on my wrist. The bones mustn't be broken, or I'd have gotten a full cast. When I flexed the muscles there, they didn't ache any worse than the rest of me did. I wasn't sure I needed the brace anymore, but what if I hurt myself all over again by taking it off?

After another bout of swearing at the driver in front of him who he felt was taking a turn too cautiously, Cam aimed the car down the highway and hit the gas. My shoulders jolted against the worn seat.

"So," my brother said after a short silence, with a wheedling note in his voice that I could recognize in an instant. My back tensed. He'd only agreed to drive me without complaint because this ride came with strings attached. "Aunt Alicia left her entire property to you, huh. I hear it's quite the place."

"It's a nice old house," I said cautiously. "But kind of in the middle of nowhere."

He nodded. "You're unloading it and all her stuff, then?"

I guessed Mom hadn't mentioned her plan with Melody to him. Not surprising.

"I haven't totally decided yet," I said. "I only had it for a few days before…" I gestured to myself to indicate the accident.

"It seems pretty unbalanced, don't you think, that she gave all that stuff just to you—and, I mean, it used to be Dad's house too. We should both have some say what happens to it."

He couldn't have been more predictable. I'd be willing to bet this was the whole reason he'd hurried over to the hospital when he'd found out I was awake. He'd probably hoped I'd be more suggestable in my weakened state. He hadn't even asked me how I was feeling after I'd just woken up from an awful accident, and he was already angling for a cut of the money from selling the house, or for me to pay him off to keep the peace if I didn't sell.

Which, yeah, maybe would have been more "balanced"—if our family had ever been balanced. If he'd ever done more than take, take, take, when he wasn't breaking other people's things and leaving me and Mom to pick up the pieces, both figuratively and sometimes literally.

The last time Aunt Alicia had visited us, he'd dented her car jumping around on the hood and then cursed her out for telling him to get off. He hadn't exactly been on his best behavior most of the visits before then either. Why the hell did he think he deserved one cent from her?

"Aunt Alicia left it to me," I said, still trying to be diplomatic. "I haven't seen much of anything around that would have been Dad's except some old toys and books, if you're interested in those. If I find anything else, something it'd make sense for you to have, I'll let you know."

Cam scoffed at the idea of taking childhood bits and pieces. It wasn't memories he wanted; it was only cash. "There've got to be a few pieces you could sell off quickly. You can see this car needs work. I'm living paycheck to paycheck here. We're family. You're not going to give me a hand when you got this huge gift dropped into your lap?"

"Cam, I just got out of the hospital. You want to give me a break?"

"Well, when am I going to get to ask you again? You hardly talk to me anymore. Like you're so much better than me."

A flare of anger went off in my chest. I didn't have the energy to put up with his bullshit right now on top of everything else. Why did I even bother trying to keep the peace anymore? My brother had shown time and time again that he couldn't care less about Mom or me.

"I don't talk to you because every time I do, you're either insulting me or looking to get something out of me, like right now," I said. "Since when have *you* ever cared about family? When you were getting yourself suspended from school and nearly sent to juvie, while Mom was working her ass off just to put food on the table? When you wrecked *her* car driving around high? When she had to empty her savings account bailing you out for the fifteenth time last year?"

Cam's face flushed red. "If you don't think I'm worth being around, I can let you out right now. Find some other schmuck to drive you." He craned his neck, looking for the next turn-off.

My hands balled into fists in my lap. The authoritative energy that had filled me earlier rose up again.

A queen's blood ran through my veins. I'd freed all of Time and challenged a mad tyrant to her face. If Cam thought I was still the same old careful, dependable Lyssa, he was in for a big fucking surprise.

"No," I said, my voice ringing from my throat. "You are going to keep driving, and we'll talk about balance. For the ten years from when Dad died to when I left for college, I was the one holding the family together, making sure Mom didn't go off the deep end, doing everything I could to see that we kept the house and had something to eat, while you ran around acting like an asshole."

Cam sucked in his breath to speak, but I cut him off. "I know. You lost your dad. Guess what—so did I. I was freaked out too. But I didn't get to go crazy, not even a little, because you took up all the space for that. So I think you owe me a hell of a lot more than I owe you. All I'm asking is for you to drive me an hour outside of town. You can do that, or you can forget it if you think we're *ever* talking again."

For a few minutes, Cam couldn't seem to speak. We drove past an exit, but he stayed in his lane. Finally, he swallowed audibly and gave a little cough as if to find his voice.

"What the hell happened to you in that coma, Lyssa? You don't sound like… you."

"It wasn't the coma," I said. "I've been figuring out a lot of things lately."

He hesitated a little longer. Then he said, "You did take care of a lot when we were kids. I was doing my best too, you know."

Because of the acknowledgment and because he was still on the highway, I didn't argue with that statement. I wasn't going to praise his efforts either, though. "Okay," I said.

"It's just easier for you," he went on. "You always seem to know what you're doing and how you're going to do it, where you're supposed to be. I… don't really ever feel that way." His voice dropped with the last sentence as if he didn't totally want to say it.

I almost laughed. Easier? But I could see how my life might have looked that way to him. He had no idea.

Maybe I hadn't really had a clue either. As I gazed at the regular fields dappled with regular trees along the side of the highway, an uncomfortable pressure wound around my heart. Had I really known where I was supposed to be any time since I was a kid? I'd spent so much time in Wonderland thinking about how I had to get back here, but what did I *have* here, really?

I had Mom and Melody, sure. But they were other people with their own lives. Beyond that… How much had I really been living, and how much had I been waiting for things to fall into place? For this boyfriend or that job to turn into the one I really wanted?

When had I let myself dream about anything other than just having a regular existence? What would I dream about if I did?

The answer was obvious now. I'd felt more alive in Wonderland than I ever had here. I wanted to see just how wonderful it could be without the Hearts crushing everyone's spirits. Wonderland needed me more than anyone in the Otherland ever had… and I needed it more than I'd ever needed anything here. *That* was where I was supposed to be. I felt it with every fiber of my being.

"I didn't really feel like I knew what I was doing either," I admitted. "I just kept going, kept following the path I thought I was supposed to, because I was too scared of what would happen if I didn't."

Cam sat with that comment for a while. I didn't expect him to apologize for anything from our past or even the conversation that had just happened, but at least he didn't snark about it.

"Are you going to be okay?" he asked, like maybe he actually wanted to know.

The start of a smile touched my lips despite the knot of tension inside me. "I think so."

We didn't talk much after that other than me giving directions when it was time to get off the highway, but the air in the car tasted at least a little clearer. To give Cam credit, he didn't bring up his interest in the inheritance again. My nerves had almost settled when Aunt Alicia's house came into view up ahead—with a big white moving truck parked out front.

I jerked forward in my seat as if that motion would propel the car faster. "Come on," I said. A couple of guys were walking from the house to the truck carrying what looked like the dining room table. Fuck. How much had they already packed up?

"What's going on?" Cam said, but he revved the engine at the same time. We sped down the driveway and jolted to a halt beside the truck. I opened the door the second the wheels stopped moving, slinging Melody's tote bag with the armored vest over my shoulder.

"Stop!" I shouted at the movers. "This is my house. I didn't give permission for anyone to move this stuff. You've got to put it all back."

The guys with the table paused and set it down on the pavement. The one with the bushy beard gave me a puzzled frown. "Look, we've got clear instructions—there was a woman here earlier who opened up the house for us—"

"She went behind my back while I was in the hospital," I said. "It's *my* house. Isn't it?"

I glanced at Cam for back-up where he was stepping out of the car. He looked a little bewildered, but he nodded automatically. The movers glanced at each other.

"Just—don't take anything else until we get it all sorted out," I said. "I have to see what's already gone."

I'd recovered a little strength during the drive, but my legs were trembling again by the time I reached the front door. I soldiered on, gripping the railing tight as I hauled myself up the stairs, freezing through a wave of nausea on the third floor, wobbling up the spiral staircase to the attic.

My head emerged into the little room at the top of the house, and my whole body stiffened.

It was empty. Everything was gone—the bookcases, the chest… My mirror to Wonderland.

I scrambled back to the ground floor as quickly as I could. I'd just reached the doorway when a car engine thrummed in the distance. When I stumbled out, Melody's bright blue Nissan raced into view along the country road heading toward us.

My stomach flipped over. After the stunt I'd just pulled running away from the hospital, she and Mom might have grounds to get me committed. They sure as hell weren't going to stand around while I had the movers haul all Aunt Alicia's stuff back into the house.

There was only one way out of this mess. And it was the way I wanted to go anyway.

One of the movers let out a shout as I dashed past him toward the open back of the truck. My legs swayed, but adrenaline carried me up the ramp and into the dark interior. Tables, chairs, and bookcases were tightly packed all around me.

A prickling pull ran over my skin and down into my chest, tugging me forward. Around a stack of boxes. Over a bedframe.

There. The mirror's glossy surface glinted faintly near the back of the truck. I gasped in relief—and heard the thump of car doors slamming outside.

No time to think. No time for doubt. I leapt at the mirror with arms outstretched.

With a hitch of my lungs, it yanked me through its cool surface and sucked me down.

CHAPTER THREE

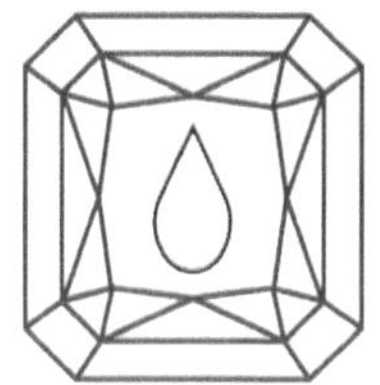

Chess

A person could move across the city of Wonderland far above the streets simply enough with the right companions. I was plenty spry on my feet, and Dum could jump from one side of an intersection to another without breaking a sweat. Here and there, Dee would vault me over with his springy arms, and I'd attach a rope for him to swing across on.

We mostly stuck to the middle of the roofs, away from any eyes on the roads below. Our destination, the Tower, gleamed silver against the sky up ahead. We didn't need any maps or signs to figure out where to go. Every time we had to cross to a new block of buildings, we scanned the street for members of the Hearts' Guard first. Their scarlet helms made them easy to pick out even amid the revelers dancing on the sidewalks.

I tugged the scarf wrapped across my lower face tighter at the sight of a heap of roses on the pavement. The palace workers had been coming through the city every morning tossing fresh blooms here and there throughout the city. Their cloying scent prickled faintly through the fabric even this far up. Down there, it seeped around door frames and down chimneys. The Clubbers couldn't escape it.

And so the whole city had become a vast version of Caterpillar's Club.

The thump of bass and a tinkling of strings carried from one of the speakers on the corners as we hurried on across the next roof. My steps fell into the beat of their own accord. The epic dance party going on all through the city would have been a welcome celebration if it'd been happening because those people *wanted* to party and not because the Queen was pulling out all the stops to keep them distracted and sedated.

At the club, at least we'd been able to choose whether we went and how long we danced, even if that choice had sometimes felt inevitable.

"It just never wears off, does it?" Dee said through his own scarf with a muffled laugh, peering over the edge. "That guy there fell asleep right in the middle of the street! Never tell a Wonderlander it's time to go to bed, right?"

He winked at me, but his cheer sounded a tad forced. The last couple weeks had been a strain on us all.

"I guess it'd be too much to wish for a blight on all the roses in the land," Dum muttered. His demeanor hadn't changed much in recent times, but then, he'd always been more on the gloomy side.

"Oh, she'd cook up some other way to screw us over." Dee shook his head. "Whatever I might say about the Queen of Hearts, she is resourceful."

"If I didn't know better, I'd say she's already lost her head," I said, matching his light-hearted tone. "A pity that isn't the case."

Dum snorted. "In every way that makes things worse for us, she has. I wonder—"

He stopped himself with a furtive glance my way. I suspected I knew what he'd been thinking of. Or rather, who. Grinning fiercely behind my scarf, more for myself than anyone else, I leapt from one set of slanted yellow singles to another of mint-green tiles veering in the opposite direction.

I wondered too. What had happened to Lyssa after she'd disappeared into the Hearts' palace those weeks ago? How long had she lived before the Queen had tired of the game of questioning her and—?

No, I wouldn't think about that part.

Mostly I wondered what Wonderland would look like right now if our lovely Otherlander had been sitting on that palace's throne. The thought stuck with me like an ache in my bones, easily forgotten if I was focused on other things, but always there if my mind wandered.

If we'd fought a little harder— If I'd gotten to her faster in the fray—

"Chess!" Dum called, as loud as he dared, and I realized the twins had gotten quite the lead on me. I picked up my pace to catch up.

The silver spire of the Tower loomed over us. We stopped on top of the building across the street from it and considered the challenges ahead.

Two guards were stationed directly outside the Tower door. The roses pinned to the collars of their pleated uniforms contained some sort of antidote to the drug the others were laced with, so that they could keep their wits, such as any of them had, while keeping an eye on the city.

A couple more guards with similar blooms beneath their chins marched by as we watched, but after a minute they passed out of view amid the dancers around the corner. I tipped my head toward the twins.

"Ready?"

"Piece of cake," Dee announced, and tied a rope around a jutting weather vane so he and his brother could scramble down into the alley on the other side of the building. I fixed one of my ropes to the random railing at the Tower side. I couldn't drop it yet, or the guards might notice it. For now, I reached toward the in-between space where I could move without being seen. The music below dulled.

The twins had to work fast once they hit the ground. Roses scattered the streets here too, more than our scarves could hope to protect us from for long up close. With a faint thump, they set their feet on the wall and skidded down one right after the other. Then they dashed through the scattered revelers toward the Tower.

Dee aimed a punch at one shop window. Dum aimed a kick at

another. The guards shouted, and the twins took off—in opposite directions. The guards charged after them, giving me my opening.

I tossed the rope and threw myself after it, only gripping it to slow my fall. The second my feet touched the ground, I sprang toward the Tower. The music and the aimless chatter farther down the street completely muted the sound of my steps. The guards hollered somewhere farther off, and I hoped the twins made it to the Spades waiting for them before the toxins in the air took over. All I could concentrate on right now was in and up.

I slipped past the Tower door—by the lands, let none of the Clubbers catch its brief swing—and hurtled into the elevator shaft.

"Twenty-seventh floor, Chess coming calling. The White Knight gives his blessing," I said quickly.

The cushion of air propelled me upward. Thank the lands the White Knight had thought to include that failsafe for his closest associates so we could still access his apartment if he wasn't in it.

Although, how close to him could I really say I'd been, current revelations taken into account?

The whisper of the elevator door closing behind me was so familiar, the gleam of the pale walls on the other side so familiar, I could almost have believed I'd find him sitting behind his big white desk in that big white room. But the White Knight's office stood empty, as did the rest of his apartment.

Would he ever come back here? I'd thought I'd seen a true joy in his expression when he'd fit the pieces of one gadget or another together to make it something real, but maybe that had all been pretense, like so much else.

For now, *we* needed those gadgets. He'd had a few days in here planning for our next efforts after Time had been freed—he'd talked about preparing equipment. Let's hope he'd prepared something that we could benefit from in our present time of need.

I started with the built-in shelves along the walls, picking up various devices and eyeballing them to determine whether they were finished or only works in progress. Ah, here was that extendable metal rope and the spinning cutting tool he'd put great use to on the

Checkerboard Plains. I stuffed those into the sack slung over my shoulder and moved on.

The drawers in the worktables offered up a few more goodies. One held a contraption in the shape of a gun that he'd assembled before, during the freeze. It could melt metal in a matter of minutes. Here was the funnel that could throw one's voice up, down, or around corners. Here some treads that could be fixed to our shoes to allow us to climb almost any surface.

None of it was exactly what I'd come for, though. But then, his most useful inventions were also the ones that would have looked too suspicious if left easily accessible. Where would he have hidden those away?

I poked around his desk feeling for secret compartments, but none revealed themselves. Perhaps not in his office at all? I prowled farther into the apartment.

I'd been in the more private areas of the White Knight's home plenty of times. When a woman at the club or in the park had particularly caught my fancy, unless I'd already had company with me I was pleased to share with, I'd generally brought her over here to "meet" the Inventor. More often than not, if he was in, he'd been game. Those might have been the only times he'd indulged himself in that side of life in general. I'd never seen him making moves on anyone on his own, although who knew how various private meetings with the other Spades might have ended, without me there to witness?

He'd been discrete, and he hadn't pursued anything continuous. Until Lyssa. How much had he already known, before the Red Knight had even laid out the Hearts' torrid history? He must have known something, mustn't he?

Because he wasn't really the White Knight or the Inventor. He was Jack, Prince of Hearts.

Even now, trying to connect the man I'd known as the White Knight to the boy I'd caught glimpses of around the palace, I couldn't quite make the pieces fit. But I *hadn't* ever seen more than occasional glimpses of Prince Jack, after all. The Queen had kept her youngest son apart from the Diamonds' leisure activities as if he were her most prized possession. Actually, not just as if. He had been. I'd seen the way the sheen in her eyes would almost glow when she so much as mentioned his name.

She's fucking obsessed with that kid, I'd murmured to the Duchess once. The Duchess had laughed and not argued even a little.

I definitely didn't want to think about either of those women. I narrowed my attention down to the task at hand, rifling through the White Knight's closets and wardrobes and cabinets, checking under the sofas and the bed. My mind did enjoy a good wander, though. Thankfully it managed to wander in a more useful direction this time. I stepped back into the hall, and my gaze came to rest on the door to the games room.

The White Knight would want to hide incriminating inventions somewhere no one would think to look for the instruments of rebellion. Like in a room devoted to play.

I didn't go much for Inventor-style games, so I hadn't spent much time in that space. I nudged open the door and considered the gray shelving units that lined one wall. The other three walls were the same blank white as in his office. All the better to not intrude on the fantasy challenges the gaming gear could invoke.

Any of the tools lying on those shelves could call up a host of translucent images at a touch. The White Knight had once told me that the White Knight before him had said this space had once been more of a training room to help people learn new skills. The younger Spades had come up with systems of ranking and points that I didn't know much about. But…

These egg-shaped devices tucked away on the back of one shelf looked familiar. I picked one up and sniffed it. Yes, that was the burnt smell of singe powder, all right. These were the White Knight's smoke bombs, which had served us well on more than one mission. I'd take all of those, thank you very much.

If any of the Queen's people had come sniffing around here themselves, he could have explained it away as part of one of the games. Very clever.

I scanned the other shelves and pocketed a few more things, my stomach starting to sink until I crouched down by the far end of the room. A real grin leapt to my face. I picked up the heavy cloth the

White Knight had wrapped across his face on our mission into the palace grounds last month.

He'd said it was to filter out the smell of the roses. As far as I knew, Prince Jack hadn't been allergic, so this might not serve our purpose after all, but it was worth a try.

There were two more of the masks folded just behind the one I'd spotted. That was a start. With a flash of victory in my chest, I dropped them into the sack with the rest of my loot.

I hurried back to the office. Leaving would be much easier than entering had been, since as soon as I was out, I could just run, and the guards wouldn't know where I'd gone. But someone might decide to come up and check on the apartment, and it wouldn't do to be caught here. The Knave had ways of making the elevator do his bidding, proper commands or no.

Stopping there by the elevator door, my momentary good mood deflated. I'd stood right here with Lyssa when I'd first brought her to meet the White Knight. *I'd* taken her to him. It'd been Hatter's suggestion, yes, but I'd gone along with it without a second thought…

How much of this catastrophe was my fault for not looking harder, not paying more attention? For having spent all those years visiting the palace lolling around and thinking only of self-satisfaction, not bothering to think much about anyone who might matter later?

How much were a few masks and other tools going to change anything now? She was *gone*. The lovely woman whose smile had lit me up inside was—

I gritted my teeth and brought back the fierce grin that had steadied me on the rooftop. Maybe this expedition would get us nowhere. Maybe it'd been pointless. But whatever had happened to Lyssa, she hadn't let us down, not one bit. I wouldn't let her down either. We'd fight until we couldn't anymore. That was the only path I cared to follow now.

CHAPTER FOUR

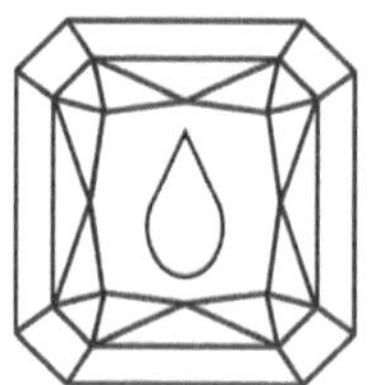

Lyssa

My body spun through the vast shifting tunnel that would spit me out into Wonderland, and I clutched the tote bag with my metal vest tight to my chest. The fall was long enough for a few pangs of guilt to find me—what would Mom and Melody think, with me fleeing the hospital and then somehow disappearing on the moving truck? How were they going to cope, not knowing what the hell had happened to me?

I'd come back. When things in Wonderland were settled and safe, when I knew I wasn't leaving everyone there in the lurch, I could hop back through the mirror and clean up the mess I'd left behind as well as I could.

Right now I had to be ready for the mess that might be waiting on Wonderland's side. I dragged in a deep breath and braced myself for the smack of the pond's salty water.

The cool liquid shot over me, and like every time before, I found myself abruptly floating upward rather than tumbling down. The muted light playing across the shifting surface above me suggested it was daytime. Harder to hide.

I spread one arm to slow my ascent and kicked toward the edge of the pond so I'd be close to the shelter of the vegetation when I emerged. The strain trembled through my weakened muscles.

Fucking truck. Fucking Wonderland mirror that had decided to drop me in the middle of the highway just because I hadn't pictured a place to arrive. Maybe a little of the Queen of Hearts' hostility had rubbed off on it.

I managed to reach the dark rocks with their glittering specks of mica before my lungs demanded air *now*. As quietly as I could, I lifted my head from the water and sucked in the tang of salt and ferns.

A figure was moving through the brush along the other side of the pond. I froze, gripping the gritty-slick side of the rock. A flash of a red helm showed between the fern fronds. It eased away farther away from the bank, out of view. I didn't see any other guards around at the moment. This might be the best chance I got.

Clenching my jaw against the protests of my limbs, I hauled myself out of the water with as careful a balance between haste and quiet as possible. After a few stumbling steps, the ferns had closed around me. I sank down on the damp soil and gave myself a moment to rest and take stock.

The vest would do me a lot more good on me rather than in this bag. I squeezed as much water as I could out of my drenched T-shirt and pulled the flexible armored bodice over my head. It was a bit of a struggle working my arm through with the brace around my wrist. I considered the padded gray fabric for a moment and decided I'd risk removing it. It would make me stand out more as someone not of this world than even the armor would, and I might need that extra bit of mobility.

I eased the brace off and tucked it into Melody's tote bag. That bag might draw attention too… After a moment's indecision, I hid it under a fallen frond.

Tentatively, I crept through the densely clustered ferns. The fronds tickled over my bare arms. My feet only made a faint murmur on the ground between them. I kept my ears perked and my body tensed to run if I had to.

Hopefully I wouldn't have to. I wasn't sure how far these legs would carry me.

Maybe I was being over-cautious. If Theo had gotten through to his mother, that guard might have been ambling around waiting to see if I'd appear so he could help me back to the city. But after everything I'd seen of the Queen of Hearts and her court, I didn't want to take any chances.

The ferns gave way to the forest of trees with jade and emerald-brilliant leaves. As I slunk on, a rustling reached my ears from up ahead. I stopped, gripping a nearby branch, every nerve on high alert.

A pale figure moved into view between the trees. I stiffened when I recognized her.

It was Mirabel, the woman the Spades had called the White Queen. She was wearing one of her typical woolly white dresses, but the fabric had grayed, patchy with smudges of dirt and other stains. Her golden curls spilled over her shoulders in disarray, only a few coils still pinned on top of her head. The curls almost hid the dark pink ridge of the scar that peaked from her hairline at her temple.

I hadn't seen Mirabel since I'd found out the truth of her identity. She was the Queen's daughter, a Princess of Hearts. It was the Queen who'd struck her and left her with that scar—and with her thoughts even more addled than they'd been already, with her ability to look both forward and backward through time.

Theo had said Mirabel wanted to see the Queen displaced as much as everyone, that she'd fled the palace and helped the rebels ever since then. I wasn't totally sure I could trust Theo's assessment of his own sister, though, especially since I still wasn't totally sure how much I could trust Theo.

He'd been trying to protect me when he'd nudged me through the mirror back to my world. He'd sworn to face his mother and fight for Wonderland head on. But he'd also spent who knew how many years hiding who he was and orchestrating the Spades' battles mostly in the background, where it was safer. He'd lied to them, and to me, more times than I could count.

Mirabel was heading straight toward me, though. Her glimpses of the future could very well have told her I was here. And *she'd* never given me any reason to distrust her. I couldn't judge her based on who her mother or her brother was.

I eased away from the tree. Mirabel's pale eyes brightened when she saw me.

"There you are!" she said, speaking in a whisper. "We only came a short way, but it seemed like a long time."

As usual, it wasn't super easy figuring out what Mirabel was talking about in her disjointed way. At least she looked happy to see me. I found myself smiling back at her.

"What are you doing out here?" I asked, matching her volume. "Why did you leave the Tower?"

Her body swayed for a second, and she wrapped her arms around herself. "They all left. And they came. The roses, everywhere—I had to find my way here. I had to find my way to you. We've already gone and come."

My throat tightened with sympathy. She sounded even more loopy than usual. How long had she been wandering around in the forest alone? I couldn't ask her and expect anything close to a straight answer.

She might be able to get us to someplace better, though. I touched the side of her arm lightly. "Do you remember where we came from? Is there somewhere we should be?"

"I—" Mirabel blinked hard. She rubbed her temple, and her mouth twisted with effort. "There is light, but I don't know how far away. The music and the stink—I didn't like it. But that's where you were needed. They always needed you. We can go, I think. We met her. She knew the way."

Okaaaay. I let the White Queen take the lead, walking half a step behind her as we wove through the woods. Mirabel's hands moved in furtive gestures by her waist. After a few minutes, I realized she was going through the motions of knitting without her needles or yarn.

Any doubts I'd had about her seemed ridiculous, watching her now. This woman wasn't *capable* of scheming or duplicity. She could barely keep track of herself in the present, let alone juggle all kinds of lies. I sure as hell couldn't blame her for not wanting to broadcast her heritage.

Maybe I couldn't blame Theo for that either. He still shouldn't have hidden so much else from me, though. He'd realized who I was, how I'd fit into Wonderland's history, long before I had, but he'd kept all that to himself for his own reasons.

"Have you seen—" I started to ask, and Mirabel raised her hand in a wave. For a second I thought she was hallucinating a friend up ahead. Then a slight figure rose from behind a bush where it'd been crouched in hiding.

The skinny woman in front of us was one of the Spades, but not one I'd really have wanted to run into. The second I looked into her pointed face with its beady, ferret-like eyes, I remembered her skeptical look at the meeting where she'd suggested I had no place in Wonderland at all. That my being there had made it worse for all of them.

None of us had known then that I had Wonderlander blood running through my veins. Unless the handful of people who'd made that discovery with me had spilled the beans since I'd been gone, she *still* didn't know. It was still hard to forget how unwelcome she'd made me feel with a few quick words. The same sensation prickled over me now as her eyes widened with what looked like horror.

"The Otherlander," she said quietly, blinking hard. "Where did you—How—Where have you *been*?"

My stomach clenched into a ball. I'd obviously been gone long enough for the Spades to assume I'd abandoned them—just like Hatter had predicted I would, back when we'd first been getting to know each other. I'd led them to that huge battle at the palace and then I'd just disappeared.

Well, I was going to have to face the rest of the Spades sometime. When I explained, when they realized I'd come as soon as I could, they'd understand, right? It was just the initial questions and hurt that I was queasily anticipating.

"I'm here now," I said. "I'm sorry."

"You take us to the others," Mirabel informed the ferrety woman in a brisk tone as if she should already have known that.

The woman left off staring with a jerky bob of her head. "Yes. All right. Yes. We have a little time before the next patrol comes around. Quickly."

She motioned to us with a twitch of her hand. I peered through the woods around us as we followed her on toward the city. From that comment about the guards, clearly the Queen was still in command and out to crush the Spades. How much more had the people of Wonderland been through while I'd been lying in a daze in that hospital bed?

The vivid walls and roofs of the buildings at the edge of the city came into view through the trees. A faint smell, sickly sweet like fresh roses dipped in corn syrup, reached my nose. The ferrety woman knelt by a boulder at the foot of a tree and heaved it up to reveal a trap door and a passage underneath. She pointed for us to head down.

Metal rungs formed a sort of ladder down into a damp tunnel. My feet hit the ground on rocky earth at the edge of an underground stream. It flowed on through a passage that was only about a foot taller than I was, the flickering blue glow of the water lighting up the rough stone walls. Where we stood, the stream stretched only a few feet across, but farther down, it doubled and then tripled in size to brush the passage walls.

The ferrety woman came down after us, closing the trap door over her head. She ushered us in the other direction, which I thought was leading us under the city. We had to leap the stream a few times when it branched with the caves, and at one wider spot we hopped across a makeshift bridge of stones. The ceiling slanted a little higher. The rose smell had faded the second we'd come underground, replaced by a crisp mineral scent.

Voices reached my ears over the hiss of the passing water. My pulse stuttered. The ferrety woman led us around a bend to an alcove at the edge of the stream, where a few of the collapsible cabins Theo had brought for our trip across the Checkerboard Plains had been set up around a heap of supplies.

One of the redheaded twins was leaning against that stack peering at a creased piece of paper. Doria and a couple other Spades I vaguely recognized were slicing bread and fruit on a makeshift table. And farther over by the cave wall, the other twin was standing with Chess in huddled conversation, Hatter listening in from where he was poised by a cabin doorway with a furrowed brow.

With the blank gap in my memory, to my mind it could have been only a day ago I'd last seen my two lovers, but my chest wrenched as if it'd been a year. The last time I'd seen them, they'd been pinned to the ground by the Queen's guards. But they were here, alive and looking reasonably well, although Hatter was going sans hat. I guessed he hadn't been able to make it back to his shop.

I wanted to fling myself at them, but my uncertainty about their reaction locked my legs. In that instant, Chess glanced up.

"Look what I found," the ferrety woman said, jabbing her thumb toward both of us. Before the words had even left her mouth, Chess bounded forward, the widest grin I'd ever seen splitting his handsome angular face. He threw his brawny arms around me and spun me around in a powerful embrace.

"Lyssa," he murmured. "My lovely." He sounded so choked up that a lump filled my throat in turn. I had to clutch the front of his shirt to keep my balance when he set me down. Then he was kissing me, and if my legs wobbled with the rush of heat from his arms and his mouth, oh well.

He eased back, still beaming, and managed to tear his gaze from me long enough to dip his head toward Mirabel. "White Queen. It's good to see you too."

Hatter had stepped toward us. He was staring, his green eyes searching my face as if for confirmation that I really was me. How long *had* I been gone?

"Hatter," I said, my voice rough, and that snapped him into action. He tugged me into his arms, his embrace as tight as Chess's had been, his head tipping next to mine. The lime-and-wood-smoke smell of him filled my nose, and tears sprang into my eyes.

They weren't angry at all. Nothing but happy to see me, just as overjoyed as I was to see them.

Still, an apology tumbled from my mouth the second Hatter released me. "I'm sorry. I came as soon as I could. There was an accident, in the Otherland—"

"You were in the Otherland?" Chess let out a breathless chuckle.

"You've got nothing to apologize for, Lyssa," Hatter said, his hand sliding down my arm to clasp my fingers. "Hearts take me, we thought you were *dead*."

Oh, God. That was why the ferrety woman had looked so unnerved by the sight of me. "I—I don't know how long it's been here —I don't know what's going on—didn't Theo manage to pass on some kind of word?"

Chess's expression turned puzzled and sad. "None of us has heard a thing from Theo—Prince Jack, I suppose we should call him now— or seen him since he walked into the palace with you two weeks ago."

CHAPTER FIVE

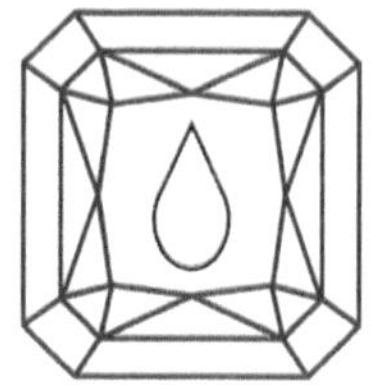

Lyssa

"Two weeks?" I said, repeating Chess's words. "And there's been no sign of Theo at all? Has the Queen even mentioned him?"

"Not where we've been able to hear," Dum muttered.

"Then…" The words stuck in my throat like a jagged rock. It hurt forcing them out. "Are you sure *he's* still alive?"

"It put the Queen over the moon to find out her precious prince wasn't murdered after all," Hatter said. "I can't imagine she'd decide to reverse that revelation."

"He made her believe he was on her side," I said. "I don't know how happy she'd have been when she found out he wasn't. He helped me escape—he took me to the mirror to the Otherland that she keeps in her chambers. He said he was going to challenge her and set things right."

But he hadn't succeeded. I'd been frustrated with him for deciding it wasn't safe for me to stay and fight alongside the Spades, but he'd probably saved my life. If the Queen hadn't shown even him any mercy…

Theo had been afraid of her rage. Afraid of what she'd do if she found out he'd left her purposely and worked with the Spades against her for years. But in the end he'd stood up to her anyway, to save *me*. To try to clear the way for me to the throne. And maybe he'd died taking that stand.

A wave of nausea rolled over me. My legs wobbled, both from that and the trek here. Chess caught my other arm.

"You look like you could stand to get off your feet for a minute or two, lovely," he said gently.

"That might be a good idea," I admitted. "I just got out of a hospital, actually. And I wasn't really supposed to leave."

"*What?*" Hatter said. He grabbed a box and helped me ease down onto it. "Were you and the prince attacked on the way to the looking-glass?"

"No," I said. "I just—I wasn't focused enough when I went through. I landed in kind of a dangerous spot, and a car hit me. I was really out of it for almost a month, Otherland time. Technically I wasn't even supposed to be up and walking around yet, but I found out my mom and my best friend had arranged to take all the furniture out of Aunt Alicia's house, and I was afraid I'd lose the mirror that could get me back here."

Chess's bright blue eyes widened a little. "As much as that devotion speaks in your favor, I'd like to speak up for self-preservation. Yours, of yourself." He motioned to the other Spades. "Bring some food over—and some of the drinking water."

With my queasiness, I wasn't sure how much food I'd be able to get down, but as soon as the plate of fresh bread and sliced fruit was in front of me, hunger gnawed right through my nausea. I hadn't had a proper meal since the last time I'd been in Wonderland. I had to restrain myself from shoving it all in my mouth, taking small slow bites instead, watching my responses to make sure I wasn't overwhelming my recently out-of-commission body.

Between the nourishment and the seat, a deeper sense of steadiness spread through me. I swallowed a mouthful of pear and glanced around at the Spades. "What else has been happening in the last two weeks? Why are you down here? This isn't all that's left of the Spades, is it?"

Hatter shook his head where he'd propped himself against the cave wall beside me. "There are a few other pockets scattered along the River Down. We thought it'd be wiser to spread ourselves out so we can't all be caught at once."

"One thing's for sure: the Queen was pretty shaken up by the way you barged in there and freed all those prisoners," the twin I thought I could now identify as Dee said, with a rough laugh. "She has guards patrolling everywhere up there, and they're bringing out fresh roses laced with the kinds of drugs the Clubbers liked to smoke at Caterpillar's—everyone's partying up there. They can't think straight enough to do anything else."

"Down here is the only place we can avoid getting caught in that high too," Dum put in. "It's made it hard to get anything done, even to follow what she's up to. Chess just picked up some equipment that'll help a little, but… we haven't been much of a rebellion since then."

"But you're here now," Dee said, smiling wide. The eager glint in his eyes looked a little desperate. "You can figure out how to topple her."

I knew why he was saying that, but a few of the people around me didn't. I glanced over at Mirabel, who'd sat herself down on the stone floor beside one of the cabins. Did she even know who I really was and what I represented to her family?

When I'd first found out, when we'd made it back to the city with the Red Knight and his revelations, I'd asked the small group who'd been with me not to say anything to anyone else. I'd needed time to figure out whether I was ready for the responsibilities that came with being the Red Queen's heir—whether I *wanted* to accept them.

Those responsibilities didn't feel like a burden now, though, not even with the news I'd just heard. There was no reason to keep the truth of my heritage quiet. After the stunt I'd pulled, growing to ten times my size to barge into the Queen of Hearts' gardens and crash her mock trial, I couldn't possibly be in any more danger from her than I already was.

"That's why I came back as quickly as I could," I said. "It might have been risky, but—I realized something that day when we freed all those people. This is my home. I belong in Wonderland. I don't want to leave my old life behind completely, but what I have here, what I need to do here, that comes first. I'm the however-many-greats granddaughter of the rightful rulers of Wonderland, and I'm going to take the throne back as the Red Queen."

After I had my bearings back, anyway. The second I finished speaking, a tremor tickled through me. I had to grip the side of the box for balance.

"Hold on, what's this about?" one of the other Spades said. Dee bounded over to exalt in a hushed voice about our adventures and discoveries on the Checkerboard Plains, and I was more than happy to let him convey that information.

Chess squeezed my shoulder. "And we need to look after our true queen. We have many fine abodes if you'd like to rest your head as well." He swept his arm toward the cabins.

"No," I said automatically. I'd spent most of the last four weeks in some sort of sleep. I wasn't in any hurry to return to that state. "I think I just…" I tugged my hair back behind my ears and grimaced at the feel of it. The brief dunk in the Pond of Tears hadn't made up for nearly four weeks with no showers. "Is there anywhere I can wash here? I think I'll feel better if I can clean myself up."

The corner of Hatter's mouth quirked up. "One thing we have plenty of down here is water."

Chess glanced from him to me and gave us a smile that looked a little sly. "Why doesn't Hatter get you where you'd like to go? I'll slip upside with our new equipment and see if I can't get a clearer answer of what happened to our White Knight turned Prince of Hearts."

My heart squeezed. It wasn't as if Chess hadn't spied on the Hearts' people plenty in the past, and I did want answers about Theo, but I'd only just gotten back here. Only just found him again. I grasped his hand for a second. "Be careful, okay?"

"I have every intention of making it back to you now that you've made it back to us," he said with a grin.

Hatter held my elbow as I got up, not insistently but just firmly enough that I knew I could lean on him if I needed to. His gaze slid to Doria, who'd come over to join the cluster around me.

"You know I'll be fine without you watching over my every move," she said, wrinkling her nose at him but smiling at the same time.

"Of course," Hatter said. He'd loosened up on his daughter as he'd become more active in the rebellion again himself, but I could imagine their current precarious situation had woken those protective parental urges right back up.

We left the camp behind, following the stream around a couple of bends in the caves and past another split.

"Here we are," Hatter said.

I stared for a moment, taking in the scene up ahead. The current of glowing blue water veered to the side, hitting the wall and then… flowing right up it. The stream coursed on in a diagonal line that reached right up to the ceiling and spiraled around back to the ground farther down the passage. Where the water crossed the cave ceiling, some of it rained down toward the floor into a pool that had formed there. But some of it defied gravity completely.

It wasn't the weirdest thing I'd seen in Wonderland. This was a place where unicorns walked around on two legs and talked, where feathered dragons might belch fire in your face, and where mirrors could transport you to other realities. But still, it was pretty freaking weird.

"That'll work," I said, already imagining the water rushing over me and washing all the lingering grime away.

"One of the few perks of our current living situation," Hatter said dryly. He started to peel off his maroon suit jacket. "It's a little slippery under the downpour. I think I'd better go with you to make sure you don't need a return trip to that hospital, so I suppose I'm getting a wash too."

Oh. Heat unfurled from low in my belly as I watched him shed his shirt and unbutton his slacks. Hatter wasn't as buff as Chess or Theo, but there was still plenty to admire about his broad-shouldered but otherwise lean form. Plenty of taut muscles I'd enjoyed running my hands over and feeling against me more than once. Um. Right. I was supposed to be getting ready to wash too.

I tugged off my woven metal vest with a twinge in my wrist when I bent it at a slightly odd angle. Note to self: Be especially careful with that arm. I set it down next to Hatter's steadily growing pile of folded clothing and reached for the hem of my shirt.

Now Hatter was watching me, everything off except for his silk boxers. A flush spread over my skin at his approving attention, especially when my small breasts jumped with the yank of my shirt over them. It wasn't as if he hadn't seen me naked before, but then it'd been in the heat of the moment. This intimacy felt much more deliberate.

When I'd stripped completely, he dropped his boxers too. He picked up a bar of what I guessed was soap, deep fuchsia in color, and guided me over to the stream's natural shower.

The first spray of the water was warmer than I expected—not as hot as I'd have usually liked to shower, but pleasantly refreshing. For the first several moments with it rushing over me like a gentle waterfall, any self-consciousness I'd been feeling was swept away with the rivulets that trickled across the rocky floor into the pool.

Hatter rubbed the soap over his dark blond hair, the pink bar's essence mingling with the blue-tinted water to create a lilac foam. He handed it to me, and I worked it all through my own much longer hair. God, that felt good. I scrubbed away every bit of oil and grease, leaving the pale strands squeaky clean.

When I'd washed my hair and face to my satisfaction, I moved to offer the soap back to Hatter, and paused with a playful spark of an idea. Instead I rubbed the bar over his chest myself.

Hatter set his hand over mine, but he didn't stop me. He just leaned close enough to speak without water streaming down between us. "Thought I could use a little help, did you?"

"Not so much that you *needed* it as that you might enjoy it," I said with a smile. "Or I will, in any case."

He made a humming sound that turned more ragged as I eased the bar of soap lower, across the flat planes of his belly. His hand came up to slide over my wet hair. I tipped my head to meet his kiss.

Hatter's mouth was hot and sweet with a hint of the water that had turned our lips slick. From the first instant of the kiss, I didn't want to stop. I didn't just belong in Wonderland. I belonged with this man.

Somewhere in the middle of that, I lost my grip on the soap. Hatter traced it over my curves as we kept kissing, teasing it under my breasts and gliding it over my nipples until I whimpered. He kissed me harder. His rigid cock brushed my belly, and a giddy tingle ran through me. I reached down to give that part of him a good rubbing too. He groaned and tugged me closer.

"I don't want you to think I'm glad to have you here just for this," he murmured by my ear in a voice full of promise. "But I did miss having you like this too. Are you sure it's not too much?"

"We'll just—take it easy," I said, with a hitch of my breath as his deft fingers grazed my clit. Fuck, none of me wanted easy right now. I wanted hard and fast and everything he had in him. Whether my body was up for that in my current state of health was another matter.

Hatter walked us to the edge of the pool where the stream's shower eased off. When he sat me on the stone ledge while he stayed in the water, he stood at the perfect height for his hips to fit between my splayed legs.

Need burned from my core, but Hatter wasn't the type to rush. He drew me into another kiss, his talented hands massaging my breasts, my ass, until my nerves were trembling for reasons that had nothing to do with any injury.

"Please," I mumbled against his mouth. My hand closed around his cock, reveling in the soft skin over that solid length before I urged it toward me. Hatter's breath stuttered.

"Here?" he said with an arch of his eyebrow. His fingers trailed down my stomach to my sex. I scooted closer with a gasp as his tip brushed my opening. Then he was pressing inside, and everything narrowed down to the hot taut slide of him filling me completely.

"Lyssa," he murmured between kisses, as if confirming to himself that I was here. "Lyssa."

"Hatter. So good." I let out a little cry as he plunged even deeper, pleasure sparking up from my core, and he paused with a look of concern so heartfelt it made my pulse skip a beat.

"I'm fine," I reassured him.

"Let's make sure you stay that way while I'm taking you someplace so much better than fine," he said, his lips grazing my cheek.

He started to move again, steady rolls of his hips, sending bliss shooting through me with each thrust. One hand slipped down between us so his thumb could settle on my clit. As I whimpered and arched against him, he braced his other arm behind me. His fingers dipped around my ass to probe my other opening where he'd filled me once before. I was held completely, penetrated in every way.

I made an inarticulate sound, overwhelmed by the sensations he was stirring all through my body. Pleasure blazed up inside me. Just like that, I was a goner. His thumb flicked over my clit, his cock plunged into me at the perfect angle, his fingers teased my ass, and I came apart in his arms.

Hatter groaned as I clenched around him. Ecstasy rippled through my body, and he propelled it higher with a few quick jerks of his hips. Then he flooded me with even more heat.

His breath seared over my chest as he held me, his head bowed, catching his breath. I clutched him in return. I was here. Maybe up there outside these caves everything was wrong, but this moment was nothing but right.

Hatter kissed me again, so tenderly it brought an ache into my chest. He stroked his hand over my back.

"You asked me some questions, that last night you were here," he said in a low voice. "I'm not sure I answered them adequately."

"Questions?" I said, searching my memory. We'd talked about an awful lot of things in the time we'd spent together here.

He pulled back far enough to meet my eyes. "Watching someone walk away from you to what you think will be their death has a way of clarifying things," he said. "And I want to say it now while I can. I love you, Lyssa."

My arms tightened around him. A smile stretched my lips. It was suddenly far easier than I'd expected to say, "I love you too."

"I don't know how this will end up, with you the Red Queen and all—"

"I'm pretty sure a queen can decide to be with whatever man she wants," I said firmly.

The corner of his mouth twitched upward. "And however many she wants?" he suggested.

"I don't think you have to worry about me bringing in *too* many others," I muttered. My thoughts leapt to Chess, and then to Theo… How could I even know what to feel about him when maybe I should be grieving him right now?

"Either way, it'll be up to you." Hatter touched his nose to mine. "I'll be here helping you make your way to that throne however I can. That's all that matters."

I hugged him to me, and we stayed locked in that embrace until my damp skin started to cool in the open air. My legs didn't wobble too much when I pulled myself back onto them.

Our little interlude must have taken longer than it'd felt like, because by the time we'd dressed and made it back to the camp, Chess was standing amid the others. I couldn't tell from his expression what he'd found, but he didn't look upset, which at least suggested it wasn't anything tragic. My spirits lifted.

"How did your expedition go?" I asked, hurrying over.

"In some ways better than others," Chess said. "I couldn't find a reasonable place to cross the palace wall. But I *did* determine that one old 'pal' of ours is still going back and forth between the city and the palace." He grinned wide enough to show his fangs. "We'll get in there and get our answers about the prince. Rabbit can be our key."

CHAPTER SIX

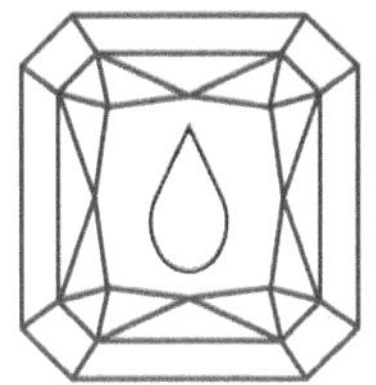

Theo

The smell of roses permeated the entire palace, but it hung particularly thick in the inner quarters. It practically colored the air in the hall the guard was hustling me down. Even when I breathed through my mouth, the odor seeped up into my nose. The sensation of fluttering petals and prickling thorns clouded my mind.

I sank as deep into my head as I could, holding onto the one thought that really mattered. The one goal I had to see through. No matter what my mother did to me, no matter what else her underlings flashed in front of my eyes or whispered in my ears or pricked my skin with, I wouldn't let myself be a victim. I'd come to the palace with a purpose, and I'd see it through. One step at a time, one piece at a time.

Lyssa was waiting for me. She and all the rest of Wonderland were counting on me.

My knees ached as we drew up in front of the door to the Queen's private chambers. They seemed to be the favorite spot of the tormentors my mother called her "doctors." Tiny pins jabbed under the knee cap. They made a lot of use of the spaces between my wrist bones and along the line of my jaw as well. Just remembering those moments brought back shards of pain.

"Come in," the Queen of Hearts commanded in her cutting voice. The guards around the door eased it open, and the one escorting me hustled me inside.

My mother was sitting on the throne of her private audience room, this seat a more subdued affair than the immensely grand throne in the public hall near the front of the palace—or even the portable one she had her attendants heft her along on when she left the palace grounds. A studied eye could tell it had been even simpler before. The Hearts' craftspeople had fixed golden panels etched with roses and vines over to the elegant lines of the cherry wood frame. No doubt the gold brocade on the velvet padding was our family's own addition too. All of it holding the throne's power in check so it couldn't burn this wrongful ruler like Lyssa's sword had rejected my hand.

The vast mauve skirts of the Queen of Hearts' dress nearly overwhelmed the throne's base. She leaned forward as I trudged along the velvet carpet toward her. The guard's grip on my arm tightened. He was nervous of her response. Even though he'd had no more to do with my "treatment" than the guards at the door had, my mother might very well take out any disappointment on him.

And disappointed I expected she'd be, once I'd seen my mission through and could speak freely.

We stopped a few feet from the throne. The Queen stayed seated, peering down at us with her coolly glinting eyes, her lips pursed. The coils of her copper hair framed the edge of her crown like foam escaping from beneath it. Her breath released with a faint hiss.

I looked back at her, keeping my expression slack. My right arm, the one the guard wasn't holding, shifted against my side. Nudging the bit of machinery I'd hidden in the loose sleeve of my shirt a little closer to the fitted cuff.

"How are you doing today, Jack?" my mother said in a tone that could have been taken as gentle if you missed the barbed edge underneath. I wasn't sure the Queen of Hearts' had the ability to be truly gentle after all these years of brutality.

Theo, I thought. *My name is Theo now.* But that detail wasn't worth arguing over, not when it would ruin the rest. I had to choose my battles wisely. And for now, I had to play to what little sympathies she possessed to get this job done.

"Rather sore," I said. "And regretful that I've caused you so much distress."

"Oh?" A gleam of hope lit in her light brown eyes.

I took a step forward, and the guard released his hold. *He* didn't want to get any closer. Which served my purposes just fine.

"I was so young, and I acted too hastily, doing what I thought I needed to do," I said. "I didn't give enough consideration to the pain my disappearance would cause you. If I could only show you how sorry I am for what I put you through…"

I took another step and knelt by the folds of her skirts. The rose scent clogged my nose as I leaned my forehead beseechingly against them. I spread my arms wide as if offering myself up to her mercy—and my right hand came to rest on the side of the throne.

There, that was the edge of the largest panel. I'd noted how the slabs of gold fit together when I'd come before the Queen in days past. Just as I'd observed the way the golden sheen in my mother's eyes shone brighter when she was sitting on this seat, the way that glow shivered over her body in fits and starts the longer she stayed there.

I'd been around the artifacts of the Red royal rule enough in recent weeks to recognize another one when I saw it now. This throne had once been the throne of the Red Queen, co-opted by the supposed Queens of Hearts for their own purposes. They had no royal magic of their own, but our history provided a clear testament that they took no concern in stealing the power of others.

With a subtle flick of my wrist, I palmed the device from my sleeve and jammed it into the small gap beside the panel as quickly as I could. I'd built the small but powerful contraption with every care I could in the spaces between the doctors' attentions, out of little offerings from my older siblings, several of whom had stopped by to ingratiate themselves with our mother's named heir. Each material on its own wouldn't have raised any suspicions. Even if they'd consulted with each other, which wasn't like the Hearts at all, I doubted they'd have the inventive instincts to guess what I'd put together.

"Enough of that, now," my mother said, urging me up with a ruffling of her skirts, but her tone was partly approving. Subservience from any quarter never failed to appeal to her. "No son of mine should lower himself to groveling. What do you have to say about this foolery you mentioned before, about letting our subjects run wild?"

Only my mother could have seen easing up on executions and offering some basic freedoms as encouraging people to "run wild." I straightened up, my mouth tightening. I'd accomplished the one small task I'd needed to carry out today. There was no need to pretend anymore, even if I'd lost any hope that my words would sway her.

The trouble was that the "treatments" she'd had her "doctors" inflict on me hadn't been entirely unsuccessful, even if they weren't curing me of the disease she thought I had. A stabbing pain ran up the fronts of my thighs and the sides of my forearms when I even thought the words I wanted to say. Sharp splinters of pain radiated from my jaw right up to my scalp, muddling my head even more than the rose smell did.

My mother thought the Spades had brainwashed me somehow. She'd ordered her doctors to wipe the rebellion's influence from mind. But I'd built that rebellion. Those principles and desires were a part of me, running right down to the core. They couldn't root them out. Their efforts only fractured who I was.

"Not run wild," I managed to say. A thudding ache spread across the back of my skull. I could have pretended to agree, but I would *not* lie simply to protect my own skin, not a single time more. If I acted the part she wanted, if I supported the horrors she'd carried out, she'd only feel more certain in them. "I merely wish to see them live under a more even hand. I've spent a lot of time among them, Mother—I know they don't wish to defy you. If you would just listen to me while I explain—"

The Queen jerked to her feet with a swish of her skirts. "Enough," she snapped. Her face had flushed crimson. "This is more of the same twaddle you spewed when you first came before me." She whipped around to aim her glare at the guard who'd brought me. "What did the doctors say of his progress? Why haven't they cleared the awful taint from my son yet?"

The guard stiffened. His face turned as white as hers had red. "I—I believe they thought they had reduced the effect, Your Highness," he stammered. "They said they'd bled out the worst of it and that he responded well to their re-education."

I'd had to play along with them before they'd willingly send me before the Queen for her consideration. A head or two might roll today. After all the bleeding and the rest, I couldn't find it in me to care very much.

"Please, Mother," I said despite the growing headache and the pains clamoring for attention all through my body. "All I want is to see Wonderland be as wondrous as it can be—as it once was. We could be the ones to bring glory and joy to the entire realm. Don't you want that?"

I didn't expect her to listen, not after everything I'd already been through, but even this one guard seeing my attempt might tip someone in the right direction. All I could do was keep trying.

The Queen of Hearts let out a ragged laugh. "Glory and joy? The only glory this place is capable of happens right here. You're still sick, Jack. I won't hear any more of this raving. Get him out of here—and tell the doctors I want them here to account for their failure immediately."

"Yes, Your Highness. Of course, Your Highness," the guard said with a frantic bob of his head. He tugged me toward the door. I stumbled as I went, a wave of dizziness throwing off my balance.

I was heading back to more of that. They'd cut deeper, bombard me harder with images and words of the rule I was supposed to believe in. The guards we passed in the hall didn't show the slightest sign of sympathy or concern. I couldn't rely on anyone but myself here.

I had to hold on. I had to fend off the worst the doctors inflicted on me and keep as much of my head as I could. My mother still maintained enough hope that I could be the son she wanted to keep me alive, and so I had to hope that I could make some difference here.

All of Wonderland was counting on me, and I'd see my neck severed before I let them down again.

CHAPTER SEVEN

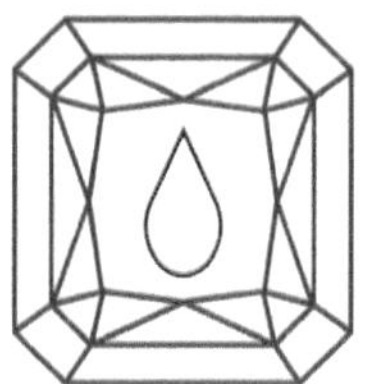

Lyssa

Wonderland's glowing underground river didn't extend beyond the city's limits in the direction of Caterpillar's club. I slunk along the darkened streets behind my sense of Chess's invisible form, my breath warm and humid inside the cloth mask he'd given me to cover the lower part of my face. A hint of the rose scent trickled in, but not enough to affect our minds—or Hatter's, beside me. Which was a good thing, because the guards had laid out heaps of their drugged flowers all along the borders of the city to ensure no one snuck out to the clearer air beyond.

There wasn't much dancing on these outer streets, but we did pass a couple slumped together next to the road with their clothes in disarray, as if they'd fallen asleep halfway to having sex. Someone was singing a tuneless, wordless song that filtered through an upper window into the cool night air.

The Queen of Hearts might not have chopped off these people's heads, but her latest tactic of control had left them pretty much out of their minds.

Chess turned visible just long enough to motion us down an alley.

The tap of a guard's footsteps marched past us on the road we'd just left. We skirted the direct route to the club and slipped into the forest of starkly green trees that sprawled around it. After the few days I'd had to continue recuperating while the Spades made their observations to construct our plan, barely any lingering pain from the accident remained in my body. I felt almost like my normal self again.

After we'd walked several minutes, even the wisp of rose that had reached my nose faded away. Hatter tugged his mask down and dragged in a deep breath, and I did the same, welcoming the rush of the crisp forest smells.

"Chess?" I murmured.

Our fanged companion shimmered into view with a brush of his hand over my shoulder. "Almost there."

"You're sure he won't have guards with him?" Hatter said under his breath.

"He hasn't the times I've watched so far," Chess said. "You'll just have to keep those hat pins of yours ready in case he's switched up his routine." His grin glinted in the dim moonlight that penetrated the leaves overhead.

Hatter made a slightly disgruntled sound, but he adjusted the sleeves of his suit jacket—an unusually subdued navy blue—where I knew he had at least a couple of those pins at the ready. We stalked on through the forest, Chess leading the way. My heart thumped louder with each rustle of the branches above us.

"Do you think the Queen took Unicorn's head for helping us?" I asked finally. The question had been rattling around my brain since Chess had said he hadn't been able to set eyes on our recent ally since the horned fighter had helped us break into the palace grounds.

"Could be," Chess said softly. "Could be she took both him and Lion, not knowing who to blame. Or they could be laying low with all appendages intact. Not many of the Diamonds are venturing far beyond the palace lately. We shook them up well, and they needed a good shaking."

Unicorn hadn't done anything all that obvious, his bashing into the gate set up to look like an accident, but the Queen had executed people for a lot less. She often executed people for nothing at all, from what I'd seen. Him simply being in the area when I'd burst into the palace grounds might have raised her suspicions.

Whether he was alive or dead, he hadn't shown any sign of being able to help more. Which was why we were on our way to chat with an even more uncertain ally.

Chess held up his hand for us to stop. I made out a narrow path of flattened grass that wove through the trees to a gnarled old oak. Its branches crisscrossed each other and wove together like a latticework, and between its arched roots lay a round mahogany door so polished you could hardly believe it had spent any time outside. I eyed it for a moment.

"Rabbit lives in an actual rabbit hole?" I said.

"I had tea with him once," Chess said with an enigmatic air. "It's rather nicer on the inside than the outside, as holes go. Which is not very far, in his case. He wants to stay put, not find himself elsewhere."

Hatter shot his friend a bemused look. Giving straight-forward answers wasn't exactly Chess's forte. But after everything I'd seen of Wonderland, I knew that hole could as easily open up into the fanciest ballroom I'd ever seen as the earthen room I'd expect.

You couldn't really expect anything to be as you'd think in Wonderland—not even when you'd seen the thing in question before.

I tugged off the blouse I'd wore to hide my armored vest and slid the ruby necklace out to rest on the interlaced metal. For this conversation, I wanted to look every bit the queen.

We stood in the shelter of the trees a few paces from the path, all of us staying silent after that. The breeze whispered through the leaves, and small creatures scampered through the brush. The buzz of a fly zipping past my ear made me flinch. Out on the Checkerboard Plains, we'd encountered some giant insects more massive than I hoped to ever have anywhere near me again. Especially since those insects had seemed to be as interested in removing our heads as the Queen was.

A chill was starting to seep through my clothes when a faint pattering reached my ears. I tensed, holding my body even more still than before.

Rabbit's white-furred form came into view down the path. Just as his home appeared to be an actual rabbit hole, he looked like an actual rabbit—one about as tall as I was, half-walking half-hopping in a trim pinstriped waistcoat. He was muttering quietly to himself. It reminded me of the one time I'd seen him before, when I'd had to dodge him in the passages beneath the club on my way to the now-broken mirror there. He'd been fussing about how Caterpillar's demands always made him late, no matter how hard he tried to keep up with them.

He hadn't sounded all that happy with his boss. There had to be something we could offer him—something I could offer him—that would sway his loyalties. Chess believed there was, anyway.

Rabbit tugged a watch out of his waistcoat pocket, glanced at it, and flattened his long furry ears closer to his head. He hop-walked a little faster. As he tucked the watch back into his pocket, Hatter and Chess stepped out onto the path to intercept him, Chess in front and Hatter behind.

Rabbit startled, his ears springing straight up. He hopped back a step and spun to see that way was blocked too. "Well, I—" he started. His voice started to rise. "It really is quite rude to hold up a person on their way. I must protest that—"

Chess held up his hand. "Before you do too much protesting, Rabbit, consider who you'd be calling for help too. The ones who've left the entire city in a daze? The ones who'd take *your* head the second you seem like a problem? Do you really think we're more dangerous than them?"

Rabbit sputtered a bit, but he didn't appear to have a coherent answer. He thumped one long foot on the ground. "Well, what do you want, then?" he asked, his dark eyes twitching from Chess to Hatter and back again.

I eased forward then, right in front of him. "We want information from the palace," I said. "And possibly a way to get in and out for that building. I'll repay you, of course."

Rabbit stared at me for a moment, his posture going rigid. He had to recognize me from the day weeks ago when I'd stomped into the palace gardens at ten times my usual height. He knew I was the "Alice" the Queen of Hearts was after.

"What makes you think I could offer you any of that?" he said tightly.

"You're the only one making his way to and fro from the palace," Chess said. "Besides the guards. All the Diamonds are staying in and all the Clubbers are staying out. You have to go right to the Queen's private chambers to get to her mirror, from what I hear. *You* must hear plenty along the way."

"I keep to my own business." Rabbit's nose twitched. "It won't do me any good to be mixed up in yours."

"It might, though," I said. "She isn't going to be queen forever. I'm the Red Queen, and I will take back the throne the Hearts stole from my family. If you help me, I'll be able to offer you an awful lot."

"And if I don't?"

I gazed back at him evenly. "I won't take your head. I won't hurt one whisker on your face. Did I hurt anyone when I came to free her prisoners, even when they were jabbing at me?"

His expression relaxed slightly. I hadn't. I'd made a point of showing how different my methods were from the Queen of Hearts'. I wasn't sure I could keep up that peacefulness through the battles ahead of us, but I'd spill as little blood as I could manage.

"The Queen of Hearts would take your head," Hatter said. "For looking at her wrong. For saying the wrong word."

"For being a tiny bit late," I added.

"Or possibly even early," Chess threw in. "It's only a matter of time now that you're brushing up so close to her, you know, Rabbit. We're trying to *save* you from the trap you're stuck in."

"It's not a trap," Rabbit said with a sniff. "It's a job. *I've* done my part for Wonderland. I've helped keep people happy and entertained."

Hatter raised his eyebrows. "Do you really think they're all that happy now?"

"The Queen is distressed. We can return to our regular club activities when she's calmed down."

"And are you treated all that well in the club either?" I said. "Caterpillar is constantly bossing you around and running you ragged. Aren't you tired of living under his thumb? Isn't there somewhere else you'd rather be?"

Rabbit bristled so quickly I could tell I'd hit a nerve—but not the way I'd wanted to. "I'm *exactly* where I want to be," he said. "I've worked within the club from the day it opened, and I've made it as good a place as any in Wonderland. Leave it to Caterpillar?" He scoffed.

The glint in his eyes and the passion in his voice lit an answering spark in me. It reminded me of how I'd felt when I'd declared that I was taking back the throne.

He'd just handed me what I'd needed—the key to his desires.

"What if we left Caterpillar out of it completely?" I said, raising my chin as if I had no doubt at all that I could fulfill the offer I was making. "What if, once I'm on that throne, the club passes into your hands as the new owner? You can run it any way you like—within reason, of course. You can make it better than he ever let you."

Rabbit's mouth opened and closed and opened again without a sound. An eager quiver ran through him. But he was hesitating.

I drew on every ounce of longing I'd felt since I'd found my way into Wonderland. "It's what you've dreamed of, isn't it? It could be yours. Don't pass up that chance. I *want* to hand you your dream on a platter. What has the Queen of Hearts ever given you except terror?"

Rabbit only wavered another half a second. "What do you want to know about the palace?" he asked in a hushed voice.

I restrained the grin that tried to spring across my face. "What have you heard about Jack, the Queen's son—the one everyone thought was dead, who was living as the Inventor? Is he in the palace?"

Is he alive? That part of the question was enough to make my urge to grin fade completely.

Rabbit rubbed his small white chin. "That matter has been kept very quiet, but I have caught a thing or two. I believe she's attempting to cure him of the Spades' influence. Has him shut away somewhere with doctors attending to him in the inner quarters of the palace."

A wave of relief rushed through me. Chess smiled wide. Hatter didn't look quite as pleased, but he didn't look upset either, which I guessed was about as good a reaction as I could have hoped for given his fraught history with Theo.

"All right," I said. "Then we're going to need you to get us into the palace and as close to where they're keeping the prince as you can without drawing too much suspicion. You're supposed to go back tomorrow, aren't you?"

The night felt even thicker as we made our way back to the entrance to the caves, but my spirits were light despite the darkness. We had a plan; we had an ally even if he was a bought one. With Theo by our side, with everything he knew about his mother, we'd be ready to topple the Queen of Hearts once and for all.

We were just slinking around the side of a building when Chess's invisible arm held me back. I froze.

A squad of the Queen's guards burst into the street out of one of the buildings, what looked like a tavern. They were herding several men and women, all of them young to middle-aged and reasonably fit, their eyes glazed with that drugged haze.

"Where are they taking them?" I murmured. An uneasy prickling filled my stomach. I couldn't see how it could be for anything *good.*

"Looks like to the palace," Chess said as the guards hustled the small crowd on past our shadowed hiding spot.

One of the guards turned his head our way, and I stiffened even more. But beneath his dented red helm, his face had almost the same vague expression as the drugged city people. His eyes slid over the street and the buildings lining on it without pausing for a second. He snapped his head back to the route ahead with the same blank expression.

Hatter must have noticed my confusion. "That's a pearl-headed one," he said softly as the guards marched out of view.

"Pearl-headed?" I repeated.

He nodded. "When the Queen beheads people, if they were reasonably physically capable, she sends them out to the sea. That's the work my 'friend' Carpenter is doing now. They have a process where they can grow a new head in the old one's place, like a pearl in a shell. They're never like they once were, though. The new person is nearly mindless."

"But he's out there with the rest of the guards," I said.

"The Queen imprints them in some way to make them see her as their one leader, and any orders she gives them, they'll follow as well as they can," Hatter said. "They have no thoughts of their own, as far as anyone's been able to tell. Mostly she uses them for servants doing menial tasks around the palace, but she's supplemented the Hearts' Guard with them too."

I hugged myself, holding back a shudder. The prickling that had filled my stomach earlier seeped through the rest of my body with a chill.

We needed to get Theo *soon.* Every moment the Queen of Hearts stayed on that throne, who knew what new horror she might commit? I just hoped we'd be in time to save those people from whatever fate she had planned for them.

"Let's go," I said. "We have preparations to make for tomorrow."

CHAPTER EIGHT

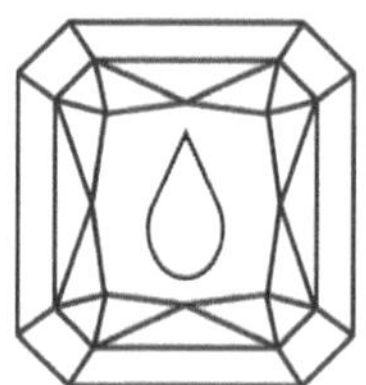

Lyssa

Rabbit's ears flattened to his head when he saw the four of us waiting in the spot just off the road to the palace where he'd told us to wait. "The more I'm bringing, the more likely they are to get suspicious," he said, shifting his weight from one foot to the other.

"It'll only look like three," Chess said brightly. He faded away to his grin, and then that blinked out of sight too. "I find our way, Hatter opens it up, and Dee can shove away any who try to block us."

"And the Otherlander?" Rabbit muttered.

Chess reappeared in a flash, his grin gone sharp with the glint of his fangs. "The Otherlander is more a Wonderlander than even we can claim, and it's her palace we're storming."

I touched his brawny arm to reassure him that I didn't need further defending. "I'm not sure Theo—Jack—will leave unless I can talk to him," I said. Theo had come to the palace with plans of his own that obviously hadn't worked out, but I wasn't sure whether he'd be willing to let go of them without a lot of convincing. And from what he'd said, he'd made those plans for me, so the convincing might need to come from me too.

Rabbit let out a huff of breath and gestured for us to follow him. "Get on your disguises now. You never know when the guards will wander."

Chess vanished. Hatter, Dee, and I pulled on the white hoodies one of the Spades had quickly sewn together for us. We tied the filtration masks over our faces and tugged the hoods tight over our hair so no one could see much but our eyes. If anyone at the palace recognized us, especially me, it was game over.

But Rabbit had clearly earned a lot of the Queen's trust. The mark of her seal still stood out starkly crimson against the thin white fur of his palm. He'd told us that she'd imbued it with enough power that it only faded once a week, to save her the hassle of approving his entrance every night.

I couldn't enjoy the warm afternoon air or the bright sun overhead. The thump of our feet against the cobblestones echoed the thudding of my pulse. We were walking right into the lion's den, and we weren't ready to fight the lion yet. But we had to get Theo out.

His mother had been trying to "cure" him, Rabbit had said, but he hadn't known more than that. What had the Queen been doing to her favorite son who'd then betrayed her?

He might be alive, but after all this time, was he okay?

We slowed as we approached the gate to the palace gardens. The gate I'd barged through like a giant a few weeks ago, as it happened. I resisted the urge to hunch my shoulders under the guards' stares. One of them frowned.

"Who's all this?" he asked Rabbit.

"With the increased demand, I'm running through my usual supply too quickly," Rabbit said. His cheek twitched, making his whiskers jitter nervously, but his voice held steady. "I need assistants to ensure I can gather the necessary ingredients in time."

"What's with their clothing?"

"To mark them quickly as my assistants, and to ensure the toxins of the Otherland don't affect them, since they haven't my experience there," Rabbit said.

The guard's frown didn't budge. "I don't know... *They* don't have the mark of the seal."

Rabbit's whiskers quivered again, but this time he managed to make them look indignant. "Shall I tell the Queen it is your fault when the club is unable to produce enough of her concoction to dose even half of the needed roses?"

The guard blanched, and the other one waved us toward the gate. "Get on with it, then."

As we passed through and the bars clanked shut behind us, I heard one murmur to the other, "I'll be glad when this whole to-do in the city is done with, won't you?"

The guards were getting frustrated with the Queen's tactics too. That was good. Every bit of leverage we had on our side was a step in the right direction.

Rabbit took us on a swift journey along the garden paths to a side door in the palace. The flowers blooming all around us formed a sickeningly sweet bouquet of scents that the mask couldn't totally shield us from.

At the door, our escort had to go through a similar song and dance about why we were with him, but shorter. I guessed these guards figured if the gate sentries had let us through, who were they to argue?

Inside, Chess brushed his fingers over my arm in a gentle gesture to let me know he was slipping ahead. The rest of us treaded carefully across the velvet-carpeted halls, past ornate tapestries and paintings with gold frames. The arched ceiling loomed high above our heads. No one much was around along the route Rabbit took. We didn't hear a sound other than the whisper of our steps.

We went up a flight of stairs and down another hall. Where it branched, Rabbit held up his hand. He'd told us last night that we'd need to part ways before we reached the Queen's private quarters—the rooms I'd been in once before, where she kept the mirror to the Otherland. Theo wasn't in her own chambers but, Rabbit suspected, somewhere not too far away.

I tipped my head in acknowledgment and thanks. Rabbit gave me a pained smile and headed onward at his halting gait. Hatter leaned against the wall, his eyes wary as he scanned our surroundings. Dee stretched his arms in front of him as if readying himself for a fight. I hoped we wouldn't end up needing his skills for that purpose, only to speed our escape.

Chess had known we'd wait for him here. He should be scouting out the halls around here invisibly, watching for a hint of Theo's location. If any guards wandered by while we were waiting for him, we'd just have to hope the excuses we could come up with worked as well as Rabbit's had.

The seconds ticked by, seeming to crawl over my skin. I crossed my arms over my chest. Hatter set a reassuring hand on my side, and I shot him a grateful glance. Dee bobbed on his feet impatiently.

Then Chess spoke out of nowhere, his playful voice right by my ear. "I've determined where we are going, so let us go forward. Straight ahead, the second left, and then a right. There's a door with two guards outside. Dee and I can deal with them."

The creeping feeling intensified with his casual acceptance of the violence he expected to come. "We don't *kill* anyone," I reminded them. "Not if we can help it."

"Of course not, lovely," Chess said. I could almost hear his smile. "I'm not partial to permanent endings myself anyway."

"Are you sure Theo is in that room?" I asked as we started down the hall. My gaze darted back and forth, every nerve on edge.

"I can't think of what else they'd be guarding there," Chess said. "And I watched for long enough to see a couple of those doctors the Queen must have working on his 'cure' emerge. I suspect we'd be better off getting to him before they get around to coming back."

We walked a little faster. The velvet carpet absorbed most of the sound of our feet. Hatter brought his hat pins into one hand, spinning them between his nimble fingers. I'd have admired his dexterity, as familiar as it was becoming, if I hadn't been so nervous.

Where we would take the right turn Chess had mentioned, we stopped. "Dee," Chess murmured. "Ready?"

The redheaded twin nodded, his eyes glinting eagerly. His spirits had seemed dampened since I'd found the Spades in their underground hideout, almost as subdued as his serious brother, but this mission had perked him up.

The air shifted as Chess sprinted down the hall. At a thump and a groan, the rest of us dashed after him.

The two guards had sprawled next to each other, pressing their hands to their foreheads. Chess must have slammed their heads together. Before they could gather their wits enough to fight back, Dee's elastic arms were jerking their uniforms up over their faces. He yanked their arms from the sleeves, knotted those and tugged them tight as a straitjacket, and tossed the guards into another room Chess had just opened the door to. Their muffled shouts fell away completely with the click of the door closing.

Hatter had already knelt by the other door, the one they'd been guarding. His fingers tensed and flexed as he worked his pins in the keyhole. The process seemed to be taking him longer than usual. He knit his brow, a curse slipping from his lips under his breath.

Voices carried from down one of the nearby halls. My pulse lurched—and the lock released with a metallic hiss. Hatter straightened up, met my eyes for just a second, and turned the knob.

The door swung open into a small room with rosy pink walls. We all darted inside to avoid notice. Then my gaze caught on the seat in the middle of the room and the figure sitting in it, and my throat constricted.

Theo was wearing clothes that presumably befitted a prince—crimson trousers and jacket over a pale pink shirt, gold detailing around the cuffs and collar—but I recognized his well-muscled body even without his usual white dress shirt and gray slacks. I *had* to recognize him from his body, which was tied to an ornate wooden chair with ropes around his wrists and ankles, because a metal helm sat over his head, completely hiding his face.

Tinny sounds seeped out of the helm. His arms and back were tensed against the chair, his hands balled into fists. A dribble of… was that blood? …streaked through the sweat beading on his throat.

Oh God. What the hell were they doing to him?

I sprang forward and grasped the helm. Dee's face had paled, but he leapt in just as quickly to fumble with ropes. Hatter hustled around to the other side of the chair.

I yanked on the helm, but it was so heavy it didn't budge, even as my muscles strained. Then Chess was beside me, a solid presence even if I still couldn't see him, setting his broad hands next to mine.

"One, two, three," he murmured, and we heaved on the helm at the same time.

With a clacking sound, it lifted up, revealing Theo's rumpled curls —the golden shade that was his natural color, not the dark brown I'd been used to—and his sweat dampened face. His cocoa-dark eyes stared at us for a few seconds as if still seeing something that was no longer there before they focused on me. He blinked, and his lips parted.

"Lyssa," he said hoarsely. "You—You were supposed to *wait*—"

A horrified laugh sputtered out of me. I tossed the helm to the side. "It's a good thing I didn't. We're getting you out of here. Can you stand?"

Hatter and Dee had snapped the ropes. Theo pushed himself to his feet and took a couple of steps. His legs held his weight steadily enough, but his head listed a little from one side to the other in a way that made me queasy, watching.

Dee grasped Theo's arm, joy shining in his face even as concern flashed through his expression. Theo had taken him in when the twins' mother had been afraid the Queen would conscript them as guards because of their valuable talents. They'd lived and breathed the Spades since they were kids—and Theo, as the White Knight, had been their sort-of king. Only right now, seeing the play of emotions on his face, did I realize how wrenching the last couple weeks without their leader must have been for all his people.

Theo had lied, yes. He'd hidden things from me and from the Spades—from everyone. But he'd meant a lot to people in spite of that. Maybe he'd been honest with them in the ways that mattered most.

We could work through the ways that mattered most to me some time when we weren't in the middle of the palace of our greatest enemy.

"You'll be all right once you're done with this place," Dee said, as if to convince himself and Theo. "We've got you."

"You do," Theo said, with a little more confidence. "You do."

"Here, you'll want to wear these. They'll help us get you out." Dee handed over a white hoodie and a strip of cloth that was a pretty close match for our masks.

Theo pulled them on, his legs swaying slightly under him. His head jerked around abruptly. He reached toward me. I grabbed his hand, he tugged me closer, and in the rush of my relief, nothing that had happened before the last five minutes seemed to matter very much at all.

I threw my arms around him and hugged him tight. Theo returned my embrace with a rasp of breath that sounded both startled and pleased. His lips brushed my cheek. His voice spilled out warm and urgent.

"I did what I could. I got it ready for you."

"What?" I said, confused, as I forced myself to pull back.

A flicker of a smile crossed his lips. "Your throne," he said. "I swore I'd see you on it. I've cleared the last part of your way there."

CHAPTER NINE

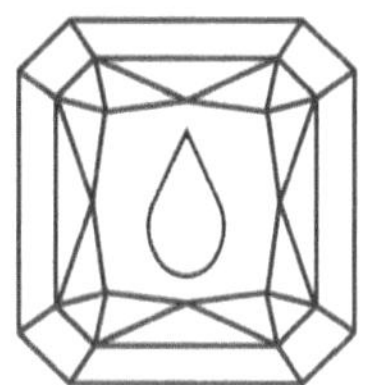

Hatter

"Does he seem quite like he did to you?" Dee asked me under his breath where we were leaning against the wall of the cave. On the other side of the alcove where we'd set up our bunch of foldable cabins, the former White Knight, now Prince of Hearts, was sitting with a plate of food one of the other Spades had brought him.

There'd been cheers and exclamations all around when we'd arrived with our supposed leader in tow. Theo—Jack?—had immediately grabbed Mirabel in a grateful hug. He'd asked for a couple of hours to recover himself before we assembled the Spades who still remained down here to hear what he had to say.

So far, that recovery had involved a shower and a change of clothes, rinsing dye powder through his hair to turn his curls back to the chestnut brown they'd been as long as I'd known him, a brief interlude in one of the cabins looking over the loot Chess had brought back from his office, and now a meal.

I supposed I couldn't fault him for needing to get his bearings after the situation we'd found him in, but there were plenty of other offences I wasn't ready to absolve him of yet.

"Whatever the Queen of Hearts had her doctors doing to him, it shook him up some," I said. Theo still held himself with the same confident posture he'd always had, but his gaze flickered more than I remembered. Sometimes he tensed for no apparent reason, as if he were controlling an impulse he didn't want to give in to.

Our White Knight had always given the impression of being perfectly in control, to the point that it'd annoyed the shit out of me. This Prince of Hearts appeared to be wavering on the edge of losing himself.

"He's only been back a little while. He'll get back to his old self soon enough," Dee said, with characteristic optimism. He couldn't quite summon a smile, though.

I wasn't sure I totally believed what he'd said either. The Theo we'd known had been the man he'd constructed for us to see, as much an invention as his various devices. Now that façade was broken. How could he ever be the exact same person he had been, when that person had always been at least in part an act?

Word had spread to the other pods of Spades in the underground caves despite Theo's request that we hold off on a real assembly. A few people drifted into our alcove, and then a few more. Doria came out of one of the cabins and lingered there, watching. Seeing my daughter hesitate to approach the man she'd followed without question just a few weeks ago set my teeth on edge.

Theo raised his head and seemed to take note of the new arrivals. His shoulders stiffened for just a second in the pale green shirt someone had lent him—even that hint of tension not quite how he'd usually have presented himself. Then he drew himself up with that assured air I now knew was a princely one.

The Queen of Hearts' fucking *son*. It was right there in the authority of his stance, the boldness of that square jaw. The youngest descendent of a line that came and took what rightfully belonged to others while squashing every sign of dissent.

Oh, yes, he had plenty of offences to account for yet.

"Spades," the prince said in his familiar rolling baritone. It filled the alcove and the passage beyond. Most of us looked sallow in the eerie glow given off by the stream, but somehow it lit him up like a supernatural aura of power. "I'm so glad to have come back to you. I wish I could take longer to relish my freedom, but we have far too pressing concerns we must address as quickly as possible."

All the Spades emerged from the cabins or turned from what they were doing to listen. Dum and Mallo left off the game of cards they'd been playing to pass the time. Lyssa looked up from where she'd been sitting with Chess.

The tension in her expression made my heart squeeze. I loved that woman, I did, with every fiber of my being, and I knew how much Theo had hurt her beyond anyone else. He'd played her like a fool, taking her on that ramble through the Checkerboard Plains as if he had no idea that the artifacts might be meant specifically for her, why she could slow the train or calm a jabberwock.

No matter what his reasons had been, my arm itched with the urge to pay him back for that pain with a punch or two where he'd hurt too. But Lyssa wouldn't like that. He was hers to deal with as she saw fit—and as queen, what she wanted to deal with, she did.

"You'll have heard a lot of things in the last few weeks," Theo went on. "I want to lay the facts as bare as possible. I *am* the son of the Queen of Hearts—I once went by the name Jack, and I faked my own murder so that I could escape from under her thumb and try to set things right on the other side of the palace walls. I kept my original identity a secret to avoid discovery that might have led to the end of the work I was doing, but I hate that I've needed to lie to you."

Murmurs carried around the camp. Everyone had heard the gist of the story by now, but some might still have hesitated to believe it until hearing it from the man's own lips.

Theo's gaze roved over the gathered rebels, as dark and steady in this moment as it had ever been. "This is the truth: I am Theo now, not Jack. I am the man you called your White Knight and your Inventor. I'm not a prince—and I never was. The Hearts stole Wonderland's throne from the queens and kings you should have had. But the Red royal family has returned to us. You can still come to me for guidance, and I hope I can offer much that is useful. When it comes to who leads us, I defer to Lyssa, the descendant of the Red Queen and the rightful ruler of Wonderland, as should all of you."

Lyssa's pose stiffened. She'd acknowledged the story of her origins with the rest of the Spades, but she hadn't tried to lord it over anyone. She obviously hadn't expected Theo to highlight her role quite that directly or emphatically. Even as I bristled on her behalf, though, I felt the rightness of his words.

Maybe he could have warned her he'd be pointing a spotlight on her, but we *should* place her word above his. He should renounce all claim on the palace or the throne in deference to her. That was the least she deserved.

Theo made a beckoning gesture, his expression softening as he met Lyssa's eyes, and Hearts take me if I couldn't see an affection and admiration there not so different from what stirred so often in my chest in her presence. Lyssa stood and took his hand to let him present her to the Spades. Despite her earlier surprise, a pleased flush had colored her cheeks. I didn't think the affection went only one way.

Well, she had always been fond of him too. If he redeemed himself, all the better for all of us. When we'd won her proper place back for her, there wasn't any doubt which of us was best suited to stand beside her at that throne, was there?

The thought niggled down my spine until I clamped my jaw and shoved it away.

"We will take back the throne," Lyssa said, her clear voice filling the room as powerfully as Theo's had. The rubies on her woven vest gleamed, but not quite as bright as those brilliant blue eyes. What a woman she was, my looking-glass girl. "We will end this reign of terror. I know I haven't been with you for very long, but I feel like I belong here. I feel connected to all of you, and there's nothing I'd like more than to see all of Wonderland as joyful as it seemed to be when I first got here—but for real this time."

A cheer rose up through the gathering. I raised my voice and clapped my hands to add to it, and so did Dee, with a hint of a furrow in his brow. He and his brother had admired the White Knight so much, I couldn't imagine how this mess had affected him.

"I believe the first step we must take toward seeing our queen to her rightful place is to take back the artifacts of the Red's rule," Theo said, his hand coming to rest tentatively on Lyssa's waist. "The ruby-marked sword and scepter are hidden away in the home belonging to our own Hatter." He tipped his head toward me with a familiarity I couldn't stop from rankling me. "I understand the Queen of Hearts has instructed her guards to keep a close watch on the premises, but I believe I have a plan that can get us to those treasures. Hatter, will you assist?"

Did he honestly expect me to refuse? "Of course," I said automatically. Perhaps I should have waited to hear his plan first, but with the way Lyssa beamed at me, it was hard to have any regrets. That was, until Theo's gaze flickered again, his mouth flattening against an involuntary twitch of his muscles.

My stomach knotted. Our Inventor had always been quick with his plans. Was the man who'd come back to us really ready to take on the Hearts' Guard already—or was he going to lead us straight back into the Queen of Hearts' clutches?

"That one?" Lyssa murmured beside me, pointing to one of the guards ambling down the street past my hat shop, keeping his distance from the wandering revelers.

Theo peered over her shoulder. All three of us were outfitted with the masks that filtered out the Queen's drug, but even with the lower half of his face covered, his gaze was penetrating.

I wished I could feel totally secure it'd stay that way. Even though his plan had made a reasonable amount of sense, we were still depending on him to pull the first part of it off.

"Yes," he said to Lyssa. "That's one. You can always tell from the slightly unnatural stiffness to the way they move. I'll take him."

He slipped away through the shadows along the street, after the pearl-headed guard. His plan required a guard's uniform, and he'd suggested we find a pearled one if we could, to make the taking easier. I couldn't deny the wisdom there.

Our White Knight had more combat skills than I'd have

suspected given his tendency to hang back behind the scenes. He whipped out a cord he'd brought with him and used it to yank the guard to him. The slam of his hand to the man's forehead left the figure slumped. He dragged the guard into an alley and returned a few minutes later in the traditional red-and-pink pleated tunic and red pants, the heart-shaped helm perched on his head and the antidote rose tucked into his collar. He'd kept his mask up as we'd discussed.

"Wish me luck," he said under his breath as he passed us. He strode into the hat shop.

Lyssa grasped my hand as we waited. The thrumming rhythm of the music playing down the street vibrated over my skin.

"Do you think we should have made him wait, or let someone else do this part?" Lyssa whispered to me. So, she'd noticed he wasn't exactly in tiptop shape too.

"He does know what demeanor the guards will respond to better than anyone else in the Spades," I said. "And he can pull off that authoritative presence. I think we should keep an eye on him, be ready to step in if he falters, but I wouldn't have agreed to go along with this plan if I'd been *that* worried."

Lyssa nodded, and I took a small particle of satisfaction from having reassured her. We braced ourselves, our eyes fixed on the doorway. Theo was meant to go in and announce to the guards that the roses just dropped on this street had been laced far too heavily with the drug, more than the antidote they all wore could stave off. They were to retreat a few blocks for an hour until it dissipated. The story would also explain the mask he was wearing, which would also stop them from identifying him.

I'd tried to find a loophole, a reason to question his judgment, but I hadn't seen one. And we hadn't been able to come up with a better plan for retrieving her sword and scepter on our own. Lyssa had been right when she'd said we needed him here, at and on our side.

At the sound of raised voices, my pulse hiccupped. It was only a stream of guards from inside the building emptying into the street. Seven of them in total, with Theo at their heels. "Three streets to the north and one west, and wait there for further instructions," he said, as if him giving commands were perfectly natural—which in a way it was. "I've got to clear everyone else out of the area."

The guards made a few puzzled sounding noises, but they headed off down the street in the direction he'd indicated. I let out my breath, but my body stayed tensed. We weren't in the clear yet.

Theo strode in the opposite direction, past us, peering through the shop windows as if looking for other comrades. Every now and then he took a quick glance over his shoulder. After the fourth of those, he glanced our way and motioned quickly to the shop.

The guards had moved out of sight. This was our chance.

Lyssa and I dashed together for the hat shop doorway. The sight of my merchandise strewn across the floor and counters made my chest twist. Ignoring that pang of discomfort, I snatched up a simple top hat as we hustled on to the stairs and set it on my head in a way that immediately set me more at ease.

I could rearrange my hats. I could make new ones. The guards hadn't hurt anything permanently.

As long as Lyssa's artifacts remained in their hiding place undiscovered.

I must have been spending too much time lurking around in the underground passages in the last few weeks and not enough getting my exercise. By the time we reached the fourth floor, I was winded. Lyssa stopped with a gasp of breath that comforted my ego a little, and we hurried down the hall to the upper apartment's master bedroom.

I sprang into the lead. The wardrobe had been my design; I knew exactly where to press the second I'd whipped the door open, exactly how much pressure to apply for the panel to swing around. Lyssa let out a sigh of relief when the gleaming sword and scepter came into view.

She lifted the scepter first, her pale fingers curling around the dark cherry wood staff. The massive ruby in its frame of gold glittered as she shoved it into the sack she'd brought. She slung the bag over her shoulder and reached for the sword. The ruby embedded in its hilt flashed as if in welcome.

Then a shout carried from the street below.

My back went rigid. Lyssa snapped up the sword and swung around. My hatpins all but leapt into my hand. Someone thumped along the street's cobblestones, raising his voice in a bellow.

"Hey! You there! What's this story you're telling? What unit are you meant to be with? Our orders were to never leave this building unguarded."

He had to be talking to Theo. Theo could flee underground, but that man stood between us and escape. I wasn't sure our former White Knight had the wherewithal to do more than save himself right now.

I looked at Lyssa—her wide eyes, her determined expression, so beautiful and so fierce at the same time—and my mouth and my body moved before I'd even really thought about it.

"I'll go down," I said, stepping toward the hall. "I'll lead him off, and you can get back to the trap door."

Before I'd even finished speaking, more footsteps thundered on the road outside. I was going to have more than one guard to distract. My gut clenched, but a surge of adrenaline overwhelmed it. I was about to race toward the stairs when Lyssa caught my arm.

"No!" she said. "Hatter—you don't need to throw yourself into the line of fire for me. We'll get out of this together. There has to be a way. We can—we can go across the rooftops."

She tugged me toward the window. I started to balk, the layout of this block unfurling in my head. Then a single sharp thought pierced the mad haze that had been rising through me.

We *could* take the roofs close enough to the underground entrance to be pretty sure of making it. All the city folk were either sleeping or reveling in their drugged state. We could slip through the window of another building farther along and go straight through a house without anyone likely to complain.

Lyssa shoved the window open just as a door banged open downstairs. I boosted her onto the shingles and scrambled out myself. The cold night air filtered through my mask, waking me up even more.

"This way," I said, grabbing her hand and trying not to think about the hasty way I'd almost run straight into danger on her behalf. "Follow me."

CHAPTER TEN

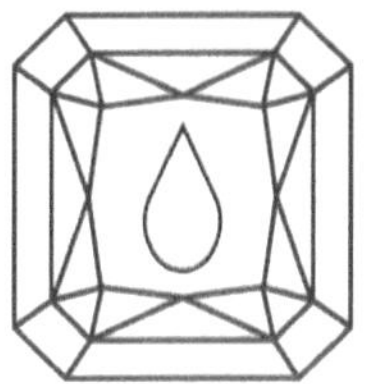

Lyssa

It felt strange just leaving the magical sword and scepter of the Red royal line sitting out in the cabin I was now sharing with Doria and the ferret-faced woman—whose name, Mallo, I'd finally gotten—but it would have felt even stranger carrying them both around in the caves. I still didn't even know how to use their magic. After the disarray when we'd fled Hatter's house last night, Theo had suggested he could help me work with them, but I wasn't sure when that would happen with so much else up in the air.

The images from the city above, the people so loopy, had haunted my dreams. They'd kept my sleep restless and short. My cabin-mates were still sleeping under their blanket, their breaths rasping faintly, as I tugged my clothes into something resembling neatness as quietly as I could.

Most of the camp was still sleeping. I knew a couple of the Spades would be standing guard farther down the caves near the closest entrances, but the only other person up near the alcove was Theo, sitting a little ways off by the edge of the stream. His head bent low as he twisted a bit of metal onto a thin black device he was holding. Still the Inventor, even now. I guessed old habits died hard.

He was so absorbed in his work that he didn't notice me coming over until I'd almost reached him. His head jerked up, and his fingers clenched around the device as if he was afraid he'd drop it. The second he saw me, the tension fled from his expression. He smiled at me, warmly but maybe not as confidently as he might have a few weeks ago.

"Couldn't sleep?" he said.

"I seem to have gotten more rest than you did." I sat down at the edge of the stream next to him, leaning to let my fingers ripple the lukewarm water. Its blue glow sharpened the angles around Theo's square jaw, the slightly crooked nose he'd purposely let heal wrong after his mentor, the previous White Knight, had broken it for him.

Even with that minor imperfection, he was handsome as a prince. Honestly, the flaw made him even more so—more real and less like a work of fiction.

But so much of our time together had been fictional. Just the story he'd wanted to tell me and not all the darker and more fraught pieces he'd wanted to keep hidden.

"I've got a lot of work to do," Theo said. He set the device down on the smooth rock beside him. "If I'm going to see you on that throne, we've got to determine a way to get more than a handful of us into the palace. Or a way to make the guards stand down no matter what my mother says. Neither is going to be easy."

"You know, you can take a little longer to recover from what she put you through," I said. "She had you trapped in there for weeks, messing with your head, hurting you…" My gaze fell on the thin pink lines of healing cuts at the corners of his jaw. I suspected there were more beneath his clothes. "No one will blame you for taking it easy for a day or two."

"I'd blame me," Theo said firmly. "I promised you I'd clear the way for you—that I'd make it safe for you to come back. But it isn't at all, and she's destroying everything that matters about this land." He rubbed his hand over his face. "I know her. I matter to her. I should be able to work out a way to turn things around."

"She has powerful magic and hundreds of people on her side, too afraid to do anything but follow her orders." Or incapable of even considering it, in the case of the "pearl-heads" Hatter had told me about. I restrained a shiver at that memory. "But I'm here now, and we've got you back, and we've managed to get the artifacts. We're already turning things around."

Theo looked at me for a long moment. The intentness of his dark brown eyes sent a tingle over my skin. My body remembered all too well what it was like to be wrapped in those strong arms, to meet the heat of his kiss with my mouth.

"I owe you so much more than this," he said. "Maybe we would have overcome her already if I hadn't let my ego and my ambitions sway my thinking. I'm not even sure how many of my decisions were practical and how many I simply convinced myself were. The only thing I do know for sure is that I haven't made up for any of it until the Queen of Hearts has fallen and you're safe in the palace that should have been yours all along."

His hand edged forward as if to take mine, but he hesitated just shy of contact. We hadn't touched since that quick hug when we'd found him in the palace. My emotions jumbled in my chest, but whatever I was feeling, however I decided our relationship played out from here, I didn't want to push him away completely.

I slid my hand the last half an inch to brush his. He wrapped his fingers around mine immediately with the same solid, comforting grasp he'd always had. A rush of warmth shot through my veins, and a large part of me wanted to scoot a little closer, to melt into his embrace like I had in the past. I held myself back.

"I think you're being too hard on yourself, like you always have," I said. "I'm still upset about the way you lied to me, but I *understand.* You were right that you weren't ready to take on the Queen of Hearts to get my throne back—no one here was. I certainly wasn't. I wish you'd trusted me with the whole truth of who I was, at least, sooner, but… You'd only known me a couple weeks. You'd seen yourself as the heir to that throne for decades. It's—it's a mess. Maybe I'm still confused and I'm going to need some time to sort out my feelings, but I know for sure that you've always truly wanted what's best for Wonderland. You don't need to prove that to me."

Theo's smile came back with a quirk of his lips. "And that generosity," he said, his gaze still holding mine, "is one of the many reasons I love you. I meant that when I said it before. I might not have proven my devotion yet, but I will. Whether you ever find you can return those feelings or not. You haven't been here long, but you've already shown me things about what a ruler should be that I'd let myself forget. I'll fight to the end, and it'll be for you as much as for Wonderland."

My breath caught. I squeezed his hand harder. Before I'd found out about his lies, I'd been falling for Theo. The qualities that had drawn me to him were still there. I wasn't ready to say the words back to him, and I didn't know when or if I would be, but hearing him talk like that made my heart sing.

"Theo," I said, not sure what to add.

He shifted a smidge closer, his other hand rising to brush over my hair. "That's all I ask for," he said. "For you to know who I am, who I'll continue being from this day forward. I'm so sorry for how I deceived you before. You have my word that I'm committed to being nothing but open with you now, and we'll just see where that takes us. You're my queen."

He said the last words so fervently I couldn't help myself. I tipped toward him, seeking out his lips. He returned my kiss in an instant, his hand coming to rest on the side of my neck, his thumb tracing a line of sparks over my cheek. His mouth moved against mine sure and eager but restrained, not the headlong passion with which we'd come together the last time we'd had sex. Still letting me lead the way.

The rose and raspberry smell of him filled my nose. I should have wondered before about that faint flowery scent that clung to him as if it were part of his essence. But it tasted sweeter on his lips than anything I'd encountered in the Queen's palace.

He wasn't his mother. He wasn't his family. That was enough for me to share this moment with him.

I curled my fingers into the fabric of his shirt, pulling myself even closer. In the back of my mind, I was conscious of the cabins in the alcove just a few steps away and of all the walls around my heart that I wasn't ready to let down.

I could still have this. Just a kiss, or maybe two, with the man who'd first made me feel like I deserved every joy Wonderland could offer.

Footsteps rapped over the stone, echoing against the cave ceiling. I drew back from Theo, and we both turned as one of the Spades from the other camps jogged into view. His expression was tight, his hands fisted. Theo sprang to his feet, and I followed.

"Whi—White Knight," the man said, coming to a stop, stumbling a bit over the title Theo had admitted wasn't entirely rightfully his. "I was scouting out around the edges of the city, like we've been doing regularly since we came under to the River Down."

The other members of our camp started to emerge from the cabins at the sound of louder voices. Theo started to speak and then looked to me. A prickling ran over my skin. I needed to lead these people now. If I told him to handle this, he would, but I had to get used to the role I was reaching for, didn't I?

"What happened?" I said, keeping my voice even but attentive. "What did you see?"

"The guards were bringing more of the Clubbers off to the palace," the sentry said. His gaze flicked between me and Theo. "A couple dozen of them this time. I don't like the looks of it at all."

"Did they say anything about what they were doing with them?" Dum asked. He and his twin had come out of the nearest cabin to join us. "Has the Queen announced anything?"

The sentry shook his head. "Not that we've heard. And the guards weren't saying anything other than to keep the Clubbers walking. They were all still drugged out of their heads—they'd just left the city."

Dee turned to Theo with a hopeful expression. "Did you hear anything about her planning a round-up while you were in the palace, boss?"

Theo's shoulders had tensed. "No," he said. "No, I—"

He flinched and clapped a hand over his eyes, hunching over for a second. My heart lurched.

"Sorry," he said quickly, jerking himself straight. His hand hadn't left his eyes, and his mouth pressed in a thin line before he went on. “Just an after-effect—the treatments—I’ve got it. I’ll be fine in a moment.”

His voice had gone ragged. I touched his arm tentatively and then more firmly when he didn’t retreat. He let out a stuttered breath and raised his head with a sheepish smile. The twins smiled back at him, but Dee’s lips wavered. He looked more frightened than reassured.

“We have to assume whatever the Queen wants with those people, it isn’t good,” I said, pitching my voice a little higher to bring everyone’s attention back to me. To get us back on track to solving this problem rather than focusing on Theo’s momentary lapse. “Is there any way to fend off the guards, to stop them from taking more people?”

The sentry sputtered a laugh. “If we could do that, we could take the whole palace.”

Fair enough. “And the city people couldn’t fight back even if they were willing to now, thanks to the drugs. Okay.” I squared my shoulders as the idea came to me. I didn’t know how well it would work, but it felt right, and that was the best we could go by. The people in the city had been trapped just as much as Theo had, and like him, they couldn’t help us unless we helped them first.

“We have the three masks. I want us going out in shifts and bringing two or three people back to the caves each time. We’ll set up another camp where they can rest while the drug leaves their system. And then they can decide whether they want to stay with us and fight for their freedom, or head back into that stupor again.”

Mallo frowned where she’d come up by the twins. “If they go back up, they might tell the guards where we’ve taken shelter.”

“I think we’ve got to take that chance,” I said. “We’ve got to believe in the people of Wonderland. The Queen has shown how far she’s willing to go. Once they’re here, and they see how much safer they are than they were up there… I think it’ll turn out we have a lot more allies than we did before.”

CHAPTER ELEVEN

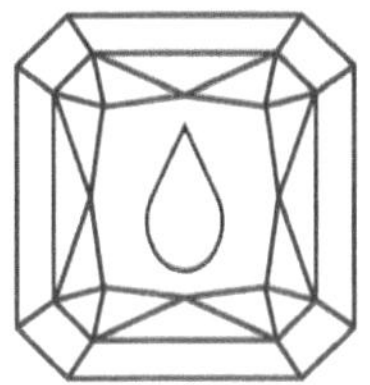

Chess

I'd had conflicted feelings about using my ability to disappear in the past, but only when it was for self-serving reasons. Prowling around the walls to the palace gardens, watching the guards' eyes slip right over my invisible form, I got nothing but satisfaction.

The knowledge of how my special powers could be of use was why I'd gone to Hatter, out of everyone, when I'd needed shelter and security after my torture at the Duchess's hand. It was why I'd asked him to introduce me to the White Knight when I was sure my head was going to stay on my shoulders, and why I'd put myself at the disposal of the leader of the Spades ever since. The Queen of Hearts and the people who carried out her will had been a poison in Wonderland long before she'd sent her guards to strew drugged roses in the city streets. In this one way, I could provide a bit of help no one else could.

It was the least and the most I could do.

There hadn't been much activity in the gardens earlier this

morning, but as I passed the west gate, the whir of what sounded like an air trolley caught my ears through the muffled atmosphere of the in-between. It came from farther along, by the north gate. I hustled along the grassy hill, glancing toward the wall to see if I could catch any glimpse of the vehicle from my slightly elevated position.

Its hunched, plated roof, like the silvered shell of an immense beetle, glinted beyond the hedges. I reached the road that stretched out from the gate just as the iron-barred door swung open. The air trolley hissed out, hovering half a foot over the ground, bits of dirt flying up in its wake.

The things could hold about fifty people if they packed in tight. This one today held maybe thirty. Several of them stood by the openings that let in the air between the silver posts, all in the uniforms of the Hearts' Guard. The others, sitting on the benches, wore garish Clubber clothes, their eyes pinkish and expressions vague enough to convince me they were still at least a little drugged.

My gaze stopped on a figure just straightening up near the back of the trolley, which the guards had otherwise kept clear. I'd never talked to Carpenter, but I recognized him from his rounded gut encased in those canvas overalls, his jowly face partly hidden by a grizzled brown beard. A chill whispered over my skin.

What was *he* doing with this crowd? And why were they heading along the road that led to the sea?

My mind was quick enough to put together the obvious answer, but the rest of me balked at accepting it. Carpenter had been looking at something at the back of the trolley. I couldn't make out what from here. That might be proof in one direction or the other.

I set off after the trolley, speeding from a jog to a lope to a sprint. I wasn't as fast on my feet as Hatter, but I could cover ground in a good amount of time when I needed to—and the trolleys didn't move all that fast anyway.

I caught up with it still in sight of the palace. Carpenter had gone to sit on a bench just behind the city folk. I pushed myself a little faster to come up beside the trolley, and then slowed to gracefully catch a bar at the back. With a hop, I swung myself onto the step at the back of the trolley without more than a slight hitch to the vehicle's constant hiss. No one looked my way.

A salty, watery, near-rotten odor reached my nose before I'd even leaned over the back wall. I braced myself.

Between the back benches lay heaps of a ridged greenish-black material. Empty oyster casings, heaped on top of one another. At least enough for every Clubber on that trolley, I'd estimate.

My stomach turned over. That was the proof I'd expected but hoped to find false. I leapt off the back of the trolley before it could carry me any farther from home and watched it whir off toward the Oyster Cove, my legs unwilling to move.

The Queen was turning all her captured city folk into pearl-heads. Fresh as possible, I guessed—their heads to be severed moments before they were shoved into those casings and cast into the workings at the sea bottom. Would the new dull heads grow faster that way? I didn't know enough about the process to have any idea.

Possibly the Queen didn't either. Possibly it was simply easier to have the bodies she'd collected walk to their doom. She wouldn't want to parade *those* heads, the heads of citizens who'd done nothing wrong but happen to be in the guards' path at an unfortunate time, through the streets, putting her clearest villainy on display for all to shudder at.

What was she pearling all those people for? I couldn't think of any purpose that sat remotely well with me.

My stomach still churning, I forced myself to turn and head back toward the city. Lyssa and Theo—and all the rest of the Spades—needed to know about this development.

As I reached the edge of the city, I pulled my mask up over my face against the stink of doctored roses. I was meant to wait for the Spades who were attempting to usher a few of the city folk down to the caves by the exit we'd decided on, in case they needed assistance. Freeing them from the Queen's influence in dribs and drabs might not make much of a difference to the larger battle, but I couldn't blame Lyssa for wanting to try. Especially after I'd seen what was happening to their neighbors.

Music warbled around me, punctuated by giggles and sighs. I

stuck to the smaller streets and alleys where the Clubber crowd wasn't generally drifting as much as I could. Even invisible, dodging those swaying, dazed bodies wasn't much fun. When I had the chance, I ducked into a shop the owner had abandoned and grabbed what food I could to bring back for our stores along the River Down.

I reached the crimson-and-blue rear end of the candy shop that had a hidden trap door in its basement just as a similarly masked figure came into view down the back alley. Doria was urging along a couple of young women who didn't look much older than she was—friends from the days when we could enjoy Caterpillar's Club at least a little, I suspected.

"I want to go back to the music!" one of them said in a slurred voice. "I wasn't done dancing, Doria."

"Mmm. I just want to lie down a moment," the other mumbled.

"There's lots of room to lie down where we're going," Doria said. She had her chin high, but even through her face mask, I could hear the waver that had crept into her voice. It was one thing to see the Clubbers in their constantly high state from the sidelines and another to try to reason with people you'd really known face-to-face. "And there's more room to dance over here. Don't you hate constantly bumping into people? Let's mix things up."

The first woman made a disgruntled sound, but she didn't appear to have the motivation to put up more of an argument. I eased back beside the building and drew myself into being fully present, the sounds sharpening and shapes steadying around me. Then I stepped out to greet them.

"This way, this way," I said with a grin, motioning them to the shop's back door with an entertainer's air. Might as well make the trip seem as appealing as possible while I could. "An exclusive lounge only for the most select patrons. Let's keep it hush hush so it stays limited to our special guests."

"Oooh," the second woman said, her eyes going overly round. "This does sound cool. How did you get in, Doria?"

Hatter's daughter shot me a grateful look. "You just have to know the right people," she said. "So aren't you lucky you know me?"

They were, more than they knew. Doria led them through the door and down to the basement. One of the other Spades would be waiting below in the caves to help take the Clubbers the rest of the way. Doria must have decided her part of that job was done, because she poked her head out a minute later.

"Should I stick around up here?" she asked. "Do you need me for anything else?"

Did *I* need her? The question sounded so bizarre that I didn't immediately know how to answer it. What did any of this work have to do with my needs?

She meant whether I thought there was any other way she could pitch in with the mission Lyssa had sent us on, of course. As I considered, Kip ducked into the alley, nudging along a middle-aged man who appeared already half-asleep. Kip's face looked pinched.

"I had two," he said under his breath as he reached us. "But a bunch of guards barged into the street while I was convincing the other—I think they're taking more people now, just over there." He jerked his head back the way he'd come, and a dazed sound of protest filtered to us at the same time.

Doria stiffened. "Should we do something?" she asked. She glanced not at Kip but at me. He did too.

I blinked at them, and it struck me like a bucketful of water in the face. Oh. She *had* been looking for actual orders—from me. It made an odd sort of sense, now that I'd cottoned on. They'd seen me at our true queen's side regularly from the moment they'd learned of Lyssa's heritage. I'd stepped up as well as I could when we'd been gathering everyone in the caves. Now the other Spades took me for one of the leaders of this rebellion.

The thought provoked much the same emotions as a dosing of water might: a discomfort at being out of my element twined with a weird sort of thrill in the new sensation.

Was I a leader? I'd never meant to be, never thought to be. I'd served as one of the White Knight's tools, and that had been plenty involvement for me.

I supposed I'd better contemplate this unexpected turn later. Right now, two of my comrades were looking to me for an answer, and I had to come up with one quick.

What would the White Knight have said? What would Lyssa want us to do? Those two guiding impulses merged into a course of action that sent a nervous quiver through me even as I felt the rightness of it.

"Send him down quickly," I said to Kip. "Then we'll scout out the street. If we see an opportunity to put the guards off, we will, but no jumping in if we're too outnumbered."

The two of them nodded as if they'd been following commands from me all along. Kip hurried his Clubber into the basement, and then the three of us set off in the direction the shout had carried from.

We stopped in the shadows at the end of the alley. The urge prickled over me to slip back into the in-between, out of view, but the awareness that my companions were looking to me for guidance kept me in place. I wasn't sure how much I liked the weight that responsibility came with, but I'd taken it at least for now, so I'd better own it.

Eight—no, nine—guards were weaving through the scattered crowd of revelers on the wide street ahead of us. A few Clubbers already paced in the back of the cart parked near the corner. My hands balled as I watched the guards grab a couple more, not too old or too young and in reasonably good health, like we'd observed before.

I couldn't see any way we could intervene that would help anyone, though. They had three times our numbers, and given the compliant way the Clubbers were going along with them, I suspected the city folk would push back against us before they'd turn on the guards. The drug hadn't made them any braver.

Hatter would never forgive me if I led Doria into a skirmish with the odds so far against us.

"I don't think we're in a position to stop them," I murmured. "But watch everything they do. It may be useful in defending against them later."

The other two nodded as if I'd offered words of great wisdom. I followed my own instructions, noting the construction of the vehicle, the way the guards moved among the Clubbers. In a matter of minutes, they'd herded several more onto the cart and jumped up themselves to move on.

"Let's go!" one shouted to the last of the helmed figures, who was still in the crowd.

"I've got one more," he called back, tugging a woman with him. At the sight of her oval face with its billow of red hair, my heart stopped. Doria flinched beside me. She grasped my arm.

"We can't just let them take *her*," she said.

"Wait," I said, holding her back. Was there a way to dislodge her without this scene turning into a bloodbath? I hesitated, trying to see it, willing my mind to narrow to tactics and logistics the way Theo's might have. My head started to ache, and the guard had already reached the cart. My lips parted as he hauled the woman up, but I had no useful words to speak.

And then they were rattling away, the remaining Clubbers swaying with the pulse of the music on as if they'd never been disturbed.

"I'm sorry," I found myself saying. "There wasn't any— I couldn't tell—"

"We'll get them back," Kip said. "When we're ready."

Whenever that would be. I swallowed hard. "Let's return to the camp," I said. "We've got a lot to report."

We trudged back to the candy shop and through the trap door into the caves. The sentry standing guard there nodded to us as we passed by. With each step toward camp, my feet grew heavier. Doria rubbed her mouth, unusually quiet.

I hadn't been quite the leader they'd wanted just now, had I?

The twins were the first people I saw when we reached the alcove. My legs stalled as they looked up from the devices Theo must have set them assembling. The former White Knight himself emerged from one of the cabins a moment later. Lyssa came just behind him, holding her ruby-marked sword. Despite the bad news I was bringing, my heart still leapt at the sight of her, so sure of herself now in the role that was meant for her.

She would lead us right. I trusted in her if not myself.

"I know why they're rounding up the Clubbers," I made myself say. The words tried to stick in my throat. I turned my gaze toward the twins. "And we've got even more reason to stop them as soon as we can. We just saw—They've taken your mother."

Dum's face grayed. Dee stared at me for a second. Then he swore and dashed the instrument he'd been working on to the ground as he leapt to his feet. He stalked off toward the cabins, but stayed within hearing.

Lyssa's lips slanted into a frown. "Tell us everything."

CHAPTER TWELVE

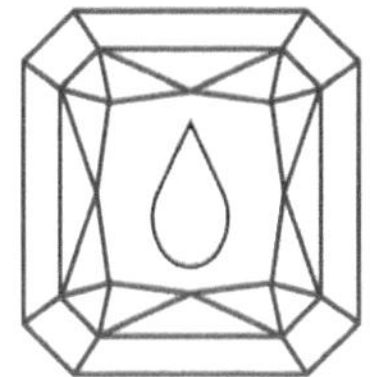

Lyssa

We walked nearly as far as the oddly shaped hills I'd passed when Hatter had taken me out to the Topsy Turvy Woods what felt like years ago. Theo stopped at the edge of a small clearing surrounded by the vibrant trees and nodded, finally declaring the spot safe enough for the training I was meant to do. Like when I'd run from Hatter's home, I had the ruby-marked scepter in a bag slung over my shoulder and the sword in my hand.

The weapon's weight didn't drag on my arm the way I remembered it doing before. My fingers seemed to fit around it perfectly. But before we started this training, I needed to address a different weight that had filled my stomach since Chess had arrived back from his patrol. I hadn't wanted to ask these questions in front of Dee and Dum.

"Why wasn't she with us—with the Spades?" I asked. "The twins' mother, I mean. She asked you to look after them from when they were kids… She obviously trusted you and believed in the cause."

Theo grimaced. Before he could answer, Chess piped up where he'd leaned against a nearby tree. "She sent Dee and Dum to the

White Knight because she was afraid of the Queen. Saving them was the most important thing. Saving herself, of lesser importance. I heard her say once that if she ran with the Spades and was identified as a rebel, the Queen's wrath might come down on all of them. Better for her to play along and not draw any additional possible ire."

And now she'd been drawn right into the palace—to be made into one of those dim "pearl-heads"? I hugged myself with one arm across my gut, my sword hand dipping. The blade brushed the grass.

"You don't have any idea how quickly the Queen is sending people out to the cove or what she's using them for after?"

Chess shook his head. "It takes at least a few days, normally, for the pearling to finish. She can't have been gathering people from the city for very long, or we'd have noticed sooner."

"No doubt we'll find out her aims soon enough," Theo said grimly. He tipped his head to me. "Which is all the more reason to help you find the full extent of your powers."

"The artifacts' powers, you mean," I couldn't help saying.

One corner of his mouth twitched upward. "They don't work for me. That sword burned my hand trying to get away from the wrong wielder. It's your power feeding them."

"So far that power hasn't done much more than light up the rubies," I muttered. I'd spent an afternoon practicing sword strokes and trying to figure out what to do with the scepter after we'd first retrieved them, with the Red Knight who'd served my however-many-greats grandmother guiding me, and hadn't gotten anywhere. The Red Knight who'd since fallen under a guard's sword, protecting me when I couldn't protect him—or even myself.

But as those doubts started to rise up inside me, a sense of iron conviction pushed back against them. I was Lyssa, the heir to the Red Queen. I *was* the Red Queen, now that anyone else who might have claimed that title was gone. This sword felt right in my hand because it was, by all rights, mine. So was the scepter, and the armored vest I wore, and the ring hanging from its chain around my neck that glowed with my blood in proof of my heritage.

This was my land, and I had thousands of people to save. I was ready to claim the role that had made me hesitate when the Red Knight had told his story.

It hadn't been safe to try out the artifacts properly in the caves around the stream—I might have hurt someone or brought the ceiling down on us. Here, far enough from the Queen's reach that my worries about discovery had faded too, anticipation hummed through my veins. I set down the scepter and hefted the sword. Warmth streamed from the grip into my palm. The ruby gleamed, and a smile crossed my lips.

"You're holding it well already," Theo said. "Maybe you won't need much of my help after all."

"The Red Knight taught me a few things," I said, with a twinge as I thought of the eccentric old man. He'd been clinging in his devotion, but he'd believed in me before I'd believed in myself. He'd given his life to save me. I wasn't sure what I believed about spirits and an afterlife, especially in a place like this, but I hoped there was some way that he was watching now. That I'd give him a victory to show his sacrifice had been worth it.

"I'll just stay here and admire the view," Chess said with a playful smirk. He'd volunteered to join us so he could stand guard while we were focused on testing the artifacts. I'd gotten the feeling he felt uncomfortable hanging around in the caves while the twins murmured together about the horrible news he'd had to bring them.

I swung my arm, the sword guiding my hand as much as my hand guided the sword. Its tingling energy spread up my arm and through my chest. Suddenly I was picturing the Queen and her tiger-headed Knave who led the Hearts' Guard, the Duchess and the other haughty Diamonds, standing across from us at the other end of the clearing.

I wanted to be rid of them. I wanted them and their influence lifted from *my* people. I wanted the joyful Wonderland I'd thought I'd landed in way back when returned to me.

My arm whipped out. The blade sang through the air. The warmth against my palm turned into a blazing heat—and a sharp ripple of magic shot from the gleaming edge.

A shimmering light raced across the clearing. It walloped the trees so hard their branches shook and the bark dented around a slash across their trunks, leaving a cut deep enough to leak sap.

The hum of power reverberated in my chest for a few seconds before it faded. I sucked in a ragged breath, staring at the damage I'd done. Excitement and horror jarred together inside me, making my lungs tighten.

"Wow," Theo said. "That was spectacular. Can you summon that magic again?"

A good question. He'd probably also like to know whether I could summon even more. I gripped the hilt harder and tried to gather the anger I'd felt in that moment, but the sight of the scored trees dampened it.

I hadn't really hurt our enemies with that slash. And even our enemies, I didn't really want to defeat by spilling their blood all over the palace, the way they'd slaughtered my ancestors centuries ago.

I sliced the sword through the air again, but this time the ruby only glowed faintly—like before. I frowned at it, but I didn't need to ask what the problem was.

"I have to be fully committed," I said. "I *am* now—to being queen. I'm just not sure I want to be the kind of queen who wins that way."

To my relief, Theo didn't push. "You know more of what you're capable of," he said. "If the moment comes when you need to use that power, you'll be ready. Do you want to go through a few basic exercises to get more comfortable with the sword in general?" He grabbed a fallen stick about the same length as my blade. "I can make do with this for training purposes. I'd like to know you can defend yourself the old-fashioned way too."

I couldn't argue with that. We circled the clearing one way and then the other, practicing parries and feints and jabs, until sweat was dampening my blouse under the metal vest. Chess was still watching us, his head cocked to listen for any sounds of approach.

"What about that ruby rod of yours?" he asked, pointing his foot toward the scepter in its bag. "Got any idea yet what magic that can stir up?"

"No, but I'd certainly like to figure it out." I set the sword down in the grass and took out the scepter. Like the sword, it felt more secure in my grasp than it had the last time I'd tested its powers. And the warm wood topped by its crown of gold and ruby spoke of a power less violent than what I'd get with a blade.

"The Red Knight said he saw his Red Queen use it once to tame… some kind of creature. I didn't recognize the word he used for it." I tipped the scepter one way and then another. Even before I'd found it, I'd worked a sort of power like that on a jabberwock on the Checkerboard Plains. An echo of that sensation quivered through me —the sense that I could connect and calm, compel the fear and anger from another being's mind, convince it to see me as a friend rather than a foe.

With that memory thrumming through me, I stepped toward the trees, looking for any animal I could test the magic out on. I held out the scepter as if the intensifying glow of the ruby might light my way —and the shadows fell back from the base of the tree trunks.

I stopped, blinking. At another wave of my hand, the patches of darkness retreated farther into the forest. It wasn't that the ruby's light fell that far. Its glow was condensed around the stone, and no red shine colored the trees or grass. No… I'd simply urged the darkness to give way. Cleared it the way I'd cleared the rage from the jabberwock's mind those weeks ago.

Chess let out a low whistle. "That's something and a half."

I didn't know how useful it would be, but I had to smile anyway. "It isn't what I meant to try. Now, where…"

A sparrow fluttered from one branch to another. It peered at me warily with beady black eyes. I raised the scepter between us, holding its gaze over the top of the ruby and its gold enclosure. A tremor of encouragement traveled over my tongue.

"Hey, there," I said. "There's nothing dangerous here. Come to me?"

The bird hopped to one side and then back again. I extended my hand slowly, willing my good intentions to flow with it the way I had with the jabberwock. Theo and Chess didn't make a sound.

The ruby glowed softly, its light drifting over the sparrow. The bird ruffled its feathers. Then it sprang off the branch and swooped down to land on my outstretched hand. Its tiny clawed feet gripped my finger.

I beamed at it with a rush of giddiness. "Thank you," I said. "Go safely."

It darted away into the forest. I let out the breath I'd been holding, and a laugh came with it.

"They work," I said. "The artifacts respond to me. I really—I really am the Red Queen."

Somehow, despite all my conviction and determination, that fact hadn't felt totally real until this moment.

Chess stepped away from his tree. He rested a hand on my waist as he lowered his head next to mine.

"Of course you are, lovely," he said. "This land will be yours, and you're going to make it the wonder it should be. I can already see how it will be every time I look at you."

His touch, his words, and the admiration in his eyes sent a flush of heat over my skin. "Is that why you're here?" I said teasingly.

"No," he said, his voice dipping. "I'm here because you're you, wondrous as that is, queen or no. Whatever you want. Whatever you need. How can I brighten your day, Your Majesty?"

I made a sound of protest at the title, and then the desire swirling through me took over. I set down the scepter, brought my hand to his jaw, and drew his mouth to mine.

Chess grinned into the kiss. Then he tucked his arm around me and pulled me right up against him, angling his head with a slide of his lips that set off sparks through my nerves. His kisses were always sweet, but there was something a little more urgent to this one.

It had been only days since we'd fallen into each other like this in my memory. For him it'd been weeks, and for most of that time he'd thought I was dead. Knowing that loosened any hesitations I might have had about seeing this moment through to the end I was already yearning for.

I curled my fingers into the rumpled waves of Chess's soft hair, kissing him harder. Aiming to make up for the time apart, to show him how much I did want him. With a pleased rumble in his throat that was almost a purr, he flicked his tongue across the seam of my lips. They parted for him. A needy whimper worked its way up my throat as his tongue twined with mine.

Chess's hand slid to my side and tugged at the base of the armored vest. As I stepped back to pull off that much too solid barrier between us, my gaze caught on the other one of my lovers here with us.

Theo was watching from a few paces away, his expression unreadable. I thought I saw hunger flash through his eyes, but he schooled them back to their usual steady warmth so quickly it was hard to be sure. He wet his lips and flipped the stick he'd been using as a makeshift sword in his hand.

"I can give you some space," he said, his attention never leaving my face. Waiting to judge my reaction so he knew what course I needed him to take. "If you'd feel more at ease without me here."

Something twisted at the base of my heart. The doubts I'd felt about getting close to him again snapped and shattered. All they left behind was a pang of longing.

What more did he have to do? He'd gone through weeks of torture rather than give in to his mother, he'd declared his loyalty to me in front of the people who'd mattered most to him, and now this man who could be so commanding was tossing away any intimate claim he might have put forward, not even asking, just assuming when I was ready, I'd let him know.

Chess's hand lingered on my side, his thumb tracing a teasing line over the silky fabric of my blouse. *He* wouldn't mind the company. He'd told me he preferred having another man there, taking some of the pressure to perform off of him. He hadn't been intimate with anyone one-on-one since the Duchess had nearly murdered him for her own gratification.

So there really wasn't any reason to deny myself.

I dropped the vest beside the other artifacts and motioned Theo over. "I'd feel best with you right *here*."

The elation that lit up his handsome face only reinforced my decision. He crossed the space between us with two swift strides. Chess eased to one side of me, trailing kisses from my cheek to my jaw, and Theo captured my mouth.

I'd never been with two men at the same time before I'd come to

Wonderland. It should have been overwhelming. But having two pairs of lips branding my skin, two sets of fingers tracing over my body, only made me feel more solidly in place.

Yes, this was where I belonged. Right here, between these two very different but oh so enticing men.

Chess's hand traveled up over my blouse to cup one breast and then the other. His thumbs circled my nipples and drew them to stiff peaks. Theo grasped my hip. He released my lips to kiss a path down my neck to my collarbone, and then Chess was devouring me again with a light pinch of his fangs. The tiny prick of pain amid the pleasure left me moaning.

Theo continued his journey downward. He yanked my blouse and bra aside and sucked the tip of my breast in his mouth. I gasped, clutching Chess's shirt, Theo's shoulder. The heat of their bodies on either side of me was like a furnace, but if I burned up, I couldn't help thinking it'd be an amazing way to go.

Theo's tongue worked some kind of magic against my skin, and Chess lifted my hair to nibble his way around to the back of my neck, and oh God, I didn't know how I'd spent so many years satisfied without this rush.

My White Knight, my prince, lifted his head just long enough to brush his lips against mine once more. "I promised you I'd worship you," he murmured in a voice rich with promise. Then he sank to his knees, charting a path farther down over my belly to my waistband. Chess nipped my shoulder and eased up my skirt, clearing the way. My hips swayed toward Theo instinctively with a desire I couldn't suppress. He smiled, tugged down my panties, and pressed his mouth to my core.

"Oh, fuck," I muttered, and then all I could get out was a sigh. Chess ground against me from behind, his cock temptingly hard against my ass. He kept one hand splayed against my thigh, holding up my skirt. The other brushed over Theo's dark curls, half caress, half urging him on. Theo didn't seem to mind, and the sight turned me on even more.

Theo grazed his teeth over my clit and swiveled his tongue around it until I was panting. Pleasure pulsed from my core, making my legs wobble. He reached past my hip to yank the fly of Chess's slacks open, and I just about caught fire right there.

Chess chuckled and slid his fingers over my slick folds. I edged my feet apart to give him more access, leaning into Theo's mouth, braced between the two men. With the utmost care, Chess aligned our bodies and eased his straining cock into me one delicious inch at a time. Theo suckled my clit harder.

The dual sensations of being filled within and worked over without tipped me over the edge. I came with a hitch of breath and stars behind my eyelids. Theo steadied me, Chess pulled back and drove into me even deeper, and I shuddered around him with a sharper cry.

Theo drew back with a gleam in his dark eyes. Chess's thumb replaced my other lover's tongue in an instant. The Prince of Hearts looked ready to rise up again, but as the aftershock of my orgasm trembled through me, another desire took hold. That wasn't where I wanted him.

I nudged him down and bent over him. Chess followed me, lowering himself to his knees as I did, adjusting his angle and driving into me far enough to hit the most sensitive spot inside. I gasped at the wave of bliss, but I wasn't going to be deterred from my current mission.

"Lyssa," Theo said as I snapped open his slacks over the bulge of his own erection. His voice was ragged. "I—You don't—"

He sounded like he was considering trying to talk me out of it. I caught his gaze. "I want to have you. Let me see how much you're mine."

Putting it that way appeared to release any concerns he'd had. He sank back on his elbows as I freed his cock. I ran my tongue up the hard, faintly salty length of it from base to tip, and a groan escaped him.

The leader of the city folk, the Spades, and the Queen of Hearts' chosen heir. I had him sprawled back and lost in pleasure, completely at my mercy.

I took him all the way into my mouth, and then I felt filled from head to toe, Theo's musky rose flavor tickled over my tongue while Chess set off fresh bursts of pleasure with each thrust behind me.

Chess's breath stuttered as he leaned closer to my back, one arm looped around my waist, the other stroking over Theo's thigh. A thought hit me, sending my desire spiking higher even as it brought a lump of emotion into my throat: We were in this together. Not just them with me, but all of us, finding bliss in each other.

"So fucking lovely," Chess said around a hitch in his voice, and then his hips were jerking, heat flooding my core. Those last few thrusts of his cock sent me crashing into my second release. Ecstasy crackled through my body, and I closed my lips tighter around Theo's length as I rode out the wave. He groaned again, bucking to meet me. Then, with a whirl of my tongue, he was flooding my mouth with his cum.

We sprawled on the grass together, me between my two lovers, but not separating them. Theo kissed me hard and then glanced over at Chess as if checking in, giving the other man's arm a brief caress before offering me the same. Chess kept his arm around my waist and nuzzled the side of my neck. He alternated between trailing his fingertips over my belly and grazing his knuckles against Theo's chest in a languid gesture of affection.

"Our queen," he said, brightly but so firmly you'd have thought I was sitting on the throne right now. I started to squirm toward him, wanting another kiss from those sweet lips, but his head snapped up. He knit his brow.

"Someone's coming this way," he said.

I scrambled up, straightening my clothes and grabbing my sword as quickly as I could. Chess had barely zipped his pants when his shoulders relaxed. "One of ours," he said.

A few moments later, one of the Spades from the secondary camps emerged through the trees. If he noticed anything odd about the three of us with our flushed cheeks and mussed hair, he was too caught up in his own concerns to react.

"We thought you'd want to know," he said, looking to Theo first, and then to me, as if he wasn't sure who he should be addressing. "It looks like Dee has gone missing."

CHAPTER THIRTEEN

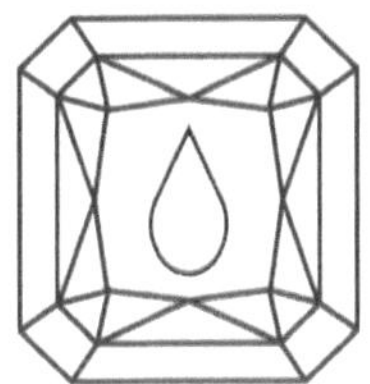

Lyssa

When we reached the main camp in the caves, a few of the Spades, including Mallo, were standing around Dum, all of their faces tense. Dum was shaking his head as if in response to something one of them had said. He looked up as the three of us came into the alcove, but his expression stayed dour.

"What exactly happened with your brother?" Theo said without preamble, his stance rigid and his voice taking on that princely commanding tone. I didn't mind him jumping in to take the lead here. He'd seen the twins as his responsibility, and he knew both of them way better than I did.

"We gave him some space, seeing as he was so upset," Mallo said. "He went into one of the cabins. But he was supposed to go up to the city with me an hour ago, and when I went to see if he was up to it, he wasn't there."

"He must have slipped off without talking to anyone," said the man beside her, a young guy who went by Kip. "No one's seen him since the morning. We looked through all the passages nearby before we thought we should let you know."

My stomach knotted. The usually cheerful twin had been distraught about his mother's capture—of course he had, especially after Chess had revealed where he'd seen the guards taking their earlier captives. Whatever he'd decided to do, he probably hadn't been thinking very clearly.

"Where do you think he'd have gone?" I asked his brother.

Dum rubbed his mouth. He glanced at his companions. "Give us a moment?" he said.

The others eased back. Chess waved them over to the other side of the alcove, asking a question about the latest Clubbers who'd been brought to our recovery area and snorting at something Kip said. Theo and I turned to Dum. He looked at the stone floor and then fixed his gaze not on Theo but on me. Somehow that choice made me proud and nervous at the same time.

He was putting his faith in me, even above the man who'd guided him since he was a kid. I had to be worthy of that trust.

"He talked to me before he left," he said in a low voice. "Tried to convince me that we should go on a mission to get Mom out of the palace. He wasn't properly in his head—he could hardly stand still, he was so agitated. I told him there'd be a mission, that we were working on it, but he didn't want to wait. He thought just the two of us should make a run at it."

The two of them against the entire Hearts' Guard? Nausea pooled in my gut. "That'd be a suicide mission."

"I know," Dum said. "I told Dee that, in softer words. I told him Mom was safer if we stuck to the plan, stuck together with the rest of the Spades, so we could see the rebellion through. If the guards caught us, which they almost definitely would, they might torture us for information before taking our heads. It'd put the whole cause at risk. I love my mother, but I don't see how that would help her. I couldn't calm Dee down, though. He was still all worked up when he walked away."

"Did you see what direction he went in?" Theo asked.

Dum shook his head. "He went back into the cabin then. It must have been later he snuck off. I never thought—I'd have stayed with him if I'd realized he was frantic enough to make a go of it on his own.

But that has to be what he's done. He must have gone off to the palace."

At the rustle of fabric, I realized we had company again. Doria had come over, Hatter right behind her, and Kip and Mallo had drifted back toward us too. From the looks on their faces, they'd heard at least the end of Dum's account.

"If they get it out of him where we've been hiding…" Mallo said, so pale her beady eyes stood out even more starkly than usual. She didn't need to finish that sentence.

"Dee wouldn't tell them anything, no matter what they did," Doria insisted. Her cheeks had flushed. She'd kind of admitted to me that she'd had a crush on the guy for a while, so I couldn't blame her for wanting to stick up for him. But it wasn't as if anyone could easily predict what they'd find themselves doing if pushed to the brink through torture.

Theo must have been thinking along similar lines. His mouth set in a grim line. "I hope that he won't, but if the guards get their hands on him and realize he's one of us, there's no telling how they'll force the issue."

"Maybe he'll think better of rushing in there once he's out at the palace alone," Kip said. "It's one thing to think about taking on the whole lot of them on his own and another to be faced with the reality."

I hoped he was right, but my stomach stayed tight. Mallo spat on the ground.

"We're all going to end up stir-crazy stuck down here like rats in a warren while the guards pick off the city folk a batch at a time."

She gave me an accusing look that might have made me wince with guilt not that long ago. But I had a queen's sword in my hand, a queen's armor over my chest, and a queen's scepter at my back. Less than an hour ago, I'd commanded more magic than most of these people had witnessed in their lifetime. I'd commanded the desires of two of the most powerful men I'd ever met.

If the Spades needed to know that we'd do more than cower in tunnels under my rule, I could show them that now. Still careful, still weighing the risks, but taking the chances we could afford to keep everyone's spirits steady.

"He might be out there working up his nerve," I said. "Let's go for him. Hatter, Chess, you come with me the shortest route through the city with the masks. Theo, you take the fastest Spades around along the fringes to meet up with us in case we end up with a fight on our hands. We'll circle the palace grounds and bring him back if we can."

Theo's eyebrows arched as if he was a little startled by my taking charge, but he didn't argue. After that split-second hesitation, he spun on his heel and swept his hand through the air.

"Mallo, Kip, you know who to round up. Grab a few small weapons too. I'll bring some of those devices we've been working on. We move out in five minutes."

He bent over the supply pile and offered me a couple of the dark metal eggs I knew would explode with a billow of smoke. "You should have some extra tools on hand too."

"I'll carry them," Chess offered. "I believe our queen has her hands full." He winked at me as he tucked a smoke bomb into each of his pant pockets.

"All right." My breath snagged in my throat now that we were putting this plan into action. It still felt like the right thing to do, for both Dee and all the people looking up to me now. "Let's go."

As we hustled to the cave entrance closest to the palace, Hatter adjusted his suit jacket sleeves where he kept his stealthy hatpins. "Isn't it about time you got yourself a real weapon, oh mad one?" Chess teased.

Hatter rolled his eyes with a tweak of his top hat. "I've got one of those too." He patted his hip, where I noticed the end of a hilt protruding, the line of a dagger visible through the fabric of his slacks. "What weapons are *you* bringing, madder one?"

Chess grinned. "My fists do well enough when the bastards can't see them coming."

The spot where the caves slanted upward into a narrower passage led us into the cellar of what Chess had told me was a pillow-stuffing factory. Stray feathers drifted through the air as we clambered up the ladder into the back room where a few heaps of fabric and bags of down lay.

We were still several blocks from the road leading from the city toward the palace. Beyond the door, music thumped and wavering voices carried back and forth. I tugged my mask tighter over my face against the chemical scent of the roses.

We eased out right by the corner of the street and darted down the alley in the opposite direction. When we had to cross the main roads, we ducked our heads and bobbed with the music as we wove between the bodies as if joining their dance.

The sun was sinking by the time we left the irregular buildings of the city behind. In the sparse forest between the city and the palace, I tugged my mask down and drank in the fresh warm air, the smell of the dry earth clearing the last lingering hints of rose from my lungs. Until we got closer to the palace, anyway.

"We need to find Theo the material to make more of these," I murmured.

"Dum's been trying to track down the supplier he used to go to," Chess said. "The woman hasn't turned up. Either the guards have taken her or she's wandered off in her reveling. He'll keep looking."

My mind started spinning through other possibilities for protecting ourselves from the rose's drug so we could move around the city more freely, but every plan that came to mind seemed more ridiculous than the last. The Queen of Hearts had the upper hand here.

We couldn't let her gain even more of one.

The tall stone walls around the palace grounds came into view up ahead. We slowed, scanning the forest and the area along the wall for both Dee and any patrolling guards.

"He might have gone to the looking spot by the laughing trees," Hatter said. "Let's head that way first."

As soon as we came near the trees with their long thin leaves that vibrated together to create an eerie chittering sound, the hairs on the back of my arms rose. It wasn't hard to figure why no one liked coming through this part of the forest, which was why it made such a good hiding spot for a rebel lookout. Hatter darted up the holds on the one tree's trunk and descended a few moments later with a frown.

"No sign of him there, and I couldn't spot him anywhere I could see from the platform. Theo's group is getting close—we could intercept them if we continue that way." He pointed in the direction we'd already been heading.

"All right," I said, my throat constricting. The platform didn't give a perfect view around the whole palace—Dee could have been around the other side, or in a particularly sheltered spot amid the trees. But every step we took without finding him, the more likely it was that he'd already gone into the palace grounds.

Hatter touched my arm as we walked on, waiting until I met his green eyes. "If he's out here, we'll find him," he said. "He was upset, but the twins aren't stupid. He'd *have* to realize rushing in there on his own would only lose him his head."

"They might have caught him even if he changed his mind," I said, and then raised my chin. "But we can't think that way. We'll cover all the grounds around the palace just in case, like we decided."

"That's our queen," Chess said, with a pleased glint in his eyes and his grin.

Hatter had directed us well. He paused and rapped on the truck of a tree three times, and an answering knock came from deeper in the forest a second later. With only the slightest rustling, Theo and the six Spades he'd assembled strode forward to join us.

He hadn't brought Dum along, I noticed. He must have been worried about the guy's emotional state, potentially losing both his mother and his brother in the same day. Dear God, please let us save at least one of them.

I pointed with my sword for us to keep along our circuit of the walls, and Theo nodded without a word. We walked on quietly, the Spades fanning out a bit between the trees to scan more ground.

The trees thinned up ahead where a road passed through the forest. As we slowed, a distant creaking sound reached my ears. I froze, my head jerking toward it. Toward the palace gate that opened onto this road.

With a shout and a thunder of booted feet, a horde of guards spilled onto the road and charged toward us. If I'd had an instant's hope that they were stampeding off to tackle some other foe, it was destroyed the second several of them veered into the forest on our side, their gazes sweeping the shadows. Someone on watch must have spotted us.

"Shit," Kip muttered, taking a step back.

The words rose in my throat to yell at the others to run. But even as my lips parted, doubt gripped me. There were dozens of guards rushing toward us. I couldn't say for sure we'd make it to one of the cave entrances without them catching any of us—and even if we did, we'd have led them straight to our shelter.

And all the Spades would have seen of their queen was a woman who turned tail and fled rather than defending them.

My legs balked for just a second, and then I leapt into the road, raising my sword high. "Go!" I said to the others. "As fast as you can. I'll slow this bunch down."

"Lyssa," Hatter said, his eyes wide, but I'd already swung around to face the onslaught of guards. Several more shouts were ringing out at the sight of me. Blades flashed in the fading sunlight, but they were nothing compared to mine.

My fingers tightened around the grip with all the conviction I had in me. The ruby flared. I didn't want to spill blood, but if it was my people or the Queen's, I had to protect mine.

When I'd sent out the sword's magic before, it'd both walloped and sliced. Maybe I could control those effects more consciously. I focused all my intent on driving the guards back, and slashed the blade through the air in a sweeping arc.

Power surged through my body and across the road, radiating into the trees. It slammed into the wave of guards, a more concentrated punch than the deflecting magic my vest had protected me with in an earlier battle. They stumbled backward, doubling over, blood springing along cuts on their arms and their pleated uniforms waving tattered where some of the cutting magic had slipped through.

"I am the true queen of Wonderland," I hollered at them, pitching my voice as forcefully as I'd heard Theo use his. "I will take back what's mine from the people who stole it from me. I will protect the people you've abused. You know I don't want to hurt you. If you'll give up your loyalty to the tyrant on the throne and join the Spades, we'll welcome you. But if you attack us, I have no choice but to push back."

The guards at the front of the rush had taken the brunt of my magical smackdown. Many more pushed past their wounded companions. Their expressions were warier now, but they raced at me with swords and daggers drawn anyway. A few of the faces I glimpsed looked more terrified than furious, so much that my heart ached.

Then the Knave appeared by the top of the wall by the gate, jabbing his sword toward me and letting out a roar from his tiger maw. "Strike them all down. Kill the usurper!"

The guards' faces hardened. They were making their choice. I'd already told them what mine would be.

I whipped my sword in front of me again, letting it sharpen this time. The magic crackled from its shining blade and sliced across the front line of the charge. The forerunners stumbled and toppled with a gush of blood down their bellies. The punch of power drove the figures behind them backward onto their asses.

My stomach turned at the sight of the men I'd likely killed, and my breath burned in my throat from just those two swings of the sword. I had to buy us a little more time to safely make our escape. Setting my jaw, I glanced around and made two swift jabs through the air toward the sides of the road.

Two massive trees toppled across the cobblestones to block the road, their emerald-green leaves shivering. As the Knave screamed at his men, I swiveled around. Chess tossed his smoke bombs over the fallen trees to cover our escape even more. Theo was waiting farther up the road. He waved us on, and Chess and I dashed to him, to flee the way he'd sent the other Spades running.

We hadn't found Dee. I guessed we'd have to hope he found his way back to us on his own. But I'd staked my claim on Wonderland, and I'd shown the Queen's defenders that I was a true force to be reckoned with.

CHAPTER FOURTEEN

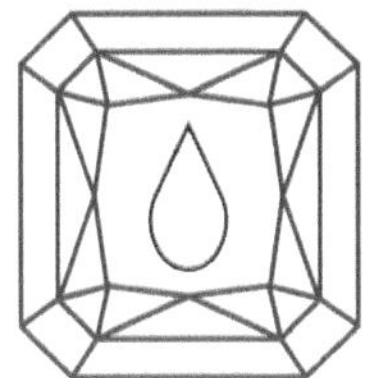

Theo

Lyssa's brainstorm had grown from a small bit of company to a crowd in the course of a day. Sixteen of the city's citizens sprawled or wandered around the shallow branch of cave where we'd laid out blankets and food for them. With only hours having passed since their last dose of that mind-muddling drug, the dazed look hadn't completely left their eyes, but a few of them were starting to register that this wasn't just some exclusive club they'd been invited to experience.

"I don't understand," said the woman I was crouched down in front of. She pulled her blanket closer around her trembling shoulders. "My head aches. I don't remember what I've been doing for… I don't know how long. How did I *get* here?"

"You know the smoke and 'shrooms you'd sometimes take in Caterpillar's Club?" I said, keeping my voice calm. "The Queen of Hearts has filled the whole city with intoxicants like that. Everyone up there has been partying like they're constantly at the club for weeks." I pointed to the stone ceiling.

The woman's chin wobbled. "Why would the Queen do *that*? I don't—I have my shop to check on. I—"

She shifted forward, and I grasped her shoulder. "You'll need to stay here a little longer," I said. "We brought you down here to get you away from the chemicals so you can clear your head. Your shop won't be safe yet. But we're working on it."

I tipped my head toward Lyssa, who was at the other side of the cave talking with an older man with a hound's head whose hands twitched in jerky movements. "The Queen of Hearts is afraid because Wonderland is finding out that she isn't a real queen after all. Her family stole the throne from the true rulers, the Red royal line. And our true queen has come back to us. The Red Queen is going to lead our way back to the world we're meant to have."

The woman peered a Lyssa with a puzzled but awed expression that brought a smile to my face. "Our true queen," she murmured.

"It's never really seemed right, having one we're afraid of, has it?" I said gently. "That's because it wasn't right at all. All along, a cruel imposter has been on the throne. We can have so much better than that."

The puzzlement melted into pure relief. I gave the woman's shoulder a light squeeze and stood up to see who else might appreciate exchanging a few words.

Looking at the people gathered there—*my* people, part of me still insisted—the impulse bubbled up to step into the middle of the room and command their attention, to guide them more like the White Knight than one of many Spades. More like a prince. The thought made me cringe inwardly.

Whatever influence my mother and the line of Hearts before her had inflicted on me, through exposure or genetics, I wanted to shed all of it. I could use those princely airs to reassure and to direct these people toward the ruler they ought to be focused on.

Lyssa caught my gaze on her and shot a small smile my way before stepping to welcome the next of the city folk. That woman's head was lolling on her shoulders, but her eyes held on Lyssa for a few seconds as the Otherlander spoke. You'd hardly know she grew up in the Otherland, seeing her now. She'd found her true self here with us.

Pride filled my chest, seeing the results of that transformation, even though I couldn't really claim much credit for it.

I helped a goat-like man whose hands were shaking around his cup drink some water and reassured a teenaged boy who was still pretty out of it but had started mumbling about where his sister might be. "We'll keep an eye out for her," I told him. "If we see her, she'll be invited here too, I promise."

Lyssa finished her rounds at about the same time I did. I stepped into the passage beyond the cave with her, blinking my eyes against the brighter glow of the water there. Then I reached for her hand, as naturally as if I had no reason to think the gesture would be anything but welcome, but ready inside to pull back if she stiffened.

She'd wanted me earlier today—she'd given herself over, and then taken me over in a way I remembered with a fresh bolt of desire through my groin. But that didn't mean every sore point between us was fully healed.

To my joy, Lyssa's hand welcomed mine, her fingers curling to grasp my palm.

"You're doing well," I told her. "Every bit a queen—all the queen they could ask for."

She smiled, but this time it looked tight. "I hope so. This afternoon… I wanted the Spades, at least, to see how committed I am. And now the Queen of Hearts knows for sure what I'm after. And I—I killed at least some of those guards…"

Her voice dropped with the last words. I stopped and turned her to face me. She hesitated, but only for a second before leaning into my embrace.

"You were brilliant out there," I said, my heart wrenching at the thought of her feeling guilty over that moment of glory. "They meant to kill as many of us as they could."

"I know." She nestled her head against my chest. I knew it was only for a moment, but I wished I could hold her like this, protect her with my arms around her, through everything that lay ahead. "I did what I had to do. It was the right choice—I'm not doubting that. I just… I hate having to make that choice."

"And that's why you're the queen we need," I said. "Just remember, we're fighting a woman who's mad as they come. Sometimes you have to get a little mad to fight back against madness. The more you can hold on to sanity in the fray, the more impressive it is."

"I'll try to keep that in mind," Lyssa said. When she exhaled, she sounded more settled. She pulled away from me and swiped her hand over the pale waves of her hair, rumpled from all the rushing around she'd been doing today. Her blue eyes still held a glow of their own even though weariness was starting to color her expression.

"How are you doing?" she asked me. "Are you sure you shouldn't be getting more rest, after the way they treated you in the palace?"

"I think all this running around has been good for me, actually," I said honestly. The spasms of my muscles, the startling flashes of images, and the pains in my head had all retreated behind adrenaline and motion as the day had gone on. "She only had me for a couple of weeks, after decades of going my own way. It shouldn't take too long for me to shake whatever she did completely."

Lyssa squeezed my hand. "All right. I don't want my White Knight running himself ragged."

"I won't," I said, with a twinge at the name I wasn't sure I could really own now. "And *you* need to rest," I said. "The guards haven't shown any sign of discovering our hide-out. We can decide how to tackle them next in the morning."

Lyssa's lips pursed, but she nodded.

Not entirely trusting her to actually get that rest once we reached the camp, I walked her all the way to the cabin she'd been sharing. She narrowed her eyes at me, but she tugged me in for a quick kiss before she opened the door. The press of her mouth against mine even for that brief moment left me hungry for more. I wasn't sure I could ever get enough of her.

When she'd ducked in, I turned away and noticed Dum's slouched posture where he was spooning up soup from a bowl outside his own cabin. The cabin he'd been sharing with Dee, as well as Chess and Hatter. Dum had always been the more down-to-earth and solemn of the twins, but he'd rarely acted outright glum. The gloom of his current situation hovered over him like a storm cloud. Even his red hair appeared to have dulled.

I'd failed him. I'd sworn to their mother I'd keep both of them from harm, and I'd lost his brother. Why hadn't I seen that Dee was shaken enough to take drastic action?

All of Mother's damned "treatments" had been addling my thoughts and my senses. Perhaps I was mostly healed now, but I'd been distracted too often since I'd returned. I needed to make sure I kept control of my mind and my body from here on.

I grabbed an apple from our food supply and hunkered down on the cool rock next to Dum. He looked up from his bowl and made an effort to straighten his stance, as if he thought I'd be offended by his downcast demeanor.

"I'm sorry," I said. Best to get that out there first, especially if he was acting as though he owed *me* something. "I really hoped we'd find him. He may return to us yet. He's never let the Hearts' Guard catch him before."

"That's true," Dum said. His lips slanted at a crooked angle. "But I think something has shifted in him. I don't know how it'll have shifted his reactions in turn."

I tipped my head to the side. "What do you mean?"

Dum shrugged. "I wouldn't have said anything to you before. It didn't matter. Maybe you already noticed anyway. But since we were kids, when we first started helping with the Spades on the sidelines, it always seemed to me like Dee saw the whole rebellion as some kind of game. An adventure where we just had to play well enough and we'd win, like the games in your apartment in the Tower. I could never get him to take things totally seriously. He didn't have to. No one we were close with ever got caught. We never got really hurt. He could always keep that delusion going to stop himself from getting too scared."

I hadn't gotten quite the same impressions Dum had, but he'd know his brother better than I did. His suggestion explained how Dee had managed to stay in such high spirits throughout the missions, even when we'd faced setbacks. In some ways, the approach had served him well.

"But you think that's changed," I prompted. "Because of your mother being taken?"

"That," Dum said. "And you being gone before that. He was

having trouble keeping up that carefree face he always wanted to show the world. He wouldn't talk to me about it, but I could see it. The fears were creeping in, and he couldn't push them back the same old ways. I'm just worried that finding out about Mom pushed him over some sort of edge. I don't know *what* he'd do if he really panicked."

"We'll do our best to find him and bring him back," I said, which was the best I could really say. "All of us. If we can save him, we will."

"I should have talked him down when he was here," Dum said. "He's *my* brother. Even I couldn't figure out the right thing to say." He raised his head. "It won't be your fault if he's gone too far for us to bring him back, is all I'm saying."

His whole family's lives were at stake, and he was trying to reassure *me*. My throat constricted. I clapped him on the back. "It won't be yours either. Don't you ever doubt that."

I left him to his meal, the talk of siblings and fear leading me across the camp to the new cabin the Spades had set up for my own sibling's use. I wasn't sure Mirabel could have tolerated sharing such close quarters with anyone else. As it was, she'd barely left the small structure since I'd arrived here.

As I'd used to when I'd arrive at her apartment in the Tower, I knocked on the door. "Come in," Mirabel said immediately, as she would have then too. I eased open the door and ducked inside to check in on my older sister.

She was sitting against the back wall, her legs drawn up under the soft white folds of her woolen skirt, a book propped against her knees. After a second, I realized the volume was upside down. I decided not to mention that fact. For all I knew, she'd managed to read it just fine like that.

"I didn't think I'd see you so soon," she said, with that dreamy air that made me wonder whether she was viewing time backwards or forwards right now. Or maybe a little of both, as seemed to becoming increasingly common these days.

"I wanted to make sure you're settling in all right," I said. "I know this is pretty different from the Tower."

Mirabel let out a light laugh. "Anywhere is fine if it's not where

Mother is." She paused, her gaze searching mine. "She comes close. I don't like her that close."

Before or after now? I swallowed hard. "I'll do whatever I can to make sure she never touches you again. You know you have my word on that."

"Yes. Yes." The urgency left her expression. She relaxed back against the wall. Then her forehead furrowed, a more melancholy shadow crossing her face. "We survived it, didn't we? As much as it hurt. As many as we lost."

A chill ran over my skin. I couldn't help asking, even though I knew my chances of getting a straight answer were slim, "What do you mean, Mirabel? What did we survive? Who did we lose?"

She rocked slightly from side to side. "Queen against Queen, Spade against Spade, family against family, friend against friend. We all turn on each other in the end. And only one can come out the other side."

CHAPTER FIFTEEN

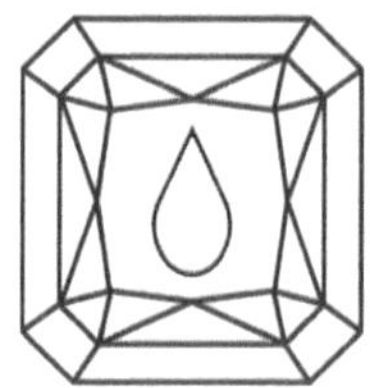

Lyssa

My mind felt more alert, if no less cluttered, after the exhausted sleep I'd toppled into. I rolled my shoulders as I considered the city people the Spades had gathered in the cave room. They seemed to be waking up in their own way too.

A few newcomers, brought in early this morning, lounged in the hazy blue light that reached the back of the cave room like they might have in one of the club's shallow pits, a faint rosy smell drifting off their clothes. The ones who'd spent the night with us were starting to ask a lot more pointed questions.

"The Inventor was here last night, wasn't he?" said one of the women Theo had talked to yesterday, peering around me as if I might be hiding him. Her gaze focused back on me, and she knit her brow. "He said you're a queen."

"I'm the Red Queen," I said. The words came more easily every time I said them. "A long time ago, my family ruled Wonderland—without anyone losing their heads. The Reds believed in spreading happiness, not fear. The Hearts slaughtered all of them except one princess who escaped to the Otherland. That was hundreds of years ago, and the Queens of Hearts wiped out every trace of us they could. But they couldn't wipe *us* out. And now I'm here, to set things right."

A woman I'd talked to yesterday stepped closer with eyes much sharper than they'd been before. "Do you really think you can do that? It's the Spades down here, isn't it? They've only made trouble the whole time I've been alive."

The man with the hound's head shuddered where he was hunched by the wall. "The Spades? If the Queen finds out we've been taken in by them, she'll have all our heads."

Several others in the cave stirred nervously. My chest tightened. Before anyone else could start fretting, I held up my hand.

"Don't you remember all those years you were stuck repeating the same day over and over? The Spades freed you from that magic. We're helping you now, bringing you down here so you can clear your head from the drug the Queen of Hearts was forcing on you."

"As if we had any choice about it," the skeptical woman said.

"*Now* you have a choice," I pointed out. "You can think properly. Do you want to go back up to the city and be taken over by that drugged daze again? You can if you want to, and the guards will never know you were gone. But you won't be able to look after yourself either. They've been stealing people from the city, you know. Grabbing cartfuls of you and shipping you out to the Oyster Cove to be pearled. Down here, you're safe from that too."

"Pearled?" the first woman repeated. She hugged herself. "Why would the Queen want *that*?"

"I don't know," I said. "We're trying to figure that out. But it can't be good for anyone. I've seen the guards with my own eyes—they were taking dancers off the street, people who hadn't done anything wrong. The guards weren't even pretending they had a good reason. Everyone up there is so out of it, they didn't even think to protest. That's what you'd be going back to."

The houndish man glanced toward the ceiling with a pensive expression. "I don't like that. But I'm not ready to join some kind of fight. That'd get us killed even faster."

I inhaled slowly, willing my nerves to settle. The most important thing was convincing the Clubbers to stay down here where they couldn't betray our location. Where we'd still have a chance of convincing them to join the cause. As long as they were with us, the rest could wait—forever, even, if that was what they wanted.

This had been my idea. I couldn't let it become the Spades' downfall.

"You don't have to join in any missions," I said. "You don't even need to help out with our camp down here if you don't want to. We'll keep you as comfortable as possible and make sure you're fed. All we want is to know you're safe. As your queen, I serve *you*. I'm not going to demand your help when you hardly know me. There'll be no pressure on you. Just stay here, stay protected, at least until we can make the city up there safe again."

The jitters that had passed through the bunch of them faded. The houndish man sucked in a breath.

"All right," he said. "I don't like how I felt up there—I don't like anything the Queen's done to us. If you're not asking anything from us, I'm in no hurry to throw myself back on *her* mercy."

The skeptical woman frowned. "I'm not either. But if you're some kind of queen, you're going to do more than this, aren't you? What about our friends? Our families? My father must be wandering around up there still. Are you going to stuff all of us down in these caves before she has the chance to pearl any more of us?"

I swallowed hard, my thoughts slipping to Dee, who I *hoped* was only wandering around up there and not already locked in the palace dungeon or being shipped to the Cove. "We're doing everything we can to stop the Queen of Hearts completely," I said. "I don't want any more people taken. If I can stop her *today*, I will."

I had no idea whether that was even remotely possible, but the answer seemed to satisfy the woman for the moment. She bobbed her head to me and sat back down on her blanket. I hurried back through the tunnels to see what kind of plans I could actually make.

As I came up on the main camp, the blue glow of the stream caught on the shiny fabric of Hatter's top hat farther down the passage. He'd been off on sentry duty, if I remembered right. It reassured me a little, seeing the bit of jaunt in his stride as if he wasn't all that fazed by the fact that we were now fighting our rebellion literally from underground. The smile he gave me warmed me even more.

"How are our refugees doing?" he asked when he reached me.

"About as well as I could have hoped, I think," I said. "I've managed to convince them they're better off staying down here for the time being."

"I happen to know you can be very persuasive," he said, an amused glint in his eyes.

"I wouldn't have needed to persuade you so much if you'd been more helpful to begin with," I reminded him.

"Fair point." He leaned in to kiss me as if he couldn't quite help himself, and I was more than happy to return it. But as much as I might have liked to lose myself in that heady sensation for longer, I had come back here with a purpose.

"Do you know where Theo is?" I asked. He normally got up early, but I didn't see him around the camp.

To my relief, Hatter nodded. "I passed him on my way here. He was heading out to take his turn guarding the entrance near the palace. I think he wanted to check up on the protections he set up last night."

After our close call with the guards, the Prince of Hearts had made whatever use he could of the materials and devices the other Spades had scavenged to hopefully buy us some time if the guards traced our path. Since they hadn't turned up yet, we seemed to have gotten off scot-free, but it couldn't hurt to have the defenses in place.

"All right," I said with a rush of purpose. "Then that's where I'm going too."

Hatter raised an eyebrow at me. "What are you up to, looking-glass girl? You almost look a little mad."

I made a face at him. "Maybe I need to be a little mad to go up against a Queen who couldn't be madder," I said, remembering Theo's words last night. "You're not exactly one to talk, Mad Hatter."

He let out a laugh, but concern had softened his gaze. "Which is exactly why I know the risks involved in letting loose that way."

"You should also know by now I'm not the type to go right off the rails. I actually have a very good track record with trains." I gave him a teasing shove. "Go do whatever else you're supposed to be doing now. Maybe I'll come back with a crown on my head."

His eyebrows rose even higher. "I'll look forward to that, then," he said, and stole one last kiss before heading into the camp.

The Spades had marked the passages around the stream with chalk symbols long before I'd made it back to Wonderland. I was becoming familiar enough with the usual routes now that I barely needed to look at them as I treaded over the rough stone beside the rippling water. Getting to the palace exit required a scramble across a makeshift bridge and a few turns.

The mineral scent in the air thickened as the stream narrowed until I could have hopped across it without any bridge at all. It veered to the right. At my left, a narrow passage slanted upward into a room about the size of my apartment kitchen back home.

Theo was standing by the far wall where carved footholds led up to the trap door, fixing slim silver rod just beneath the door with a faint squeak. He gave the base one last twist and turned to face me as I slipped into the small space.

"Everything's still as you wanted it?" I asked.

"I made a few adjustments I thought of overnight," he said. "I may not be the Inventor anymore, but my mind still leaps into those ways of thinking automatically."

"Good for us that it does," I said with a smile.

Theo studied me. "You didn't come out here just to find out about that," he said. "What is it, Lyssa?"

He'd always been able to take a quick read of my mood. I guessed there wasn't any point in beating around the bush.

"I want us to move on the palace as soon as we can," I said. "Too many people are being hurt. I want the hold the Queen of Hearts has over Wonderland severed as quickly as possible, not with a drawn out war. When we found you, in the palace, you said something about clearing the way to the throne for me. What exactly did you do? What do we need if we're going to see that plan through?"

I'd thought Theo had recovered his balance yesterday. Now, with the abrupt clenching of his jaw, I knew he hadn't completely shaken the effects of his mother's torment yet. He closed his eyes for a second, his throat working as he composed himself. The obvious strain made my heart ache for him.

"My apologies," he said, his voice only slightly rough. "Yes. I— The Queen of Hearts has more than one throne. There's one most people never get to see her sitting on, farther into her inner chambers than the looking-glass I sent you through. Seeing it while I was there these past weeks, I realized it's another artifact of the Red royal rule. I believe my family has harnessed the magic in it somehow to their own ends—it's the source of her magic. If you can reclaim it, I don't think defeating her will be difficult after that."

My heart leapt, but only for an instant before I thought of all the obstacles still in the way. "How do I reclaim it?"

"Once you get to it, I managed to fix a small device to one of the panels, that when triggered should crack through the cage of sorts she's built around it to control it. Then all you should need to do is sit on it and let it welcome you." Theo gave me a crooked smile. "Of course, the greater trouble is getting you that far into the palace to begin with. And not just you, but enough of us to protect you while we subdue my mother. Even without any magical power, some of the guards will still listen to her. You couldn't take her and them on alone."

"Okay," I said, mulling her words over. "So we really just have one problem—how to get me and at least a few Spades into the Queen's inner quarters. That's a *tricky* problem, but at least it only needs one solution, and then we're ready to go."

Theo chuckled. "You do know how to look on the bright side. We'll get you there. *I'll* get you there. Those city folk you've been collecting may sway the balance too."

"I don't know. They didn't seem too enthusiastic about the cause this morning." But that could change. I opened my mouth to ask another question, and a raised voice filtered through the trap door above us, far too close for comfort.

"This is it. I'm telling you."

My mouth snapped shut. Even muffled by the layer of wood, it sounded like… Dee. Another, deeper voice was already answering him.

"You'd better not be yanking us around. If this is a trick, your head will be on a pike within the hour."

That growl was the Knave—I was almost sure of it. My eyes caught Theo's and found his expression was as distraught as I felt. Then Dee spoke up again.

"Why would I come to you and make this offer if I was lying? I just want the deal we made—I want my mother freed—you promised that, didn't you?"

A dismissive guffaw from one of the other men above didn't dislodge the horror that swelled inside me in an instant.

The Hearts' Guard hadn't forced Dee into giving us up. He'd gone to them intending to betray us.

CHAPTER SIXTEEN

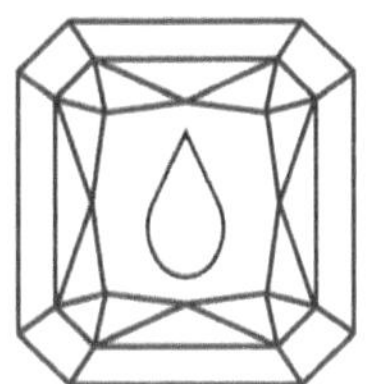

Lyssa

Theo grabbed my arm. "Let's get out of here," he said under his breath. "*Fast.* We have to warn the others."

As I scrambled after him into the longer passage with the glowing stream, the trap door's latch was already grating to the side. Shit. My heart thumped with a lurching beat. How could Dee have given us all up like that—even his own brother?

We broke into a run along the side of the stream. "What are we going to do?" I said to Theo.

His mouth had gone tight. "The measures I put in place will slow them down exactly as I intended. I just didn't expect one of our own to be helping set them off. Damn it."

Nausea coiled around my stomach. "What else do you think he might have told them? What if there are guards at all the exits?"

Theo shook his head. "I have to believe he still had some concern for us and the cause. The way he was talking up there—he'd have known that by pitching his voice that loud, anyone standing guard down below would hear it. And he knew there'd be a sentry at that entrance. He sold us out, but he purposely gave us a little warning. I don't think he wants us dead. He just wanted a big enough bargaining chip to save his mother."

It was hard to picture the happy-go-lucky guy I'd been getting to know scheming like that, but I hoped Theo was right. "Do you think the Queen will keep up her end of the deal she made with him?"

Theo's lips curled into a grimace. "I wouldn't count on it. Even if he'd served us all up on a platter, she'd probably enjoy laughing in his face and sending him off to be pearled with the rest of them. He'll have admitted he was a Spade. That's a death sentence right there. She'll never trust him to stay in 'her' kingdom."

Then we'd better make it my kingdom before it came to that. My breath ragged in my throat, I pushed my legs even harder.

A crashing sound echoed through the passage behind me. I startled, nearly tripping over my feet. Theo steadied me.

"That's the main trap," he said with grim satisfaction. "It'll take them at least a few minutes to work their way through that."

A sentry from one of the smaller secondary camps came into view up ahead. "Get everyone to move out!" I hollered to her. "Right away, take only what you have to. The guards have found the way into the River Down." I paused for a second, searching my whirling thoughts for the right strategy. "Leave through the forest exit. We'll regroup on the other side of the mushroom fields." Please, let that be far enough.

Between our fight and flight yesterday and the stress my body had been through in the weeks before that, I couldn't keep up the same pace as Theo for much longer. A burn nibbled at my legs and chest. He slowed as I did, but I nudged him onward. "I'll catch up. You get to the main camp and sound the alarm there. As soon as I've got my sword, I can push back anyone who comes at us down here."

We still had to leave, though. Now that the guards knew that the Spades were using these underground passages, we'd never be safe down here again.

Theo squeezed my hand and forced himself to let go. I kept up a steady lope as he pulled ahead. The prickling burn spread on through the muscles in my calves.

When I made it to the main camp, everyone was already grabbing their things and heading farther along the stream. Theo had retrieved my sword and my scepter from my cabin where I'd left them. I didn't have anything else here that mattered all that much to me. Theo handed the artifacts to me and gripped Mirabel's arm where she was standing wide-eyed next to him to urge her along. Chess fell in with us at my other side. Hatter glanced back from up ahead where he was hurrying Doria along, and the mass of us hustled on through the caves.

The stream's blue glow wavered over our bodies. The Spades stayed quiet, but the noise of so many hurrying footsteps echoed through the cave. I kept glancing back over my shoulder, waiting to see a flash of red-and-pink tunic. How long would it take the Knave and the other guards to break through Theo's defenses?

He was fiddling now with a round device about the size of a coaster, with a shell of dark gray metal and a clump of tiny wires protruding from its upper edge.

"What's that?" I asked him in a hushed voice.

"Something to cover our escape," he said. "I didn't think I was going to be using it down here, but if I adjust the intensity of the shock..."

That sounded a little ominous. We passed the third camp and stirred everyone there into action. My pulse stuttered at the thought of the city people we'd brought down here, the ones I'd been talking to no more than an hour ago. I'd promised them they'd be safe, and now the guards were coming right down here.

"The Clubbers," I said. "We can't leave them."

"Of course not," Theo said. "Chess and I will get them. That'll be the perfect place to cut off the charge anyway."

The fork in the passage opened up ahead of us, one side leading to the Clubbers' room, the other to the forest exit. Theo motioned to my sword. "Hold off anyone who comes this way. We'll be back as soon as we can, and then I'll blockade the guards completely."

There wasn't time to ask him how he was going to do that. He motioned to Chess, and the two of them dashed down the left passage toward the cave where the Clubbers had been recovering. In front of me, the other Spades kept running. I stopped at the fork and spun around, sword at the ready.

The hasty footsteps on either side of me faded away. I stood braced, my fingers clutching the sword's hilt, my ears pricked for the slightest sound of our pursuers.

It didn't take long. Theo's traps might have slowed the guards down, but they hadn't needed to stop to warn anyone or grab anything. The distant rasp of dozens of boots scraping the rocky ground carried to me, getting louder by the second. My gut knotted. I raised my sword a little higher.

They emerged into the hazy light like a mass of crimson, the mix of red and pink reminding me of butcher's meat. At first it was hard to pick apart individual forms. They barrelled toward me along both sides of the street, their blades flashing with the blue light, and I made out the Knave's tiger head at the front of the pack. He wasn't hanging back shouting orders today. No doubt after yesterday's embarrassment, he wanted to sever my head from my body himself.

Too bad, buddy. I intended to keep it right where it belonged.

My muscles ached with tension, but I held myself still, poised. The thunder of their feet and the warble of harsh breaths and muttered curses filled the passage. There was no point in playing my hand too soon. I didn't want to wear myself out. Only when I had to, I'd press them back.

Chess and Theo had better get those city people over here fast.

There was no sign of Dee in the midst of the guards. They must have left him behind, either suspecting he might try to sabotage their efforts at the last second or not wanting him to get in the way. It wasn't as if the guy was a fighter.

Something else struck me about the faces scattered around the Knave as the horde came more clearly into view. Not just a few but at least a dozen of those I could see had the glazed look of the pearl-heads I'd noticed before. Their expressions were slack, their eyes fogged, as dazed as the Clubbers were when under the influence of the rosy drug. Their bodies moved in a relentless forward charge as if nothing existed inside them except the impulse to carry out the orders they'd been given.

No doubt those orders included slicing through any Spades they encountered.

I shivered with a sudden, chilly certainty. *This* was why the Queen of Hearts had commanded her guards to round up people from the city—people healthy and strong. She was expanding her army by the day with unwilling soldiers. With innocents she'd murdered.

If I'd lacked conviction before to strike back with all the power I had in me, that realization would have summoned it. I adjusted my grip on the sword and tensed my muscles. They were only thirty feet away now. Twenty. Fifteen—

I lashed out, snapping the blade in a swift arc, the need to defend all the people fleeing behind me rolling off me and surging out through the air.

The sword's power smacked into the advancing force as if a sheet of metal had slammed into their middles. The guards buckled over and heaved backward at the same time, knocking into each other in a domino effect down several rows. Some stumbled and fell into the stream. Blood spilled across the floor where the sharpest edge of the magical blow had hit them.

I sucked the still air into my lungs and readied myself for another strike. The sound of pounding feet reached my ears again—from the passage beside me this time. Theo and Chess were urging our twenty or so recovered Clubbers toward me.

"Go!" I called to them. "Hurry! I can hold them off for now."

The woman who'd expressed so many doubts when I'd talked to her earlier glanced past me down the caves toward the horde of guards. Panic washed across her face, followed by a startled expression as she realized the men were struggling just to get up. Her gaze fell to my sword and then rose to my face. In that instant, for the first time, she looked at me like I really was a queen. Similar surprised relief lit up the expressions of her companions.

I waved them on down the tunnel, and they dashed the same way the Spades had gone. Chess loped with them, calling directions. Theo came to a halt beside me. He reached into his pocket and yanked out the coaster-shaped device he'd been tweaking earlier.

"It's time for you to go too," he said. "Let's see how well this works underground. Get ready to run."

He flipped a switch on the device and jammed it into a nook in the rocky wall. Hooking his hand around my elbow, he tugged me down the passage. I raced with him, but I couldn't stop myself from looking back over my shoulder at the eerie crackling that reverberated through the cave.

Sparks were shooting from the device. A bolt of searing white electricity leapt from its top and arced across the cave ceiling. Everywhere it touched, the stone cracked and split open.

The Knave roared on the other side of the device's path. He rushed toward us, one arm pressed against his abdomen where my sword's magic must have cut him, the other gesturing for his men to follow. He wasn't fast enough.

The ceiling shattered. Rocks rained down with a boom that rattled my ear drums. In an instant, that entire section of cave had collapsed in on itself, cutting us off from the rest of the underground.

Pebbles plummeted down even where we stood. At Theo's noise of warning, I started running again.

We darted through increasingly narrow passages until a familiar top hat came into sight in a streak of sunlight spilling down from an opening above. Hatter let out a relieved sound at the sight of us. "Everyone else is up," he said. "Come on, slow-pokes." He paused as he gripped the rungs of the ladder. "What in the lands was that noise back there?"

"I carried out a minor renovation to the caves' layout," Theo said, breathlessly wry. "There's now a wall where there once was a passage heading this way. If the guards want to catch us, they'll have to find their way back aboveground first."

Hatter's lips curled into a smirk. He scrambled nimbly up the ladder. Unwilling to let go of the sword that had saved us twice now, I heaved myself after him one-handed, the blade clinking against the rungs.

In the thick forest above, the fresh green smells of the vivid leaves filled my nose. Most of the Spades were already hustling off between the trees, aiming for the land beyond the mushroom field like I'd told them.

When I turned in the other direction, all I could see of the city amid the foliage was a sliver here and there of bright paint. My legs locked for a second. That city was part of *my* Wonderland. We were fleeing it, leaving it behind—abandoning all the people there who still needed my protection.

"We should get moving," Theo said, firmly but with sympathy in his eyes. "The Knave knows which direction we fled in; he'll suspect we came to ground somewhere. He'll send troops this way as soon as he can."

"I know." I did, but turning my back on the city still wrenched at me. I set my jaw and strode toward the mushrooms. We'd regroup and sort ourselves out, and then we'd come up with a plan for how to reclaim the ground we'd lost—and more.

No workers chattered and giggled in the mushroom field today. The giant orange-and-pink spotted forms loomed beside the path completely untended. I guessed Caterpillar didn't have any need to harvest his crop when the Queen was getting the entire city high with her doctored roses and the ingredients Rabbit was bringing from the Otherland.

More forest sprawled beyond the mushrooms. A cloud drifted over the sun as we tramped along, and a cool breeze tickled over my skin. How far did we need to go to make sure the Hearts' Guard didn't find us? *Could* we go far enough? They might track us all the way to the Topsy Turvy Woods with its massive upside down trees. The Queen wanted us all dead, one way or another.

I needed to make sure I could protect the people already with me before I could even think about the rest of the city.

Our companions had gathered in a clearing just out of view of the mushrooms. It might have been the same one where I'd trained with my sword and scepter the other day. The city people paced or swayed in the middle of the meadow while the Spades stalked along the perimeter as if on patrol, but they were here. A few of them had even picked up spare weapons the Spades had brought with them, watching the forest just as warily. A little awe touched me, looking at them.

The Clubbers might not be all the way ready to fight yet, but they were coming around to the cause. They'd chosen to stay with us rather than take their chances heading back to the city. We had more than twice the number of allies we could have counted on a few days ago. It was the start of a real army.

The thought sent a quiver of nausea down to my gut, but it steadied me at the same time. We *needed* an army. That much was clear. Even what we had now wasn't going to be enough.

"Where to now?" Dum asked, his gaze on me expectantly. "What should we do?"

Oh, fuck. It was up to me to figure that out too, of course. I had the urge to glance at Theo for guidance, but that might destroy the confidence I'd spent the last two days building in all these people watching. They'd want to know their queen could make her own call.

The guards might be coming behind us. Ahead of us lay that stretch of bizarrely shaped hills and then the Topsy Turvy Woods. Would it be easier to hide out there? Of course, I also had to consider that the last time I'd ventured that far, Hatter and I had nearly been lunch for a jabberwock…

Oh.

A smile leapt to my face with the spark of inspiration that had just lit in my head. I wanted to laugh, but I hadn't pulled my new plan off yet.

I reached behind me and tugged my scepter from its carry bag. Theo watched me with obvious curiosity.

"What are you going to do with that?" he asked.

"We don't want the guards catching up with us here," I said. "I'm going to put something between us and them that they won't want to tangle with. I'm going to call a jabberwock."

CHAPTER SEVENTEEN

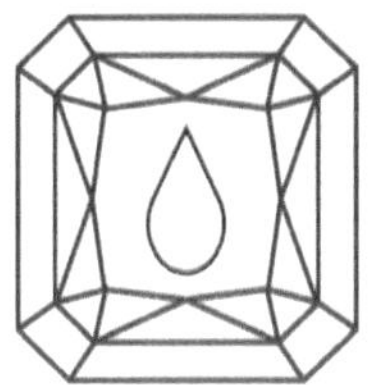

Hatter

"This is fucking *amazing*," Doria said, her face glowing with excitement as we moved through the forest. She bent to grab another stick to add to the pile of firewood in her arms. "Isn't it? Can you imagine the looks on their faces when they realized they'd have to go through a jabberwock to get to us?"

"It's pretty incredible," I said, maybe a little more dryly than she'd have hoped to get from my response. The truth was that an anxious twitch had been tugging at my ribs from the moment Lyssa had declared her intentions. Not even the evergreen tang in the warm summer air or the brightness of the sun—more sun than I'd gotten to experience in weeks—had managed to soothe it.

I was the one who'd once earned the name "Mad." If anyone around here could say a plan was completely bonkers, it should be me. Ordering jabberwocks to serve as our guard dogs was one hundred percent, beyond a doubt, utterly insane.

And yet our queen's first attempt had worked out so well, she was summoning a few more of the monsters right now.

I scooped another two thick branches into my arms and judged I wasn't going to be able to carry much more back to the camp without my arms falling off. Also, it was a good thing I'd become accustomed to my suits getting ruined on a regular basis, because this one's sleek blue fabric was now polka-dotted with bits of bark.

My daughter's arms looked heavily laden too. "I think this is enough for now," I said to her. "Let's head back before they start thinking a stray jabberwock has eaten us."

Doria gave me an amused look as we tramped through the brush toward the clearing where we'd set up a new sort of camp. "Once Lyssa brings more of them, she's going to start pushing the guards right out of the city, you know. That's what she said. But she'll need people on the ground helping the Clubbers stay out of the way and watching her back. I'm planning on going with her."

She kept eyeing me warily as she said the last bit. I didn't need any psychic powers to know she suspected I was going to argue about her plans.

A month ago, I probably *would* have argued. Even now, after everything all of us had been through together, after everything we'd survived, something deep in my chest screamed *No!* at the thought of Doria going up against the Hearts' Guard directly, even with a bunch of us and a herd of jabberwocks at her side.

I swallowed that scream down. If I'd learned anything from all those close calls, it was that these days hearing a "No" only made Doria more determined to follow through. She was coming up on fifteen, coming up on adulthood soon after. I'd taken plenty of mad risks with the Spades at her age.

March and May had wanted me to look after her, not lock her in a cage.

"Of course you do, Mouse," I said fondly. I'd have ruffled her hair for good measure if my arms hadn't been occupied with the heap of firewood. Doria made a face at me for the childhood nickname, but I wasn't done yet. There were things I should say that maybe I should have said even earlier.

"You don't need permission from me to run missions or pitch in however you think you best can," I went on. "I've seen how well you can handle yourself, especially in the last few weeks since we've come underground. I'm still going to worry, because as far as I know that's what parents are for, but I'll try not to inflict those worries on you too often. All I ask is that you make sure you're working *with* us, not running off to try something on your own like you did with that fiery sign outside the club."

Doria blinked at me. A slow smile spread across her face. "Yeah. Okay, I can handle that. I'm not in any hurry to revisit the palace dungeon anyway." She paused, and her voice softened. "Thanks, Dad."

Damn, she had grown into a capable young woman right in front of me, hadn't she? I found I had to add, "I'm proud of you, you know."

She brightened even more, and then a teasing glint lit in her dark eyes. "I'm proud of you too, Pops," she said, bumping her elbow against my arm. "You proved you're not just a stick in the mud after all."

I laughed. "I suppose I deserve that."

She grinned, but a moment later a shadow crossed her expression. Her gaze slipped away toward the forest ahead. I knew her well enough to guess what she might be thinking about.

"You and Dee were good friends," I said. "I know it must be hard—if you want to talk about anything to do with that, you can."

Her mouth tensed. "I'm not even totally sure what happened. Did he really sell us out? He *offered* to bring the guards to the River Down?"

The twins had been not just good friends but her best friends in the Spades. I wished I could save her from the pain of that kind of betrayal, but I had to be honest.

"I wasn't there, but from what Lyssa and Theo have said, there isn't much doubt. He didn't have anything else to bargain with, and he was frantic to save his mother." And he'd been shaken, no doubt, by all the revelations about the man he'd looked to as a leader. None of that excused him turning traitor, but the circumstances explained his betrayal at least a little. "Theo did say it sounded as if he tried to give warning, to make sure we'd get out in time. And that worked."

"Still." Doria kicked at a fallen twig. "I would never have

thought… We could all have been *killed.* How could he trust the Queen's people enough to even try to make a deal?"

"I don't know." I'd run missions with the twins and joked around with them afterward for a few years before my life had become focused on parenthood, but I couldn't say we'd really been close. "People can always surprise you. Sometimes in good ways, but sometimes in bad ways too."

She let out a sharp chuckle. "I still hope he makes it back to us in one piece. If only so I can shout his head off myself."

"Well, I don't think anyone would blame you for that—either part of it."

To my relief, the conversation appeared to have taken a small weight off her shoulders. She strode over to the pile of firewood in the camp with her usual energy.

Most of the city folk we'd taken in were sitting near the fire, gnawing on pieces of roast pigeon. Dum and a couple of the others had gone off on a hunting trip not long after we'd set down here. A prickle of annoyance passed over me looking at the bunch of Clubbers as I set down my wood in the pile too.

They were sitting on their asses enjoying our efforts, happy enough that we'd gotten them away from the Queen's influence but too scared of the consequences to really join in.

It was going to take time, I reminded myself. A lifetime of playing along and following the rules couldn't be switched off in an instant. It'd taken me long enough to recover my sense of righteous courage after holding back in caution for twelve years, and I'd had plenty of years of running wild before that.

Chess strolled over to meet us, the bright sun sparking in his auburn hair. He rubbed his hands together with one of his familiar grins.

"Are you ready?" he asked Doria. "We're heading out now."

Despite the way I'd talked myself down when she'd mentioned the impending mission, a flicker of panic shot through me. "Are you going to the city already?"

Chess tipped his head in that direction. "Our queen headed over with her first jabberwock not that long ago. She said she expected she could summon a few more before too long. They do move rather quickly when they're motivated. She wanted us to be ready to press on toward the city right away."

I supposed that was better than having a horde of jabberwocks prowling around *here*. I worked my jaw for a second and then said, "I'm coming along too."

"The more the merrier," Chess said. "We'll show the guards how the Spades throw a party." He beckoned, and a few more of the Spades joined us: Dum and Kip and a newer woman whose name I couldn't recall. There wasn't any sign of Theo around, but probably our former Inventor was conjuring up new tools for us wherever he could find the means.

With at least one monster making sure no guards came this way, we could take the faster path of the road rather than weaving out of sight through the forest and the mushroom stands. I spotted the jabberwock before I made out Lyssa. Or rather, jabberwock*s*. One sat right at the side of the road, its searing violet gaze aimed at the city as if daring anyone to try to travel this way. Another stood closer to the nearest buildings, ruffling its gold and scarlet feathers impatiently.

A third of the immense creatures was leaning right over Lyssa where she stood in the middle of the cobblestone lane. Streams of smoke trailed up from the jabberwock's wide nostrils as it nudged its snout against the scepter she was holding up. Its lips drew back, revealing the jagged teeth I'd seen another clamp around a guard's body just a few weeks ago.

Lyssa's lips were moving too, forming words too soft for me to make out across the distance. As we approached, her attention didn't waver from the beast in front of her. My pulse kicked up a notch as the sour stench of the creatures' breath reached my nose.

I'd watched Lyssa tame jabberwocks before, but I'd also seen one snap from her hold in an instant. That one was so close, it could have snatched her in its maw before she could so much as blink.

Just as that thought crossed my mind, the beast's head jerked up and then down again. My heart outright stopped. Before I had a chance to think anything else, my feet were already flinging me forward to grab Lyssa, to fling myself between the monster and the woman I loved if I had to.

The moment I leapt, a shudder passed through the jabberwock's bulky body. Its eyes flashed, and its head jerked again—toward me.

"Hey!" Lyssa said, a little louder now but still gentle. "Hey. Here. With me."

I stopped in my tracks. My heart thumped so hard it echoed through my head, every nerve insisting I had to get my queen, my lover, to safety, but I clenched my hands against the urge.

Lyssa knew what she was doing, I reminded myself. I had to trust her. My attempt to intervene had only incited the creature.

Chess came up beside me, touching my shoulder. I forced myself to take a slow step backward, and then another. The jabberwock shifted its focus to Lyssa again, and Doria let out a shaky breath, as much excited as relieved.

Lyssa rubbed the creature's muzzle with the gold-and-ruby end of the scepter, and the muscles coiled beneath its feathered skin appeared to relax. The jabberwock exhaled with a putrid huff. A satisfied sound reverberated in its throat. It blinked slowly and gazed down at the new Red Queen with a look I'd almost call adoring.

Now that we were closer, I could see there was a fourth jabberwock, already tamed, waiting amid the trees on the other side of the road. Its gaze was trained on Lyssa with a similar expression. She had won them over well, hadn't she? I never would have thought I'd see a jabberwock look at anything like that.

If she could keep them that loyal, we might really get somewhere.

Lyssa slid her scepter into the bag at her back and pulled her sword from the belted leather sheath Theo had hastily constructed for her. She pointed the blade toward the city. "We destroy the roses and clear off the men in the uniforms of the Hearts. Everyone else is our friend. Watch me and listen."

She glanced back at us and gave a quick nod. I couldn't blame her for not being able to spare us more than that brief gesture. By all means, let her stay focused on the massive beasts that could slaughter us all in a matter of seconds.

Three of the jabberwocks lumbered toward the city with our

queen. The one farthest back stayed in place to watch over the path to our camp. It narrowed its eyes at us as we passed, but apparently we passed muster. I wasn't keen to find out what it was going to do to anyone who didn't. How well could they identify the guards' uniforms, exactly?

As we passed the first few buildings, the revelers up ahead caught sight of the jabberwocks. Even in their dazed state, a few of the Clubbers shrieked.

"Go inside," Lyssa called out. "They won't hurt you, but it'll be easier for us to protect you if you're off the street. As soon as we've passed by, you can come back out. The Red Queen is here to take your city back for you and free you from the spell of the Queen of Hearts' roses."

With her last words, she pointed her sword toward a nearby heap of roses. One of the jabberwocks snorted and spewed out a spurt of flame. In an instant, only cinders and a faint burnt smell remained.

If we could burn up all the drugged roses and stop the guards from bringing more, the whole city *would* be freed.

I walked on with lightening spirits, pausing to reassure a trembling woman who'd frozen by the door of a shop, carefully slipping past the monsters to usher a few gaping kids into the shelter of a nearby house. In the Clubbers' current state, no one was likely to care which building belonged to whom.

Lyssa strode on between the jabberwocks without a hint of nerves. My gaze kept sliding back to her, wanting to revel myself—in the power she commanded, in the confidence she was finding in herself. She'd always been pretty, but now, with her eyes bright and her mouth set in a determined smile, she was more beautiful than I'd ever seen her.

It made me want to offer her more than meandering along here dealing with the stragglers.

When we reached the street with my hat shop, a tiny inspiration hit me. It wasn't much, but hopefully it'd give her a little comfort when she took a break from her work.

A few of the guards who'd been stationed there charged out and then fled with jabberwock fire scorching their heels. Lyssa directed one of the beasts to bring its head to an open second floor window, and I heard more scampering out the back of the building with shouts of alarm. I exchanged a glance with Chess.

"Let's make sure they're all cleared out?" I said. "We don't want any enemies lurking at our backs."

Chess nodded, and I pushed past the shop door. "Everyone out," I hollered, "or the jabberwocks will have you. This building belongs to the Spades now."

It turned out only one guard had stood his ground. He rushed at us on the stairs, and Chess heaved him on past us, leaving him crumpled in a heap at the bottom.

"Off with you," he said. "And run fast, or the beasts with have you for dinner."

I brandished my dagger in one hand and a hatpin in the other. The guard looked from one of us to the other, and then out the shop window at the feathered beasts beyond, and must have recalculated how much he valued his life. He darted out the back door.

A couple of now-stale scones sat on a plate in the kitchen. The bakery would be closed, the baker as muddled by drugs as the rest of the city, or I'd have grabbed more of those to bring back to the camp. Too bad.

On the top floor, I opened up the wardrobe Lyssa had been using and picked out a couple of the dresses I thought she'd favored. Since she'd arrived here, she'd been relying on her Otherlander clothes and a blouse and skirt one of the Spades had been able to lend her. Something clean and familiar should give her a least a bit of joy.

"For Lyssa?" Chess said from where he was leaning against the doorframe.

"It's the least I can think to do." I stared at the fabric in my hands, and suddenly this effort seemed ridiculous. "She's out there with jabberwocks looming over her on all sides, taking on all the guards in the city practically on her own. Doesn't it bother you that she's having to put herself through so much, and there's hardly a thing we can do to protect her?"

"I don't think Lyssa takes more onto her shoulders than her

shoulders can hold," Chess said in his typical offhand way. "When she needs us, we're here."

"It doesn't seem right to simply wait on the sidelines." Not for the woman I loved. Not when there was so much danger still ahead of us.

"It's hardly right to jump into the line of fire either, I expect." Chess cocked his head, and his tone turned more serious. "You know, when our queen heard of threats still hanging over me, the best thing she did for me was to simply ask what I needed and give me that. She didn't go charging off trying to take on the spirits of my past as if she didn't believe I could attend to them myself. She has my back, and I have hers, but we don't step in front of each other in our eagerness to prove our devotion. Treat her like she's whole, not like she's broken."

I couldn't help thinking of the state Chess had been in when he'd first come to me, years and years ago, after his torture at the Duchess's hands. The resetting of the day had ensured his body had returned to its previous state, but he'd flinched at almost every touch, at random noises. He'd spent five days holed up in my guest bedroom before he'd come back to himself enough to join myself and March and May even for dinner outside those four walls.

The buoyant, carefree man I'd always seen him as hadn't taken long to re-emerge, but perhaps that wasn't the whole story. The pain of the past could haunt a person a long time—I should know. Had he still felt broken?

However much he was speaking from his side of the experience as well, his words rang true. I'd only diminish the confidence I'd been admiring in our queen if I hovered around Lyssa braced for any possible catastrophe. Trying to guard Doria that avidly certainly hadn't helped anyone.

"That sounds… very reasonable," I said. "Even if I wish I could take more of the blows to come."

"Ah," Chess said, his smile coming back, "but she wouldn't wish that, don't you see?"

Perhaps not well enough, but I'd have plenty of time to practice shifting my inclinations during the battles to come. I bundled up the dresses and headed back down the stairs, stopping only to duck into my bedroom and grab a fresh suit for myself as well.

My gaze roved over the shelves beside my bed automatically and halted. I frowned, stepping closer to check the floor.

The sketch of Alicia's house—the house Lyssa had since inherited—wasn't sitting where I'd left it. It didn't appear to have fallen, either. Where had that slip of paper gotten to?

A roar echoed through the walls, and the hairs on the backs of my arms jumped up. That minor mystery could wait for another day. I dashed toward the street to see how I might have my queen's back now.

CHAPTER EIGHTEEN

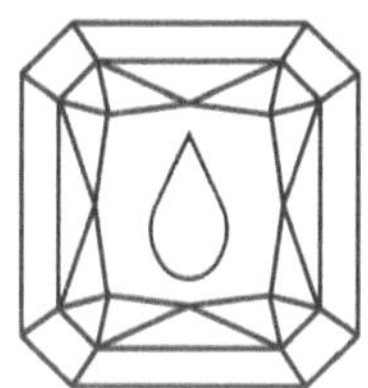

Lyssa

In the morning, we'd fled the city. Now, between streaks of amber lamplight, I was bringing the Clubbers home. While I watched their faces as we walked past the first buildings, as they breathed in the clearing air and took in the burnt piles the jabberwocks had reduced the Queen's roses to, a glow lit up inside me—a sense of accomplishment more potent than anything I'd felt before.

In some ways, the Queen of Hearts had stolen these people's home from them. She'd turned it into a place where they had no choice but to live in a drug-addled daze. I'd freed them from her and given back everything she'd taken from them.

Almost everything she'd taken from them. I couldn't say they really had their freedom until I'd managed to strip her guards of their weapons and her of all her power. But for now, this felt like a pretty epic victory.

The jabberwock lumbering along beside me let out a faint snort. I patted its feathered leg. When I'd first called out to the creatures I'd thought of as monsters, I'd been terrified underneath. But the connection I'd been able to form with the ones we'd encountered on the Checkerboard Plains, to calm them and tame them, had come even more easily now that I held the scepter and believed in my right to use it.

As the cleansing glow of the scepter's ruby had dispelled the storming emotions behind the blazing eyes and the teeth like shards of glass, I'd gotten a taste of their turmoil. The jabberwocks were more anxious than raging. I had to wonder whether they'd always been monstrous or if the tyranny of the Hearts' rule had driven them to viciousness like it had warped so much else in Wonderland.

I sensed a faint impression of the other three I'd summoned, which I'd asked to patrol the fringes of the city on the palace side and to frighten off any guards who tried to journey along those roads. If the guards didn't frighten, they might find themselves barbequed or skewered. I was leaving the choice up to them.

A thin wail caught my ears. The jabberwock shivered but stayed at my side. I peered down a side-street and spotted a little girl, no more than six or seven, hugging her knees where she sat at the side of the road.

The jabberwock would probably only scare her more. I looked into the violet eye closest to me and made a motion for it to stay put. Then I hurried over to the girl.

"What's wrong?" I asked, crouching down in front of her. "Do you need help?"

She swiped at her damp cheeks. Her hair was tangled and her face smudged with dirt, presumably from weeks of roaming around amid the revelers. The drug had left the city people barely able to look after themselves.

"I don't know where my mom and dad are," she said, and jabbed her thumb at the building behind her, a spindly yellow structure that zigzagged back and forth across its five storeys. "This is my house. I came back a couple hours ago, but they aren't here. Maybe they went off somewhere without me. Everything's gone so confusing." She rubbed her forehead.

An ache closed around my heart. "We'll try to find your parents," I said. It was possible they were among the Clubbers the guards had taken to be pearled. I couldn't bring myself to mention that to her, though.

One of the city people, the woman who'd been so hesitant to trust the Spades before, came up beside me. "I can help her look," she said, with a tight but warm smile at me. "And if we can't find them tonight, I'll make sure she has somewhere comfortable to sleep."

"Thank you," I said, with a swell of resolve. I hadn't been totally sure what to say to the city people we'd rescued now that we were here. Why not give them a purpose?

I let my gaze sweep over the crowd when I came back into the main street we'd been walking along. "You can all go back to your homes, of course," I said. "If you want to help the city recover, though, I'd be grateful if you could check in on your friends and neighbors and help anyone in need as much as you're able too. We've destroyed all the roses, but the effects of the drug aren't likely to wear off completely until sometime tomorrow, and even once people's heads have cleared, they're going to be confused. Let's really take back the city."

A murmur of agreement spread through the Clubbers. A few of them headed off down other streets right then, I guessed toward their own neighborhoods.

The man with the hound's head sidled closer to me. "Are you sure the guards won't come back to take some sort of revenge?"

"They won't know any of you were ever with us once you're back at home," I reassured him. "And I've got more of my new friends protecting the city for us so that the guards can't get this far anyway."

He gave the jabberwock a glance that was both awed and horrified. I'd take that combination.

Most of the Spades had come back to the city with us too, some of them scouting along the edges to make sure we hadn't missed any guards and others here with me. Theo ambled over as more of the Clubbers dispersed.

"Where are you planning on spending the night?" he asked. "We'll want to make sure *you're* fully protected."

"I haven't decided yet," I admitted. He'd probably like it if I joined him in his Tower, assuming that was where he was going, but like often before, it felt too claustrophobic to me. Too difficult to escape from if the guards managed to break through. And now, on top of that, I couldn't help thinking of how distant it would put me from the people I wanted to have faith in me.

It'd be better if they could see me as much as possible, better if they knew I was standing right here with them, ready to defend them the moment any threat raised its head.

"I have a few ideas for adding to our protections along the city borders," the former Inventor went on. He rubbed his jaw, his eyes going distant with thought. "I think some of the Clubbers who came with us are ready to take on some minor responsibilities now. We can get more people on rotation around the most vulnerable points of entry. I'll equip them as well as I can."

"I don't plan on us having to hold the city like this for very long," I said, lowering my voice. "Once everyone in the city has had time to recover, we're going to gather as many willing volunteers as we can, and then we're marching on the palace. I'm sure a lot of them will be ready to step up after how the Queen of Hearts has treated them and after we've saved them. Between them and the jabberwocks, we've got to be able to make it to the throne."

Theo nodded, the corners of his lips curling upward. "I believe we will," he said. "If not tomorrow, maybe the next day. We just want to be sure of holding the city that long."

His vote of confidence gave me another burst of assurance. It lasted about half a minute. Then Chess came dashing down the street toward us, his face flushed, running so fast he'd lost most of the grace his brawny body usually held. My heart skipped a beat.

"We scouted closer to the palace, keeping a safe distance," he said between pants for breath after he'd reached us. "We saw—they're preparing fresh carts of the roses. The first ones were already heading out when I left. They've assembled some new weaponry, too—arrows and a few catapults—I think they mean to try to fight the jabberwocks directly."

A memory flashed through my head of the previous Knave, the one with the sharkish face, charging at one of the jabberwocks on the Checkerboard Plain after I'd distracted it in my attempt at calming it.

I was pretty sure he'd killed the poor creature. I couldn't let the ones I'd summoned, the ones who'd offered me their help at the sight of my scepter and the sound of my voice, meet the same fate now.

At the thought of projectiles flying through the air, heat crept over my chest. The rubies on my armored vest had started to glow. I gazed down at them, a tingle of power racing over my skin. Before I'd been sure of myself as queen, before I'd been able to get the Red royal artifacts to work for me consistently, this vest had propelled back a bunch of guards who'd been racing to attack me. It'd protected me from the worst of a speeding truck's impact.

I didn't let myself second-guess the idea that had popped into my head. I rubbed the jabberwock's leg, and it lowered its head to peer at me.

"So, they're not scared of the jabberwocks anymore," I said. "I'll give them something even more terrifying to deal with."

Chess raised his eyebrows, and Theo cocked his head. "What's that?" the Prince of Hearts asked.

I shot him a nervous grin. "An avenging queen *on* a jabberwock."

It was probably a good thing that Hatter was off on patrol elsewhere in the city, because I suspected he'd have had a few critical remarks to make about this decision. I slid my hand up to the jabberwock's shoulder above my head and tugged lightly on the gold feathers there, holding its gaze at the same time.

"I'd like to ride you," I said. "We're going to take on more of the people who'd want to hurt you. But I'll make sure they can't touch us at all. We'll send them all running or burn them up. What do you say?"

I wasn't sure how much the creature comprehended my words or just could read my meaning in my expression or tone. One way or another, it understood me enough. It sank down until its broad belly rested on the cobblestones. The Clubbers still with us stared as I climbed onto the massive feathered form using the bends in its front leg for leverage.

A rumble trembled through the jabberwock's body when I'd settled into what felt like the most secure position I could find, between its stunted wings just above its shoulder blades. My legs dangled on either side of its long sinewy neck, and the scabbard with my sword rested on the feathers beside me. I rubbed the beast's tensed muscles. "I'm ready. Let's go teach them a lesson."

The jabberwock heaved itself to its feet at those words. I swayed a little but kept my balance with a squeeze of my legs and my hands gripping the coarse feathers in front of me. My pulse thumped faster as the beast rose to its full height. I was level with the third floor windows on the building beside me.

Oh, yes, those guards had better be afraid.

At my nudge, the jabberwock lurched forward. It fell into a shuffling jog, a little faster than its earlier walk. But Chess had said the guards were already on their way, and we had a lot of ground to cover. As soon as I felt stable enough at that speed, I patted the creature's back behind me to urge it faster.

It broke into a full-out run. The buildings in all their vivid colors whipped by on either side of us. The wind tossed my hair.

When we came to the next major cross-street, I directed the jabberwock in the direction of the palace with another light nudge. The thrum of its pulse and the anticipation shivering through its body echoed into me. I wasn't sure it needed my touch at all to pick up on where I wanted it to go.

We rushed on, taking another turn, and another, the quickest route to the palace road I knew where my unusual steed would fit. Ahead of us, the buildings gave way to the sparse forest where I'd spent more time than I'd have liked in the last couple months. I urged the jabberwock even faster.

We charged past the last of the buildings in time to see a swarm of guards who'd just come up over the crest of the hill. Several clusters of them pulled carts of roses and others were hauling the catapults Chess had mentioned.

The jabberwocks I'd sent on patrol prowled closer at the sight of me. One of them looked toward the guards and hissed through its jagged teeth. Blood seeped over the golden feathers on its neck where it must have taken a hit. They were hanging back now, waiting for my instructions.

I didn't think I could shield all of them, and I didn't want to send them forward to be battered. We'd have to see if my steed and I could manage this on our own.

I stroked the jabberwock's shoulder encouragingly. "Go for it," I said. "Burn up the flowers, the carts, the weapons. Burn the guards up too if they won't fall back. I'll keep you safe."

The rubies on my vest flared hotter and brighter. A ripple of energy ruffled the jabberwock's feathers. It hummed through the air around us.

Please let it be enough to ward off their attacks.

The jabberwock barrelled up the road toward the guards. The ones at the forefront gave a shout. Panic blanched some of their faces—and others just trudged on with the same dull expression. How many pearl-heads did the Queen of Hearts have fighting for her now? Had Carpenter sent back even more since this morning?

My gut twisted, but I couldn't focus on that now. The people they'd once been had already been murdered. I had to protect the city's people, the ones still living, first.

I pointed toward the nearest cart. "Light them up!"

My body swayed with the hitch of the jabberwock's stride. A burst of flame shot from its mouth to swallow up an entire cart and all its contents. The guards hollered to each other, the ones at the catapults fumbling with the controls. A line of pearl-heads strung bows with arrows and raised them toward us with robotic precision.

The jabberwock managed to cough out another spurt of flame that turned one of the catapults into charred wood. Three more of the massive weapons launched spiky metal balls at us while the arrows whined through the air. I dug my fingers into the jabberwock's feathers and willed all the power I had in me through the rubies on my vest.

The weapons hurtled toward us—and the energy of my vest slammed them backward a few inches from the jabberwock's snout. One of the spiked balls smacked a guard in the chest, knocking him over with its force. The arrows rattled against the ground. The jabberwock released a furious belch that lit up another of the catapults—and a couple of the guards scrambling around it.

Their screams made me cringe, but I held on with my jaw

clenched. "This city is under the Red Queen's protection," I shouted. "You cannot touch us. I don't want to hurt you, but if it's that or see my people hurt, I will. Go, before I have to."

The other jabberwocks sprang to my side without any orders, emboldened by our success. The guards might have taken them out, but they didn't know that, and the sight of their enemy suddenly quadrupled must have been too great a test for their resolve. The hollers turned more frantic. A couple of pearl-heads tried to launch one of the remaining catapults, and my jabberwock scorched them in an instant.

"Retreat and regroup!" a call went up. The remaining guards dashed for the palace grounds, leaving their carts rather than be slowed down hauling them. I gestured to the jabberwocks, and they turned the rest of the drugged roses into a massive flaming pyre.

My whole body was quivering with exhilaration when I had my jabberwock turn back toward the city. I hadn't expected to see anyone there except maybe a Spade or two who'd been patrolling with Chess.

A small crowd of Clubbers, a few Spades mixed in with them, had gathered at the edge of the city. They all stood stock-still in shock. As the reality of our victory must have sunk in, one and then another raised their hands with a breathless cheer.

A smile stretched across my face that had nothing but joy in it. We hadn't won the war yet, but damn, winning this battle had felt fucking good.

I could beat the guards on our ground. Now I just had to figure out how to beat them on theirs.

CHAPTER NINETEEN

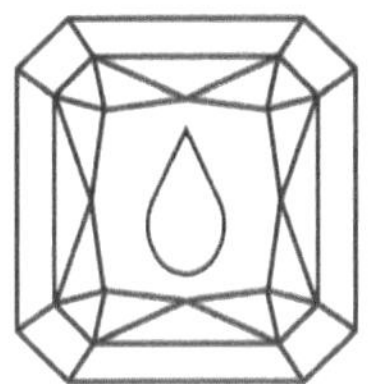

Lyssa

Chess was waiting for me on the road when I slid down off the jabberwock—a little less gracefully than I'd have preferred. He caught my elbow when I landed off balance. I shot him a grateful smile and patted the creature's side. It studied me with its fiery violet eyes. They were actually kind of pretty amid the gold and scarlet feathers, once you got used to their intensity.

"Keep watch on the palace," I told it. "Come looking for me if more like that bunch head this way."

I could feel in the quiver of energy that had summoned the jabberwocks to me that they would be able to seek me out the same way. No further guards had emerged from the palace grounds as evening had darkened into night, but I doubted that attack would be their last.

The jabberwock bobbed its head in apparent understanding. Chess gave me an amused grin when I turned back to him.

"When we first met, you told me you didn't have many interesting stories to share, lovely. I can't imagine anyone will ever top the one you just gave me."

"We'll see about that by the time this rebellion is over," I said, but under my bravado I was way too worn out to even imagine attempting any more epic activities today. I let out my breath, my shoulders sinking from their tensed stance, and Chess slipped his arm around me.

"I heard some of the Spades were going to meet up in the city park. It would be my pleasure to escort you there."

"Sounds good," I said. My hands instinctively moved to check my sword at my hip and my scepter at my back. My vest's rubies had cooled again against my chest. Everything was where it should be.

The crowd of city people who'd gathered to watch me scare off the guards from the jabberwock's back parted to let us through. Their faces still shone with the elation I'd seen when they'd cheered, but they looked awfully weary underneath that too. For nearly three weeks, they'd been partying and only sleeping in brief spells when they'd gotten exhausted enough to overshadow the high of the Queen's drug.

But they seemed unwilling to head off to bed even now. As Chess and I headed toward the park, most of the Clubbers drifted after us.

I'd just saved them twice over in one day. Maybe they were taking comfort from keeping me in sight. Hopefully that meant Theo was right about more of the city people taking up arms with us, even if right now I found their devotion a little uncomfortable.

I didn't want them to swap their blind fear of the Queen of Hearts for blind loyalty to me. I wanted them to believe I'd have their best interests at heart even if they were off doing whatever made them happy.

Lights glowed on posts here and there throughout the sprawling park, which was where I'd first met Chess ages ago. It didn't look as if any of the revelers had bothered with the chessboard other than to fling around the pieces, most of which were now missing. Someone's dress fluttered where it hung from a branch it'd been tossed over. The ashes of burnt roses floated off in the breeze like dark snow. A lingering hint of smoke mingled with the crisp scent of the grass.

I recognized a few of the figures already in the park from the Spades—Kip was there, and a couple others from one of the side camps, as well as a few of the city people who'd fully recovered in our care. It wasn't much of a meeting, though. Really, we all needed to get some sleep at this point. I could figure out where Hatter and Theo had gotten to in the morning.

Kip and the others were moving among the Clubbers who were slumped or meandering here and there across the park's lawns, most of them hazy but waking up enough to look confused. The bunch who'd followed Chess and me ambled into the park and glanced around uncertainly, their posture wary.

The excitement I'd been able to generate in the battle with the guards had waned, and now there wasn't much left but fatigue and anxiety around me. That was about all I had left in me, too.

I groped for something to say, some gesture to make, that might put them at ease enough that they'd find somewhere to rest. Nothing emerged from my tired brain.

Chess peered around us and at me, and a wider grin stretched his lips. He bounded away from me and leapt onto a nearby hedge, catching the attention of everyone around the park as he teetered on the landing. He caught his balance and dipped into a bow as if that had been part of the performance—which knowing him, maybe it had.

"What a day!" he called out in his playful tenor. He sauntered along the top of the hedge with a bit of a sway as he found his footing. "Did you see all the exploits of our Red Queen? It's enough to make you wonder why we've been dodging the Hearts' Guard all this time, isn't it? The look on their faces when the jabberwocks came trotting into the city…"

He let his jaw drop and clutched his chest in mock panic before scrambling backward so frantically leaves flitted off the hedge from under his feet. A tittering spread through his audience. A smile slipped across my face.

"And then," Chess said, righting himself, "they think, 'Ah, well, we can handle a few jabberwocks if we come out with every bit of weaponry we own.'" He lumbered forward with shoulders up to his ears in a joking imitation of the guards' march. "No match for our queen, though. She just hops right up on one of those jabberwocks and sends them running back home like they've got fire at their heels.

Because they do." He made a panicked dash across the hedge and spun around with a wink.

The crowd watched him avidly, clapping in encouragement. Chess gave another little bow. "I think we deserve to enjoy ourselves while they're shivering in their pretty palace," he said. "Take a load off and make the most of what true freedom can be."

He tipped over, falling onto his back with a delighted smile as if he meant to fall asleep right there. The second he hit the hedge, he blinked out of sight. Then his grin appeared, gleaming as it floated against the night.

More laughter carried through the gathered Clubbers. Someone found a guitar leaning against a nearby tree and started playing it—not the frenetic music that had filled the city before, but soft strums of a city at peace. People sank down on the grass, talking in quiet voices, their faces light again.

Chess turned visible again as he hopped down from the hedge. He strolled back to me with his light blue eyes twinkling. I beamed back at him, a surge of affection washing away every other emotion inside me.

I might have protected these people from the guards, but Chess was already bringing them back to the joy they deserved. The joy I wanted Wonderland to be made of.

"It's amazing what you can accomplish by playing a fool," he said. "Make much of how little our enemies really are, and we feel like a whole lot more."

"I don't think there's anything foolish about that," I said, and then I couldn't help myself. I gripped the front of his shirt and bobbed up on my toes to kiss him.

This intimacy didn't feel as urgent as yesterday's, that first real coming together after a painful separation. This time, his kiss and his touch was all another sort of joy. I leaned into his well-muscled body, wanting to soak in his warmth and his tenderness with every particle in me. Chess teased his fingers into my hair and tipped my head to claim my lips at an even more enticing angle.

There were people all around us who might be watching, but I found I didn't care one bit. Wonderlanders didn't appear to have any qualms about enjoying each other where their neighbors could see. I wasn't about to do the full horizontal tango in front of dozens of them, but I had no problem with letting them see how much I wanted this man.

They should know their queen had as much love in her as she did defiance.

Desire unfurled through me with the heat of Chess's mouth against mine. I gripped his shirt harder, the ache of need in my core bringing my hips against his. He hummed low in his throat, his tongue darting out to part my lips, and I knew I wasn't going to want to stop.

But he might. I couldn't make assumptions, not when the last woman he'd dedicated much of himself to had torn him apart so badly. He'd told me, the first night we'd come together—when he'd surreptitiously arranged for Hatter to join our interlude—that he didn't trust himself to be able to offer enough on his own.

I kissed him back hard, my tongue tangling with his, and then I eased back a few inches. It took me a moment to recover my words.

"Is there somewhere nearby we can talk without any spectators?" I asked quietly.

Chess's eyebrows rose, but after a pause, he nodded. "Why don't you come see the closest thing I've had to a home, for many years past?"

He had a home—near here? I'd gotten the impression he just roamed around, resting wherever he felt like it with whatever company he felt like keeping.

He tucked his hand around mine and led me beyond the hedge and past a stand of saplings. Not far from the park's fountain, we reached a dense thicket, nearly as tall as Chess and maybe fifteen feet across, the spiny leaves such a dark green they were almost black.

Chess prodded his fingers into the brambles and opened up a gap with some careful shifting. I followed him through the narrow gap into a hollow in the center of the thicket. The brambles pulled back over a stretch of grass only slightly larger than Chess would have been lying down.

He sat on the thin grass at one end of the hollow and motioned for me to join him. I sank down tentatively. A faint glow from the nearest lamp seeped over us.

"This is where I'd taken a mind to sleep the night the Queen froze time," Chess said, his gaze drifting over the brambles around him. "I suppose it was for decades I woke up here every morning. Not a bad bit of shelter, as shelter went in times like that."

Oh. That was what he'd meant about it being his "home."

My throat tightened in sympathy. Hatter might have ended up in his armchair every morning rather than a bed, but at least he'd been inside his apartment, on a cushioned surface. Theo had managed to arrange a bed of his choosing inside the Tower. Chess had cycled back to a bit of ground in the middle of the park every morning.

Maybe it wasn't so surprising he'd had trouble believing he deserved better than the Duchess. Or that he'd been tempted by the extravagances of the palace in the first place.

I took off my sword and set down my scepter at the far end of the hollow, and then scooted closer to him. Chess wrapped me in his embrace from behind. With his intoxicating licorice-and-wine smell making my mouth water, it felt perfectly natural to tilt my head back against his shoulder so he could recapture my lips. He kissed me so easily I started to think we might not need to talk at all.

Chess claimed my mouth slow and sweet, deeper with each kiss, his fingers trailing along my jaw. Fresh desire quivered through my body. I turned in his arms to face him, just slightly taller than him when I knelt between his thighs. He ran his hands down my side as I kissed him again, but only a hint of that contact carried through the woven metal of my armor. *That* definitely needed to come off.

As I leaned back and pulled the vest up over my head, hunger darkened Chess's eyes, but his shoulders stiffened at the same time. I tossed the vest over to join the rest of my royal equipment and hesitated. When he leaned in for another kiss, I stopped him with a gentle hand on his cheek.

"I want you," I said. "I want— It's been good, before, with Hatter and Theo joining in. I'll be happy to do that again. But I want us to have our moments that we don't share with anyone else. I love you, Chess. Every bit as much as I love them. You don't have to give some perfect performance. I want *you*, nothing more or less. If you're not ready to be with just me, that's okay. It's up to you how far we go. I just thought you should know."

Chess stared at me. His throat worked. For a second, like in the moment weeks ago when I'd first asked to kiss him, I thought he was going to turn me away. Then in one swift motion, he slid his hand over my hair and tugged me to him, rising to meet me at the same time.

We kissed with a hot tangle of tongues, his other hand roaming under my dress, searing my skin with need. When he tipped me over on my back, looming over me, I settled into the grass eagerly. He gazed down at me, the light in his eyes giddy if a bit frantic.

"My queen should have everything she desires," he said, his voice gone smoky with his own desire.

Something in me balked at those words. "I don't want you to have sex with me because I'm your *queen*."

His gaze softened. "No," he said. "You're right. I'm here because you're my lovely. My Lyssa."

Then he was kissing me again, urging my hips to arch toward him. The hard length of his erection fit against my core through our clothes, and an eager noise burst from my throat. Chess smiled against my mouth. He pressed against me with soft, rhythmic hitches that sent pleasure and longing sparking through every inch of me. I scrabbled at his shirt, needing more of him.

Chess peeled his shirt off and eased up my dress. As he reclaimed my lips, one of his hands traveled over my chest with a teasing flick over my breasts, across my belly, to settle between my legs. He stroked over my clit with a more precise pressure than the bulge in his pants had offered and then dipped his fingers beneath the fabric of my panties, lower, until they could slick right up inside the place where I was most wanting.

I whimpered into his mouth. He groaned in response at the feel of me, already soaked with desire. His fingers worked deeper, the heel of his hand rubbing my clit. I squirmed as I ran my fingers over the planes of bare muscle down his back, solid and smooth and coiled with effort focused completely on me in this moment.

"Mmm," he murmured, and ducked his head down to kiss my neck with a scrape of his fangs. A gasp escaped me, and his fingers plunged right to the sweet spot inside me. I came with a burst of bliss and a cry I couldn't contain.

Chess beamed down at me, looking the very picture of satisfied, as if it didn't matter to him at all that his cock was still straining for attention.

"Happy with that, are you?" I asked, breathless and teasing.

He chuckled. "I think it'll do for a start."

"In that case…"

I yanked at the button on his pants, and he kicked them off. Somewhere in the middle of another scorching kiss, I lost my panties. Good riddance. I slid my hand between us and gripped his erection through his boxer-briefs. Chess growled, and a moment later his undergarments were no longer in the picture either. I raised my legs to his hips instinctively, and he drove into me so hard and fast I saw stars.

"Chess," I gasped, and he chuckled again, rawer this time. We rocked together in a blissful muddle of stuttered kisses and shifting limbs, his cock thrusting deeper with each brilliant pulse, his heat and his scent engulfing me. If it wasn't perfect, then it was perfectly Chess, unpredictable and jubilant. Another wave of ecstasy built up inside me sharp and swift, as much as I wanted to linger in this pleasure.

My peak shuddered through me, and my core clamped around him. As I rode out the wave of bliss, my head tipping back against the grass, Chess let out another groan. He came with me, his face buried against the crook of my neck, his hand clamped on my thigh to lock us even more tightly together.

He stayed braced over me as I came trembling down from that high. A grin I suspected looked rather goofy curled my lips. Chess grinned back at me.

"*Now* I'm happy," he said, in a voice that held nothing but joy.

CHAPTER TWENTY

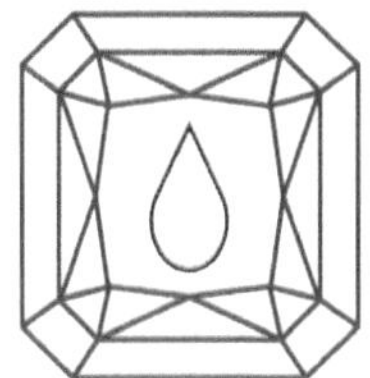

Chess

Somehow the Tower apartment looked more familiar with its owner in it. Although perhaps Theo wasn't truly its owner anymore. I supposed the city would have to sort out the matter of whether a Prince of Hearts could also be the Inventor once we could say the city was fully ours.

Theo rifled through the drawers of his worktables and the bins on the shelves with the efficiency you'd expect from a man who could construct a bomb—a small one, anyway—in fifteen minutes flat. The contacts rattled and clicked. We'd already filled one sack, now slung over my shoulder, with materials he thought he could make good use of. All the rifling had sent a sharp metallic sent into the air. Familiar as they were, the blank white walls around us left me uneasy.

All right, it might not have been *just* them causing my uneasiness. I shifted my weight from one foot to the other. The pleasure I'd shared with Lyssa yesterday night had started my thoughts off on other tracks, some more welcome than others. But even as I'd dodged the memories of less pleasant intimacies, it had occurred to me that tools used once could serve fresh purposes.

"Theo?" I said. His claimed name tasted odd on my tongue after all those years referring to him by the title White Knight, but I'd noticed he got a bit twitchy when anyone directed that label at him since his return.

He swiped his dark curls back from his face and fixed his gaze on me, puzzled but with his full attention. That was why he'd made a good White Knight—and a good Inventor, I supposed. No matter what else was occupying him, he could pick up on how important a matter was to someone else, and then it became important to him too.

He could have been the Prince of Razorweed Town for all I cared, as long as he was still that same man.

"Is something wrong, Chess?" he asked.

"Not exactly," I said. "Possibly the opposite. I only—I got thinking last night… Do you remember, quite a lot of years ago, Hatter asked you to make a device that could siphon a memory from a person's mind?"

Theo straightened up. "He told you about that? It was an experiment. It seemed to work somewhat on the Spades who volunteered for testing, minor memories I constructed and then removed, and I assumed it ended up working well enough, since Hatter was never arrested for the crime he said he had to wipe, but I wouldn't have tried if he hadn't said the situation was dire. I don't like meddling with minds."

Ah. I supposed it was too late to retreat from this line of inquiry now.

"The dire situation was actually mine," I admitted. "One of the Diamonds, one who had shown an interest in hurting me, knew something about me that would have made me a very wanted man if she'd chosen to share it with the Queen. Hatter said you might be able to help." I had the cat-like urge to swipe my hand across my face in embarrassment. "I would have come to you myself, but we hadn't exactly moved in the same circles back then."

And then, as our lives had shifted, I'd ended up one of the White Knight's most regular companions, and Hatter had withdrawn from the Spades into domesticity. Funny how these things turned around.

Theo considered me for a long moment. "I have to wonder what you had to hide before you were involved with the Spades, but I'd imagine if you wanted to tell me, you would have. It doesn't really matter who used the device. I'm glad it helped you. Why do you bring it up now?"

My innards unclenched. Part of me had been expecting him to ask the question he'd just dodged for me. That wasn't how Theo usually operated, though. He wasn't his mother's son, not really.

"I just thought—there was a lot of power in that device. And what Lyssa wants to do is change people's minds, not bludgeon them into submission or slaughter dissenters. I'm not sure what other ways you could use the general concept, but perhaps there's something useful there."

Theo's expression turned thoughtful. "That's a good point. Let me make sure I have the supplies I used for that. I think there were a few things Dum had to pick up specially…"

He rummaged through the drawers and then wandered off to his other rooms. When he returned, the sack he'd been carrying was bulging even larger than mine. His mouth was curved in a subdued but pleased smile.

"I think we've got everything I'm likely to use in the next few days."

"You don't expect to move back in here any time soon?" I asked as we headed for the elevator.

Theo grimaced. "We'll see what the future holds when we get there. For the time being, the people I want to be helping are down on the ground. I spent too long watching over the city from afar up here, I think. I'll be back to visit Mirabel, since I think she'll be happiest here for now, but otherwise I'd like to stay close to the streets."

When we came out into the warm mid-morning sun at the base of the Tower, Mallo was waiting for us. She darted over with furtive twitches of her eyes along the road, even though there'd been no sign of a renewed attack from the palace since the one Lyssa had pushed back last night. The only sounds I could hear were relaxed voices of recovering city folk chatting with each other down the street, but I braced myself for bad news all the same.

"The Otherlan—The Red Queen already knows," she said, looking at Theo. "But I thought you should be part of the discussion too. A representative has snuck out of the palace to try to strike a deal with us —between us and the Diamonds."

At the word "Diamonds," my blood ran cold. "What representative?" I said, even though she hadn't been directing her comments at me. "Who came?"

Mallo's gaze jerked to me, startled. "It's—you know. Unicorn." She gestured over her head as if indicating the gentleman's shiny horn. "I know he helped us before, but I still don't entirely like it."

"It's good that you told us, although I'm sure the Red Queen would have asked to consult with us before making any decisions anyway," Theo said.

My mind was still whirling. "Unicorn came alone?" I said.

Mallo nodded. "He said it was a lot of trouble getting out without the Queen catching on. I'd imagine it'd have been harder with more."

"Did he say which other Diamonds were involved in the offer?"

"I didn't hear much," Mallo said. "It sounded like all of them."

I could think of a large number of the Queen's pampered courtiers who would have sooner chopped their own heads off than ally themselves with the common city dwellers. Unicorn *had* helped us—I trusted him well enough. But so many of the others… My gut couldn't quite sit right with the idea.

"Do you think this is some kind of ploy?" Theo asked. "They have plenty of reasons to want to see the Queen of Hearts overthrown. Who knows how she's been terrorizing them during this latest furor."

"All true, all true," I said, taking a step away. "But having spent as much time among them as I have… I think I'd like to look into a few things before I report back to our queen."

I slipped into the in-between without another word. If I was going to make it to the palace and back in time to share any news I could bring, I'd have to hustle.

The Duchess had rambled on sometimes in a bragging tone when I'd gone to her rooms with her. Back then, she'd known a little stone cottage near the edge of the palace grounds that was overgrown with vines as if no one ever went there. Which made it, she'd told me, the perfect place for her to meet with other Diamonds if they wanted to have discussions without any fear of the Queen overhearing.

They'd just sent Unicorn off to us. Where else would they be waiting for him to return with the answer we gave him but there?

I jogged through the streets, speeding up as I left the city behind. One of the first things we would need to do once we had our land back was replenish our stock of horses and carts. Maybe we could even claim some air trolleys for city use. I didn't think Lyssa would object to speedier transportation options.

I skirted the wall around the palace grounds until I was in the area of the cottage, between the west and the north gates. Getting over the wall would have been easier with Dee along. But he was somewhere on the other side of that wall already, making his own deals. My hackles rose at the thought.

In the end, I took a running start and simply flung myself toward the top. My fingers managed to hook around the edge of the highest stones. I hauled myself up, hoping no guards inside had been close enough to hear my scramble even if they couldn't see me.

To my relief, no one was in earshot. I stalked along the top of the wall until I spotted the viney mass, only the door, a window, a chimney, and patches of worn marble stones visible amid the leafy tendrils.

I leapt down from the wall and hurried over to the wooden door. In my invisible state, I leaned my ear close.

Someone was in there. Muffled voices reached my ears, but the door was thick enough to muddle their words. I couldn't make out a thing they were saying.

I frowned and stalked to the window, but it had been covered with some kind of fabric on the other side to prevent any outside eyes from peering in. The stuff dampened their voices too. I circled the whole building, but there was no way I was finding out what was going on in there short of opening the door and strolling in. Somehow I didn't think I'd get a particularly warm welcome. The Duchess had gone to some effort in recent months to see my head ended up on one of the Queen's pikes.

My gaze drifted up to the roof and settled on the chimney. My chest tightened.

There was another way I could get into the building—a way that, if I was careful, would ensure they'd never know their center of conspiring had been breached. The trouble was that even the idea of doing it made my skin prickle with discomfort.

I sucked in a breath. I'd shifted before, to save Lyssa, even though the sensation had brought too many awful memories back to the surface. It had been easier to make the leap in that moment of panic, though. I might not hear anything useful in there. Lyssa hadn't asked this of me.

She shouldn't have to. Whether I'd planned it or not, I was more than just a rambler helping the rebellion on the side. I was at the fore of the struggle now, and I had to act like it. It wasn't just Lyssa but all the people in that city back there whose lives could rest on the information I discovered.

A hero wasn't someone who only pitched in when it was easy. I hadn't seen myself as a hero before, hadn't wanted the title particularly, but when I remembered the way my queen had looked at me last night, I wanted to earn it. For her sake and mine.

Holding myself in the in-between, I hunched down on the ground and gritted my teeth. With a mental shove, the change rippled through my body. I seemed to contract and expand at once, shrinking but changing shape, fur sprouting all over my suddenly rotund body. My whiskers twitched. My tail lashed behind me instinctively.

The ghosts of long ago fingers, pins, knives traced over my skin. I shuddered and sprang at the vines.

If I just thought about Lyssa—if I could let those better, fresher memories drown out the old ones, even if they came from my human form…

As my claws dug into the tendrils and I clambered up the side of the cottage, I urged my mind back to last night. To the gentle caress of her hands, the eager slide of her mouth. The fondness so clear in her voice and in her eyes…

Fondness? No, I should be honest. It'd been love. Love that she'd spoken of, love that she'd shown.

Even my cat heart in my cat chest thumped eagerly in response to those recollections. The words to return her sentiment had been there at the back of my throat. But I hadn't said them. Even now, a shiver passed through my nerves imagining doing so.

The shiver rippled deeper in this form. It connected with the older memories and sparked a flare of understanding that burned all the way to my bones with the phantom echoes of ropes tied tight and slicing knives.

I did love her. Oh, how I loved her. More than I'd ever cared for anyone in my entire existence. It was fucking terrifying.

Saying those words, admitting the depth of that emotion out loud… somehow that felt like tying myself to her in a way I might not be able to break.

Why in the lands would I *want* to break it? Hearts take me, I should be honored if she wanted me by her side for as long as we both did live. I didn't enjoy the roaming. I got nothing but joy at her side. The Duchess would have the ultimate triumph if I let her perversions sour everything good in my future.

I needed to be brave for Lyssa, and not just here, in this private mission.

My resolve coursed through me. I climbed up the side of the chimney with a steady grip. Then I eased my way down inside, thanking the powers that be that it was far too warm a season for a fire.

It was slow going, because while no one would see me if they looked up the chimney, they'd catch the scrape of my claws if I wasn't careful. Also, it wasn't the widest chimney in the world, and I had plenty of bulk for a cat. After several tight and tense minutes, I'd edged down far enough to make out the voices in the room.

"Do you really think that's wise?" a man was saying.

The laugh that answered made my fur stand up all across my back. "Make what you will of it," the Duchess said. "We can always leave you behind."

Were they talking about going to the city, as if they truly meant to go through with that plan? It was impossible to tell from a comment that vague. I wasn't inclined to trust a word that came out of her mouth, besides.

There sounded to be at least a dozen people in the room. A few murmurs went around about the chocolates someone had brought for snacking on. "How long will they take to hash it out, do you think?" someone asked.

Apparently the Duchess was leading this endeavor, because she answered immediately again. "The poor things, no doubt the offer has sent them into quite a tizzy, picturing an alliance with us. We must give them time."

Her patronizing tone set my teeth even more on edge.

"It is a gamble," another voice pointed out. "Either way you slice it."

"You wouldn't be here if you didn't agree that appeasing her is our only hope of survival," the Duchess replied. "*Any* way you slice it, we all know what the greater threat is here. "

The greater threat. A prickle ran over my skin as the words sunk in. Was that the place they were making this offer from? Their sense of a great threat?

Knowing the Duchess, knowing the Diamonds, I couldn't imagine them fearing anyone more than the Queen of Hearts.

CHAPTER TWENTY-ONE

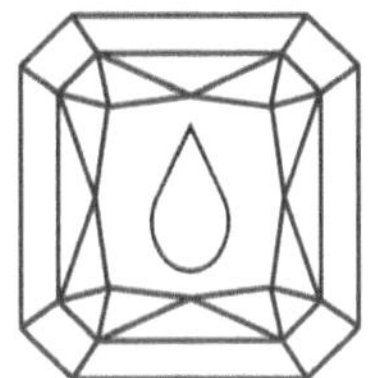

Lyssa

It should have been totally bizarre seeing a horse-like figure sitting at a table like a man, but somehow Unicorn perched on his chair, resting his hooved arms on the tabletop, as if it was a perfectly natural pose. Here in Wonderland, I guessed it was.

He shook back his glinting mane with a quiver of the muscles in his graceful white neck. He didn't look totally at ease with the proposal he was making, but then, I wasn't sure I'd ever seen Unicorn really relaxed. Every time I'd talked to him, we'd been making illicit plans behind the Queen's back, after all.

The woman who owned the ice cream café that'd been a convenient spot for our sit-down lingered by the back counter, watching us with wide eyes. Several of the Spades, including Theo and Hatter, stood along the walls around us. Hatter periodically whirled the hatpin he was holding with a faint hiss of motion. Having them at my back put me a little more at ease, but my heart was thudding harder than usual anyway.

The decision I made here could win or lose us the war.

"All of the Diamonds would help us push back the guards?" I said, turning over what Unicorn had already told me about the theoretical alliance in my head. The flavor of the shop's sweet cream laced my tongue. "How many of you are there?"

"Around a hundred," Unicorn said. "Not as many as there are guards, but combined with your numbers here, and the jabberwocks, and the fact that we can move on the inside to stem the charge before it truly begins… I think we could make a useful contribution."

I did too, though I wasn't sure how much of that impression I wanted to share with him. Even though Unicorn had helped us before, he'd spent most of his life at the Queen's beck and call. How far could we really trust him?

And if I couldn't completely trust him, how could I trust the Diamonds who'd never shown any interest in supporting our cause at all?

"What exactly would I need to promise in return for that contribution?" I asked, watching him carefully and paying careful attention to my ring. So far it hadn't woken up as if there was danger to combat, but it had been pretty selective in what it decided to respond to in the past, so that wasn't a total comfort.

"We'd ask for forgiveness for our association with and prior support of the Hearts' rule," Unicorn said. "No charges laid, no punishments dealt out. Those who wish to will keep their homes in and around the palace until equivalent accommodations are found or built."

That didn't sound unreasonable, even though the idea of living in the palace with the glammed up Diamonds all around made my skin crawl. We'd have to come up with those "equivalent" accommodations quickly. Let the Spades have the run of the palace for a change.

"And they'll trust my word?" I said.

Unicorn shrugged. "I trust it. I vouched for your credibility. They were all there when you broke the prisoners free—they know you're not the bloodthirsty type by nature."

I ran my thumb over my chin. "Why would they take this risk at all, though? They've had an extravagant life living the way they do under the Queen of Hearts."

"I don't see that any amount of extravagance is worth the constant tension having her right at our backs," Unicorn said. "If I could put you on that throne right now in her place, I'd happily do it. Her latest strategies... We can't be sure how long she'll even let us keep our free minds as her paranoia grows."

His shudder as he said that convinced me that he meant every word. But he was speaking for an awful lot of others.

"Do you trust all of the Diamonds you're here on behalf of?" I asked. "You believe that they'll follow through? They haven't always been all that considerate of you, from what I've seen."

Unicorn grimaced, but he nodded at the same time. "All the talk that happened when I was part of their discussions sounded genuine enough. I wouldn't have come to you if I doubted them."

"Fair enough." I exhaled slowly, trying to hide my tangled emotions, and eased back my chair. "I'd like to discuss the offer with my companions, and we might have more questions after that. Do you mind waiting here?"

"That's fine," Unicorn said. "But I'd like to bring your answer back as quickly as possible. The Diamonds may have meant the offer, but they do tend toward impatience... If they start to feel you're not committed to working with them, I don't know what directions their minds will go in next."

Well, that wasn't exactly reassuring. I got up, and most of the Spades followed me out, Kip and Dum staying behind to keep an eye on Unicorn.

We walked across the sunny street into the shadows of the buildings on the other side. Hatter passed his hatpin from one hand to the other, his expression tight. I could guess how he felt about the possibility of allying with the Diamonds. Theo looked more thoughtful.

"What do you think?" I said. "Is it worth trusting them?"

The Prince of Hearts rested his dark gaze on me. "I think we should hear what you make of this first, my queen," he said. "Better that you have a chance to sway my judgment before I give it than the other way around."

I wasn't so sure about that, considering he'd spent way more time around the Diamonds and the palace than I had, even if that'd been decades ago. But I *was* supposed to be queen here. I still had to get used to acting like it.

"I'm thinking that *if* we can trust them, allying would give us a huge advantage. We'd have people helping open the way for us on the inside. And with more numbers, with people who can step in early on, we might be able to avoid a lot of the violence that'd be inevitable otherwise if we're going to get to the throne. I like all of that."

"If we can trust them," Hatter muttered.

"Exactly." I wet my lips. "They haven't found the courage to stand up to the Queen in an awfully long time, even though they were in the best position to do it. They might resent her, but they've always enjoyed the benefits they get from sucking up to her a lot more. But they *could* have been shaken up enough by the way I challenged her during the trial and the way she retaliated afterward to rethink their position. I'm not sure how we could tell."

"I'm inclined to think we should take the chance," Theo said. "The Diamonds, from what I knew of them—my mother didn't have me mingle very much—are selfish but often smart. If they see more benefit in supporting you than her now, they'll switch sides in an instant. If they're lying, then we're in exactly the same position we were before. We'll just have to be prepared to make the full push ourselves, and any way they assist will be a welcome gift."

My gaze slid to Hatter. "Do you feel okay about that?"

His mouth twisted. "I don't like making any promises to those boot-lickers. Why should they get to keep everything as they've had it at the expense of everyone else, just for finally doing what they should have done ages ago? If they really cared about setting things right, they wouldn't put conditions on their help."

Theo spread his hands. "Like I said, they're selfish."

"I don't like that part either," I said to Hatter. "But at least we can put specific conditions on how they need to help, and if they don't do enough, then we don't have to keep our end of the deal either."

"It may be worth it, then," he admitted. "I know how much you'd like to reclaim the throne without bloodshed."

My stomach knotted. "I realize there'll end up being some no matter what I do." I just had to keep reminding myself of all the blood the Queen of Hearts would continue shedding if I didn't take this stand. "All right. Let's work out exactly what we want the Diamonds to do for us, and see what Unicorn—"

"Wait." Chess's voice leapt from the air a second before his form blinked into sight. Sweat dampened his rumpled auburn hair, and his broad chest was heaving as if he'd run all the way from the palace. A chill raced through me. Theo had said Chess had gone to do some scouting. Obviously he hadn't liked whatever he'd seen.

"What's wrong?" I said.

Half a dozen pairs of eyes fixed on Chess. He tensed a bit under that scrutiny, and a flicker of uncertainty crossed his face.

"I—I'm not entirely sure," he said in a careful tone. "I was able to listen in on some of the Diamonds' conversation, but they'd already discussed the particulars of their plan, of course. They didn't say anything that clearly revealed their intentions." He studied my face. "You want to accept the alliance."

"I think it would make the battle ahead much easier if it's real," I said. "But if you heard or saw anything that made you uneasy, Chess, I want you to tell me. You know those people better than anyone, even Theo. I trust your judgment."

His mouth twitched, as if caught between smiling and frowning. He wasn't used to people relying on his judgment, was he? All this time, it'd always been him following Theo's directions—or not caring what anyone thought at all. It seemed like a simple request I was making of him, but maybe it wasn't after all.

"It doesn't sit right with me," he said after that momentary hesitation. "The Duchess sounded as if she's in charge, and she's never cared about anyone other than herself in all the time I've known her. And… they were talking about appeasing someone, about avoiding the greater threat. They didn't say enough for me to be sure what they meant, but… I think they're more likely to assume the Queen of Hearts will win against you and to be coming up with a scheme to prove their loyalty to her, than to be afraid of you beating her. They don't know you like we do. They've always been terrified of her."

"They saw how Lyssa took her on during the trial," Theo pointed out. "And how could they hope to turn this in the Hearts' favor?"

"I don't know," Chess admitted, his head ducking. "If they know when we mean to march or what signal to look for, they could betray us. But that was only my impression. I'll admit I may have biases at play."

I didn't think his feelings about the Duchess were biases. They were instincts created through experience—horrible experience. An ache crept through my chest at the thought of giving up this chance, but I believed in *him*. He wouldn't have tried to sway my hopes if he hadn't been awfully worried.

"All right," I said. "We do this without the Diamonds. That way we don't owe them anything. A little more bloodshed on the Hearts' is worth it if it means we don't have to worry about getting stabbed in the back. Come on. We'd better let Unicorn know." I paused, my mind spinning. The ache dug deeper, but I felt the rightness of my next thought all the way down to my bones.

I glanced at Theo. "Do you have enough of your devices ready for us to have a real shot at making it to the throne?"

His eyebrows rose, but he nodded. "I haven't put together everything I was thinking of, but I started with the most important pieces."

I dragged in a breath. "Then *I'll* tell Unicorn. Chess, you stay with me—you've done enough running. Everyone else, round up all the city people who are willing to march on the palace, and set them up with whatever weapons and armor you can. Right now the Diamonds expect us to be considering their offer, not already marching. So we march now and take them all by surprise."

Unicorn looked briefly startled when I told him my decision, but his expression quickly steadied with determination. "I can't blame you for hesitating," he said. "If we're not fighting alongside them, then I'm staying here to fight on this side with you. If you'll have me."

It was my turn to be startled. "Of course," I said. "We'll need all the help we can get. Thank you."

A hint of a smile curled his equine lips. "Thank *you*, Red Queen, for coming back to us before the Hearts completely destroyed Wonderland."

Outside the ice cream café, a crowd was already gathering. Spades ran this way and that, bringing equipment to the city folk. Most of the Clubbers had shaken off their drugged daze, but those who'd agreed to join us for the march shifted nervously as they shrugged on makeshift armor and tested the weapons the Spades had found for them.

We were really doing this. We were going to take back the palace, take back the throne the Hearts family had viciously stolen all those years ago. Despite my nerves, a rush of exhilaration filled me. *Now* my ruby necklace glowed against my chest, but its heat was encouraging, not alarming.

Chess had followed me out. He touched my arm to draw me to the side. "Can I talk to you for a moment before we rush into the fray?" he said.

Did he have some other concern he hadn't wanted to mention in front of the others? I followed him to the edge of an alley away from the noisy activity on the main street. Chess stopped in front of me. He touched the side of my face, bowing his head so his nose brushed mine. My pulse hiccupped giddily as his breath grazed my lips.

"I should have said this last night," he said. "But precision has never been my specialty. Let's just pretend I did."

"Chess," I said, meaning to reassure him, but he shook his head gently to stop me.

"This is what's true," he said. "For most of my life, I've never known where I was going, so the path didn't matter much. You changed that. From here on, the only way I want to go is where I'll find you, for as long as you want me with you. I love you too."

I hadn't needed to hear the words, but the sincerity in his voice washed everything away except the love I felt in return. I tipped my head up to kiss him hard. He kissed me back just as passionately. Then his arms slid around me to hug me close.

"Now let's see you all the way to that throne," he murmured.

"I wouldn't have a chance of getting there without you," I said.

He made a dismissive sound, but he was beaming when we rejoined our growing army.

The crowd was ready within an hour. I hopped up on a crate to look out over the swarm of figures who'd joined our cause. Yes, we could do this. And we would do it now.

"We'll march together up the road to the palace as quickly as we can. I'll take the lead with the jabberwocks to blast open the gate and push back the nearest guards. The Spades will handle as many of the others as they can. All the rest of you need to do is defend yourselves and keep going until we reach the palace. This will be the last day the Queen of Hearts reigns through fear!"

A nervous cheer rose up. I caught Theo's eye at the other end of the crowd, and he nodded.

We set off through the streets, the thump of footsteps behind me gaining confidence with each block. When I held up my hand and the jabberwocks moved to join us at the edge of the city, another cheer rose up, more forceful this time. We barreled on toward the palace.

Guards massed around the main gate as we approached. Some of them were no doubt pearl-headed Clubbers. My stomach twisted at the thought of them charred or sliced by my sword's magic, but I squared my shoulders. There was no way to help them now, and I'd given the guards who still had their real heads plenty of opportunities to come over to our side.

Our charge sped up. I slid my sword free from its hilt. Just as I was about to order the jabberwocks forward, the striped head of the Knave appeared on the parapet next to the gate.

"Halt, Red Queen," he hollered, "or lose what you love most."

What I loved most? I had no idea what he was talking about, but he sounded so sure my pace faltered.

A guard hauled a man into view beside him—a bearded guy in a logo-etched polo shirt who looked only vaguely familiar at that distance. Then the Knave's comrades shoved two more figures into view, and my heart stopped.

Standing side by side, their faces bruised and arms bound behind their backs, my best friend and my mother stared back at me.

CHAPTER TWENTY-TWO

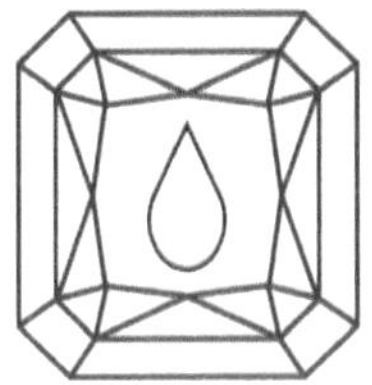

Lyssa

My sword arm sagged, dropping my weapon to my side. At the same time, the Knave gestured, and the guards brought the blades of their daggers to the throats of the three hostages along the wall. They weren't careful about it. A bead of blood streaked down Melody's pale throat. She winced.

Around me, the jabberwocks shuddered with uneasiness. "Hold," I murmured, my voice coming out hoarse. I could hardly pay attention to them, hardly think of anything except the faces of my mother and my best friend in the last place I'd ever have expected to see them. The last place I'd ever have *wanted* to see them.

The guy next to them… It was one of the movers who'd been helping haul the furniture out of Aunt Alicia's house. The Knave must have gone back there and grabbed whoever he could find.

How had he— *Where* had he— When—

The questions jostled in my head, but none of them really mattered. All that mattered was getting those deadly edges away from Mom and Melody's throats. And the mover guy's. He didn't deserve to be here anymore than they did.

I had no idea how to save them, though. The guards could slit their throats in an instant. No one, not even Hatter, could move that fast. Fuck. The smell of the roses in the palace garden drifted over the wall, clogging my nose and making me want to vomit.

The army behind me was stirring restlessly, the metal pieces of their makeshift armor clinking. They had no idea what was going on. I didn't know what to say. The Knave must already be able to tell he'd landed his blow well. Did I want him to know just how much?

He'd managed to get his hands on the two people on the other side of the looking-glass I cared about most.

"Not so hasty now, are you?" the Knave called down. His tiger mouth pulled back into a sneer, his fangs glinting in the midday sun. "Will you sacrifice these three in your bid for the throne?"

He didn't know that only two of them were particularly important to me, then. I didn't see how I could use that fact either. My thoughts were too scattered; my chest clenched tight.

Theo eased closer behind me. "Lyssa?" he said under his breath.

"My mother and my best friend, from back home," I said, just as quietly. "The guy, I don't really know." My gaze didn't leave them for a second. The words "back home" felt strange coming out of my mouth. I'd claimed Wonderland as my home. My bond with the ground beneath my feet rang through me even now when I reached for it.

But the Otherworld had been my home for much longer. I'd already been torn up with guilt over running off on Mom and Melody, leaving them wondering where I'd vanished to. Now they knew where I was, and that was so much worse.

I was a queen here. I had to remember that. I was *the* queen. I tried to summon the resolve and certainty that had carried me to the palace.

"If you have any honor at all, you'll release those three," I said, raising my chin. "You know they have nothing to do with our conflict. Or is your supposed queen so afraid of me that threatening random civilians is the only way she can think to protect herself?"

Some of the Clubbers snickered at the jab. The Knave's sneer tensed, but he didn't care about the Queen of Hearts' pride half as much as she did.

"It looks as though you're the one afraid now," he shot back. "You call yourself a queen, do you? Interloper. Otherlander. What do you think the ones you left behind feel about the danger you've brought down on them?"

He motioned to the guard holding my mom. My stomach dropped as the guy eased his sword a little lower and shoved her right up to the edge of the wall. Mom blinked hard, her face sickly pale. Her shoulders trembled.

"Lyssa?" she said. "What on Earth… What is this place? Who are these people? What have you gotten yourself caught up in?"

A lump filled my throat. "There's too much to explain right now. I'm so sorry. I had no idea… I'm sorry."

"Can you make them stop? Tell them we're not part of… whatever this is. Give them whatever it is they want. Whatever you're doing here, it can't be worth it."

Her voice wavered with the last sentence. I swallowed hard. She had no idea how much rested on my shoulders. What the men holding her and the woman who commanded them wanted was to crush every person behind me, every person in the city. They wanted another two hundred years of battering Wonderland's spirit, if this place survived that long.

It was worth almost anything. But how could I say it was worth these three lives? Mom had raised me, even if she'd needed some help along the way. Melody had been there for me every time I'd turned to her, even if she'd turned to me more often. I'd shared so much of my life with them. I loved them.

The guard behind Melody shoved her forward next. "This is crazy, Lyss," Melody said. "These fucking people—whatever they think they're doing, they've gone way over the top. I really think they'll kill us. This is some scary shit. I don't know what to do."

I didn't know what to tell her either.

Was I a queen or wasn't I? The answer felt suddenly out of reach. How could I say I was the Red Queen, the ruler of all Wonderland, if I'd give up the whole battle for three people who weren't even of this place?

How could I say I was a human being worth living if I let them die?

The moving guy sputtered when the guard nudged him. "She's right, this is fucking crazy," he said. "I don't even know who *you* are. Why the hell am I even here?" He twisted his head toward the Knave. "You've got to let me go. I was just there on a job."

The Knave raised his hand with a jerk, and the guard silenced the guy with the touch of his dagger to the guy's throat.

Another restless rustling spread through the crowd behind me. A prickle ran over my skin. The Knave hadn't made any demands. He hadn't even told me to stop fighting in so many words. His threat was obvious, but he wasn't pushing the issue—why?

My heart started pounding even faster. What else could he want from this stand-off?

"Well?" he shouted. "What will you do, little queen? Would you like to chat with them some more about how they've been treated here? Get a better idea of their fate?"

Of the men I trusted most, Hatter was the only one I could see nearby now. He might know where Theo had moved to in the crowd —Theo could get a better read on the Knave. "Hatter," I said in a low voice. "I have a bad feeling. Can you—"

I was cut off by a torrent of motion. A squad of guards burst from the trees along the side of the road, swinging swords and spears at my army of Clubbers.

I whirled around, my fingers clutching the grip of my sword. The force must have left through a farther gate and slunk through the woods while the Knave distracted us. *No.*

A woman near me shrieked. A teen in a metal helm that looked like it'd once been a pot toppled as a guard stabbed him. More cries rang out from the other side of the road where a matching force was charging at us. We were boxed in by enemies on both sides.

I slashed out with my sword instinctively, but my heart was heavy, my emotions in disarray. The ruby didn't flare to life. No magic leapt from the blade. I only managed to cut a tear through the red-and-pink tunic of a guard right in front of me.

The royal artifacts didn't respond unless I was completely committed.

My shaken confidence rippled through the other connections I'd forged. The jabberwocks spun around, their violet eyes flashing with a testy light, their maws snapping. One lashed out at the incoming wave of guards, but another sent a frantic spurt of flame into the crowd of Clubbers. Someone screamed.

No. I had to get control of the beasts I'd summoned. Planting my feet on the cobblestones, bracing myself in the midst of the chaos, I grasped my scepter and held it up over my head.

Maybe I was afraid of the consequences of this battle, but I knew this land belonged to me. I knew every creature living on it should respond to my command.

"Jabberwocks! Only the ones in pink and red. Only the guards with their helms. The rest of us fight with you, not against you. Please."

The last word dropped from my throat as the jabberwocks wheeled and groaned in clear confusion. The road had turned into a mass of struggling bodies. Billows of smoke puffed up where someone had tossed several of Theo's smoke bombs. The creature closest to me gouged its claws through the road, wrenching up cobblestones in its wake. Another whipped this way and that, more flame dancing over its lips.

They were trying to listen, but the commotion was too much for me to get a proper hold. One snapped its jaws around a woman from the city, and my heart wrenched.

The best I could do was get them out of here before they did our side any more damage.

I waved the scepter in the air. "Jabberwocks—away! Into the trees! Leave us until I call on you again."

Smoke coated my throat. I coughed and stumbled as a body collided with mine. I could barely make out who was friend and foe with the haze swirling around us and sunlight glancing off blades in every dircction.

We'd lost our advantage. The thought of abandoning Mom and Melody to the Queen of Hearts made me queasy all over again, but I'd really have abandoned them if I died here and there was no one left to fight for them at all. All I could think to do was pull away, retreat from the crush of guards on either side, back to the shelter of the city where we could regroup and decide how to deal with this new threat.

If we even could make it back.

"Retreat!" I cried out raggedly. "Spades and Clubbers, back to the city, now, as quickly as you can move!"

The crowd shifted one way and another. I smacked aside a lunging guard with the flat of my sword. The mass of bodies heaved a few steps in the direction of the city, but it was hard to tell if that was even on purpose or just part of the turmoil of the fray. More smoke surged up from somewhere to my left.

My straining eyes couldn't make out anyone I recognized. Theo, Hatter, Chess—they were all lost to me in the chaos. If my heart had been heavy before, now it weighed on my gut like a boulder.

I'd led all these people here, and if I didn't pull them together fast, this march would turn out to have been an invitation to a slaughter.

CHAPTER TWENTY-THREE

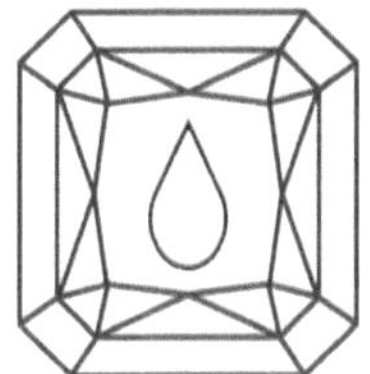

Theo

The Knave on the wall today might not have been the Knave I'd grown up with—my mother had gone through at least a couple in the time I'd lived in the palace, and more since then—but I could sense from his stance as he had the guards prod their captives to call out to Lyssa that there was more at stake here than rubbing his ruthlessness in my queen's face. He was making some kind of play.

I took a step back from Lyssa, scanning the road. We were surrounded by sparsely forested hills on both sides with the main palace gate looming straight ahead. I couldn't see far enough along the wall to make out the next gates farther away. While we'd been charging forward, our force had seemed unstoppable. Now, as the gathered city folk waited on restless feet for further orders, the sensation of being boxed in crawled over my skin.

We'd lost our element of surprise. Our enemies could watch our every move while our line of sight was cut off in every direction except behind us. No, this didn't feel secure at all. I didn't like it one bit.

We'd stopped closer to the wall than I'd usually come on my furtive missions in days past. The smell of the roses grew more pungent, trickling down my throat with every moment we stood here. Flashes of images and the doctors' muttering voices jostled my mind, with an undercurrent of more distant impressions from the pomp and callousness of my childhood. Rich fabrics. Raised voices. The crimson splash of fine wine and the scarlet of fresh-spilled blood.

I stiffened my shoulders, holding myself in the present. I had to focus. I had to *think*.

Breathing shallowly, I eased through the crowd toward a head of red hair that stood out amid the Clubbers. Dum caught my eye and drew himself straighter the second he saw my expression. The Knave was taunting Lyssa again, but I tuned his voice out. He was trying to keep our attention on him—to distract us from other things.

"Go along the east side of the road, watching the woods," I said, and handed Dum a few of my smoke bombs. He closed his fingers carefully around the egg-shaped devices. "If you see any movement, shout a warning and slow them down with the smoke and those sprightly legs."

A tight smile curled Dum's lips. "I can do that."

"And the west side?" a light voice said at my shoulder. Chess's grin flashed for a second before he shimmered into view.

Just the man I'd wanted to talk to next. I gave him a few smoke bombs too. "You can put those stealthy fighting skills to good use, if you need to."

"Here's to the very slim chances I don't," Chess said with a salute, and vanished.

I was just turning on my heel, watching Dum reach the edge of the road and feeling decently satisfied with my preparations, when the forest on either side of us exploded with a flurry of movement.

Guards careened down the slopes on either side, red and pink flooding toward us between the trees. There wasn't time for Dum or Chess to really slow them down. Smoke burst on either side of the road, but too close to our haphazard army. It flowed over us as well as through the trees, and the guards were already on us.

I caught glimpses of my Spades dashing to the defense, wielding the electrically charged batons I'd given out. Sparks flitted through the smoke. The city folk, who'd never really had to or been inclined to fight before, jostled against each other with panicked faces. A few steps away from me, one of the guards speared a young man straight through. My gut lurched.

"Hold tight!" I shouted, even though I wasn't sure they'd even know what to make of that suggestion. I squeezed through churning crowd to zap and smack aside a few of the closest guards with my own baton. My other hand wrenched my short sword from my belt, but I hardly had room to use it without risking slicing through my own people too.

With a warbling roar, one of the jabberwocks reared up over the clouds of smoke. Its head shot into our midst and snatched up a guard. Before I could feel grateful for that, another of the feathered monsters let loose a stream of fire over a clot of Clubbers. Shrieks and the odor of burnt flesh mingled with the rose stink in the air.

Lyssa's bright voice, fraught with tension now, broke through the chaos. I couldn't make out anything more than the word "jabberwocks," but whatever she'd said and done, it at least made them back off from the fray.

I snapped my baton left and right, sending one guard to the ground and another wheeling backward, but more were battering us from all around the road. Farther down, Mallo's hair clung to her sweaty forehead as she exchanged blows with a guard holding a spiked club. Unicorn pummeled another pleated figure with his hooves. Hatter's hands whipped out, one with his narrow dagger and the other with a hatpin. He caught one guard in mid stab, but he wasn't quite fast enough to stop another from slashing through a woman's stomach.

My pulse rattled through my veins. What if they got to Lyssa? Hearts take me, what if they took down all of us? The rebellion we'd built over so many years might fall apart in the space of an hour. And then what would Wonderland be left with?

Lyssa's voice rang out again, this time clear enough to split through the clatter of the battle.

"Retreat! Back to the city, now, as quickly as you can move!"

The idea made me balk down to my core, but in the same moment, I understood it was our only real option. We were hemmed in here—we had no real chance of making it through the gate, let alone across the grounds to the palace. Our best hope was to pull back and regroup.

The Clubbers around me bumped against each other as they tried to orient themselves. Fear still whitened their faces. "This way!" I hollered with a sweep of my arm. Several of those anxious gazes locked onto me.

"Inventor!" one woman said, with a sob. "What do we do?"

Even more of the city folk turned toward me, a hint of relief touching their expressions.

"The Inventor will know what to do."

"Should we go?"

"You've got to help us!"

My stomach twisted at the barrage of hopeful but frantic voices. Their queen—their *true* queen—had just told them what to do, but that wasn't enough.

They'd known me, turned to me for help, for ages. She'd only revealed who she was a few days ago. How could I blame them?

I dragged in a breath, and the scent of roses saturated my lungs. A cool thread of thought bloomed in the back of my head and curled tight around every other intention.

I could spin this in my favor—have all the power I'd once assumed was mine in the space of a few heartbeats. Win their loyalty now even more than I'd ever had it before, and they'd turn to me every time afterward too. Lyssa might sit on the throne, but I'd be the one truly in command.

Even as the idea crossed through my mind, the rest of me rebelled. Nausea coiled in my stomach. A chill raced over my skin.

Lyssa and the others hadn't really rescued me when they'd hustled me out of the palace a few days ago, had they? Its hooks had been in me still. If I was going to be free of the horrors of my family's reign, I was going to have to rescue myself, once and for all.

My gaze sought out Lyssa's form through the haze and the turmoil. Her pale hair streamed around her, tinted with the reddish glow from the rubies on her vest. My mother's treachery had battered and overwhelmed her just like my family's had all of Wonderland, but she was still standing, unbroken.

Like Wonderland itself.

The understanding clicked into place like a wire into its slot. I'd wanted to champion Wonderland, to build it back into the realm it had once been. I could still do that with everything I had in me. Our queen *was* Wonderland. The realm's fate lay within her. Being her champion was all I could ever have wanted.

With that realization, the treacherous urge inside me crumbled away. The poison laced through my bloodline disintegrated. I raised my voice with all the conviction I had in me.

"Friends!" I called out. "We must follow the Red Queen. Retreat toward the city, quickly, as she said! Listen for her commands. She'll guide us true. We can overcome our enemies yet if we stand with her and do not falter."

I moved down the road, jabbing at the guards who tried to stop us as I went. One knocked my sword from my hand as I swiped at him, but I sent him stumbling backward with a thrust of my baton. The crowd surged around me, really moving now, displacing the guards from the road just with the force of so many bodies. We'd lost some, but most were still standing.

I dug into my pouch and produced a handful of skitter cubes. "Toss them at the ground by the guards," I shouted, passing some along to the figures around me. "It'll slow them down." I hurled one of my own, and several of the new guards running at us skidded and fell on the silvery shards of metal that slipped beneath their feet.

Our army swarmed along the road back toward the city, pulling away from the main force of the guards as they stumbled and tripped and our batons forced them back. The Hearts' force gathered together between us and the palace, but we had no intention of making another attempt at it now.

They pressed forward as we kept hustling on. They'd follow us all the way to the city if we let them.

That realization sent a fresh chill through me. Lyssa's jabberwocks had dispersed. There was nothing to stop the Hearts' Guard from pushing any advantage they gained today even farther. We'd needed this retreat, but we couldn't outright flee, not if we wanted to keep our freedom after.

I wove through the crowd, gripping shoulders here and there to offer words of encouragement, toward where the sunlight glanced off Lyssa's white-blond hair near the edge of the fray. The rubies on her armored vest still cast her with their ruddy glow, and relief rushed through me to see her unharmed other than a shallow cut near her elbow. Several of the Spades had gathered around her to help fend off the guards following our retreat.

I motioned to Chess, and he leapt in front of her to shield her completely. Lyssa glanced back at me, her face so stark with tension it made my heart ache for her. I grasped her arm and leaned close to speak over the clang of blades.

"We've survived the worst of it. We can hold our ground here. We have to show the guards they can't push us back completely. *You* can show your people that this retreat isn't a full-out loss."

"I don't want any more of the Clubbers getting hurt because of me," Lyssa said, doubt coloring her voice. My heart squeezed tighter.

"Not because of you," I said fiercely. "Because of the villains we're fighting. No matter what else happens, you've been amazing, Lyssa. You're our queen. You're *my* queen, as long as I live. It's an honor to stand here with you. Don't let the bastards take what belongs to you."

Her grip on her sword tightened. I felt the power moving through her body as her spirit stirred to action. She shot me a quick glance, grateful and determined, and raised her sword to catch the sunlight, high enough that our whole force should have seen it.

"We stand here!" she cried. "Fall in behind me, protect each other's backs, and don't give up your ground. They can't move us if we won't be moved."

Then she sprang forward, sweeping the sword down and across. A crackling wave of magic surged from the blade. It slammed the guards several feet back, blood welling through the rents in their uniforms, bodies crashing into those behind. When the ones farther back tried to surge past their injured companions, Lyssa lashed out again, toppling them too.

The crowd pulled tight around me. The Clubbers still looked

nervous, but their chins were high, their eyes bright. We'd survived this long, and they weren't so scared any more that we wouldn't survive longer.

They believed in our queen.

The guards spread out, attempting to circle our army again, but the Spades along the edges battered them with stones and tossed skitter cubes into their midst. Those still on the road between us and the palace milled around uncertainly.

Our Clubber allies probably should have still been scared. The guards wouldn't hesitate much before they came at us again, and we would run out of tricks like the skitter cubes soon. But for now, we'd shown we weren't that easily cowed. That might just be enough.

I wove through the crowd once, handing out my last few skitter cubes, nodding to my Spade companions. My pulse thumped with a ragged rhythm driven by adrenaline and hope. Then a choked hush fell over the fray.

A grand figure had appeared on the wall by the gate, her tall crown gleaming and her eyes glimmering even across that distance. I stopped in my tracks. My innards tangled into knots at the sight of my mother, but my feet held steady against the ground.

She knew what I was now. I'd only lied to her before to get where I needed to go. That time was past. All that mattered now was how to stop her from dealing out even more terror.

She grazed her elegant hand over the heads of the Otherlander hostages the Knave had gathered. Her lips pursed into a tense smile. When she let them part, her cudgel of a voice carried all the way up the road.

"False queen and false queen's disciples, you have twelve hours to make your surrender. If the one of the line of Alice does not present herself to me for my justice within that time, the three on the wall will meet their deaths instead. And then the rest of you will follow them. Guards, to me!"

She spun with a whirl of her massive skirts, and the guards drew back to congregate by the gate, leaving us with her ultimatum and her threat ringing in our ears.

CHAPTER TWENTY-FOUR

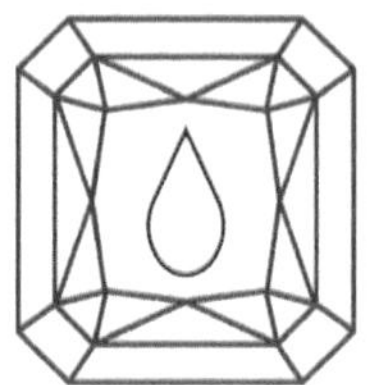

Lyssa

A couple of days ago, Wonderland's city streets had been filled with partiers. Maybe those people had been caught up in drug-fueled whims they couldn't control, but they'd given some appearance of being happy.

Now we were laying out the wounded along the road beneath the gleaming silver tower. Dozens of Clubbers and Spades sprawled on blankets and mats or simply pieces of clothing laid out for a bit of comfort. Mallo, it turned out, had some medical skill, so she was moving from person to person checking on their needs, bandaging or sewing up wounds as need be, with Doria acting as her assistant. A few of the city people had volunteered their services too. Dum passed around tubes of the healing cream Theo had used on my bad cut weeks ago.

The scent of the roses, even the smoke of their burning, had dispersed completely. A fresh bready smell wafted from the bakery on the corner, where the owner was hard at work making loaves to feed this crowd.

I walked along the street with my sword at my hip and my

scepter at my back, my nerves jumping despite the comforting warmth of the afternoon sun. But even though no music was playing and I heard more groans than laughter, this was better. These people had made their own choice, and they'd fought for what they believed in.

They'd believed in me.

The patients sat up a little straighter when I approached. Their faces lit up in spite of whatever pain they were feeling. Any friends or relatives keeping them company gazed at me with no hint of blame for the injuries dealt under my watch, only awe and an eager sort of hope.

"Red Queen," one woman said. "Thank you. We're going to take Wonderland back for ourselves."

"Yes, we will," I said, with all the confidence I had in me. "And thank *you*. I couldn't do it on my own. We're only succeeding because we're willing to face the danger together."

"We were always in danger before," the man beside her muttered. "It doesn't matter how hard we tried not to notice. *She* was always looming over us—one wrong step, one wrong word…"

"It won't be like that when I take back the throne," I promised him. "I don't want anyone hurt. This isn't about power or vengeance. When we free Wonderland, you'll truly be *free*. A ruler is supposed to serve their country and their people, not the other way around."

"No one could watch you and not know you're doing all you can for us," another woman said, cradling the sling around her broken arm. "I'll fight again if I can."

I went on down one side of the street and then up the other like that, giving everyone a chance to talk to me, letting them see how much I cared. My heart still weighed heavy in my chest, but I tried not to let that tension show on my face. I smiled and kept my voice mild. I thanked everyone for the risks they'd faced in the battle. It was all I could think to do, right now.

It was hardest when the questions came. "Red Queen, when will we march again?"

"What will we bring to the Hearts' doorstep next?"

"How will we finally bring her down?"

"I'll talk with my advisors in the Spades, and we'll have a new plan soon," I told everyone. "Before the end of the day, we'll hold the palace."

Or the palace would hold me, probably without my head. I didn't think it'd help spirits any to comment on that possibility, though.

Dum came over to me as I finished my circuit. His mouth was twisted as if he wasn't sure he should be saying what he was going to.

I paused. "What is it?"

"I just—" He sighed. "You'd probably have said something if you had, but I have to ask: Did you see any sign of Dee when we were out by the palace?"

His anguish for his brother showed all across his face. He had loved ones in the Queen's grip too. I couldn't imagine it was any easier knowing one of them had put himself there purposefully.

"I'm sorry," I said. "I didn't. When we take the palace, the first thing we'll do is search for him, all right?"

"You don't need— I understand he's a traitor." He looked down at his hands. "I'm not asking you for anything. It's just hard for me not to wonder."

"Of course it is," I said. "And I *want* to find him, so we can hear his explanation for himself. He doesn't deserve whatever the Queen has in store for him—I'm sure of that."

Dum let out his breath. "Okay. Thank you."

He still looked pained. "*You* did everything you could to keep him safe," I said, remembering how he'd always looked out for his brother. "You know that, right?"

"Did I?" Dum said. "I've thought a lot about our last conversation, things I might have said differently or could have said but didn't… I should have found some way to convince him to stay with us. Or maybe I should have gone with him and we could have found another way that wouldn't have hurt the Spades, even if it was the death of both of us. He was ready to give up everything for family, and I wasn't."

"Hey," I said firmly, and waited until he raised his head. "You didn't know what he was going to do. And *you* did what you thought was best for everyone that matters to you. It was a horrible position to be in—it still is—but he made his own choices. Try to remember that and to keep hope."

Dum nodded, the tension in him relaxing only a little. I resisted the urge to hug myself as he went to talk with Doria about something.

My loved ones in the palace hadn't made any choice. The only reason they were there was because of the Queen's vendetta against me and the war I was waging against her.

Theo emerged from the tower just then with an armful of supplies. He caught my eye with a tip of his head, and I waited for him while he distributed more tubes and thread and a substance Wonderlanders apparently used to make casts. Then he strode over to meet me.

With his head high and the sun glancing off his chestnut curls, he looked every bit the prince. Even heavy, my heart still fluttered seeing his commanding presence, even though technically I held more authority than he did now.

"How are you holding up?" he asked, coming to a stop a few feet away from me. That was the one area where he wasn't so assured anymore—navigating his closeness with me. He wouldn't have felt he needed to leave that much space before. I'd appreciated the consideration at first, but suddenly it made me weary.

We had so many enemies and troubles in front of us. Why let the past hurts linger on any more? I knew why he'd done what he had; I knew how honorable and devoted he was at heart despite it.

"Well enough," I said, which was the most I wanted to admit where the wounded Clubbers could hear me. "I just wanted to see how everyone here is holding up. I thought I owed them that."

"I'm sure your concern helped raise their spirits," Theo said with a smile.

Mallo passed us and paused to bob her head to me. For the first time, even though her former leader was standing right next to me, her gaze fixed on me instead of Theo.

"I think we've taken care of all the injured as well as we can, Red Queen," she said. "What else can I do that would be useful?"

There was no irony or bitterness in her tone. She actually wanted my opinion. I guessed she was glad now that the Spades hadn't offered me up to the Queen of Hearts in sacrifice all those weeks ago. Part of me wanted to laugh, but all of me was glad to see I'd managed to make an impression on one of my harshest critics along with the Clubbers.

"Are there any other supplies we need gathered?" I asked Theo.

He shook his head. "I have that covered."

I turned back to Mallo. "We can't trust the Queen of Hearts to stick to the timeline she gave us. The more people we have patrolling the edge of the city, the better. Sound the warning if you see anything at all that worries you, okay?"

"Of course," she said, and darted off.

"Winning over hearts and minds," Theo said after she'd disappeared from view, sounding amused. He motioned for me to walk with him farther down the street, away from the resting patients. "You didn't need much time."

His praise brought a flush into my cheeks that was probably not very regal. "Apparently I was born for this. And it's not all that hard to look better than my counterpart, is it?" That being his mother. Maybe not the best point to raise.

Theo didn't look insulted. It wasn't as if he liked the Queen of Hearts' methods any more than I did.

"You sell yourself short," he said. "I know it's been hard. I know it must be even harder now, with the Knave's new plot. You've held your own better than most people would have. Born for it or not, this is you."

I swallowed thickly. "Thank you for helping me get my focus back during the battle. Seeing people from back home here—seeing how he was treating them—it was hard to think clearly."

"I only said what was true," Theo said simply. "I've been part of this struggle for ages longer than you have. I'll always speak my mind if I see a strategy I think we should use. And then you get to decide whether you listen to me, my queen." The corner of his lips curled slyly with that last comment.

We ambled around the corner onto a quieter street, and I stopped him with a hand on his arm. "Theo… You know I'm not at all angry with you anymore, don't you? I don't have any doubts about which side you're on. I don't have any doubts about whether you care about me. It's never going to be the same as when you were the White Knight and I was an Otherlander, lost and confused, but you don't have to hold yourself back with me. In case that wasn't clear."

Theo's smile softened. He stepped closer, setting his hands on my waist. "It is different now," he said, his voice low. "You *are* my queen. And I'm from the family that destroyed yours."

I made a dismissive sound. "At least one member of my family abandoned Wonderland instead of taking up the crown she was meant to. I'm pretty sure we're past judging each other by our ancestors. And I'm not just the queen. I'd better not ever be just the queen. I'm still the woman who was falling in love with you."

"Was?" Theo repeated lightly.

"I think we can say I'm finished falling."

He closed the last few inches between us and kissed me, one hand rising to trace his fingertips over my cheek. I leaned into him, wishing I could enjoy this connection for more than just a moment, knowing I couldn't.

Theo pulled back only slightly, his head still bowed. "I'm not perfect," he said. "I'm still her son, along with everything else I am. I think I'll have to grapple with the impulses of that heritage as long as I live. But after today… I have no fears at all that I can't overcome them. The rest of me is stronger."

"I know," I said. "You wouldn't be here at all if that wasn't true. Did you only just figure that out?"

His lips twitched with another smile. "I suppose it's taken me a little while to find my feet again. A prince never shows his weaknesses, you know. It simply isn't done."

I wrinkled my nose at that comment and gave him another quick kiss on the mouth. "Maybe not, but Theo had better know he can." I glanced down the street. "Where are we heading? I've got an awful lot of plans to make." The weight of the Queen's timeline and the threat that came with it pressed back down on me.

"I asked Hatter and Chess to meet us at the hat shop," Theo said. "I thought maybe, in light of the stakes, you'd prefer to talk things through first with those of us you know best rather than a whole crowd of Spades. Although if you'd prefer more or less or to be left alone to think it through, just say the word."

"No," I said, wrapping my hand around his. "Talking it through with you three sounds just right. I think it's going to take a lot of talking."

Anxiety crept back through my body as we made our way through the streets. It loosened a little when we stepped into the shop to the sight of the other two men I loved. Chess was perched on the edge of the counter, his legs dangling, and Hatter leaned against the glass display case next to him. He nudged today's bowler hat up over his spiky blond hair as he straightened up to greet us.

"So," he said. "We have quite the conundrum. I'm sorry, Lyssa."

The apology sounded like more than just an expression of sympathy. I blinked at him. "It's not your fault."

He grimaced. "It might be, in part. I noticed when we took this place back from the guards that Alicia's sketch of her house—your house—was missing. It never occurred to me the guards would have taken it, but… That has to be how they got to your mother and your friend. Whoever went through the looking-glass used it to focus on their destination and arrive there."

And Mom and Melody—and the mover—had still been at the house in the aftermath of my disappearance. It might have been only hours for them since I'd leapt back into Wonderland.

"It doesn't matter," I said. "You couldn't have predicted the Knave would use it that way. What matters is he's got them now, and I don't know what to do about it."

"What have you been thinking, lovely?" Chess said. "Ramble on all you want. I find I often make my way to an answer if I just keep talking toward it."

I wasn't sure any of my thoughts so far would get us anywhere. "I don't know. I just feel torn." I raked my fingers through my hair. "We can't surrender. The Queen of Hearts will slaughter me and all the Spades and who knows how many of the Clubbers—and I'm not naïve enough to think she'd even spare Mom or Melody once she's gotten her way. But I can't just march right back to the palace and risk her killing them to punish me. They never asked to be part of this. They *shouldn't* be part of this. It's my world, but it isn't theirs."

"I wouldn't put it past her to order them killed as promised," Theo said. "Not at all. But I will say that she's clearly scared of you. If she'd truly felt she had the upper hand, she'd have demanded your surrender immediately. But then you could have called her bluff, and if she'd killed them right away, she'd have lost her only bargaining chip. She didn't believe her guards could hold our forces back if we'd taken up the charge with full commitment again."

"So she left me to stew on it," I said.

"And she bought herself more time to rally her own defenses," Hatter said. "No doubt she's got another cartload of pearl-heads on the way."

"Then if we're going to strike again, we should strike as soon as we can, before she has much chance to think up other ways to screw us over." I let out my breath. "But we can't get any prisoners out of the palace without storming it and forcing her hand in the first place. It doesn't matter how scared she is—I still have to make sure Mom and Melody get out of this."

Theo set his hand on my shoulder. "We've only just started talking. Between the four of us, and the minds of all the Spades and the city folk if we need to turn to them, we'll find an answer. That's what being a leader is—finding an answer that satisfies every side of the equation. The land itself is on your side. I know you can find your way through."

Hatter's eyes gleamed bright as he took my other hand in his. "And we have advantages the Queen of Hearts will never even think of," he said. "She approaches every problem in the same old standard ways. Make threats, try to bully everyone into submission. We're ready to do anything. All we have to do is find the right wild, mad plan, and she'll never know what hit her."

Chess scooted closer along the counter and bent over to brush a kiss to the top of my head. "And no matter what comes, you *do* have all of us. The Queen of Hearts orders everyone from a distance because she rules with fear. You've already got all the respect and love you need to put you on that throne. I'll think with you in whatever which way we need to until the right idea sparks."

My throat tightened with all the faith and affection surrounding me. I gripped Hatter's hand harder, leaned into Theo's touch, and squeezed Chess's knee as I glanced around at all of them. Even with the massive threat looming over me, it felt important to take a moment to say this one thing to the three so different but all so important men who owned my heart.

"I'm going to want you all to stay with me, you know. If—no, *when*—I take that throne. I don't know if any queen of Wonderland has had three partners before, but I don't really care what's normal. I want all of you by my side. We'll make Wonderland wondrous again together."

"Lyssa..." Hatter kissed my cheek, his voice abruptly choked. Chess embraced me from behind. Theo just beamed at me. That was all I needed to know they wanted to be with me as much as I wanted them.

Maybe they would have said more, except right then the door burst open to reveal a panting Kip.

"One of the jabberwocks came back," he said. "We need our queen before it charbroils the whole street."

CHAPTER TWENTY-FIVE

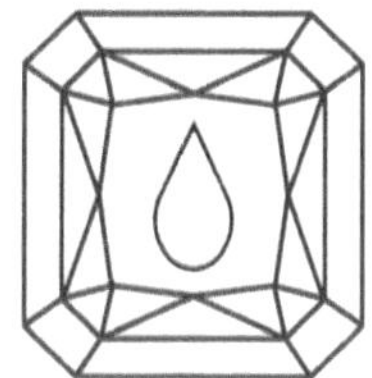

Lyssa

The jabberwock's burbling moans carried several blocks from the edge of the city where it had started its rampage. I picked up my pace to a run, sliding my scepter from its carry bag as my feet smacked the cobblestones. Kip sped up too, waving his arm to show me the right direction. My three lovers loped along just behind me.

An all-too familiar sickly sweet scent tickled my nose. I hesitated, my fingers tensing around the scepter's staff.

"Did the guards dump more roses here?" I asked.

Kip shook his head, wrinkling his nose. "There was an old batch in an alley out here we managed to miss. The drug is mostly faded by now, but some of the residents are still pretty dazed. We figure the smell is what drew the jabberwock. It's the palace folk they're really not happy with. Wish this one had taken its anger out on the guards instead."

No kidding. As we dashed closer, the faint prickle of smoke reached my nose as well. If the jabberwocks I'd encouraged to come to the city had hurt anyone else here… Guilt twisted my gut.

We came around a bend to the scattered buildings along the edge of the city. The jabberwock fluttered its frail, useless wings and let out a belch that sent flames licking over the side of the nearest house. Its head wove from side to side on its feathered, serpentine neck, and its clawed feet clattered against the group. I could tell at a glance it wasn't angry so much as distressed. Although an unhappy jabberwock didn't look very different from a raging one.

The Spades and a few of the Clubbers were hustling residents out of their houses and away down the street. Some of the locals, like Kip had suggested, swayed on their feet, their expressions dazed with growing confusion. This was not a sight I'd have wanted anyone to wake up from a drug-haze to.

My nerves shivered when the jabberwock swung its maw toward us with a rasp of its jagged teeth, but I clenched my jaw and strode into the middle of the street. Figures amid the trees caught my eyes with a stutter of my pulse. A couple of the drug-dazed Clubbers had wandered into the forest instead of deeper into the city. One stumbled over a branch just a few feet from the jabberwock's lashing tail. Its head snapped in their direction at the sound.

"Jabberwock!" I called out quickly, raising the scepter in the air. The tingle of its calming, clarifying energy washed over me and flowed out toward the massive creature with the ruby's crimson glow.

At my voice, the jabberwock turned back to face me. As the glow touched it, its body stilled, its gaze focusing completely on me. It let out another moan, but this one sounded more questioning than distraught.

One of the Clubbers behind it scrambled onward through the forest on unsteady feet. The one closer to us had stopped. The woman rubbed her eyes as if she'd just woken from a sound sleep. Her gaze settled on me, her eyes abruptly sharp with attention. Then she registered the jabberwock and leapt backwards with a squeak of shock. Despite being startled, she managed to keep her balance.

I glanced from her to the jabberwock. How had she come out of her daze?

A suspicion crept up through my mind. The scepter's energy might have washed over her too as I'd sent it toward the jabberwock. Had it cleared the drug's effects from her mind, just like it'd cleared the jabberwock's frantic impulses?

If I'd known that was possible, our job recovering the city would have been a whole lot simpler. Of course, maybe I'd have worn out the scepter's magic if I'd tried to bring the entire population out of their daze in the course of a day.

Right now, I had to deal with the jabberwock first. Keeping the scepter held up between us, I took a step closer to the creature. It bowed its head to meet me.

"Hey," I said in a soothing voice. "There's no danger here. There's nothing to fight. But it's good that you came back to us. We can still use your protection from the ones in the red-and-pink uniforms—the Queen of Hearts' men. Will you help us again?"

The jabberwock let out a sound that was closest to a sigh and nudged its muzzle against my extended hand. A smile touched my lips. It wanted to serve this land, to free it, just as much as I did. The creatures just needed a push in the right direction and guiding words to keep them on track.

"Will you call the other ones back before we march on the palace again?" Theo asked from where he'd stopped a little behind me.

I patted the jabberwock's nose and pointed along the line of the forest. "Go to the road and keep watch there. You know how to warn me."

As the creature lumbered off, I turned back to my companions. Chess was grinning, Hatter's eyes gleaming with a mix of awe and worry for me. Theo studied me, waiting for my answer.

"If we come up with a plan where I'm sure I can keep control of them, I will," I said. "They've been valuable allies. It wasn't their fault that they got confused during the battle. *I* was confused."

The woman who'd come out of her drugged state eased tentatively toward the buildings now that the jabberwock had left. "Is it safe?" she said, sounding totally alert.

"It should be," I said, and remembered the possibility that had occurred to me earlier. "Where are the rest of the Clubbers who are still recovering from the drug?" I asked Kip. "I want to see them—I think I might be able to help."

"The others were just taking them a couple of streets over," he said. "We figured staying out in the fresh air was the best thing if they're going to come out of it soon."

"Let's see if I can bring them out of it right now."

I brandished my scepter, and he led the way. Theo fell into step next to me. "What are you thinking?" he said.

"The scepter calms creatures down and brings them to me by clearing all the distractions out of their minds," I said. "The same way it can push back literal darkness. I think it accidentally had the same effect on one of the Clubbers who was still under the drug's influence. I'd like to see if I can do it again."

And if I could… The start of another idea trembled eagerly at the back of my mind.

Like Kip had said, the other Spades had ushered the drugged city people to a nearby street. They drifted over the cobblestones looking aimless and anxious at the same time. I adjusted my fingers around my scepter and held it out again, picturing the drug's tendrils retreating from all those minds.

"People of Wonderland," I said steadily but gently. "Remember what matters to you. Remember yourselves. Come through the fog and back to me."

The ruby's glow grew, filling my eyes and spilling out across the street. My breath caught with the energy streaming through that light. Gasps and startled cries sounded all down the street.

When the light faded, I peered, blinking, at the Clubbers it had touched. They were staring around, bewildered but present, like the woman I'd woken up by the jabberwock. A rush of triumph filled my chest. As the Spades started answering their barrage of questions, I spun around to face the three men who'd followed me this far.

"Is there somewhere we could get to quickly where we could ambush just a few guards?"

Chess's eyebrows leapt up. "And where will you go with them after you get them?"

Theo considered my scepter, his gaze going thoughtful. When he spoke up, I knew he'd guessed my intention. "Is there any particular kind of guard you want to ambush?"

I dropped my voice, not wanting to get any hopes up outside our small circle in case this gambit didn't work. "I want to see what this scepter's magic can do for a pearl-head."

Hatter stared at me for a second. "You think—" He shook his head. "No. Their minds are gone. There's no one there to save."

"Maybe not, but we won't know that for sure until we try. Do you have any idea how pearling even works?"

"There's some kind of magic to it, but no, I've got no idea how it all comes together," he admitted.

"Then there's a chance I can help them," I said. "And even if I can't bring back any of the people they used to be… at least I can try to wipe the Queen of Hearts' influence from their minds. Free them from serving her."

Theo nodded. "It's worth a try. It could make a huge difference in our plans. Come on. I think I know a spot where they'll be stationed. We don't want to lose much time to this."

The Queen's deadline was hanging over all our heads, but mine especially, if I wanted to make sure my mother and my best friend kept *their* heads. I dragged in a breath. "You show me the way. Chess, why don't you come too in case we need help grabbing the one I'm going to try to wake up? Hatter, can you see if we can equip the people still willing to fight for us with some better armor in the meantime? You've got to have some good helmet techniques up your sleeve at least."

Hatter's mouth quirked upward. "I might have an idea or two. Don't get up to anything too exciting without me."

"I'll be right back." I stepped in to give him a quick kiss as if to make those words a promise.

Chess set off with a bounce in his step as if he was eager to get back into action. "Where are we off to, Whi—ah, Theo?"

"Through the forest," Theo said with a sweeping motion. "I know some of the favorite posts outside the palace grounds."

We stayed quiet as we moved between the trees. When we got close to the spot Theo expected to find guards on the look-out, he sent Chess ahead invisibly to scope out the lay of the land. Chess returned after a few minutes with a smirk.

"Three of them," he murmured to us. "One a pearl-head. What are we going to do with the other two while our queen is working her magic on him?"

Theo smiled. "I'm sure between the two of us we can come up with something."

"Don't hurt them any more than you need to," I reminded them. "We're trying to set the opposite example from the current rule."

Chess saluted me, and Theo pulled a length of metallic rope from his pocket. The two of them set off ahead of me. I trailed along behind, waiting for my turn to play a part. Stealthy attacks didn't seem to correspond with any of my queenly powers. I guessed it'd be a little much if I had the magic to handle every situation in the world.

Was it possible my scepter might bring back the people who'd lost their heads and then been pearled? Hope fluttered through my heart. If I could manage that, then all the innocent people the Queen had ordered taken and killed for her use—I could restore them to the friends and family they'd been stolen from. I could give them their lives back.

Theo and Chess sprang forward. There was a thump and a grunt, followed by a brief rustling. When I reached the guard post, two men who looked fully conscious sat against a tree trunk, gagged and wrists bound, another loop of rope around their chests tying them in to the tree. Other than a red mark on the verge of a bruise on one's forehead, they didn't appear to have suffered much damage.

Chess was holding the arms of the pearl-headed guard, his hand clamped over the man's mouth. From the puff of the young guy's cheeks, he was trying to yell anyway. His gaze floated dimly over us, his body jerking with a repetitive attempt to dislodge his captor.

My throat constricted. He barely understood what was happening, clearly—he was simply following the orders the Queen had given him as well as he could. No thought seemed to pass behind those glazed eyes. He might as well have been an actual pearl for all the independent consciousness he showed.

There was no point in prolonging his distress. We led him several paces away where the other guards couldn't observe us. Then I drew out my scepter and held the ruby level with his eyes. All the longing in me to undo the damage the Queen had done to him radiated through me into the warm wood in my hand. The ruby lit up with its soft glow.

"What the Queen of Hearts said, it can leave your mind," I said. "You don't need to follow her orders or those of her men. You can be who you were before. Follow who you want to follow. Everything they told you, everything they commanded you to do, let it fall away."

The pearl-headed man's body gradually relaxed. Chess eased up his hold, and the guy stood there without any resistance. He pursed his lips but didn't speak when Chess removed his hand. His eyes still looked glazed, but not quite as blankly as before. Or maybe that was just my wishful thinking.

"Hey," I said, lowering the scepter to my side. "Do you know who you are? What's your name?"

The man's eyelids twitched. He focused on me as if he were seeing me from a great distance away. "Name," he repeated slowly. "I— Who are you?"

"I'm the Red Queen," I said. "The rightful ruler of Wonderland."

His face brightened. "*You* are the one I should listen to. I hear it—I feel it."

He still sounded pretty vague. My stomach tightened. "I'm not going to order you to do anything. I just wanted you to be free. The Queen of Hearts was treating you like a slave. Do you remember anything from before? You probably lived in the city once…" I didn't know whether he was one of the recent people she'd snatched or someone who'd served her for a while.

His head drifted from one side to the other. "I saw a yellow house," he said dreamily. "I liked it. And there was… chocolate?" A pleased chuckle escaped his lips.

Theo and Chess exchanged a glance. My heart sank. Maybe there were a few fragments of the man this guy used to be that had survived the pearling process, but no more than that.

I wasn't bringing anyone back, not really.

But I'd still broken him from his subservience to the Queen. He was no longer her slave. And if I could do that with him…

"Come on," I said, giving him a gentle nudge. "Let's get you someplace safer."

"You accomplished the most important part," Theo said as we started walking. "He *is* free."

"And I can free the others. A lot of the Queen's army is made of pearl-heads now." How far could the scepter's glow reach? I guessed I was going to find out. "That'll make the battle easier, but it doesn't solve all of our problems."

"No," Theo said. "But it's given me an idea. And seeing you with the jabberwock gave me another one. Let's see if I can't invent our way to victory one last time."

CHAPTER TWENTY-SIX

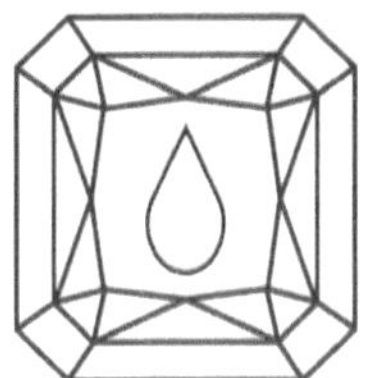

Hatter

"It doesn't seem quite right that you all have turned out to be more mad than I ever was," I said, eyeing the beast that Theo had just presented me with on the outskirts of the city.

Jabberwocks weren't the most reassuring sight on the best of days. The creature's red and gold feathers ruffled as it shifted its considerable weight, its searing violet eyes watching me from far over my head. I caught a whiff of its sour, meaty breath. But the worst part about the sight in front of me was the broad, metal-framed strips of fabric that Theo had slid over the creature's stumpy natural wings and strapped around its broad chest. It flapped them tentatively as I watched.

"The line between brilliance and madness is rather thin, in my experience," Theo said with a crooked smile. "*It* doesn't seem to mind."

"Do the wings actually work?" I asked, even though I found it hard to believe we'd be standing here discussing this in the first place if he hadn't tested and confirmed as much already. "Can the beast fly?"

"We took a few trial runs over the mushroom stands once it got dark," Theo said. "I'm not sure how long the contraptions will last, but we don't need it to fly a marathon. Maybe ten minutes to fly to and around the palace, a matter of seconds to pull off the rescue—I expect it to go off without a hitch."

"Easy for you to say when you're not the one who'll be riding on it," I muttered. I would have asked why me, but I already knew that too. I was Hatter of the nimble fingers. If anyone was going to snatch Lyssa's loved ones to safety in time, it was me.

I just hadn't been counting on doing it from the back of a monster that had only just discovered proper flight.

"There are additional straps attached to the ones holding the artificial wings in place." Theo pointed. "You can wrap them around your legs to keep you secure, so you won't have to worry about falling when you let go with your hands. The loose straps at the back are for your passengers. Lyssa has told the jabberwock to listen to you. The rest of the plan is as we discussed with the group."

I crossed my arms over my chest and eyed the creature. "You're going to let me be the boss, huh?" I said to it. "Even without a fancy scepter? Let's see that head of yours down here where I can look at you face to face, then."

Even though I'd seen how well Lyssa could persuade the creatures, my pulse leapt with a hint of surprise when the jabberwock lowered its snout to my level. It cocked its head to one side and clicked its jagged teeth together with a sound that wasn't exactly reassuring.

"Good… boy," I said, and patted it on the muzzle the way I'd seen Lyssa do. "We've got an important job to do for our queen. We'll make sure we pull it off, you hear?"

The jabberwock emitted a huff that suggested it thought *I* was a lot more likely to screw this mission up than it was and hunkered down on its belly, ready for me to clamber on.

We had to get going soon. The sliver of a moon was high in the night sky, the air cooling around us. Only two hours remained before the Queen of Hearts' deadline.

If we couldn't pull this attempt off, we weren't going to get another chance.

"We should be ready to move out in ten minutes," Theo said. "If you're ready."

I made myself nod. I'd be ready. This was what Lyssa needed from me. And maybe it wasn't all that much madder than some of my exploits way back when.

"I suppose this is payback for turning my back on you and the Spades for the last twelve years," I said, raising an eyebrow at Theo.

He gave me that crooked smile again. I trusted it more than the smooth, confident one he'd always put on in his role as the White Knight. A princely smile, it'd been—I must have sensed it even if I hadn't known enough to consciously recognize what it meant.

"You're the best man for the job, Hatter," he said. "And even if I did think from time to time that you'd made the wrong decision by backing away from the Spades… that wasn't really my call to make. I didn't understand the position you were in."

I wasn't sure what to make of that admission. "And you do now?"

Theo glanced toward the city. "Until recently, I never had anyone that mattered to me as much as Wonderland did. I couldn't imagine putting anything else first." His gaze slid back to me. "Now I know what it's like to want to protect someone with all of your being. I'm not going to tell you that being a great father was less important than being a great Spade."

There was no denying the earnestness in his words. If I'd had any lingering doubts about his intentions toward Lyssa, they disintegrated in that instant.

I tipped my head in acknowledgment. "And sometimes, on the other hand, what or who you care about means you end up taking some crazy risks trying to make things better for them. It's easier for me to see now why you felt so much urgency about setting Wonderland right."

"Yes. I suppose we both know a lot more than we did back then."

The jabberwock shifted its weight impatiently. I looked up at it, and my throat constricted. "If this goes wrong somehow, you'll watch out for Doria? I know she doesn't need someone at her heels every second, but just, in general…"

"Of course," Theo said, sounding honestly startled. "You don't even have to ask that."

I exhaled. "Okay. Good."

He clapped me on the back and wished me luck before he left, and that felt just about right. I patted the jabberwock's neck and pondered whether I wanted to get settled on its back just yet or to wait until the last minute when the signal came. I hadn't quite decided when the rasp of footsteps sounded on the cobblestones.

Lyssa emerged from one of the side streets, sword at her hip and scepter at her back, the rubies on her armored vest gleaming as bright as her blue eyes. So much power emanated from her stride that my heart skipped a beat, watching her approach. I tugged at my hat with a fidgety twitch of my fingers.

"Shouldn't you be off preparing for your part in this grand battle?" I said lightly.

"I think we're as prepared as anyone could be," Lyssa said. "You didn't know exactly what you were signing up for. Are you okay with this?" She nodded to the jabberwock.

Did she really think I was going to say no at this late hour? The idea seemed absurd, and yet at the same time I was sure she'd accept it if I did. I forced a smile.

"I've got to remind everyone why I'm Mad Hatter, don't I?"

I obviously hadn't completely erased my nerves from my voice. Lyssa peered at me in the dim glow that seeped from the lamps on the streets behind her. "All you have to do is scatter the guards around the hostages and get the three of them onto the jabberwock, and then get the hell out of there. We'll take care of the rest. I'll have your back."

Those last words reminded me of Chess's comments. My smile relaxed a little. "And I'll have yours."

She stepped closer, her hand coming up to curl around my tie the way she'd grasped it the first time she'd kissed me, the way that made my heart thump harder in an instant. "I also remembered that the last time I kissed you for good luck, things turned out pretty much perfectly. Let's see if we can pull that off again."

I didn't need more invitation than that. I slipped my arm around her and tugged her to me, and for a few seconds everything was her fresh sweet smell and the hint of the tea we'd drunk during that last meeting, sharp and hot on her lips. Hearts take me, I'd ride a hundred jabberwocks if I got moments like this in between.

She pulled back reluctantly. "I'd better get back. I'll see you after it's over."

"Let's make that a promise," I said.

When she'd jogged back to where the rest of our sort-of army was preparing, I finally gathered my courage and scrambled up to my perch between the jabberwock's extended wings. The straps Theo had pointed out weren't hard to fix in place. I secured my legs, trying not to think of the possible negative consequences of being strapped to a deadly fire-breathing monster.

"Fucking wow," a voice murmured as I finished up. Doria eased out of the shadows where she must have been lurking. Her eyes were round as she took in me and the beast I was perched on. "I thought they were kidding. You're really topping your old exploits, aren't you, Pops."

My fingers tightened around the feathers between my mount's shoulders. "I wouldn't get too close, Mouse."

She let out a faint laugh. "I'm good here. I just wanted to see… And I figured someone should tell you to be careful. Since that strategy always worked so well with me."

I couldn't contain a laugh of my own. "So it did. Worried about your old man, are you?"

She crossed her skinny arms over her chest, hugging herself. "I'm allowed to, right? It can go both ways."

How long had she been watching—and listening? Had she heard my comment to Theo about watching out for her?

"Doria," I started.

"I'm going to do that," she said before I could go on, with a familiar defiant raise of her chin. "I'm going to worry about you too. And… maybe sometimes it's nice to know you're around to worry about me, even if it bugs me in the moment. Okay?"

I wished I wasn't up here in this ridiculous saddle so I could have hugged her if she'd let me. I had to settle for smiling with all the fatherly fondness I had in me. "I'll remind you that you said that the next time you complain."

She wrinkled her nose at me, but she was smiling too.

The first chime rang out. Doria glanced toward the city where the others had assembled and back at me. "I'll see you out there. Good luck!"

"To you too," I called after her as she darted away. *I'll only take as much as you can spare.* Then I tapped the jabberwock's shoulder, and it pushed onto its feet. "Almost our time."

It answered with a little snort and a puff of smoke.

The second chime sounded a minute later. Lyssa had instructed the jabberwock well. It didn't even wait for a signal from me, just leapt into the air with a flap of its new artificial wings. I could have sworn from the glimpse of its face I got as it shot a quick look toward the city that it was grinning.

The cool wind warbled against the taut material of the wings and licked over my clothes. My fingers tightened around the feathers along the creature's shoulders as we rose up toward the sky. The lights of the city and the palace up ahead fell away beneath us. My pulse raced, but as much from exhilaration as nerves.

This was… actually pretty amazing.

The jabberwock soared forward, its body hitching slightly with each flap. After the first couple minutes, I adjusted to the rhythm enough to release my death grip on its feathery shoulders.

We left the city behind, making straight for the glittering lanterns that dotted the royal gardens. Lights glowed from several of the palace windows and along the parapet over its main door. I could already make out dozens of guards patrolling the grounds, as aware as we were that the deadline was fast approaching.

Beneath me, Lyssa would be making her way up the road with Theo and Chess and a handful of other Spades. Dum was leading the rest of our force, including Doria, through the forest, stealing the guards' tactic from this morning. Lyssa would present herself supposedly for surrender but would demand to see that her loved ones were still alive before she came through the gate.

I wouldn't be able to hear any of that conversation, as far up as we needed to stay to avoid the lights catching on the jabberwock's form, but the moment the three Otherlanders stepped out of the palace, we'd have to move in an instant.

The road between the city and the palace was so shadowed I

couldn't even track Lyssa's progress that way. The jabberwock wheeled high above the palace, its wings holding steady as Theo had promised. What did it make of this, deep in that strange monster brain of its?

"Good work," I said, giving its neck an encouraging rub like I might have a horse. Then more lights flared on below around the gate.

As we circled back that way, figures darted between the gate and the palace. The lights along the wall glinted starkly in Lyssa's white blond hair where she stood on the road just outside. My lungs constricted. If they laid one harsh hand on my lover, my queen…

The main doors to the palace were opening. This was our moment. I leaned forward, peering down as the jabberwock swept in a tighter circle.

The Knave strode out, flicking a hand over the striped fur of his face. Several guards joined him, the three Otherlanders held between them. They strode forward and halted where Lyssa would have been able to make them out from the now-open gate, but not close enough that she could have hoped to reach them.

They weren't prepared for me.

"Now!" I said with a nudge of my fingers.

The jabberwock dove. The wind shrieked past my ears and whisked away my hat, but I didn't have time to miss it. We were hurtling toward the ground, so fast I left my stomach behind. For an instant I thought we might smash right into the hedges.

The jabberwock banked at the last second. Its feet slammed into the ground just a foot from the nearest Otherlander, crushing at least one guard under it, kicking others to the side, spewing a burst of flame at a couple more.

"Here, here," I shouted, grasping the older woman's elbow, the younger's wrist, heaving them and the man onto the jabberwock's back and fastening the straps around them so quickly my arms ached with the effort. The man almost fell when the jabberwock lurched around to belch more fire at the Knave, but I snapped the buckle in place just in time.

"Go!" I cried, tapping the creature's shoulders. As it shoved off the ground, a shriek rang out above us. My head jerked up.

The Queen had come out onto the parapet over the palace's front door. Her face blanched white with rage at the sight of her bargaining chips being swept away from her.

Seeing her, it occurred to me with a thump of my pulse that I could end this right now. My hand darted to the straps holding my legs.

The jabberwock knew where to go with its precious cargo. As it soared upward, I could spring from its back onto the parapet, stab the Queen of Hearts through the heart she barely knew how to use with one of the hatpins up my sleeve, like I had the old Knave before, and there'd be no one to stand between Lyssa and her throne. The guards she must have nearby would kill me for it in turn, but wouldn't that sacrifice be worth it?

Except I couldn't guarantee killing the Queen would stop the guards swarming the gardens, not in the crucial early moments when the most blood would be shed anyway. I couldn't even guarantee that I'd land my leap in time and close enough to end the Queen's life before her guards took mine.

And I promised Lyssa I'd see her again, after.

Get the hell out of there, she'd said. *We'll handle the rest.* I'd had her back, and now she had mine, like Chess had said. Lyssa had her own plan, a plan that didn't involve my death if she could help it, and that was the plan she'd want me to follow.

She'd want me to trust her that she could bring down the Queen without me throwing my life away. She'd want me to be by her side when the battle was over.

Damn it, I wanted that too. I wanted to be there to worry about Doria and banter with Chess and love my rising queen.

My hand stilled on the strap. The jabberwock soared up, past the palace, into the night sky. A pang filled my chest, but I welcomed the sensation, the strange sense of having lost and gained something at the same time.

Perhaps this was what love was meant to be, really. Not holding the one you loved back from the fray or throwing yourself in front of them, but facing it together, side by side, with all the faith you had.

CHAPTER TWENTY-SEVEN

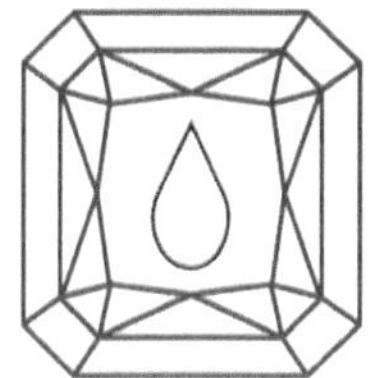

Lyssa

The jabberwock's bright feathers flashed against the night, lit up by the palace's lanterns. The smoke of its fiery attack tainted the thick scent of the garden's roses. As the creature rose up, Hatter's form showed as a dark silhouette between its crafted wings with three figures clinging on just behind him.

That was all I needed to see. I yanked my sword from its scabbard and swung it toward the gate.

"Now!"

The Spades and Clubbers who'd been gathering behind the treed slope beside the road broke from that shelter and rushed down to join me with a volley of cries. I charged ahead toward the gate with Theo and Chess at my side. The guards who'd eased it open so I could see the Knave's hostages leapt forward to shove it closed again, but I slashed out with my sword before they'd heaved it more than a couple of steps.

The blade's power thrummed through the air and smacked into the gate and the guards. The door careened open, the men in their pleated uniforms toppling in its wake. I barreled onward with the thumping of hundreds of determined feet behind me—and the burbling moan of the other jabberwocks I'd summoned, now loping over from where they'd been waiting by the city.

The guards from all across the palace grounds raced to meet us. I stopped with a hitch of breath and thrust my scepter out in front of me. My gaze caught dozens of glazed eyes and blank faces beneath those helms. I focused on them, on the need to wash away the Hearts' horrible influence.

"I am the Red Queen," I called out with all the force of my lungs. "The guardian and ruler of Wonderland. I dismiss every order you've been given from the tyrant who stole my throne. May your heads clear and your minds go free. Get yourselves away from here, to the ends of the garden, to as much safety as you can find!"

A pulse of energy rolled off the scepter. The ruddy glow flowed over the horde of guards descending on us. Within the space of a breath, many of them stumbled and lurched to the side. They wavered on their feet for a second before my last command sunk in. Their heart-shaped helms tumbled off their heads as they dashed out of the fray.

When we'd discussed this plan earlier, Theo had suggested that I could ask the pearl-headed guards to fight for me instead of the false queen who'd made them. Maybe that would have made this battle a little easier. But most of those people had never asked to serve the Queen of Hearts; had given their lives to her cruelty only to be battered with blades all over again. I wasn't going to use them the same callous way she had.

I did not intend to build my reign on a foundation of suffering.

I shoved my scepter back into its bag and tightened my grip on my sword as I hurried onward. The city people who'd joined our cause flooded into the gardens around me, everyone with some kind of weapon in their hands. The Spades wove along the edges of the crowd, tossing smoke bombs and skitter cubes to disorient the guards that were closing in. The jabberwocks dove into the mass of uniformed figures with slashes of their claws and gnashing teeth.

Theo, Chess, and Dum moved to flank me as we pushed down the center of the path. Some of the guards skirted the wider fray to come down the middle of it at us. I knocked them back with the power of my sword. Dum sprang ahead to kick the ones who'd toppled to the side with his elastic legs. Theo and Chess fended off the few who sprang closer, Theo with the sword he'd found for himself and Chess with his fists flashing in and out of sight.

Despite the cool night air, sweat was trickling down my back by the time the palace doors came into sight through the chaos. I readied my sword and fixed my gaze on the dozen or so guards assembled in front of the entrance.

"I don't want to hurt anyone. I'm just here to take back what was stolen from my family. Go, and I won't have to go through you."

The furor of the battle and the powers they'd already seen me demonstrate must have finally overcome their fear of the Queen of Hearts. Half of them scattered. The others charged at us, weapons drawn. I propelled them backward with a slice of my blade. Its power rattled the hinges and sent the door bursting open.

Theo stepped into the lead, pointing the way with his sword. "This hall will get us to the Queen's chambers fastest," he said. The rest of us hustled after him, leaving the worst of the fray behind.

We dashed down the hall, dispatching a few more guards who rushed at us along the way. Theo gestured us up a staircase.

Just as we reached the top, the Knave marched out to meet us. His tiger lips were curled in a sneer that showed his vicious teeth, and he was shoving Dee in front of him, his dagger pressed against the young man's throat.

The once-cheerful twin's red hair lay lank on his head. His face sported a black eye and a split lip. Whether the Queen had ever planned to keep up her end of the bargain or had decided their deal was forfeit when the Spades had escaped the tunnels, I didn't know, but it looked like he'd spent the last two days in the dungeons.

"There are no jabberwocks to swoop down in here," the Knave snarled, looking at Dum. "How much is your brother worth to you?"

He hadn't even gotten his final words out when Dum was springing at him with all the force of his sprightly legs. Theo gave a shout of warning, too late. Another guard had been waiting in the shadows. He leapt out in front of the Knave and stabbed his sword into Dum's gut.

A cry broke from my lips. As Dum's body slumped on the floor, the pool of blood spreading beneath his belly stark red against the mauve carpet, more guards threw themselves at us. And Dee threw himself against the Knave's hold.

He slammed his fist, driven by his springy arm, into the Knave's hand. The dagger still raked across his throat, drawing a gush of blood, but the wound wasn't deep enough to stop Dee. The Knave stumbled backward, and Dee hurtled toward his brother, pummeling every guard in the way.

"No," he rasped out. "Brother, stay with me, dammit." The last word came out with a choked sob. He gripped his brother's shoulders, but Dum's head only lolled against the ground.

My heart wrenched. Dum had loved his brother so much, even after that traitorous turn. He'd given up everything for him after all.

With my teeth gritted, I lashed out at the rest of the guards. The sword's magic slammed them back into the wall. Theo flung himself ahead of me, his face tight with anguish, his sword singing in the air. He rammed it straight into the Knave's heart.

The Knave barely managed to spit out one last gasp of a snarl before his body crumpled. Theo yanked out his sword, looking no more satisfied for the kill. The Prince of Hearts wasn't one for revenge. But nothing we did was going to bring back the young man he'd promised to protect from childhood.

We didn't even have a moment to grieve the loss. Every minute that passed before I ended this war, more of my people were dying out there while the guards fought on.

I had to get to the Queen.

We left Dee hunched over his brother's body and hustled down the hall. I knew we were almost at the Queen's quarters when the rose smell thickened again. Theo's shoulders stiffened, but his steps didn't falter.

"Out of the way!" I shouted when the door came into view up ahead, more guards clustered around it. "I'd rather go around you than through you. It's your choice."

I brandished my sword. A few of the guard's expressions wavered, and they broke from the bunch. The others braced themselves, knuckles whitening where they clutched their weapons. My stomach clenched, but my resolve didn't shake. I swung the sword's sharp magic into them.

The door flew open, the guards doubling over around it, the ones who'd been right in front tumbling through. Chess darted ahead to shove and yank them out of my path. More guards charged toward us as we hurried through the interconnected rooms with all their ornate furniture and paintings, but I dispatched them with a few swipes of my sword. The thump of my pulse filled my body.

I was here. I was so close I could feel it, taste it. This was the palace I should have grown up in, the home that had always belonged to me even while I struggled to find my place in the Otherland, not knowing Wonderland even existed.

Chess battered through one more squad of guards, blinking invisible and then visible again when they'd fallen. We strode through one last doorway, and I found myself face to face with the Queen of Hearts.

I'd never seen her this close before. She perched on a throne carved from the same red-brown cherry wood as the staff of the scepter at my back, but fitted with the gold plates Theo had mentioned to me, as if she'd bound the royal seat itself. Magic rippled through the air around her, stirring the copper coils of her hair and the ruffles of her expansive pink dress. Her eyes sparked with their eerie sheen.

But now, for the first time, I noticed the lines around those eyes that make-up couldn't completely conceal. The veins that stood out on her hands where they clutched the arms of the throne.

She'd held onto her illegitimate rule for a long time. And now that time was over.

"Don't take one more step!" she snapped at us as I stepped forward. My feet halted. Theo tipped his head. I reached to my belt to press the switch on the device my Inventor had made just for me, to set off the chain reaction he'd planned before he'd even known if he'd make it out of this palace alive or if I'd make it back to Wonderland.

A sharp hiss cut through the air, and the gold plates burst from the sides and back of the throne. The Queen screeched, lunging forward, and the seat seemed to wallop her at the same time. She staggered rather than flying at us and fell to her knees.

I was already sprinting forward. I bounded right over her and dropped onto the throne. As if drawn by the power humming through the wood, one of my hands rose to set the sword against the right arm and the other reached to place the scepter against the left.

The rubies blazed on those artifacts, all across my armored vest, and on the ring beneath it too, if I was going by the blast of heat that washed over my chest. In that instant, I felt all of Wonderland stretching out around me through the base of the throne. I saw the train streaking around the Checkerboard Plains and heard the breeze whispering through the Topsy Turvy wood, smelled the scones baking in the city and tasted the salt of the sea. The sensations soaked into my skin and quivered around me with a wash of warmth that made me gasp with joy.

I was home. I was exactly where I belonged, in a way I'd never experienced before this moment.

With all those impressions colliding around and inside me, I could hardly focus on what was happening right in front of me in the room. The Queen of Hearts threw herself to her feet and spun on me with a screech. But before she could lunge at me, Theo caught her, clamping her elbows to her sides with his strong arms.

"No, Mother," he said, his voice low and firm. "It's over. The time of the Hearts is done. This rule was never meant to be ours at all."

He glanced at Chess, who lifted the crown from the former queen's head. Chess flashed a brief grin at me. "I think we'll find or make a new one for our rightful queen."

"No," the Queen of Hearts protested, squirming against Theo's hold. "It was mine. This was all *mine*." But the power that had once reverberated through her had faded the moment I'd claimed my throne. Even the sheen in her eyes had faded, leaving them an ordinary light brown.

Theo sat his mother back on the ground, keeping one hand on her shoulder to restrain her, and fished a web of dark strands from the pouch he'd been carrying. Chess knelt down to hold her still as Theo set the contraption over the Queen of Hearts' head. He caught my eye, and I lifted my scepter again, ready for when he gave the cue.

He pressed a button at the base of the web, and a faint hum carried through the room. "Mother," he said, his voice even softer now. "I want you to forget all the reasons you think you have to hate and fear. Forget your greed for the throne."

"Let it all go," I murmured, my throat tight and my fingers gripping the scepter's staff. "Let it fade away."

The scepter's glow spread out to mingle with the device's hum. The sound rose, the air vibrating against my skin. Theo stared down at his mother, his eyes worried but his expression determined.

The glow contracted back into the ruby. The hum died off as well. The Queen of Hearts slumped where she sat, the tension seeping from her stout body. She lifted her head. One of her stiff curls fell loose across her forehead. Her gaze fixed on Theo, her brow furrowing.

"Jack?" she said hesitantly. "What am I doing here?"

Theo's mouth formed a tight smile. "You're setting things right, Mother. Come with me. We're going to end a war."

The throne called to me to stay, but I'd be back soon. I pushed myself off of it, taking up my sword as well as my scepter. The power that had flowed into me kept tingling through my nerves as we made our way out of the royal chambers, along the hall, and to the parapet where the Queen had watched the beginnings of the battle before it had started to turn against her. A battle that would now be finally done.

We stepped out into the cool night. Clangs and shouts clashed in the gardens below. "Stop!" I shouted at the top of my lungs. "The fighting ends now! The throne is mine. The Hearts have fallen."

"Tell them," Theo said to his mother, gripping her arm.

The guards had fallen back at the sight of their former queen, who stood shaken and crown-less before them. She blinked, her chin trembling before she found the words.

"There's nothing to fight for," she said. "The throne isn't mine. I give it up."

"And the Red Queen claims what was rightfully hers!" Chess called out.

The Spades and Clubbers whooped, excited laughter spilling through the gardens. The palace guards dropped their weapons. I gazed out over them in my first act as Wonderland's official queen and felt the breeze wash over me like a wave of peace spreading across the land all around me.

CHAPTER TWENTY-EIGHT

One month later

Lyssa

"Do you really have to go already?" Melody asked as the waitress cleared our lunch dishes from the café table. My best friend gave me a pleading look that was offset by her wry smile.

There was something comforting about the muted colors and the soft melody of normal Otherland music in the room around me, but coming to this world already felt like taking a trip, not coming home.

"A queen's work is never done," I said with a grin. "But I promise I'll do my best to make it for your big fashion show next week. We're still studying the whole mirror connection thing to figure out how to predict the passing of time."

"Well, until you do have it figured out, I'm happy to stay on call for spontaneous meals whenever you happen to drop in." Melody shook her head, still smiling. "I just tell myself that you've relocated to some other actual country. That's a whole lot easier to wrap my head around. The less said about that crazy place you're actually going back to, the better."

I laughed as we stood up. All three of the Otherlanders the Knave had held hostage had been pretty shaken up by the experience, to say the least, but Melody had bounced back the fastest. We had an unspoken deal that I didn't talk too much about the weirdness of my new life and she wouldn't hassle me about how much danger I'd put myself in, and we'd continue on like friends who just didn't live as close to one another anymore.

"Have you heard anything else from your mom?" Melody asked.

I grimaced as I pushed past the café door into the parking lot. "Her last few texts were still in full freak-out mode. I'm sticking with the whole no-contact thing until she can talk to me without having a breakdown." The last time I'd seen Mom—as well as the last time I'd talked to her, a week after that visit—she'd sobbed and cajoled and demanded that I go back to a hospital or at least come "home" so she'd know I was okay. The way she was acting, she needed help a whole lot more than I did.

The same old sense of duty had prickled over me. But I had other people counting on me now—and I shouldn't have had to be the one to support Mom back when I was a kid either. At a certain point, enough was enough.

I'd told her I loved her, that I was happy, and that I couldn't keep talking to her until she could accept those facts without constant reassurance. I'd also nudged her to get in touch with the therapist she'd seen a few times. If she could turn to a counselor instead of to me with all her worries, maybe we could have a better relationship down the road.

"I'm sorry," Melody said. "Even if I kind of get where she's coming from."

"It's only been a few weeks," I said. "I think she'll come around with enough time."

What the moving guy had made of the whole experience, I wasn't totally sure. He'd stammered something about needing to get home the second I'd brought them all back through to my house and practically torn a hole in the driveway getting out of there.

When we stopped at our cars, which were parked side-by-side, Melody touched my arm. "You know, even if I kind of get where your mom is coming from, I'm really happy for you at the same time, Lyss. There's something about you… Like you're lit up from the inside in a way you weren't before. Maybe I don't understand this whole situation, but I can tell you're doing the right thing for you. That's the best I could ask for, for my best friend."

Affection for her swelled in my throat. I gave her a hug, and she squeezed me back tightly.

"I'll give you a call as soon as I make it here again," I said.

"I'll be looking forward to it," Melody said. "Bring me a couple more of those Wonderland dresses if you can spare them, all right? I got some great inspiration from the first one."

I gave her a thumbs up and got into my car.

My spirits lifted as I drove through the dreary weather toward Aunt Alicia's old house—my house now, not that I spent much time in it these days. Mrs. Plisby, the woman I'd hired to take care of the place during my absences, was out in the front yard pulling up weeds. I waved to her before heading inside. I paid her well enough that she didn't ask any questions about where I disappeared to during those absences.

All the furniture Mom and Melody had ordered packed up was now back in place, other than a little rearranging to suit my tastes. The mirror to Wonderland stood in the master bedroom, freshly polished. Even now, a giddy sensation raced over my skin as I stepped close to it and watched my reflection fade away. I touched the glass and reached through it to the surface on the other side.

After some trial and error, I'd found that I could direct my journey through the Otherland side looking-glass just like I could when I traveled from the Wonderland side. No more pond dunkings every time I slipped through. With a whisk of wind and a whoosh of darkness, I popped out into the entrance hall off my royal chambers.

A lot of the grandeur the Queen of Hearts had decorated her rooms with had been stripped away. I'd discovered the cherry wood floor under the thick carpeting and stripped the gold-gilded paper from the walls. The plaster was now painted a subdued moss-green that happened to be one of my favorite shades. On it I'd hung not fancy oils but sketches and paintings the city folk had made in celebration of their newfound freedom.

Out in the rest of the palace, people were still at work removing the unwanted traces of the Hearts' rule. Afternoon sunlight streamed through windows no longer choked by thick velvet curtains. The smell of fresh paint tinged the air. The workers smiled and waved at me from where they were swiping their brushes over the wall farther down.

I hadn't checked on two of the former royals in residence today. I stopped by a second-floor room and knocked on the door. Mirabel's voice rang out on the other side. "Do come again soon!"

She was looking mainly backwards today, it sounded like. I eased open the door to find her sitting on one of the sofas we'd moved to this set of rooms from her Tower apartment. In the last few weeks, she'd decided to put aside her knitting to give embroidery a try. Beside her, the former Queen of Hearts was stitching away at her own strip of cloth.

The older woman looked up at me and offered a faint smile. She always gave the impression that she didn't entirely remember me but suspected that she was supposed to. Whatever the combined effects of Theo's memory gadget and my scepter had accomplished, it'd both wiped the violence from the tyrant's mind and left her a little vacant. But Mirabel seemed to find her mother's company pleasant enough in her new state. It was easier keeping an eye on her here in the palace than off where the rest of her children might nudge her in less positive directions.

Like every day, I asked, "How are you doing?" and "Is there anything you need?" Today Mirabel asked if she could have some silver thread sent up, but otherwise she showed nothing but contentment. I didn't ask her to try to pry into the future or dredge up the past. We'd left her head aching with enough of those requests in the past.

Besides, everything around me told me the future was bright.

As I came past the grand staircase into the wide front hall, I caught sight of Doria slipping away into one of the side rooms with

Kip and Mallo, all of them laughing. A figure shifted in the shadows beside the staircase—Dee, watching them go, his expression so fraught it sent a twinge through my heart.

He'd apologized profusely for his betrayal, and his guilt over his brother's death hung over him like a cloud. I wasn't sure any of the Spades would ever feel comfortable treating him like a real friend again, though. As someone who'd once sacrificed a lot trying to save her mother from going under, I wasn't going to keep kicking him while he was down, but I wasn't sure when I'd be ready to give him much responsibility either.

He hadn't even managed to save his mother. We'd found her body in a pile of what Carpenter had called "discards" out at the Oyster Cove, her reformed head stalled in mid-growth. Apparently they'd lost nearly a quarter of the new pearl-heads thanks to the hasty adjustments to speed up the process. I couldn't imagine how painful that loss must be for Dee on top of the other.

"I can take a little comfort knowing the Queen of Hearts couldn't force Mom into being her slave," he'd said when I'd delivered the news. We'd held a memorial for her and all the other fallen city folk not long after the battle.

I followed the railing around to the door that led to the parapet. From that high vantage point, I could see across the palace grounds all the way to the little town the Diamonds and the remains of the Hearts family were building for themselves on the opposite side of the club from the main city. We'd never found any definite proof that the Duchess and her allies had meant to betray us, and I'd wanted to give everyone a blank slate for the beginning of my rule.

They *did* have to build the homes they wanted for themselves, though, since they preferred not to mingle too much with the city folk, and I wasn't keeping them in the palace.

The rough scrape of stone sliding against stone reached my ears from their construction site. Caterpillar's hulking, segmented form came into view briefly between the trees, lugging a slab the size of a boulder. He'd decided to look to them for new career possibilities now that I'd relieved him of his club.

"I think we need new management all around," I'd told him,

remembering the way he'd leered at me when he'd thought I was just a Dreamer who'd stumbled into Wonderland. Rabbit hadn't been able to hide his giddiness when I'd handed him the keys.

Closer by, Unicorn had just finished a run around the lawn we'd set down where the mass of rose bushes used to be. Chess ambled over with a remark I could tell was bantering from his tone even if I couldn't make out most of the words, and Unicorn chuckled in response.

The bright feathers of the royal jabberwocks gleamed as they meandered between the freshly planted flowerbeds—every sort of flower Wonderland had to offer, other than roses. One of the creatures sprawled on its side, soaking up the sun. Since the Hearts had fallen, all the aggression had seeped out of their temperaments. They acted like overgrown feathery puppies most of the time. But if a bunch of Diamonds, say, got it into their heads to storm the palace, then the teeth and the fire would come out.

The main gate opened, and Theo strode into the garden with a couple of the Spades he'd been making the rounds with. A queen needed a royal guard of some sort, and I'd asked the former White Knight to take charge of that area of my rule. No more oddly shaped helms or pleated uniforms, though. He'd gone back to his preferred white dress shirts and gray slacks. They did suit him, after all.

I left the parapet and headed down to meet him. As I came out into the courtyard beyond the front doors, Hatter approached a couple of women sitting on a granite bench at the edge of the garden path. He held out a hat with a tuft of jabberwock feathers to the younger one.

"Fully customized to your requests," he said with a tip of his own hat. He'd restarted his business out of one of the rooms in the palace, and in the celebratory mood after our victory, there'd been plenty of call for eye-catching hats among the Clubbers.

"It's gorgeous," the woman said, setting it on her braided hair. "Thank you so much." She turned to show it to her companion. The older woman considered it with clear but wandering eyes. She was a pearl-head—maybe the woman's mother.

"Very nice," she said in a quiet voice. None of the pearl-heads I'd freed from the Queen of Hearts' commands had really recovered, but they had some sort of lives still. People had reported a few memories and little signs of their loved ones' original personalities surfacing. Maybe over time they'd become more themselves.

Theo reached the courtyard as I came down the steps outside the palace. He gave me his assured smile and dipped into a bow as he kissed my hand. "How was your visit, my queen?"

"It was good," I said. "But I'm always glad to come back home. Have there been any problems today?"

"Nothing major," he said. "A minor dispute between a couple of the city folk, a complaint from one of the Diamonds." He arched his eyebrow wryly with the latter comment. "All of it easily taken care of."

"It's a good thing I've got you to be where I can't be."

"You've certainly been covering a lot of ground yourself. Every time I see you you're either coming or going. Where are you off to now?"

There were plenty more things on my to-do list. We'd started Wonderland on the path back to joy, and the atmosphere here already felt so much lighter, but we still had a lot of distance to cover. The thought of all the responsibilities on my extensive list rose up in my head.

Having Theo's warm eyes on me reminded me that my royal blood wasn't the only connection that had kept me here. I *had* been running around a lot in the last few weeks. As his fingers twined with mine, a tingle raced up my arm. It had been days since I'd taken the time to fuel that other, more private connection. None of the items on my to-do list were so urgent I couldn't put them off for a little while.

I didn't ever want to get too busy for, er, getting busy.

"There's actually a matter in the palace you could assist me with," I said with a sly smile, squeezing his hand. "If you have a moment."

"Anything for my queen," Theo replied, his voice dipping low, full of promise.

Chess had turned from his chat with Unicorn to look our way. I made a quick beckoning gesture as I caught his eye, and he bounded over with a grin. Hatter was just heading back into the palace at the same time we reached the doors. I grasped the lapel of his suit jacket —deep green, today—with a playful tug.

"I require the use of your nimble fingers," I said with a twitch of my eyebrows.

He took the three of us in, and amusement and hunger lit together in his eyes. He tipped his hand to me. "As you wish, Your Highness."

I did have some sense of propriety. I didn't touch more than Theo's hand or Hatter's jacket as we walked—fairly quickly—through the halls to the Queen's chambers. Somehow the heat between us flickered higher all the same, fueled by anticipation.

Theo's thumb traced over my knuckles, sparking a tingle of desire. Chess teased his fingers down my back as I opened the door. It was all I could do to push past that door and make sure it'd shut behind us before I pulled my three lovers to me.

Theo's mouth crashed into mine. Hatter kissed the side of my neck. Chess eased the straps of my dress down, nibbling my shoulder in the first one's wake. I gave myself over to the rising passion, kissing Theo back hard, knocking Hatter's hat aside as my fingers tangled with his spiky hair, whimpering when Chess's mouth dipped lower to the swell of my breast.

We didn't always come together at the same time. It was nice to have just one or two men to focus on now and then. But there was nothing more delicious than the rush of having all three of them around me.

I tore my mouth from Theo's and yanked Hatter's lips to mine. My other hand fumbled with Chess's shirt. He tossed it to the side and jerked the zipper of my dress to send it pooling at my feet. Theo sucked in a breath and set to work lapping my nipples into peaks with his tongue. Pleasure shivered through my chest.

Hatter wrenched off his jacket at my tug. His hot mouth trailed to my earlobe, and Chess captured my lips. Hatter dipped his hand between my legs as Theo continued working over my breasts, and need flooded every part of me. My hips arched into Hatter's touch. My core was aching to be filled.

We'd barely made it two feet from the door. I spun myself and

Theo around, shoving him up against a mahogany end table. He grinned, yanking down my panties as I loosened his pants. I freed his cock and stroked the silky skin over that rigid length, but I was too hungry for much teasing.

Theo must have felt the same way. With a shift of his arm, he hefted me up to straddle him, braced against the side table. "Whatever my queen desires," he said, his dark brown eyes glinting as he gazed at me.

I slid down onto his cock with a gasp that turned into a satisfied moan. Theo's breath hitched. He thrust up into me, gripping my side to hold me in place, bringing his lips to my throat.

I turned my head, my skin blazing everywhere Theo pressed his mouth. "Hatter," I said breathlessly.

He didn't need more encouragement than that. I'd chosen this position for a reason. Faster than should have been humanly possible, the swiftest man I knew slipped into the royal bathroom and returned with the oil I'd obtained an ample supply of. He kissed my back, and Chess reclaimed my lips.

Hatter slicked the oil over my other opening. His fingers circled and slid into my ass with the same slow, building rhythm as Theo pumped up into me. I shuddered with longing. The muscles relaxed to give way. Then the head of Hatter's cock slid into me, filling me doubly.

I clung to Theo's half-open shirt, to Chess's arm as he tweaked my breast. A cry tumbled out of me. I loved this, but every time that sensation of total fullness somehow shocked me.

Bliss rang through my nerves. I bucked against Theo, Hatter matching my pace with his own thrusts. Chess stroked down my side and up Theo's.

My third lover needed attention too. I groped at his pants, and he dropped them for me with a smirk. His expression melted into a dreamy smile when my fingers closed around his straining cock.

Chess leaned closer, pumping into my grasp, as Theo and Hatter pounded into me in time. Their hands gripped my thighs, my waist; the jerk of their hips as they filled me sent me higher and higher. As pleasure swelled from my core all through my body, for a moment before I reached my peak, I felt raised up between the three of them, lifted to great heights by their love and their desire.

I soared on and on, riding that ecstasy until it burst inside me like a firecracker. My muscles tightened with the surge of bliss, and Hatter groaned. He came with a stuttered motion, and then Theo made a choked sound and followed him over. Chess pressed his face against mine as I pumped him faster, and found his release with a hot spurt over my arm.

I came back to earth cradled between the three of them, my skin damp with sweat I didn't remember forming, giddiness racing through me. For a few minutes, we just basked in the afterglow with soft lingering kisses. Then reality started to seep back in with its reminders of all my queenly duties.

I eased off Theo and found my footing on the floor. "I guess I should get back to my royal work. I was going to check on the reconstruction of those buildings the jabberwocks burned—and I've been meaning to get out to the Topsy Turvy Woods sometime—and—"

Theo cut me off with a laugh and another kiss. "My queen," he said, his voice bright with fondness, "all of that can wait a little longer."

"We had a little talk," Chess said, walking his fingers up my side. "Made some plans for our queen who's full of plans."

"What plans?" I said, glancing around.

Hatter smiled and trailed his thumb along my jaw in a gentle caress. "You, looking-glass girl, have a bad habit of putting all your energy into taking care of everyone around you and none into taking care of yourself. Consider this an intervention. If you're not going to take care of you, then that's obviously our job."

"Come here," Theo said, guiding me deeper into my chambers to my bedroom. He nudged me onto the airy surface of the feather duvet.

Hatter vanished. Chess sat down on the bed next to me and set his broad hands on my shoulders. "If anyone can teach you how to relax, it should be me," he practically purred. His thumbs dug into the tense muscles along my spine. A different sort of pleasure radiated out from those pressure points. I sighed, letting myself sink into the massage.

"Okay, I can spare a few minutes for this."

He chuckled and kissed the spot just behind my ear as his hands continued their kneading. "We have music ready too," he said. "When you're loosened up, you can let loose on a dance floor all your own, if you'd like, like old times."

Hatter ducked into the room a moment later. I recognized the smell that came with him before I'd even gotten a look at the plate in his hands.

"Vanilla-cranberry-pine scones!" I said with delight I couldn't restrain. Various chefs and bakers had been volunteering their services in the palace, but nothing I'd tasted yet compared to my very first favorite food in Wonderland.

Hatter offered one to me with a twinkle in his eyes. As the sweet buttery dough melted in my mouth, Theo bent down beside the bed.

"I had a little Inventor inspiration," he said. "If you want the full experience, we'll have to adjourn to the Tower one of these days, but for now…"

Something under the bed clicked. With a faint hum, the frame lifted off the floor. It hovered there, drifting gently to the side. A giggle tumbled from my lips. We were flying on it as if it were weightless, like in Theo's anti-gravity room.

Hatter and Theo scrambled up onto the bed. I sank into the warmth of my lovers, pleased from head to toe.

No matter what awaited us, I believed I could safely say that Wonderland was in very good hands—and so was I.

ABOUT THE AUTHOR

Eva Chase is an Amazon bestselling author of urban fantasy and paranormal romance. She grew up on a steady diet of magic, mayhem, and romantic angst, and brings plenty of all three to her stories. But no need to fear the dreaded love triangle—Eva's heroines never have to choose. She lives in Ontario, Canada with her family and one velcro-like cat.

Along with the Looking-Glass Curse trilogy, she is the author of the Royal Spares series, the Rites of Possession series, the Shadowblood Souls series, the Heart of a Monster series, the Gang of Ghouls series, the Bound to the Fae series, the Flirting with Monsters series, the Cursed Studies trilogy, the Royals of Villain Academy series, the Moriarty's Men series, the Their Dark Valkyrie series, the Witch's Consorts series, the Dragon Shifter's Mates series, the Demons of Fame Romance series, the Legends Reborn trilogy, and the Alpha Project Psychic Romance series.

Connect with Eva online:
www.evachase.com
eva@evachase.com

www.ingramcontent.com/pod-product-compliance
Lightning Source LLC
Chambersburg PA
CBHW020347310726
48979CB00015B/2533/J
* 9 7 8 1 9 9 8 5 8 2 1 2 9 *